Also by Joe Abercrombie

The First Law Trilogy
The Blade Itself
Before They Are Hanged
Last Argument of Kings

Best Served Cold

THE FIRST LAW: BOOK THREE

JOE ABERCROMBIE

LAST ARGUMENT OF KINGS

First published in Great Britain in 2008 by
Gollancz
An imprint of the Orion Publishing Group
Orion House, 5 Upper St Martin's Lane,
London WC2H 9EA

An Hachette UK company

This edition published in Great Britain in 2010
by Gollancz

5 7 9 10 8 6 4

A CIP catalogue record for this book is available
from the British Library

ISBN 978 0 575 09111 5

Typeset at The Spartan Press Ltd,
Lymington, Hants

Printed in Great Britain by
Clays Ltd, St Ives plc

The Orion Publishing Group's policy is to use papers
that are natural, renewable and recyclable products and
made from wood grown in sustainable forests. The logging
and manufacturing processes are expected to conform to
the environmental regulations of the country of origin.

www.joeabercrombie.com
www.orionbooks.co.uk

For the Four Readers
You know who you are

PART I

'Life being what it is,
one dreams of revenge.'

Paul Gauguin

The Poison Trade

Superior Glokta stood in the hall, and waited. He stretched his twisted neck out to one side and then to the other, hearing the familiar clicks, feeling the familiar cords of pain stretching out through the tangled muscles between his shoulder-blades. *Why do I do it, when it always hurts me? Why must we test the pain? Tongue the ulcer, rub the blister, pick the scab?*

'Well?' he snapped.

The marble bust at the foot of the stairs offered only its silent contempt. *And I get more than enough of that already.* Glokta shuffled away, his useless foot scraping over the tiles behind him, the tapping of his cane echoing amongst the mouldings on the faraway ceiling.

When it came to the great noblemen on the Open Council, Lord Ingelstad, the owner of this oversized hall, was an under-sized man indeed. The head of a family whose fortunes had declined with the passing years, whose wealth and influence had shrivelled to almost nothing. *And the more shrivelled the man, the more swollen his pretensions must become. Why do they never realise? Small things only seem smaller in large spaces.*

Somewhere in the shadows a clock vomited up a few sluggish chimes. *Good and late already. The more shrivelled the man, the longer the wait on his pleasure. But I can be patient, when I must. I have no dazzling banquets, no ecstatic crowds, no beautiful women waiting breathlessly for my arrival, after all. Not any more. The Gurkish saw to that, in the darkness beneath the Emperor's prisons.* He pressed his tongue into his empty gums and grunted as he shifted his leg, needles from it shooting up his back and making his eyelid flicker. *I can be patient. The one good thing about every step being an ordeal. You soon learn how to tread carefully.*

3

The door beside him opened sharply and Glokta snapped his head round, doing his best to hide a grimace as his neck bones crunched. Lord Ingelstad stood in the doorway: a big, fatherly man with a ruddy complexion. He offered up a friendly smile as he beckoned Glokta into the room. *Quite as though this were a social call, and a welcome one at that.*

'I must apologise for keeping you waiting, Superior. I have had so many visitors since I arrived in Adua, my head is in quite a spin!' *Let us hope it doesn't spin right off.* 'So very many visitors!' *Visitors with offers, no doubt. Offers for your vote. Offers for your help in choosing our next king. But my offer, I think, you will find painful to refuse.* 'Will you take wine, Superior?'

'No, my Lord, thank you.' Glokta hobbled over the threshold. 'I will not stay long. I, too, have a great deal of business to attend to.' *Elections don't rig themselves, you know.*

'Of course, of course. Please be seated.' Ingelstad dropped happily into one of his chairs and gestured to another. It took Glokta a moment to get settled, lowering himself carefully, then shifting his hips until he discovered a position in which his back did not give him constant pain. 'And what did you wish to discuss with me?'

'I have come on behalf of Arch Lector Sult. I hope you will not be offended if I am blunt, but his Eminence wants your vote.'

The nobleman's heavy features twisted in feigned puzzlement. *Very badly feigned, as it goes.* 'I am not sure that I understand. My vote on what issue?'

Glokta wiped some wet from beneath his leaking eye. *Must we engage in such undignified dancing? You have not the build for it, and I have not the legs.* 'On the issue of who will next occupy the throne, Lord Ingelstad.'

'Ah. That.' *Yes, that. Idiot.* 'Superior Glokta, I hope I will not disappoint you, or his Eminence, a man for whom I have nothing but the highest respect,' and he bowed his head with an exaggerated show of humility, 'when I say that I could not, in all good conscience, allow myself to be influenced in any one direction. I feel that I, and all the members of the Open

4

Council, have been given a sacred trust. I am duty bound to vote for the man who seems to me to be the very finest candidate, from the many excellent men available.' And he assumed a grin of the greatest self-satisfaction.

A fine speech. A village dunce might have even believed it. How often have I heard it, or its like, the past few weeks? Traditionally, the bargaining would come next. The discussion of how much, exactly, a sacred trust is worth. How much silver outweighs a good conscience. How much gold cuts through the bindings of duty. But I am not in a bargaining mood today.

Glokta raised his eyebrows very high. 'I must congratulate you on a noble stand, Lord Ingelstad. If everyone had your character we would be living in a better world. A noble stand indeed . . . especially when you have so much to lose. No less than everything, I suppose.' He winced as he took his cane in one hand and rocked himself painfully forward towards the edge of the chair. 'But I see you will not be swayed, and so I take my leave—'

'What can you refer to, Superior?' The nobleman's unease was written plainly across his plump face.

'Why, Lord Ingelstad, to your corrupt business dealings.'

The ruddy cheeks had lost much of their glow. 'There must be some mistake.'

'Oh no, I assure you.' Glokta slid the papers of confession from the inside pocket of his coat. 'You are mentioned often in the confessions of senior Mercers, you see? Very often.' And he held the crackling pages out so they both could see them. 'Here you are referred to as – and not my choice of words, you understand – an "accomplice". Here as the "prime beneficiary" of a most unsavoury smuggling operation. And here, you will note – and I almost blush to mention it – your name and the word "treason" appear in close proximity.'

Ingelstad sagged back into his chair and set his glass rattling down on the table beside him, a quantity of wine sloshing out onto the polished wood. *Oh, we really should wipe that up. It could leave an awful stain, and some stains are impossible to remove.*

5

'His Eminence,' continued Glokta, 'counting you as a friend, was able to keep your name out of the initial enquiries, for everybody's sake. He understands that you were merely trying to reverse the failing fortunes of your family, and is not without sympathy. If you were to disappoint him in this business of votes, however, his sympathy would be quickly exhausted. Do you take my meaning?' *I feel that I have made it abundantly clear.*

'I do,' croaked Ingelstad.

'And the bonds of duty? Do they feel any looser, now?'

The nobleman swallowed, the flush quite vanished from his face. 'I am eager to assist his Eminence in any way possible, of course, but . . . the thing is—' *What now? A desperate offer? A despairing bribe? An appeal to my conscience, even?* 'A representative of High Justice Marovia came to me yesterday. A man called Harlen Morrow. He made very similar representations . . . and not dissimilar threats.' Glokta frowned. *Did he now? Marovia, and his little worm. Always just one step ahead, or just one step behind. But never far away.* A shrill note crept into Ingelstad's voice. 'What am I to do? I cannot support you both! I will leave Adua, Superior, and never return! I will . . . I will abstain from voting—'

'You'll do no such fucking thing!' hissed Glokta. 'You'll vote the way I tell you and Marovia be damned!' *More prodding? Distasteful, but so be it. Are my hands not filthy to the elbow? Rummaging through another sewer or two will scarcely make the difference.* He let his voice soften to an oily purr. 'I observed your daughters in the park, yesterday.' The nobleman's face lost its last vestige of colour. 'Three young innocents on the very cusp of womanhood, dressed all in the height of fashion, and each one lovelier than the last. The youngest would be . . . fifteen?'

'Thirteen,' croaked Ingelstad.

'Ah.' And Glokta let his lips curl back to display his toothless smile. 'She blooms early. They have never before visited Adua, am I correct?'

'They have not,' he nearly whispered.

'I thought not. Their excitement and delight as they toured the gardens of the Agriont were perfectly charming. I swear, they must have caught the eye of every eligible suitor in the capital.' He allowed his smile slowly to fade. 'It would break my heart, Lord Ingelstad, to see three such delicate creatures snatched suddenly away to one of Angland's harshest penal institutions. Places where beauty, and breeding, and a gentle disposition, attract an entirely different and far less enjoyable kind of attention.' Glokta gave a carefully orchestrated shudder of dismay as he leaned slowly forward to whisper. 'I would not wish that life on a dog. And all on account of the indiscretions of a father who had the means of reparation well within his grasp.'

'But my daughters, they were not involved—'

'We are electing a new king! Everyone is involved!' *Harsh, perhaps. But harsh times demand harsh actions.* Glokta struggled to his feet, hand wobbling on his cane with the effort. 'I will tell his Eminence that he can count on your vote.'

Ingelstad collapsed, suddenly and completely. *Like a stabbed wine-skin.* His shoulders sagged, his face hung loose with horror and hopelessness. 'But the High Justice . . .' he whispered. 'Have you no pity?'

Glokta could only shrug. 'I did have. As a boy I was soft-hearted beyond the point of foolishness. I swear, I would cry at a fly caught in a spider's web.' He grimaced at a brutal spasm through his leg as he turned for the door. 'Constant pain has cured me of that.'

It was an intimate little gathering. *But the company hardly inspires warmth.* Superior Goyle glared at Glokta from across the huge, round table in the huge, round office, his beady eyes staring from his bony face. *And not with tender feelings, I rather think.*

The attention of his Eminence the Arch Lector, the head of his Majesty's Inquisition, was fixed elsewhere. Pinned to the curving wall, taking up perhaps half of the entire chamber, were three hundred and twenty sheets of paper. *One for every great heart on our noble Open Council.* They crackled gently in the breeze from the great windows. *Fluttering little papers for fluttering little votes.* Each one was marked with a name. *Lord this, Lord that, Lord someone of wherever. Big men and little men. Men whose opinions, on the whole, no one cared a damn for until Prince Raynault fell out of his bed and into his grave.*

Many of the pages had a blob of coloured wax on their corner. Some had two, or even three. *Allegiances. Which way will they vote? Blue for Lord Brock, red for Lord Isher, black for Marovia, white for Sult, and so on. All subject to change, of course, depending which way the wind blows them.* Below were written lines of small, dense script. Too small for Glokta to read from where he was sitting, but he knew what they said. *Wife was once a whore. Partial to young men. Drinks too much for his good. Murdered a servant in a rage. Gambling debts he cannot cover. Secrets. Rumours. Lies. The tools of this noble trade. Three hundred and twenty names, and just as many sordid little stories, each one to be picked at, and dug out, and jabbed our way. Politics. Truly, the work of the righteous.*

So why do I do this? Why?

The Arch Lector had more pressing concerns. 'Brock still leads,' he murmured in a dour drone, staring at the shifting papers with his white gloved hands clasped behind his back. 'He has some fifty votes, more or less certain.' *As certain as we can be in these uncertain times.* 'Isher is not far behind, with forty or more to his name. Skald has made some recent gains, as far as we can tell. An unexpectedly ruthless man. He has the Starikland delegation more or less in his hand, which gives him thirty votes, perhaps, and Barezin about the same. They are the four main contenders, as things stand.'

But who knows? Perhaps the King will live another year, and by the time it comes to a vote we'll all have killed each other. Glokta had to stifle a grin at the thought. *The Lords' Round heaped with richly-dressed corpses, every great nobleman in the Union and all twelve members of the Closed Council. Each stabbed in the back by the man beside. The ugly truth of government . . .*

'Did you speak to Heugen?' snapped Sult.

Goyle tossed his balding head and sneered at Glokta with seething annoyance. 'Lord Heugen is still struggling under the delusion that he could be our next king, though he cannot certainly control more than a dozen chairs. He barely had time to hear our offer he was so busy scrabbling to coax out more votes. Perhaps in a week, or two, he will see reason. Then he might be encouraged to lean our way, but I wouldn't bet on it. More likely he'll throw in his lot with Isher. The two of them have always been close, I understand.'

'Good for them,' hissed Sult. 'What about Ingelstad?'

Glokta stirred in his seat. 'I presented him with your ultimatum in very blunt terms, your Eminence.'

'Then we can count on his vote?'

How to put this? 'I could not say so with absolute certainty. High Justice Marovia was able to make threats almost identical to our own, through his man Harlen Morrow.'

'Morrow? Isn't he some lickspittle of Hoff's?'

'It would seem he has moved up in the world.' *Or down, depending on how you look at it.*

'He could be taken care of.' Goyle wore a most unsavoury expression. 'Quite easily—'

'No!' snapped Sult. 'Why is it, Goyle, that no sooner does a problem appear than you want to kill it! We must tread carefully for now, and show ourselves to be reasonable men, open to negotiation.' He strode to the window, the bright sunlight glittering purple through the great stone on his ring of office. 'Meanwhile the business of actually running the country is ignored. Taxes go uncollected. Crimes go unpunished. This bastard they call the Tanner, this demagogue, this traitor, speaks in public at village fairs, urging open rebellion! Daily now, peasants leave their farms and turn to banditry, perpetrating untold theft and damage. Chaos spreads, and we have not the resources to stamp it out. There are only two regiments of the King's Own left in Adua, scarcely enough to maintain order in the city. Who knows if one of our noble Lords will tire of waiting and decide to try to seize the crown prematurely? I would not put it past them!'

'Will the army return from the North soon?' asked Goyle.

'Unlikely. That oaf Marshal Burr has spent three months squatting outside Dunbrec, and given Bethod ample time to regroup beyond the Whiteflow. Who knows when he'll finally get the job done, if ever!' *Months spent destroying our own fortress. It almost makes one wish we'd put less effort into building the place.*

'Twenty-five votes.' The Arch Lector scowled at the crackling papers. 'Twenty-five, and Marovia has eighteen? We're scarcely making progress! For every vote we gain we lose one somewhere else!'

Goyle leaned forwards in his chair. 'Perhaps, your Eminence, the time has come to call again on our friend at the University—'

The Arch Lector hissed furiously, and Goyle snapped his mouth shut. Glokta looked out the great window, pretending that he had heard nothing out of the ordinary. The six crumbling spires of the University dominated the view. *But what help could anyone possibly find there? Amongst the decay, and the dust, from those old idiots of Adepti?*

Sult did not give him long to consider it. 'I will speak to Heugen myself.' And he jabbed one of the papers with a finger. 'Goyle, write to Lord Governor Meed and try to elicit his support. Glokta, arrange an interview with Lord Wetterlant. He has yet to declare himself one way or the other. Get out there, the pair of you.' Sult turned from his sheets full of secrets and fixed on Glokta with his hard blue eyes. 'Get out there and get . . . me . . . votes!'

Being Chief

'Cold night!' shouted the Dogman. 'Thought it was meant to be summer!'

The three of 'em looked up. The nearest was an old man with grey hair and a face that looked like it had seen some weather. Just past him was a younger man, missing his left arm above the elbow. The third was no more'n a boy, stood down the end of the quay and frowning out at the dark sea.

Dogman faked a nasty limp as he walked over, dragging one leg behind him and wincing like he was in pain. He shuffled under the lamp, dangling on its high pole with the warning bell beside it, and held up the jar so they could all see.

The old man grinned, and leaned his spear against the wall. 'Always cold, down by the water.' He came up, rubbing his hands together. 'Just as well we got you to keep us warm, eh?'

'Aye. Good luck all round.' Dogman pulled out the stopper and let it dangle, lifted one of the mugs and poured out a slosh.

'No need to be shy, eh, lad?'

'I guess there ain't at that.' Dogman sloshed out some more. The man with one arm had to set his spear down when he got handed his mug. The boy came up last, and looked Dogman over, wary.

The old one nudged him with an elbow. 'You sure your mother'd care for you drinking, boy?'

'Who cares what she'd say?' he growled, trying to make his high voice sound gruff.

Dogman handed him a mug. 'You're old enough to hold a spear, you're old enough to hold a cup, I reckon.'

'I'm old enough!' he snapped, snatching it out o' Dogman's hand, but he shuddered when he drank from it. Dogman remembered his first drink, feeling mighty sick and wondering what all the fuss was about, and he smiled to himself. The boy thought he was being laughed at, most likely. 'Who are you anyway?'

The old man tutted. 'Don't mind him. He's still young enough to think that rudeness wins respect.'

''S alright,' said Dogman, pouring himself a mug then setting the jar down on the stones, taking time to think out what to say, make sure he didn't make no mistakes. 'My name's Cregg.' He'd known a man called Cregg once, got killed in a scrap up in the hills. Dogman hadn't liked him much, and he'd no idea why that name came to mind, but one was about as good as another right then, he reckoned. He slapped his thigh. 'Got poked in the leg up at Dunbrec and it ain't healed right. Can't march no more. Reckon my days at holding a line are over, so my chief sent me down here, to watch the water with you lot.' He looked out at the sea, flapping and sparkling under the moon like a thing alive. 'Can't say I'm too sorry about it, though. Being honest, I had a skin full o' fighting.' That last bit was no lie, at least.

'Know how you feel,' said One-Arm, waving his stump in Dogman's face. 'How're things up there?'

'Alright. Union are still sat outside their own walls, trying everything to get in, and we're on the other side o' the river, waiting for 'em. Been that way for weeks.'

'I heard some boys have gone over to the Union. I heard old Threetrees was up there, got killed in that battle.'

'He was a great man, Rudd Threetrees,' said the old boy, 'great man.'

'Aye.' Dogman nodded. 'That he was.'

'Heard the Dogman took his place, though,' said One-Arm. 'That a fact?'

'So I heard. Mean bastard, that. Huge big lad. They call him Dogman 'cause he bit some woman's teats off one time.'

Dogman blinked. 'Do they now? Well, I never saw him.'

'I heard the Bloody-Nine was up there,' whispered the boy, eyes big like he was talking about a ghost.

The other two snorted at him. 'The Bloody-Nine's dead,

boy, and good riddance to that evil fucker.' One-Arm shuddered. 'Damn it but you get some fool notions!'

'Just what I heard, is all.'

The old man swilled down some more grog and smacked his lips. 'Don't much matter who's where. Union'll most likely get bored once they've got their fort back. Get bored and go home, across the sea, and everything back to normal. None of 'em will be coming down here to Uffrith, anyway.'

'No,' said One-Arm happily. 'They'll not be coming here.'

'Then why we out here watching for 'em?' whined the boy.

The old man rolled his eyes, like he'd heard it ten times before and always made the same answer. ''Cause that's the task we been given, lad.'

'And once you got a task, you best do it right.' Dogman remembered Logen telling him the same thing, and Threetrees too. Both gone now, and back in the mud, but it was still as true as it ever was. 'Even if it's a dull task, or a dangerous, or a dark one. Even if it's a task you'd rather not do.' Damn it, but he needed to piss. Always did, at a time like this.

'True enough,' said the old man, smiling down into his mug. 'Things've got to get done.'

'That they do. Shame, though. You seem a nice enough set o' lads.' And the Dogman reached behind his back, just like he was scratching his arse.

'Shame?' The boy looked puzzled. 'How d'you mean a—'

That was when Dow came up behind him and cut his neck open.

Same moment, almost, Grim's dirty hand clamped down on One-Arm's mouth and the bloody point of a blade slid out the gap in his cloak. Dogman jumped forward and gave the old man three quick stabs in the ribs. He wheezed, and stumbled, eyes wide, mug still hanging from his hand, groggy drool spilling out his open mouth. Then he fell down.

The boy crawled a little way. He had one hand to his neck, trying to keep the blood in, the other reaching out towards the pole the warning bell was hung on. He had some bones, the Dogman reckoned, to be thinking of the bell with a slit

13

throat, but he didn't drag himself more'n a stride before Dow stomped down hard on the back of his neck and squashed him flat.

Dogman winced as he heard the boy's neck bones crunch. He hadn't deserved to die like that, most likely. But that's what war is. A lot of folk getting killed that don't deserve it. The job had needed doing, and they'd done it, and were all three still alive. About as much as he could've hoped for from a piece of work like that, but somehow it still left a sour taste on him. He'd never found it easy, but it was harder than ever, now he was chief. Strange, how it's that much easier to kill folk when you've got someone telling you to do it. Hard business, killing. Harder than you'd think.

Unless your name's Black Dow, of course. That bastard would kill a man as easy as he'd take a piss. That was what made him so damn good at it. Dogman watched him bend down, strip the cloak from One-Arm's limp body and pull it round his own shoulders, then roll the corpse off into the sea, careless as dumping rubbish.

'You got two arms,' said Grim, already with the old man's cloak on.

Dow looked down at himself. 'What're you saying exactly? I ain't cutting my arm off to make for a better disguise, y'idiot!'

'He means keep it out o' sight.' Dogman watched Dow wipe out a mug with a dirty finger, pour himself a slug and knock it back. 'How can you drink at a time like this?' he asked, pulling the boy's bloody cloak off his corpse.

Dow shrugged as he poured himself another. 'Shame to waste it. And like you said. Cold night.' He broke a nasty grin. 'Damn it, but you can talk, Dogman. Name's Cregg.' He took a couple of limping steps. 'Stabbed in me arse up at Dunbrec! Where d'you get it from?' He slapped Grim's shoulder with the back of his hand. 'Fucking lovely, eh? They got a word for it, don't they? What's that word, now?'

'Plausible,' said Grim.

Dow's eyes lit up. 'Plausible. That's what y'are, Dogman. You're one plausible bastard. I swear, you could've told 'em

14

you was Skarling Hoodless his own self and they'd have believed it. Don't know how you can keep a straight face!'

Dogman didn't feel too much like laughing. He didn't like looking at them two corpses, still laid out on the stones. Kept worrying that the boy'd get cold without his cloak. Damn fool thing to think about, given he was lying in a pool of his own blood a stride across.

'Never mind about that,' he grunted. 'Dump these two here and get over by the gate. Don't know when there'll be others coming.'

'Right y'are, chief, right y'are, whatever you say.' Dow heaved the two of them off into the water, then he unhooked the clapper from inside the bell and tossed that into the sea for good measure.

'Shame,' said Grim.

'What is?'

'Waste of a bell.'

Dow blinked at him. 'Waste of a bell, I swear! You got yourself a lot to say all of a sudden, and you know what? I think I liked you better before. Waste of a bell? You lost your mind, boy?'

Grim shrugged. 'Southerners might want one, when they get here.'

'They can fucking take a dive for the clapper then, can't they!' And Dow snatched up One-Arm's spear and strode over to the open gate, one hand stuffed inside his stolen cloak, grumbling to himself. 'Waste of a bell . . . by the fucking dead . . .'

The Dogman stretched up on his toes and unhooked the lamp, held it up, facing the sea, then he lifted one side of his cloak to cover it, brought it down again. Lifted it up, brought it down. One more time and he hooked it flickering back on the pole. Seemed a tiny little flame right then, to warm all their hopes at. A tiny little flame, to be seen all the way out there on the water, but the only one they had.

He was waiting all the time for the whole business to go wrong, for the clamour to go up in the town, for five dozen

Carls to come pouring out that open gate and give the three o' them the killing they deserved. He was bursting to piss, thinking about it. But they didn't come. No sound but the empty bell creaking on its pole, the cold waves slapping on stone and wood. It was just the way they'd planned it.

The first boat came gliding out the darkness, Shivers grinning in the prow. A score of Carls were pressed into the boat behind him, working the oars real careful, white faces tensed up, teeth gritted with the effort of keeping quiet. Still, every click and clank of wood and metal set the Dogman's nerves to jumping.

Shivers and his boys hung some sacks of straw over the side as they brought the boat in close, stopping the wood scraping on the stones, all thought out the week before. They tossed up ropes and Dogman and Grim caught 'em, dragged the boat up tight and tied it off. Dogman looked over at Dow, leaning still and easy against the wall by the gate, and he shook his head gently, to say no one was moving in the town. Then Shivers was up the steps, smooth and quiet, squatting down in the darkness.

'Nice work, chief,' he whispered, smiling right across his face. 'Nice and neat.'

'There'll be time to slap each others' backs later. Get the rest o' them boats tied off.'

'Right y'are.' There were more boats coming now, more Carls, more sacks of straw. Shivers' boys pulled them in, started dragging men up onto the quay. All kinds of men who'd come over the last few weeks. Men who didn't care for Bethod's new way of doing things. Soon there was a good crowd of 'em down by the water. So many Dogman could hardly believe they weren't seen.

They formed up into groups, just the way they'd planned, each one with their own chief and their own task. A couple of the lads knew Uffrith and they'd made a plan of the place in the dirt, the way Threetrees used to. Dogman had every one of 'em learn it. He grinned when he thought of how much Black Dow had carped about that, but it was worth it now. He squatted by the gate, and they came past, one dark and silent group at a time.

Tul was first up, a dozen Carls behind him. 'Alright, Thunderhead,' said Dogman, 'you got the main gate.'

'Aye,' nodded Tul.

'Biggest task o' the lot, so try and get it done quiet.'

'Quiet, you got it.'

'Luck then, Tul.'

'Won't need it.' And the giant hurried off into the dark streets with his crew behind.

'Red Hat, you got the tower by the well and the walls beside.'

'That I have.'

'Shivers, you and your boys are keeping a watch on the town square.'

'Like the owl watches, chief.'

And so on, past they went, through the gate and into the dark streets, making no more noise than the wind off the sea and the waves on the dock, Dogman giving each crew their task and slapping 'em off on their way. Black Dow came up last, and a hard-looking set of men he had behind him.

'Dow, you got the headman's hall. Stack it up with some wood, like we said, but don't set fire to it, you hear? Don't kill anyone you don't have to. Not yet.'

'Not yet, fair enough.'

'And Dow.' He turned back. 'Don't go bothering any womenfolk either.'

'What do you think I am?' he asked, teeth gleaming in the darkness. 'Some kind of an animal?'

And that was it done. There was just him and Grim, and a few others to watch the water. 'Uh,' said Grim, nodding his head slowly. That was high praise indeed from him.

Dogman pointed over at the pole. 'Get us that bell, would you?' he said. 'Might have a use for it after all.'

By the dead, but it made a sound. Dogman had to half close his eyes, his whole arm trembling as he whacked at the bell with the handle of his knife. He didn't feel too comfortable in amongst all those buildings, squashed in by walls and fences. He hadn't spent much time in towns in his life, and what he had spent he hadn't much enjoyed. Either burning things and causing mischief after a siege, or lying around in Bethod's prisons, waiting to be killed.

He blinked round at the jumble of slate roofs, the walls of old grey stone, black wood, dirty grey render, all greasy with the thin rain. Seemed a strange way to live, sleeping in a box, waking all your days in the exact same spot. The idea alone made him restless, as though that bell hadn't got him twitchy enough already. He cleared his throat and set it down on the cobbles beside him. Then he stood there waiting, one hand on the hilt of his sword in a way that he hoped meant business.

Some flapping footfalls came from down a street and a little girl ran out into the square. Her jaw dropped open when she saw them standing there, a dozen men all bearded and armed, Tul Duru in their midst. Probably she never saw a man half so big. She turned around sharp to run the other way, almost slipping over on the slick cobbles. Then she saw Dow sitting on a pile of wood just behind her, leaning back easy against the wall, his drawn sword on his knees, and she froze stone still.

'That's alright, girl,' growled Dow. 'You can stay where y'are.'

There were more of 'em coming now, hurrying down into the square from all around, all getting that same shocked look when they saw Dogman and his lads stood waiting. Women and boys, mostly, and a couple of old men. Dragged out o' their beds by the bell and still half asleep, eyes red and faces puffy, clothes tangled, armed with whatever was to hand. A boy with a butcher's cleaver. An old man all stooped over with a sword looked even older than he was. A girl at the front with a pitch-fork and a lot of messy dark hair had a look on her face reminded Dogman of Shari. Hard and thoughtful, the way she used to look at him before they started lying together. Dogman frowned down at her dirty bare feet, hoping that he wouldn't have to kill her.

Getting 'em good and scared would be the best way to get things done quick and easy. So Dogman tried to talk like someone to be feared, rather than someone who was shitting himself. Like Logen might've talked. Or maybe that was more fear than was needful. Like Threetrees, then. Tough but fair, wanting what was best for everyone.

'The headman among you?' he growled.

'I'm him,' croaked the old man with the sword, his face all slack with shock at finding a score of well-armed strangers standing in the middle of his town square. 'Brass is my name. Who the hell might you be?'

'I'm the Dogman, and this here is Harding Grim, and the big lad is Tul Duru Thunderhead.' Some eyes went wide, some folk muttered to each other. Seemed they'd heard the names before. 'We're here with five hundred Carls and last night we took your city off you.' A few gasps and squeals at that. It was closer to two hundred, but there was no point telling 'em so. They might've got the notion that fighting was a good idea and he'd no wish to end up stabbing a woman, or getting stabbed by one either. 'There's plenty more of us, round about, and your guards are all trussed up, those we didn't have to kill. Some o' my boys, and you ought to know I'm talking of Black Dow—'

'That's me.' Dow flashed his nasty grin, and a few folk shuffled fearfully away from him like they'd been told hell itself was sat there.

'. . . Well, they were for putting the torch straight to your houses and getting some killing done. Do things like we used to with the Bloody-Nine in charge, you take my meaning?' Some child in amongst the rest started to cry a bit, a wet kind of snuffling. The boy stared round him, cleaver wobbling in his hand, the dark-haired girl blinked and clung on tighter to her pitch-fork. They got the gist, alright. 'But I thought I'd give you a fair chance to give up, being as the town's full with womenfolk and children and all the rest. My score's with Bethod, not with you people. The Union want to use this place as a port, bring in men and supplies and whatever.

They'll be here inside an hour, in their ships. A lot of 'em. It's happening with or without your say so. I guess my point is we can do this the bloody way, if that's the way you want it. The dead know we've had the practice. Or you can give up your weapons, if you've got 'em, and we can all get along, nice and . . . what's the word for it?'

'Civilised,' said Grim.

'Aye. Civilised. What d'you say?'

The old man fingered his sword, looking like he'd rather have leant on it than swung it, and he stared up at the walls, where a few of the Carls were looking down, and his shoulders slumped. 'Looks like you got us cold. The Dogman, eh? I always heard you was a clever bastard. No one much left here to fight you, anyway. Bethod took every man could hold a spear and a shield at once.' He looked round at the sorry crowd behind him. 'Will you leave the women be?'

'We'll leave 'em be.'

'Those that want to be left be,' said Dow, leering at the girl with the pitch-fork.

'We'll leave 'em be,' growled Dogman, giving him a hard look. 'I'll see to it.'

'Well then,' wheezed the old man, shuffling up and wincing as he knelt and dropped his rusty blade at Dogman's feet. 'You're a better man than Bethod, far as I'm concerned. I suppose I ought to be thanking you for your mercy, if you keep your word.'

'Uh.' Dogman didn't feel too merciful. He doubted the old boy he'd killed on the dock would be thanking him, or the one-armed man stabbed through from behind, or the lad with the cut throat who'd had his whole life stolen.

One by one the rest of the crowd came forward, and one by one the weapons, if you could call 'em that, got dropped in a heap. A pile of old rusty tools and junk. The boy came up last and let his cleaver clatter down with the rest, gave a scared look at Black Dow, then hurried back to the others and clung to the dark-haired girl's hand.

They stood there, in a wide-eyed huddle, and Dogman

could almost smell their fear. They were waiting for Dow and his Carls to set to hacking 'em down where they stood. They were waiting to get herded in a house and locked in and the place set fire to. Dogman had seen all that before. So he didn't blame 'em one bit as they all crowded together like sheep pressed up in a field in winter. He'd have done the same.

'Alright!' he barked. 'That's it! Back to your houses, or whatever. Union'll be here before midday, and it'd be better if the streets were empty.'

They blinked at Dogman, and at Tul, and at Black Dow, and at each other. They swallowed and trembled, and muttered their thanks to the dead. They broke up, slowly, and spread out, and went off their own ways. Alive, to everyone's great relief.

'Nicely done, chief,' said Tul in Dogman's ear. 'Threetrees himself couldn't have done it no better.'

Dow sidled up from the other side. 'About the women, though, if you're asking my opinion—'

'I'm not,' said Dogman.

'Have you seen my son?' There was one woman who wasn't going home. She was coming up from one man to another, half-tears in her eyes and her face all wild from worry. The Dogman put his head down and looked the other way. 'My son, he was on guard, down by the water! You seen him?' She tugged at Dogman's coat, her voice cracked and wet-sounding. 'Please, where's my son?'

'You think I know where everyone's at?' he snapped in her weepy face. He strode away like he had a load of important stuff to do, and all the while he was thinking – you're a coward, Dogman, you're a bastard bloody coward. Some hero, pulling a neat trick on a bunch of women, and children, and old men.

It ain't easy, being chief.

This Noble Business

The great moat had been drained early in the siege, leaving behind a wide ditch full of black mud. At the far end of the bridge across it four soldiers worked by a cart, dragging corpses to the bank and rolling them flopping down to the bottom. The corpses of the last defenders, gashed and burned, spattered with blood and dirt. Wild men, from past the River Crinna far to the east, tangle-haired and bearded. Their limp bodies seemed pitifully withered after three months sealed up behind the walls of Dunbrec, pitifully starved. Scarcely human. It was hard for West to take much joy in the victory over such sorry creatures as these.

'Seems a shame,' muttered Jalenhorm, 'after they fought so bravely. To end like that.'

West watched another ragged corpse slither down the bank and into the tangled heap of muddy limbs. 'This is how most sieges end. Especially for the brave. They'll be buried down there in the muck, then the moat will be flooded again. The waters of the Whiteflow will surge over them, and their bravery, or lack of it, will have meant nothing.'

The fortress of Dunbrec loomed over the two officers as they crossed the bridge, black outlines of walls and towers like great, stark holes in the heavy white sky. A few ragged birds circled above. A couple more croaked from the scarred battlements.

It had taken General Kroy's men a month to make this same journey, bloodily repulsed time and again, and to finally break through the heavy doors under a steady rain of arrows, stones, and boiling water. Another week of claustrophobic slaughter to force the dozen strides down the tunnel beyond, to burst through the second gate with axe and fire and finally seize control of the outer wall. Every advantage had lain with the defenders. The place had been most carefully designed to ensure that it was so.

And once they had made it through the gatehouse, their problems were only just beginning. The inner wall was twice the height and thickness of the outer, dominating its walkways at every point. There had been no shelter from missiles from the six monstrous towers.

To conquer that second wall Kroy's men had tried every strategy in the manual of siege. They had worked with pick and crowbar, but the masonry was five strides thick at the base. They had made an effort at a mine but the ground was waterlogged outside the fortress and solid Angland rock beneath. They had bombarded the place with catapults, but scarcely scratched the mighty bastions. They had come with scaling ladders, again and again, in waves and in parties, by surprise at night or brazenly in the day, and in the darkness and the light the straggling lines of Union wounded had shuffled away from their failed attempts, the dead dragged solemnly behind. They had finally tried reasoning with the wild defenders, through the medium of a Northern translator, and the unfortunate man had been pelted with night soil.

It had been pure fortune, in the end. After studying the movements of the guards, one enterprising sergeant had tried his luck with a grapple under cover of night. He had climbed up and a dozen other brave men had followed him. They took the defenders by surprise, killed several of them and seized the gatehouse. The whole effort took ten minutes and cost one Union life. It was a fitting irony, to West's mind, that having tried every roundabout method and been bloodily repulsed, the Union army had finally entered the inner fortress by its open front gate.

A soldier was bent over near that archway now, being noisily sick onto the stained flagstones. West passed him with some foreboding, the sound of his clicking boot heels echoing around the long tunnel, and emerged into the wide courtyard at the centre of the fortress. It was a regular hexagon, echoing the shape of the inner and outer walls, all part of the perfectly symmetrical design. West doubted that the architects would have approved, however, of the state in which the Northmen had left the place.

A long wooden building at one side of the yard, perhaps a stables, had caught fire in the attack and was now reduced to a mass of charred beams, the embers still glowing. Those clearing away the mess had too much work outside the walls, and the ground was still scattered with fallen weapons and tangled corpses. The Union dead had been stretched out in rows near one corner and covered up with blankets. The Northmen lay in every attitude, on their faces or on their backs, curled up or stretched out where they fell. Beneath the bodies the stone flags were deeply scored, and not just with the random damage of a three-month siege. A great circle had been chiselled from the rock, and other circles within it, strange marks and symbols laid out in an intricate design. West did not care for its look in the least. Worse still, he was becoming aware of a repulsive stench to the place, more pungent even than the tang of burned wood.

'What ever is that smell?' muttered Jalenhorm, putting one hand over his mouth.

A sergeant nearby overheard him. 'Seems that our Northern friends chose to decorate the place.' He pointed up above their heads, and West followed the gauntleted finger with his eyes.

They were so decayed that it took him a moment to realise he was looking at the remains of men. They had been nailed, spread-eagled, to the inside walls of each of the towers, high above the lean-to buildings round the courtyard. Rotting offal hung down from their bellies, crawling with flies. Cut with the Bloody Cross, as the Northmen would say. Tattered shreds of brightly-coloured Union uniforms were still vaguely visible, fluttering in the breeze among the masses of putrefying flesh.

Clearly they had been hanging there some time. Since before the siege began, certainly. Perhaps since the fortress first fell to the Northmen. Corpses of the original defenders, nailed there, rotting, for all those months. Three appeared to be without their heads. The companion pieces, perhaps, to those three gifts that had been sent to Marshal Burr all that time ago. West found himself wondering, pointlessly, whether any of them had been alive when they were nailed up. Spit rushed into his mouth, the sound of flies buzzing seeming suddenly, sickeningly loud.

Jalenhorm had gone pale as a ghost. He did not say anything. He did not have to. 'What happened here?' muttered West through his gritted teeth, as much to himself as anything.

'Well, sir, we think they were hoping to get help.' The sergeant grinned at him, clearly possessed of a very strong stomach. 'Help from some unfriendly gods, we've been guessing. Seems that no one was listening down below though, eh?'

West frowned at the ragged markings on the ground. 'Get rid of them! Tear up the flags and replace them if you have to.' His eyes strayed to the decaying cadavers above, and he felt his stomach give a painful squeeze. 'And offer a ten-mark bounty to the man with guts enough to climb up there and cut those corpses down.'

'Ten marks, sir? Bring me over that ladder!'

West turned and strode out through the open gates of the fortress of Dunbrec, holding his breath and hoping like hell that he never had occasion to visit the place again. He knew that he would be back, though. If only in his dreams.

Briefings with Poulder and Kroy were more than enough to sicken the healthiest of men, and Lord Marshal Burr was by no means in that category. The commander of His Majesty's armies in Angland was as pitifully shrunken as the defenders of Dunbrec had been, his simple uniform hanging loose around him while his pale skin seemed stretched too tight over the bones. In a dozen short weeks he had aged as many years. His hand shook, his lip trembled, he could not stand for long, and could not ride at all. From time to time he would grimace and shiver as though he was racked by unseen pangs. West hardly knew how he was able to carry on, but carry on he did, fourteen hours a day and more. He attended to his duties with all his old diligence. Only now they seemed to eat him up, piece by piece.

Burr frowned grimly up at the great map of the border region, his hands resting on his belly. The Whiteflow was a winding blue line down the middle, Dunbrec a black hexagon marked in swirly script. On its left, the Union. On its right, the North. 'So,' he croaked, then coughed and cleared his throat, 'the fortress is back in our hands.'

General Kroy gave a stiff nod. 'It is.'

'Finally,' observed Poulder under his breath. The two generals still appeared to regard Bethod and his Northmen as a minor distraction from the real enemy; each other.

Kroy bristled, his staff muttering around him like a flock of angry crows. 'Dunbrec was designed by the Union's foremost military architects, and no expense was spared in its construction! Capturing it has been no mean task!'

'Of course, of course,' growled Burr, doing his best to mount a diversion. 'Damned difficult place to take. Do we have any notion of how the Northmen managed it?'

'None survived to tell us what trickery they employed, sir. They fought, without exception, to the death. The last few barricaded themselves in the stables and set fire to the structure.'

Burr glanced at West, and slowly shook his head. 'How can one understand such an enemy? What is the condition of the fortress now?'

'The moat was drained, the outer gatehouse partly destroyed, considerable damage done to the inner wall. The defenders tore down some buildings for wood to burn and stones to throw and left the rest in . . .' Kroy worked his lips as though struggling to find the words. 'A very poor condition. Repairs will take some weeks.'

'Huh.' Burr rubbed unhappily at his stomach. 'The Closed Council are anxious that we cross the Whiteflow into the North as soon as possible, and take the fight to the enemy. Positive news for the restless populace, and so on.'

'The capture of Uffrith,' leaped in Poulder, with a grin of

towering smugness, 'has left our position far stronger. We have gained at a stroke one of the best ports in the North, perfectly situated to supply our forces as we push into enemy territory. Before, everything had to come the length of Angland by cart, over bad roads in bad weather. Now we can bring in supplies and reinforcements by ship and almost straight to the front! And the whole thing managed without a single casualty!'

West was not about to allow him to steal the credit for that. 'Absolutely,' he droned in an emotionless monotone. 'Our northern allies have once again proved invaluable.'

Poulder's red-jacketed staff frowned and grumbled. 'They played a part,' the General was forced to admit.

'Their leader, the Dogman, came to us with the original plan, executed it himself using his own men, and delivered the town to you, its gates open and its people compliant. That was my understanding.'

Poulder frowned angrily across at Kroy, who was now allowing himself the very thinnest of smiles. 'My men are in possession of the city and are already building up a stockpile of supplies! We have outflanked the enemy and forced him to fall back towards Carleon! That, Colonel West, is surely the issue here, and not precisely who did what!'

'Indeed!' cut in Burr, waving one big hand. 'You have both done great services for your country. But we must now look forward to future successes. General Kroy, arrange for work parties to be left behind to complete the repairs to Dunbrec, and a regiment of levies to man the defences. With a commander that knows his business, please. It would be embarrassing, to say the least, if we were to lose the fortress for a second time.'

'There will be no mistake,' snarled Kroy at Poulder, 'you can depend on it.'

'The rest of the army can cross the Whiteflow and form up on the far bank. Then we can begin to press east and northward, towards Carleon, using the harbour at Uffrith to bring in our supplies. We have driven the enemy out of Angland. Now we must press forward and grind Bethod to his knees.' And the

27

Marshal twisted a heavy fist into his palm by way of demonstration.

'My division will be across the river by tomorrow evening,' hissed Poulder at Kroy, 'and in good order!'

Burr grimaced. 'We must move carefully, whatever the Closed Council say. The last time a Union army crossed the Whiteflow was when King Casamir invaded the North. I need hardly remind you that he was forced to withdraw in some disarray. Bethod has caught us out before, and will only grow stronger as he falls back into his own territory. We must work together. This is not a competition, gentlemen.'

The two generals immediately competed with each other to be the one to agree most. West gave a long sigh, and rubbed at the bridge of his nose.

The New Man

'**A**nd so we return.' Bayaz frowned towards the city: a bright, white crescent spread out around the glittering bay. Slowly but decisively it came closer, reaching out and wrapping Jezal in its welcoming embrace. The features grew distinct, green parks peeping out between the houses, white spires thrusting up from the mass of buildings. He could see the towering walls of the Agriont, sunlight glinting from burnished domes above. The House of the Maker loomed high over all, but even that forbidding mass now seemed, somehow, to speak of warmth and safety.

He was home. He had survived. It felt like a hundred years since he had stood at the stern of a not dissimilar ship, miserable and forlorn, watching Adua slide sadly away into the distance. Over the surging water, the snapping sailcloth, the cries of the seabirds, he began to distinguish the distant rumble of the city. It sounded like the most wonderful music he had ever heard. He closed his eyes and dragged the air in hard through his nostrils. The rotten salt tang of the bay was sweet as honey on his tongue.

'One takes it you enjoyed the trip, then, Captain?' asked Bayaz, with heavy irony.

Jezal could only grin. 'I'm enjoying the end of it.'

'No need to be downhearted,' offered Brother Longfoot. 'Sometimes a difficult journey does not deliver its full benefit until long after one returns. The trials are brief, but the wisdom gained lasts a lifetime!'

'Huh.' The First of the Magi curled his lip. 'Travel brings wisdom only to the wise. It renders the ignorant more ignorant than ever. Master Ninefingers! Are you determined to return to the North?'

Logen took a brief break from frowning at the water. 'I've got no reason to stay.' He glanced sideways at Ferro, and she glared back.

'Why look at me?'

Logen shook his head. 'Do you know what? I've no fucking idea.' If there had been anything vaguely resembling a romance between them, it appeared now to have collapsed irreparably into a sullen dislike.

'Well,' said Bayaz, raising his brows, 'if you are decided.' He held his hand out to the Northman and Jezal watched them shake. 'Give Bethod a kick from me, once you have him under your boot.'

'That I will, unless he gets me under his.'

'Never easy, kicking upwards. My thanks for your help, and for your manners. Perhaps you will be my guest again, one day, at the library. We will look out at the lake, and laugh about our high adventures in the west of the World.'

'I'll hope for it.' But Logen hardly looked as if there was much laughter in him, or much hope either. He looked like a man who had run out of choices.

In silence Jezal watched as the ropes were thrown down to the quay and made fast, the long gangplank squealed out to the shore and scraped onto the stones. Bayaz called out to his apprentice. 'Master Quai! Time for us to disembark!' And the pale young man followed his master down from the ship without a backward glance, Brother Longfoot behind them.

'Good luck, then,' said Jezal, offering his hand to Logen.

'And to you.' The Northman grinned, ignored the hand and folded him in a tight and unpleasant-smelling embrace. They stayed there for a somewhat touching, somewhat embarrassing moment, then Ninefingers clapped him on the back and let him go.

'Perhaps I'll see you, up there in the North.' Jezal's voice was just the slightest bit cracked, in spite of all his efforts. 'If they send me . . .'

'Maybe, but . . . I think I'll hope not. Like I said, if I was you I'd find a good woman and leave the killing to those with less sense.'

'Like you?'

'Aye. Like me.' He looked over at Ferro. 'So that's it then, eh, Ferro?'

'Uh.' She shrugged her scrawny shoulders, and strode off down the gangplank.

Logen's face twitched at that. 'Right,' he muttered at her back. 'Nice knowing you.' He waggled the stump of his missing finger at Jezal. 'Say one thing for Logen Ninefingers, say he's got a touch with the women.'

'Mmm.'

'Aye.'

'Right.' Jezal was finding actually leaving strangely difficult. They had been almost constant companions for the last six months. To begin with he had felt nothing but contempt for the man, but now that it came to it, it was like leaving a much-respected older brother. Far worse, in fact, for Jezal had never thought too highly of his actual brothers. So he dithered on the deck, and Logen grinned at him as though he guessed just what he was thinking.

'Don't worry. I'll try to get along without you.'

Jezal managed half a smile. 'Just try to remember what I told you, if you get in another fight.'

'I'd say, unfortunately, that's pretty much a certainty.'

Then there was really nothing Jezal could do but turn away and clatter down to the shore, pretending that something had blown into his eye on the way. It seemed a long walk to the busy quay, to stand next to Bayaz and Quai, Longfoot and Ferro.

'Master Ninefingers can look after himself, I daresay,' said the First of the Magi.

'Oh, yes indeed,' chuckled Longfoot, 'few better!'

Jezal took a last look back over his shoulder as they headed off into the city. Logen raised one hand to him from the rail of the ship, and then the corner of a warehouse came between them, and he was gone. Ferro loitered for a moment, frowning back towards the sea, her fists clenched and a muscle working on the side of her head. Then she turned and saw Jezal watching her.

'What are you looking at?' And she pushed past him and followed the others, into the swarming streets of Adua.

The city was just as Jezal remembered it, and yet everything was different. The buildings seemed to have shrunk and huddled in meanly together. Even the wide Middleway, the great central artery of the city, felt horribly squashed after the huge open spaces of the Old Empire, the awe-inspiring vistas of ruined Aulcus. The sky had been higher, out there on the great plain. Here everything was reduced, and, to make matters worse, had an unpleasant smell he had never before noticed. He went with his nose wrinkled, dodging between the buffeting flow of passers-by with bad grace.

It was the people that were strangest of all. It had been months since Jezal had seen more than ten at one time. Now there were suddenly thousands pressed in all around him, furiously intent on their own doings. Soft, and scrubbed, and decked out in gaudy colours, as freakish to him now as circus performers. Fashions had moved on while he was away facing death in the barren west of the World. Hats were worn at a different angle, sleeves had swollen to a wider cut, shirt collars had shrivelled to a length that would have been thought preposterously short a year before. Jezal snorted to himself. It seemed bizarre that such nonsense could ever have interested him, and he watched a group of perfumed dandies strutting past with the highest contempt.

Their group dwindled as they passed on through the city. First Longfoot made his effusive farewells with much pressing of hands, talk of honours and privileges, and promises of reunion that Jezal suspected, and indeed rather hoped, were insincere. Near the great market square of the Four Corners, Quai was dispatched on some errand or other with all his habitual sullen silence. That left only the First of the Magi as a companion, with Ferro slouching angrily along behind.

Being honest, Jezal would not have minded had the group

dwindled considerably further. Ninefingers might have proved himself a staunch companion, but the rest of the dysfunctional family would hardly have been among Jezal's chosen dinner guests. He had long ago given up any hope that Ferro's armour of scowls would crack to reveal a caring soul within. But at least her abysmal temper was predictable. Bayaz, if anything, was an even more unnerving companion: one half grandfatherly good humour, the other half who knew what? Whenever the old man opened his mouth Jezal flinched in anticipation of some ugly surprise.

But he chatted pleasantly enough for the time being. 'Might I ask what your plans are now, Captain Luthar?'

'Well, I suppose I will be sent to England, to fight against the Northmen.'

'I imagine so. Although we never know what turns fate may take.'

Jezal did not much care for the sound of that. 'And you? Will you be going back to . . .' He realised he had not the slightest idea of where the Magus had appeared from in the first place.

'Not quite yet. I will remain in Adua for the moment. Great things are afoot, my boy, great things. Perhaps I will stay to see how they turn out.'

'Move, bitch!' came a yell from the side of the road.

Three members of the city watch had gathered round a dirty-faced girl in a tattered dress. One was leaning down over her with a stick clenched in his fist, shouting in her face while she cringed back. An unhappy-seeming press had gathered to watch, workmen and labourers mostly, scarcely cleaner than the beggar herself.

'Why don't you let her be?' one grumbled.

One of the watchmen took a warning step at them, raising his stick, while his friend seized hold of the beggar by her shoulder, kicking over a cup in the road, sending a few coins tinkling into the gutter.

'That seems excessive,' said Jezal under his breath.

'Well,' Bayaz watched down his nose, 'these sort of things

happen all the time. Are you telling me you've never seen a beggar moved along before?'

Jezal had, of course, often, and never raised an eyebrow. Beggars could not simply be left to clutter up the streets, after all. And yet for some reason the process was making him uncomfortable. The unfortunate waif kicked and cried, and the guardsman dragged her another stride on her back with entirely unnecessary violence, clearly enjoying himself. It was not so much the act itself that Jezal objected to, as that they would do it in front of him without a thought for his feelings. It rendered him somehow complicit.

'That is a disgrace,' he hissed through gritted teeth.

Bayaz shrugged. 'If it bothers you that much, why not do something about it?'

The watchman chose that moment to seize the girl by her scruffy hair and give her a sharp blow with his stick, and she squealed and fell, her arms over her head. Jezal felt his face twist. In a moment he had shoved through the crowd and dealt the man a resounding boot to his backside, sending him sprawling in the gutter. One of his companions came forward with his stick out, but stumbled back a moment later. Jezal realised he had his steels drawn, the polished blades glinting in the shadows beside the building.

The audience gasped and edged back. Jezal blinked. He had not intended the business to go anything like this far. Damn Bayaz and his idiotic advice. But there was nothing for it now but to carry it through. He assumed his most fearless and arrogant expression.

'One step further and I'll stick you like the swine you are.' He looked from one of the watchmen to the other. 'Well? Do any of you care to test me?' He earnestly hoped that none of them did, but he need not have worried. They were predictably cowardly in the face of determined resistance, and loitered just out of range of his steels.

'No one deals with the watch like that. We'll find you, you can depend on—'

'Finding me will present no difficulty. My name is Captain

Luthar, of the King's Own. I am resident in the Agriont. You cannot miss it. It is the fortress that dominates the city!' And he jabbed up the street with his long steel, making one of the watchmen stumble away in fear. 'I will receive you at your convenience and you can explain to my patron, Lord Marshal Varuz, your disgraceful behaviour towards this woman, a citizen of the Union guilty of no greater crime than being poor!'

A ludicrously overblown speech, of course. Jezal found himself almost flushing with embarrassment at that last part. He had always despised poor people, and he was far from sure his opinions had fundamentally changed, but he got carried away halfway through and had no choice but to finish with a flourish.

Still, his words had their effect on the city watch. The three men backed away, for some reason grinning as if the whole business had gone just as they planned, leaving Jezal to the unwanted approval of the crowd.

'Well done, lad!'

'Good thing someone's got some guts.'

'What did he say his name was?'

'Captain Luthar!' roared Bayaz suddenly, causing Jezal to jerk round halfway through sheathing his steels. 'Captain Jezal dan Luthar, the winner of last year's Contest, just now returned from his adventures in the west! Luthar, the name!'

'Luthar, did he say?'

'The one who won the Contest?'

'That's him! I saw him beat Gorst!'

The whole crowd was staring, wide-eyed and respectful. One of them reached out, as though to touch the hem of his coat, and Jezal stumbled backwards, almost tripping over the beggar-girl who had been the cause of the whole fiasco.

'Thank you,' she gushed, in an ugly commoner's accent rendered still less appealing by her bloody mouth. 'Oh, thank you, sir.'

'It was nothing.' Jezal edged away, deeply uncomfortable. She was extremely dirty, at close quarters, and he had no wish

35

to contract an illness. The attention of the group as a whole was, in fact, anything but pleasant. He continued to shuffle backwards while they watched him, all smiles and admiring mutterings.

Ferro was frowning at him as they moved away from the Four Corners. 'Is there something?' he snapped.

She shrugged. 'You're not as much of a coward as you were.'

'My thanks for that epic praise.' He rounded on Bayaz. 'What the hell was that?'

'That was you carrying out a charitable act, my boy, and I was proud to see it. It would seem my lessons have not been entirely wasted on you.'

'I meant,' growled Jezal, who felt himself to have gained less than nothing from Bayaz' constant lecturing, 'what were you about, proclaiming my name to all and sundry? The story will now spread all over town!'

'I had not considered that.' The Magus gave a faint smile. 'I simply felt that you deserved the credit for your noble actions. Helping those less fortunate, the aid of a lady in distress, protecting the weak and so forth. Admirable, truly.'

'But—' muttered Jezal, unsure whether he was being taken for a fool.

'Here our paths diverge, my young friend.'

'Oh. They do?'

'Where are you going?' snapped Ferro suspiciously.

'I have a few matters to attend to,' said the Magus, 'and you will be coming with me.'

'Why would I do that?' She appeared to be in a worse mood even than usual since they left the docks, which was no mean achievement.

Bayaz' eyes rolled to the sky. 'Because you lack the social graces necessary to function for longer than five minutes on your own in such a place as this. Why else? You will be going back to the Agriont, I assume?' he asked Jezal.

'Yes. Yes, of course.'

'Well, then. I would like to thank you, Captain Luthar, for the part you played in that little adventure of ours.'

'How dare you, you magical arsehole? The entire business was a colossal, painful, disfiguring waste of my time, and a failure to boot.' But what Jezal really said was, 'Of course, yes.' He took the old man's hand, preparing to give it a limp shake. 'It has been an honour.'

Bayaz' grip was shockingly firm. 'That is good to hear.' Jezal found himself drawn very close to the old man's face, staring into his glittering green eyes at unnervingly close quarters. 'We may have the need to collaborate again.'

Jezal blinked. Collaborate really was an ugly choice of word. 'Well then . . . er . . . perhaps I will . . . see you later?' Never would have been preferable, in his opinion.

But Bayaz only grinned as he let go of Jezal's buzzing fingers. 'Oh, I feel sure we shall meet again.'

The sun shone pleasantly through the branches of the aromatic cedar, casting a dappled shade on the ground beneath, just as it used to. A pleasant breeze fluttered through the courtyard and the birds twittered in the branches of the trees, just as they always had. The old buildings of the barracks had not changed, crowding in, coated with rustling ivy on all sides of the narrow courtyard. But there the similarity to Jezal's happy memories ended. A dusting of moss had crept up the legs of the chairs, the surface of the table had acquired a thick crust of bird droppings, the grass had gone unclipped for weeks on end and seed-heads thrashed at Jezal's calves as he wandered past.

The players themselves were long gone. He watched the shadows shifting on the grey wood, remembering the sound of their laughter, the taste of smoke and strong spirits, the feel of the cards in his hand. Here Jalenhorm had sat, playing at being tough and manly. Here Kaspa had laughed at jokes at his own expense. Here West had leaned back and shaken his head with resigned disapproval. Here Brint had shuffled nervously at his hand, hoping for big wins that never came.

And here had been Jezal's place. He dragged the chair out from the clutching grass, sat down in it with one boot up on the table and rocked it onto its rear legs. It seemed hard to believe, now, that he had sat here, watching and scheming, thinking about how best to make his friends seem small. He told himself he would never have engaged in any such foolishness now. No more than a couple of hands, anyway.

If he had thought that a thorough wash, a careful shave, a plucking of bristles and a long-winded arranging of hair would make him feel at home, he was disappointed. The familiar routines left him feeling like a stranger in his own dusty rooms. It was hard to become excited over the shining of the boots and buttons, or the arrangement of the gold braid just so.

When he finally stood before the mirror, where long ago he had whiled away so many delightful hours, he found his reflection decidedly unnerving. A lean and weather-worn adventurer stared bright-eyed from the Visserine glass, his sandy beard doing little to disguise the ugly scar down his bent jaw. His old uniforms were all unpleasantly tight, scratchily starched, chokingly constricted round the collar. He no longer felt like he belonged in them to any degree. He no longer felt like a soldier.

He scarcely even knew who he should report to, after all this time away. Every officer he was aware of, more or less, was with the army in Angland. He supposed he could have sought out Lord Marshal Varuz, had he really wanted to, but the fact was he had learned enough about danger now to not want to rush at it. He would do his duty, if he was asked. But it would have to find him first.

In the meantime, he had other business to attend to. The very thought made him terrified and thrilled at once, and he pushed a finger inside his collar and tugged at it in an effort to relieve the pressure in his throat. It did not work. Still, as Logen Ninefingers had been so very fond of saying: it was better to do it, than to live with the fear of it. He picked up his dress sword, but after a minute of staring at the absurd brass scrollwork on the hilt, he tossed it on the floor and kicked it under his bed. Look less than you are, Logen would have said. He retrieved his travel-worn long steel and slid it through the clasp on his belt, took a deep breath, and walked to the door.

*

There was nothing intimidating about the street. It was a quiet part of town, far off from chattering commerce and rumbling industry. In the next road a knife sharpener was throatily proclaiming his trade. Under the eaves of the modest houses a pigeon coo-cooed half-heartedly. Somewhere nearby the sound of clopping hooves and crackling carriage-wheels rose and faded. Otherwise all was quiet.

He had already walked past the house once in each direction, and dared not do so again for fear that Ardee would see him through a window, recognise him, and wonder what the hell he was up to. So he made circuits of the upper part of the street, practising what he would say when she appeared at the door.

'I am returned.' No, no, too high-blown. 'Hello, how are you?' No, too casual. 'It's me, Luthar.' Too stiff. 'Ardee . . . I've missed you.' Too needy. He saw a man frowning at him from an upstairs window, and he coughed and made off quickly towards the house, murmuring to himself over and over. 'Better to do it, better to do it, better to do it . . .'

His fist pounded against the wood. He stood and waited, heart thumping in his teeth. The latch clicked and Jezal put on his most ingratiating smile. The door opened and a short, round-faced and highly unattractive girl stared at him from the doorway. There could be no doubt, however things had changed, that she was not Ardee. 'Yes?'

'Er . . .' A servant. How could he have been such a fool as to think Ardee would open her own front door? She was a commoner, not a beggar. He cleared his throat. 'I am returned . . . I mean to say . . . does Ardee West live here?'

'She does.' The maid opened the door far enough for Jezal to step through into the dim hallway. 'Who shall I say is calling?'

'Captain Luthar.'

Her head snapped round as though it had an invisible string attached to it and he had given it a sudden jerk. 'Captain . . . Jezal dan Luthar?'

'Yes,' he muttered, mystified. Could Ardee have been discussing him with the help?

39

'Oh . . . oh, if you wait . . .' The maid pointed to a doorway and hurried off, eyes wide, quite as if the Emperor of Gurkhul had come calling.

The dim living room gave the impression of having been decorated by someone with too much money, too little taste, and not nearly enough space for their ambitions. There were several garishly upholstered chairs, an over-sized and over-decorated cabinet, and a monumental canvas on one wall which, had it been any bigger, would have required the room to be knocked through into the neighbouring house. Two dusty shafts of light came in through the gaps in the curtains, gleaming on the highly polished, if slightly wonky, surface of an antique table. Each piece might have passed muster on its own, but crowded together the effect was quite suffocating. Still, Jezal told himself as he frowned round at it all, he had come for Ardee, not for her furniture.

It was ridiculous. His knees were weak, his mouth was dry, his head was spinning, and with every moment that passed it got worse. He had not felt this scared in Aulcus, with a crowd of screaming Shanka bearing down on him. He took a nervous circuit of the room, fists clenching and unclenching. He peered out into the quiet street. He leaned over a chair to examine the massive painting. A muscular-seeming king lounged in an outsize crown while fur-trimmed lords bowed and scraped around his feet. Harod the Great, Jezal guessed, but the recognition brought him little joy. Bayaz' favourite and most tiresome topic of conversation had been the achievements of that man. Harod the Great could be pickled in vinegar for all Jezal cared. Harod the Great could go—

'Well, well, well . . .'

She stood in the doorway, bright light from the hall beyond glowing in her dark hair and down the edges of her white dress, her head on one side and the faintest ghost of a smile on her shadowy face. She seemed hardly to have changed. So often in life, moments that are long anticipated turn out to be profound disappointments. Seeing Ardee again, after all that time apart, was undoubtedly an exception. All his carefully prepared conversation evaporated in that one instant, leaving him as empty-headed as he had been when he first laid eyes on her.

'You're alive, then,' she murmured.

'Yes . . . er . . . just about.' He managed half an awkward smile. 'Did you think I was dead?'

'I hoped you were.' That wiped the grin off his face with sharp effect. 'When I didn't get so much as a letter. But really I thought you'd just forgotten about me.'

Jezal winced. 'I'm sorry I didn't write. Very sorry. I wanted to . . .' She swung the door shut and leaned against it with her hands behind her, frowning at him all the while. 'There wasn't a day I didn't want to. But I was called for, and never had the chance to tell anyone, not even my family. I was . . . I was far away, in the west.'

'I know you were. The whole city is buzzing with it, and if I've heard, it must be common knowledge indeed.'

'You've heard?'

Ardee jerked her head towards the hall. 'I had it from the maid.'

'From the maid?' How the hell could anyone in Adua have heard anything about his misadventures, let alone Ardee West's maid? He was assailed with sudden unpleasing images. Crowds of servants giggling at the thought of him lying around crying over his broken face. Everyone who was anyone gossiping about what a fool he must have looked being fed with a spoon by a scarred brute of a Northman. He felt himself blushing to the tips of his ears. 'What did she say?'

'Oh, you know.' She wandered absently into the room. 'That you scaled the walls at the siege of Darmium, was it? Opened the gates to the Emperor's men and so on.'

'What?' He was even more baffled than before. 'Darmium? I mean to say . . . who told her . . .'

She came closer, and closer, and he grew more and more flustered until he stammered to a stop. Closer yet, and she was looking slightly upwards into his face with her lips parted. So close that he was sure she was going to take him in her arms and kiss him. So close that he leaned forward slightly in

41

anticipation, half-closing his eyes, his lips tingling . . . Then she passed him, her hair nearly flicking in his face, and went on to the cabinet, opening it and taking out a decanter, leaving him behind, marooned on the carpet.

In gormless silence he watched her fill two glasses and offer one out, wine slopping and trickling stickily down the side. 'You've changed.' Jezal felt a sudden surge of shame and his hand jerked up to cover his scarred jaw on an instinct. 'I don't mean that. Not just that, anyway. Everything. You're different, somehow.'

'I . . .' The effect she had on him was, if anything, stronger now than it used to be. Then there had not been all the weight of expectation, all the long day-dreaming and anticipation out in the wilderness. 'I've missed you.' He said it without thinking, then found himself flushing and had to try and change the subject. 'Have you heard from your brother?'

'He's been writing every week.' She threw her head back and drained her glass, started to fill it again. 'Ever since I found out he was still alive, anyway.'

'What?'

'I thought he was dead, for a month or more. He only just escaped from the battle.'

'There was a battle?' squeaked Jezal, just before remembering there was a war on. Of course there had been battles. He brought his voice back under control. 'What battle?'

'The one where Prince Ladisla was killed.'

'Ladisla's dead?' he squealed, voice shooting up into a girlish register again. The few times he had seen the Crown Prince the man had seemed so self-absorbed as to be indestructible. It was hard to believe he could simply be stabbed with a sword, or shot with an arrow, and die, like anyone else, but there it was.

'And then his brother was murdered—'

'Raynault? Murdered?'

'In his bed in the palace. When the king dies, they'll choose a new one by a vote in Open Council.'

'A vote?' His voice rose so high at that he almost felt some sick at the back of his throat.

42

She was already filling her glass again. 'Uthman's emissary was hanged for the murder, despite most likely being innocent, and so the war with the Gurkish is dragging on—'

'We're at war with the Gurkish as well?'

'Dagoska fell at the start of the year.'

'Dagoska . . . fell?' Jezal emptied his glass in one long swallow and stared at the carpet, trying to fit it all into his head. He should not have been surprised, of course, that things had moved on while he was away, but he had hardly expected the world to turn upside down. War with the Gurkish, battles in the North, votes to choose a new king?

'You need another?' asked Ardee, tilting the decanter in her hand.

'I think I'd better.' Great events, of course, just as Bayaz had said. He watched her pour, frowning down intently, almost angrily, as the wine gurgled out. He saw a little scar on her top lip that he had never noticed before, and he felt a sudden compulsion to touch it, and push his fingers in her hair, and hold her against him. Great events, but it all seemed of small importance compared to what happened now, in this room. Who knew? The course of his life might turn on the next few moments, if he could find the right words, and make himself say them.

'I really did miss you,' he managed. A miserable effort which she dismissed with a bitter snort.

'Don't be a fool.'

He caught her hand, making her look him in the eye. 'I've been a fool all my life. Not now. There were times, out there on the plain, the only thing that kept me alive was the thought that . . . that I might be with you again. Every day I wanted to see you . . .' She did nothing but frown back at him, entirely unmoved. Her failure to melt into his arms was highly frustrating, after all he had been through. 'Ardee, please, I didn't come here to argue.'

She scowled at the floor as she threw down another glass. 'I don't know why you did come here.'

'Because I love you, and I want never to be separated from

you again! Please, tell me that you will be my wife!' He almost said it, but at the last moment he saw her scornful sneer, and he stopped himself. He had entirely forgotten how difficult she could be. 'I came here to say that I'm sorry. I let you down, I know. I came as soon as I could, but I see that you're not in the mood. I'll come back later.'

He brushed past her and made for the door but Ardee got there first, twisted the key in the lock and snatched it out. 'You leave me all alone here, without so much as a letter, then when you come back you want to leave without even a kiss?' She took a lurching step at him and Jezal found himself backing off.

'Ardee, you're drunk.'

She flicked her head with annoyance. 'I'm always drunk. Didn't you say you missed me?'

'But,' he muttered, starting for some reason to feel slightly scared, 'I thought—'

'There's your problem, you see? Thinking. You're no good at it.' She herded him back against the edge of the table, and he got his sword so badly tangled up with his legs he had to put a hand down to stop himself falling.

'Haven't I been waiting?' she whispered, and her breath on his face was hot and sour-sweet with wine. 'Just like you asked me?' Her mouth brushed gently against his, and the tip of her tongue slipped out and lapped against his lips, and she made soft gurgling sounds in her throat and pressed herself up against him. He felt her hand slide down onto his groin, rubbing at him gently through his trousers.

The feeling was pleasant, of course, and caused an instant stiffening. Pleasant in the extreme, but more than slightly worrying. He looked nervously towards the door. 'What about the servants?' he croaked.

'If they don't like it they can find another fucking job, can't they? They weren't my idea.'

'Then whose—ah!'

She twisted her fingers in his hair and dragged his head painfully round so she was speaking right into his face. 'Forget about them! You came here for me, didn't you?'

'Yes . . . yes, of course!'

'Say it, then!' Her hand pressed up hard against his trousers, almost painful, but not quite.

'Ah . . . I came for you.'

'Well? Here I am.' And her fingers fumbled with his belt and dragged it open. 'No need to be shy now.'

He tried to catch her wrist. 'Ardee, wait—' Her other hand caught him a stinging slap right across the face and knocked his head sideways, hard enough to make his ears ring.

'I've been sitting here for six months doing *nothing*!' she hissed in his face, words slightly slurred. 'Do you know how bored I've been? And now you're telling me to *wait*? Fuck yourself!' She dug roughly into his trousers and dragged his prick out, rubbing at him with one hand, squeezing at his face with the other while he closed his eyes and gasped shallow breaths into her mouth, nothing in his mind but her fingers.

Her teeth nipped at his lip, almost painful, and then harder. 'Ah,' he grunted. 'Ah!' She was decidedly biting him. Biting with a will, as though his lip were a piece of gristle to be chewed through. He tried to pull away but the table was at his back and she had him fast. The pain was almost as great as the shock, and then, as the biting went on, considerably greater.

'Aargh!' He grabbed hold of her wrist with one hand and twisted it behind her back, yanked her arm and shoved her down onto the table. He heard her gasp as her face cracked hard against the polished wood.

He stood over her, frozen with dismay, his mouth salty with blood. He could see one dark eye through Ardee's tangled hair, expressionless, watching him over her twisted shoulder. The hair moved round her mouth as she breathed, fast. He let go of her wrist, suddenly, saw her arm move, the marks left by his fingers angry pink on her skin. Her hand slid down and took hold of a fistful of her dress and pulled it up, took another fistful and pulled it up, until her skirts were all tangled around her waist and her bare, pale arse was sticking up at him.

Well. He might have been a new man, but he was still a man.

45

With each thrust her head tapped against the plaster, and his skin slapped against the backs of her thighs, and his trousers sagged further and further down his legs until his sword-hilt was scraping against the carpet. With each thrust the table made an outraged creaking, louder and louder every time, as though they were fucking over the back of some disapproving old man. With each thrust she made a grunt, and he made a gasp, not of pleasure or pain in particular, but a necessary moving of air in response to vigorous exercise. It was all over with merciful swiftness.

So often in life, moments that are long anticipated prove to be a profound disappointment. This was undoubtedly one of those occasions. When he had spent all those interminable hours out on the plain, saddle-sore and in fear of his life, dreaming of seeing Ardee again, a quick and violent coupling on the table in her tasteless living-room had not been quite what he'd had in mind. When they were done he pushed his wilting prick back inside his trousers, guilty, and ashamed, and miserable in the extreme. The sound of his belt-buckle clinking made him want to smash his face against the wall.

She got up, and let her skirts drop, and smoothed them down, her face to the floor. He reached for her shoulder. 'Ardee—' She shook him angrily off, and walked away. She tossed something on the floor behind her and it rattled on the carpet. The key to the door.

'You can go.'

'I can what?'

'Go! You got what you wanted, didn't you?'

He licked disbelieving at his bloody lip. 'You think this is what I wanted?' Nothing but silence. 'I love you.'

She gave a kind of cough, as if she was about to be sick, and she slowly shook her head. 'Why?'

He wasn't sure he knew. He wasn't sure what he meant, or how he felt any more. He wanted to start again, but he didn't know how. The whole thing was an inexplicable nightmare from which he hoped soon to wake. 'What do you mean, why?'

She bent over, fists clenched, and screamed at him. 'I'm

fucking nothing! Everyone who knows me hates me! My own father hated me! My own brother!' Her voice cracked, and her face screwed up, and her mouth spat with anger and misery. 'Everything I touch I ruin! I'm nothing but shit! Why can't you see it?' And she put her hands over her face, and turned her back on him, and her shoulders shook.

He blinked at her, his own lip trembling. The old Jezal dan Luthar would most likely have made a quick grab for that key, sprinted from the room and off down the street, never to come back, and counted himself lucky to have got away so easily. The new one thought about it. He thought about it hard. But he had more character than that. Or so he told himself.

'I love you.' The words tasted like lies in his bloody mouth, but he had gone far too far now to turn back. 'I still love you.' He crossed the room, and though she tried to push him off he put his arms around her. 'Nothing's changed.' He pushed his fingers into her hair, and held her head against his chest while she cried softly, sobbing snot down the front of his garish uniform.

'Nothing's changed,' he whispered. But of course it had.

Feeding Time

They did not sit so close that it was obvious they were together. *Two men who, in the course of their daily business, happen to have placed their arses on the same piece of wood.* It was early morning, and although the sun cast a stinging glare in Glokta's eyes and lent the dewy grass, the rustling trees, the shifting water in the park a golden glow, there was still a treacherous nip to the air. Lord Wetterlant was evidently an early riser. *But then so am I. Nothing encourages a man to leave his bed like being kept awake all night by searing cramps.*

His Lordship reached into a paper bag, drew out a pinch of bread dust between thumb and forefinger, and tossed it at his feet. A mob of self-important ducks had already gathered, and now they fussed at each other furiously in their efforts to get at the crumbs while the old nobleman watched them, his lined face a slack and emotionless mask.

'I am under no illusions, Superior,' he droned, almost without moving his lips and without looking up at all. 'I am not a big enough man to compete in this contest, even should I wish to. But I am big enough to get something from it. I intend to get what I can.' *Straight to business, then, for once. No need to talk about the weather, or how the children are, or the relative merits of different-coloured ducks.*

'There is no shame in that.'

'I do not think so. I have a family to feed, and it grows by the year. I strongly advise against too many children.' *Hah, that shouldn't be a problem.* 'And then I keep dogs, and they must be fed also, and have great appetites.' Wetterlant gave a long, wheezing sigh, and tossed the birds another pinch of bread.

'The higher you rise, Superior, the more dependents cry at you for scraps; that is a sad fact.'

'You carry a large responsibility, my Lord.' Glokta grimaced at a spasm in his leg, and cautiously stretched it out until he felt his knee click. 'How large, might I ask?'

'I have my own vote, of course, and control the votes of three other chairs on the Open Council. Families tied to my own by bonds of land, of friendship, of marriage, and of long tradition.' *Such bonds may prove insubstantial in times such as these.*

'You are certain of those three?'

Wetterlant turned his cold eyes on Glokta. 'I am no fool, Superior. I keep my dogs well chained. I am certain of them. As certain as we can be of anything, in these uncertain times.' He tossed more crumbs into the grass and the ducks quacked, and pecked, and beat at each other with their wings.

'Four votes in total, then.' *No mean share of the great pie.*

'Four votes in total.'

Glokta cleared his throat, checked quickly that there was no-one within earshot. A girl with a tragic face stared listlessly into the water just down the path. Two dishevelled officers of the King's Own sat on a bench as far away on the other side, holding forth to each other loudly about who had been drunker the night before. *Might the tragic girl be listening for Lord Brock? Might the two officers report to High Justice Marovia? I see agents everywhere, and it is just as well. There are agents everywhere.* He lowered his voice to a whisper. 'His Eminence would be willing to offer fifteen thousand marks for each vote.'

'I see.' Wetterlant's hooded eyes did not so much as twitch. 'So little meat would scarcely satisfy my dogs. It would leave nothing for my own table. I should tell you that Lord Barezin, in a highly roundabout manner, already offered me eighteen thousand a vote, as well as an excellent stretch of land that borders my own estates. Deer hunting woods. Are you a hunting man, Superior?'

'I was.' Glokta tapped his ruined leg. 'But not for some time.'

'Ah. My commiserations. I have always loved the sport. But

then Lord Brock came to visit me.' *How charming for you both.*
'He was good enough to make an offer of twenty thousand, and a very suitable match of his youngest daughter for my eldest son.'

'You accepted?'

'I told him it was too early to accept anything.'

'I am sure his Eminence could stretch to twenty-one, but that would have to be—'

'High Justice Marovia's man already offered me twenty-five.'

'Harlen Morrow?' hissed Glokta through his remaining teeth.

Lord Wetterlant raised an eyebrow. 'I believe that was the name.'

'I regret that I can only match that offer at present. I will inform his Eminence of your position.' *His delight, I am sure, will know no bounds.*

'I look forward to hearing from you, Superior.' Wetterlant turned back to his ducks and permitted them a few more crumbs, a vague smile hovering round his lips as he watched them tussle with each other.

Glokta hobbled painfully up to the ordinary house in the unexceptional street, something resembling a smile on his face. *A moment free of the suffocating company of the great and the good. A moment in which I do not have to lie, or cheat, or watch for a knife in my back. Perhaps I'll even find a room that doesn't still stink of Harlen Morrow. That would be a refreshing—*

The door opened sharply even as he raised his fist to knock, and he was left staring into the grinning face of a man wearing the uniform of an officer in the King's Own. It was so unexpected that Glokta did not recognise him at first. Then he felt a surge of dismay.

'Why, Captain Luthar. What a surprise.' *And a thoroughly unpleasant one.*

He was considerably changed. Where once he had been boyish and smooth, he had acquired a somewhat angular, even a weather-beaten look. Where once he had carried his chin with an arrogant lift, he now had an almost apologetic tilt to his face. He had grown a beard too, perhaps in an unsuccessful attempt to disguise a vicious-looking scar through his lip and down his jaw. *Though it has far from rendered him ugly, alas.*

'Inquisitor Glokta . . . er . . .'

'Superior.'

'Really?' Luthar blinked at him for a moment. 'Well . . . in that case . . .' The easy smile reappeared, and Glokta was surprised to find himself being shaken warmly by the hand. 'Congratulations. I would love to chat but duty calls. I haven't long in the city, you see. Off to the North, and so on.'

'Of course.' Glokta frowned after him as he stepped jauntily off up the street, with just the one furtive glance over his shoulder as he rounded the corner. *Leaving only the question of why he was here in the first place.* Glokta hobbled through the open door and shut it quietly behind him. *Although honestly, a young man leaving a young woman's house in the early morning? One scarcely requires his Majesty's Inquisition to solve that particular mystery. Did I not leave more than my share of residences in the early hours, after all? Pretending to hope that I wasn't observed, but really rather hoping that I was?* He passed through the doorway into the living room. *Or was that a different man?*

Ardee West stood with her back to him, and he heard the sound of wine trickling into a glass. 'Did you forget something?' she asked over her shoulder, voice soft and playful. *Not a tone I often get to hear women use. Horror, disgust, and the slightest touch of pity are more common.* There was a clinking as she put the bottle away. 'Or did you decide you really couldn't live without another—' She had a crooked smile on her face as she turned, but it slid off suddenly when she saw who was standing there.

Glokta snorted. 'Don't worry, I get that reaction from everyone. Even myself, every morning, when I look into the mirror.' *If I can even manage to stand up in front of the damn thing.*

'It's not like that, and you know it. I just wasn't expecting you to wander in.'

'We've all had quite the shock this morning, then. You'll never guess who I passed in your hallway.'

She froze for just a moment, then tossed her head dismissively and slurped wine from her glass. 'Aren't you going to give me a clue?'

'Alright, I will.' Glokta winced as he lowered himself into a chair, stretching his aching leg out in front of him. 'A young officer in the King's Own, no doubt with a scintillating future ahead of him.' *Though we can all hope otherwise.*

Ardee glared at him over the rim. 'There are so many officers in the King's Own I can scarcely tell one from another.'

'Really? This one won last year's Contest, I believe.'

'I hardly remember who was in the final. Every year is like the last, don't you find?'

'True. Since I competed it's been straight downhill. But I thought you might remember this particular fellow. Looked as if someone might have hit him in the face since we last met. Quite hard, I would say.' *Though not half as hard as I'd have liked.*

'You're angry with me,' she said, but without the appearance of the slightest concern.

'I'd say disappointed. But what would you expect? I thought you were cleverer than this.'

'Cleverness is no guarantee of sensible behaviour. My father used to say so all the time.' She finished her wine with a practised flick of her head. 'Don't worry. I can look after myself.'

'No you can't. You've made that abundantly clear. You realise what will happen if people find out? You'll be shunned.'

'What would be the difference?' she sneered at him. 'Perhaps you'll be surprised to learn I get few invitations to the palace now. I barely even qualify as an embarrassment. No one speaks to me.' *Apart from me, of course, but I'm hardly the type of company young women hope for.* 'No one cares a shit what I do. If they find out it will be no worse than they expect from a slattern like me. Damn commoners, no more self-control than animals, don't you know. Anyway, didn't you tell me I could fuck who I pleased?'

'I also told you the less fucking the better.'

'And I suppose that's what you told all your conquests, is it?'

Glokta grimaced. *Not exactly. I coaxed and I pleaded, I threatened and I bullied. Your beauty has wounded me, wounded me in the heart! I am wretched, I will die without you! Have you no pity? Do you not love me? I did everything short of display the instruments, then when I got what I wanted I tossed them aside and went merrily on to the next with never a backward glance.*

'Hah!' snorted Ardee, as though she guessed what he was thinking. 'Sand dan Glokta, giving lectures on the benefits of chastity? Please! How many women did you ruin before the Gurkish ruined you? You were notorious!'

A muscle began to tremble in his neck, and he worked his shoulder round until he felt it soften. *She makes a fair point. Perhaps a soft word with the gentleman in question will do the trick. A soft word, or a hard night with Practical Frost.* 'Your bed, your business, I suppose, as they say in Styria. How does the great Captain Luthar come to be among the civilians in any case? Doesn't he have Northmen to rout? Who will save Angland, while he's here?'

'He wasn't in Angland.'

'No?' *Father find him a nice, out of the way spot, did he?*

'He's been in the Old Empire, or some such. Across the sea to the west and far away.' She sighed as though she had heard a great deal about it and was now thoroughly bored of the subject.

'Old Empire? What the hell was he up to out there?'

'Why don't you ask him? Some journey. He talked a lot about a Northman. Ninefingers, or something.'

Glokta's head jerked up. 'Ninefingers?'

'Mmm. Him and some old bald man.'

A flurry of twitches ran down Glokta's face. 'Bayaz.' Ardee shrugged and swigged from her glass again, already developing a slight drunken clumsiness to her movements. *Bayaz. All we need, with an election coming, is that old liar sticking his hairless head in.* 'Is he here, now, in the city?'

'How should I know?' grumbled Ardee. 'Nobody tells me anything.'

So Much in Common

Ferro stalked round the room, and scowled. She poured her scorn out into the sweet-smelling air, onto the rustling hangings, over the great windows and the high balcony beyond them. She sneered at the dark pictures of fat pale kings, at the shining furniture scattered about the wide floor. She hated this place, with its soft beds and its soft people. She infinitely preferred the dust and thirst of the Badlands of Kanta. Life there was hard, and hot, and brief.

But at least it was honest.

This Union, and this city of Adua in particular, and this fortress of the Agriont especially, were all packed to bursting with lies. She felt them on her skin, like an oily stain she could not rub off. And Bayaz was sunk in the very midst of it. He had tricked her into following him across the world for nothing. They had found no ancient weapon to use against the Gurkish. Now he smiled, and laughed, and whispered secrets with old men. Men who came in sweating from the heat outside, and left sweating even more.

She would never have admitted it to anyone else. She despised having to admit it to herself. She missed Ninefingers. Though she had never been able to show it, it had been a reassurance, having someone she could halfway trust.

Now she had to look over her own shoulder.

All she had for company was the apprentice, and he was worse than nothing. He sat and watched her in silence, his book ignored on the table beside him. Watching and smiling without joy, as though he knew something she should have guessed. As though he thought her a fool for not seeing it. That only made her angrier than ever. So she prowled round the room, frowning at everything, her fists clenched and her jaw locked tight.

'You should go back to the South, Ferro.'

She stopped in her tracks, and scowled at Quai. He was right, of course. Nothing would have pleased her more than to leave these Godless pinks behind forever and fight the Gurkish with weapons she understood. Tear vengeance from them with her teeth, if she had to. He was right, but that changed nothing. Ferro had never been much for taking advice. 'What do you know about what I should do, scrawny pink fool?'

'More than you think.' He did not take his slow eyes away from her for a moment. 'We are much alike, you and I. You may not see it, and yet we are. So much in common.' Ferro frowned. She did not know what the sickly idiot meant by that, but she did not like the sound of it. 'Bayaz will bring you nothing you need. He cannot be trusted. I found out too late, but you still have time. You should find another master.'

'I have no master,' she snapped at him. 'I am free.'

One corner of Quai's pale lips twitched up. 'Neither of us will ever be free. Go. There is nothing for you here.'

'Why do you stay, then?'

'For vengeance.'

Ferro frowned deeper. 'Vengeance for what?'

The apprentice leaned forward, his bright eyes fixed on hers. The door creaked open and he snapped his mouth shut, sat back and looked out of the window. Just as if he had never meant to speak.

Damn apprentice with his damn riddles. Ferro turned her scowl towards the door.

Bayaz came slowly through into the room, a teacup held carefully level in one hand. He did not so much as look in Ferro's direction as he swept past and out the open door onto the balcony. Damn Magus. She stalked after, narrowing her eyes at the glare. They were high up, and the Agriont was spread out before them, as it had been when she and Nine-fingers climbed over the rooftops, long ago. Groups of idle pinks lazed on the shining grass below, just as they had done before Ferro left for the Old Empire. And yet not everything was the same.

Everywhere in the city, now, there was a kind of fear. She could see it in each soft, pale face. In their every word and gesture. A breathless expectation, like the air before the storm breaks. Like a field of dry grass, ready to burst into flame at the slightest spark. She did not know what they were waiting for, and she did not care.

But she had heard a lot of talk about votes.

The First of the Magi watched her as she stepped through the door, the bright sun shining on the side of his bald head. 'Tea, Ferro?'

Ferro hated tea, and Bayaz knew it. Tea was what the Gurkish drank when they had treachery in mind. She remembered the soldiers drinking it while she struggled in the dust. She remembered the slavers drinking it while they talked prices. She remembered Uthman drinking it while he chuckled at her rage and her helplessness. Now Bayaz drank it, little cup held daintily between his thick thumb and forefinger, and he smiled.

Ferro ground her teeth. 'I am done here, pink. You promised me vengeance and have given me nothing. I am going back to the South.'

'Indeed? We would be sorry to lose you. But Gurkhul and the Union are at war. There are no ships sailing to Kanta at present. There may not be for some time to come.'

'Then how will I get there?'

'You have made it abundantly clear that you are not my responsibility. I have put a roof over your head and you show scant gratitude. If you wish to leave, you can make your own arrangements. My brother Yulwei should return to us shortly. Perhaps he will be prepared to take you under his wing.'

'Not good enough.' Bayaz glared at her. A fearsome look, perhaps, but Ferro was not Longfoot, or Luthar, or Quai. She had no master, and would never have another. 'Not good enough, I said!'

'Why is it that you insist on testing the limits of my patience? It is not without an end, you know.'

'Neither is mine.'

Bayaz snorted. 'Yours scarcely even has a beginning, as Master Ninefingers could no doubt testify. I do declare, Ferro, you have all the charm of a goat, and a mean-tempered goat at that.' He stuck his lips out, tipped up his cup and sucked delicately from the rim. Only with a mighty effort was Ferro able to stop herself from slapping it out of his hand, and butting the bald bastard in the face into the bargain. 'But if fighting the Gurkish is still what you have in mind—'

'Always.'

'Then I am sure that I can still find a use for your talents. Something that does not require a sense of humour. My purposes with regard to the Gurkish are unchanged. The struggle must continue, albeit with other weapons.' His eyes slid sideways, towards the great tower that loomed up over the fortress.

Ferro knew little about beauty and cared still less, but that building was a beautiful thing to her mind. There was no softness, no indulgence in that mountain of naked stone. There was a brutal honesty in its shape. A merciless precision in its sharp, black angles. Something about it fascinated her.

'What is that place?' she asked.

Bayaz narrowed his eyes at her. 'The House of the Maker.'

'What is inside?'

'None of your business.'

Ferro almost spat with annoyance. 'You lived there. You served Kanedias. You helped the Maker with his works. You told us all this, out on the plains. So tell me, what is inside?'

'You have a sharp memory, Ferro, but you forget one thing. We did not find the Seed. I do not need you. I do not need, in particular, to answer your endless questions any longer. Imagine my dismay.' He sucked primly at his tea again, raising his brows and peering out at the lazy pinks in the park.

Ferro forced a smile onto her own face. Or as close as she could get to a smile. She bared her teeth, at least. She remembered well enough what the bitter old woman Cawneil had said, and how much it had annoyed him. She would do the same. 'The Maker. You tried to steal his secrets. You tried to steal his daughter. Tolomei was her name. Her father threw her from the roof. In return for her betrayal, in opening his gates to you. Am I wrong?'

Bayaz angrily flicked the last drops from his cup over the balcony. Ferro watched them glitter in the bright sun, tumbling downwards. 'Yes, Ferro, the Maker threw his daughter from the roof. It would seem that we are both unlucky in love, eh? Bad luck for us. Worse luck for our lovers. Who would have dreamed we have so much in common?' Ferro wondered about shoving the pink bastard off the balcony after his tea. But he still owed her, and she meant to collect. So she only scowled, and ducked back through the doorway.

There was a new arrival in the room. A man with curly hair and a wide smile. He had a tall staff in his hand, a case of weathered leather over one shoulder. There was something strange about his eyes – one light, one dark. There was something about his watchful gaze that made Ferro suspicious. Even more than usual.

'Ah, the famous Ferro Maljinn. Forgive my curiosity, but it is not every day that one encounters a person of your . . . remarkable ancestry.'

Ferro did not like that he knew her name, or her ancestry, or anything about her. 'Who are you?'

'Where are my manners? I am Yoru Sulfur, of the order of Magi,' and he offered his hand. She did not take it but he only smiled. 'Not one of the original twelve, of course, not I. Merely an afterthought. A late addition. I was once apprentice to great Bayaz.'

Ferro snorted. That hardly qualified him for trust in her estimation. 'What happened?'

'I graduated.'

Bayaz tossed his cup down rattling on a table by the window. 'Yoru,' he said, and the newcomer humbly bowed his head. 'My thanks for your work thus far. Precise and to the point, as always.'

Sulfur's smile grew broader. 'A small cog in a large machine, Master Bayaz, but I try to be a sturdy one.'

'You have yet to let me down. I do not forget that. How is your next little game progressing?'

'Ready to begin, at your command.'

'Let us begin now. There is nothing to be gained by delay.'

'I shall make the preparations. I have also brought this, as you asked.' He swung the bag down from his shoulder and gingerly reached inside. He slowly drew out a book. Large and black, its heavy covers hacked, and scarred, and charred by fire. 'Glustrod's book,' he murmured softly, as though afraid to say the words.

Bayaz frowned. 'Keep it, for now. There was an unexpected complication.'

'A complication?' Sulfur slid the book back into its case with some relief.

'What we sought . . . was not there.'

'Then—'

'As regards our other plans, nothing is changed.'

'Of course.' Sulfur bowed his head again. 'Lord Isher will already be on his way.'

'Very well.' Bayaz glanced over at Ferro, as though he had only just remembered that she was there. 'For the time being, perhaps you would be good enough to give us the room? I have a visitor that I must attend to.'

She was happy to leave, but she took her time moving, if only because Bayaz wanted her gone quickly. She unfolded her arms, stood on the spot and stretched. She strolled to the door by a roundabout route, letting her feet scuff against the boards and fill the room with their ugly scraping. She stopped on the way to gaze at a picture, to poke at a chair, to flick at a shiny pot, none of which interested her at all. All the while Quai watched, and Bayaz frowned, and Sulfur grinned his knowing little grin. She stopped in the doorway.

'Now?'

'Yes, now,' snapped Bayaz.

She looked round the room one more time. 'Fucking Magi,' she snorted, and slid through the door.

She almost walked into a tall old pink in the room beyond. He wore a heavy robe, even in the heat, and had a sparkling chain around his shoulders. A big man loomed behind him, grim and watchful. A guard. Ferro did not like the old pink's look. He stared down his nose at her, chin tilted up, as though she were a dog.

As though she were a slave.

'Ssssss.' She hissed in his face as she shouldered past him. He gave an outraged snort and his guard gave Ferro a hard look. She ignored it. Hard looks mean nothing. If he wanted her knee in his face he could try and touch her. But he did not. The two of them went in through the door.

'Ah, Lord Isher!' she heard Bayaz saying, just before it shut. 'I am delighted that you could visit us at short notice.'

'I came at once. My grandfather always said that—'

'Your grandfather was a wise man, and a good friend. I would like to discuss with you, if I may, the situation in the Open Council. Will you take tea . . . ?'

Honesty

Jezal lay on his back, his hands behind his head, the sheets around his waist. He watched Ardee looking out of the window, her elbows on the sill, her chin on her hands. He watched Ardee, and he thanked the fates that some long-forgotten designer of military apparel had seen fit to provide the officers of the King's Own with a high-waisted jacket. He thanked them with a deep and earnest gratitude, because his jacket was all she was wearing.

It was amazing how things had changed between them, since that bitter, bewildering reunion. For a week they had not spent a night apart, and for a week the smile had barely left his face. Occasionally the memory would wallow up, of course, unbidden and horribly surprising, like a bloated corpse bobbing to the surface of the pond while one enjoys a picnic on the shore, of Ardee biting and hitting him, crying and screaming in his face. But when it did so he would fix his grin, and see her smile at him, and soon enough he would be able to shove those unpleasant thoughts back down again, at least for now. Then he would congratulate himself on being a big enough man to do it, and on giving her the benefit of the doubt.

'Ardee,' he wheedled at her.

'Mmm?'

'Come back to bed.'

'Why?'

'Because I love you.' Strange, how the more he said it, the easier it became.

She gave a bored sigh. 'So you keep saying.'

'It's true.'

She turned round, hands on the sill behind, her body a dark outline against the bright window. 'And what does that mean, exactly? That you've been fucking me for a week and you haven't had enough yet?'

'I don't think I'll ever get enough.'

'Well,' and she pushed herself away from the window and padded across the boards. 'I don't suppose there's any harm in finding out, is there? No more harm, anyway.' She stopped at the foot of the bed. 'Just promise me one thing.'

Jezal swallowed, worried at what she might ask him, worried at what he might say in reply. 'Anything,' he murmured, forcing himself to smile.

'Don't let me down.'

His smile grew easier. That was not so hard to say yes to. He was a changed man, after all. 'Of course, I promise.'

'Good.' She crept up on to the bed, on her hands and knees, eyes fixed on his face while he wriggled his toes in anticipation under the sheet. She knelt up, one leg on either side of him, and jerked the jacket smooth across her chest. 'Well then, Captain, do I pass muster?'

'I would say . . .' and he grabbed the front of the jacket and pulled her down on top of him, slipped his hands inside it, 'that you are without a doubt . . .' and he slid his hand under her breast and rubbed at her nipple with his thumb, 'the finest-looking soldier in my company.'

She pressed her groin against his through the sheet, and worked her hips back and forward. 'Ah, the Captain is already at attention . . .'

'For you? Constantly . . .'

Her mouth licked and sucked at his, smearing spit on his face, and he pushed his hand between her legs and she rubbed herself against it for a while, his sticky fingers squelching in and out of her. She grunted and sighed in her throat, and he did the same. She reached down and dragged the sheet out of the way. He took hold of his prick and she wriggled her hips until they found the right spot and worked her way down onto him, her hair tickling at his face, her rasping breath tickling at his ear.

There were two heavy knocks at the door, and they both froze. Another two knocks. Ardee put her head up, pushing her hair out of her flushed face. 'What is it?' she called, voice thick and throaty.

'There's someone for the Captain.' The maid. 'Is he . . . is he still here?'

Ardee's eyes rolled down to Jezal's. 'I daresay I could get a message to him!' He bit on his lip to stifle a laugh, reached up and pinched at her nipple and she slapped his hand away. 'Who is it?'

'A Knight Herald!' Jezal felt his smile fading. Those bastards never seemed to bring good news, and always at the worst possible times. 'Lord Marshal Varuz needs to speak to the Captain urgently. They're all over town looking for him.' Jezal cursed under his breath. It seemed that the army had finally realised he was back.

'Tell him that when I see the Captain I will let him know!' shouted Ardee, and the sound of footsteps retreated down the corridor outside.

'Fuck!' Jezal hissed as soon as he was sure the maid was gone, not that she could have been in too much doubt about what had been going on for the past few days and nights. 'I'll have to go.'

'Now?'

'Now, curse them. If I don't they'll just keep looking, and the sooner I go, the sooner I can get back.'

She sighed and rolled over onto her back while he slithered off the bed and started hunting round the room for his scattered clothes. His shirt had a wine stain down the front, his trousers were creased and rumpled, but they would have to do. Cutting the perfect figure was no longer his one goal in life. He sat down on the bed to pull his boots on and he felt her kneel behind him, her hands sliding across his chest, her lips brushing at his ear as she whispered to him. 'So you'll be leaving me all alone again, will you? Heading off to Angland, to slaughter Northmen with my brother?'

Jezal leaned down with some difficulty and heaved one boot on. 'Perhaps. Perhaps not.' The idea of the soldiering life no longer inspired him. He had seen enough of violence, close up, to know it was extremely frightening and hurt like hell. Glory and fame seemed like meagre rewards for all the risks involved. 'I'm giving serious thought to the idea of resigning my commission.'

'You are? And doing what?'

'I'm not sure.' He turned his head and raised an eyebrow at her. 'Maybe I'll find a good woman and settle down.'

'A good woman? Do you know any?'

'I was hoping you might have some suggestions.'

She pressed her lips together. 'Let me think. Does she have to be beautiful?'

'No, no, beautiful women are always so bloody demanding. Plain as ditchwater, please.'

'Clever?'

Jezal snorted. 'Anything but that. I am notorious for my empty-headedness. A clever woman would only make me look the dunce the whole time.' He dragged the other boot on, peeled her hands away and stood up. 'A wide-eyed and thoughtless calf would be ideal. Someone to endlessly agree with me.'

Ardee clapped her hands. 'Oh yes, I can see her on you now, trailing from your arm like an empty dress, a kind of echo at a higher pitch. Noble blood though, I imagine?'

'Of course, nothing but the best. One point on which I could never compromise. And fair hair, I have a weakness for it.'

'Oh, I entirely agree. Dark hair is so commonplace, so very much the colour of dirt, and filth, and muck.' She shuddered. 'I feel sullied just thinking of it.'

'Above all,' as he pushed his sword through the clasp on his belt, 'a calm and even temper. I have had my fill of surprises.'

'Naturally. Life is difficult enough without a woman making trouble. So terribly undignified.' She raised her eyebrows. 'I will think through my acquaintances.'

'Excellent. In the meantime, and although you wear it with far greater dash than I ever could, I will need my jacket.'

'Oh, yes, sir.' She pulled it off and flung it at him, then

stretched out on the bed, stark naked, back arched, hands above her head, wriggling her hips slowly back and forth, one knee in the air, the other leg stretched out, big toe pointing at him. 'You aren't going to leave me alone for too long, though, are you?'

He watched her for a moment. 'Don't you dare move a fucking inch,' he croaked, then he pulled the jacket on, wedged his prick between his thighs and waddled out the door, bent over. He hoped it would go down before he had his briefing with the Lord Marshal, but he was not entirely sure it would.

Once again, Jezal found himself in one of High Justice Marovia's cavernous chambers, standing all alone on the empty floor, facing the enormous, polished table while three old men regarded him grimly from the other side.

As the clerk shut the high doors with an echoing boom, he had a deeply worrying sense of having lived through this very experience before. The day he had been summoned from the boat for Angland, torn from his friends and his ambitions, to be sent on a madcap, doomed journey into the middle of nowhere. A journey that had cost him some of his looks and nearly his life. It was safe to say that he did not entirely relish being back here, and hoped most fervently for a better outcome.

From that point of view, the absence of the First of the Magi was something of a tonic, even if the panel was otherwise far from comforting. Facing him were the hard old faces of Lord Marshal Varuz, High Justice Marovia, and Lord Chamberlain Hoff.

Varuz was busy waxing on about Jezal's fine achievements in the Old Empire. He had, evidently, heard a very different version of events from the one that Jezal himself remembered.

'. . . great adventures in the west, as I understand it, bringing honour to the Union on foreign fields. I was particularly impressed by the story of your charge across the bridge at Darmium. Did that really happen the way I have been told?'

'Across the bridge, sir, well, truthfully, er . . .' He should probably have asked the old fool what the hell he was talking about, but he was far too busy thinking of Ardee, stretched out naked. Shit on his country. Duty be damned. He could resign his commission now and be back in her bed before the hour was out. 'The thing is—'

'That was your favourite, was it?' asked Hoff, lowering his goblet. 'It was the one about the Emperor's daughter that most caught my fancy.' And he looked at Jezal with a twinkle in his eye that implied a story of a saucy tone.

'Honestly, your Grace, I've not the slightest idea how that rumour began. Nothing of the kind occurred, I assure you. The whole business appears somehow to have become greatly exaggerated—'

'Well, one glorious rumour is worth ten disappointing truths, would you not agree?'

Jezal blinked. 'Well, er, I suppose—'

'In any case,' cut in Varuz, 'the Closed Council have received excellent reports of your conduct while abroad.'

'They have?'

'Many and various reports, and all glowing.'

Jezal could not help grinning, though he had to wonder from whom such reports might have come. He could scarcely imagine Ferro Maljinn gushing about his fine qualities. 'Well, your lordships are very kind, but I must—'

'As a result of your dedication and courage in this difficult and vital task, I am delighted to announce that you have been elevated to the rank of Colonel, with immediate effect.'

Jezal's eyes opened up very wide. 'I have?'

'You have indeed, my boy, and no one could deserve it more.'

To rise two ranks in one afternoon was an unprecedented honour, especially when he had fought in no battle, carried out no recent deeds of valour, and made no ultimate sacrifices. Unless you counted leaving off the most recent bedding of his best friend's sister halfway. A sacrifice, no doubt, but scarcely the kind that usually earned the King's favour.

'I, er, I . . .' He could not escape a glow of satisfaction. A new uniform, and more braid, and so forth, and more people to tell what to do. Glory and fame were meagre rewards, perhaps, but he had taken the risks already, and now had only to say yes. Had he not suffered? Had he not earned it?

He did not have to think about it for so very long. He scarcely had to think about it at all. The idea of leaving the army and settling down receded rapidly into the far distance. 'I would be entirely honoured to accept this exceptional . . . er . . . honour.'

'Then we are all equally delighted,' said Hoff sourly. 'Now to business. You are aware, *Colonel* Luthar, that there has been some trouble with the peasants of late?'

Surprisingly, no news had reached Ardee's bedroom. 'Nothing serious, surely, your Grace?'

'Not unless you call a full-blown revolt serious.'

'Revolt?' Jezal swallowed.

'This man, the Tanner,' spat the Lord Chamberlain. 'He has been touring the countryside for months, whipping up dissatisfaction, sowing the seeds of disobedience, inciting the peasantry to crimes against their masters, against their lords, against their king!'

'No one ever suspected it would reach the point of open rebellion.' Varuz worked his mouth angrily. 'But following a demonstration near Keln a group of peasants encouraged by this Tanner armed themselves and refused to disband. They won a victory over the local landowner, and the insurrection spread. Now we hear they crushed a significant force under Lord Finster yesterday, burned his manor house and hung three tax collectors. They are in the process of ravaging the countryside in the direction of Adua.'

'Ravaging?' murmured Jezal, glancing at the door. Ravaging really was a very ugly word.

'It is a most regrettable business,' bemoaned Marovia. 'Half of them are honest men, faithful to their king, pushed to this through the greed of their landlords.'

Varuz sneered his disgust. 'There can be no excuse for

treason! The other half are thieves, and blackguards, and malcontents. They should be whipped to the gallows!'

'The Closed Council has made its decision,' cut in Hoff. 'This Tanner has declared his intention to present a list of demands to the King. To the King! New freedoms. New rights. Every man the equal of his brother and other such dangerous nonsense. Soon it will become known that they are on their way and there will be panic. Riots in support of the peasants, and riots against them. Things are balanced on a knife edge already. Two wars in progress and the king in fading health, with no heir?' Hoff bashed at the table with his fist, making Jezal jump. 'They must not be allowed to reach the city.'

Marshal Varuz clasped his hands before him. 'The two regiments of the King's Own that have remained in Midderland will be sent out to counter this threat. A list of concessions,' and he scowled as he said the word, 'has been prepared. If the peasants will accept negotiation, and return to their homes, their lives can be spared. If this Tanner will not see reason, then his so-called army must be destroyed. Scattered. Broken up.'

'Killed,' said Hoff, rubbing at a stain on the table with his heavy thumb. 'And the ringleaders delivered to his Majesty's Inquisition.'

'Regrettable,' murmured Jezal, without thinking, feeling a cold shiver at the very mention of that institution.

'Necessary,' said Marovia, sadly shaking his head.

'But hardly straightforward.' Varuz frowned at Jezal across the table. 'In each village, in each town, in every field and farm they have passed through they have picked up more recruits. The country is alive with malcontents. Ill-disciplined, of course, and ill-equipped, but at our last estimate they numbered some forty thousand.'

'Forty . . . thousand?' Jezal shifted his weight nervously. He had supposed they were perhaps discussing a few hundred, and those without proper footwear. There was no danger here, of course, safe behind the walls of the Agriont, the walls of the city. But forty thousand was an awful lot of very angry men. Even if they were peasants.

'The King's Own are making their preparations: one regiment of horse and one of foot. All that is missing now is a commander for the expedition.'

'Huh,' grunted Jezal. He did not begrudge that unfortunate man his position, commanding a force outnumbered five to one against a bunch of savages buoyed up by righteousness and petty victories, drunk on hatred of noblemen and monarchy, thirsty for blood and loot . . .

Jezal's eyes went wider still. 'Me?'

'You.'

He fumbled for the words. 'I do not wish to seem . . . ungrateful, you understand, but, surely, I mean to say, there must be men better suited to the task. Lord Marshal, you yourself have—'

'This is a complicated time.' Hoff glared sternly at Jezal from beneath his bushy brows. 'A very complicated time. We need someone without . . . affiliations. We need someone with a clean slate. You fit the bill admirably.'

'But . . . negotiating with peasants, your Grace, your Worship, Lord Marshal, I have no understanding of the issues! I have no understanding of law!'

'We are not blind to your deficiencies,' said Hoff. 'That is why there will be a representative from the Closed Council with you. Someone who possesses unchallenged expertise in all those areas.'

A heavy hand slapped suddenly down on Jezal's shoulder. 'I told you it would be sooner rather than later, my boy!' Jezal slowly turned his head, a feeling of terrible dismay boiling up from his stomach, and there was the First of the Magi, grinning into his face from a distance of no more than a foot, very much present after all. It was no surprise, really, that the bald old meddler was involved in this. Strange and painful events seemed to follow in his wake like stray dogs barking behind the butcher's wagon.

'The peasants' army, if we can call it such, is camped within four days' slovenly march of the city, spread out across the country, seeking for forage.' Varuz craned forward, poking at the table with a finger. 'You will proceed immediately to intercept them. Our hopes hang on this, Colonel Luthar. Do you understand your orders?'

'Yes, sir,' he whispered, trying and utterly failing to sound enthusiastic.

'The two of us, back together?' Bayaz chuckled. 'They'd better run, eh, my boy?'

'Of course,' murmured Jezal, miserably. He had had his own chance to escape, his chance to start a new life, and he had given it up in return for an extra star or two on his jacket. Too late he realised his awful blunder. Bayaz' grip tightened round his shoulder, drew him to a fatherly distance, and did not feel like releasing him. There really was no way out.

Jezal stepped out of the door to his quarters in a great hurry, cursing as he dragged his box behind him. It really was an awful imposition that he had been obliged to carry his own luggage, but time was extremely pressing if he was to save the Union from the madness of its own people. He had given only the briefest consideration to the idea of sprinting for the docks and taking passage on the first ship to distant Suljuk, before angrily dismissing it. He had taken the promotion with his eyes open, and now he supposed he had no choice but to see it through. Better to do it, than to live with the fear of it, and so forth. He twisted his key in the lock, turned around, and recoiled with a girlish gasp of shock. There was someone in the shadows opposite his door, and the feeling of horror only worsened when he realised who it was.

The cripple Glokta stood against the wall, leaning heavily on his cane and grinning his repulsive, toothless grin. 'A word, Colonel Luthar.'

'If you are referring to this business with the peasants, it is well in hand.' Jezal was unable to keep the sneer of disgust entirely off his face. 'You need not trouble yourself on that—'

'I am not referring to that business.'

'Then what?'

'Ardee West.'

The corridor seemed suddenly very empty, very quiet. The soldiers, the officers, the servants, all away in Angland. There were just the two of them, for all Jezal knew, in the entire barracks. 'I fail to see how that is any concern of—'

'Her brother, our mutual friend Collem West, you do remember him? Worried-looking fellow, losing his hair. Bit of a temper.' Jezal felt a guilty flush across his face. He remembered the man well enough, of course, and his temper in particular. 'He came to me shortly before departing for the war in Angland. He asked me to look to his sister's welfare while he was away, risking his life. I promised to do so.' Glokta shuffled slightly closer and Jezal's flesh crept. 'A responsibility which, I assure you, I take as seriously as any task the Arch Lector might choose to give me.'

'I see,' croaked Jezal. That certainly explained the cripple's presence at her house the other day, which had, until then, been causing him some confusion. He felt no easier in his mind, however. Considerably less, in fact.

'I hardly think that Collem West would be best pleased with what has been transpiring these last few days, do you?'

Jezal shifted guiltily from one foot to the other. 'I admit that I have visited her—'

'Your visits,' whispered the cripple, 'are not good for that girl's reputation. We are left with three options. Firstly, and this is my personal favourite, you walk away, and you pretend you never met her, and you never see her again.'

'Unacceptable,' Jezal found himself saying, his voice surprisingly brash.

'Secondly, then, you marry the lady, and all's forgotten.'

A course that Jezal was considering, but he was damned if he'd be bullied into it by this twisted remnant of a man. 'And third?' he enquired, with what he felt was fitting contempt.

'Third?' A particularly disgusting flurry of twitches crawled up the side of Glokta's wasted face. 'I don't think you want to know too much about number three. Let us only say that it will include a long night of passion with a furnace and a set of razors, and an even longer morning involving a sack, an anvil, and the bottom of the canal. You might find that one of the other two options suits you better.'

Before he knew what he was doing Jezal had taken a step forward, forcing Glokta to rock back, wincing, against the wall. 'I do not have to explain myself to you! My visits are between me and the lady in question, but for your information, I long ago resolved to marry her, and am merely waiting for the right moment!' Jezal stood there in the darkness, hardly able to believe what he had heard himself say. Damn his mouth, it still landed him in all manner of trouble.

Glokta's narrow left eye blinked. 'Ah, lucky her.'

Jezal found himself moving forward again, almost butting the cripple in the face and crushing him helpless against the wall. 'That's right! So you can shove your threats up your crippled arse!'

Even squashed against the wall, Glokta's surprise only lasted an instant. Then he leered his toothless grin, his eyelid fluttering and a long tear running down his gaunt cheek. 'Why, Colonel Luthar, it is difficult for me to concentrate with you so very close.' He stroked the front of Jezal's uniform with the back of his hand. 'Especially given your unexpected interest in my arse.' Jezal jerked back, mouth sour with disgust. 'It seems that Bayaz succeeded where Varuz failed, eh? He taught you where your spine is! My congratulations on your forthcoming wedding. But I think I'll keep my razors handy, just in case you don't follow through. I'm so glad we had this chance to talk.' And Glokta limped off towards the stairs, his cane tapping on the boards, his left boot scraping along behind.

'As am I!' shouted Jezal after him. But nothing could have been further from the truth.

Ghosts

Uffrith didn't look much like it used to. Of course, the last time Logen had seen the place had been years ago, at night, after the siege. Crowds of Bethod's Carls wandering the streets – shouting, and singing, and drinking. Looking for folk to rob and rape, setting fire to anything that would hold a flame. Logen remembered lying in that room after he'd beaten Threetrees, crying and gurgling at the pain all through him. He remembered scowling out the window and seeing the glow from the flames, listening to the screams over the town, wishing he was out there making mischief and wondering if he'd ever stand up again.

It was different now, with the Union in charge, but it wasn't so very much more organised. The grey harbour was choked with ships too big for the wharves. Soldiers swarmed through the narrow streets, dropping gear all over. Carts and mules and horses, all loaded down and piled up, tried to shove a way through the press. Wounded limped on crutches down towards the docks, or were carried on stretchers through the spotting drizzle, bloody bandages stared at wide-eyed by the fresh-faced lads going the other way. Here and there, looking greatly puzzled at this mighty flood of strange people sweeping through their town, some Northerner was standing in a doorway. Women mostly, and children, and old men.

Logen walked fast up the sloping streets, pushing through the crowds with his head down and his hood up. He kept his fists bunched at his sides, so no one would see the stump of his missing finger. He kept the sword that Bayaz had given him wrapped up in a blanket on his back, under his pack, where it wouldn't make anyone nervous. All the same, his shoulders prickled every step of the way. He was waiting to hear someone shout, 'It's the Bloody-Nine!' He was waiting for folk to start running, screaming, pelting him with rubbish, faces all stamped with horror.

But no one did. One more figure that didn't belong was nothing to look at in all that damp chaos, and if anyone might have known him here, they weren't looking for him. Most likely they'd all heard he went back to the mud, far away, and were good and glad about it too. Still, there was no point staying longer than he had to. He strode up to a Union officer who looked as if he might be in charge of something, pushed his hood back and tried to put a smile on his face.

He got a scornful look for his trouble. 'We've no work for you, if that's what you're looking for.'

'You don't have my kind of work.' Logen held out the letter that Bayaz had given him.

The man unfolded it and looked it over. He frowned and read it again. Then he looked doubtfully up at Logen, mouth working. 'Well then. I see.' He pointed towards a crowd of young men, standing nervous and uncertain a few strides away, huddled miserably together as the rain started to thicken up. 'There's a convoy of reinforcements leaving for the front this afternoon. You can travel with us.'

'Fair enough.' They didn't look like they'd be much reinforcement, those scared-seeming lads, but that didn't matter to him. He didn't much care who he travelled with, as long as they were pointed at Bethod.

The trees clattered by on either side of the road – dim green and black, full of shadows. Full of surprises, maybe. It was a tough way to travel. Tough on the hands from clinging to the rail all the way, even tougher on the arse from bouncing and jolting on that hard seat. But they were getting there, gradually, and Logen reckoned that was the main thing.

There were more carts behind, spread out in a slow line along the road, loaded down with men, food, clothes, weapons, and all the stuff you need to make a war. Each one had a lamp lit, hanging up near the front, so there was a trail of bobbing lights in the dull dusk, down into the valley and up the far slope, marking out the path of the road they'd followed through the woods.

Logen turned and looked at the Union boys, gathered up in a clump near the front of the cart. Nine of them, all jolting and swaying about together with the jumping of the axles, and all keeping as well clear of him as they could.

'You seen scars like that on a man before?' one muttered, not guessing he could speak their tongue.

'Who is he anyway?'

'Dunno. A Northman, I guess.'

'I can see he's a Northman, idiot. I mean what's he doing here with us?'

'Maybe he's a scout.'

'Big bastard for a scout, ain't he?'

Logen grinned to himself as he watched the trees roll past. He felt the cool breeze on his face, smelled the mist, the earth, the cold, wet air. He never would have thought he'd be happy to be back in the North, but he was. It was good, after all that time a stranger, to be in a place where he knew the rules.

They camped out on the road, the ten of them. One group out of many, strung out through the woods, each one clustered close to their cart. Nine lads on one side of a big fire, a pot of stew bubbling over the top of it and giving off a fine-smelling steam. Logen watched them stirring it, talking to each other about home, and what was coming, and how long they'd be out there.

After a while one of them started spooning the food out into bowls and handing them round. He looked over at Logen, once he was done with the rest, then served up one more. He edged over like he was coming at a wolf's cage.

'Er . . .' He held the bowl out at arm's length. 'Stew?' He opened his mouth up wide and pointed into it with his free hand.

'Thanks, friend,' said Logen as he took the bowl, 'but I know where to put it.'

The lads all stared at him, a row of worried-looking faces, lit up flickering yellow on the far side of the fire, more suspicious than ever at him speaking their language. 'You talk common? You kept that quiet, didn't you?'

'Best to seem less than you are, in my experience.'

'If you say so,' said the lad who'd given him the bowl. 'What's your name, then?'

Logen wondered for a moment if he should make up a lie. Some nothing name that no one could have heard of. But he was who he was, and sooner or later someone would know him. That, and he'd never been much at lying. 'Logen Ninefingers, they call me.'

The lads looked blank. They'd never heard of him, and why would they have? A bunch of farmers' sons from far away, in the sunny Union. They looked like they barely knew their own names.

'What are you here for?' one of them asked him.

'Same as you. I'm here to kill.' The boys looked a bit nervy at that. 'Not you, don't worry. I've got some scores to settle.' He nodded off up the road. 'With Bethod.'

The lads exchanged some glances, then one of them shrugged. 'Well. Long as you're on our side, I guess.' He got up and dragged a bottle out of his pack. 'You want a drink?'

'Well, now.' Logen grinned and held out his cup. 'I've never yet said no to that.' He knocked it down in one, smacked his lips as he felt it warming his gullet. The lad poured him another. 'Thanks. Best not give me too much, though.'

'Why?' he asked. 'Will you kill us then?'

'Kill you? If you're lucky.'

'And if we're not?'

Logen grinned over his mug. 'I'll sing.'

The lad cracked a smile at that, and one of his mates started laughing. Next moment an arrow hissed into his side and he coughed blood down his shirt, the bottle dropping on the grass, wine gurgling out in the dark. Another boy had a shaft sticking in his thigh. He sat there, frozen, staring down at it. 'Where did that . . .' Then everyone was shouting, fumbling for weapons or throwing themselves flat on their faces. A couple more arrows whizzed over, one clattering into the fire and sending up a shower of sparks.

Logen threw his stew away, snatched up his sword and started running. He blundered into one of the boys on the way and knocked him on his face, slipped and slid, righted himself and ran full tilt for the trees where the arrow came from. It was run right at them, or run away, and he made the choice without thinking. Sometimes it doesn't matter too much what choice you make, as long as you make it quick and stick to it. Logen saw one of the archers as he rushed up close, a flash of his pale skin in the darkness as he reached for another arrow. He pulled the Maker's sword from its tattered sheath and let go a fighting roar.

The bowman could've got his arrow away before Logen was on him, most likely, but it would've been a close thing, and in the end he didn't have the bones to stand there waiting. Not many men can weigh their choices properly while death comes racing up at them. He dropped the bow too late and turned to run, and Logen hacked him in the back before he got more than a stride or two, knocked him screaming into the bushes. He dragged himself round face up, all tangled in the brush, screeching and fumbling for a knife. Logen lifted the sword to finish the job. Then blood sprayed out of the archer's mouth and he trembled, fell back and was quiet.

'Still alive,' Logen mouthed to himself, squatting down low beside the corpse, straining into the darkness. It would probably have been better for all concerned if he'd run the other way, but it was a bit late for that. Probably have been better if he'd stayed in Adua, but it was a bit late for that too.

'Bloody North,' he cursed in a whisper. If he let these bastards go they'd be making mischief all the way to the front and Logen wouldn't get a wink of sleep for worrying, aside from the good chance of an arrow in his face. Better odds coming for them, than waiting for them to come to him. A lesson he'd learned from hard experience.

He could hear the rest of the ambush crashing away through the brush and he set out after them, fist clenched tight round the grip of his sword. He felt his way between the trunks, keeping his distance. The light of the fire and the noise of the Union boys shouting dwindled behind him until he was deep in the woods, smelling of pines and wet earth, only the sound of men's hurrying feet to guide him. He made himself part of the forest, the way he had in the old days. It wasn't so hard to do. The knack came right back as though he'd been creeping in the trees every night for years. Voices echoed through the night, and Logen pressed himself still and silent up behind a pine-trunk, listening.

'Where's Dirty-Nose?'

There was a pause. 'Dead, I reckon.'

'Dead? How?'

'They had someone with 'em, Crow. Some big fucker.' Crow. Logen knew the name. Knew the voice too, now that he heard it. A Named Man who'd fought for Littlebone. You couldn't have called them friends, him and Logen, but they'd known each other. They'd been close together in the line at Carleon, fighting side by side. And now here they were again with no more than a few strides between them, more than willing to kill each other. Strange, the turns fate can take. Fighting with a man and fighting against him are only a whisker apart. Far closer together than not fighting at all.

'Northman, was he?' came Crow's voice.

'Might've been. Whoever it was he knew his business. Came up real quick. I didn't have time to get a shaft away.'

'Bastard! We ain't letting that pass. We'll camp out here and follow 'em tomorrow. Might be we'll get him then, this big one.'

'Oh aye, we'll fucking get him. Don't you worry about that none. I'll cut his neck for him, the bastard.'

'Good for you. 'Til then you can keep an eye open for him while the rest of us catch some sleep. Might be the anger'll keep you awake this time, eh?'

'Aye, chief. Right y'are.'

Logen sat and watched, catching glimpses through the trees as four of them spread out their blankets and rolled up to sleep.

The fifth took his place, back to the others, and looked out the way they'd come, sitting guard. Logen waited, and he heard one begin to snore. Some rain started up, and it tapped and trickled on the branches of the pines. After a while it spattered into his hair, into his clothes, ran down his face and fell to the wet earth, drip, drip, drip. Logen sat, still and silent as a stone.

It can be a fearsome weapon, patience. One that few men ever learn to use. A hard thing, to keep your mind on killing once you're out of danger and your blood's cooled off. But Logen had always had the trick of it. So he sat and let the slow time sneak by, and thought about long ago, until the moon was high, and there was pale light washing down between the trees with the tickling rain. Pale light enough for him to see his tasks by.

He uncurled his legs and started moving, working his way between the tree trunks, planting his feet nice and gentle in the brush. The rain was his ally, patter and trickle masking the soft sounds his boots made as he circled round behind the guard.

He slid out a knife, wet blade glinting once in the patchy moonlight, and he padded out from the trees and through their camp. Between the sleeping men, close enough to touch them. Close as a brother. The guard sniffed and shifted unhappily, dragging his wet blanket round his shoulders, all beaded up with twinkling rain drops. Logen stopped and waited, looked down at the pale face of one of the sleepers, turned sideways, eyes closed and mouth wide open, breath making faint smoke in the clammy night.

The guard was still now, and Logen slipped up close behind him, holding his breath. He reached out with his left hand, fingers working in the misty air, feeling for the moment. He reached out with his right hand, fist clenched tight round the hard grip of his knife. He felt his lips curling back from his gritted teeth. Now was the time, and when the time comes, you strike with no backward glances.

Logen reached round and clamped his hand tight over the guard's mouth, cut his throat quick and hard, deep enough that he felt the blade scraping on his neck bones. He jerked and struggled for a moment, but Logen held him tight, tight as a lover, and he made no more than a quiet gurgle. Logen felt blood over his hands, hot and sticky. He didn't worry yet about the others. If one of them woke all they'd see would be the outline of one man in the darkness, and that was all they were expecting.

It wasn't long before the guard went limp, and Logen laid him down gently on his side, head flopping. Four shapes lay there under their wet blankets, helpless. Maybe there'd been a time when Logen would've had to work himself up to a job like this. When he'd have had to think about why it was the right thing to do. But if there had been, it was long gone. Up in the North, the time you spend thinking will be the time you get killed in. All they were now were four tasks to get done.

He crept up to the first, lifted his bloody knife, overhand, and stabbed him clean in the heart right through his coat, hand pressed over his mouth. He died quieter than he slept. Logen came up on the second one, ready to do the same. His boot clattered into something metal. Water flask, maybe. Whatever it was, it made quite the racket. The sleeping man's eyes worked open, he started to lift himself up. Logen rammed the knife in his gut and dragged at it, slitting his belly open. He made a kind of a wheeze, mouth and eyes wide, clutching at Logen's arm.

'Eh?' The third one sat straight up and staring. Logen tore his hand free and heaved his sword out. 'Wha' the—' The man lifted his arm up, on an instinct, and the dull blade took his hand off at the wrist and chopped deep into his skull, sending black spots of blood showering into the wet air and knocking him down on his back.

But that gave the last of them time enough to roll out of his blanket and grab up an axe. Now he stood hunched over, hands spread out, fighting ready like a man who'd had plenty of practice at it. Crow. Logen could hear his breath hissing, see it smoking in the rain.

'You should've started wi' me!' he hissed.

Logen couldn't deny it. He'd been concentrating on getting

81

them all killed, and hadn't paid much mind to the order. Still, it was a bit late to worry now. He shrugged. 'Start or finish, ain't too much difference.'

'We'll see.' Crow weighed his axe in the misty air, shifting around, looking for an opening. Logen stood still and caught his breath, the sword hanging down by his side, the grip cold and wet in his clenched fist. He'd never been much of a one for moving until it was time. 'Best tell me your name, while you still got breath in you. I like to know who I've killed.'

'You already know me, Crow.' Logen held his other hand up, and he let the fingers spread out, and the moonlight glinted black on his bloody hand, and on the bloody stump of his missing finger. 'We were side by side in the line at Carleon. Never thought you'd all forget me so soon. But things don't often turn out the way we expect, eh?'

He'd stopped moving now, had Crow. Logen couldn't see more than a gleam of his eyes in the dark, but he could tell the doubt and the fear in the way he stood. 'No,' he whispered, shaking his head in the darkness. 'Can't be! Ninefingers is dead!'

'That so?' Logen took a deep breath and pushed it out, slow, into the wet night. 'Reckon I must be his ghost.'

They'd dug some sort of a hole to squat in, the Union lads, sacks and boxes up on the sides as a rampart. Logen could see the odd face moving over the top, staring off into the trees, the dull light from the guttering fire glinting on an arrow head or a spear tip. Dug in, watching for another ambush. If they'd been nervy before, they were most likely shitting themselves now. Probably one of them would get scared and shoot him as soon as he made himself known. Damn Union bows had a trigger that went off at a touch, once they were drawn. Would have been just about his luck, to get killed over nothing in the middle of nowhere, and by his own side too, but he didn't have much of a choice. Not unless he wanted to walk up to the front.

So he cleared his throat and called out. 'Now no one shoot

or anything!' A string went and a bolt thudded into a tree a couple of strides to his left. Logen hunched down against the wet earth. 'No one shoot, I said!'

'Who's out there?'

'It's me, Ninefingers!' Silence. 'The Northman who was on the cart!'

A long pause, and some whispering. 'Alright! But come out slow, and keep your hands where we can see them!'

'Fair enough!' He straightened up and crept out from the trees, hands held high. 'Just don't shoot me, eh? That's your end of the deal!'

He walked across the ground towards the fire, arms spread out, wincing at the thought of getting a bolt in his chest any minute. He recognised the faces of the lads from before, them and the officer who had charge of the supply column. A couple of them followed him with their bows as he stepped slowly over the makeshift parapet and down into the trench. It had been dug along in front of the fire, but not that well, and there was a big puddle in the bottom.

'Where the hell did you get to?' demanded the officer angrily.

'Tracking them that ambushed us tonight.'

'Did you catch 'em?' one of the boys asked.

'That I did.'

'And?'

'Dead.' Logen nodded at the puddle in the bottom of the hole. 'So you needn't sleep in the water tonight. Any of that stew left?'

'How many were there?' snapped the officer.

Logen poked around the embers of the fire, but the pot was empty. Just his luck, again. 'Five.'

'You, on your own, against five?'

'There were six to begin with, but I killed one at the start. He's in the trees over there somewhere.' Logen dug a heel of bread out of his pack and rubbed it round the inside of the pot, trying to get a bit of meat grease on there, at least. 'I waited until they were sleeping, so I only had to fight one of 'em, face to face. Always been lucky that way, I guess.' He didn't feel that lucky. Looking at his hand in the firelight, it was still stained with blood. Dark blood under his fingernails, dried into the lines in his palm. 'Always been lucky.'

The officer hardly looked convinced. 'How do we know that you aren't one of them? That you weren't spying on us? That they aren't waiting out there now, for you to give them a signal when we're vulnerable?'

'You've been vulnerable the whole way,' snorted Logen. 'But it's a fair question. I thought you might ask it.' He pulled the canvas bag out from his belt. 'That's why I brought you this.' The officer frowned as he reached out for it, shook it open, peered suspiciously inside. He swallowed. 'Like I said, there were five. So you got ten thumbs in there. That satisfy you?'

The officer looked more sick than satisfied, but he nodded, lips squeezed together, and held the bag back out to him at arm's length.

Logen shook his head. 'Keep it. It's a finger I'm missing. I got all the thumbs I need.'

The cart lurched to a stop. For the last mile or two they'd moved at a crawl. Now the road, if you could use the word about a sea of mud, was choked up with floundering men. They squelched their way from one near solid spot to another, flowing through the thin rain between the press of mired carts and unhappy horses, the stacks of crates and barrels, the ill-pitched tents. Logen watched a group of filth-caked lads straining at a wagon stuck up to its axles in the muck, without much success. It was like seeing an army sink slowly into a bog. A vast shipwreck, on land.

Logen's travelling companions were down to seven now, hunched and gaunt, looking mighty tired from sleepless nights and bad weather on the trail. One dead, one sent back to Uffrith already with an arrow in his leg. Not the best start to their time in the North, but Logen doubted it would get any better from here on. He clambered down off the back of the

84

cart, boots sinking into the well-rutted mud, arched his back and stretched his aching legs out, dragged his pack down.

'Luck, then,' he said to the lads. None of them spoke. They'd hardly said a word to him since the night of the ambush. Most likely that whole business with the thumbs had got them worried. But if that was the worst they saw while they were up here they'd have done alright, Logen reckoned. He shrugged and turned away, started floundering through the muck.

Just up ahead the officer from the supply column was being dealt a talking-to by a tall, grim-looking man in a red uniform, seemed like the closest thing they had in all this mess to someone in charge. It took Logen a minute to recognise him. They'd sat together at a feast, in very different surroundings, and they'd talked of war. He looked older, leaner, tougher, now. He had a hard frown on his face and a lot of hard grey in his wet hair, but he grinned when he saw Logen standing there, and walked up to him with his hand out.

'By the dead,' he said in good Northern, 'but fate can play some tricks. I know you.'

'Likewise.'

'Ninefingers, wasn't it?'

'That's right. And you're West. From Angland.'

'That I am. Sorry I can't give you a better welcome, but the army only got up here a day or two ago and, as you can see, things aren't quite in order yet. Not there, idiot!' he roared at a driver trying to get his cart between two others, the space between them nowhere near wide enough. 'Do you have such a thing as summer in this bloody country?'

'You're looking at it. Didn't you see winter?'

'Huh. You've a point there. What brings you up here, anyway?'

Logen handed West the letter. He hunched over to shield it from the rain and read it, frowning.

'Signed by Lord Chamberlain Hoff, eh?'

'That a good thing?'

West pursed his lips as he handed the letter back. 'I suppose that depends. It means you've got some powerful friends. Or some powerful enemies.'

'Bit of both, maybe.'

West grinned. 'I find they go together. You've come to fight?'

'That I have.'

'Good. We can always use a man with experience.' He watched the recruits clambering down off the carts and gave a long sigh. 'We've still got far too many here without. You should go up and join the rest of the Northmen.'

'You've got Northmen with you?'

'We have, and more coming over every day. Seems that a lot of them aren't too happy with the way their King has been leading them. About his deal with the Shanka in particular.'

'Deal? With the Shanka?' Logen frowned. He'd never have thought that even Bethod would stoop that low, but it was hardly the first time he'd been disappointed. 'He's got Flatheads fighting with him?'

'He certainly does. He's got Flatheads, and we've got Northmen. It's a strange world, alright.'

'That it surely is,' said Logen, shaking his head. 'How many do you have?'

'About three hundred, I'd say, at last count, though they don't take too well to being counted.'

'Reckon I'll make it three hundred and one, then, if you'll have me.'

'They're camped up there, on the left wing,' and he pointed towards the dark outline of trees against the evening sky.

'Right enough. Who's the chief?'

'Fellow called the Dogman.'

Logen stared at him for a long moment. 'Called the what?'

'Dogman. You know him?'

'You could say that,' whispered Logen, a smile spreading right across his face. 'You could say that.'

Dusk was pressing on fast and night was pressing in fast behind, and they'd just got the long fire burning as Logen walked up. He could see the shapes of the Carls taking their places down each side of it, heads and shoulders cut out black against the flames. He could hear their voices and their laughter, loud in the still evening now the rain had stopped.

It had been a long time since he heard a crowd of men all speaking Northern, and it sounded strange in his ears, even if it was his own tongue. It brought back some ugly memories. Crowds of men shouting at him, shouting for him. Crowds charging into battle, cheering their victories, mourning their dead. He could smell meat cooking from somewhere. A sweet, rich smell that tickled his nose and made his gut grumble.

There was a torch set up on a pole by the path, and a bored-looking lad stood underneath it with a spear, frowning at Logen as he walked up. Must've drawn the short straw, to be on guard while the others were eating, and he didn't look too happy about it.

'What d'you want?' he growled.

'You got the Dogman here?'

'Aye, what of it?'

'I'll need to speak to him.'

'Will you, now?'

Another man walked up, well past his prime, with a shock of grey hair and a leathery face. 'What we got here?'

'New recruit,' grumbled the lad. 'Wants to see the chief.'

The old man squinted at Logen, frowning. 'Do I know you, friend?'

Logen lifted up his face so the torchlight fell across it. Better to look a man in the eye, and let him see you, and show him you feel no fear. That was the way his father had taught him. 'I don't know. Do you?'

'Where did you come over from? Whitesides' crew, is it?'

'No. I've been working alone.'

'Alone? Well, now. Seems like I recognise—' The old boy's eyes opened up wide, and his jaw sagged open, and his face went white as cut chalk. 'By all the fucking dead,' he whispered, taking a stumbling step back. 'It's the Bloody-Nine!'

Maybe Logen had been hoping no-one would know him.

That they'd all have forgotten. That they'd have new things to worry them, and he'd be just a man like any other. But now he saw that look on the old boy's face – that shitting-himself look, and it was clear enough how it would be. Just the way it used to be. And the worst of it was, now that Logen was recognised, and he saw that fear, and that horror, and that respect, he wasn't sure that he didn't like seeing it. He'd earned it, hadn't he? After all, facts are facts.

He was the Bloody-Nine.

The lad didn't quite get it yet. 'Having a joke on me are yer? You'll be telling me it's Bethod his self come over next, eh?' But no one laughed, and Logen lifted his hand up and stared through the gap where his middle finger used to be. The lad looked from that stump, to the trembling old man and back.

'Shit,' he croaked.

'Where's your chief, boy?' Logen's own voice scared him. Flat, and dead, and cold as the winter.

'He's . . . he's . . .' The lad raised a quivering finger to point towards the fires.

'Well then. Guess I'll sniff him out myself.' The two of them edged out of Logen's way. He didn't exactly smile as he passed. More he drew his lips back to show them his teeth. There was a certain reputation to be lived up to, after all. 'No need to worry,' he hissed in their faces. 'I'm on your side, ain't I?'

No one said a word to him as he walked along behind the Carls, up towards the head of the fire. A couple of them glanced over their shoulders, but nothing more than any newcomer in a camp might get. They'd no idea who he was, yet, but they soon would have. That lad and that old man would be whispering, and the whispers would spread around the fire, as whispers do, and everyone would be watching him.

He started as a great shadow moved beside him, so big he'd taken it for a tree at first. A huge, big man, scratching at his beard, smiling at the fire. Tul Duru. There could be no mistaking the Thunderhead, even in the half-light. Not a man that size. Made Logen wonder afresh how the hell he'd beaten him in the first place.

He felt a strange urge, right then, just to put his head down and walk past, off into the night and never look back. Then he wouldn't have to be the Bloody-Nine again. It would just have been a fresh lad and an old man, swore they saw a ghost one night. He could've gone far away, and started new, and been whoever he wanted. But he'd tried that once already, and it had done him no good. The past was always right behind him, breathing on his neck. It was time to turn around and face it.

'Alright there, big lad.' Tul peered at him in the dusk, orange light and black shadow shifting across his big rock of a face, his big rug of a beard.

'Who . . . hold on . . .' Logen swallowed. He'd no idea, now he thought about it, what any of them might make of seeing him again. They'd been enemies long before they were friends, after all. Each one of them had fought him. Each one had been keen to kill him, and with good reasons too. Then he'd run off south and left them to the Shanka. What if all he got after a year or more apart was a cold look?

Then Tul grabbed hold of him and folded him in a crushing hug. 'You're alive!' He let go of him long enough to check he had the right man, then hugged him again.

'Aye, I'm alive,' wheezed Logen, just enough breath left in him to say it. Seemed he'd get one warm welcome, at least.

Tul was grinning all over his face. 'Come on.' And he beckoned Logen after. 'The lads are going to shit!'

He followed Tul, his heart beating in his mouth, up to the head of the fire, where the chief would sit with his closest Named Men. And there they were, sat around on the ground. Dogman was in the middle, muttering something quiet to Dow. Grim was on the other side, leaning on one elbow, fiddling with the flights on his arrows. It was just like nothing had changed.

'Got someone here to see you, Dogman,' said Tul, his voice squeaky from keeping the surprise in.

'Have you, now?' Dogman peered up at Logen, but he was hidden in the shadows behind Tul's great shoulder. 'Can't it wait 'til after we've eaten?'

'Do you know, I don't think it can.'

'Why? Who is it?'

'Who is it?' Tul grabbed Logen's shoulder and shoved him lurching out into the firelight. 'It's only Logen fucking Ninefingers!' Logen's boot slid in the mud and he nearly pitched on his arse, had to wave his arms around all over to keep his balance. The talk around the fire all sputtered out in a moment and every face was turned towards him. Two long, frozen rows of them, slack in the shifting light, no sound but the sighing wind and the crackling fire. The Dogman stared up at him as though he was seeing the dead walk, his mouth hanging wider and wider open with every passing moment.

'I thought you was all killed,' said Logen as he got his balance back. 'Guess there's such a thing as being too realistic.'

Dogman got to his feet, slowly. He held out his hand, and Logen took hold of it.

There was nothing to say. Not for men who'd been through as much as the two of them had together – fighting the Shanka, crossing the mountains, getting through the wars, and after. Years of it. Dogman pressed his hand and Logen slapped his other hand on top of it, and Dogman slapped his other hand on top of that. They grinned at each other, and nodded, and things were back the way they had been. Nothing needed saying.

'Grim. Good to see you.'

'Uh,' grunted Grim, handing him up a mug then looking back to his shafts, just as though Logen had gone for a piss a minute ago and come back a minute later like everyone had expected. Logen had to grin. He'd have hoped for nothing else.

'That Black Dow hiding down there?'

'I'd have hidden better if I knew you were coming.' Dow looked Logen up and down with a grin not entirely welcoming. 'If it ain't Ninefingers his self. Thought you said he went over a cliff?' he barked at Dogman.

'That's what I saw.'

'Oh, I went over.' Logen remembered the wind in his mouth, the rock and the snow turning around him, the crash as the water crushed his breath out. 'I went on over and I washed up whole, more or less.' Dogman made room for him on the stretched-out hides by the fire, and he sat down, and the others sat near him.

Dow was shaking his head. 'You always was a lucky bastard when it came to staying alive. I should've known you'd turn up.'

'I thought the Flatheads had got you all sure,' said Logen. 'How'd you get out of there?'

'Threetrees got us out,' said Dogman.

Tul nodded. 'Led us out and over the mountains, and hunted through the North, and all the way down into Angland.'

'Squabbling all the way like a bunch of old women, no doubt?'

Dogman grinned across at Dow. 'There was some moaning on the trail.'

'Where's Threetrees now, then?' Logen was looking forward to having a word with that old boy.

'Dead,' said Grim.

Logen winced. He'd guessed that might be the way, since Dogman was in charge. Tul nodded his big head. 'Died fighting. Leading a charge, into the Shanka. Died fighting that thing. That Feared.'

'Bastard fucking thing.' And Dow hawked some spit into the mud.

'What about Forley?'

'Dead n'all,' barked Dow. 'He went into Carleon, to warn Bethod that the Shanka were coming over the mountains. Calder had him killed, just for the sport of it. Bastard!' And he spat again. He'd always been a great one for spitting, had Dow.

'Dead.' Logen shook his head. Forley dead, and Threetrees dead, it was a damn shame. But it wasn't so long since he thought the whole lot of them were back in the mud, so four still going was quite the bonus, in a way. 'Well. Good men both. The best, and died well, by the sound of it. As well as men can, anyway.'

'Aye,' said Tul, lifting up a mug. 'As well as you can. Here's to the dead.'

They all drank in silence, and Logen smacked his lips at the taste of beer. Too long away. 'So, a year gone by,' grunted Dow. 'We done some killing, and we walked a damn long way, and we fought in a bastard of a battle. We lost two men and we got us a new chief. What the hell you been up to, Ninefingers?'

'Well . . . that there is some kind of a tale.' Logen wondered what kind, exactly, and found he wasn't sure. 'I thought the Shanka got you all, since life's taught me to expect the worst, so I went south, and I fell in with this wizard. I went a sort of journey with him, across the sea and far away, to find some kind of a thing, which when we got there . . . weren't there.' It all sounded more than a bit mad now he said it.

'What kind of a thing?' asked Tul, his face all screwed up with puzzlement.

'Do you know what?' Logen sucked at his teeth, tasting of drink. 'I can't say that I really know.' They all looked at each other as if they never heard such a damn-fool story, and Logen had to admit they probably hadn't. 'Still, it hardly matters now. Turns out life ain't quite the bastard I took it for.' And he gave Tul a friendly clap on the back.

The Dogman puffed out his cheeks. 'Well, we're glad you're back, anyway. Guess you'll be taking your place again now, eh?'

'My place?'

'You'll be taking over, no? I mean to say, you were chief.'

'Used to be, maybe, but I've no plans to go back to it. Seems as if these lads are happy enough with things the way they are.'

'But you know a sight more than me about leading men—'

'I don't know that's a fact. Me being in charge never worked out too well for anyone, now did it? Not for us, not for those who fought with us, not for them we fought against.' Logen hunched his shoulders at the memories. 'I'll put my word in, if you want it, but I'd sooner follow you. I did my time, and it wasn't a good one.'

Dogman looked like he'd been hoping for a different outcome. 'Well . . . if you're sure . . .'

'I'm sure.' And Logen slapped him on the shoulder. 'Not easy, is it, being chief?'

'No,' grumbled Dogman. 'It bloody ain't.'

'Besides, I reckon a lot of these lads have been on the other side of an argument with me before, and they're not altogether pleased to see me.' Logen looked down the fire at the hard faces, heard the mutterings with his name in them, too quiet to tell the matter for sure, but he could guess that it wasn't complimentary.

'They'll be glad enough to have you alongside 'em when the fighting starts, don't worry about that.'

'Maybe.' Seemed an awful shame that he'd have to set to killing before folk would give him so much as a nod. Sharp looks came at him from out the dark, flicking away when he looked back. There was only one man, more or less, who met his eye. A big lad with long hair, halfway down the fire.

'Who's that?' asked Logen.

'Who's what?'

'That lad down there staring at me.'

'That there is Shivers.' Dogman sucked at his pointed teeth. 'He's got a lot of bones, Shivers. Fought with us a few times now, and he does it damn well. First of all I'll tell you he's a good man and we owe him. Then I ought to mention that he's Rattleneck's son.'

Logen felt a wave of sickness. 'He's what?'

'His other son.'

'The boy?'

'Long time ago now, all that. Boys grow up.'

A long time ago, maybe, but nothing was forgotten. Logen could see that straight away. Nothing was ever forgotten, up here in the North, and he should've known better than to think it might be. 'I should say something to him. If we have to fight together . . . I should say something.'

Dogman winced. 'Might be better that you don't. Some wounds are best not picked at. Eat, and talk to him in the morning. Everything sounds fairer in the daylight. That or you can decide against it.'

'Uh,' grunted Grim.

Logen stood up. 'You're right, most likely, but it's better to do it—'

'Than to live with the fear of it.' Dogman nodded into the fire. 'You been missed, Logen, and that's a fact.'

'You too, Dogman. You too.'

He walked down through the darkness, smelly with smoke and meat and men, along behind the Carls sitting at the fire. He felt them hunching their shoulders, muttering as he passed. He knew what they were thinking. The Bloody-Nine, right behind me, and there's no worse man in the world to have your back to. He could see Shivers watching him all the way, one eye cold through his long hair, lips pressed together in a hard line. He had a knife out for eating, but just as good for stabbing a man. Logen watched the firelight gleaming on its edge as he squatted down beside him.

'So you're the Bloody-Nine.'

Logen grimaced. 'Aye. I reckon.'

Shivers nodded, still staring at him. 'This is what the Bloody-Nine looks like.'

'Hope you're not disappointed.'

'Oh no. Not me. Good to have a face on you, after all this time.'

Logen looked down at the ground, trying to think of some way to come at it. Some way to move his hands, or set his face, some words that might start to make the tiniest part of it right. 'Those were hard times, back then,' he ended up saying.

'Harder'n now?'

Logen chewed at his lip. 'Well, maybe not.'

'Times are always hard, I reckon,' said Shivers between gritted teeth. 'That ain't an excuse for doing a runny shit.'

'You're right. There ain't any excuses for what I did. I'm not proud of it. Don't know what else I can say, except I hope you can put it out of the way, and we can fight side by side.'

'I'll be honest with you,' said Shivers, and his voice was strangled-sounding, like he was trying not to shout, or trying not to cry, or both at once, maybe. 'It's a hard thing to just put behind me. You killed my brother, when you'd promised him mercy, and you cut his arms and legs off, and you nailed his head on Bethod's standard.' His knuckles were trembling white round the grip of his knife, and Logen saw that it was taking all he had not to stab him in the face, and he didn't blame him. He didn't blame him one bit. 'My father never was the same after that. He'd nothing in him any more. I spent a lot of years dreaming of killing you, Bloody-Nine.'

Logen nodded, slowly. 'Well. You'll never be alone with that dream.'

He caught other cold looks from across the flames, now. Frowns in the shadows, grim faces in the flickering light. Men he didn't even know, afraid to their bones, or nursing scores against him. A whole lot of fear and a whole lot of scores. He could count on the fingers of one hand the folk who were pleased to see him alive. Even missing a finger. And this was supposed to be his side of the fight.

Dogman had been right. Some wounds are best not picked at. Logen got up, his shoulders prickling, and walked back to the head of the fire, where the talk came easier. He'd no doubt Shivers wanted to kill him just as much as he ever had, but that was no surprise.

You have to be realistic. No words could ever make right the things he'd done.

Bad Debts

Superior Glokta,

Though I believe that we have never been formally introduced, I have heard your name mentioned often these past few weeks. Without causing offence, I hope, it seems as if every room I enter you have recently left, or are due soon to arrive in, and every negotiation I undertake is made more complicated by your involvement.

Although our employers are very much opposed in this business, there is no reason why we should not behave like civilised men. It may be that you and I can hammer out between us an understanding that will leave us both with less work and more progress.

I will be waiting for you at the slaughter-yard near the Four Corners tomorrow morning from six. My apologies for such a noisy choice of spot but I feel our conversation would be better kept private.

I daresay that neither one of us is to be put off by a little ordure underfoot.

Harlen Morrow,
Secretary to High Justice Marovia.

Being kind, the place stank. *It would seem that a few hundred live pigs do not smell so sweet as one would expect.* The floor of the shadowy warehouse was slick with their stinking slurry, the thick air full of their desperate noise. They honked and squealed, grunted and jostled each other in their writhing pens, sensing, perhaps, that the slaughterman's knife was not so very far away. But, as Morrow had observed, Glokta was not one to be put off by the noise, or the knives, or, for that matter, an unpleasant odour. *I spend my days wading through the metaphorical filth, after all. Why not the real thing?* The slippery footing was more of a problem. He hobbled with tiny steps, his leg burning. *Imagine arriving at my meeting caked in pig dung. That would hardly project the right image of fearsome ruthlessness, would it?*

He saw Morrow now, leaning on one of the pens. *Just like a farmer admiring his prize-winning herd.* Glokta limped up beside him, boots squelching, wincing and breathing hard, sweat trickling down his back. 'Well, Morrow, you know just how to make a girl feel special, I'll give you that.'

Marovia's secretary grinned up at him, a small man with a round face and eyeglasses. 'Superior Glokta, may I first say that I have nothing but the highest respect for your achievements in Gurkhul, your methods in negotiation, and—'

'I did not come here to exchange pleasantries, Morrow. If that's all your business I can think of sweeter-smelling venues.'

'And sweeter companions too, I do not doubt. To business, then. These are trying times.'

'I'm with you there.'

'Change. Uncertainty. Unease amongst the peasantry—'

'A little more than unease, I would say, wouldn't you?'

'Rebellion, then. Let us hope that the Closed Council's trust in Colonel Luthar will be justified, and he will stop the rebels outside the city.'

'I wouldn't trust his corpse to stop an arrow, but I suppose the Closed Council have their reasons.'

'They always do. Though, of course, they do not always agree with each other.' *They never agree about anything. It's practically a rule of the damn institution.* 'But it is those that serve them,' and Morrow peered significantly over the rims of his eye-glasses, 'that carry the burden for their lack of accord. I feel that we, in particular, have been stepping on each other's toes rather too much for either of our comfort.'

'Huh,' sneered Glokta, working his numb toes inside his boot. 'I do hope your feet aren't too bruised. I could never live with myself if I caused you to limp. Might you have a solution in mind?'

'You could say that.' He smiled down at the pigs, watching

97

them squirm and grunt and clamber over one another. 'We had hogs on the farm, where I grew up.' *Mercy. Anything but the life story.* 'It was my responsibility to feed them. Rising in the morning, so early it was still dark, breath smoking in the cold.' *Oh, he paints a vivid picture! Young Master Morrow, up to his knees in filth, watching his pigs gorge themselves, and dreaming of escape. A brave new life in the glittering city!* Morrow grinned up at him, dim light twinkling on the lenses of his spectacles. 'You know, these things will eat anything. Even cripples.'

Ah. So that's it.

It was then that Glokta became aware of a man moving furtively towards them from the far end of the shed. A burly-looking man in a ragged coat, keeping to the shadows. He had his arm pressed tightly by his side, hand tucked up in his sleeve. *Just as if he were hiding a knife up there, and not doing it very well. Better just to walk up with a smile on your face and the knife in plain view. There are a hundred reasons to carry a blade in a slaughterhouse. But there can only ever be one reason to try and hide one.*

He glanced over his shoulder, wincing as his neck clicked. Another man, much like the first, was creeping up from that direction. Glokta raised his eyebrows. 'Thugs? How very unoriginal.'

'Unoriginal, perhaps, but I think you will find them quite effective.'

'So I'm to be slaughtered in the slaughterhouse, eh, Morrow? Butchered at the butchers! Sand dan Glokta, breaker of hearts, winner of the Contest, hero of the Gurkish war, shat out the arses of a dozen different pigs!' He snorted with laughter and had to wipe some snot off his top lip.

'I'm so glad you enjoy the irony,' muttered Morrow, looking slightly put out.

'Oh, I do. Fed to the swine. So obvious I can honestly say it's not what I expected.' He gave a long sigh. 'But not expected and not planned for are two quite different things.'

The bowstring made no sound over the clamour of the hogs. The thug seemed at first to slip, to drop his shining knife and

98

fall on his side for no reason. Then Glokta saw the bolt poking from his side. *Not too great a surprise, of course, and yet it always seems like magic.*

The hired man at the other end of the warehouse took a shocked step back, never seeing Practical Vitari slip silently over the rail of the empty pen behind him. There was a flash of metal in the darkness as she slashed the tendons at the back of his knee and brought him down, his cry quickly shut off as she pulled her chain tight round his neck.

Severard dropped down easily from the rafters off to Glokta's left and squelched into the muck. He sauntered over, flatbow across his shoulder, kicked the fallen knife off into the darkness and looked down at the man he had shot. 'I owe you five marks,' he called to Frost. 'Missed his heart, damn it. Liver, maybe?'

'Lither,' grunted the albino, emerging from the shadows at the far end of the warehouse. The man struggled up to his knees, clutching at the shaft through his side, twisted face half crusted with filth. Frost lifted his stick as he passed and dealt him a crunching blow on the back of the head, putting a sharp end to his cries and knocking him face down in the muck. Vitari, meanwhile, had wrestled her man onto the floor and was kneeling on his back, dragging at the chain round his neck. His struggling grew weaker, and weaker, and stopped. *A little more dead meat on the floor of the slaughterhouse.*

Glokta looked back to Morrow. 'How quickly things can change, eh, Harlen? One minute everyone wants to know you. The next?' He tapped sadly at his useless foot with the filthy toe of his cane. 'You're fucked. It's a tough lesson.' *I should know.*

Marovia's secretary backed away, tongue darting over his lips, one hand held out in front of him. 'Now hold on—'

'Why?' Glokta pushed out his bottom lip. 'Do you really think we can grow to love each other again after all this?'

'Perhaps we can come to some—'

'I'm not upset that you tried to kill me. But to make such a pathetic effort at it? We're professionals, Morrow. It's an insult, that you thought this might work.'

'I'm hurt,' muttered Severard.

'Wounded,' sang Vitari, chain jingling in the darkness.

'Deethly othended,' grunted Frost, herding Morrow back towards the pen.

'You should have stuck to licking Hoff's big drunk arse. Or maybe you should have stayed on the farm, with your pigs. Tough work, perhaps, in the early morning, and so on. But it's a living.'

'Just wait! Just wuurgh—'

Severard grabbed Morrow's shoulder from behind, stabbed him through the side of his neck and chopped his throat out as calmly as if he was gutting a fish.

Blood showered over Glokta's boots and he stumbled back, wincing as pain shot up his ruined leg. 'Shit!' he hissed through his gums, nearly stumbling and falling on his arse in the filth, only managing to stay upright by clinging desperately to the fence beside him. 'Couldn't you just have strangled him?'

Severard shrugged. 'Same result, isn't it?' Morrow slid to his knees, eye-glasses skewed across his face, one hand clutching at his cut neck while blood bubbled out into his shirt collar.

Glokta watched the clerk tip onto his back, one leg kicking at the floor, his scraping heel leaving long streaks in the stinking muck. *Alas for the pigs on the farm. They will never now see young master Morrow coming back over the hill, returned from his brave life in the glittering city, his breath smoking in the cold, cold morning . . .*

The secretary's convulsions grew gentler, and gentler, and he lay still. Glokta clung to the rail for a moment, watching the corpse. *When was it exactly that I became . . . this? By small degrees, I suppose. One act presses hard upon another, on a path we have no choice but to follow, and each time there are reasons. We do what we must, we do what we are told, we do what is easiest. What else can we do but solve one sordid problem at a time? Then one day we look up and find that we are . . . this.*

He looked at the blood gleaming on his boot, wrinkled his nose and wiped it off on Morrow's trouser leg. *Ah, well. I would love to spend more time on philosophy, but I have officials to bribe, and noblemen to blackmail, and votes to rig, and secretaries to murder, and lovers to threaten. So many knives to juggle. And as one clatters to the filthy floor, another must go up, blade spinning razor sharp above our heads. It never gets any easier.*

'Our magical friends are back in town.'

Severard lifted his mask and scratched behind it. 'The Magi?'

'The First of the bastards, no less, and his bold company of heroes. Him, and his slinking apprentice, and that woman. The Navigator too. Keep an eye on them, and see if there's a piglet we can separate from the herd. It's high time we knew what they were about. Do you still have your charming house, by the water?'

'Of course.'

'Good. Perhaps for once we can get ahead of the game, and when his Eminence demands answers we can have them to hand.' *And I can finally earn a pat on the head from my master.*

'What shall we do with these?' asked Vitari, jerking her spiky head towards the corpses.

Glokta sighed. 'The hogs will eat anything, apparently.'

The city was growing dark as Glokta dragged his ruined leg through the emptying streets and up towards the Agriont. The shopkeepers were closing their doors, the householders were lighting their lamps, candlelight spilling out into the dusky alleyways through chinks around the shutters. *Happy families settling down to happy dinners, no doubt. Loving fathers with their lovely wives, their adorable children, their full and meaningful lives. My heartfelt congratulations.*

He pressed his remaining teeth into his sore gums with the effort of maintaining his pace, sweat starting to dampen his shirt, his leg burning more and more with every lurching step. *But I'm not stopping for this useless lump of dead meat.* The pain crept up from ankle to knee, from knee to hip, from hip all the way up his twisted spine and into his skull. *All this effort just to kill a mid-level administrator, who worked no more than a few buildings away from the House of Questions in any case. It's a damn waste of my time, is what it is, it's a damn—*

'Superior Glokta?'

A man had stepped up, respectfully, his face in shadow. Glokta squinted at him. 'Do I—'

It was well done, there was no denying it. He was not even aware of the other man until the bag was over his head and one of his arms was twisted behind his back, pushing him helplessly forward. He stumbled, fumbled his cane and heard it clatter to the cobbles.

'Aargh!' A searing spasm shot through his back as he tried unsuccessfully to drag his arm free, and he was forced to hang limp, gasping with pain inside the bag. In a moment they had his wrists tied and he felt a powerful hand shoved under each of his armpits. He was marched away with great speed, one man on each side, his feet barely scraping on the cobbles as they went. *The fastest I've walked in a good long while, anyway.* Their grip was not rough, but it was irresistible. *Professionals. An altogether better class of thug than Morrow stretched to. Whoever ordered this is no fool. So who did order it?*

Sult himself, or one of Sult's enemies? One of his rivals in the race for the throne? High Justice Marovia? Lord Brock? Anyone on the entire Open Council? Or could it be the Gurkish? They have never been my closest friends. The banking house of Valint and Balk, perhaps, chosen finally to call in their debt? Might I have seriously misjudged young Colonel Luthar, even? Or could it simply be Superior Goyle, no longer keen to share his job with the cripple? It was quite the list, now that he was forced to consider it.

He heard the footfalls slapping around him. Narrow alleys. He had no idea how far they had come. His breath echoed in the bag, rasping, throaty. *The heart thumps, the skin prickles with cold sweat. Excited. Scared, even. What might they want with me? People are not snatched from the street in order to be given promotions, or confections, or tender kisses, more's the pity. I know why people are snatched from the street. Few better.*

Down a set of steps, the toes of his boots scuffing helplessly against the treads. The sound of a heavy door being heaved shut. Footsteps echoing in a tiled corridor. Another door closing. He felt himself dumped unceremoniously in a chair. *And now, no doubt, for better or worse, we shall find out . . .*

The bag was snatched suddenly from his head and Glokta blinked as harsh light stabbed at his eyes. A white room, too bright for comfort. *A type of room with which I am sadly familiar. And yet it looks so much uglier from this side of the table.* Someone was sitting opposite. *Or the blurry outline of a someone.* He closed one eye and peered through the other as his vision adjusted.

'Well,' he murmured. 'What a surprise.'

'A pleasant one, I hope.'

'I suppose we'll see.' Carlot dan Eider had changed. *And it would seem that exile has not entirely disagreed with her.* Her hair had grown back, not all the way, perhaps, but more than far enough to manage a fetching style. The bruises round her throat had faded, there were only the very faintest of marks where her cheek had been covered in scabs. She had swapped traitor's sack-cloth for the travelling clothes of a lady of means, and looked extremely well in them. Jewels twinkled on her fingers, and around her neck. She seemed every bit as rich and sleek as when they first met. That, and she was smiling. *The smile of the player who holds all the cards. Why is it that I cannot learn? Never do a good turn. Especially not for a woman.*

A small pair of scissors lay on the table before her, within easy reach. Of the type that rich women use to trim their nails. *But just as good for trimming the skin from the soles of a man's feet, for trimming his nostrils wider, for trimming his ears off, strip by slow strip . . .*

Glokta found it decidedly difficult to move his eyes away from those polished little blades, shining in the bright lamp-light. 'I thought I told you never to come back,' he said, but his voice lacked its customary authority.

'You did. But then I thought . . . why ever not? I have assets in the city that I was not willing to relinquish, and some business opportunities that I am keen to take advantage of.' She took up the scissors, trimmed the thinnest scrap from the corner of one already perfectly-shaped thumbnail, and frowned at the results. 'And it's hardly as though you'll be telling anyone I'm here, now, is it?'

'My concerns for your safety are all laid to rest,' grunted Glokta. *My concerns for my own, alas, grow with every moment. A man is never so crippled, after all, that he could not be more so.* 'Did you really need to go to all this trouble just to share your travel arrangements?'

Her smile grew somewhat broader, if anything. 'I hope my men didn't hurt you. I did ask them to be gentle. At least for the time being.'

'A gentle kidnapping is still a kidnapping, though, don't you find?'

'Kidnapping is such an ugly word. Why don't we think of it as an invitation difficult to resist? At least I let you keep your clothes, no?'

'That particular favour is a mercy to us both, believe me. An invitation to what, might I ask, beyond a painful manhandling and a brief conversation?'

'I'm hurt that you need more. But there was something else, since you mention it.' She pared away another sliver of nail with her scissors, and her eyes rolled up to his. 'A little debt left over, from Dagoska. I fear that I will not sleep easily until it is repaid.'

A few weeks in a black cell and a choking to the point of death? What form of repayment might that earn me? 'Please, then,' hissed Glokta through his gums, his eyelid flickering as he watched those blades snip, snip, snip. 'I can scarcely stand the suspense.'

'The Gurkish are coming.'

He paused for a moment, wrong-footed. 'Coming here?'

'Yes. To Midderland. To Adua. To you. They have built a fleet, in secret. They began building it after the last war, and now it is complete. Ships to rival anything the Union has.' She tossed her scissors down on the table and gave a long sigh. 'Or so I hear.'

The Gurkish fleet, just as my midnight visitor Yulwei told me.

Rumours and ghosts, perhaps. But rumours are not always lies. 'When will they arrive?'

'I really couldn't say. The mounting of such an expedition is a colossal work of organisation. But then the Gurkish have always been so very much better organised than us. That's what makes doing business with them such a pleasure.'

My own dealings with them have been less than delightful, but still. 'In what numbers will they come?'

'A very great number, I imagine.'

Glokta snorted. 'Forgive me if I regard the words of a proven traitor with a certain scepticism, especially as you are rather thin on the details.'

'Have it your way. You're here to be warned, not convinced. I owe you that much, I think, for giving me my life.'

How wonderfully old-fashioned of you. 'And that is all?'

She spread her hands. 'Can a lady not trim her nails without giving offence?'

'Could you not simply have written?' snapped Glokta, 'and spared me the chafing on my under-arms?'

'Oh, come now. You never struck me as a man to bridle at a little chafing. Besides, it has given us the chance to renew a thoroughly enjoyable friendship. And you have to allow me my little moment of triumph, after what you put me through.'

I suppose that I can. I've had less charming threats, and at least she has better taste than to meet in a pig sty. 'I can simply walk away, then?'

'Did anyone pick up a cane?' No one spoke. Eider gave a happy smile, showing Glokta her perfect white teeth. 'You can crawl away, then. How does that sound?'

Better than floating to the top of the canal after a few days on the bottom, bloated up like a great pale slug and smelling like all the graves in the city. 'As good as I'll get, I suppose. I do wonder, though. What is to stop me having my Practicals follow the scent of expensive perfume after we are done here and finish what they started?'

'It is so very like you to say such a thing.' She sighed. 'I should inform you that an old and trustworthy business acquaintance of mine has a sealed letter in his possession. In the event of my death, it will be sent to the Arch Lector, laying out to him the exact nature of my sentence in Dagoska.'

Glokta sucked sourly at his gums. *Just what I need, another knife to juggle.* 'And what will occur if, entirely independently from my actions, you succumb to the rot? Or a house falls on you? Or you choke on a slice of bread?'

She opened her eyes very wide, as though the thought had only just occurred. 'In any of those cases . . . I suppose . . . the letter would be sent anyway, despite your innocence.' She gave a helpless laugh. 'The world is nothing like as fair a place as it should be, in my opinion, and I daresay that the natives of Dagoska, the enslaved mercenaries, and the butchered Union soldiers who you made fight for your lost cause would concur.' She smiled as sweetly as if they were discussing gardening. 'Things would probably have been far simpler for you if you'd had me strangled, after all.'

'You read my mind.' *But it is far too late now. I did a good thing, and so, of course, there is a price to be paid.*

'So tell me, before we part ways again, for what, we can both only hope, will be the last time – are you involved with this business of the vote?'

Glokta felt his eye twitch. 'My duties would seem to touch upon it.' *Indeed it occupies my every waking hour.*

Carlot dan Eider leaned forward to a conspiratorial distance, her elbows on the table, her chin in her hands. 'Who will be the next king of the Union, do you suppose? Will it be Brock? Isher? Will it be someone else?'

'A little early to say. I'm working on it.'

'Off you hobble, then.' She pushed out her bottom lip. 'And it's probably better if you don't mention our meeting to his Eminence.' She nodded, and Glokta felt the bag forced back over his face.

A Ragged Multitude

J ezal's command post, if you could use the phrase in relation to a man as utterly confused and clueless as he felt, was at the crest of a long rise. It offered a splendid view of the shallow valley below. At least, it would have been a splendid view in happier times. As things stood, it had to be admitted, the spectacle was far from pleasant.

The main body of the rebels entirely covered several large fields further down the valley, and a dark, and grubby, and threatening infestation they seemed, glinting in places with bright steel. Farming implements and tradesman's tools, perhaps, but sharp ones.

Even at this distance there was disturbing evidence of organisation. Straight, regular gaps through the men for the quick movement of messengers and supplies. It was plain, even to Jezal's unpractised eye, that this was as much an army as a mob, and that someone down there knew his business. A great deal better than he did, most likely.

Smaller, less organised groups of rebels were scattered far and wide across the landscape, each one a considerable body in its own right. Men sent foraging for food and water, picking the country clean. That crawling black mass on the green fields reminded Jezal of a horde of black ants crawling over a pile of discarded apple peelings. He had not the slightest idea how many of them there were, but it looked at this distance as though forty thousand might have been a considerable underestimate.

Down in the village in the bottom of the valley, behind the main mass of rebels, fires were burning. Bonfires or buildings it was hard to say, but Jezal rather feared the latter. Three tall columns of dark smoke rose up and drifted apart high above, giving to the air a faint and worrying tang of fire.

It was a commander's place to set a tone of fearlessness which his men would not be able to help but follow. Jezal knew that, of course. And yet, looking down that long, sloping field, he could not help but reflect on the very great number of men at the other end, so ominously purposeful. He could not stop his eyes from darting back towards their own lines, so thin, meagre, and uncertain-seeming. He could not avoid wincing and tugging uncomfortably at his collar. The damn thing still felt far too tight.

'How do you wish the regiments deployed, sir?' asked his adjutant, Major Opker, with a look which somehow managed to be both condescending and sycophantic all at once.

'Deployed? Er . . . well . . .' Jezal racked his brains for something vaguely appropriate, let alone correct, to say. He had discovered early in his military career that if one has an effective and experienced officer above, coupled with effective and experienced soldiers below, one need do, and know, nothing. This strategy had stood him in fine stead for several comfortable peacetime years, but its one shortcoming was now starkly laid bare. If by some miracle one rises to complete command, the system collapses entirely.

'Deployed . . .' he growled, furrowing his brow and trying to give the impression he was surveying the ground, though he had only a hazy idea what that even meant. 'Infantry in double line . . .' he ventured, remembering a fragment of some story Collem West had once told him. 'Behind this hedgerow here.' And he slashed his baton portentously across the landscape. The use of a baton, at least, he was expert in, having practiced extensively before the mirror.

'In front of the hedgerow, the Colonel means to say, of course,' threw in Bayaz smoothly. 'Infantry deployed in double line to either side of that milestone. The light cavalry in the trees there, heavy cavalry in a wedge on the far flank, where they can use the open field to their advantage.' He displayed an uncanny familiarity with military parlance. 'Flatbows in a single line behind the hedgerow where they will at first be hidden from the enemy, and can give them plunging fire from the high ground.' He winked at Jezal. 'An excellent strategy, Colonel, if I may say.'

'Of course,' sneered Opker, turning away to give the orders.

Jezal gripped tight to his baton behind his back, rubbing nervously at his jaw with the other hand. Evidently there was a lot more to command than simply being called 'sir' by everyone. He would really have to read some books when he got back to Adua. If he got back.

Three small dots had detached themselves from the crawling mass of humanity down in the valley and started moving up the rise toward them. Shading his eyes with his hand, Jezal could just see a shred of white moving in the air above them. A flag of parley. He felt Bayaz' decidedly uncomforting hand on his shoulder.

'Don't worry, my boy, we are well prepared for violence. But I feel confident it will not come to that.' He grinned down at the vast mass of men below. 'Very confident.'

Jezal ardently wished he could have said the same.

For a famous demagogue, traitor, and inciter of riots, there was nothing in the least remarkable about the man known as the Tanner. He sat calmly in his folding chair at the table in Jezal's tent, an ordinary face under a mop of curly hair, a man of medium size in a coat of unexceptional style and colour, a grin on his face that implied he knew very well that he held the upper hand.

'They call me the Tanner,' he said, 'and I have been nominated to speak for the alliance of the oppressed, and the exploited, and the put-upon down in the valley. These are two of my partners in this righteous and entirely patriotic venture. My two generals, one might say. Goodman Hood,' and he nodded sideways at a burly man with a shovel beard, a ruddy complexion, and a seething frown, 'and Cotter Holst,' and he jerked his head the other way towards a weasely type with a long scar on his cheek and a lazy eye.

'Honoured,' said Jezal warily, though they looked more like brigands than Generals as far as he was concerned. 'I am Colonel Luthar.'

'I know. I saw you win the Contest. Fine swordplay, my friend, very fine.'

'Oh, well, er . . .' Jezal was caught off guard, 'thank you. This is my adjutant, Major Opker, and this is . . . Bayaz, the First of the Magi.'

Goodman Hood snorted his disbelief, but the Tanner only stroked thoughtfully at his lip. 'Good. And you have come to fight, or negotiate?'

'We have come for either one.' Jezal embarked on his statement. 'The Closed Council, while condemning the method of your demonstration, concede that you may have legitimate demands—'

Hood made a rumbling snort. 'What choice have they got, the bastards?'

Jezal pressed on. 'Well, er . . . they have instructed me to offer you these concessions.' He held up the scroll that Hoff had prepared for him, a huge thing with elaborately carved handles and a seal the size of a saucer. 'But I must caution you,' doing his very best to sound confident, 'should you refuse, we are quite ready to fight, and that my men are the best trained, best armed, best prepared in the King's service. Each one of them is worth twenty of your rabble.'

The burly farmer gave a threatening chuckle. 'Lord Finster thought the same, and our rabble kicked his arse all the way from one end of his estates to the other. He would have got himself hung for his trouble if he'd had a slower horse. How fast is your horse, Colonel?'

The Tanner touched him gently on the shoulder. 'Peace, now, my fiery friend. We came to get terms, if we can get terms we can accept. Why not show us what you have there, Colonel, and we'll see if there is any need for threats.'

Jezal held out the weighty document and Hood snatched it angrily from his hand, tore it open and began to read, the thick paper crackling as it unrolled. The more he read, the grimmer grew his frown.

'An insult!' he snapped when he was done, giving Jezal a brooding stare. 'Lighter taxes and some shit about the use of common land? And that much they'll most likely never honour!' He tossed the scroll sideways to the Tanner, and Jezal swallowed. He had not the leanest understanding of the concessions or their possible shortcomings, of course, but Hood's response hardly seemed to promise an early agreement.

The Tanner's eyes moved lazily over the parchment. Different-coloured eyes, Jezal noticed: one blue, one green. When he got to the bottom he laid the document down and gave a theatrical sigh. 'These terms will do.'

'They will?' Jezal's eyes opened wide with surprise, but nowhere near as far as Goodman Hood's.

'But these are worse than the last terms we were offered!' shouted the farmer. 'Before we sent Finster's men running! You said then we could accept nothing but land for every man!'

The Tanner screwed his face up. 'That was then.'

'That was then?' muttered Hood, gaping with disbelief. 'What happened to honest wages for honest work? What happened to shares in the profit? What happened to equal rights no matter the cost? You stood there, and you promised me!' He shoved his hand towards the valley. 'You promised all of them! What's changed, except that Adua's within our grasp? We can take all we want! We can—'

'I say these terms will do!' snarled the Tanner with a sudden fury. 'Unless you care to fight the King's men on your own! They follow me, Hood, not you, in case you hadn't noticed.'

'But you promised us freedom, for every man! I trusted you!' The farmer's face hung slack with horror. 'We all trusted you.'

Jezal had never seen a man look so utterly indifferent as the Tanner did now. 'I suppose I must have that kind of face that people trust,' he droned, and his friend Holst shrugged and stared at his fingernails.

'Damn you, then! Damn you all!' And Hood turned and shoved angrily out through the tent flap.

Jezal was aware of Bayaz leaning sideways to whisper to Major Opker. 'Have that man arrested before he leaves the lines.'

'Arrested, my Lord, but . . . under a flag of parley?'

'Arrested, placed in irons, and conducted to the House of Questions. A shred of white cloth can be no hiding place from the King's justice. I believe Superior Goyle is handling the investigations.'

'Er . . . of course.' Opker rose to follow the Goodman out of the tent, and Jezal smiled nervously. There was no doubt that the Tanner had heard the exchange, but he grinned on as though the future of his erstwhile companion was no longer any of his concern.

'I must apologise for my associate. In a matter like this, you can't please everyone.' He gave a flamboyant wave of his hand. 'But don't worry. I'll give the little people a big speech, and tell them we have all we fought for, and they'll soon be off back to their homes with no real harm done. Some few will be determined to make trouble perhaps, but I'm sure you can round them up without much effort, eh, Colonel Luthar?'

'Er . . . well,' mumbled Jezal, left without the slightest idea of what was going on. 'I suppose that we—'

'Excellent.' The Tanner sprang to his feet. 'I fear I must now take my leave. All kinds of errands to be about. Never any peace, eh, Colonel Luthar? Never the slightest peace.' He exchanged a long glance with Bayaz, then ducked out into the daylight and was gone.

'If anyone should ask,' murmured the First of the Magi in Jezal's ear, 'I would tell them that it was a testing negotiation, against sharp and determined opponents, but that you held your nerve, reminded them of their duty to king and country, implored them to return to their fields, and so forth.'

'But . . .' Jezal felt like he wanted to cry, he was so baffled. Hugely baffled and hugely relieved at once. 'But I—'

'If anyone should ask.' There was an edge to Bayaz' voice that implied the episode was now finished with.

Beloved of the Moon

The Dogman stood, squinting into the sun, and watched the Union lads all shuffling past the other way. There's a certain look the beaten get, after a fight. Slow-moving, hunched-up, mud-spattered, mightily interested in the ground. Dogman had seen that look before often enough. He'd had it himself more'n once. Sorrowful they'd lost. Shamed they'd been beaten. Guilty, to have given up without getting a wound. Dogman knew how that felt, and a gnawing feeling it could be, but guilt was a sight less painful than a sword-cut, and healed a sight quicker.

Some of the hurt weren't so badly off. Bandaged or splinted, limping with a stick or with their arm round a mate's shoulders. Enough to get light duty for a few weeks. Others weren't so lucky. Dogman thought he knew one. An officer, hardly old enough for a beard, his smooth face all twisted up with white pain and shock, his leg off just above the knee, his clothes, and the stretcher, and the two men carrying him, all specked and spattered with dark blood. He was the one who'd sat on the gate, when Dogman and Threetrees had first come to Ostenhorm to join up with the Union. The one who'd looked at 'em like they were a pair of turds. He didn't sound so very clever now, squealing with every jolt of his stretcher, but it hardly made the Dogman smile. Losing a leg seemed like harsh punishment for a sneering manner.

West was down there by the path, talking to an officer with a dirty bandage round his head. Dogman couldn't hear what they were saying, but he could guess the gist. From time to time one of 'em would point up towards the hills they'd come from. A steep and nasty-looking pair, wooded mostly, with a few hard faces of bare rock showing. West turned and caught the Dogman's eye, and his face was grim as a gravedigger's. It hardly took a quick mind to see that the war weren't won quite yet.

'Shit,' muttered the Dogman, under his breath. He felt that sucking feeling in his gut. That low feeling he used to get whenever he had to scout out a new piece of ground, whenever Threetrees called for weapons, whenever there was nothing for breakfast but cold water. Since he was chief, though, he seemed to have it pretty much all the time. Everything was his problem now. 'Nothing doing?'

West shook his head as he walked up. 'Bethod was waiting for us, and in numbers. He's dug in on those hills. Well dug in and well prepared, between us and Carleon. More than likely he was ready for this before he even crossed the border.'

'He always did like to be ready, did Bethod. No way round him?'

'Kroy's tried both the roads and had two maulings. Now Poulder's tried the hills head on and had a worse one.'

Dogman sighed. 'No way round.'

'No way that won't give Bethod a nice chance to stick the knife right into us.'

'And Bethod won't be missing no chance like that. It's what he'll be hoping for.'

'The Lord Marshal agrees. He wants you to take your men north.' West glared out at the grey whispers of other hills, further off. 'He wants you to look for a weakness. There's no way Bethod can cover the whole range.'

'Is there not?' asked Dogman. 'I guess we'll see.' Then he headed off into the trees. The boys were going to love this.

He strode up the track, soon came up on where his crew were camped out. They were growing all the time. Might've been four hundred now, all counted, and a tough crowd too. Those who'd never much cared for Bethod in the first place, mostly, who'd fought against him in the wars. Who'd fought against the Dogman as well, for that matter. The woods were choked up with 'em, sat round fires, cooking, polishing at weapons and working at gear, a couple having a practice at each other with blades. Dogman winced at the sound of steel clashing. There'd be more of that later, and with bloodier results, he didn't doubt.

'Chief!' they shouted at him. 'Dogman! The chief! Hey hey!' They clapped their hands and tapped their weapons on the rocks they sat on. Dogman held up his fist, and gave the odd half-grin, and said 'aye, good, good,' and all that. He still didn't have the slightest clue how to act like a chief, if the truth be told, so he just acted like he always had. The band all seemed happy enough, though. He guessed they always did. Until they started losing fights, and decided they wanted a new chief.

He came up on the fire where the pick of his Named Men were passing the day. No sign of Logen, but the rest of the old crew were sat round it, looking bored. Those that were still alive, leastways. Tul saw him coming. 'The Dogman's back.'

'Uh,' said Grim, trimming at some feathers with a razor.

Dow was busy mopping grease out of a pan with a chunk o' bread. 'How'd the Union get on with them hills, then?' And he had a sneer to his voice that said he knew the answer already. 'Make a shit from it, did they?'

'Well, they came out second, if that's what you're asking.'

'Second o' two sides is what I call shit.'

Dogman took a deep breath and let it pass. 'Bethod's dug in good, watching the roads to Carleon. No one can see an easy way to come at him, or an easy way around him neither. He was good and ready for this, I reckon.'

'I could've bloody told you that!' barked Dow, spraying out greasy crumbs. 'He'll have Littlebone on one o' them hills, and Whitesides on the other, then he'll have Pale-as-Snow and Goring further out. Those four won't be giving anyone any chances, but if they decide to, Bethod'll be sat behind with the rest, and his Shanka, and his fucking Feared, ready to snuff 'em out double-time.'

'More'n likely.' Tul held his sword up to the light, peered at it, then set to polishing up the blade again. 'Always liked to have a plan, did Bethod.'

'And what do them that hold our leash have to say?' sneered Dow. 'What sort of work's the Furious got for his animals?'

'Burr wants us to move north a way, through the woods, see if Bethod's left a weak spot up there.'

'Huh,' snorted Dow. 'Bethod ain't in the habit of leaving holes. Not unless he's left one he means for us to fall into. Fall into and break our necks.'

'Well I guess we'd better be careful where we tread then, eh?'

'More bloody errands.'

Dogman reckoned he was getting about as sick of Dow's moaning as Threetrees used to be. 'And just what else would it be, eh? That's what life is. A bunch of errands. If you're worth a shit you do your best at 'em. What's got up your arse anyway?'

'This!' Dow jerked his head into the trees. 'Just this! Nothing's changed that much, has it? We might be over the Whiteflow, and back in the North, but Bethod's dug in good and proper up there, with no way for the Union to get round him that won't leave their arses hanging out. And if they do knock him off them hills, what then? If they get to Carleon and they get in, and they burn it just as good as Ninefingers did the last time, so what? Don't mean nothing. Bethod'll keep going, just like he always does, fighting and falling back, and there'll always be more hills to sit on, and more tricks to play. Time'll come, the Union will have had their fill and they'll piss off south and leave us to it. Then Bethod's going to turn around, and what d'you know? He'll be the one chasing us all the way across the fucking North and back. Winter, summer, winter, summer, and it's more of the same old shit. Here we are, fewer of us than there used to be, but still pissing around in the woods. Feel familiar?'

It did, somewhat, now it was mentioned, but Dogman didn't see what he could do about it. 'Logen's back, now, eh? That'll help.'

Dow snorted again. 'Hah! Just when did the Bloody-Nine bring anything but death along with him?'

'Steady now,' grunted Tul. 'You owe him, remember? We all do.'

'There's a limit on what a man should owe, I reckon.' Dow tossed his pan down by the fire and stood up, wiping his hands on his coat. 'Where's he been, eh? He left us up in the valleys without a word, didn't he? Left us to the Flatheads and pissed off halfway across the world! Who's to say he won't wander off again, if it suits him, or go over to Bethod, or set to murder over nothing, or the dead know what?'

Dogman looked at Tul, and Tul looked back, guilty. They'd all seen Logen do some damn dark work, when the mood was on him. 'That was a long time ago,' said Tul. 'Things change.'

Dow only grinned. 'No. They don't. Tell yourselves that tale if it makes you sleep easier, but I'll be keeping one eye open, I can tell you that! It's the Bloody-Nine we're talking of! Who knows what he'll do next?'

'I've one idea.' The Dogman turned round and saw Logen, leaning up against a tree, and he was starting to smile when he saw the look in his eye. A look Dogman remembered from way back, and dragged all kind of ugly memories up after it. That look the dead have, when the life's gone out of 'em, and they care for nothing any more.

'You got a thing to say then you can say it to my face, I reckon.' Logen walked up, right up close to Dow, with his head falling on one side, scars all pale on his hanging-down face. The Dogman felt the hairs on his arms standing up, cold feeling even though the sun was warm.

'Come on, Logen,' wheedled Tul, trying to sound like the whole business was all a laugh when it was plain as a slow death it was no such thing. 'Dow didn't mean nothing by it. He's just—'

Logen spoke right over him, staring Dow in the face with his corpse's eyes all the long while. 'I thought when I gave you the last lesson that you'd never need another. But I guess some folk have short memories.' He came in even closer, so close that their faces were almost touching. 'Well? You need a learning, boy?'

Dogman winced, sure as sure they'd set to killing one another, and how the hell he'd stop 'em once they started he hadn't the faintest clue. A tense moment all round, it seemed to last for ever. He wouldn't have taken that from any other man, alive or dead, Black Dow, not even Threetrees, but in the end he just split a yellow grin.

'Nah. One lesson's all I need.' And he turned his head sideways, hawked up and spat onto the ground. Then he backed off, no hurry, that grin still on his face, like he was saying he'd take a telling this time, maybe, but he might not the next.

Once he was gone, and no blood spilled, Tul blew out hard like they'd got away with murder. 'Right then. North, was it? Someone better get the lads ready to move.'

'Uh,' said Grim, sliding the last arrow into his quiver and following him off through the trees.

Logen stood there for a moment, watching 'em walk. When they'd got away out of sight he turned round, and he squatted down by the fire, hunched over with his arms resting on his knees and his hands dangling. 'Thank the dead for that. I nearly shit myself.'

Dogman realised he'd been holding onto his breath the whole while, and he let it rush out in a gasp. 'I think I might've, just a bit. Did you have to do that?'

'You know I did. Let a man like Dow take liberties and he won't ever stop. Then all the rest of these lads will get the idea that the Bloody-Nine ain't anything like so frightening as they heard, and it'll be a matter of time before someone with a grudge decides to take a blade to me.'

Dogman shook his head. 'That's a hard way of thinking about things.'

'That's the way they are. They haven't changed any. They never do.'

True, maybe, but they weren't ever going to change if no one gave 'em half a chance. 'Still. You sure all that's needful?'

'Not for you maybe. You got that knack that folk like you.' Logen scratched at his jaw, looking sadly off into the woods. 'Reckon I missed my chance at that about fifteen years ago. And I ain't getting another.'

*

The woods were warm and familiar. Birds twittered in the branches, not caring a damn for Bethod, or the Union, or any o' the doings of men. Nowhere had ever seemed more peaceful, and Dogman didn't like that one bit. He sniffed at the air, sifting it through his nose, over his tongue. He was double careful these days, since that shaft came over and killed Cathil in the battle. Might have been he could've saved her, if he'd trusted his own nose a mite more. He wished he had saved her. But wishing don't help any.

Dow squatted down in the brush, staring off into the still forest. 'What is it, Dogman? What d'you smell?'

'Men, I reckon, but kind of sour, somehow.' He sniffed again. 'Smells like—'

An arrow flitted up out of the trees, clicked into the tree trunk just beside Dogman and stuck there, quivering.

'Shit!' he squealed, sliding down on his arse and fumbling his own bow off his shoulder, much too late as always. Dow slithered down cursing beside him and they got all tangled up with each other. Dogman nearly got his eye poked out on Dow's axe before he managed to push him off. He shoved his palm out at the men behind to say stop, but they were already scattering for cover, crawling for trees and rocks on their bellies, pulling out weapons and staring into the woods.

A voice drifted over from the forest ahead. 'You with Bethod?' Whoever it was spoke Northern with some strange-sounding accent.

Dow and Dogman looked at each other for a minute, then shrugged. 'No!' Dow roared back. 'And if you are, you'd best make ready to meet the dead!'

A pause. 'We're not with that bastard, and never will be!'

'Good enough!' shouted Dogman, putting his head up no more'n an inch, his bow full drawn and ready in his hands. 'Show yourselves, then!'

A man stepped out from behind a tree maybe six strides distant. Dogman was that shocked he nearly fumbled the string and let the shaft fly. More men started sliding out of the woods all round. Dozens of 'em. Their hair was tangled, their faces were smeared with streaks of brown dirt and blue paint, their clothes were ragged fur and half-tanned hides, but the heads of their spears, and the points of their arrows, and the blades of their rough-forged swords all shone bright and clean.

'Hillmen,' Dogman muttered.

'Hillmen we are, and proud of it!' A great big voice, echoing out from the woods. A few of 'em started to shuffle to one side, like they were making way for someone. Dogman blinked. There was a child coming between them. A girl, maybe ten years old, with dirty bare feet. She had a huge hammer over one shoulder, a thick length of wood a stride long with a scarred lump of iron the size of a brick for a head. Far and away too big for her to swing. It was giving her some trouble even holding it up.

A little boy came next. He had a round shield across his back, much too wide for him, and a great axe he was lugging along in both hands. Another boy was at his shoulder with a spear twice as high as he was, the bright point waving around above his head, gold twinkling under the blade in the strips of sunlight. He kept having to look up to make sure he didn't catch it on a branch.

'I'm dreaming,' muttered the Dogman. 'Aren't I?'

Dow frowned. 'If y'are it's a strange one.'

They weren't alone, the three children. Some huge bastard was coming up behind. He had a ragged fur round his great wide shoulders, and some big necklace hanging down on his great fat belly. A load of bones. Fingerbones, the Dogman saw as he got closer. Men's fingers, mixed up with flat bits of wood, strange signs cut into them. He had a great yellow grin hacked out from his grey-brown beard, but that didn't put the Dogman any more at ease.

'Oh shit,' groaned Dow, 'let's go back. Back south and enough o' this.'

'Why? You know him?'

Dow turned his head and spat. 'Crummock-i-Phail, ain't it.'

Dogman almost wished it had turned out to be an ambush,

now, rather than a chat. It was a fact that every child knew. Crummock-i-Phail, chief of the hillmen, was about the maddest bastard in the whole damn North.

He pushed the spears and the arrows gently out of his way as he came. 'No need for that now, is there, my beauties? We're all friends, or got the same enemies, at least, which is far better, d'you see? We all have a lot of enemies up in them hills, don't we, though? The moon knows I love a good fight, but coming at them great big rocks, with Bethod and all his arse-lickers stuck in tight on top? That's a bit too much fight for anyone, eh? Even your new Southern friends.'

He stopped just in front of them, fingerbones swinging and rattling. The three children stopped behind him, fidgeting with their great huge weapons and frowning up at Dow and the Dogman.

'I'm Crummock-i-Phail,' he said. 'Chief of all the hillmen. Or all the ones as are worth a shit.' He grinned as though he'd just turned up to a wedding. 'And who might be in charge o' this merry outing?'

Dogman felt that hollow feeling again, but there was nothing for it. 'That'd be me.'

Crummock raised his brows at him. 'Would it now? You're a little fellow to be telling all these big fellows just what to be about, are you not? You must have quite some name on your shoulders, I'm thinking.'

'I'm the Dogman. This is Black Dow.'

'Some strange sort of a crew you got here,' said Dow, frowning at the children.

'Oh it is! It is! And a brave one at that! The lad with my spear, that's my son Scofen. The one with my axe is my son Rond.' Crummock frowned at the girl with the hammer. 'This lad's name I can't remember.'

'I'm your daughter!' shouted the girl.

'What, did I run out of sons?'

'Scenn got too old and you give him 'is own sword, and Sceft's too small to carry nothing yet.'

Crummock shook his head. 'Don't hardly seem right, a bloody woman taking the hammer.'

The girl threw the hammer down on the ground and booted Crummock in his shin. 'You can carry it yourself then, y'old bastard!'

'Ah!' he squawked, laughing and rubbing his leg at once. 'Now I remember you, Isern. Your kicking's brought it all back in a rush. You can take the hammer, so you can. Smallest one gets the biggest load, eh?'

'You want the axe, Da?' The smaller lad held the axe up, wobbling.

'You want the hammer?' The girl dragged it up out the brush and shouldered her brother out the way.

'No, my loves, all I need for now is words, and I've plenty of those without your help. You can watch your father work some murder soon, if things run smooth, but there'll be no need for axes or hammers today. We didn't come here to kill.'

'Why did you come here?' asked Dogman, though he wasn't sure he even wanted the answer.

'Right to business is it, and no time to be friendly?' Crummock stretched his neck to the side, his arms over his head, and lifted one foot and shook it around. 'I came here because I woke in the night, and I walked out into the darkness, and the moon whispered to me. In the forest, d'you see? In the trees, and in the voices of the owls in the trees, and d'you know what the moon said?'

'That you're mad as fuck?' growled Dow.

Crummock slapped his huge thigh. 'You've a pretty way of talking for an ugly man, Black Dow, but no. The moon said . . .' And he beckoned to the Dogman like he had some secret to share. 'You got the Bloody-Nine down here.'

'What if we do?' Logen came up quiet from behind, left hand resting on his sword. Tul and Grim came with him, frowning at all the painted-face hillmen stood about, and at the three dirty children, and at their great fat father most of all.

'There he is!' roared Crummock, sticking out one great sausage of a trembling finger. 'Take your fist off that blade,

Bloody-Nine, before I piss my breaks!' He dropped down on his knees in the dirt. 'This is him! This is the one!' He shuffled forward through the brush and he clung to Logen's leg, pressing himself up against it like a dog to his master.

Logen stared down at him. 'Get off my leg.'

'That I will!' Crummock jerked away and dropped down on his fat arse in the dirt. Dogman had never seen such a performance. Looked like the rumours about him being cracked were right enough. 'Do you know a fine thing, Bloody-Nine?'

'More'n one, as it goes.'

'Here's another, then. I saw you fight Shama Heartless. I saw you split him open like a pigeon for the pot, and I couldn't have done it better my blessed self. A lovely thing to see!' Dogman frowned. He'd been there too, and he didn't remember much lovely about it. 'I said then,' and Crummock rose up to his knees, 'and I said since,' and he stood up on his feet, 'and I said when I came down from the hills to seek you out,' and he lifted up his arm to point at Logen. 'That you're a man more beloved of the moon than any other!'

Dogman looked over at Logen, and Logen shrugged. 'Who's to say what the moon likes or doesn't? What of it?'

'What of it, he says! Hah! I could watch him kill the whole world, and a thing of beauty it would be! The what of it is, I have a plan. It flowed up with the cold springs under the mountains, and was carried along in the streams under the stones, and washed up on the shore of the sacred lake right beside me, while I was dipping my toes in the frosty.'

Logen scratched at his scarred jaw. 'We've got work to be about, Crummock. You got something worth saying you can get to it.'

'Then I will. Bethod hates me, and the feeling's mutual, but he hates you more. Because you've stood against him, and you're living proof a man of the North can be his own man, without bending on his knee and tonguing the arse of that golden-hat bastard and his two fat sons and his witch.' He frowned. 'Though I could be persuaded to take my tongue to her. D'you follow me so far?'

'I'm keeping up,' said Logen, but Dogman weren't altogether sure that he was.

'Just whistle if you drop behind and I'll come right back for you. My meaning's this. If Bethod were to get a good chance at catching you all alone, away from your Union friends, your crawling-like-ants sunny-weather lovers over down there yonder, then, well, he might give up a lot to take it. He might be coaxed down from his pretty hills for a chance like that, I'm thinking, hmmm?'

'You're betting that he hates me a lot.'

'What? Do you doubt that a man could hate you that much?' Crummock turned away, spreading his great long arms out wide at Tul and Grim. 'But it's not just you, Bloody-Nine! It's all of you, and me as well, and my three sons here!' The girl threw the hammer down again and planted her hands on her hips, but Crummock blathered on regardless. 'I'm thinking your boys join up with my boys and it might be we'll have eight hundred spears. We'll head up north, like we're going up into the High Places, to get around behind Bethod and play merry mischief with his arse end. I'm thinking that'll get his blood up. I'm thinking he won't be able to pass on a chance to put all of us back in the mud.'

The Dogman thought it over. Chances were that a lot of Bethod's people were jumpy about now. Worried to be fighting on the wrong side of the Whiteflow. Maybe they were hearing the Bloody-Nine was back, and thinking they'd picked the wrong side. Bethod would love to put a few heads on sticks for everyone to look at. Ninefingers, and Crummock-i-Phail, Tul Duru and Black Dow, and maybe even the Dogman too. He'd like that, would Bethod. Show the North there was no future in anything but him. He'd like it a lot.

'Supposing we do wander off north,' asked Dogman. 'How's Bethod even going to know about it?'

Crummock grinned wider than ever. 'Oh, he'll know because his witch'll know.'

'Bloody witch,' piped up the lad with the spear, his thin arms trembling as he fought to keep it up straight.

'That spell-cooking, painted-face bitch Bethod keeps with him. Or does she keep him with her? There's a question, though. Either way, she's watching. Ain't she, Bloody-Nine?'

'I know who you mean,' said Logen, and not looking happy. 'Caurib. A friend o' mine once told me she had the long eye.' Dogman didn't have the first clue about all that, but if Logen was taking it to heart he reckoned he'd better too.

'The long eye, is it?' grinned Crummock. 'Your friend's got a pretty name for an ugly trick. She sees all manner of goings-on with it. All kind of things it'd be better for us if she didn't. Bethod trusts her eyes before he trusts his own, these days, and he'll have her watching for us, and for you in particular. She'll have both her long eyes open for it, that she will. I may be no wizard,' and he spun one of the wooden signs around and around on his necklace, 'but the moon knows I'm no stranger to the business neither.'

'And what if it goes like you say?' rumbled Tul, 'what happens then? Apart from we give Bethod our heads?'

'Oh, I like my head where it is, big lad. We draw him on, north by north, that's what the forest told me. There's a place up in the mountains, a place well loved by the moon. A strong valley, and watched over by the dead of my family, and the dead of my people, and the dead of the mountains, all the way back until when the world was made.'

Dogman scratched his head. 'A fortress in the mountains?'

'A strong, high place. High and strong enough for a few to hold off a many until help were to arrive. We lure him on up into the valley, and your Union friends follow up at a lazy distance. Far enough that his witch don't see 'em coming, she's so busy looking at us. Then, while he's all caught up in trying to snuff us out for good and all, the Southerners creep up behind, and—' He slapped his palms together with an echoing crack. 'We squash him between us, the sheep-fucking bastard!'

'Sheep-fucker!' cursed the girl, kicking at the hammer on the ground.

They all looked at each other for a moment. Dogman didn't much like the sound of this for a plan. He didn't much like the notion of trusting their lives to the say-so o' this crazy hillman. But it sounded like some kind of a chance. Enough that he couldn't just say no, however much he'd have liked to. 'We got to talk on this.'

'Course you do, my new best friends, course you do. Don't take too long about it though, eh?' Crummock grinned wide. 'I been down from the High Places for way too long, and the rest o' my beautiful children, and my beautiful wives, and the beautiful mountains themselves will all of them be missing me. Think on the sunny side o' this. If Bethod don't follow, you get a few nights sat up in the High Places as the summer dies, warming yourselves at my fire, and listening to my songs, and watching the sun going down over the mountains. That sound so bad? Does it?'

'You thinking of listening to that mad bastard?' muttered Tul, once they'd got out of earshot. 'Witches and wizards and all that bloody rubbish? He makes it up as he goes along!'

Logen scratched his face. 'He's nowhere near as mad as he sounds. He's held out against Bethod all these years. The only one who has. Twelve winters is it now, he's been hiding, and raiding, and keeping one foot ahead? Up in the mountains maybe, but still. He'd have to be slippery as fishes and tough as iron to make that work.'

'You trust him, then?' asked Dogman.

'Trust him?' Logen snorted. 'Shit, no. But his feud with Bethod's deeper even than ours is. He's right about that witch, I seen her, and I seen some other things this past year . . . if he says she'll see us, I reckon I believe him. If she doesn't, and Bethod don't come, well, nothing lost is there?'

Dogman had that empty feeling, worse'n ever. He looked over at Crummock, sitting on a rock with his children round him, and the madman smiled back a mouthful of yellow teeth. Hardly the man you'd want to hang all your hopes on, but Dogman could feel the wind changing. 'We'd be taking one bastard of a risk,' he muttered. 'What if Bethod caught up to us and got his way?'

'We move fast, then, don't we!' growled Dow. 'It's a war. Taking risks is what you do if you reckon on winning!'

'Uh,' grunted Grim.

Tul nodded his big head. 'We've got to do something. I didn't come here to watch Bethod sit on a hill. He needs to be got down.'

'Got down where we can set to work on him!' hissed Dow.

'But it's your choice.' Logen clapped his hand down on the Dogman's shoulder. 'You're the chief.'

He was the chief. He remembered them deciding on it, gathered round Threetrees' grave. Dogman had to admit, he'd much rather have told Crummock to fuck himself, then turned round and headed back, and told West they never found a thing except woods. But once you've got a task, you get it done. That's what Threetrees would've said. Dogman gave a long sigh, that feeling in his gut bubbling up so high he was right on the point of puking. 'Alright. But this plan ain't going to get us anything but dead unless the Union are ready to do their part, and in good time too. We'll take it to Furious, and let their chief Burr know what we're about.'

'Furious?' asked Logen.

Tul grinned. 'Long story.'

Flowers and Plaudits

J ezal still did not have the slightest idea why it was necessary for him to wear his best uniform. The damn thing was stiff as a board and creaking with braid. It had been designed for standing to attention in rather than riding, and, as a result, dug painfully into his stomach with every movement of his horse. But Bayaz had insisted, and it was surprisingly difficult to say no to the old fool, whether Jezal was supposed to be in command of this expedition or not. It had seemed easier, in the end, just to do as he was told. So he rode at the head of the long column in some discomfort, constantly tugging at his tunic and sweating profusely in the bright sun. The one consolation was that he got to breathe fresh air. Everyone else had to eat his dust.

To further add to his pain, Bayaz was intent on continuing the themes that had made Jezal so very bored all the way to the edge of the World and back.

'. . . it is vital for a king to maintain the good opinion of his subjects. And it is not so very hard to do. The lowly have small ambitions, and are satisfied with small indulgences. They need not get fair treatment. They need only think that they do . . .'

Jezal found that after a while he could ignore the droning of the old man's voice, in the same way that one could ignore the barking of an old dog that barked all the time. He slumped into his saddle and allowed his thoughts to wander. And where else would they find their way, but to Ardee?

He had landed himself in quite a pickle, alright. Out on the plain, things had seemed so very simple. Get home, marry her, happily ever after. Now, back in Adua, back among the powerful, and back in his old habits, they grew more complicated by the day. The possibility of damage to his reputation and his prospects were issues that could not simply be dismissed. He was a Colonel in the King's Own, and that meant certain standards to uphold.

'. . . Harod the Great always had respect for the common man. More than once, it was the secret of his victories over his peers . . .'

And then Ardee herself was so much more complicated in person than she had been as a silent memory. Nine parts witty, clever, fearless, attractive. One part a mean and destructive drunk. Every moment with her was a lottery, but perhaps it was that sense of danger that struck the sparks when they touched, made his skin tingle and his mouth go dry . . . his skin was tingling now, even at the thought. He had never felt like this about a woman before, not ever. Surely it was love. It had to be. But was love enough? How long would it last? Marriage, after all, was forever, and forever was a very long time.

An indefinite extension of their current not-so secret romance would have been his preferred choice, but that bastard Glokta had stuck his ruined foot through that possibility. Anvils, and sacks, and canals. Jezal remembered that white monster shoving his bag over a prisoner's head on a public thoroughfare, and shuddered at the thought. But he had to admit that the cripple was right. Jezal's visits were not good for that girl's reputation. One should treat others the way one would want to be treated, he supposed, just as Ninefingers had once said. But it certainly was a damned inconvenience.

'. . . are you even listening, my boy?'

'Eh? Er . . . yes, of course. Harod the Great, and so forth. The high respect he had for the common man.'

'Appeared to have,' grumbled Bayaz. 'And he knew how to take a lesson too.'

They were getting close to Adua now, passing out of the farmland and through one of the huddles of shacks, impromptu dwellings, cheap inns and cheaper brothels that had grown up around each of the city's gates, huddling about the road, each one almost a town in its own right. Up into the long shadow of Casamir's Wall, the outermost of the city's lines of defence. A dour guardsmen stood on either side of the high archway, gates marked with the golden sun of the Union standing open. They passed through the darkness and out into the light. Jezal blinked.

A not inconsiderable number of people had gathered in the cobbled space beyond, pressing in on either side of the road, held back by members of the city watch. They burst into a chorus of happy cheers as they saw him ride through the gate. Jezal wondered for a moment if it was a case of mistaken identity, and they had been expecting someone of actual importance. Harod the Great, perhaps, for all he knew. He soon began to make out the name 'Luthar' repeated amongst the noise, however. A girl at the front flung a flower at him, lost under his horse's hooves, and shouted something he could not make out. But her manner left Jezal with no doubts. All these people had gathered for him.

'What's happening?' he whispered to the First of the Magi.

Bayaz grinned as though he, at least, had expected it. 'I imagine the people of Adua wish to celebrate your victory over the rebels.'

'They do?' He winced and gave a limp-wristed wave, and the cheering grew noticeably in volume. The crowd only thickened as they made their way into the city and the space reduced. There were people scattered up and down the narrow streets, people at the downstairs windows and people higher up, whooping and cheering. More flowers were thrown from a balcony high above the road. One stuck in his saddle and Jezal picked it up, turned it round and round in his hand.

'All this . . . for me?'

'Did you not save the city? Did you not stop the rebels, and without spilling a drop of blood on either side?'

'But they gave up for no reason. I didn't do anything!'

Bayaz shrugged, snatched the flower from Jezal's hand and sniffed at it, then tossed it away and nodded his head towards a clump of cheering tradesmen crowding a street corner. 'It would seem they disagree. Just keep your mouth shut and smile. That's always good advice.'

Jezal did his best to oblige, but the smiles were not coming easily. Logen Ninefingers, he was reasonably sure, would not have approved. If there was an opposite to trying to look like less than you were, then this, surely, was its very definition. He glanced nervously around, convinced that the crowds would suddenly recognise him for the utter fraud he felt, and replace the flowers and calls of admiration with angry jeers and the contents of their chamber pots.

But it did not happen. The cheering continued as Jezal and his long column of soldiers worked their slow way through the Three Farms district. With each street Jezal passed down he relaxed a little more. He slowly began to feel as if he must indeed have achieved something worthy of the honour. To wonder if he might, in fact, have been a dauntless commander, a masterful negotiator. If the people of the city wished to worship him as their hero, he began to suppose it would be churlish to refuse.

They passed through a gate in Arnault's Wall and into the central district of the city. Jezal sat up tall in his saddle and puffed out his chest. Bayaz dropped behind to a respectful distance, allowing him to lead the column alone. The cheering mounted as they tramped down the wide Middleway, as they crossed the Four Corners towards the Agriont. It was like the feeling of victory at the Contest, only it had involved considerably less work, and was that really such an awful thing? What harm could it do? Ninefingers and his humility be damned. Jezal had earned the attention. He plastered a radiant smile across his face. He lifted his arm with self-satisfied confidence, and began to wave.

The great walls of the Agriont rose up ahead and Jezal crossed the moat to the looming south gatehouse, rode up the long tunnel into the fortress, the crackling hooves and tramping boots of the King's Own echoing in the darkness behind him. He processed slowly down the Kingsway, approvingly observed by the great stone monarchs of old and their advisers, between high buildings crammed with onlookers, and into the Square of Marshals.

Crowds had been carefully arranged on each side of the vast open space, leaving a long track of bare stone down the middle. At the far end a wide stand of benches had been erected, a crimson canopy in the centre denoting the presence of royalty. The noise and spectacle were breathtaking.

Jezal remembered the triumph laid on for Marshal Varuz when he returned from his victory over the Gurkish, remembered staring wide-eyed, little more than a child. He had caught one fleeting glimpse of the Marshal himself, seated high on a grey charger, but never imagined that one day he might ride in the place of honour. It still seemed strange, if he was honest. After all, he had defeated a bunch of peasants rather than the most powerful nation in the Circle of the World. Still, it was hardly his place to judge who was worthy of a triumph and who was not, was it?

And so Jezal spurred his horse forwards, passing between the rows of smiling faces, waving arms, through air thick with support and approval. He saw that the great men of the Closed Council were arranged across the front row of benches. He recognised Arch Lector Sult in shining white, High Justice Marovia in solemn black. His erstwhile fencing master, Lord Marshal Varuz, was there, Lord Chamberlain Hoff just beside him. All applauding, mostly with a faint disdain which Jezal found rather ungracious. In the midst, well propped up on a gilded chair, was the King himself.

Jezal, now fully adjusted to his role of conquering hero, dragged hard on the bridle making his steed rear up, front hooves thrashing theatrically at the air. He vaulted from the saddle, approached the royal dais, and sank gracefully down on one knee, head bowed, the applause of the crowd echoing around him, to await the King's gratitude. Would it be too much to hope for a further promotion? Perhaps even a title of his own? It seemed suddenly hard to believe that he had been forced to consider a quiet life in obscurity, not so very long ago.

'Your Majesty . . .' he heard Hoff saying, and he peered up from under his brows. The King was asleep, his eyes firmly closed, his mouth hanging open. Hardly a great surprise in its own way, the man was long past his best, but Jezal could not help being galled. It was the second time, after all, that he had slumbered through one of Jezal's moments of glory. Hoff nudged the monarch as subtly as possible with an elbow, but when he did not wake, was forced to lean close to whisper in his ear.

'Your Majesty—' He got no further. The King leaned sideways, his head slumping, and fell all of a sudden from his gilded chair, sprawling on his back before the stricken members of the Closed Council like a landed whale. His scarlet robe flopped open to reveal a great wet stain across his trousers and the crown tumbled from his head, bounced once and clattered across the flags.

There was a collective gasp, punctuated by a shriek from a lady near the back. Jezal could only stare, open mouthed, as the Lord Chamberlain flung himself down on his knees, bending over the stricken King. A silent moment passed, a moment in which every person in the Square of Marshals held their breath, then Hoff got slowly to his feet. His face had lost all of its redness.

'The King is dead!' he wailed, the tortured echoes ringing from the towers and buildings around the square. Jezal could only grimace. It was just his luck. Now no one would be cheering for him.

Too Many Knives

Logen sat on a rock, twenty strides from the track that Crummock was leading them up. He knew all the ways, Crummock-i-Phail, all the ways in the North. That was the rumour, and Logen hoped it was a fact. He didn't fancy being led straight into an ambush. They were heading north, towards the mountains. Hoping to draw Bethod down off his hills and up into the High Places. Hoping the Union would come up behind him, and catch him in a trap. An awful lot of hoping, that.

It was a hot, sunny day, and the earth under the trees was broken with shadow and slashed with bright sunlight, shifting as the branches moved in the wind, the sun slipping through and stabbing in Logen's face from time to time. Birds tweeted and warbled, trees creaked and rustled, insects floated in the still air, and the forest floor was spattered with clumps of flowers, white and blue. Summer, in the North, but none of it made Logen feel any better. Summer was the best season for killing, and he'd seen plenty more men die in good weather than in bad. So he kept his eyes open, looking out into the trees, watching hard and listening harder.

That was the task Dogman had given him. Staying out on the right flank, making sure none of Bethod's boys crept up while they were all spread out in file down that goat track. It suited Logen well enough. Kept him on the edge, where none of his own side might get tempted to try and kill him.

Watching men moving quiet through the trees, voices kept down low, weapons at the ready, brought back a rush of memories. Some good, some bad. Mostly bad, it had to be said. One man came away from the others as Logen watched, started walking towards him through the trees. He had a big grin on his face, just as friendly as you like, but that meant nothing, Logen had known plenty of men who could grin while they planned to kill you. He'd done it himself, and more than once.

He turned his body sideways a touch, sliding his hand down out of sight and curling it tight round the grip of a knife. You can never have too many knives, his father had told him, and that was strong advice. He looked around, slow and easy, just to make sure there was no one at his back, but there were only empty trees. So he shifted his feet for a better balance and stayed sitting, trying to look as if nothing worried him, but with every muscle tensed and ready to spring.

'My name's Red Hat.' The man stopped no more than a stride away, still grinning, his left hand slack on the pommel of his sword, the other just hanging.

Logen's mind raced, thinking over all the men he'd wronged, or hurt, or got bound up in a feud with. Those he'd left alive, anyway. Red Hat. He couldn't find a place for it anywhere, but that was no reassurance. Ten men with ten big books couldn't have kept track of all the enemies he'd made, and the friends and the family and the allies of all his enemies. And that was without a man trying to kill him without much of a reason, just to make his own name bigger. 'Can't say I recognise the name.'

Red Hat shrugged. 'No reason you should do. I fought for Old Man Yawl, way back. He was a good man, was Yawl, a man you could respect.'

'Aye,' said Logen, still watching hard for a sudden move.

'But when he went back to the mud I got a place with Littlebone.'

'Never saw eye to eye with Littlebone, even when we were on the same side.'

'Neither did I, being honest. A right bastard. All bloated up with victories that Bethod won for him. Didn't sit well with me. That's why I came over, you know? When I heard Threetrees was here.' He sniffed and looked down at the earth. 'Someone needs to do something about that fucking Feared.'

'So they tell me.' Logen was hearing a lot about this Feared, and none of it good, but it'd take more than a few words in the right direction to get his hand off his knife.

'Still, the Dogman's a good chief, I reckon. One of the best I've had. Knows his business. Careful, like. Thinks about things.'

'Aye. Always thought he would be.'

'You think Bethod's following us?'

Logen didn't take his eyes from Red Hat's. 'Maybe he is, maybe he isn't. Don't reckon we'll know 'til we get up in the mountains and hear him knocking at the door.'

'You think the Union'll keep to their end of it?'

'Don't see why not. That Burr seems to know what he's about, far as I can tell, and his boy Furious as well. They said they'll come, I reckon they'll come. Not much we can do about it either way now, though, is there?'

Red Hat wiped some sweat from his forehead, squinting off into the trees. 'I reckon you're right. Anyway, all's I wanted to say was, I was in the battle, at Ineward. I was on the other side from you, but I saw you fight, and I kept well away, I can tell you that.' He shook his head, and grinned. 'Never saw anything like that, before or since. I suppose what I'm saying is, I'm happy to have you with us. Real happy.'

'Y'are?' Logen blinked. 'Alright, then. Good.'

Red Hat nodded. 'Well. That's all. See you in the fight, I reckon.'

'Aye. In the fight.' Logen watched him stride away through the trees, but even when Red Hat was well out of sight, he somehow couldn't make his hand uncurl from the grip of his knife, still couldn't lose the feeling that he had to watch his back.

Seemed he'd let himself forget what the North was like. Or he'd let himself pretend it would be different. Now he saw his mistake. He'd made a trap for himself, years ago. He'd made a great heavy chain, link by bloody link, and he'd bound himself up in it. Somehow he'd been offered the chance to get free, a chance he didn't come near to deserving, but instead he'd blundered back in, and now things were apt to get bloody.

He could feel it coming. A great weight of death, like the shadow of a mountain falling on him. Every time he said a word, or took a step, or had a thought, even, it seemed he'd somehow brought it closer. He drank it down with every swallow, he sucked it in with every breath. He hunched his shoulders up and stared down at his boots, strips of sunlight across the toes. He should never have let go of Ferro. He should have clung to her like a child to its mother. How many things halfway good had he been offered in his life? And now he'd turned one down, and chosen to come back and settle some scores. He licked his teeth, and he spat sour spit out onto the earth. He should've known better. Vengeance is never halfway as simple, or halfway as sweet, as you think it's going to be.

'I bet you're wishing you didn't come back at all, eh?'

Logen jerked his head up, on the point of pulling the knife and setting to work. Then he saw it was only Tul standing over him. He pushed the blade away and let his hands drop. 'Do you know what? The thought had occurred.'

The Thunderhead squatted down beside him. 'Sometimes I find my own name's a heavy weight to carry. Dread to think how a name like yours must drag at a man.'

'It can seem a burden.'

'I bet it can.' Tul watched the men moving past, single file, down on the dusty track. 'Don't mind 'em. They'll get used to you. And if things get low, well, you've always got Black Dow's smile to fall back on, eh?'

Logen grinned. 'That's true. It's quite the smile he has, that man. It seems to light up the whole world, don't it?'

'Like sunshine on a cloudy day.' Tul sat down on the rock next to him, pulled the stopper from his canteen and held it out. 'I'm sorry.'

'You're sorry? For what?'

'That we didn't look for you, after you went over that cliff. Thought you were dead.'

'Can't say I hold much of a grudge for that. I was pretty damn sure I was dead myself. I'm the one should have gone looking for you lot, I reckon.'

137

'Well. Should've looked for each other, maybe. But I guess you learn to stop hoping, after a while. Life teaches you to expect the worst, eh?'

'You have to be realistic, I reckon.'

'That you do. Still, it came out alright. Back with us now, aren't you?'

'Aye.' Logen sighed. 'Back to warring, and bad food, and creeping through woods.'

'Woods,' grunted Tul, and he split a big grin. 'Will I ever get tired of 'em?'

Logen took a drink from the canteen, then handed it back, and Tul took a swig himself. They sat there, silent, for a minute.

'I didn't want this, you know, Tul.'

'Course not. None of us wanted this. Don't mean we don't deserve it, though, eh?' Tul slapped his big hand down on Logen's shoulder. 'You need to talk it over, I'm around.'

Logen watched him go. He was a good man, the Thunderhead. A man that could be trusted. There were still a few left. Tul, and Grim, and the Dogman. Black Dow too, in his own way. It almost gave Logen some hope, that did. Almost made him glad that he chose to come back to the North. Then he looked back at the file of men and he saw Shivers in there, watching him. Logen would have liked to look away, but looking away wasn't something the Bloody-Nine could do. So he sat there on his rock, and they stared at each other, and Logen felt the hatred digging at him until Shivers was lost through the trees. He shook his head again, and sucked his teeth again, and spat.

You can never have too many knives, his father had told him. Unless they're pointed at you, and by people who don't like you much.

Best of Enemies

'T ap, tap.'

'Not now!' stormed Colonel Glokta. 'I have all these to get through!' There must have been ten thousand papers of confession for him to sign. His desk was groaning with great heaps of them, and the nib of his pen was soft as butter. What with the red ink, his marks looked like dark bloodstains sprayed across the pale paper. 'Damn it!' he raged as he knocked over the bottle with his elbow, splashing ink out over the desk, soaking into the piles of papers, dripping to the floor with a steady tap, tap, tap.

'There will be time later for you to confess. Ample time.'

The Colonel frowned. The air had grown decidedly chill. 'You again! Always at the worst times!'

'You remember me, then?'

'I seem to . . .' In truth, the Colonel was finding it hard to recall from where. It looked like a woman in the corner, but he could not make out her face.

'The Maker fell burning . . . he broke upon the bridge below . . .' The words were familiar, but Glokta could not have said why. Old stories and nonsense. He winced. Damn it but his leg hurt.

'I seem to . . .' His usual confidence was all ebbing away. The room was icy cold now, he could see his breath smoking before his face. He stumbled up from his chair as his unwelcome visitor came closer, his leg aching with a vengeance. 'What do you want?' he managed to croak.

The face came into the light. It was none other than Mauthis, from the banking house of Valint and Balk. 'The Seed, Colonel.' And he smiled his joyless smile. 'I want the Seed.'

'I . . . I . . .' Glokta's back found the wall. He could go no further.

'The Seed!' Now it was Goyle's face, now Sult's, now Severard's, but they all made the same demand. 'The Seed! I lose patience!'

'Bayaz,' he whispered, squeezing his eyes closed, tears running out from underneath his lids. 'Bayaz knows—'

'Tap, tap, torturer.' The woman's hissing voice again. A finger-tip jabbed at the side of his head, painfully hard. 'If that old liar knew, it would be mine already. No. You will find it.' He could not speak for fear. 'You will find it, or I will tear the price from your twisted flesh. So tap, tap, time to wake.'

The finger stabbed at his skull again, digging into the side of his head like a dagger blade. 'Tap, tap, cripple!' hissed the hideous voice in his ear, breath so cold it seemed to burn his bare cheek. 'Tap, tap!'

Tap, tap.

For a moment Glokta hardly knew where he was. He jerked upright, struggling with the sheets, staring about him, hemmed in on every side by threatening shadows, his own whimpering breath hissing in his head. Then everything fell suddenly into place. *My new apartments.* A pleasant breeze stirred the curtains in the sticky night, washing through the one open window. Glokta saw its shadow shifting on the rendered wall. It swung shut against the frame, open, then shut again.

Tap, tap.

He closed his eyes and breathed a long sigh. Winced as he sagged back in his bed, stretching his legs out, working his toes against the cramps. *Those toes the Gurkish left me, at least. Only another dream. Everything is—*

Then he remembered, and his eyes snapped wide open. *The King is dead. Tomorrow we elect a new one.*

The three hundred and twenty papers were hanged, lifeless, from their nails. They had grown more and more creased, battered, greasy and grubby over the past few weeks. *As the business itself has slid further into the filth.* Many were ink smudged, covered with angrily scrawled notes, with fillings-in and crossings-out. *As men were bought and sold, bullied and blackmailed, bribed and beguiled.* Many were torn where wax had been removed, added, replaced with other colours. *As the allegiances shifted, as the promises were broken, as the balance swung this way and that.*

Arch Lector Sult stood glaring at them, like a shepherd at his troublesome flock, his white coat rumpled, his white hair in disarray. Glokta had never before seen him look anything less than perfectly presented. *He must, at last, taste blood. His own. I would almost want to laugh, if my own mouth were not so terribly salty.*

'Brock has seventy-five,' Sult was hissing to himself, white gloved hands fussing with each other behind his back. 'Brock has seventy-five. Isher has fifty-five. Skald and Barezin, forty a piece. Brock has seventy-five . . .' He muttered the numbers over and over, as though they were a charm to protect him from evil. *Or from good, perhaps.* 'Isher has fifty-five . . .'

Glokta had to suppress a smile. *Brock, then Isher, then Skald and Barezin, while the Inquisition and Judiciary struggle over scraps. For all our efforts, the shape of things is much the same as when we began this ugly dance. We might as well have fled the country then and saved ourselves the trouble. Perhaps it is still not too late . . .*

Glokta noisily cleared his throat and Sult's head jerked round. 'You have something to contribute?'

'In a manner of speaking, your Eminence.' Glokta kept his tone as servile as he possibly could. 'I received some rather . . . troubling information recently.'

Sult scowled, and nodded his head at the papers. 'More troubling than this?'

Equally, at any rate. After all, whoever wins the vote will have but a brief celebration if the Gurkish arrive and slaughter the lot of us a week later. 'It has been suggested to me . . . that the Gurkish are preparing to invade Midderland.'

There was a brief, uncomfortable pause. *Scarcely a promising* reception, but we have set sail now. What else to do but steer straight for the storm? 'Invade?' sneered Goyle. 'With what?'

'It is not the first time I have been told they have a fleet.' *Trying desperately to patch my foundering vessel.* 'A considerable fleet, built in secret, after the last war. We could easily make some preparations, then if the Gurkish do come—'

'And what if you are wrong?' The Arch Lector was frowning mightily. 'From whom did this information come?'

Oh, dear me no, that would never do. Carlot dan Eider? Alive? But how? Body found floating by the docks . . . 'An anonymous source, Arch Lector.'

'Anonymous?' His Eminence glowered through narrowed eyes. 'And you would have me go to the Closed Council, at a time like this, and put before them the unproven gossip of your anonymous source?' *The waves swamp the deck . . .*

'I merely wished to alert your Eminence to the possibility—'

'When are they coming?' *The torn sailcloth flaps in the gale . . .*

'My informant did not—'

'Where will they land?' *The sailors topple screaming from the rigging . . .*

'Again, your Eminence, I cannot—'

'What will be their numbers?' *The wheel breaks off in my shaking hands . . .*

Glokta winced, and decided not to speak at all.

'Then kindly refrain from distracting us with rumours,' sneered Sult, his lip twisted with contempt. *The ship vanishes beneath the merciless waves, her cargo of precious warnings consigned to the deep, and her captain will not be missed.* 'We have more pressing concerns than a legion of Gurkish phantoms!'

'Of course, your Eminence.' *And if the Gurkish come, who will we hang? Oh, Superior Glokta, of course. Why ever did that damn cripple not speak up?*

Sult's mind had already slipped back into its well-worn circles. 'We have thirty-one votes and Marovia has something over twenty. Thirty-one. Not enough to make the difference.' He shook his head grimly, blue eyes darting over the papers. *As if there were some new way to look at them that would alter the terrible mathematics.* 'Nowhere near enough.'

'Unless we were to come to an understanding with High Justice Marovia.' Again, a pause, even more uncomfortable than last time. *Oh dear. I must have said that out loud.*

'An understanding?' hissed Sult.

'With Marovia?' squealed Goyle, his eyes bulging with triumph. *When the safe options are all exhausted, we must take risks. Is that not what I told myself as I rode down to the bridge, while the Gurkish massed upon the other side? Ah well, once more into the tempest . . .*

Glokta took a deep breath. 'Marovia's seat on the Closed Council is no safer than anyone else's. We may have been working against each other, but only out of habit. On the subject of this vote our aims are the same. To secure a weak candidate and maintain the balance. Together you have more than fifty votes. That might well be enough to tip the scales.'

Goyle sneered his contempt. 'Join forces with that peasant-loving hypocrite? Have you lost your reason?'

'Shut up, Goyle.' Sult glared at Glokta for a long while, his lips pursed in thought. *Considering my punishment, perhaps? Another tongue-lashing? Or a real lashing? Or my body found floating—* 'You are right. Go and speak to Marovia.'

Sand dan Glokta, once more the hero! Goyle's jaw hung open. 'But . . . your Eminence!'

'The time for pride is far behind us!' snarled Sult. 'We must seize any chance of keeping Brock and the rest from the throne. We must find compromises, however painful, and we must take whatever allies we can. Go!' he hissed over his shoulder, folding his arms and turning back to his crackling papers. 'Strike a deal with Marovia.'

Glokta got stiffly up from his chair. *A shame to leave such lovely company, but when duty calls . . .* He treated Goyle to the briefest of toothless smiles, then took up his cane and limped for the door.

'And Glokta!' He winced as he turned back into the room.

'Marovia's aims and ours may meet for now. But we cannot trust him. Tread carefully.'

'Of course, your Eminence.' *I always do. What other choice, when every step is agony?*

The private office of the High Justice was as big as a barn, its ceiling covered in festoons of old moulding, riddled with shadows. Although it was only late afternoon, the thick ivy outside the windows, and the thick grime on the panes, had sunk the place into a perpetual twilight. Tottering heaps of papers were stacked on every surface. Wedges of documents tied with black tape. Piles of leather-bound ledgers. Stacks of dusty parchments in ostentatious, swirling script, stamped with huge seals of red wax and glittering gilt. A kingdom's worth of law, it looked like. *And, indeed, it probably is.*

'Superior Glokta, good evening.' Marovia himself was seated at a long table near the empty fireplace, set for dinner, a flickering candelabra making each dish glisten in the gloom. 'I hope you do not mind if I eat while we talk? I would rather dine in the comfort of my rooms, but I find myself eating here more and more. So much to do, you see? And one of my secretaries appears to have taken a holiday unannounced.' *A holiday to the slaughterhouse floor, in fact, by way of the intestines of a herd of swine.* 'Would you care to join me?' Marovia gestured at a large joint of meat, close to raw in the centre, swimming in bloody gravy.

Glokta licked at his empty gums as he manoeuvred himself into a chair opposite. 'I would be delighted, your Worship, but the laws of dentistry prevent me.'

'Ah, of course. Those laws there can be no circumventing, even by a High Justice. You have my sympathy, Superior. One of my greatest pleasures is a good cut of meat, and the bloodier the better. Just show them the flame, I always tell my cook. Just show it to them.' *Funny. I tell my Practicals to start the same way.* 'And to what do I owe this unexpected visit? Do you come on your own initiative, or at the urging of your employer, my esteemed colleague from the Closed Council, Arch Lector Sult?'

Your bitter mortal enemy from the Closed Council, do you mean? 'His Eminence is aware that I am here.'

'Is he?' Marovia carved another slice and lifted it dripping onto his plate. 'And with what message has he sent you? Something relating to tomorrow's business in the Open Council, perhaps?'

'You spoil my surprise, your Worship. May I speak plainly?'

'If you know how.'

Glokta showed the High Justice his empty grin. 'This affair with the vote is a terrible thing for business. The doubt, the uncertainty, the worry. Bad for everyone's business.'

'Some more than others.' Marovia's knife squealed against the plate as he slit a ribbon of fat from the edge of his meat.

'Of course. At particular risk are those that sit on the Closed Council, and those that struggle on their behalf. They are unlikely to be given such a free hand if powerful men such as Brock or Isher are voted to the throne.' *Some of us, indeed, are unlikely to live out the week.*

Marovia speared a slice of carrot with his fork and stared sourly at it. 'A lamentable state of affairs. It would have been preferable for all concerned if Raynault or Ladisla were still alive.' He thought about it for a moment. 'If Raynault were still alive, at least. But the vote will take place tomorrow, however much we might tear our hair. It is hard now to see our way to a remedy.' He looked from the carrot to Glokta. 'Or do you suggest one?'

'You, your Worship, control between twenty and thirty votes on the Open Council.'

Marovia shrugged. 'I have some influence, I cannot deny it.'

'The Arch Lector can call on thirty votes himself.'

'Good for his Eminence.'

'Not necessarily. If the two of you oppose each other, as you always have, your votes will mean nothing. One for Isher, the other for Brock, and no difference made.'

Marovia sighed. 'A sad end to our two glittering careers.'

'Unless you were to pool your resources. Then you might have sixty votes between you. As many, almost, as Brock controls. Enough to make a King of Skald, or Barezin, or Heugen, or even some unknown, depending on how things go. Someone who might be more easily influenced in the future. Someone who might keep the Closed Council he has, rather than selecting a new one.'

'A King to make us all happy, eh?'

'If you were to express a preference for one man or another, I could take that back to his Eminence.' *More steps, more coaxing, more disappointments. Oh, to have a great office of my own, and to sit all day in comfort while cringing bastards slog up my stairs to smile at my insults, lap up my lies, beg for my poisonous support.*

'Shall I tell you what would make me happy, Superior Glokta?'

Now for the musings of another power-mad old fart. 'By all means, your Worship.'

Marovia tossed his cutlery onto his plate, sat back in his chair and gave a long, tired sigh. 'I would like no King at all. I would like every man equal under the law, to have a say in the running of his own country and the choosing of his own leaders. I would like no King, and no nobles, and a Closed Council selected by, and answerable to, the citizens themselves. A Closed Council open to all, you might say. What do you think of that?'

I think some people would say that it sounds very much like treason. The rest would simply call it madness. 'I think, your Worship, that your notion is a fantasy.'

'Why so?'

'Because the vast majority of men would far rather be told what to do than make their own choices. Obedience is easy.'

The High Justice laughed. 'Perhaps you are right. But things will change. This rebellion has convinced me of it. Things will change, by small steps.'

'I am sure Lord Brock on the throne is one small step none of us would like to see taken.'

'Lord Brock does indeed have very strong opinions, mostly

relating to himself. You make a convincing case, Superior.' Marovia sat back in his chair, hands resting on his belly, staring at Glokta through narrowed eyes. 'Very well. You may tell Arch Lector Sult that this once we have common cause. If a neutral candidate with sufficient support presents themselves, I will have my votes cast along with his. Who could have thought it? The Closed Council united.' He slowly shook his head. 'Strange times indeed.'

'They certainly are, your Worship.' Glokta struggled to his feet, wincing as he put his weight on his burning leg, and shuffled across the gloomy, echoing space towards the door. *Strange, though, that our High Justice is so philosophical on the subject of losing his position tomorrow. I have scarcely ever seen a man look calmer.* He paused as he touched the handle of the door. *One would almost suppose that he knows something we do not. One might almost suppose that he already has a plan in mind.*

He turned back. 'Can I trust you, High Justice?'

Marovia looked sharply up, the carving knife poised in his hand. 'What a beautifully quaint question from a man in your line of work. I suppose that you can trust me to act in my own interests. Just as far as I can trust you to do the same. Our deal goes no further than that. Nor should it. You are a clever man, Superior, you make me smile.' And he turned back to his joint of meat, prodding at it with a fork and making the blood run. 'You should find another master.'

Glokta shuffled out. *A charming suggestion. But I already have two more than I'd like.*

The prisoner was a scrawny, sinewy specimen, naked and bagged as usual, with hands manacled securely behind his back. Glokta watched as Frost dragged him into the domed room from the cells, his stumbling bare feet flapping against the cold floor.

'He wasn't too hard to get a hold of,' Severard was saying. 'He left the others a while ago, but he's been hanging round the city like the smell of piss ever since. We picked him up yesterday night.'

Frost flung the prisoner down in the chair. *Where am I? Who has me? What do they want? A horrifying moment, just before the work begins. The terror and the helplessness, the sick tingling of anticipation. My own memory of it was sharply refreshed, only the other day, at the hands of the charming Magister Eider. I was set free unmolested, however.* The prisoner sat there, head tilted to one side, the canvas on the front of the bag moving back and forth with his hurried breath. *I very much doubt that he will be so lucky.*

Glokta's eyes crept reluctantly to the painting above the prisoner's bagged head. *Our old friend Kanedias.* The painted face stared grimly down from the domed ceiling, the arms spread wide, the colourful fire behind. *The Maker fell burning . . .* He weighed the heavy hammer reluctantly in his hand. 'Let's get on with it, then.' Severard snatched the canvas bag away with a showy flourish.

The Navigator squinted into the bright lamplight, a weather-beaten face, tanned and deeply lined, head shaved, like a priest. *Or a confessed traitor, of course.*

'Your name is Brother Longfoot?'

'Indeed! Of the noble Order of Navigators! I assure you that I am innocent of any crime!' The words came out in rush. 'I have done nothing unlawful, no. That would not be my way at all. I am a law-abiding man, and always have been. I can think of no possible reason why I should be manhandled in this way! None!' His eyes swivelled down and he saw the anvil, gleaming on the floor between him and Glokta, where the table would usually have been. His voice rose an entire octave higher. 'The Order of Navigators is well respected, and I am a member in good standing! Exceptional standing! Navigation is the foremost of my many remarkable talents, it is indeed, the foremost of—'

Glokta cracked his hammer against the top of the anvil with a clang to wake the dead. 'Stop! Talking!' The little man blinked, and gaped, but he shut up. Glokta sank back in his chair, kneading at his withered thigh, the pain prickling up his back. 'Do you have any notion of how tired I am? Of how much I have to do? The agony of getting out of bed each morning leaves me a broken man before the day even begins, and the present moment is an exceptionally stressful one. It is therefore a matter of the most supreme indifference to me whether you can walk for the rest of your life, whether you can see for the rest of your life, whether you can hold your shit in for the rest of your intensely short, intensely painful life. Do you understand?'

The Navigator looked wide-eyed up at Frost, looming over him like an outsize shadow. 'I understand,' he whispered.

'Good,' said Severard.

'Ve' gooth,' said Frost.

'Very good indeed,' said Glokta. 'Tell me, Brother Longfoot, is one among your remarkable talents a superhuman resistance to pain?'

The prisoner swallowed. 'It is not.'

'Then the rules of this game are simple. I ask a question and you answer precisely, correctly, and, above all, briefly. Do I make myself clear?'

'I understand completely. I do not speak other than to—'

Frost's fist sunk into his gut and he folded up, eyes bulging. 'Do you see,' hissed Glokta, 'that your answer there should have been *yes*?' The albino seized the wheezing Navigator's leg and dragged his foot up onto the anvil. *Oh, cold metal on the sensitive sole. Quite unpleasant, but it could be so much worse. And something tells me it probably will be.* Frost snapped a manacle shut around Longfoot's ankle.

'I apologise for the lack of imagination.' Glokta sighed. 'In our defence, it's difficult to be always thinking of something new. I mean, smashing a man's feet with a lump hammer, it's so . . .'

'Pethethrian?' ventured Frost.

Glokta heard a sharp volley of laughter from behind Severard's mask, felt his own mouth grinning too. *He really should have been a comedian, rather than a torturer.* 'Pedestrian! Precisely so. But don't worry. If we haven't got what we need by the time we've crushed everything below your knees to pulp, we'll see if we can think of something more inventive for the rest of your legs. How does that sound?'

'But I have done nothing!' squealed Longfoot, just getting his breath back. 'I know nothing! I did—'

'Forget . . . about all that. It is meaningless now.' Glokta leaned slowly, painfully forwards, let the head of the hammer tap gently against the iron beside the Navigator's bare foot. 'What I want you to concentrate on . . . are my questions . . . and your toes . . . and this hammer. But don't worry if you find that difficult now. Believe me when I say – once the hammer starts falling, you will find it easy to ignore everything else.'

Longfoot stared at the anvil, nostrils flaring as his breath snorted quickly in and out. *And the seriousness of the situation finally impresses itself upon him.*

'Questions, then,' said Glokta. 'You are familiar with the man who styles himself Bayaz, the First of the Magi?'

'Yes! Please! Yes! Until recently he was my employer.'

'Good.' Glokta shifted in his chair, trying to find a more comfortable position while bending forwards. 'Very good. You accompanied him on a journey?'

'I was the guide!'

'What was your destination?'

'The Island of Shabulyan, at the edge of the World.'

Glokta let the head of the hammer click against the anvil again. 'Oh come, come. The edge of the World? A fantasy, surely?'

'Truly! Truly! I have seen it! I stood upon that island with my own feet!'

'Who went with you?'

'There was . . . was Logen Ninefingers, from the distant North.' *Ah, yes, he of the scars and the tight lips.* 'Ferro Maljinn, a Kantic woman.' *The one that gave our friend Superior Goyle so much trouble.* 'Jezal dan Luthar, a . . . a Union officer.' *A posturing dolt.* 'Malacus Quai, Bayaz' apprentice.' *The skinny liar with the troglodyte's complexion.* 'And then Bayaz himself!'

'Six of you?'

'Only six!'

'A long and a difficult journey to undertake. What was at the edge of the World that demanded such an effort, besides water?'

Longfoot's lip trembled. 'Nothing!' Glokta frowned, and nudged at the Navigator's big toe with the head of the hammer. 'It was not there! The thing that Bayaz sought! It was not there! He said he had been tricked!'

'What was it that he thought would be there?'

'He said it was a stone!'

'A stone?'

'The woman asked him. He said it was a rock . . . a rock from the Other Side.' The Navigator shook his sweating head. 'An unholy notion! I am glad we found no such thing. Bayaz called it the Seed!'

Glokta felt the grin melting from his face. *The Seed. Is it my imagination, or has the room grown colder?* 'What else did he say about it?'

'Just myths and nonsense!'

'Try me.'

'Stories, about Glustrod, and ruined Aulcus, and taking forms, and stealing faces! About speaking to devils, and the summoning of them. About the Other Side.'

'What else?' Glokta dealt Longfoot's toe a firmer tap with the hammer.

'Ah! Ah! He said the Seed was the stuff of the world below! That it was left over from before the Old Time, when demons walked the earth! He said it was a great and powerful weapon! That he meant to use it, against the Gurkish! Against the Prophet!' *A weapon, from before the Old Time. The summoning of devils, the taking of forms.* Kanedias seemed to frown down from the wall more grimly than ever, and Glokta flinched. He remembered his nightmare trip into the House of the Maker, the patterns of light on the floor, the shifting rings in the darkness. He remembered stepping out onto the roof, standing high above the city without climbing a single stair.

'You did not find it?' he whispered, his mouth dry.

'No! It was not there!'

'And then?'

'That was all! We came back across the mountains. We made a raft and rode the great Aos back to the sea. We took a ship from Calcis and I sit before you now!'

Glokta narrowed his eyes, studying carefully his prisoner's face. *There is more. I see it.* 'What are you not telling me?'

'I have told you everything! I have no talent for dissembling!' *That, at least, is true. His lies are plain.*

'If your contract is ended, why are you still in the city?'

'Because . . . because . . .' The Navigator's eyes darted round the room.

'Oh, dear me, no.' The heavy hammer came down with all of Glokta's crippled strength and crushed Longfoot's big toe flat with a dull thud. The Navigator gaped at it, eyes bulging from his head. *Ah, that beautiful, horrible moment between stubbing your toe and feeling the hurt. Here it comes. Here it comes. Here it—* Longfoot let vent a great shriek, squirmed around in his chair, face contorted with agony.

'I know the feeling,' said Glokta, wincing as he wriggled his own remaining toes around in his sweaty boot. 'I truly, truly do, and I sympathise. That blinding flash of pain, then up washes the sick and dizzy faintness of the shattered bone, then the slow pulsing up the leg that seems to drag the water from your eyes and make your whole body tremble.' Longfoot gasped, and whimpered, tears glistening on his cheeks. 'And what comes next? Weeks of limping? Months of hobbling, crippled? And if the next blow is to your ankle?' Glokta prodded at Longfoot's shin with the end of the hammer. 'Or square on your kneecap, what then? Will you ever walk again? I know the feelings well, believe me.' *So how can I inflict them now, on someone else?* He shrugged his twisted shoulders. *One of life's mysteries.* 'Another?' And he raised the hammer again.

'No! No! Wait!' wailed Longfoot. 'The priest! God help me, a priest came to the Order! A Gurkish priest! He said that one day the First of the Magi might ask for a Navigator, and that he wished to be told of it! That he wished to be told what happened afterward! He made threats, terrible threats, we had no choice but to obey! I was waiting in the city for another Navigator, who will convey the news! Only this morning I told him everything I have told you! I was about to leave Adua, I swear!'

'What was the name of this priest?' Longfoot said nothing, his wet eyes wide, the breath hissing in his nose. *Oh, why must they test me?* Glokta looked down at the Navigator's toe. It was already starting to swell and go blotchy, streaks of black blood-blisters down each side, the nail deep, brooding purple, edged with angry red. Glokta ground the end of the hammer's handle savagely into it. 'The name of the priest! His name! His name! His—'

'Aargh! Mamun! God help me! His name was Mamun!' *Mamun. Yulwei spoke of him, in Dagoska. The first apprentice of the Prophet himself. Together they broke the Second Law, together they ate the flesh of men.*

'Mamun. I see. Now.' Glokta craned further forward, ignoring an ugly tingling up his twisted spine. 'What is Bayaz doing here?'

Longfoot gaped, a long string of drool hanging from his bottom lip. 'I don't know!'

'What does he want with us? What does he want in the Union?'

'I don't know! I have told you everything!'

'Leaning forwards is a considerable ordeal for me. One that I begin to tire of.' Glokta frowned, and lifted the hammer, its polished head glinting.

'I just find ways from here to there! I only navigate! Please! No!' Longfoot squeezed his eyes shut, tongue wedged between his teeth. *Here it comes. Here it comes. Here it comes . . .*

Glokta tossed the hammer clattering down on the floor and leaned back, rocking his aching hips left and right to try and squeeze away the aches. 'Very well,' he sighed. 'I am satisfied.'

The prisoner opened first one grimacing eye, and then the other. He looked up, face full of hope. 'I can go?'

Severard chuckled softly behind his mask. Even Frost made a

kind of hissing sound. 'Of course you can go.' Glokta smiled his empty smile. 'You can go back in your bag.'

The Navigator's face went slack with horror. 'God take pity on me.'

If there is a God, he has no pity in him.

Fortunes of War

Lord Marshal Burr was in the midst of writing a letter, but he smiled up as West let the tent flap drop.

'How are you, Colonel?'

'Well enough, thank you, sir. The preparations are well underway. We should be ready to leave at first light.'

'As efficient as ever. Where would I be without you?' Burr gestured at the decanter. 'Wine?'

'Thank you, sir.' West poured himself a glass. 'Would you care for one?'

Burr indicated a battered canteen at his elbow. 'I believe it would be prudent if I was to stick to water.'

West winced, guiltily. He hardly felt as if he had the right to ask, but there was no escaping it now. 'How are you feeling, sir?'

'Much better, thank you for asking. Much, much better.' He grimaced, put one fist over his mouth, and burped. 'Not entirely recovered, but well on the way.' As though to prove the point he got up easily from his chair and strode to the map, hands clasped behind his back. His face had indeed regained much of its colour. He no longer stood hunched over, wobbling as though he were about to fall.

'Lord Marshal . . . I wanted to speak to you . . . about the battle at Dunbrec.'

Burr looked round. 'About what feature of it?'

'When you were sick . . .' West teetered on the brink of speaking, then let the words bubble out. 'I didn't send for a surgeon! I could have, but—'

'I'm proud that you didn't.' West blinked. He had hardly dared to hope for that answer. 'You did what I would have wanted you to do. It is important that an officer should care, but it is vital that he should not care too much. He must be able to place his men in harm's way. He must be able to send them to their deaths, if he deems it necessary. He must be able to make sacrifices, and to weigh the greatest good, without emotion counting in his choice. That is why I like you, West. You have compassion in you, but you have iron too. One cannot be a great leader without a certain . . . ruthlessness.'

West found himself lost for words. The Lord Marshal chuckled, and slapped the table with his open hand. 'But as it happens, no harm done, eh? The line held, the Northmen were turned out of Angland, and I tottered through alive, as you can see!'

'I am truly glad to see you feeling better, sir.'

Burr grinned. 'Things are looking up. We are free to move again, with our lines of supply secure and the weather finally dry. If your Dogman's plan works then we have a chance of finishing Bethod within a couple of weeks! They've been a damn courageous and useful set of allies!'

'They have, sir.'

'But this trap must be carefully baited, and sprung at just the right moment.' Burr peered at the map, rocking energetically back and forward on his heels. 'If we're too early Bethod may slip away. If we're too late our Northern friends could be crushed before we can reach them. We have to make sure bloody Poulder and bloody Kroy don't drag their bloody feet!' He winced and put a hand on his stomach, reached for his canteen and took a swig of water.

'I'd say you finally have them house-trained, Lord Marshal.'

'Don't you believe it. They're only waiting for their chance to put the knife in me, the pair of them! And now the King is dead. Who knows who will replace him? Voting for a monarch! Have you ever heard of such a thing?'

West's mouth felt unpleasantly dry. It was almost impossible to believe that the whole business had been partly his own doing. It would hardly have done to take credit for it however, given that his part had been to murder the heir to the throne in cold blood. 'Who do you think they will choose, sir?' he croaked.

'I'm no courtier, West, for all I have a seat on the Closed Council. Brock, maybe, or Isher? I'll tell you one thing for sure – if you think there's violence going on up here, it'll be twice as brutal back home in Midderland, with half the mercy shown.' The Marshal burped, and swallowed, and laid a hand on his stomach. 'Gah. No Northman's anything like as ruthless as those vultures on the Closed Council when they get started. And what will change when they have their new man in his robes of state? Not much, I'm thinking. Not much.'

'Very likely, sir.'

'I daresay there's nothing that we can do about it either way. A pair of blunt soldiers, eh, West?' He stepped up close to the map again, and traced their route northwards towards the mountains, his thick forefinger hissing over the paper. 'We must make sure we are ready to move at sunup. Every hour could be vital. Poulder and Kroy have had their orders?'

'Signed and delivered, sir, and they understand the urgency. Don't worry, Lord Marshal, we'll be ready to go in the morning.'

'Don't worry?' Burr snorted. 'I'm the commander of his Majesty's army. Worrying is what I do. But you should get some rest.' He waved West out of the tent with one thick hand. 'I'll see you at first light.'

They played their cards by torchlight on the hillside, in the calm night under the stars, and by torchlight below them the Union army made its hurried preparations to advance. Lamps bobbed and moved, soldiers cursed in the darkness. Bangs, and clatters, and the ill-tempered calls of men and beasts floated through the still air.

'There'll be no sleep for anyone tonight.' Brint finished dealing and scraped up his cards with his fingernails.

'I wish I could remember the last time I got more than three good hours together,' said West. Back in Adua, most likely, before his sister came to the city. Before the Marshal put him on his staff. Before he came back to Angland, before he met Prince Ladisla, before the freezing journey north and the things he had done on it. He hunched his shoulders and frowned down at his dog-eared cards.

'How's the Lord Marshal?' asked Jalenhorm.

'Much better, I'm pleased to say.'

'Thank the fates for that.' Kaspa raised his brows. 'I don't much fancy the idea of that pedant Kroy in charge.'

'Or Poulder either,' said Brint. 'The man's ruthless as a snake.'

West could only agree. Poulder and Kroy hated him almost as much as they hated each other. If one of them took command he'd be lucky if he found himself swabbing latrines the following day. Probably he'd be on a boat to Adua within the week. To swab latrines there.

'Have you heard about Luthar?' asked Jalenhorm.

'What about him?'

'He's back in Adua.' West looked up sharply. Ardee was in Adua, and the idea of the two of them together again was not exactly a heartening thought.

'I had a letter from my cousin Ariss.' Kaspa squinted as he clumsily fanned out his cards. 'She says Jezal was far away somewhere, on some kind of mission for the king.'

'A mission?' West doubted anyone would have trusted Jezal with anything important enough to be called a mission.

'All of Adua is buzzing with it, apparently.'

'They say he led some charge or other,' said Jalenhorm, 'across some bridge.'

West raised his eyebrows. 'Did he now?'

'They say he killed a score of men on the battlefield.'

'Only a score?'

'They say he bedded the Emperor's daughter,' murmured Brint.

West snorted. 'Somehow I find that the most believable of the three.'

Kaspa spluttered with laughter. 'Well whatever the truth of it, he's been made up to Colonel.'

'Good for him,' muttered West, 'he always seems to fall on his feet, that boy.'

'Did you hear about this revolt?'

'My sister mentioned something about it in her last letter. Why?'

'There was a full-scale rebellion, Ariss tells me. Thousands of peasants, roaming the countryside, burning and looting, hanging anyone with a 'dan' in their name. Guess who was given command of the force sent to stop them?'

West sighed. 'Not our old friend Jezal dan Luthar, by any chance?'

'The very same, and he persuaded them to go back to their homes, how about that?'

'Jezal dan Luthar,' murmured Brint, 'with the common touch. Who could have thought it?'

'Not me.' Jalenhorm emptied his glass and poured himself another. 'But they're calling him a hero now, apparently.'

'Toasting him in the taverns,' said Brint.

'Congratulating him in the Open Council,' said Kaspa.

West scraped the jingling pile of coins towards him with the edge of his hand. 'I wish I could say I was surprised, but I always guessed I'd be taking my orders from Lord Marshal Luthar one of these days.' It could have been worse, he supposed. It could have been Poulder or Kroy.

The first pink glow of dawn was creeping across the tops of the hills as West walked up the slope towards the Lord Marshal's tent. It was past time to give the word to move. He saluted grimly to the guards beside the flap and pushed on through. One lamp was still burning in the corner beyond, casting a ruddy glow over the maps, over the folding chairs and the folding tables, filling the creases in the blankets on Burr's bed with black shadows. West crossed to it, thinking over all the tasks he had to get done that morning, checking that he had left nothing out.

'Lord Marshal, Poulder and Kroy are waiting for your word to move.' Burr lay upon his camp bed, his eyes closed, his mouth open, sleeping peacefully. West would have liked to leave him there, but time was already wasting. 'Lord Marshal!' he snapped, walking up close to the bed. Still he did not respond.

That was when West noticed that his chest was not moving.

He reached out with hesitant fingers and held them above Burr's open mouth. No warmth. No breath. West felt the horror slowly spreading out from his chest to the very tips of his fingers. There could be no doubt. Lord Marshal Burr was dead.

It was grey morning when the coffin was carried from the tent on the shoulders of six solemn guardsmen, the surgeon walking along behind with his hat in his hand. Poulder, Kroy, West, and a scattering of the army's most senior men lined the path to watch it go. Burr himself would no doubt have approved of the simple box in which his corpse would be shipped back to Adua. The same rough carpentry in which the Union's lowest levies were buried.

West stared at it, numb.

The man inside had been like a father to him, or the closest he had ever come to having one. A mentor and protector, a patron and a teacher. An actual father, rather than the bullying, drunken worm that nature had cursed him with. And yet he did not feel sorrow as he stared at that rough wooden box. He felt fear. For the army and for himself. His first instinct was not to weep, it was to run. But there was nowhere to run to. Every man had to do his part, now more than ever.

Kroy lifted his sharp chin and stood up iron rigid as the shadow of the casket passed across them. 'Marshal Burr will be much missed. He was a staunch soldier, and a brave leader.'

'A patriot,' chimed in Poulder, his lip trembling, one hand pressed against his chest as though it might burst open with emotion. 'A patriot who gave his life for his country! It was my honour to serve under his orders.'

West wanted to vomit at their hypocrisy, but the fact was he desperately needed them. The Dogman and his people were out in the hills, moving north, trying to lure Bethod into a trap. If the Union army did not follow, and soon, they would have no help when the King of the Northmen finally caught up to them. They would only succeed in luring themselves into their graves.

'A terrible loss,' said West, watching the coffin carried slowly down the hillside, 'but we will honour him best by fighting on.'

Kroy gave a regulation nod. 'Well said, Colonel. We will make these Northmen pay!'

'We must. To that end, we should make ready to advance. We are already behind schedule, and the plan relies on precise—'

'What?' Poulder stared at him as though he suspected West of having gone suddenly insane. 'Move forward? Without orders? Without a clear chain of command?'

Kroy gave vent to an explosive snort. 'Impossible.'

Poulder violently shook his head. 'Out of the question, entirely out of the question.'

'But Marshal Burr's orders were quite specific—'

'Circumstances have very plainly altered.' Kroy's face was an expressionless slab. 'Until I receive explicit instructions from the Closed Council, no one will be moving my division so much as a hair's breadth.'

'General Poulder, surely you—'

'In this particular circumstance, I cannot but agree with General Kroy. The army cannot move an inch until the Open Council has selected a new king, and the king has appointed a new Lord Marshal.' And he and Kroy eyed each other with the deepest hatred and distrust.

West stood stock still, his mouth hanging slightly open, unable to believe his ears. It would take days for news of Burr's death to reach the Agriont, and even if the new king decided on a replacement immediately, days for the orders to come back. West pictured the long miles of forested track to Uffrith, the long leagues of salt water to Adua. A week, perhaps, if the decision was made at once, and with the government in chaos that hardly seemed likely.

In the meantime the army would sit there, doing nothing,

the hills before them all but undefended, while Bethod was given ample time to march north, slaughter the Dogman and his friends, and return to his positions. Positions which, no doubt, untold numbers of their own men would be killed assaulting once the army finally had a new commander. All an utterly pointless, purposeless waste. Burr's coffin had only just passed out of sight but already, it seemed, it was quite as if the man had never lived. West felt the horror creeping up his throat, threatening to strangle him with rage and frustration. 'But the Dogman and his Northmen, our allies . . . they are counting on our help!'

'Unfortunate,' observed Kroy.

'Regrettable,' murmured Poulder, with a sharp intake of breath, 'but you must understand, Colonel West, that the entire business is quite out of our hands.'

Kroy nodded stiffly. 'Out of our hands. And that is all.'

West stared at the two of them, and a terrible wave of powerlessness swept over him. The same feeling that he had when Prince Ladisla decided to cross the river, when Prince Ladisla decided to order the charge. The same feeling that he had when he floundered up in the mist, blood in his eyes, and knew the day was lost. That feeling that he was nothing more than an observer. That feeling that he had promised himself he would never have again. His own fault, perhaps.

A man should only make such promises as he is sure he can keep.

The Kingmaker

It was a hot day outside, and sunlight poured in through the great stained-glass windows, throwing coloured patterns across the tiled floor of the Lords' Round. The great space usually felt airy and cool, even in the summer. Today it felt stuffy, suffocating, uncomfortably hot. Jezal tugged his sweaty collar back and forth, trying to let some breath of air into his uniform without moving from his attitude of stiff attention.

The last time he had stood in this spot, back to the curved wall, had been the day the Guild of Mercers was dissolved. It was hard to imagine that it was little more than a year ago, so much seemed to have happened since. He had thought then that the Lords' Round could not possibly have been more crowded, more tense, more excited. How wrong he had been.

The curved banks of benches that took up the majority of the chamber were crammed to bursting with the Union's most powerful noblemen, and the air was thick with their expectant, anxious, fearful whispering. The entire Open Council was in breathless attendance, wedged shoulder to fur-trimmed shoulder, each man with the glittering chain that marked him out in gold or silver as the head of his family. Jezal might have had little more understanding of politics than a mushroom, but even he had to be excited by the importance of the occasion. The selection of a new High King of the Union by open vote. He felt a flutter of nerves in his throat at the thought. As occasions went, it was difficult to imagine one bigger.

The people of Adua certainly knew it. Beyond the walls, in the streets and squares of the city, they were waiting eagerly for news of the Open Council's decision. Waiting to cheer their new monarch, or perhaps to jeer him, depending on the choice. Beyond the high doors of the Lords' Round, the Square of

Marshals was a single swarming crowd, each man and woman in the Agriont desperate to be the first to hear word from inside. Futures would be decided, great debts would be settled, fortunes won and lost on the result. Only a lucky fraction had been permitted into the public gallery, but still enough that the spectators were crushed together around the balcony, in imminent danger of being shoved over and plunging to the tiled floor below.

The inlaid doors at the far end of the hall opened with a ringing crash, the echoes rebounding from the distant ceiling and booming around the great space. There was a rustling as every one of the councillors swivelled in his seat to look towards the entrance, and then a clatter of feet as the Closed Council approached steadily down the aisle between the benches. A gaggle of secretaries, and clerks, and hangers-on hurried after, papers and ledgers clutched in their eager hands. Lord Chamberlain Hoff strode at their head, frowning grimly. Behind him walked Sult, all in white, and Marovia, all in black, their faces equally solemn. Next came Varuz, and Halleck, and . . . Jezal's face fell. Who else but the First of the Magi, attired once again in his outrageous wizard's mantle, his apprentice skulking at his elbow. Bayaz grinned as though he were doing nothing more than attending the theatre. Their eyes met, and the Magus had the gall to wink. Jezal was far from amused.

To a swelling chorus of mutterings, the old men took their high chairs behind a long, curved table, facing the noblemen on their banked benches. Their aides arranged themselves on smaller chairs and laid out their papers, opened their books, whispered to their masters in hushed voices. The tension in the hall rose yet another step towards outright hysteria.

Jezal felt a sweaty shiver run up his back. Glokta was there, beside the Arch Lector, and the familiar face was anything but a reassurance. Jezal had been at Ardee's house only that morning, and all night too. Needless to say, he had neither forsworn her nor proposed marriage. His head spun from going round and round the issue. The more time he spent with her, the more impossible any decision seemed to become.

Glokta's fever-bright eyes swivelled to his, held them, then flicked away. Jezal swallowed, with some difficulty. He had landed himself in a devil of a spot, alright. What ever was he to do?

Glokta gave Luthar one brief glare. *Just to remind him of where we stand.* Then he swivelled in his chair, grimacing as he stretched out his throbbing leg, pressing his tongue hard into his empty gums as he felt the knee click. *We have more important business than Jezal dan Luthar. Far more important business.*

For this one day, the power lies with the Open Council, not the Closed. With the nobles, not the bureaucrats. With the many, not the few. Glokta looked down the table, at the faces of the great men who had guided the course of the Union for the last dozen years and more: Sult, Hoff, Marovia, Varuz, and all the rest. Only one member of the Closed Council was smiling. *Its newest and least welcome addition.*

Bayaz sat in his tall chair, his only companion his pallid apprentice, Malacus Quai. *And he looks scant companionship for anyone.* The First of the Magi seemed to revel in the bowel-loosening tension as much as his fellows were horrified by it, his smile absurdly out of place among the frowns. Worried faces. Sweaty brows. Nervous whispers to their cronies. *They perch on razors, all of them. And I too, of course. Let us not forget poor Sand dan Glokta, faithful public servant! We cling to power by our fingernails – slipping, slipping. We sit like the accused, at our own trials. We know the verdict is about to come down. Will it be an ill-deserved reprieve?* Glokta felt a smile twitch the corner of his mouth. *Or an altogether bloodier sentence? What say the gentlemen of the jury?*

His eyes flickered over the faces of the Open Council on their benches. *Three hundred and twenty faces.* Glokta pictured the papers nailed to the Arch Lector's wall, and he matched them to the men sitting before him. *The secrets, the lies, and the allegiances. The allegiances most of all. Which way will they vote?*

He saw some whose support he had made certain of. *Or as certain as we can be in these uncertain times.* He saw Ingelstad's pink face among the press, near to the back, and the man swallowed and looked away. *As long as you vote our way, you can look where you like.* He saw Wetterlant's slack features a few rows back, and the man gave him an almost imperceptible nod. *So our last offer was acceptable. Four more for the Arch lector? Enough to make the difference, and keep us in our jobs? To keep us all alive?* Glokta felt his empty grin widen. *We shall soon see . . .*

In the centre of the front row, among the oldest and best families of Midderland's nobility, Lord Brock sat, arms folded, with a look of hungry expectation. *Our front runner, keen to spring from the gate.* Not far from him was Lord Isher, old and stately. *The second favourite, still with every chance.* Barezin and Heugen sat nearby, wedged uncomfortably together and occasionally looking sideways at each other with some distaste. *Who knows? A late spurt and the throne could be theirs.* Lord Governor Skald sat on the far left, at the front of the delegations from Angland and Starikland. *New men, from the provinces. But a vote is still a vote, however we might turn our noses up.* Over on the far right twelve Aldermen of Westport sat, marked as outsiders by the cut of their clothes and the tone of their skin. *Yet a dozen votes still, and undeclared.*

There were no representatives of Dagoska today. *There are none left at all, alas. Lord Governor Vurms was relieved of his post. His son lost his head and could not attend. As for the rest of the city – it was conquered by the Gurkish. Well. Some wastage is inevitable. We will struggle on without them. The board is set, the pieces ready to be moved. Who will be the winner of this sordid little game, do we suppose? We shall soon see . . .*

The Announcer stepped forwards into the centre of the circular floor, lifted his staff high above his head and brought it down with a series of mighty crashes that echoed from the polished marble walls. The chatter faded, the magnates shuffled round to face the floor, every face drawn with tension. A pregnant silence settled over the packed hall, and Glokta felt a flurry of twitches slink up the left side of his face and set his eyelid blinking.

'I call this meeting of the Open Council of the Union to order!' thundered the Announcer. Slowly, and with the grimmest of frowns, Lord Hoff rose to face the councillors.

'My friends! My colleagues! My Lords of Midderland, Angland, and Starikland, Aldermen of Westport! Guslav the Fifth, our King . . . is dead. His two heirs . . . are dead. One at the hands of our enemies in the north, the other, our enemies in the south. Truly, this is a time of troubles, and we are left without a leader.' He held his arms up imploringly to the councillors. 'You are now faced with a grave responsibility. The selection, from among your number, of a new High King of the Union. Any man who holds a chair on this Open Council is a potential candidate! Any of you . . . could be our next King.' A volley of near-hysterical whispers floated down from the public gallery, and Hoff was obliged to raise his voice to shout over them.

'Such a vote has only been taken once before in the long history of our great nation! After the civil war and the fall of Morlic the Mad, when Arnault was raised to the throne by near-unanimous accord. He it was who sired the great dynasty that lasted until a few short days ago.' He let fall his arms and stared sadly down at the tiles. 'Wise was the choice your forebears made that day. We can only hope that the man elected here this morning, by and in full view of his peers, will found a dynasty just as noble, just as strong, just as even-handed, and just as long-lived!'

We can only hope for someone who will do as he's damn well told.

Ferro shoved a woman in a long gown out of her way. She elbowed past a fat man, his jowls trembling with outrage. She forced her way through to the balcony and glared down. The wide chamber below was crammed with fur-trimmed old men, crowded together on high banks of seating, each with a sparkling chain round his shoulders and a sparkling sheen of sweat across his pale face. Opposite them, behind a curved table, were another set of men, fewer in number. She scowled as she saw Bayaz sitting at one end of them, smiling as if he knew some secret that no one else could guess.

Just like always.

Beside him stood a fat pink with a face full of broken veins, shouting something about each man voting with his conscience. Ferro snorted. She would have been surprised if the few hundred men down there had five whole consciences between them. It seemed as if they were all attending carefully to the fat man's address, but Ferro saw differently.

The room was full of signals.

Men glanced sideways at one another and gave subtle nods. They winked with one eye or the other. They touched forefingers to noses and ears. They scratched in strange ways. A web of secrets, spreading out to every part of the chamber, and with Bayaz sitting grinning in the midst of it. Some way behind him, with his back to the wall, Jezal dan Luthar was standing in a uniform festooned with shiny thread. Ferro curled her lip. She could see it in the way he stood.

He had learned nothing.

The Announcer stabbed at the floor with his stick again. 'Voting will now begin!' There was a ragged groan and Ferro saw the woman she had pushed past earlier slide to the floor in a faint. Someone dragged her away, flapping a piece of paper in her face, and the ill-tempered press closed in tight behind. 'In the first round the field will be narrowed to three choices! There will be a show of hands for each candidate in order of the most extensive lands and holdings!'

Down below on their benches, the richly dressed sweated and trembled like men before a battle.

'Firstly!' shrieked a clerk, voice cracking as he consulted an enormous ledger, 'Lord Brock!'

Up in the gallery people mopped their faces, muttering and gasping as if they were facing death. Perhaps some of them were. The whole place reeked of doubt, and excitement, and terror. So strong it was contagious. So strong that even Ferro, who did not care a shit for the pinks and their damn vote, felt her mouth dry, her fingers itching, her heart thumping fast.

The Announcer turned to face the chamber. 'The first candidate will be Lord Brock! All those members of the Open Council who wish to vote for Lord Brock as the next High King of the Union, will you please raise your—'

'One moment, my Lords!'

Glokta jerked his head round, but his neck-bones stuck halfway and he had to peer from the corner of one dewy eye. He need hardly have bothered. *I could have guessed without looking who spoke.* Bayaz had risen from his chair and was now smiling indulgently towards the Open Council. *With perfect timing.* A volley of outraged calls rose up from its members in response.

'This is no time for interruptions!'

'Lord Brock! I vote for Brock!'

'A new dynasty!'

Bayaz' smile did not slip a hair's breadth. 'But what if the old dynasty could continue? What if we could make a new beginning,' and he glanced significantly across the faces of his colleagues on the Closed Council, 'while keeping all that is good in our present government? What if there was a way to heal wounds, rather than to cause them?'

'How?' came the mocking calls.

'What way?'

Bayaz' smile grew broader yet, 'Why, a royal bastard.'

There was a collective gasp. Lord Brock bounced from his seat. *Quite as if he had a spring under his arse.* 'This is an insult to this house! A scandal! A slur on the memory of King Guslav!' *Indeed, he now seems not only a drooling vegetable, but a lecherous one.* Other councillors rose to join him, faces red with outrage, white with fury, shaking fists and making angry calls. The whole sweep of benches seemed to honk and grunt and wriggle. *Just like the pig pens at the slaughterhouse, clamouring for any swill on offer.*

'Wait!' shrieked the Arch Lector, his white-gloved hands raised in entreaty. *Sensing some faint glimmer of hope in the*

169

darkness, perhaps? 'Wait, my Lords! There is nothing to be lost by listening! We shall have the truth here, even if it is painful! The truth should be our only concern!' Glokta had to chomp his gums down on a splutter of laughter. *Oh, of course, your Eminence! The truth has ever been your only care!*

But the babble gradually subsided. Those councillors who were on their feet were shamed back into line. *Their habit of obedience to the Closed Council is not easily broken. But then habits never are. Especially of obedience. Only ask my mother's dogs.* They grumbled their way back into their seats, and allowed Bayaz to continue.

'Your Lordships have perhaps heard of Carmee dan Roth?' A swell of noise from the gallery above confirmed that the name was not unfamiliar. 'She was a great favourite with the King, when he was younger. A very great favourite. So much so that she became pregnant with a child.' Another wave of muttering, louder. 'I have always carried a sentimental regard for the Union. I have always had one eye on its welfare, despite the scant thanks I have received for it.' And Bayaz gave the very briefest curl of his lip towards the members of the Closed Council. 'So, when the lady died in childbirth, I took the King's bastard into my care. I placed him with a noble family, to be well raised and well educated, in case the nation should one day find itself without an heir. My actions now seem prudent indeed.'

'Lies!' someone shrieked. 'Lies!' But few voices joined in. Their tone instead was one of curiosity.

'A natural son?'

'A bastard?'

'Carmee dan Roth, did he say?'

They have heard this tale before. Rumours, perhaps, but familiar ones. Familiar enough to make them listen. To make them judge whether it will be in their interests to believe.

But Lord Brock was not convinced. 'A blatant fabrication! It will take more than rumour and conjecture to sway this house! Produce this bastard, if you can, so-called First of the Magi! Work your magic!'

'No magic is needful,' sneered Bayaz. 'The King's son is already with us in the chamber.' Gasps of consternation from the gallery, sighs of amazement from the councillors, stunned silence from the Closed Council and their aides, every eye fixed on Bayaz' pointing finger as he swept out his hand towards the wall. 'No other man than Colonel Jezal dan Luthar!'

The spasm began in Glokta's toeless foot, shot up his ruined leg, set his twisted spine shivering from his arse right to his skull, made his face twitch like an angry jelly, made his few teeth rattle in his empty gums, set his eyelid flickering fast as a fly's wings.

The echoes of Bayaz' last utterance whispered round the suddenly silent hall. 'Luthar, Luthar, Luthar . . .'

You must be fucking joking.

The pale faces of the councillors were frozen, hanging in wide-eyed shock, squashed up in narrow-eyed rage. The pale men behind the table gaped. The pale people at the balcony pressed their hands over their mouths. Jezal dan Luthar, who had wept with self-pity while Ferro had stitched his face. Jezal dan Luthar, that leaky piss-pot of selfishness, and arrogance, and vanity. Jezal dan Luthar, who she had called the princess of the Union, had a chance of ending the day as its King.

Ferro could not help herself.

She let her head drop back and she hacked, and coughed, and gurgled with amusement. Tears sprung up in her eyes, her chest shook and her knees trembled. She clung to the rail of the balcony, she gasped, blubbered, drooled. Ferro did not laugh often. She could scarcely remember the last time. But Jezal dan Luthar, a King?

This was funny.

High above, in the public gallery, someone had started laughing. A jagged cackling completely inappropriate to the solemnity of the moment. But Jezal's first impulse, when he realised that it was his name that Bayaz had called out, when he realised that it was him the outstretched finger was pointing to, was to join in. His second, as every face in the entire vast space turned instantly towards him, was to vomit. The result was an ungainly cough, a shame-faced grin, an unpleasant burning at the very back of the mouth, and an instant paling of the complexion.

'I . . .' he found himself croaking, but without the slightest idea of how he would continue his sentence. What words could possibly help at a time like this? All he could do was stand there, sweating profusely, trembling under his stiff uniform, as Bayaz continued in ringing tones, his voice cutting over the laughter bubbling down from above.

'I have the sworn statement of his adoptive father here, attesting that all I say is true, but does it matter? The truth of it is plain for any man to see!' His arm shot out towards Jezal again. 'He won a Contest before you all, and accompanied me on a journey full of peril with never a complaint! He charged the bridge at Darmium, without a thought for his own safety! He saved Adua from the revolt without a drop of blood spilled! His valour and his prowess, his wisdom and his selflessness are well known to all! Can it be doubted that the blood of kings flows in his veins?'

Jezal blinked. Odd facts began to bob to the surface of his sluggish mind. He was not much like his brothers. His father had always treated him differently. He had got all the looks in the family. His mouth was hanging open, but he found he could not close it. When his father had seen Bayaz, at the Contest, he had turned white as milk, as though he recognised him.

He had done, and he was not Jezal's father at all.

When the king had congratulated Jezal on his victory, he had mistaken him for his own son. Not such blinding folly, evidently, as everyone might have thought. The old fool had been closer to the mark than anyone. Suddenly, it all made horrible sense.

He was a bastard. Literally.

He was the natural son of a king. What was much more, he

was slowly and with increasing terror beginning to realise, he was now being seriously considered as his replacement.

'My Lords!' shouted Bayaz over the disbelieving chatter gaining steadily in volume with every passing moment. 'You sit amazed! It is a difficult fact to accept, I can understand. Especially with the suffocating heat in here!' He signalled to the guards at both ends of the hall. 'Open the gates, please, and let us have some air!'

The doors were heaved open and a gentle breeze washed into the Lords' Round. A cooling breeze, and something else with it. Hard to make out at first, and then coming more clearly. Something like the noise of the crowd at the Contest. Soft, repetitive, and more than a little frightening.

'Luthar! Luthar! Luthar!' The sound of his own name, chanted over and over from a multitude of throats beyond the walls of the Agriont, was unmistakable.

Bayaz grinned. 'It would seem that the people of the city have already chosen their favoured candidate.'

'This is not their choice!' roared Brock, still on his feet but only now regaining his composure. 'Any more than it is yours!'

'But it would be foolish to ignore their opinion. The support of the commoners cannot be lightly dismissed, especially in these restless times. If they were to be disappointed, in their current mood, who knows what might occur? Riots in the streets, or worse? None of us wants that, surely, Lord Brock?'

Several of the councillors shifted nervously on their benches, glancing towards the open doors, whispering to their neighbours. If the atmosphere in the Round had been confused before, it was flabbergasted now. But the worry and surprise of the Open Council was nothing compared to Jezal's own.

A fascinating tale, but if he supposes that the Union's greediest men will simply take his word for it and give the crown away he has made a staggering blunder, whether commoners wet themselves at the name of Luthar or not. Lord Isher rose from the front row for the first time, stately and magnificent, the jewels on his chain of office flashing. *And so the furious objections, the outraged denials, the demands for punishment begin.*

'I wholeheartedly believe!' called Isher in ringing tones, 'that the man known as Colonel Jezal dan Luthar is none other than the natural child of the recently deceased King Guslav the Fifth!' Glokta gawped. So, it seemed, did almost everyone else in the chamber. 'And that he is further fitted for rule on account of his exemplary character and extensive achievements, both within the Union and outside it!' Another peal of ugly laughter gurgled down from above, but Isher ignored it. 'My vote, and the votes of my supporters, are wholeheartedly for Luthar!'

If Luthar's eyes had gone any wider they might have dropped from his skull. *And who can blame him?* Now one of the Westport delegation was on his feet. 'The Aldermen of Westport vote as one man for Luthar!' he sang out in his Styrian accent. 'Natural son and heir to King Guslav the Fifth!'

A man jumped up a few rows back. He glanced quickly and somewhat nervously at Glokta. None other than Lord Ingelstad. *The lying little shit, what's he about?* 'I am for Luthar!' he shrieked.

'And I, for Luthar!' Wetterlant, his hooded eyes giving away no more emotion than they had when he fed the ducks. *Better offers, eh, gentlemen? Or better threats?* Glokta glanced at Bayaz. He had a faint smile on his face as he watched others spring from their benches to declare their support for the so-called natural son of Guslav the Fifth. Meanwhile, the chanting of the crowds out in the city could still be heard.

'Luthar! Luthar! Luthar!'

As the shock drained away, Glokta's mind began to turn. *So that is why our First of the Magi cheated in the Contest on Luthar's behalf. That is why he has kept him close, all this time. That is why he procured for him so notable a command. If he had presented some nobody as the King's son, he would have been laughed from the chamber. But Luthar, love him or hate him, is one of us. He is known, he is familiar, he is . . . acceptable.* Glokta looked at Bayaz with something close to admiration.

Pieces of a puzzle, patient years in the preparation, calmly slotted into place before our disbelieving eyes. And not a thing that we can do, except, perhaps, to dance along to his tune?

Sult leaned sideways in his chair and hissed urgently in Glokta's ear. 'This boy, Luthar, what manner of a man is he?'

Glokta frowned over at him, standing dumbstruck by the wall. He looked at that moment as if he could scarcely be trusted to control his own bowels, let alone a country. *Still, you could have said much the same for our previous King, and he discharged his duties admirably. His duties of sitting and drooling, while we ran the country for him.* 'Before his trip abroad, your Eminence, he was as empty-headed, spineless and vain a young fool as one might hope to find in the entire nation. The last time I spoke to him, though—'

'Perfect!'

'But, your Eminence, you must see that this is all according to Bayaz' plans—'

'We will deal with that old fool later. I am taking advice.' Sult turned to hiss at Marovia without waiting for a reply. Now the two old men looked out at the Open Council, now they gave their nods and their signals to the men they controlled. All the while, Bayaz smiled. *The way an engineer might smile as his new machine works for the first time, precisely according to his design.* The Magus caught Glokta's eye, and gave the faintest of nods. There was nothing for Glokta to do but shrug, and give a toothless grin of his own. *I wonder if the time may come when we all wish we had voted for Brock.*

Now Marovia was speaking hurriedly to Hoff. The Lord Chamberlain frowned, nodded, turned towards the house and signalled to the Announcer, who beat furiously on the floor for silence.

'My Lords of the Open Council!' Hoff roared, once something resembling quiet had been established. 'The discovery of a natural son plainly changes the complexion of this debate! Fate would appear to have gifted us the opportunity to continue the dynasty of Arnault without further doubt or conflict!' *Fate gifts us? I rather think we have a less disinterested benefactor.*

'In view of these exceptional circumstances, and the strong support already voiced by members of this house, the Closed Council judges that an exceptional vote should now be taken. A single vote, on whether the man previously known as Jezal dan Luthar should be declared High King of the Union forthwith!'

'No!' roared Brock, veins bulging from his neck. 'I strongly protest!' But he might as well have protested against the incoming tide. The arms were already shooting up in daunting numbers. The Aldermen of Westport, the supporters of Lord Isher, the votes that Sult and Marovia had bullied and bribed their way. Glokta saw many more, now, men he had thought undecided, or firmly declared for one man or another. *All lending their support to Luthar with a speed that strongly implies a previous arrangement.* Bayaz sat back, arms folded, as he watched the hands shoot skywards. It was already becoming terribly clear that over half of the room was in favour.

'Yes!' hissed the Arch Lector, a smile of triumph on his face. 'Yes!'

Those who had not raised their arms, men committed to Brock, or Barezin, or Heugen, stared about them, stunned and not a little horrified at how quickly the world seemed to have passed them by. *How quickly the chance at power has slipped through their fingers. And who can blame them? It has been a surprising day for us all.*

Lord Brock made one last effort, raising a finger to stab at Luthar, still goggling by the wall. 'What proof have you that he is the son of anyone in particular, beside the word of this old liar?' and he gestured at Bayaz. 'What proof, my Lords? I demand proof!'

Angry mutterings swept up and down the benches, but no one made themselves conspicuous. *The second time Lord Brock has stood before this Council and demanded proof, and the second time no one has cared. What proof could there be, after all? A birthmark on Luthar's arse in the shape of a crown? Proof is boring. Proof is tiresome. Proof is an irrelevance. People would far rather be handed an easy lie than search for a difficult truth, especially if it suits their own purposes. And most of us would far rather have a King with no friends and no enemies, than a King with plenty of both. Most of us would rather have things stay as they are, than risk an uncertain future.*

More hands were raised, and more. Luthar's support had rolled too far for any one man to stop it. *Now it is like a great boulder hurtling down a slope. They dare not stand in its way in case they are squashed to gravy. So they crowd in behind, and add their own weight to it, and hope to snatch the scraps up afterward.*

Brock turned, a deadly frown across his face, and he stormed down the aisle and out of the chamber. Probably he had hoped that a good part of the Open Council would storm out with him. *But in that, as in so much else today, he must be harshly disappointed.* No more than a dozen of his most loyal followers accompanied him on the lonely march out of the Lords' Round. *The others have better sense.* Lord Isher exchanged a long look with Bayaz, then raised his pale hand. Lords Barezin and Heugen watched the best part of their support flocking to the cause of the young pretender, glanced at each other, retreated back into their seats and stayed carefully silent. Skald opened his mouth to call out, looked about him, thought better of it, and with evident reluctance, slowly lifted his arm.

There were no further protests.

King Jezal the First was raised to the throne by near-unanimous accord.

The Trap

Coming up into the High Places again, and the air felt crisp and clear, sharp and familiar in Logen's throat. Their march had begun gently as they came up through the woods, a rise you'd hardly notice. Then the trees thinned out and their path took them up a valley between grassy fells, cracked with trickling streams, patched with sedge and gorse. Now the valley had narrowed to a gorge, hemmed in on both sides with slopes of bare rock and crumbling scree, getting always steeper. Above them, on either side of that gorge, two great crags rose up. Beyond, the hazy hints of mountain peaks – grey, and light grey, and even lighter grey, melted in the distance into the heavy grey sky.

The sun was out, and meaning business, and it was hot to walk in, bright to squint into. They were all weary from climbing, and worrying, and looking behind them for Bethod. Four hundred Carls, maybe, and as many painted-face hillmen, all spread out in a great long column, cursing and spitting, boots crunching and sliding in the dry dirt and the loose stones. Crummock's daughter was struggling up ahead of Logen, bent double under the weight of her father's hammer, hair round her face dark with sweat. Logen's own daughter would have been older than that, by now. If she hadn't been killed by the Shanka, along with her mother and her brothers. That thought gave Logen a hollow, guilty feeling. A bad one.

'You want a hand with that mallet, girl?'

'No I fucking don't!' she screamed at him, then dropped it off her shoulder and dragged it away up the slope by the handle, scowling at him all the way, the hammer's head clattering along and leaving a groove in the stony soil. Logen blinked after her. Seemed his touch with the women went all the way down to ones ten years old.

Crummock came up behind him, fingerbones swinging round his neck. 'Fierce, ah? Y'ave to be fierce, to get on in my family!' He leaned close and gave a wink. 'And she's the fiercest of the lot, that little bitch. If I'm honest, she's my favourite.' He shook his head as he watched her dragging at that hammer. 'She'll make some poor bastard one hell of a wife one day. We're here, in case you were wondering.'

'Eh?' Logen wiped sweat from his face, frowning as he stared about. 'Where's the—'

Then he realised. Crummock's fortress, if you could call it that, was right ahead of them.

The valley was no more than a hundred strides now from one cliff to the other, and a wall was built across it. An ancient and crumbling wall of rough blocks, so full of cracks, so coated with creeper, brambles, seeding grass, that it seemed almost part of the mountains. It wasn't a whole lot steeper than the valley itself, and as tall as three men on each other's shoulders at its highest, sagging here and there as if it was about to fall down on its own. In the centre was a gate of weathered grey planks, splattered with lichen, managing to seem rotten and dried-out both at once.

To one side of the wall there was a tower, built up against the cliff. Or at least there was a great natural pillar sticking out from the rock with half-cut chunks of stone mortared to the top, making a wide platform on the cliff-side, overlooking the wall from high above. Logen looked at the Dogman as he trudged up, and the Dogman squinted at that wall as if he couldn't believe what he was seeing.

'This is it?' growled Dow, coming up next to them, his lip curling. A few trees had taken root at one side, just under the tower, must have been fifty years ago at least. Now they loomed up over the wall. A man could have climbed them easily, and stepped inside the place without even stretching far.

Tul stared up at the ragged excuse for a fortress. 'A strong place in the mountains, you said.'

'Strong . . . ish.' Crummock waved his hand. 'We hillmen have never been much for building and so on. What were you expecting? Ten marble towers and a hall bigger'n Skarling's?'

'I was expecting a halfway decent wall, at least,' growled Dow.

'Bah! Walls? I heard you were cold as snow and hot as piss, Black Dow, and now you want walls to hide behind?'

'We'll be outnumbered ten to one if Bethod does turn up, you mad fuck! You're damn right I want a wall, and you told us there'd be one!'

'But you said it yourself, friend.' Crummock spoke soft and slow as though he was explaining it to a child, and he tapped at the side of his head with one thick finger. 'I'm mad! Mad as a sack of owls, and everyone says so! I can't remember the names of my own children. Who knows what I think a wall looks like? I hardly know what I'm talking of myself, most of the time, and you're fool enough to listen to me? You must be mad yourselves!'

Logen rubbed at the bridge of his nose and he gave a groan. The Dogman's Carls were gathering near them now, looking up at that mossy heap of stones and muttering to each other, far from happy. Logen could hardly blame them. It was a long, hot walk they'd had to find this at the end of it. But they had no choices, as far as he could see. 'It's a bit late to build a better one,' he grumbled. 'We'll have to do what we can with what we've got.'

'That's it Bloody-Nine, you need no wall and you know it!' Crummock clapped Logen on the arm with his great fat hand. 'You cannot die! You're beloved of the moon, my fine new friend, above all others! You cannot die, not with the moon looking over you! You cannot—'

'Shut up,' said Logen.

They crunched sourly across the slope towards the gate. Crummock called out and the old doors wobbled open. A pair of suspicious hillmen stood on the other side, watching them come in. They slogged up a steep ramp cut into the rock, all tired and grumbling, and came out into a flat space above. A saddle between the two crags, might have been a hundred strides wide and two hundred long, sheer cliffs of stone all round. There were a few wooden shacks and sheds scattered about the edges, all green with old moss, a slumping stone hall built against the rock face with smoke rising out of a squat chimney. Just next to it a narrow stair was cut into the cliff, climbing up to the platform at the top of the tower.

'Nowhere to run to,' Logen muttered, 'if things turn sour.'

Crummock only grinned the wider. 'Course not. That's the whole point, ain't it? Bethod'll think he's got us like beetles in a bottle.'

'He will have,' growled the Dogman.

'Aye, but then your friends will come up behind him and won't he get the father of all shocks, though? It'll almost be worth it for the look on his face, the shit-eating bastard!'

Logen worked his mouth and spat onto the stony ground. 'I wonder what the looks on our faces'll be by then? All slack and corpse-like would be my guess.' A herd of shaggy sheep were pressed in tight together in a pen, staring around wide-eyed, bleating to each other. Hemmed in and helpless, and Logen knew exactly how they felt. From inside the fort, where the ground was a good deal higher, there was hardly a wall at all. You could've stepped up onto its walkway, if you'd got long legs, and stood at its crumbling, moss-ridden excuse for a parapet.

'Don't you worry your beautiful self about nothing, Bloody-Nine,' laughed Crummock. 'My fortress could be better built, I'll grant you, but the ground is with us, and the mountains, and the moon, all smiling on our bold endeavour. This is a strong place, with a strong history. Do you not know the story of Laffa the Brave?'

'Can't say that I do.' Logen wasn't altogether sure he wanted to hear it now, but he was in the long habit of not getting what he wanted.

'Laffa was a great bandit chief of the hillmen, a long time ago. He raided all the clans around for years, him and his brothers. One hot summer the clans had enough, so they banded together and hunted him in the mountains. Here's where he made his last stand. Right here in this fortress. Laffa and his brothers and all his people.'

'What happened?' asked Dogman.

'They all got killed, and their heads cut off and put in a sack, and the sack was buried in the pit they used to shit in.' Crummock beamed. 'Guess that's why they call it a last stand, eh?'

'That's it? That's the story?'

'That's all of it that I know, but I'm not right sure what else there could be. That was pretty much the end for Laffa, I'd say.'

'Thanks for the encouragement.'

'That's alright, that's alright! I've more stories, if you need more!'

'No, no, that's enough for me.' Logen turned and started walking off, the Dogman beside him. 'You can tell me more once we've won!'

'Ha ha, Bloody-Nine!' shouted Crummock after him, 'that'll be a story in itself, eh? You can't fool me! You're like I am, beloved of the moon! We fight hardest when our backs are to the mountains and there's no way out! Tell me it ain't so! We love it when we got no choices!'

'Oh aye,' Logen muttered to himself as he stalked off towards the gate. 'There's nothing better than no choices.'

Dogman stood at the foot o' the wall, staring up at it, and wondering what to do to give him and the rest a better chance at living out the week.

'It'd be a good thing to get all this creeper and grass cleared off it,' he said. 'Makes it a damn sight easier to climb.'

Tul raised an eyebrow. 'You sure it ain't all that plant that's holding it together?'

Grim tugged at a vine and a shower of dried-out mortar came with it.

'Might be you're right.' Dogman sighed. 'Cut off what we can, then, eh? Some work at the top would be time well spent and all. Be nice to have a decent stack o' stones to hide behind when Bethod starts shooting arrows at us.'

'That it would,' said Tul. 'And we could dig us a ditch down here in front, plant some stakes round the bottom, make it harder for 'em to get up close.'

'Then close that gate, nail it shut, and wedge a load of rocks in behind it.'

'We'll have trouble getting out,' said Tul.

Logen snorted. 'Us getting out won't be the pressing problem, I'm thinking.'

'You've a point right there,' laughed Crummock, ambling up with a lit pipe in his fat fist. 'It's Bethod's boys getting in that we should worry on.'

'Getting these walls patched up would be a good start at settling my mind.' Dogman pointed at the trees grown up over the wall. 'We need to get these cut down and cut up, carve us out some stone, mix us some mortar and all the rest. Crummock, you got people can do that? You got tools?'

He puffed at his pipe, frowning at Dogman all the long while, then blew brown smoke. 'I might have, but I won't take my orders from such as you, Dogman. The moon knows my talents, and they're for murder, not mortaring.' Grim rolled his eyes.

'Who will you take orders from?' asked Logen.

'I'll take 'em from you, Bloody-Nine, and from no other! The moon loves you, and I love the moon, and you're the man for—'

'Then get your people together and get to fucking cutting wood and stone. I'm bored o' your blather.'

Crummock knocked out his ashes sourly against the wall. 'You're no fun at all, you boys, you do nothing but worry. You need to think on the sunny side o' this. The worst that can happen is that Bethod don't show!'

'The worst?' Dogman stared at him. 'You sure? What about if Bethod does come, and his Carls kick your wall over like a pile o' turds and kill every last one of us?'

Crummock's brow furrowed. He frowned down at the

ground. He squinted up at the clouds. 'True,' he said, breaking out in a smile. 'That is worse. You got a fast mind, lad.'

Dogman gave a long sigh, and stared down into the valley. The wall might not have been all they'd hoped for, but you couldn't knock the position. Coming up that steep slope against a set of hard men, high above and with nothing to lose, ready and more'n able to kill you. That was no one's idea o' fun.

'Tough to get organised down there,' said Logen, speaking Dogman's own thoughts. 'Specially with arrows plunging on you from above and nothing to hide behind. Hard to make numbers count. I wouldn't much fancy trying it myself. How are we going to work it, if they come?'

'I reckon we'll make three crews.' Dogman nodded to the tower. 'Me up there with five score or so o' the best archers. Good spot to shoot from, that. Nice and high, and a good view of the front o' the wall.'

'Uh,' said Grim.

'Maybe some strong lads to throw a rock or two.'

'I'll lob a rock,' said Tul.

'Fair enough. Then the pick of our lads up on the wall, ready to take 'em on hand to hand, if they get up there. That'll be your crew, I reckon, Logen. Dow and Shivers and Red Hat can be your seconds.'

Logen nodded, not looking all that happy. 'Aye, alright.'

'Then Crummock up behind with his hillmen, ready to charge if they make it through the gate. If we last more'n a day, maybe you can swap over. Hillmen on the wall, Logen and the rest behind.'

'That's quite the plan for a little man!' Crummock clapped him on the shoulder with a huge hand and damn near knocked him on his face. 'Like as not you had it from the moon while you slept! Ain't one thing in it I'd change!' He slapped his meaty fist into his palm. 'I love a good charge! I hope the Southerners don't come, and leave more for the rest of us! I want to charge now!'

'Good for you,' grunted Dogman. 'Maybe we can find you a

cliff to charge off.' He squinted into the sun, taking another look up at the wall that held all of their hopes. He wouldn't have cared to try and climb it, not from this side, but it wasn't halfway as high, or as thick, or as strong as he'd have liked. You don't always get things the way you like, Threetrees would have said. But just once would've been nice.

'The trap is ready,' said Crummock, grinning down into the valley.

The Dogman nodded. 'The only question is who'll get caught in it. Bethod? Or us?'

Logen walked through the night, between the fires. Some fires had Carls round them, drinking Crummock's beer, and smoking his chagga, and laughing at stories. Others had hillmen, looking like wolves in the shifting light with their rough furs, their tangled hair, their half-painted faces. One was singing, somewhere. Strange songs in a strange tongue that yapped and warbled like the animals in the forest, rose and fell like the valleys and the peaks. Logen had to admit he'd been smoking, for the first time in a while, and drinking too. Everything felt warm. The fires, and the men, and the cool wind, even. He wove his way through the dark, looking for the fire where the Dogman and the rest were sitting, and not having a clue which way to find it. He was lost, and in more ways than one.

'How many men you killed, Da?' Had to be Crummock's daughter. There weren't too many high voices round that camp, more was the pity. Logen saw the hillman's great shape in the darkness, his three children sitting near him, their outsize weapons propped up in easy reach.

'Oh, I've killed a legion of 'em, Isern.' Crummock's great deep voice rumbled out at Logen as he came closer. 'More'n I can remember. Your father might not have all his wits all the time, but he's a bad enemy to have. One of the worst. You'll see the truth of that close up, when Bethod and his arse-lickers come calling.' He looked up and saw Logen coming through the night. 'I swear, and I don't doubt Bethod would swear with me, there's only one bastard in all the North who's nastier, and bloodier, and harder than your father.'

'Who's that?' asked the boy with the shield. Logen felt his heart sinking as Crummock's arm lifted up to point towards him.

'Why, that's him there. The Bloody-Nine.'

The girl glared at Logen. 'He's nothing. You could have him, Da!'

'By the dead, not me! Don't even say it girl, in case I make a piss-puddle big enough to drown you in.'

'He don't look like much.'

'And there's a lesson for all three of you. Not looking much, not saying much, not seeming much, that's a good first step in being dangerous, eh, Ninefingers? Then when you let the devil go free it's twice the shock for whatever poor bastard's on the end of it. Shock and surprise, my little beauties, and quickness to strike, and lack of pity. These are the things that make a killer. Size, and strength, and a big loud voice are alright in their place, but they're nothing to that murderous, monstrous, merciless speed, eh, Bloody-Nine?'

It was a hard lesson for children, but Logen's father had taught it to him young, and he'd kept it in mind all these years. 'It's a sorry fact. He who strikes first often strikes last.'

'That he does!' shouted Crummock, slapping his great thigh. 'Well said! But it's a happy fact, not a sorry one. You remember old Wilum, don't you, my children?'

'Thunder got him!' shouted the boy with the shield. 'In a storm, up in the High Places!'

'That it did! One moment he's standing there, the next there's a noise like the world falling and a flash like the sun, and Wilum's dead as my boots!'

'His feet was on fire!' laughed the girl.

'That they were, Isern. You saw how fast he died, how much the shock, how little mercy that the lightning showed, well.' And Crummock's eyes slid across to Logen. 'That's what it'd be to cross that man there. One moment you'd say your hard word, the next?' He clapped his hands together with a crack and made the three children jump. 'He'd send you back to the mud. Faster than the sky killed Wilum, and with no more regret. Your life hangs on a thread, every moment you stand within two strides of that nothing-looking bastard there, does it not, Bloody-Nine?'

'Well . . .' Logen wasn't much enjoying this.

'How many men you killed then?' the girl shouted at him, sticking her chin out.

Crummock laughed and rubbed his hand in her hair. 'The numbers aren't made to count that high, Isern! He's the king of killers! No man made more deadly, not anywhere under the moon.'

'What about that Feared?' asked the boy with the spear.

'Ohhhhhh,' cooed Crummock, smiling right across his face. 'He's not a man, Scofen. He's something else. But I wonder. Fenris the Feared and the Bloody-Nine, setting to kill one another?' He rubbed his hands together. 'Now *that* is a thing I would like to see. *That* is a thing the moon would love to shine upon.' His eyes rolled up towards the sky and Logen followed them with his own. The moon was up there, sitting in the black heavens, big and white, glowing like new fire.

Horrible Old Men

The tall windows stood open, allowing a merciful breeze to wash through the wide salon, to give the occasional cooling kiss to Jezal's sweating face, to make the vast, antique hangings flap and rustle. Everything in the chamber was outsized – the cavernous doorways were three times as high as a man, and the ceiling, painted with the peoples of the world bowing down before an enormous golden sun, was twice as high again. The immense canvases on the walls featured life-size figures in assorted majestic poses, whose warlike expressions would give Jezal uncomfortable shocks whenever he turned around.

It seemed a space for great men, for wise men, for epic heroes or mighty villains. A space for giants. Jezal felt a tiny, meagre, stupid fool in it.

'Your arm, if it please your Majesty,' murmured one of the tailors, managing to give Jezal orders while remaining crushingly sycophantic.

'Yes, of course . . . I'm sorry.' Jezal raised his arm a little higher, inwardly cursing at having apologised yet again. He was a king now, as Bayaz was constantly telling him. If he had shoved one of the tailors out of the window, no apology would have been necessary. The man would probably have thanked him profusely for the attention as he plummeted to the ground. As it was he merely gave a wooden smile, and smoothly unravelled his measuring tape. His colleague was crawling below, doing something similar around Jezal's knees. The third was punctiliously recording their observations in a marbled ledger.

Jezal took a long breath, and frowned into the mirror. An uncertain-seeming young idiot with a scar on his chin gazed back at him from the glass, draped with swatches of glittering cloth as though he were a tailor's dummy. He looked, and certainly felt, more like a clown than a king. He looked a joke, and undoubtedly would have laughed, had he not himself been the ridiculous punch-line.

'Perhaps something after the Osprian fashion, then?' The Royal Jeweller placed another wooden nonsense carefully on Jezal's head and examined the results. It was far from an improvement. The damn thing looked like nothing so much as an inverted chandelier.

'No, no!' snapped Bayaz, with some irritation. 'Far too fancy, far too clever, far too big. He will scarcely be able to stand in the damn thing! It needs to be simple, to be honest, to be light. Something a man could fight in!'

The Royal Jeweller blinked. 'He will be fighting in the crown?'

'No, dolt! But he must look as if he might!' Bayaz came up behind Jezal, snatched the wooden contraption from his head and tossed it rattling on the polished floor. Then he seized Jezal by the arms and stared grimly at his reflection from over his shoulder. 'This is a warrior king in the finest tradition! The natural heir to the Kingdom of Harod the Great! A peerless swordsman, who has dealt wounds and received them, who has led armies to victory, who has killed men by the score!'

'Score?' murmured Jezal, uncertainly.

Bayaz ignored him. 'A man as comfortable with saddle and sword as with throne and sceptre! His crown must go with armour. It must go with weapons. It must go with steel. Now do you understand?'

The Jeweller nodded slowly. 'I believe so, my Lord.'

'Good. And one more thing.'

'My Lord has but to name it.'

'Give it a big-arsed diamond.'

The Jeweller humbly inclined his head. 'That goes without saying.'

'Now out. Out, all of you! His Majesty has affairs of state to attend to.'

The ledger was snapped shut, the tapes were rolled up in a moment, the swatches of cloth were whisked away. The tailors and the Royal Jeweller bowed their way backwards from the room with a range of servile mutterings, whisking the huge, gilt-encrusted doors silently shut. Jezal had to stop himself from leaving with them. He kept forgetting that he was now his Majesty.

'I have business?' he asked, turning from the mirror and trying his best to sound offhand and masterful.

Bayaz ushered him out into the great hallway outside, its walls covered in beautifully rendered maps of the Union. 'You have business with your Closed Council.'

Jezal swallowed. The very name of the institution was daunting. Standing in marble chambers, being measured for new clothes, being called your Majesty, all of this was bemusing, but hardly required a great effort on his part. Now he was expected to sit at the very heart of government. Jezal dan Luthar, once widely celebrated for his towering ignorance, would be sharing a room with the twelve most powerful men in the Union. He would be expected to make decisions that would affect the lives of thousands. To hold his own in the arenas of politics, and law, and diplomacy, when his only areas of true expertise were fencing, drink, and women, and he was forced to concede that, in that last area at least, he did not seem to be quite the expert he had once reckoned himself.

'The Closed Council?' His voice shot up to a register more girlish than kingly, and he was forced to clear his throat. 'Is there some particular matter of importance?' he growled in an unconvincing bass.

'Some momentous news arrived from the North earlier today.'

'It did?'

'I am afraid that Lord Marshal Burr is dead. The army needs a new commander. Argument on that issue will probably take up a good few hours. Down here, your Majesty.'

'Hours?' muttered Jezal, his boot-heels clicking down a set of wide marble steps. Hours in the company of the Closed Council. He rubbed his hands nervously together.

Bayaz seemed to guess his thoughts. 'There is no need for you to fear those old wolves. You are their master, whatever they may have come to believe. At any time you can replace them, or have them dragged away in irons, for that matter, should you desire. Perhaps they have forgotten it. It might be that we will need to remind them, in due course.'

They stepped through a tall gateway flanked by Knights of the Body, their helmets clasped under their arms but their faces kept so carefully blank they might as well have had their visors down. A wide garden lay beyond, lined on all four sides by a shady colonnade, its white marble pillars carved in the likenesses of trees in leaf. Water splashed from fountains, sparkling in the bright sunlight. A pair of huge orange birds with legs as thin as twigs strutted self-importantly about a perfectly clipped lawn. They stared haughtily at Jezal down their curved beaks as he passed them, evidently in no more doubt than him that he was an utter impostor.

He gazed at the bright flowers, and the shimmering greenery, and the fine statues. He stared up at the ancient walls, coated with red, white, and green creeper. Could it really be that all this belonged to him? All this, and the whole Agriont besides? Was he walking now in the mighty footsteps of the kings of old? Of Harod, and Casamir, and Arnault? It boggled the mind. Jezal had to blink and shake his head, as he had a hundred times already that day, simply to prevent himself from falling over. Was he not the same man as he had been last week? He rubbed at his beard, as if to check, and felt the scar beneath it. The same man who had been soaked out on the wide plain, who had been wounded among the stones, who had eaten half-cooked horsemeat and been glad to get it?

Jezal cleared his throat. 'I would like very much . . . I don't know whether it would be possible . . . to speak to my father?'

'Your father is dead.'

Jezal cursed silently to himself. 'Of course he is, I meant . . . the man I thought was my father.'

'What is it that you suppose he would tell you? That he made bad decisions? That he had debts? That he took money from me in return for raising you?'

'He took money?' muttered Jezal, feeling more forlorn than ever.

'Families rarely take in orphans out of good will, even those with a winning manner. The debts were cleared, and more than cleared. I left instructions that you should have fencing lessons as soon as you could hold a steel. That you should have a commission in the King's Own, and be encouraged to take part in the summer Contest. That you should be well prepared, in case this day should come. He carried out my instructions to the letter. But you can see that a meeting between the two of you would be an extremely awkward scene for you both. One best avoided.'

Jezal gave a ragged sigh. 'Of course. Best avoided.' An unpleasant thought crept across his mind. 'Is . . . is my name even Jezal?'

'It is now that you have been crowned.' Bayaz raised an eyebrow. 'Why, would you prefer another?'

'No. No, of course not.' He turned his head away and blinked back the tears. His old life had been a lie. His new one felt still more so. Even his own name was an invention. They walked in silence through the gardens for a moment, their feet crunching in the gravel, so fresh and perfect that Jezal wondered if every stone of it was daily cleaned by hand.

'Lord Isher will make many representations to your Majesty over the coming weeks and months.'

'He will?' Jezal coughed, and sniffed, and put on his bravest face. 'Why?'

'I promised him that his two brothers would be made Lords Chamberlain and Chancellor on the Closed Council. That his family would be preferred above all others. That was the price of his support in the vote.'

'I see. Then I should honour the bargain?'

'Absolutely not.'

Jezal frowned. 'I am not sure that I—'

'Upon achieving power, one should immediately distance oneself from all allies. They will feel they own your victory, and no rewards will ever satisfy them. You should elevate your enemies instead. They will gush over small tokens, knowing they do not deserve them. Heugen, Barezin, Skald, Meed, these are the men you should bring into your circle.'

'Not Brock?'

'Never Brock. He came too close to wearing the crown to ever feel himself beneath it. Sooner or later he must be kicked back into his place. But not until you are safe in your position, and have plentiful support.'

'I see,' Jezal puffed out his cheeks. Evidently there was more to being king than fine clothes, a haughty manner, and always getting the biggest chair.

'This way.' Out of the garden and into a shadowy hallway panelled with black wood and lined with an array of antique arms to boggle the mind. Assorted suits of full armour stood to glittering attention: plate and chain-mail, hauberk and cuirass, all stamped and emblazoned with the golden sun of the Union. Ceremonial greatswords as tall as a man, and halberds considerably taller, were bolted to the wall in an elaborate procession. Under them were mounted an army's worth of axes, maces, morningstars and blades curved and straight, long and short, thick and thin. Weapons forged in the Union, weapons captured from the Gurkish, weapons stolen from Styrian dead on bloody battlefields. Victories and defeats, commemorated in steel. High above, the flags of forgotten regiments, gloriously slaughtered to a man in the wars of long ago, hung tattered and lifeless from charred pikestaffs.

A heavy double door loomed at the far end of this collection, black and unadorned, as inviting as a scaffold. Knights Herald stood on either side of it, solemn as executioners, winged helmets glittering. Men taxed not only with guarding the centre of government, but with carrying the King's Orders to whatever corner of the Union was necessary. His orders, Jezal realised with a sudden further lurch of nerves.

'His Majesty seeks audience with the Closed Council,'

intoned Bayaz. The two men reached out and pulled the heavy doors open. An angry voice surged out into the corridor. 'There must be further concessions or there will only be further unrest! We cannot simply—'

'High Justice, I believe we have a visitor.'

The White Chamber was something of a disappointment after the magnificence of the rest of the palace. It was not that large. There was no decoration on the plain white walls. The windows were narrow, almost cell-like, making the place seem gloomy even in the sunshine. There was no draught and the air was uncomfortably close and stale. The only furniture was a long table of dark wood, piled high with papers, and six plain, hard chairs arranged down either side with another at the foot and one more, noticeably higher than the others, at the head. Jezal's own chair, he supposed.

The Closed Council rose as he ducked reluctantly into the room. As frightening a selection of old men as could ever have been collected in one place, and every man of them staring right at Jezal in expectant silence. He jumped as the door was heaved shut behind him, the latch dropping with an unnerving finality.

'Your Majesty,' and Lord Chamberlain Hoff bowed deep, 'may I and my colleagues first congratulate you on your well-deserved elevation to the throne. We all feel that we have in you a worthy replacement for King Guslav, and look forward to advising you, and carrying out your orders, over the coming months and years.' He bowed again, and the collection of formidable old men clapped their hands in polite applause.

'Why, thank you all,' said Jezal, pleasantly surprised, however little he might feel like a worthy replacement for anything. Perhaps this would not be so painful as he had feared. The old wolves seemed tame enough to him.

'Please allow me to make the introductions,' murmured Hoff. 'Arch Lector Sult, head of your Inquisition.'

'An honour to serve, your Majesty.'

'High Justice Marovia, chief Law Lord.'

'Likewise, your Majesty, an honour.'

'With Lord Marshal Varuz, I believe you are already well acquainted.'

The old soldier beamed. 'It was a privilege to train you in the past, your Majesty, and will be a privilege to advise you now.'

So they went on, Jezal smiling and nodding to each man in turn. Halleck, the Lord Chancellor. Torlichorm, the High Consul. Reutzer, Lord Admiral of the Fleet, and so on, and so on. Finally Hoff ushered him to the high chair at the head of the table and Jezal enthroned himself while the Closed Council smiled on. He grinned gormlessly up at them for a moment, and then realised. 'Oh, please be seated.'

The old men sat, a couple of them with evident winces of pain as old knees crunched and old backs clicked. Bayaz dropped carelessly into the chair at the foot of the table, opposite Jezal, as though he had been occupying it all his life. Robes rustled as old arses shifted on polished wood, and gradually the room went silent as a tomb. One chair was empty at Varuz' elbow. The chair where Lord Marshal Burr would have sat, had he not been assigned to duty in the North. Had he not been dead. A dozen daunting old men waited politely for Jezal to speak. A dozen old men who he had thought of until recently as occupying the pinnacle of power, all now answerable to him. A situation he could never have imagined in his most self-indulgent daydreams. He cleared his throat.

'Pray continue, my Lords. I will try and catch up as we go.'

Hoff flashed a humble smile. 'Of course, your Majesty. If at any time you require explanation, you have but to ask.'

'Thank you,' said Jezal, 'thank—'

Halleck's grinding voice cut over him. 'Back to the issue of discipline among the peasantry, therefore.'

'We have already prepared concessions!' snapped Sult. 'Concessions which the peasants were happy to accept.'

'A shred of bandage to bind a suppurating wound!' returned Marovia. 'It is only a matter of time before rebellion comes again. The only way we can avoid it is by giving the common man what he needs. No more than is fair! We must involve him in the process of government.'

'Involve him!' sneered Sult.

'We must transfer the burden of tax to the landowners!'

Halleck's eyes rolled to the ceiling. 'Not this nonsense again.'

'Our current system has stood for centuries,' barked Sult.

'It has failed for centuries!' threw back Marovia.

Jezal cleared his throat and the heads of the old men snapped round to look at him. 'Could each man not simply be taxed the same proportion of his income, regardless of whether he is a peasant or a nobleman . . . and then, perhaps . . .' He trailed off. It had seemed a simple enough idea to him, but now all eleven bureaucrats were staring at him, shocked, quite as if a domestic pet had been ill-advisedly allowed into the room, and it had suddenly decided to speak up on the subject of taxation. At the far end of the table, Bayaz silently examined his finger-nails. There was no help there.

'Ah, your Majesty,' ventured Torlichorm in soothing tones, 'such a system would be almost impossible to administer.' And he blinked in a manner that said, 'How do you manage to dress yourself, given your incredible ignorance?'

Jezal flushed to the tips of his ears. 'I see.'

'The subject of taxation,' droned Halleck, 'is a stupendously complex one.' And he gave Jezal a look that said, 'It is far too complex a subject to fit inside your tiny fragment of a mind.'

'It would perhaps be better, your Majesty, if you were to leave the tedious details to your humble servants.' Marovia had an understanding smile that said, 'It would perhaps be better if you kept your mouth shut and avoided embarrassing the grown-ups.'

'Of course.' Jezal retreated shame-facedly into his chair. 'Of course.'

And so it went on, as the morning ground by, as the strips of light from the windows slunk slowly over the heaps of papers across the wide table. Gradually, Jezal began to work out the rules of this game. Horribly complex, and yet horribly simple. The ageing players were split roughly into two teams. Arch Lector Sult and High Justice Marovia were the captains, fighting viciously over every subject, no matter how small, each with three supporters who agreed with their every utterance. Lord Hoff, meanwhile, ineffectually assisted by Lord Marshal Varuz, played the role of referee, and struggled to build bridges across the unbridgeable divide between these two entrenched camps.

Jezal's mistake had not been to think that he would not know what to say, though of course, he did not. His mistake had been to think that anyone would want him to say anything. All they cared about was continuing their own profitless struggles. They had become used, perhaps, to conducting the affairs of state with a drooling halfwit at the head of the table. Jezal now realised that they saw in him a like-for-like trade. He began to wonder if they were right.

'If your Majesty could sign here . . . and here . . . and here . . . and there . . .'

The pen scratched against paper after paper, the old voices droned on, and held forth, and bickered one with the other. The grey men smiled, and sighed, and shook their heads indulgently whenever he spoke, and so he spoke less and less. They bullied him with praise and blinded him with explanation. They bound him up in meaningless hours of law, and form, and tradition. He sagged slowly lower and lower into his uncomfortable chair. A servant brought wine, and he drank, and became drunk, and bored, and even more drunk and bored. Minute by stretched-out minute, Jezal began to realise: there was nothing so indescribably dull, once you got down to the nuts and bolts of it, as ultimate power.

'Now to a sad matter,' observed Hoff, once the most recent argument had sputtered to a reluctant compromise. 'Our colleague, Lord Marshal Burr, is dead. His body is on its way back to us from the North, and will be interred with full honours. In the meantime, however, it is our duty to recommend a replacement. The first chair to be filled in this room since the death of the esteemed Chancellor Feekt. Lord Marshal Varuz?'

The old soldier cleared his throat, wincing as though he realised he was about to open a floodgate that might very well drown them all. 'There are two clear contenders for the post.

Both are men of undoubted bravery and experience, whose merits are well known to this council. I have no doubt that either General Poulder or General Kroy would—'

'There can be not the slightest doubt that Poulder is the better man!' snarled Sult, and Halleck immediately voiced his assent.

'On the contrary!' hissed Marovia, to angry murmurs from his camp, 'Kroy is transparently the better choice!'

It was an area in which, as an officer of some experience, Jezal felt he might have been of some minuscule value, but not one of the Closed Council seemed even to consider seeking his opinion. He sagged back sulkily into his chair, and took another slurp of wine from his goblet while the old wolves continued to snap viciously at one another.

'Perhaps we should discuss this matter at greater length later!' cut in Lord Hoff over the increasingly acrimonious debate. 'His Majesty is growing fatigued with the fine points of the issue, and there is no particular urgency!' Sult and Marovia glared at each other, but did not speak. Hoff gave a sigh of relief. 'Very well. Our next point of business relates to the supply of our army in Angland. Colonel West writes in his dispatches—'

'West?' Jezal sat up sharply, his voice rough with wine. The name was like smelling salts to a fainting girl, a solid and dependable rock to cling to in the midst of all this chaos. If only West had been there now, to help him through, things would have made so much more sense . . . he blinked at the chair that Burr had left behind him, sitting empty at Varuz' shoulder. Jezal was drunk, perhaps, but he was king. He cleared his wet throat. 'Colonel West shall be my new Lord Marshal!'

There was a stunned silence. The twelve old men stared. Then Torlichorm chuckled indulgently, in a manner that said, 'How will we shut him up?'

'Your Majesty, Colonel West is known to you personally, and a brave man, of course . . .'

The entire Council, it seemed, had finally found one issue on which they could all agree. 'First through the breach at

Ulrioch and so on,' muttered Varuz, shaking his head, 'but really—'

'. . . he is junior, and inexperienced, and . . .'

'He is a commoner,' said Hoff, eyebrows raised.

'An unseemly break with tradition,' lamented Halleck.

'Poulder would be far superior!' snarled Sult at Marovia.

'Kroy is the man!' Marovia barked back.

Torlichorm gave a syrupy smile, of the kind a wet-nurse might use while trying to calm a troublesome infant. 'So you see, your Majesty, we cannot possibly consider Colonel West as—'

Jezal's empty goblet bounced off Torlichorm's bald forehead with a loud crack and clattered away into the corner of the room. The old man gave a wail of shock and pain and slid from his chair, blood running from a long gash across his face.

'Cannot?' screamed Jezal, on his feet, eyes starting from his head. 'You dare to give me fucking "cannot", you old bastard? You belong to me, all of you!' His finger stabbed furiously at the air. 'You exist to advise me, not to dictate to me! I rule here! Me!' He snatched up the ink bottle and hurled it across the room. It burst apart against the wall, spraying a great black stain across the plaster and spattering the arm of Arch Lector Sult's perfect white coat with black spots. 'Me! Me! The tradition we need here is one of fucking obedience!' He grabbed a sheaf of documents and flung them at Marovia, filling the air with fluttering paper. 'Never again give me "cannot!" Never!'

Eleven sets of dumbstruck eyes stared at Jezal. One set smiled, down at the very end of the table. That made him angrier than ever. 'Collem West shall be my new Lord Marshal!' he screeched, and kicked his chair over in a fury. 'At our next meeting I will be treated with the proper respect, or I'll have the pack of you in chains! In fucking chains . . . and . . . and . . .' His head was hurting, now, rather badly. He had thrown everything within easy reach, and was becoming desperately unsure of how to proceed.

Bayaz rose sternly from his chair. 'My Lords, that will be all for today.'

The Closed Council needed no further encouragement. Papers flapped, robes rustled, chairs squealed as they scrambled to be first out of the room. Hoff made it into the corridor. Marovia followed close behind and Sult swept after him. Varuz helped Torlichorm up from the floor and guided him by his elbow. 'I apologise,' he was wheezing as he was hustled, bloody-faced, through the door, 'your Majesty, I apologise profusely . . .'

Bayaz stood sternly at the end of the table, watching the councillors hurry from the room. Jezal lurked opposite, frozen somewhere between further anger and mortal embarrassment, but increasingly tending towards the latter. It seemed to take an age for the last member of the Closed Council to finally escape from the room, and for the great black doors to be dragged shut.

The First of the Magi turned towards Jezal, and a broad smile broke suddenly out across his face. 'Richly done, your Majesty, richly done.'

'What?' Jezal had been sure that he had made an ass of himself to a degree from which he could never recover.

'Your advisers will think twice before taking you lightly again, I think. Not a new strategy, but no less effective for that. Harod the Great was himself possessed of a fearsome temper, and made excellent use of it. After one of his tantrums no one would dare to question his decisions for weeks.' Bayaz chuckled. 'Though I suspect that even Harod would have balked at dealing a wound to his own High Consul.'

'That was no tantrum!' snarled Jezal, his temper flickering up again. If he was beset by horrible old men, then Bayaz was himself the worst culprit by far. 'If I am a king I will be treated like one! I refuse to be dictated to in my own palace! Not by anyone . . . not by . . . I mean . . .'

Bayaz glared back at him, his green eyes frighteningly hard, and spoke with frosty calm. 'If your intention is to lose your temper with me, your Majesty, I would strongly advise against it.'

Jezal's rage had been on the very verge of fading already, and now, under the icy gaze of the Magus, it wilted away entirely. 'Of course . . . I'm sorry . . . I'm very sorry.' He closed his eyes and stared numbly down at the polished tabletop. He never used to say sorry for anything. Now that he was a king, and needed to apologise to no man, he found he could not stop. 'I did not ask for this,' he muttered weakly, flopping down in his chair. 'I don't know how it happened. I did nothing to deserve it.'

'Of course not.' Bayaz came slowly around the table. 'No man can ever deserve the throne. That is why you must strive to be worthy of it now. Every day. Just as your great predecessors did. Casamir. Arnault, Harod himself.'

Jezal took a long breath, and blew it out. 'You're right, of course. How can you always be right?'

Bayaz held up a humble hand. 'Always right? Scarcely. But I have the benefit of long experience, and am here to guide you as best I can. You have made a fine start along a difficult road, and you should be proud, as I am. There are certain steps we cannot delay, however. Chief among them is your wedding.'

Jezal gaped. 'Wedding?'

'An unmarried king is like a chair with three legs, your Majesty. Apt to fall. Your rump has only just touched the throne, and it is far from settled there. You need a wife who brings you support, and you need heirs so that your subjects may feel secure. All that delay will bring is opportunities for your enemies to work against you.'

The blows fell so rapidly that Jezal had to grasp his head, hoping to stop it flying apart. 'My enemies?' Had he not always tried to get on with everyone?

'Can you be so naïve? Lord Brock is doubtless already plotting against you. Lord Isher will not be put off indefinitely. Others on the Open Council supported you out of fear, or were paid to do so.'

'Paid?' gasped Jezal.

'Such support does not last forever. You must marry, and your wife must bring you powerful allies.'

'But I have . . .' Jezal licked his lips, uncertain of how to broach the subject. 'Some commitments . . . in that line.'

'Ardee West?' Jezal half opened his mouth to ask Bayaz how he knew so much about his romantic entanglements, but quickly thought better of it. The old man seemed to know far more about him than he did himself, after all. 'I know how it is, Jezal. I have lived a long life. Of course you love her. Of course you would give up anything for her, now. But that feeling, trust me, will not last.'

Jezal shifted his weight uncomfortably. He tried to picture Ardee's uneven smile, the softness of her hair, the sound of her laugh. The way that had given him such comfort, out on the plain. But it was hard to think of her now without remembering her teeth sinking into his lip, his face tingling from her slap, the sound of the table creaking back and forward underneath them. The shame, and the guilt, and the complexity. Bayaz' voice continued: mercilessly calm, brutally realistic, ruthlessly reasonable.

'It is only natural that you made commitments, but your past life is gone, and your commitments have gone with it. You are a king, now, and your people demand that you behave like one. They need something to look up to. Something effort-lessly higher than themselves. We are talking of the High Queen of the Union. A mother to kings. A farmer's daughter with a tendency towards unpredictable behaviour and a pen-chant for heavy drinking? I think not.' Jezal flinched to hear Ardee described that way, but he could hardly argue the point.

'You are a natural son. A wife of unimpeachable breeding would lend your line far greater weight. Far greater respect. There is a world full of eligible women, your Majesty, all born to high station. Dukes' daughters, and kings' sisters, beautiful and cultured. A world of princesses to choose from.'

Jezal felt his eyebrows rising. He loved Ardee, of course, but Bayaz made a devastating argument. There was so much more to think of now than his own needs. If the idea of himself as a king was absurd, the idea of Ardee as a queen was triply so. He loved her, of course. In a way. But a world of princesses to choose from? That was a phrase it was decidedly hard to find fault with.

'You see it!' The First of the Magi snapped his fingers in triumph. 'I will send to Duke Orso of Talins, that his daughter Terez should be introduced to you.' He held up a calming hand. 'Just to begin with, you understand. Talins would make a powerful ally.' He smiled, and leaned forward to murmur in Jezal's ear. 'But you need not leave everything behind, if you truly are attached to this girl. Kings often keep mistresses, you know.'

And that, of course, decided the matter.

Prepared for the Worst

Glokta sat in his dining room, staring down at his table, rubbing at his aching thigh with one hand. His other stirred absently at the fortune in jewels spread out on the black leather case.

Why do I do this? Why do I stay here, and ask questions? I could be gone on the next tide, and no one any worse off. Perhaps a tour of the beautiful cities of Styria? A cruise round the Thousand Isles? Finally to faraway Thond, or distant Suljuk, to live out my twisted days in peace among people who do not understand a word I say? Hurting no one? Keeping no secrets? Caring no more for innocence or guilt, for truth or for lies, than do these little lumps of rock.

The gems twinkled in the candlelight, clicking against each other, tickling at his fingers as he pushed them through one way, and back the other. *But his Eminence would weep and weep at my sudden disappearance. So, one imagines, would the banking house of Valint and Balk. Where in all the wide Circle of the World would I be safe from the tears of such powerful masters? And why? So I can sit on my crippled arse all the long day, waiting for the killers to come? So I can lie in bed, and ache, and think about all that I've lost?*

He frowned down at the jewels: clean, and hard, and beautiful. *I made my choices long ago. When I took Valint and Balk's money. When I kissed the ring of office. Before the Emperor's prisons, even, when I rode down to the bridge, sure that only magnificent Sand dan Glokta could save the world . . .*

A thumping knock echoed through the room and Glokta jerked his head up, toothless mouth hanging open. *As long as it is not the Arch Lector—*

'Open up, in the name of his Eminence!'

He grimaced at a spasm through his back as he dragged

himself out of his chair, clawing the stones into a heap. Priceless, glittering handfuls of them. Sweat had broken out across his forehead.

What if the Arch Lector were to discover my little treasure trove? He giggled to himself as he snatched at the leather case. *I was going to mention all this, really I was, but the timing never seemed quite right. A small matter, after all – no more than a king's ransom.* His fingers fumbled with the jewels, and in his haste he flicked one astray and it dropped sparkling to the floor with a sharp click, click.

Another knock, louder this time, the heavy lock shuddering from the force of it. 'Open up!'

'I'm just coming!' He forced himself down onto his hands and knees with a moan, casting about across the floor, his neck burning with pain. He saw it – a flat green one sitting on the boards, shining bright in the firelight.

Got you, you bastard! He snatched it up, pulled himself to his feet by the edge of the table, folded up the case, once, twice. *No time to hide it away.* He shoved it inside his shirt, right down so it was behind his belt, then he grabbed his cane and limped towards the front door, wiping his sweaty face, adjusting his clothes, doing his best to present an unruffled appearance.

'I'm coming! There's no need to—'

Four huge Practicals shoved past him into his apartments, almost knocking him over. Beyond them, in the corridor outside, stood his Eminence the Arch Lector, frowning balefully, two more vast Practicals at his back. *A surprising hour for such a gratifying visit.* Glokta could hear the four men stomping around his apartments, throwing open doors, pulling open cupboards. *Never mind me, gentlemen, make yourself at home.* After a moment they marched back in.

'Empty,' grunted one, from behind his mask.

'Huh,' sneered Sult, moving smoothly over the threshold, staring about him with a scowl of contempt. *My new lodgings, it would seem, are scarcely more impressive than my old ones.* His six Practicals took up positions around the walls of Glokta's dining room, arms folded across their chests, watching. *An awful lot of great big men, to keep an eye on one little cripple.*

Sult's shoes stabbed at the floor as he strode up and down, his blue eyes bulging, a furious frown twisting his face. *It does not take a masterful judge of character to see that he is not a happy man. Might one of my ugly secrets have come to his attention? One of my little disobediences?* Glokta felt a sweaty trembling slink up his bent spine. *The non-execution of Magister Eider, perhaps? My agreement with Practical Vitari to tell less than the whole truth?* The corner of the leather pouch dug gently into his ribs as he shifted his hips. *Or merely the small matter of the large fortune with which I was purchased by a highly suspect banking house?*

An image sprang unbidden into Glokta's mind, of the jewel-case suddenly splitting behind his belt, gems spilling from his trouser legs in a priceless cascade while the Arch Lector and his Practicals stared in amazement. *I wonder how I'd try to explain that one?* He had to stifle a giggle at the thought.

'That bastard Bayaz!' snarled Sult, his white-gloved hands curling into shaking fists.

Glokta felt himself relax by the smallest hair. *I am not the problem, then. Not yet, at least.* 'Bayaz?'

'That bald liar, that smirking impostor, that ancient charlatan! He has stolen the Closed Council!' *Stop, thief!* 'He has that worm Luthar dictating to us! You told me he was a spineless nothing!' *I told you he used to be a spineless nothing, and you ignored me.* 'This cursed puppy-dog proves to have teeth, and is not afraid to use them, and that First of the bastard Magi is holding his leash! He is laughing at us! He is laughing at me! At me!' screamed Sult, stabbing at his chest with a clawing finger.

'I—'

'Damn your excuses, Glokta! I am drowning in a sea of damned excuses, when what I need are answers! What I need are solutions! What I need is to know more about this liar!'

Then perhaps this will impress you. 'I have already, in fact, taken the liberty of some steps in that direction.'

'What steps?'

'I was able to take his Navigator into custody,' said Glokta, allowing himself the smallest of smiles.

'The Navigator?' Sult gave no sign of being impressed. 'And what did that stargazing imbecile tell you?'

Glokta paused. 'That he journeyed across the Old Empire to the edge of the World with Bayaz and our new king, before his enthronement.' He struggled for words that would fit cleanly into Sult's world of logic, and reasons, and neat explanations. 'That they were seeking for . . . a relic, of the Old Time—'

'Relics?' asked Sult, his frown deepening. 'Old Time?'

Glokta swallowed. 'Indeed, but they did not find it—'

'So we now know one of a thousand things that Bayaz *did not* do? Bah!' Sult ripped angrily at the air with his hand. 'He is nobody, and told you less than nothing! More of your myths and rubbish!'

'Of course, your Eminence,' muttered Glokta. *There really is no pleasing some people.*

Sult frowned down at the squares board under the window, his white-gloved hand hovering over the pieces as if to make a move. 'I lose track of how often you have failed me, but I will give you a final chance to redeem yourself. Look into this First of the Magi once more. Find some weakness, some weapon we can use against him. He is a disease, and we must burn him out.' He prodded angrily at one of the white pieces. 'I want him destroyed! I want him finished! I want him in the House of Questions, in chains!'

Glokta swallowed. 'Your Eminence, Bayaz is ensconced in the palace, and well beyond my reach . . . his protégé is now our King . . .' *Thanks in part to our own desperate efforts.* Glokta almost winced, but he could not stop himself from asking the question. 'How am I to do it?'

'How?' shrieked Sult. 'How, you crippled worm?' He swept his hand furiously across the board and dashed the pieces spinning across the floor. *And I wonder who will have to bend down to pick those up?* The six Practicals, as though controlled by the pitch of the Arch Lector's voice, detached themselves from the walls and loomed menacingly into the room. 'If I wished to attend to every detail myself I would have no need of your worthless services! Get out there and get it done, you twisted slime!'

'Your Eminence is too kind,' muttered Glokta, humbly inclining his head once more. *But even the lowest dog needs a scratch behind the ears, from time to time, or he might go for his master's throat . . .*

'And look into his story while you're about it.'

'Story, Arch Lector?'

'This fairytale of Carmee dan Roth!' Sult's eyes went narrower still, hard creases cutting into the bridge of his nose. 'If we cannot take the leash ourselves, we must have the dog put down, do you understand?'

Glokta felt his eye twitching, in spite of his efforts to make it be still. *We find a way to bring King Jezal's reign to an abrupt end. Dangerous. If the Union is a ship, it has but lately come through a storm, and is listing badly. We have lost one captain. Replace another now, and the boat might break apart entirely. We will all be swimming in some deep, cold, unknown waters then. Civil War, anyone?* He frowned down at the squares pieces scattered across his floor. *But his Eminence has spoken. What is it that Shickel said? When your master gives you a task, you do your best at it. Even if the task is a dark one. And some of us are only suited to dark tasks . . .*

'Carmee dan Roth, and her bastard. I shall find the truth of it, your Eminence, you can depend on me.'

Sult's sneer curled to even greater heights of contempt. 'If only!'

The House of Questions was busy, for an evening. Glokta saw no-one as he limped down the corridor, his excuses for teeth pressed into his lip, his hand clenched tight around the handle of his cane, slippery with sweat. He saw no-one, but he heard them.

Voices bubbled from behind the iron-bound doors. Low and insistent. *Asking the questions.* High and desperate. *Spilling the answers.* From time to time a shriek, or a roar, or a howl of pain would cut through the heavy silence. *Those hardly need explaining.* Severard was leaning against the dirty wall as Glokta limped towards him, one foot up on the plaster, whistling tunelessly behind his mask.

'What's all this?' asked Glokta.

'Some of Lord Brock's people got drunk, then they got noisy. Fifty of 'em, made quite a mess up near the Four Corners. Moaning about rights, whining on how the people were cheated, mouthing off how Brock should've been king. They say it was a demonstration. We say it was treason.'

'Treason, eh?' *The definition is notoriously flexible.* 'Pick out some ringleaders and get some paper signed. Angland is back in Union hands. High time we started filling the place up with traitors.'

'They're already at it. Anything else?'

'Oh, of course.' *Juggling knives. One comes down, two go up. Always more blades spinning in the air, and each one with a deadly edge.* 'I had a visit from his Eminence earlier today. A brief visit, but too long for my taste.'

'Work for us?'

'Nothing that will make you a rich man, if that's what you're hoping for.'

'I'm always hoping. I'm what you call an optimist.'

'Lucky for you.' *I rather tend the other way.* Glokta took a deep breath and let it out in a long sigh. 'The First of the Magi and his bold companions.'

'Again?'

'His Eminence wants information.'

'This Bayaz, though. Isn't he tight with our new king?'

Glokta raised an eyebrow as a muffled roar of pain echoed down the corridor. *Tight? He might as well have made him out of clay.* 'That is why we must keep our eyes upon him, Practical Severard. For his own protection. Powerful men have powerful enemies, as well as powerful friends.'

'Think that Navigator knows anything else?'

'Nothing that will do the trick.'

'Shame. I was getting used to having the little bastard around. He tells a hell of a story about a huge fish.'

Glokta sucked at his empty gums. 'Keep him where he is for now. Perhaps Practical Frost will appreciate his tall tales.' *He has a fine sense of humour.*

'If the Navigator's no use, who do we squeeze?'

Who indeed? Ninefingers is gone. Bayaz himself is tucked up tight in the palace, and his apprentice hardly leaves his side. The erstwhile Jezal dan Luthar, we must concede, is now far beyond our reach . . . 'What about that woman?'

Severard looked up. 'What, that brown bitch?'

'She's still in the city, isn't she?'

'Last I heard.'

'Follow her, then, and find out what she's about.'

The Practical paused. 'Do I have to?'

'What? You scared?'

Severard lifted up his mask and scratched underneath it. 'I can think of people I'd rather follow.'

'Life is a series of things we would rather not do.' Glokta looked up and down the corridor, making sure there was no one there. 'We also need to ask some questions about Carmee dan Roth, supposed mother of our present king.'

'What sort of questions?'

He leaned towards Severard and hissed quietly in his ear. 'Questions like – did she really bear a child before she died? Was that child really the issue of the overactive loins of King Guslav? Is that child truly the same man that we now have on the throne? You know the kind of questions.' *Questions that could land us in a great deal of trouble. Questions that some people might call treason. After all, the definition is notoriously flexible.*

Severard's mask looked the same as ever, but the rest of his face was decidedly worried. 'You sure we want to go digging there?'

'Why don't you ask the Arch Lector if he's sure? He sounded sure to me. Get Frost to help you if you're having trouble.'

'But . . . what are we looking for? How will we—'

'How?' hissed Glokta. 'If I wished to attend to every detail myself I would have no need of your services. Get out there and get it done!'

When Glokta had been young and beautiful, quick and promising, admired and envied, he had spent a great deal of time in the taverns of Adua. *Though I never remember falling this far, even in my darkest moods.*

He scarcely felt out of place now, as he hobbled among the customers. To be crippled was the norm here, and he had more teeth than average. Nearly everyone carried unsightly scars or debilitating injuries, sores or warts to make a toad blush. There were men with faces rough as the skin on a bowl of old porridge. Men who shook worse than leaves in a gale and stank of week-old piss. Men who looked as if they'd slit a child's throat just to keep their knives sharp. A drunken whore slouched against a post in an attitude that could hardly have been arousing to the most desperate sailor. *That same reek of sour beer and hopelessness, sour sweat and early death that I remember from the sites of my worst excesses. Only stronger.*

There were some private booths at one end of the stinking common room, vaulted archways full of miserable shadows and even more miserable drunks. *And who might one expect to find in such surroundings?* Glokta shuffled to a stop beside the last of them.

'Well, well, well. I never thought I'd see you alive again.'

Nicomo Cosca looked even worse than when Glokta first met him, if that was possible. He was spread out against the slimy wall, his hands dangling, his head hanging over to one side, his eyes scarcely open as he watched Glokta work his painful way into a chair opposite. His skin was soapy pale in the flickering light from the single mean candle flame, dark pouches under his eyes, dark shadows shifting over his pinched and pointed face. The rash on his neck had grown angrier, and spread up the side of his jaw like ivy up a ruin. *With just a little more effort he might look nearly as ill as me.*

'Superior Glokta,' he wheezed, in a voice as rough as tree-bark, 'I am delighted that you received my message. What an honour to renew our acquaintance, against all the odds. Your masters did not reward your efforts in the South with a cut throat, eh?'

'I was as surprised as you are, but no.' *Though there is still ample time.* 'How was Dagoska after I left?'

The Styrian puffed out his hollow cheeks. 'Dagoska was a real mess, since you are asking. A lot of men dead. A lot of men made slaves. That's what happens when the Gurkish come to dinner, eh? Good men with bad endings, and the bad men did little better. Bad endings for everyone. Your friend General Vissbruck got one of them.'

'I understand he cut his own throat.' *To rapturous approval from the public.* 'How did you get away?'

The corner of Cosca's mouth curled up, as though he would have liked to smile but had not the energy. 'I disguised myself as a servant girl, and I fucked my way out.'

'Ingenious.' *But far more likely you were the one who opened the gates to the Gurkish, in return for your freedom. I wonder if I would have done the same, in that position? Probably.* 'And lucky for us both.'

'They say that luck is a woman. She's drawn to those that least deserve her.'

'Perhaps so.' *Though I appear to be both undeserving and un-lucky.* 'It is certainly fortunate that you should appear in Adua at this moment. Things are . . . unsettled.'

Glokta heard a squeaking, rustling sound and a large rat dashed out from under his chair and paused for a moment in full view. Cosca delved a clumsy hand into his stained jacket and whipped it out. A throwing knife flew out with it, flashed through the air. It shuddered into the boards a good stride or two wide of the mark. The rat sat there for a moment longer, as though to communicate its contempt, then scurried away between the table and chair legs, the scuffed boots of the patrons.

Cosca sucked at his stained teeth as he slithered from the

booth to retrieve his blade. 'I used to be dazzling with a throwing knife, you know.'

'Beautiful women used to hang from my every word.' Glokta sucked at his own empty gums. 'Times change.'

'So I hear. All kinds of changes. New rulers mean new worries. Worries mean business, for people in my trade.'

'It might be that I will have a use for your particular talents, before too long.'

'I cannot say that I would turn you down.' Cosca tipped his bottle up and stuck his tongue into the neck, licking out the last trickle. 'My purse is empty as a dry well. So empty, in fact, that I don't even have a purse.'

There, at least, I am able to assist. Glokta checked that they were not observed, then tossed something across the rough table top and watched it bounce with a click and a spin to a halt in front of Cosca. The mercenary picked it up between finger and thumb, held it to the candle flame and stared at it through one bloodshot eye. 'This seems to be a diamond.'

'Consider yourself on retainer. I daresay you could find some like-minded men to assist you. Some reliable men, who tell no tales and ask no questions. Some good men, to help out.'

'Some bad men, do you mean?'

Glokta grinned, displaying the gaps in his teeth. 'Well. I suppose that all depends on whether you're the employer, or you're the job.'

'I suppose it does at that.' Cosca let his empty bottle drop to the ill-formed floorboards. 'And what is the job, Superior?'

'For now, just to wait, and stay out of sight.' He leaned from the booth with a wince and snapped his fingers at a surly serving girl. 'Another bottle of what my friend is drinking!'

'And later?'

'I'm sure I can find something for you to do.' He shuffled painfully forward in his chair to whisper. 'Between you and me, I heard a rumour that the Gurkish are coming.'

Cosca winced. 'Them again? Must we? Those bastards don't play by the rules. God, and righteousness, and belief.' He shuddered. 'Makes me nervous.'

'Well, whoever it is banging on the door, I'm sure I can organise a heroic last stand, against the odds, without hope of relief.' *I am not lacking for enemies, after all.*

The mercenary's eyes glinted as the girl thumped a full bottle down on the warped table before him. 'Ah, lost causes. My favourite.'

The Habit of Command

West sat in the Lord Marshal's tent and stared hopelessly into space. For the past year he had scarcely had an idle moment. Now, suddenly, there was nothing for him to do but wait. He kept expecting to see Burr push through the flap and walk to the maps, his fists clenched behind him. He kept expecting to feel his reassuring presence around the camp, to hear his booming voice call the wayward officers to order. But of course he would not. Not now and not ever again.

On the left sat General Kroy's staff, solemn and sinister in their black uniforms, as rigidly pressed as ever. On the right lounged Poulder's men, top buttons carelessly undone in an open affront to their opposite numbers, as puffed-up as peacocks displaying their tail feathers. The two great Generals themselves eyed each other with all the suspicion of rival armies across a battlefield, awaiting the edict that would raise one of them to the Closed Council and the heights of power, and dash the other's hopes for ever. The edict that would name the new King of the Union, and his new Lord Marshal.

It was to be Poulder or Kroy, of course, and both anticipated their final, glorious victory over the other. In the meantime the army, and West in particular, sat paralysed. Powerless. Far to the north the Dogman and his companions, who had saved West's life in the wilderness more times than he could remember, were no doubt fighting for survival, watching desperately for help that would never come.

For West, the entire business was very much like being at his own funeral, and one attended chiefly by sneering, grinning, posturing enemies. It was to be Poulder or Kroy, and whichever one it was, he was doomed. Poulder hated him with a flaming passion, Kroy with an icy scorn. The only fall swifter and more complete than his own would be that of Poulder, or of Kroy, whichever of them was finally overlooked by the Closed Council.

There was a dim commotion outside, and heads turned keenly to look. There was a scuffle of feet up to the tent, and several officers rose anxiously from their chairs. The flap was torn aside and the Knight Herald finally burst jingling through it. He was immensely tall, the wings on his helmet almost poking a hole in the tent's ceiling as he straightened up. He had a leather case over one armoured shoulder, stamped with the golden sun of the Union. West stared at it, holding his breath.

'Present your message,' urged Kroy, holding out his hand.

'Present it to me!' snapped Poulder.

The two men jostled each other with scant dignity while the Knight Herald frowned down at them, impassive. 'Is Colonel West in attendance?' he demanded, in a booming bass. Every eye, and most especially those of Poulder and Kroy, swivelled round.

West found himself rising hesitantly from his chair. 'Er . . . I am West.'

The Knight Herald stepped carelessly around General Kroy and advanced on West, spurs rattling. He opened his dispatch case, pulled out a roll of parchment and held it up. 'On the king's orders.'

The final irony of West's unpredictable career, it seemed, was that he would be the one to announce the name of the man who would dismiss him in dishonour moments later. But if he was to fall on his sword, delay would only increase the pain. He took the scroll from the Knight's gauntleted hand and broke the heavy seal. He unrolled it halfway, a block of flowing script coming into view. The room held its breath as he began to read.

West gave vent to a disbelieving giggle. Even with the tent as tense as a courtroom waiting for judgement, he could not help himself. He had to go over the first section twice more before he came close to taking it in.

'What is amusing?' demanded Kroy.

'The Open Council has elected Jezal dan Luthar as the new King of the Union, henceforth known as Jezal the First.' West had to stifle more laughter even though, if it was a joke, it was not a funny one.

'Luthar?' someone asked. 'Who the hell is Luthar?'

'That boy who won the Contest?'

It was all, somehow, awfully appropriate. Jezal had always behaved as though he was better than everyone else. Now, it seemed, he was. But all of that, momentous though it might have been, was a side-issue here.

'Who is the new Lord Marshal?' growled Kroy, and the two staffs shuffled forward, all on their feet now, forming a half-circle of expectation.

West took a deep breath, gathered himself like a child preparing to plunge into an icy pool. He pulled the scroll open and his eyes scanned quickly over the lower block of writing. He frowned. Neither Poulder's name nor Kroy's appeared anywhere. He read it again, more carefully. His knees felt suddenly very weak.

'Who does it name?' Poulder nearly shrieked. West opened his mouth, but he could not find the words. He held the letter out, and Poulder snatched it from his hand while Kroy struggled unsuccessfully to look over his shoulder.

'No,' breathed Poulder, evidently having reached the end.

Kroy wrestled the dispatch away and his eyes flickered over it. 'This must be a mistake!'

But the Knight Herald did not think so. 'The Closed Council are not in the habit of making mistakes. You have the King's orders!' He turned to West and bowed. 'My Lord Marshal, I bid you farewell.'

The army's best and brightest all gawped at West, jaws dangling. 'Er . . . yes,' he managed to stammer. 'Yes, of course.'

An hour later, the tent was empty. West sat alone at Burr's writing desk, nervously arranging and rearranging the pen, ink, paper, and most of all the large letter he had just sealed with a blob of red wax. He frowned down at it, and up at the maps on the boards, and back down at his hands sitting idle on the scarred leather, and he tried to understand what the hell had happened.

As far as he could tell, he had been suddenly elevated to one of the highest positions in the Union. Lord Marshal West. With the possible exception of Bethod himself, he was the most powerful man on this side of the Circle Sea. Poulder and Kroy would be obliged to call him 'sir'. He had a chair on the Closed Council. Him! Collem West! A commoner, who had been scorned, and bullied, and patronised his entire life. How could it possibly have happened? Not through merit, certainly. Not through any action or inaction on his part. Through pure chance. A chance friendship with a man who, in many ways, he did not particularly like, and had certainly never expected to do him any favours. A man who, in a stroke of fortune that could only be described as a miracle, had now ascended to the throne of the Union.

His disbelieving laughter was short-lived. A most unpleasant image was forming in his head. Prince Ladisla, lying somewhere in the wilderness with his head broken open, half-naked and unburied. West swallowed. If it had not been for him, Ladisla would now be king, and he would be swabbing latrines instead of preparing to take command of the army. His head was starting to hurt and he rubbed uncomfortably at his temples. Perhaps he had played a crucial part in his own advancement after all.

The tent flap rustled as Pike came through with his burned-out ruin of a grin. 'General Kroy is here.'

'Let him sweat a moment.' But it was West who was sweating. He wiped his moist palms together and tugged the jacket of his uniform smooth, his Colonel's insignia but recently cut from the shoulders. He had to appear to be in complete and effortless control, just as Marshal Burr had always done. Just as Marshal Varuz had used to, out in the dry wastelands of Gurkhul. He had to squash Poulder and Kroy while he had the chance. If he did not do it now, he would be forever at their mercy. A piece of meat, torn between two furious dogs. He reluctantly picked up the letter and held it out to Pike.

'Could we not just hang the pair of them, sir?' asked the convict as he took it.

'If only. But we cannot do without them, however troublesome they may be. A new King, a new Lord Marshal, both men that, by and large, no one has ever heard of. The soldiers need leaders they know.' He took a long breath through his nose, puffing out his chest. Each man had to do his part, and that was all. He let it hiss out. 'Show in General Kroy, please.'

'Yes, sir.' Pike held the tent flap open and roared out, 'General Kroy!'

Kroy's black uniform, chased about the collar with embroidered golden leaves, was so heavily starched that it was a surprise he could move at all. He drew himself up and stood to vibrating attention, eyes fixed on the middle distance. His salute was impeccable, every part of his body in regulation position, and yet he somehow managed to make his contempt and disappointment plain to see.

'May I first offer my congratulations,' he grated, 'Lord Marshal.'

'Thank you, General. Graciously said.'

'A considerable promotion, for one so young, so inexperienced—'

'I have been a professional soldier some dozen years, and fought in two wars and several battles. It would seem his Majesty the King deems me sufficiently seasoned.'

Kroy cleared his throat. 'Of course, Lord Marshal. But you are new to high command. In my opinion you would be wise to seek the assistance of a more experienced man.'

'I agree with you absolutely.'

Kroy lifted one eyebrow a fraction. 'I am glad to hear that.'

'That man should, without the slightest doubt, be General Poulder.' To give him credit, Kroy's face did not move. A small squeak issued from his nose. The only indication of what, West did not doubt, was his boundless dismay. He had been hurt when he arrived. Now he was reeling. The very best time to plunge the blade in to the hilt. 'I have always been a great admirer of General Poulder's approach to soldiering. His dash. His vigour. He is, to my mind, the very definition of what an officer should be.'

'Quite so,' hissed Kroy through gritted teeth.

'I am taking his advice in a number of areas. There is only one major issue upon which we differed.'

'Indeed?'

'You, General Kroy.' Kroy's face had assumed the colour of a plucked chicken, the trace of scorn replaced quick-time by a definite tinge of horror. 'Poulder was of the opinion that you should be dismissed immediately. I was for giving you one more chance. Sergeant Pike?'

'Sir.' The ex-convict stepped forward smartly and held out the letter. West took it from him and displayed it to the General.

'This is a letter to the king. I begin by reminding him of the happy years we served together in Adua. I go on to lay out in detail the reasons for your immediate dismissal in dishonour. Your unrepentant stubbornness, General Kroy. Your tendency to steal the credit. Your bloodless inflexibility. Your insubordinate reluctance to work with other officers.' If it was possible for Kroy's face to grow yet more drawn and pale it did so, steadily, as he stared at the folded paper. 'I earnestly hope that I will never have to send it. But I will, at the slightest provocation to myself or to General Poulder, am I understood?'

Kroy appeared to grope for words. 'Perfectly understood,' he croaked in the end, 'my Lord Marshal.'

'Excellent. We are extremely tardy in setting off for our rendezvous with our Northern allies and I hate to arrive late to a meeting. You will transfer your cavalry to my command, for now. I will be taking them north with General Poulder, in pursuit of Bethod.'

'And I, sir?'

'A few Northmen still remain on the hills above us. It will be your task to sweep them away and clear the road to Carleon, giving our enemies the impression that our main body has not moved north. Succeed in that and I may be willing to trust you with more. You will make the arrangements before first light.' Kroy opened his mouth, as though about to complain at the impossibility of the request. 'You have something to add?'

The General quickly thought better of it. 'No, sir. Before first light, of course.' He even managed to force his face into a shape vaguely resembling a smile.

West did not have to try too hard to smile back. 'I am glad you are embracing this chance to redeem yourself, General. You are dismissed.' Kroy snapped to attention once more, spun on his heel, caught his leg up with his sabre and stumbled from the tent in some disarray.

West took a long breath. His head was pounding. He wanted nothing more than to lie down for a few moments, but there was no time. He tugged the jacket of his uniform smooth again. If he had survived that nightmare journey north through the snow, he could survive this. 'Send in General Poulder.'

Poulder swaggered into the tent as though he owned the place and stood to slapdash attention, his salute as flamboyant as Kroy's had been rigid. 'Lord Marshal West, I would like to extend to you my earnest congratulations on your unexpected advancement.' He grinned unconvincingly, but West did not join him. He sat there, frowning up at Poulder as if he was a problem that he was considering a harsh solution to. He sat there for some time, saying nothing. The General's eyes began to dart nervously around the tent. He gave an apologetic cough. 'Might I ask, Lord Marshal, what you had to discuss with General Kroy?'

'Why, all manner of things.' West kept his face stony hard. 'My respect for General Kroy on all matters military is bound-less. We are much alike, he and I. His precision. His attention to detail. He is, to my mind, the very definition of what a soldier should be.'

'He is a most accomplished officer,' Poulder managed to hiss.

'He is. I have been elevated with great rapidity to my position, and I feel I need a senior man, a man with a wealth of experience, to act as a . . . as a mentor, if you will, now that Marshal Burr is gone. General Kroy has been good enough to agree to serve in that capacity.'

'Has he indeed?' A sheen of sweat was forming across Poulder's forehead.

'He has made a number of excellent suggestions which I am already putting into practice. There was only one issue on which we could not agree.' He steepled his fingers on the desk before him and looked sternly at Poulder over the top of them. 'You were that issue, General Poulder. You.'

'I, Lord Marshal?'

'Kroy pressed for your immediate dismissal.' Poulder's fleshy face was rapidly turning pink. 'But I have decided to extend to you one final opportunity.'

West picked up the very same paper that he had displayed to Kroy. 'This is a letter to the king. I begin by thanking him for my promotion, by enquiring after his health, by reminding him of our close personal friendship. I go on to lay out in detail the reasons for your immediate cashiering in disgrace. Your unbecoming arrogance, General Poulder. Your tendency to steal the credit. Your reluctance to obey orders. Your stubborn inability to work with other officers. I earnestly hope that I will never have to send it. But I will, at the slightest provocation. The slightest provocation to myself or to General Kroy, am I understood?'

Poulder swallowed, sweat glistening all over his ruddy face. 'You are, my Lord Marshal.'

'Good. I am trusting General Kroy to seize control of the hills between us and Carleon. Until you prove yourself worthy of a separate command you will stay with me. I want your division ready to move north before first light, and the swiftest units to the fore. Our Northern allies are relying on us, and I do not mean to let them down. At first light, General, and with the greatest speed.'

'The greatest speed, of course. You can rely on me . . . sir.'

'I hope so, in spite of my reservations. Every man must do his part, General Poulder. Every man.'

Poulder blinked and worked his mouth, half turned to leave, remembered belatedly to salute, then strode from the tent. West watched the flap moving ever so gently in the wind outside, then he sighed, crumpled the letter up in his hand and tossed it away into the corner. It was nothing but a blank sheet of paper, after all.

Pike raised one pink, mostly hairless brow. 'Sweetly done, sir, if I may say. Even in the camps, I never saw better lying.'

'Thank you, Sergeant. Now that I begin, I find I warm to the work. My father always warned me against untruths, but between you and me the man was a shit, a coward, and a failure. If he was here now I'd spit in his face.'

West rose and walked to the largest-scale of the maps, stood before it, his hands clasped behind his back. In just the way that Marshal Burr would have done, he realised. He examined the dirty finger-smudge in the mountains where Crummock-i-Phail had indicated the position of his fortress. He traced the route to the Union army's own current position, far to the south, and frowned. It was hard to believe that a Union cartographer could ever have come close to surveying that terrain in person, and the flamboyant shapes of the hills and rivers had an undoubted flavour of make-believe about them.

'How long do you think it will take to get there, sir?' asked Pike.

'Impossible to say.' Even if they got started immediately, which was unlikely. Even if Poulder did as he was told, which was doubly so. Even if the map was halfway accurate, which he knew it was not. He shook his head grimly. 'Impossible to say.'

The First Day

The eastern sky was just catching fire. Long strips of pink cloud and long strips of black cloud were stretched out across the pale blue, the hazy grey shapes of mountains notched and jagged as a butcher's knife underneath. The western sky was a mass of dark iron still – cold and comfortless.

'Nice day for it,' said Crummock.

'Aye.' But Logen wasn't sure there was any such a thing.

'Well, if Bethod don't show, and we get nothing killed at all, at least you lot will have done wonders for my wall, eh?'

It was amazing how well and how fast a man could patch a wall when it was the pile of stones that might save his own life. A few short days and they had the whole stretch of it built up and mortared, most of the ivy cut away. From inside the fort, where the ground was that much higher, it didn't look too fearsome. From outside it was three times the height of a tall man up to the walkway. They'd made new the parapet neck-high at the top, with plenty of good slots for shooting and throwing rocks from. Then they'd dug out a decent ditch in front, and lined it with sharp stakes.

They were still digging, over on the left where the wall met the cliff and it was easiest to climb over. That was Dow's stretch, and Logen could hear him shouting at his boys over the sound of shovels. 'Get digging, you lazy fucks! I'll not be killed for your lack of work! Put your back into it, you bastards!' and so on, all day long. One way of getting work out of a man, Logen reckoned.

They'd dug the ditch out especially deep right in front of the old gate. A nice reminder to everyone that there were no plans to leave. But it was still the weakest spot, and there was no missing it. That was where Logen would be, if Bethod came.

Right in the middle, on Shivers' stretch of wall. He was standing above the archway now, not far from Logen and Crummock, his long hair flapping about in the breeze, pointing out some cracks that still needed mortaring.

'Wall's looking good!' Logen shouted at him.

Shivers looked round, worked his mouth, then spat over his shoulder. 'Aye,' he growled, and turned away.

Crummock leaned close. 'If it comes to a battle you'll have to watch your back with that one, Bloody-Nine.'

'I reckon so.' The middle of a fight was a good place to settle a score with a man on your own side. No one ever checked too carefully if the corpses got it in the back or the front once the fighting was done. Everyone too busy crying at their cuts, or digging, or running away. Logen gave the big hillman a long stare. 'I'll have a lot of men to watch if it comes to a battle. We ain't so very friendly that you won't be one of 'em.'

'Likewise,' said Crummock, grinning all the way across his big, bearded face. 'We both got a reputation for being none too picky who gets killed, once the killing starts. But that's no bad thing. Too much trust makes men sloppy.'

'Too much trust?' It had been a while since Logen had too much of anything except enemies. He jerked his thumb towards the tower. 'I'm going up, check if they've seen anything.'

'I hope they have!' said Crummock, rubbing his fat palms together. 'I hope that bastard comes today!'

Logen hopped down from the wall and walked out across the fort, if you could call it that, past Carls and hillmen, sat in groups eating, or talking, or cleaning weapons. A few who'd been on guard through the night wrapped up in blankets, asleep. He passed the pen where the sheep were huddled together, a good deal fewer than there had been. He passed the makeshift forge set up near the stone shed, a couple of soot-smeared men working a bellows, another pouring metal into moulds for arrow heads. They'd need a damn lot of arrow-heads if Bethod came calling. He came to the narrow steps cut into the rock-face and took them two at a time, up above the fort to the top of the tower.

There was a big pile of rocks for throwing up there, on that shelf on the mountainside, and six big barrels wedged full of shafts. The pick of the archers stood at the new-mortared parapets, the men with the best eyes and the best ears keeping watch for Bethod. Logen saw the Dogman in amongst the rest, with Grim on one side of him and Tul on the other.

'Chief!' It still made Logen smile to say it. A long time, they'd done things the other way around, but it worked a lot better like this, to his mind. At least no-one was scared all the time. Not of their own chief, anyway. 'See anything?'

The Dogman grinned round, and offered him out a flask. 'A lot, as it goes.'

'Uh,' said Grim. The sun was getting up above the mountains now, slitting the clouds with bright lines, eating into the shadows across the hard land, burning away the dawn haze. The great fells loomed up bold and careless on either side, smeared with yellow green grass and fern on the slopes, strips of bare rock breaking through the brown summits. Below, the bare valley was quiet and still. Spotted with thorn bushes and clumps of stunted trees, creased with the paths of dried-out streams. Just as empty as it had been the day before, and the day before that, and ever since they'd got there.

It reminded Logen of his youth, climbing up in the High Places, alone. Days at a time, testing himself against the mountains. Before his was a name that anyone had heard of. Before he married, or had children, and before his wife and his children went back to the mud. The happy valleys of the past. He sucked in a long, cold breath of the high air, and he blew it out. 'It's quite a spot for a view, alright, but I meant have we seen anything of our old friend.'

'You mean Bethod, the right royal King of the Northmen? No, no sign of him. Not a hair.'

Tul shook his big head. 'Would've expected there to be some sign by now, if he was coming.'

Logen sloshed some water round his mouth and spat it out over the side of the tower, watched it splatter on the rocks way down below. 'Maybe he won't fall for it.' He could see the

226

happy side of Bethod not coming. Vengeance is a nice enough notion at a distance, but the getting of it close up isn't so very pretty. Especially when you're outnumbered ten to one with nowhere to run to.

'Maybe he won't at that,' said Dogman, wistful. 'How's the wall?'

'Alright, long as they don't bring such a thing as a ladder with 'em. How long do you reckon we wait, before we—'

'Uh,' grunted Grim, his long finger pointing down into the valley.

Logen saw a flicker of movement down there. And again. He swallowed. A couple of men, maybe, creeping through the boulders like beetles through gravel. He felt the men tense up all around him, heard them muttering. 'Shit,' he hissed. He looked sideways at the Dogman, and the Dogman looked back. 'Seems like Crummock's plan worked.'

'Seems that way. Far as getting Bethod to follow us, at least.'

'Aye. The rest is the tricky bit.' The bit that was more than likely to get them all killed, but Logen knew they were all thinking it without him saying a word.

'Now we just hope that the Union keeps their end of the deal,' said Dogman.

'We hope.' Logen tried to smile, but it didn't come out too good. Hoping had never turned out that well for him.

Once they'd started coming, the valley had filled up quick, right in front of Dogman's eyes. Nice and clean, just the way Bethod had always done things. The standards were set out between the two rock faces, three times a good bowshot distant, and the Carls and the Thralls were pressed in tight around 'em, all looking up towards their wall. The sun was getting up high in a blue sky with just a few shreds of cloud to cast a shadow, and all that weight of steel flashed and sparked like the sea under the moon.

Their signs were all there, all Bethod's best from way back – Whitesides, Goring, Pale-as-Snow, Littlebone. Then there were others – sharp and ragged marks from out past the Crinna.

Wild men, made dark and bloody deals with Bethod. Dogman could hear them whooping and calling to each other, strange sounds like animals might make in the forest.

Quite a gathering, all in all, and the Dogman could smell the fear and the doubt thick as soup up on the wall. A lot of weapons being fingered, a lot of lips being chewed. He did his best to keep his face hard and careless, the way that Threetrees would've done. The way a chief should. However much his own knees wanted to tremble.

'How many now, you reckon?' asked Logen.

Dogman let his eyes wander over 'em, thinking about it. 'Eight thousand do you think, or ten, maybe?'

A pause. 'That's about what I was thinking.'

'A lot more'n us, anyway,' Dogman said, keeping his voice low.

'Aye. But fights aren't always won by the bigger numbers.'

'Course not.' Dogman worked his lips as he looked at all them men. 'Just mostly.' There was plenty going on down there, up at the front, shovels glinting, a ditch and an earth rampart taking shape, all across the valley.

'Doing some digging o' their own,' grunted Dow.

'Always was thorough, was Bethod,' said Dogman. 'Taking his time. Doing it right.'

Logen nodded. 'Make sure none of us get away.'

Dogman heard the sound of Crummock's laughter behind him. 'Getting away wasn't ever the purpose o' this, though, eh?'

Bethod's own standard was going up now, near to the back but still towering over the others. Huge great thing, red circle on black. Dogman frowned at it, flapping in the breeze. He remembered seeing it months ago, back in Angland. Back when Threetrees had still been alive, and Cathil too. He worked his tongue round his sour mouth.

'King o' the fucking Northmen,' he muttered.

A few men came out from the front, where they were digging, started walking up towards the wall. Five of 'em, all in good armour, the one at the front with his arms spread out wide.

'Jawing time,' muttered Dow, then gobbed down into the ditch. They came up close, the five, up in front of the patched-up gate, mail coats shining dull in the brightening sun. The first of 'em had long white hair and one white eye, and weren't too hard to remember. White-Eye Hansul. He looked older than he used to, but didn't they all? He'd been the one to ask Threetrees to surrender, at Uffrith, and been told to piss off. He'd had shit thrown down on him at Heonan. He'd offered duels to Black Dow, and to Tul Duru, and to Harding Grim. Duels against Bethod's champion. Duels against the Bloody-Nine. He'd done a lot of talking for Bethod, and he'd told a lot o' lies.

'That Shite-Eye Hansul down there?' jeered Black Dow at him. 'Still sucking on Bethod's cock, are you?'

The old warrior grinned up at them. 'Man's got to feed his family somehow, don't he, and one cock tastes pretty much like another, if you ask me! Don't pretend like your mouths ain't all tasted salty enough before!'

He had some kind of point there, the Dogman had to admit. They'd all fought for Bethod themselves, after all. 'What're you after, Hansul?' he shouted. 'Bethod want to surrender to us, does he?'

'You'd have thought so, wouldn't you, outnumbered like he is, but that's not why I'm here. He's ready to fight, just like always, but I'm more of a talker than a fighter, and I talked him into giving you all a chance. I got two sons down there, in with the rest, and call me selfish but I'd rather not have 'em in harm's way. I'm hoping we can maybe talk our way clear of this.'

'Don't seem too likely!' shouted Dogman. 'But give it a go if you must, I've got nothing else pressing on today!'

'Here's the thing, then! Bethod don't particularly want to waste time, and sweat, and blood on climbing your little shit-pile of a wall. He's got business with the Southerners he wants to get settled. It's scarcely worth the breath of pointing out the bastard of a fix you're in. We've got the numbers more'n ten to one, I reckon. Much more, and you've no way out. Bethod says any man wants to give up now can go in peace. All he has to do is give over his weapons.'

'And his head soon afterwards, eh?' barked Dow.

Hansul took a big breath in, like he hardly expected to be believed. 'Bethod says any man wants to can go free. That's his word.'

'Fuck his word!' Dow sneered at him, and down the walls men jeered and spat their support. 'D'you think we ain't all seen him break it ten times before? I done shits worth more!'

'Lies, o' course,' chuckled Crummock, 'but it's traditional, no? To get a bit o' lying done, before we get started on the hard work. You'd feel insulted if he didn't give it some kind of a try at least. Any man, is it?' he called down. 'What about Crummock-i-Phail, can he go free? What about the Bloody-Nine?'

Hansul's face sagged at the name. 'It's true then? Ninefingers is up there, is he?'

Dogman felt Logen come up beside and show himself on the wall. White-Eye turned pale, and his shoulders slumped. 'Well,' Dogman heard him saying quiet, 'it has to be blood, then.'

Logen leaned lazily on the parapet, and he gave Hansul and his Carls a look. That hungry, empty look, like he was picking which one of a herd o' sheep to slaughter first. 'You can tell Bethod we'll come out.' He left a pause. 'Once we've killed the fucking lot o' you.'

A ripple of laughter went down the walls, and men jeered and shook their weapons in the air. Not funny words, particularly, but hard ones, which was what they all needed to hear, Dogman reckoned. Good way to get rid of their fear, for a moment. He even managed half a smile himself.

White-Eye just stood there, in front of their rickety gate, and he waited for the boys to go quiet. 'I heard you was chief of this crowd now, Dogman. So you don't have to take your orders from this blood-mad butcher no more. That your answer as well? That the way it is?'

Dogman shrugged. 'Just what other way did you think it'd

be? We didn't come here to talk, Hansul. You can piss off back, now.'

Some more laughter, and some more cheers, and one lad down at Shivers' end of the wall pulled his trousers down and stuck his bare arse over the parapet. So that was that for the negotiations.

White-Eye shook his head. 'Alright, then. I'll tell him. Back to the mud with the lot o' you, I reckon, and well earned. You can tell the dead I tried, when you meet 'em!' He started picking his way back down the valley, the four Carls behind him.

Logen loomed forward, all of a sudden. 'I'll be looking for your sons, Hansul!' he screamed, spit flying out his snarling, grinning mouth and away into the wind, 'When the work begins! You can tell Bethod I'm waiting! Tell 'em all I'll be waiting!'

A strange stillness fell on the wall and the men upon it, on the valley and the men within it. That kind of stillness that comes sometimes, before a battle, when both sides know what to expect. The same stillness that Logen had felt at Carleon, before he drew his sword and roared for the charge. Before he lost his finger. Before he was the Bloody-Nine. Long ago, when things were simpler.

Bethod's ditch was deep enough for him, and the Thralls had put away their shovels and moved behind it. The Dogman had climbed the steps back to the tower, no doubt taken up his bow beside Grim and Tul, and was waiting. Crummock was behind the wall with his Hillmen, lined up fierce and ready. Dow was with his lads on the left. Red Hat was with his boys on the right. Shivers wasn't far from Logen, both of them stood above the gate, waiting.

The standards down in the valley flapped and rustled gently in the wind. A hammer clanged once, twice, three times in the fortress behind them. A bird called, high above. A man whispered, somewhere, then was still. Logen closed his eyes, and tipped his face back, and he felt the hot sun and the cool breeze of the High Places on his skin. All as quiet as if he'd been alone, and there were no ten thousand men about him eager to set to killing one another. So still, and calm, he almost smiled. Was this what life would have been, if he'd never held a blade?

For the length of three breaths or so, Logen Ninefingers was a man of peace.

Then he heard the sound of men moving, and he opened his eyes. Bethod's Carls shuffled to the sides of the valley, rank after rank of them, with a crunching of feet and a rattling of gear. They left a rocky path, an open space through their midst. Out of that gap black shapes came, swarming over the ditch like angry ants from a broken nest, boiling up the slope towards the wall in a formless mass of twisted limbs, and snarling mouths and scraping claws.

Shanka, and even Logen had never seen half so many in one place. The valley crawled with them – a gibbering, clattering, squawking infestation.

'By the fucking dead,' someone whispered.

Logen wondered if he should shout something to the men on the walls around him. If he should cry, 'Steady!', or 'Hold!'. Something to help put some heart in his lads, the way a leader was meant to. But what would have been the point? Every one of them had fought before and knew his business. Every one of them knew that it was fight or die, and there was no better spur to a man's courage than that.

So Logen gritted his teeth, and he curled his fingers tight round the cold grip of the Maker's sword, and he slid the dull metal from its scarred sheath, and he watched the Flatheads come. A hundred strides away now, maybe, the front runners, and coming on fast.

'Ready your bows!' roared Logen.

'Bows!' echoed Shivers.

'Arrows!' came Dow's harsh scream from down the wall, and Red Hat's bellow from the other side. All around Logen the bows creaked as they were drawn, men taking their aim, jaws clenched, faces grim and dirty. The Flatheads came on, heedless, teeth shining, tongues lolling, bitter eyes bright with hate. Soon, now, very soon. Logen spun the grip of the sword round in his hand.

'Soon,' he whispered.

'Start fucking shooting, then!' And the Dogman loosed his shaft into the crowd of Shanka. Strings buzzed all round him and the first volley went hissing down. Arrows missed their marks, bounced off rock and spun away, arrows found their marks and brought Flatheads squealing down in a tangle of black limbs. Men reached for more, calm and solid, the best archers in the whole crew and knowing it.

Bows clicked and shafts twittered and Shanka died down in the valley, and the archers took aim, nice and easy, loosing 'em off and on to the next. Dogman heard the order from down below and he saw the twitch and flicker of shafts flying from the walls. More Flatheads dropped, thrashing and struggling in the dirt.

'Easy as squashing ants in a bowl!' someone shouted.

'Aye!' growled the Dogman, 'except ants won't climb up out of that bowl and cut your fucking head off! Less talk and more arrows!' He watched the first Shanka come up to their fresh-dug ditch, start floundering in, trying to drag the stakes down, scrabbling about at the bottom of the wall.

Tul heaved a great stone up over his head, leaned out and flung it spinning down with a roar. Dogman saw it crash into a Shanka's head below in the ditch and dash its brains out, red against the rocks, saw it bounce and tumble into others, send a couple reeling. More fell, screeching as shafts flitted down into them, but there were plenty behind, sliding into the ditch, swarming over each other. They crushed up to the wall, spreading out down its length, a few of them hurling spears up at the men on top, or shooting clumsy arrows.

Now they were starting to climb, claws digging into pitted stone, hauling themselves up, and up. Slow across most of the wall, and getting torn off by rocks and arrows from above. Quicker on the far side, over on the left, furthest from the

Dogman and his boys, where Black Dow had the watch. Even quicker round the gate, where there was still some ivy stuck to the stone.

'Damn it, but those bastards can climb!' hissed the Dogman, fumbling out his next shaft.

'Uh,' grunted Grim.

The Shanka's hand slapped down on the top of the parapet, a twisted claw, scratching at the stones. Logen watched the arm come after, bent and ugly, patched with thick hair and squirming with thick sinew. Now came the flattened top of its bald head, a hulking lump of heavy brow, great jaw yawning wide, sharp teeth slick with spit. The deep set eyes met his. Logen's sword split its skull down to its flat stub of nose and popped one eye from its socket.

Men shot arrows and ducked down as arrows bounced from stone. A spear went twittering past over Logen's head. Down below he could hear the Shanka scratching and tearing at the gates, beating at them with clubs and hammers, could hear them shrieking with rage. Shanka hissed and squawked as they tried to pull themselves over the parapet and men hacked at them with sword and axe, poked them off the wall with spears.

He could hear Shivers roaring, 'Get 'em away from the gate! Away from the gate!' Men bellowed curses. One Carl who'd been leaning out over the parapet fell back, coughing. He had a Shanka's spear through him, just under his shoulder, the point making the shirt stick right up off his back. He blinked down at the warped shaft, opened his mouth to say something. He groaned, took a couple of wobbling steps, and a big Flathead started dragging itself over the parapet behind him, its arm stretched out on the stone.

The Maker's sword chopped deep into it just below the elbow, spattering sticky spots across Logen's face. The blade caught stone and made his hand sing, sent him stumbling long enough for the Shanka to drag itself over, its flopping arm only just held on by a flap of skin and sinew, dark blood drooling out in long spurts.

It came for Logen with its other claw but he caught its wrist, kicked its knee sideways and brought it down. Before it could get up he'd chopped a long gash out of its back, splinters of white bone showing in the great wound. It thrashed and struggled, splattering blood around, and Logen caught it tight under the throat, heaved it back over the wall and flung it off. It fell, and crashed into another just starting to climb. Both of them went sprawling in the ditch, one scrabbling around with a broken stake in its throat.

A young lad stood there, gawping, bow hanging limp from his hand.

'Did I tell you to stop fucking shooting?' Logen roared at him, and he blinked and nocked a shaft with a trembling hand, hurried back to the parapet. There were men everywhere fighting, and shouting, shooting arrows and swinging blades. He saw three Carls stabbing at a Flathead with their spears. He saw Shivers plant a blow in the small of another's back, blood leaping in the air in dark streaks. He saw a man smash a Flathead in the face with his shield, just as it got to the top of the wall, and knock it into the empty air. Logen slashed at a Shanka's hand, slipped in some blood and fell on his side, nearly stabbed himself. He crawled a stride or two and fumbled his way up. He hacked a Shanka's arm off that was already spitted thrashing on a Carl's spear, chopped halfway through another's neck as it showed itself over the parapet. He lurched after it and stared over.

One Shanka was still on the wall, and Logen was just pointing to it when an arrow from off the tower took it in the back. It crashed down into the ditch, stuck on a stake. The ones round the gate were all done, crushed with rocks and bristling with broken arrows. That was it for the centre, and Red Hat's side was already clear. Over on the left there were still a few up on the walls, but Dow's boys were getting well on top of them now. Even as Logen watched he saw a couple flung down bloody into the ditch.

In the valley they started wavering, edging away, squeaking and shrieking, arrows still falling among them from the

Dogman's archers. Seemed that even Shanka could have enough. They started to turn, to scuttle back towards Bethod's ditch.

'We done 'em!' someone bellowed, and then everyone was cheering and screaming. The boy with the bow was waving it over his head now, grinning like he'd beaten Bethod all by himself.

Logen didn't celebrate. He frowned out at the great crowd of Carls beyond the ditch, the standards of Bethod's host flapping over them in the breeze. Brief and bloody, that one might have been, but the next time they came it was likely to be a lot less brief, and a lot more bloody. He made his aching fist uncurl from round the Maker's sword, leaned it up against the parapet, and he pressed one hand with the other to stop them shaking. He took a long breath.

'Still alive,' he whispered.

Logen sat sharpening his knives, the firelight flashing on the blades as he turned them this way and that, stroking them with the whetstone, licking his fingertip and wiping a smudge away, getting them nice and clean. You could never have too many, and that was a fact. He grinned as he remembered what Ferro's answer to that had been. Unless you fall into a river and drown for all that weight of iron. He wondered for an idle moment if he'd ever see her again, but it didn't look likely. You have to be realistic, after all, and getting through tomorrow seemed like quite the ambition.

Grim sat opposite, trimming some straight sticks to use as arrow shafts. There'd still been the slightest glimmer of dusk in the sky when they'd sat down together. Now it was dark as pitch but for the dusty stars, and neither one of them had said a word the whole time. That was Harding Grim for you, and it suited Logen well enough. A comfortable silence was much preferable to a worrisome conversation, but nothing lasts forever.

The sound of angry footsteps came out of the darkness and Black Dow stalked up to the fire, Tul and Crummock just behind him. He had a frown on his face black enough to have earned his name, and a dirty bandage round his forearm, a long streak of dark blood dried into it.

'Pick up a cut, did you?' asked Logen.

'Bah!' Dow dropped down beside the fire. 'Nothing but a scratch. Fucking Flatheads! I'll burn the lot of 'em!'

'How about the rest of you?'

Tul grinned. 'My palms are terrible chafed from hefting rocks, but I'm a tough bastard. I'll live through it.'

'And I still find myself miserably idle,' said Crummock, 'with my children looking to my weapons, and cutting arrows from the dead. Good work for children, that, gets 'em comfortable round a corpse. The moon's keen to see me fight, though, so she is, and so am I.'

Logen sucked at his teeth. 'You'll get your chance, Crummock, I'd not worry about that. Bethod's got plenty for everyone, I reckon.'

'I never seen Flatheads come on like that,' Dow was musing. 'Right at a well-manned wall with no ladders, no tools. It ain't too clever, your Flathead, but it ain't stupid either. They like ambushes. They like cover, and hiding, and creeping around. They can be mad fearless, when they have to be, but to come on like that, by choice? Not natural.'

Crummock chuckled, a great raspy rumbling. 'Shanka fighting for one set of men against another ain't natural either. These aren't natural times. Might be Bethod's witch has worked some charm to get 'em all stirred up. Cooked herself a chant and a ritual to fill those things with hate of us.'

'Danced naked round a green fire and all the rest, I don't doubt,' said Tul.

'The moon will see us right, my friends, don't worry yourself on that score!' Crummock rattled the bones around his neck. 'The moon loves us all, and we cannot die while there's—'

'Tell it to those as went back to the mud today.' Logen jerked his head over towards the fresh dug graves at the back of the fortress. There was no seeing them in the darkness, but they were there. A score or so long humps of turned and pressed-down earth.

But the big hillman only smiled. 'I'd call them the happy ones, though, wouldn't you? Least they all get their own beds, don't they? We'll be lucky if we don't go in pits for a dozen each once the work gets hot. There'll be nowhere for the living to sleep otherwise. Pits for a score! Don't tell me you ain't seen that before, or dug the holes your own sweet self.'

Logen got up. 'Maybe I have, but I didn't like it any.'

'Course you did!' Crummock roared after him. 'Don't give me that, Bloody-Nine!'

Logen didn't look back. There were torches set on the wall, every ten paces or so, bright flames in the darkness, white specks of insects floating around them. Men stood in their light, leaning on their spears, bows clenched in their hands, swords drawn, watching the night for surprises. Bethod had always loved surprises, and Logen reckoned they'd have some before they were through, one way or another.

He came up to the parapet and set his hands on the clammy stone, frowned down at the fires burning in the blackness of the valley. Bethod's fires, far away in the dark, and their own ones, bonfires built up and lit just below the wall to try and catch any clever bastards trying to sneak up. They cast flickering circles across the shadowy rocks, with here or there the twisted corpse of a Flathead, hacked and flung from the wall or stuck with arrows.

Logen felt someone move behind him and his back prickled, eyes sliding to the corners. Shivers, maybe, come to settle their score and shove him off the wall. Shivers, or one of a hundred others with some grudge that Logen had forgotten but they never would. He made sure his hand was close to a blade, and he bared his teeth, and he made ready to spin and strike.

'We did good today, though, eh?' said the Dogman. 'Lost less than twenty.'

Logen breathed easy again, and he let his hand drop. 'We did alright. But Bethod's just getting started. He's prodding, to see where we're weakest, see if he can wear us down. He knows that time's the thing. Most valuable thing there is, in war. A day or two's worth more to him than a load of Flatheads. If he can crush us quick he'll take the losses, I reckon.'

'Best thing might be to hold out, then, eh?'

Off in the darkness, far away and echoing, Logen could just hear the clang and clatter of smithing and carpentry. 'They're building down there. All the stuff they'll need to climb our wall, fill in our ditch. Lots of ladders, and all the rest. He'll take us quick if he can, Bethod, but he'll take us slow if he has to.'

Dogman nodded. 'Well, like I said. Best thing to do would be to hold out. If all goes to plan, the Union'll be here soon.'

'They'd better be. Plans have a way of coming apart when you lean on 'em.'

Such Sweet Sorrow

'**H**is Resplendence, the Grand Duke of Ospria, desires only the best of relations . . .'

Jezal could do little but sit and smile, as he had been sitting and smiling all the whole interminable day. His face, and his rump, were aching from it. The burbling of the ambassador continued unabated, accompanied by flamboyant hand gestures. Occasionally he would dam the river of blather for a moment, so that his translator could render his platitudes into the common tongue. He need scarcely have bothered.

'. . . the great city of Ospria was always honoured to count herself among the closest friends of your illustrious father, King Guslav, and now seeks nothing more than the continuing friendship of the government and people of the Union . . .'

Jezal had sat and smiled through the long morning, in his bejewelled chair, on his high marble dais, as the ambassadors of the world came to pay their ingratiating respects. He had sat as the sun rose in the sky and poured mercilessly through the vast windows, glinting on the gilt mouldings that encrusted every inch of wall and ceiling, flashing from the great mirrors, and silver candlesticks, and grand vases, striking multi-coloured fire from the tinkling glass beads on the three monstrous chandeliers.

'. . . the Grand Duke wishes once again to express his brotherly regret at the minor incident last spring, and assures you that nothing of the kind will happen again, provided the soldiers of Westport stay on their side of the border . . .'

He had sat through the endless afternoon as the room grew hotter and hotter, squirming as the representatives of the world's great leaders bowed in and scraped out with identical bland congratulations in a dozen different languages. He had sat as the sun went down, and hundreds of candles were lit and hoisted up, twinkling at him from the mirrors, and the darkened windows, and the highly polished floor. He sat, smiling, and receiving praise from men whose countries he had scarcely even heard of before that endless day began.

'. . . His Resplendence furthermore hopes and trusts that the hostilities between your great nation and the Empire of Gurkhul may soon come to an end, and that trade may once more flow freely around the Circle Sea.'

Both ambassador and translator paused politely for a rare instant and Jezal managed to stir himself into sluggish speech. 'We have a similar hope. Please convey to the Grand Duke our thanks for the wonderful gift.' Two lackeys, meanwhile, heaved the huge chest to one side and placed it with the rest of the gaudy rubbish Jezal had accumulated that day.

Further Styrian chatter flowed out into the room. 'His Resplendence wishes to convey his heartfelt congratulations on your August Majesty's forthcoming marriage to the Princess Terez, the Jewel of Talins, surely the greatest beauty alive in all the wide Circle of the World.' Jezal could only fight to maintain his stretched grin. He had heard the match spoken of as a settled thing so often that day that he had lost the will to correct the misconception, and had in fact almost started to think of himself as engaged. All he cared about was that the audiences should finally be finished with, so he might steal a moment to drown himself in peace.

'His Resplendence has further instructed us to wish your August Majesty a long and happy reign,' explained the translator, 'and many heirs, that your line may continue undiminished in glory.' Jezal forced his smile a tooth wider, and inclined his head. 'I bid you good evening!'

The Osprian ambassador bowed with a theatrical flourish, sweeping off his enormous hat, its multicoloured feathers thrashing with enthusiasm. Then he shuffled backwards, still bent over, across the gleaming floor. He somehow made it out into the corridor without pitching over on his back, and the great doors, festooned with gold leaf, were smoothly shut upon him.

Jezal snatched the crown from his head and tossed it onto the cushion beside the throne, rubbing at the chafe marks round his sweaty scalp with one hand while he tugged his embroidered collar open with the other. Nothing helped. He still felt dizzy, weak, oppressively hot.

Hoff was already ingratiating himself onto Jezal's left side. 'That was the last of the ambassadors, your Majesty. Tomorrow will be occupied by the nobility of Midderland. They are eager to pay homage—'

'Lots of homage and little help, I'll be bound!'

Hoff managed a chuckle of suffocating falseness. 'Ha, ha, ha, your Majesty. They have sought audiences from dawn, and we would not wish to offend them by—'

'Damn it!' hissed Jezal, jumping up and shaking his legs in a vain effort to unstick his trousers from his sweaty backside. He jerked his crimson sash over his head and flung it away, tore his gilded frock coat open and tried to rip it off, but in the end he got his hand caught in one cuff and had to turn the bloody thing inside out before he could finally get free of it.

'Damn it!' He hurled it down on the marble dais with half a mind to stamp it to rags. Then he remembered himself. Hoff had taken a cautious step back, and was frowning as if he had discovered his fine new mansion was afflicted with a terrible case of rot. The assorted servants, pages, and Knights, both Herald and of the Body, were all staring studiously ahead, doing their best to imitate statues. Over in the dark corner of the room, Bayaz was standing. His eyes were sunk in shadow, but his face was stony grim.

Jezal blushed like a naughty schoolboy called to account, and pressed one hand over his eyes, 'A terribly trying day . . .' He hurried down the steps of the dais and out of the audience chamber with his head down. The blaring of a belated and slightly off-key fanfare pursued him down the hallway. So, unfortunately, did the First of the Magi.

'That was not gracious,' said Bayaz. 'Rare rages render a man frightening. Common ones render him ridiculous.'

'I apologise,' growled Jezal through gritted teeth. 'The crown is a mighty burden.'

'A mighty burden and a mighty honour both. We had a discussion, as I recall, about your striving to be worthy of it.' The Magus left a significant pause. 'Perhaps you might strive harder.'

Jezal rubbed at his aching temples. 'I just need a moment to myself is all. Just a moment.'

'Take all the time you need. But we have business in the morning, your Majesty, business we cannot avoid. The nobility of Midderland will not wait to congratulate you. I will see you at dawn, brimful with energy and enthusiasm, I am sure.'

'Yes, yes!' Jezal snapped over his shoulder. 'Brimful!'

He burst out into a small courtyard, surrounded on three sides by a shadowy colonnade, and stood still in the cool evening. He shook himself, squeezed his eyes shut, let his head tip back and took a long, slow breath. A minute alone. He wondered if, aside from pissing or sleeping, it was the first he had been permitted since that day of madness in the Lords' Round.

He was the victim, or perhaps the beneficiary, of the most almighty blunder. Somehow, everyone had mistaken him for a king, when he was very clearly a selfish, clueless idiot who had scarcely in his life thought more than a day ahead. Every time someone called him, 'your Majesty' he felt more of a fraud, and with each moment that passed he was more guiltily surprised not to have been found out.

He wandered across the perfect lawn, giving vent to a long, self-pitying sigh. It caught in his throat. There was a Knight of the Body beside a doorway opposite, standing to attention so rigidly that Jezal had hardly noticed him. He cursed under his breath. Could he not be left alone for five minutes together? He frowned as he walked closer. The man seemed somehow familiar. A great big fellow with a shaved head and a noticeable lack of neck . . .

243

'Bremer dan Gorst!'

'Your Majesty,' said Gorst, his armour rattling as he clashed his meaty fist against his polished breastplate.

'It is a pleasure to see you!' Jezal had disliked the man from the first moment he had laid eyes on him, and being bludgeoned round a fencing circle by him, whether Jezal had won in the end or no, had not improved his opinion of the neckless brute. Now, however, anything resembling a familiar face was like a glass of water in the desert. Jezal actually found himself reaching out and squeezing the man's heavy hand as though they were old friends, and had to make himself let go of it.

'Your Majesty does me too much honour.'

'Please, you need not call me that! How did you come to be part of the household? I thought that you served with Lord Brock's guard?'

'That post did not suit me,' said Gorst in his strangely high, piping voice. 'I was lucky enough to find a place with the Knights of the Body some months ago, your Maj—' He cut himself off.

An idea slunk into Jezal's head. He looked over his shoulder, but there was no one else nearby. The garden was still as a graveyard, its shadowy arcades as quiet as crypts. 'Bremer . . . I may call you Bremer, may I?'

'I suppose that my king may call me whatever he wishes.'

'I wonder . . . could I ask you for a favour?'

Gorst blinked. 'Your Majesty has only to ask.'

Jezal spun around as he heard the door open. Gorst stepped out into the colonnade with the soft jingle of armour. A cloaked and hooded figure followed him, silently. The old excitement was still there as she pushed back her hood and a chink of light from a window above crept across the lower part of her face. He could see the bright curve of her cheek, one side of her mouth, the outline of a nostril, the gleam of her eyes in the shadows, and that was all.

'Thank you, Gorst,' said Jezal. 'You may leave us.' The big man thumped his chest and backed through the archway, pulling the door to behind him. Hardly the first time they had met in secret, of course, but things were different now. He wondered if it would end with kisses and soft words between them, or if it would simply end. The start was far from promising.

'Your August Majesty,' said Ardee with the very heaviest of irony. 'What a towering honour. Should I grovel on my face? Or do I curtsey?'

However hard her words, the sound of her voice still made the breath catch in his throat. 'Curtsey?' he managed to say. 'Do you even know how?'

'In truth, not really. I have not had the training for polite society, and now the lack of it quite crushes me.' She stepped forward, frowning into the darkened garden. 'When I was a girl, in my wildest flights of fancy, I used to dream of being invited to the palace, a guest of the king himself. We would eat fine cakes, and drink fine wine, and talk fine talk of important things, deep into the night.' Ardee pressed her hands to her chest and fluttered her eyelashes. 'Thank you for making the pitiful dreams of one poor wretch come true, if only for the briefest moment. The other beggars will never believe me when I tell them!'

'We are all more than a little shocked by the turn events have taken.'

'Oh, we are indeed, your Majesty.'

Jezal flinched. 'Don't call me that. Not you.'

'What should I call you?'

'My name. Jezal, that is. The way you used to . . . please.'

'If I must. You promised me, Jezal. You promised me you would not let me down.'

'I know I did, and I meant to keep my promise . . . but the fact is . . .' King or not, he fumbled with the words as much as he ever had, then blurted them out in an idiotic spurt. 'I cannot marry you! I surely would have done, had not . . .' He raised his arms and hopelessly let them drop. 'Had not all this happened. But it has happened, and there is nothing that I can do. I cannot marry you.'

'Of course not.' Her mouth gave a bitter twist. 'Promises are for children. I never thought it very likely, even before. Even in my most unrealistic moments. Now the notion seems ridiculous. The king and the peasant-girl. Absurd. The most hackneyed story-book would never dare suggest it.'

'It need not mean that we never see each other again.' He took a hesitant step towards her. 'Things will be different, of course, but we can still find moments . . .' He reached out, slowly, awkwardly. 'Moments when we can be together.' He touched her face, gently, and felt the same guilty thrill he always had. 'We can be to each other just as we were. You would not need to worry. Everything would be taken care of . . .'

She looked him in the eye. 'So . . . you'd like me to be your whore?'

He jerked his hand back. 'No! Of course not! I mean . . . I would like you to be . . .' What did he mean? He fumbled desperately for a better word. 'My lover?'

'Ah. I see. And when you take a wife, what will I be then? What word do you think your queen might use to describe me?' Jezal swallowed, and looked at his shoes. 'A whore is still a whore, whatever word you use. Easily tired of, and even more easily replaced. And when you tire of me, and you find other lovers? What will they call me then?' She gave a bitter snort. 'I'm scum, and I know it, but you must think even less of me than I do.'

'It's not my fault.' He felt tears in his eyes. Pain, or relief, it was hard to tell. A bitter alloy of both, perhaps. 'It's not my fault.'

'Of course it isn't. I don't blame you. I blame myself. I used to think I had bad luck, but my brother was right. I make bad choices.' She looked at him with that same judging expression in her dark eyes that she had when they first met. 'I could have found a good man, but I chose you. I should have known better.' She reached up and touched his face, rubbed a tear from his cheek with her thumb. Just as she had when they parted before, in the park, in the rain. But then there had been the hope that they would meet again. Now there was none. She sighed, and let her arm drop, and stared sulkily out into the garden.

Jezal blinked. Could that really be all? He yearned to say some last tender word, at least, some bitter-sweet farewell, but his mind was empty. What words could there possibly be that could make any difference? They were done, and more talk would only have been salt in the cuts. Wasted breath. He set his jaw, and wiped the last damp streaks from his face. She was right. The king and the peasant-girl. What could have been more ridiculous?

'Gorst!' he barked. The door squealed open and the muscle-bound guardsman emerged from the shadows, his head humbly bowed. 'You may escort the lady back to her home.'

He nodded, and stood away from the dark archway. Ardee turned and walked towards it, pulling up her hood, and Jezal watched her go. He wondered if she would pause on the threshold and look back, and their eyes would meet, and there would be one last moment between them. One last catching of his breath. One last tugging at his heart.

But she did not look back. Without the slightest pause she stepped through and was gone, and Gorst after her, and Jezal was left in the moonlit garden. Alone.

Picked Up A Shadow

Ferro sat on the warehouse roof, her eyes narrowed against the bright sun, her legs crossed underneath her. She watched the boats, and the people flowing off them. She watched for Yulwei. That was why she came here every day.

There was war between the Union and Gurkhul, a meaningless war with a lot of talk and no fighting, and so no ships went to Kanta. But Yulwei went where he pleased. He could take her back to the South, so she could have her vengeance on the Gurkish. Until he came, she was trapped with the pinks. She ground her teeth, and clenched her fists, and grimaced at her own uselessness. Her boredom. Her wasted time. She would have prayed to God for Yulwei to come.

But God never listened.

Jezal dan Luthar, fool that he was, for reasons she could not comprehend, had been given a crown and made king. Bayaz, who Ferro was sure had been behind the whole business, now spent every hour with him. Still trying to make him a leader of men, no doubt. Just as he had all the long way across the plain and back, with small results.

Jezal dan Luthar, the King of the Union. Ninefingers would have laughed long and hard at that, if he could have heard it. Ferro smiled to think of him laughing. Then she realised that she was smiling, and made herself stop. Bayaz had promised her vengeance, and given her nothing, and left her mired here, powerless. There was nothing to smile at.

She sat, and watched the boats for Yulwei.

She did not watch for Ninefingers. She did not hope to see him slouch onto the docks. That would have been a foolish, childish hope, belonging to the foolish child she had been when the Gurkish took her for a slave. He would not change his mind and come back. She had made sure of it. Strange, though, how she kept thinking that she saw him, in amongst the crowds.

The dockers had come to recognise her. They had shouted at her, for a while. 'Come down here, my lovely, and give me a kiss!' one of them had called, and his friends had laughed. Then Ferro had thrown half a brick at his head and knocked him in the sea. He had nothing to say to her once they fished him out. None of them had, and that suited her well enough.

She sat, and watched the boats.

She sat until the sun was low, casting a bright glare across the bottoms of the clouds, making the shifting waves sparkle. Until the crowds thinned out, and the carts stopped moving, and the shouting and bustle of the docks faded to a dusty quiet. Until the breeze grew cool against her skin.

Yulwei was not coming today.

She climbed down from the roof of the warehouse and worked her way through the back streets towards the Middleway. It was as she was walking down that wide road, scowling at the people who passed her, that she realised. She was being followed.

He did it well, and carefully. Sometimes closer, sometimes further back. Staying out of plain sight, but never hiding. She took a few turns to make sure, and he always followed. He was dressed all in black, with long, lank hair and a mask covering part of his face. All in black, like a shadow. Like the men that had chased her and Ninefingers, before they left for the Old Empire. She watched him out of the corners of her eyes, never looking straight at him, never letting him know that she knew.

He would find out soon enough.

She took a turn down a dingy alley, stopped and waited behind the corner. Pressed up against the grimy stonework, holding her breath. Her bow and her sword might be far away, but shock was the only weapon she needed. That and her hands, and her feet, and her teeth.

She heard the footsteps coming. Careful footsteps, padding down the alley, so soft she could barely hear them. She found that she was smiling. It felt good to have an enemy, to have a purpose. Very good, after so long without one. It filled the empty space inside her, even if it was only for a moment. She gritted her teeth, feeling the fury swelling up in her chest. Hot and exciting. Safe and familiar. Like the kiss of an old lover, much missed.

When he rounded the corner her fist was already swinging. It crunched into his mask and sent him reeling. She pressed in close, cracking him in the face with each hand and knocking his head right and left. He fumbled for a knife, but he was slow and dizzy and the blade was barely out of its sheath before she had his wrist tight. Her elbow snapped his head back, jabbed into his throat and left him gurgling. She tore the knife out of his limp hand, spun around and kicked him in the gut so he bent over. Her knee thudded into his mask and sent him onto his back in the dirt. She followed him down, her legs wrapping tight around his waist, her arm across his chest, his own knife pressed up against his throat.

'Look at this,' she whispered in his face. 'I have picked up a shadow.'

'Glugh,' came from behind his mask, his eyes still rolling.

'Hard to talk with that on, eh?' And she slashed the straps of his mask with a jerk of the knife, the blade leaving a long scratch down his cheek. He did not look so dangerous without it. Much younger than she had thought, with a rash of spots around his chin and a growth of downy hair on his top lip. He jerked his head and his eyes came back into focus. He snarled, tried to twist free, but she had him fast, and a touch of the knife against his neck soon calmed him.

'Why are you following me?'

'I'm not fucking—'

Ferro had never been a patient woman. Straddling her shadow as she was it was an easy thing to rear up and smash her elbow into his face. He did his best to ward her off, but all her weight was on his hips and he was helpless. Her arm crashed through his hands and into his mouth, his nose, his cheek, cracking his head back against the greasy cobbles. Four of those and the fight was out of him. His head lolled back, and she crouched down over him again and tucked the knife up under his neck. Blood bubbled out of his nose and his mouth and ran down the side of his face in dark streaks.

'Following me now?'

'I just watch.' His voice clicked in his bloody mouth. 'I just watch. I don't give the orders.'

The Gurkish soldiers did not give the orders to kill Ferro's people and make her a slave. That did not make them innocent. That did not make them safe from her. 'Who does?'

He coughed, and his face twitched, bubbles of blood blew out of his swollen nostrils. Nothing else. Ferro frowned.

'What?' She moved the knife down and pricked at his thigh with the point. 'You think I never cut a cock off before?'

'Glokta,' he mumbled, closing his eyes. 'I work . . . for Glokta.'

'Glokta.' The name meant nothing to her, but it was something to follow.

She slid the knife back up, up to his neck. The lump on his throat rose and fell, brushing against the edge of the blade. She clenched her jaw, and worked her fingers round the grip, frowning down. Tears had started to glitter in the corners of his eyes. Best to get it done, and away. Safest. But her hand was hard to move.

'Give me a reason not to do it.'

The tears welled up and ran down the sides of his bloody face. 'My birds,' he whispered.

'Birds?'

'There'll be no one to feed them. I deserve it, sure enough, but my birds . . . they've done nothing.' She narrowed her eyes at him.

Birds. Strange, the things that people have to live for.

Her father had kept a bird. She remembered it, in a cage, hanging from a pole. A useless thing, that could not even fly, only cling to a twig. He had taught it words. She remembered watching him feeding it, when she was a child. Long ago, before the Gurkish came.

'Sssss,' she hissed in his face, pressing the knife up against his neck and making him cower. Then she pulled the blade away, got up and stood over him. 'The moment when I see you again will be your last. Back to your birds, shadow.'

He nodded, his wet eyes wide, and she turned and stalked off down the dark alleyway, into the dusk. When she crossed a bridge she tossed the knife away. It vanished with a splash, and ripples spread out in growing circles across the slimy water. A mistake, most likely, to have left that man alive. Mercy was always a mistake, in her experience.

But it seemed she was in a merciful mood today.

Questions

Colonel Glokta was a magnificent dancer, of course, but with his leg feeling as stiff as it did it was difficult for him to truly shine. The constant buzzing of flies was a further distraction, and his partner was not helping. Ardee West looked well enough, but her constant giggling was becoming quite the irritation.

'Stop that!' snapped the Colonel, whirling her around the laboratory of the Adeptus Physical, the specimens in the jars pulsing and wobbling in time to the music.

'Partially eaten,' grinned Kandelau, one eye enormously magnified through his eyeglass. He pointed downwards with his tongs. 'This is a foot.'

Glokta pushed the bushes aside, one hand pressed over his face. The butchered corpse lay there, glistening red, scarcely recognisable as human. Ardee laughed and laughed at the sight of it. 'Partially eaten!' she tittered at him. Colonel Glokta did not find the business in any way amusing. The sound of flies was growing louder and louder, threatening to drown out the music entirely. Worse yet, it was getting terribly cold in the park.

'Careless of me,' said a voice from behind.

'How do you mean?'

'Just to leave it there. But sometimes it is better to move quickly, than to move carefully, eh, cripple?'

'I remember this,' murmured Glokta. It had grown colder yet, and he was shivering like a leaf. 'I remember this!'

'Of course,' whispered the voice. A woman's voice, but not Ardee. A low and hissing voice, that made his eye twitch.

'What can I do?' The Colonel could feel his gorge rising.

The wounds in the red meat yawned. The flies were so loud he could hardly hear the reply.

'Perhaps you should go to the University, and ask for advice.' Icy breath brushed his neck and made his back shiver. 'Perhaps while you are there . . . you could ask them about the Seed.'

Glokta lurched to the bottom of the steps and staggered sideways, falling back against the wall, the breath hissing over his wet tongue. His left leg trembled, his left eye twitched, as though the two were connected by a cord of pain that cut into his arse, guts, back, shoulder, neck, face, and tightened with every movement, however small.

He forced himself to be still. To breathe long and slow. He made his mind move off the pain and on to other things. *Like Bayaz, and his failed quest for this Seed. After all, his Eminence is waiting, and is not known for his patience.* He stretched his neck out to either side and felt the bones clicking between his twisted shoulder-blades. He pressed his tongue into his gums and shuffled away from the steps, into the cool darkness of the stacks.

They had not changed much in the past year. *Or probably in a few centuries before that.* The vaulted spaces smelled of fust and age, lit only by a couple of flickering, grimy lamps, sagging shelves stretching away into the shifting shadows. *Time to go digging once again through the dusty refuse of history.* The Adeptus Historical did not appear to have changed much either. He sat at his stained desk, poring over a mouldy-looking pile of papers in the light from a single squirming candle flame. He squinted up as Glokta hobbled closer.

'Who's there?'

'Glokta.' He peered up suspiciously towards the shadowy ceiling. 'What happened to your crow?'

'Dead,' grunted the ancient librarian sadly.

'History, you might say!' The old man did not laugh. 'Ah, well. It happens to us all.' *And some sooner than others.* 'I have questions for you.'

The Adeptus Historical craned forward over his desk, peering dewily up at Glokta as though he had never seen another human before. 'I remember you.' *Miracles do happen, then?* 'You asked me about Bayaz. First apprentice of great Juvens, first letter in the alphabet of the—'

'Yes, yes, we've been over this.'

The old man gave a sulky frown. 'Did you bring that scroll back?'

'The Maker fell burning, and so on? I'm afraid not. The Arch Lector has it.'

'Gah. I hear far too much about that man these days. Them upstairs are always carping on him. His Eminence this, and his Eminence that. I'm sick of hearing it!' *I know very much how you feel.* 'Everyone's in a spin, these days. A spin and a ruckus.'

'Lots of changes upstairs. We have a new king.'

'I know that! Guslav, is it?'

Glokta gave a long sigh as he settled himself in the chair on the other side of the desk. 'Yes, yes, he's the one.' *Only thirty years out of date, or so. I'm surprised he didn't think Harod the Great was still on the throne.*

'What do you want this time?'

Oh, to fumble in the darkness for answers that are always just out of reach. 'I want to know about the Seed.'

The lined face did not move. 'The what?'

'It was mentioned in your precious scroll. That thing that Bayaz and his magical friends searched for in the House of the Maker, after the death of Kanedias. After the death of Juvens.'

'Bah!' The Adeptus waved his hand, the saggy flesh under his wrist wobbling. 'Secrets, power. It's all a metaphor.'

'Bayaz does not seem to think so.' Glokta shuffled his chair closer, and spoke lower. *Though there cannot be anyone to hear, or to care if they did.* 'I heard it was a piece of the Other Side, left over from the Old Time, when devils walked our earth. The stuff of magic, made solid.'

The old man wheezed with papery laughter, displaying a rotten cavern of a mouth with fewer teeth even than Glokta's own. 'I did not take you for a superstitious man, Superior.' *Nor was I one, when I last came here with questions. Before my visit to the House of the Maker, before my meeting with Yulwei, before I saw Shickel smile while they burned her. What happy times they were, before I had heard of Bayaz, when things still made sense.* The Adeptus wiped his runny eyes with his palsied mockery of a hand. 'Where did you hear that?'

Oh, from a Navigator with his foot on an anvil. 'Never you mind from where.'

'Well, you know more about it than me. I read once that rocks sometimes fall out of the sky. Some say they are fragments of the stars. Some say they are splinters, flung out from the chaos of hell. Dangerous to touch. Terribly cold.'

Cold? Glokta could almost feel that icy breath upon his neck, and he wriggled his shoulders at it, forcing himself not to glance behind him. 'Tell me about hell.' *Though I think I already know more than most on the subject.*

'Eh?'

'Hell, old man. The Other Side.'

'They say it is where magic comes from, if you believe in such things.'

'I have learned to keep an open mind on the subject.'

'An open mind is like to an open wound, apt to—'

'So I have heard, but we are speaking of hell.'

The librarian licked at his sagging lips. 'Legend has it that there was a time when our world and the world below were one, and devils roamed the earth. Great Euz cast them out, and spoke the First Law – forbidding all to touch the Other Side, or to speak to devils, or to tamper with the gates between.'

'The First Law, eh?'

'His son Glustrod, hungry for power, ignored his father's warnings, and he sought out secrets, and summoned devils, and sent them against his enemies. It is said his folly led to the destruction of Aulcus and the fall of the Old Empire, and that when he destroyed himself, he left the gates ajar . . . but I am not the expert on all that.'

'Who is?'

The old man grimaced. 'There were books here. Very old.

Beautiful books, from the time of the Master Maker. Books on the subject of the Other Side. The divide between. The gates and the locks. Books on the subject of the Tellers of Secrets, and of their summoning and sending. A load of invention if you ask me. Myth and fantasy.'

'There *were* books?'

'They have been missing from my shelves for some years now.'

'Missing? Where are they?'

The old man frowned. 'Strange, that you of all people should ask that—'

'Enough!' Glokta turned as quickly as he could to look behind him. Silber, the University Administrator, stood at the foot of the steps, with a look of the strangest horror and surprise on his rigid face. *Quite as if he had seen a ghost. Or even a demon.* 'That will be quite enough, Superior! We thank you for your visit.'

'Enough?' Glokta gave a frown of his own. 'His Eminence will not be—'

'I know what his Eminence will or will not be . . .' *An unpleasantly familiar voice.* Superior Goyle worked his way slowly down the steps. He strolled around Silber, across the shadowy floor between the shelves. 'And I say enough. We most heartily thank you for your visit.' He leaned forwards, eyes popping furiously from his head. 'Make it your last!'

There had been some startling changes in the dining hall since Glokta went downstairs. The evening had grown dark outside the dirty windows, the candles had been lit in their tarnished sconces. *And, of course, there is the matter of two dozen widely assorted Practicals of the Inquisition.*

Two narrow-eyed natives of Suljuk sat staring at Glokta over their masks, as like as if they had been twins, their black boots up on the ancient dining table, four curved swords lying sheathed on the wood before them. Three dark-skinned men stood near one dark window, heads shaved, each with an axe at his belt and a shield on his back. A great tall Practical loomed up by the fireplace, long and thin as a birch tree with blond hair hanging over his masked face. Beside was a short one, almost dwarfish, his belt bristling with knives.

Glokta recognised the huge Northman called the Stone-Splitter from his previous visit to the University. *But it looks as if he has been attempting to split stones with his face since we last met, and with great persistence.* His cheeks were uneven, his brows were wonky, the bridge of his nose pointed sharply to the left. His ruin of a face was almost as disturbing as the enormous mallet he had clenched in his massive fists. *But not quite.*

So it went on, as strange and worrying a collection of murderers as could ever have been collected together in one place, and all heavily armed. *And it seems that Superior Goyle has restocked his freak show.* In the midst of them, and seeming quite at home, stood Practical Vitari, pointing this way and that, giving orders. *You would never have thought she was the mothering type, seeing her now, but I suppose we all have our hidden talents.*

Glokta threw his right arm up in the air. 'Who are we killing?'

All eyes turned towards him. Vitari stalked over, a frown across the freckled bridge of her nose. 'What the hell are you doing here?'

'I could ask you the same question.'

'If you know what's good for you, you'll ask no questions at all.'

Glokta leered his empty smile at her. 'If I knew what was good for me I'd never have lost my teeth, and questions are all I have left. What's in this old pile of dust that's of interest to you?'

'That's none of my business, and even less of yours. If you're looking for traitors, maybe you should look in your own house first, eh?'

'And what is that supposed to mean?'

Vitari leaned close to him and whispered through her mask. 'You saved my life, so let me return the favour. Get away from here. Get away, and keep away.'

*

Glokta shuffled down the passageway and up to his heavy door. *As far as Bayaz goes, we are no further on. Nothing that will bring a rare smile to the face of his Eminence. Summonings and sendings. Gods and devils. Always more questions.* He turned his key impatiently in the lock, desperate to sit down and take the weight from his trembling leg. *What was Goyle doing at the university? Goyle, and Vitari, and two dozen Practicals, all armed as if they were going to war?* He took a wincing step over the threshold. *There must be some—*

'Gah!' He felt his cane snatched away and he lurched sideways, clutching at the air. Something crunched into his face and filled his head with blinding pain. The next moment the floor thumped him in the back and drove his wind out in a long sigh. He blinked and slobbered, mouth salty with blood, the dark room swaying madly around him. *Oh dear, oh dear. A fist in the face, unless I am much mistaken. It never loses its impact.*

A hand grabbed the collar of his coat and dragged him up, the cloth cutting into his throat and making him squawk like a strangled chicken. Another had him by the belt and he was hauled bodily along, his knees and the toes of his boots scraping limp over the boards. He struggled weakly on a reflex, but only managed to send a stab of pain through his own back.

The bathroom door cracked against his head and banged open on the wall, he was dragged powerless across the darkened room towards the bath, still full of dirty water from that morning. 'Wait!' he croaked as he was wrestled over the edge. 'Who are—blurghhhh!'

The cold water closed around his head, the bubbles rushed around his face. He was held there, struggling, eyes bulging open with shock and panic, until it seemed his lungs would burst. Then he was yanked up by the hair, water pouring from his face and splattering into the bath. *A simple technique, but undeniably effective. I am greatly discomfited.* He took in a gasping breath. 'What do you—blarghhh!'

Back into the darkness, such air as he had managed to drag

in gurgling out into the dirty water. *But whoever it is let me breathe. I am not being murdered. I am being softened up. Softened up for questions. I would laugh at the irony . . . were there any breath . . . left in my body . . .* He shoved at the bath and thrashed at the water. His legs kicked pointlessly, but the hand on the back of his neck was made of steel. His stomach clenched and his ribs heaved, desperate to drag in air. *Do not breathe . . . do not breathe . . . do not breathe!* He was just sucking in a great lungful of dirty water as he was snatched up from the bath and flung onto the boards, coughing, gasping, vomiting all at once.

'You are Glokta?' A woman's voice, short and hard, with a rough Kantic accent.

She squatted down in front of him, balanced on the balls of her feet, her wrists resting on her knees, her long brown hands hanging limp. She wore a man's shirt, loose around her scrawny shoulders, wet sleeves rolled up around her bony wrists. Her black hair was hacked off short and stuck from her head in greasy clumps. She had a thin, pale scar down her hard face, a scowl on her thin lips, but it was her eyes that were most off-putting, gleaming yellow in the half light from the corridor. *Small wonder that Severard was reluctant to follow her. I should have listened to him.*

'You are Glokta?'

There was no point denying it. He wiped the bitter drool from his chin with a shaking hand. 'I am Glokta.'

'Why are you watching me?'

He pushed himself painfully up to sitting. 'What makes you think I will have anything to say to—'

Her fist struck him on the point of his chin and snapped his head back, tore a gasp out of him. His jaws banged together and one tooth punched a hole in the bottom of his tongue. He sagged back against the wall, the dark room lurching, his eyes filling up with tears. When things came back into focus she was staring at him, yellow eyes narrowed. 'I will keep hitting you until you give me answers, or you die.'

'My thanks.'

'Thanks?'

'I think you might have loosened my neck up just a fraction.'
Glokta smiled, showing her his few bloody teeth. 'For two
years I was a captive of the Gurkish. Two years in the darkness
of the Emperor's prisons. Two years of cutting, and chiselling,
and burning. Do you think the thought of a slap or two scares
me?' He chuckled bloody laughter in her face. 'It hurts more
when I piss! Do you think I'm scared to die?' He grimaced at
the stabbing through his spine as he leaned towards her. 'Every
morning . . . that I wake up alive . . . is a disappointment! If
you want answers you'll have to give me answers. Like for like.'

She stared at him for a long moment, not blinking. 'You
were a prisoner of the Gurkish?'

Glokta swept a hand over his twisted body. 'They gave me
all this.'

'Huh. We have both lost something to the Gurkish, then.'
She slid down onto crossed legs. 'Questions. Like for like. But
if you try to lie to me—'

'Questions, then. I would be failing in my duties as a host if
I did not allow you to go first.'

She did not smile. *But then she does not seem the joking type.*
'Why are you watching me?'

I could lie, but for what? I might as well die telling the truth. 'I
am watching Bayaz. The two of you seem friendly, and Bayaz is
hard to watch these days. So I am watching you.'

She scowled. 'He is no friend of mine. He promised me
vengeance, that is all. He has yet to deliver.'

'Life is full of disappointments.'

'Life is made of disappointments. Ask your question,
cripple.'

*Once she has her answers, will it be bath-time again, and this
time my last?* Her flat yellow eyes gave nothing away. Empty,
like the eyes of an animal. *But what are my choices?* He licked
the blood from his lips, and leaned back against the wall. *I
might as well die a little wiser.* 'What is the Seed?'

Her frown deepened by the smallest fraction. 'Bayaz said it is
a weapon. A weapon of very great power. Great enough to turn

Shaffa to dust. He thought it was hidden, at the edge of the World, but he was wrong. He was not happy to be wrong.' She frowned at him for a silent moment. 'Why are you watching Bayaz?'

'Because he stole the crown and put it on a spineless worm.'

She snorted. 'There at least we can agree.'

'There are those in my government who worry about the direction in which he might take us. Who worry profoundly.' Glokta licked at one bloody tooth. 'Where is he taking us?'

'He tells me nothing. I do not trust him, and he does not trust me.'

'There too we can agree.'

'He planned to use the Seed as a weapon. He did not find it, so he must find other weapons. My guess is he is taking you to war. A war against Khalul, and his Eaters.'

Glokta felt a flurry of twitches run up the side of his face and set his eyelid fluttering. *Damn treacherous jelly!* Her head jerked to the side. 'You know of them?'

'A passing acquaintance.' *Well, where's the harm?* 'I caught one, in Dagoska. I asked it questions.'

'What did it tell you?'

'It talked of righteousness and justice.' *Two things that I have never seen.* 'It talked of war and sacrifice.' *Two things that I have seen too much of.* 'It said that your friend Bayaz killed his own master.' The woman did not move so much as an eyelash. 'It said that its father, the Prophet Khalul, still seeks vengeance.'

'Vengeance,' she hissed, her hands bunching into fists. 'I will show them vengeance!'

'What did they do to you?'

'They killed my people.' She uncrossed her legs. 'They made me a slave.' She rose smoothly to her feet, looming over him. 'They stole my life from me.'

Glokta felt the corner of his mouth twitch up. 'One more thing we have in common.' *And I sense my borrowed time is up.*

She reached down and grabbed two fistfuls of his wet coat. She dragged him from the floor with fearsome strength, his back sliding up the wall. *Body found floating in the bath . . . ?* He felt his nostrils opening wide, the air hissing fast in his bloody nose, his heart thumping in anticipation. *No doubt my ruined body will struggle, as best it can. An irresistible reaction to the lack of air. The unconquerable instinct to breathe. No doubt I will thrash and wriggle, just as Tulkis, the Gurkish ambassador, thrashed and wriggled when they hanged him, and dragged his guts out for nothing.*

He did his twisted best to stay up under his own power, to stand as close to straight as he could manage. *After all, I was a proud man once, even if that is all far behind me. Hardly the end that Colonel Glokta would have hoped for. Drowned in the bath by a woman in a dirty shirt. Will they find me slumped over the rim, my arse in the air? But what does it matter? It is not how you die, but how you lived, that counts.*

She let go of his coat, flattened the front with a slap of her hand. *And what has my life been, these past years? What do I have that I might truly miss? Stairs? Soup? Pain? Lying in the darkness with the memories of the things I have done digging at me? Waking in the morning to the stink of my own shit? Will I miss tea with Ardee West? A little perhaps. But will I miss tea with the Arch Lector? It almost makes you wonder why I didn't do it myself, years ago.* He stared into his killer's eyes, as hard and bright as yellow glass, and he smiled. A smile of the purest relief. 'I am ready.'

'For what?' She pressed something into his limp hand. The handle of his cane. 'If you have more business with Bayaz, leave me out of it. I will not be so gentle next time.' She backed slowly towards the doorway, a bright rectangle against the shadowy wall. She turned, and the sound of her boots receded down the corridor. Aside from the soft tip-tap of water dripping from his wet coat, all fell silent.

And so, it seems, I survive. Again. Glokta raised his eyebrows. *Perhaps the trick is not wanting to.*

The Fourth Day

He was an ugly bastard, this Easterner. A huge big one, dressed all in stinking, half-tanned furs and a bit of rusted chain-mail, more ornament than protection. Greasy black hair, bound up here and there with rough-forged silver rings, dripped with the thin rain. He had a great scar down one cheek and another across his forehead, and the countless nicks and pittings of lesser wounds and boils as a lad, nose flattened and bent sideways like a dented spoon. His eyes were screwed up tight with effort, his yellow teeth were bared, the front two missing, his grey tongue pressed into the gap. A face that had seen war all its days. A face that had lived by sword, and axe, and spear, and counted every day alive a bonus.

For Logen, it was almost like looking in a mirror.

They held each other as tight as a pair of bad lovers, blind to everything around them. They lumbered back and forward, lurching like feuding drunkards. They plucked and tugged, bit and gouged, gripped and tore, strained in frozen fury, blasting sour breath in each other's faces. An ugly, and a wearying, and a fatal dance, and all the while the rain came down.

Logen took a painful dig in the gut and had to twist and wriggle to smother a second. He gave a half-hearted head-butt and did nothing more then scuff Ugly's face with his forehead. He nearly got tripped, stumbled, felt the Easterner shift his weight, trying to find a set to throw him. Logen managed to dig him in the fruits with his thigh before he could do it, enough to make his arms go weak for a moment, enough so he could slide his hand up onto Ugly's neck.

Logen forced that hand up, inch by painful inch, his stretched-out forefinger creeping over the Easterner's pitted face while he peered down at it, cross-eyed, trying to tip his head out of the way. His hand gripped painful tight round Logen's wrist, trying to haul it back, but Logen had his shoulder dipped, his weight set right. The finger edged past his grimacing mouth, over his top lip, into Ugly's bent nose, and Logen felt his broken nail digging at the flesh inside. He crooked his finger, and bared his teeth, and twisted it about as best he could.

The Easterner hissed and thrashed around, but he was hooked. He'd no choice but to grab at Logen's wrist with his other hand and try to drag that tearing finger out of his face. But that left Logen one hand free.

He snatched a knife out and grunted as he stabbed, his arm jerking in and out. Quick punches, but with steel on the end of them. The blade squelched in the Easterner's gut, and his thigh, and his arm, and his chest, blood coming out in long streaks, splattering them both and trickling into the puddles under their boots. Once he was stabbed enough Logen caught him by his coat, hauled him into the air with a jaw-clenched effort, and roared as he flung him over the battlements. He plummeted away, limp as a carcass and soon to be one, crashed to the ground in among his fellows.

Logen bent over the parapet, gasping at the wet air, the rain drops flitting down away from him. There were hundreds of them, it seemed like, milling around in the sea of mud at the base of the wall. Wild men, from out past the Crinna, where they hardly spoke right and cared nothing for the dead. They all were rain-soaked and filth-spattered, hiding under rough-made shields and waving rough-forged weapons, barbed and brutal. Their standards stood flapping in the rain behind them, bones and ragged hides, ghostly shadows in the downpour.

Some were carrying rickety ladders forwards, or lifting those that had been thrown down, trying to foot them near the wall and haul them up while rocks and spears and sodden arrows flapped and splattered into the mud. Others were climbing, shields held over their heads, two ladders up at Dow's side, one on Red Hat's side, one just to Logen's left. A pair of big savages were swinging great axes against the scarred gates, chopping wet splinters out with every blow. Logen pointed at them, screamed uselessly into the wet. No one heard him, or could have over the great noise of drumming rain, of crashing, thudding, scraping, blades on shields, shafts in flesh, battle cries and shrieks of pain.

He fumbled his sword up from the puddles on the walkway, dull metal glistening with beads of water. Just near him one of Shivers' Carls was facing off against an Easterner who'd scrambled from the top of a ladder. They traded a couple of blows, axe against shield then sword swishing at the empty air. The Easterner's axe-arm went up again and Logen hacked it off at the elbow, stumbled into his back and knocked him screaming on his face. The Carl finished him with a chop to the back of the skull, pointed his bloody sword over Logen's shoulder.

'There!'

Another Easterner with a big hook nose just getting to the top of the ladder, leaning forward over the battlements, right arm going back with a spear ready. Logen bellowed as he came for him.

His eyes went wide and the spear wobbled, too late to throw. He tried to swing out of the way, clinging to the wet wood with his free hand, but only managed to drag the ladder grating across the battlements. Logen's sword stabbed him under the arm and he flailed back with a grunt, dropping his spear behind him. Logen stabbed at him again, slipped and lunged too far, near falling into his arms. Big-Nose clawed at him, trying to bundle him over the parapet. Logen smashed him in the face with the pommel of his sword and knocked his head back, took some teeth out with a second blow. The third one knocked him senseless and he fell back off the ladder, plummeting down and taking one of his friends into the mud with him.

'Bring that pole!' Logen roared at the Carl with the sword.

'What?'

'Pole, you fucker!'

The Carl snatched the wet length of wood up and threw it through the rain. Logen dropped his sword and wedged the branched end against one upright of the ladder, started pushing for all he was worth. The Carl came and added his weight to it, and the ladder creaked, wobbled, and started tipping back. An Easterner's face came up over the battlements, surprised-looking. He saw the pole. He saw Logen and the Carl growling at it. He tumbled off as the ladder dropped away, down on the heads of the bastards below.

Further along the wall another ladder had just been pushed back up and the Easterners were starting to climb it, shields up over their heads while Red Hat and his boys chucked rocks at them. Some had got to the top over on Dow's bit of the wall, and he could hear the shouting from there, the sounds of murder. Logen gnawed at his bloody lip, wondering whether to push on down there and give them some help, but he decided against. He'd be needed here before long.

So he took up the Maker's sword, and he nodded to the Carl who'd helped him, and he stood and caught his breath. He waited for the Easterners to come again, and all around him men fought, and killed, and died.

Devils, in a cold, wet, bloody hell. Four days of it, now, and it felt as if he'd been there forever. As if he'd never left. Perhaps he never had.

Like the Dogman's life weren't difficult enough already, there had to be rain.

Wet was an archer's worst fear, alright. Apart from being ridden down by horsemen, maybe, but that weren't so likely up a tower. The bows were slippery, the strings were stretchy, the feathers were sodden, which all made for some ineffective shooting. Rain was costing them their advantage, and that was a worry, but it could cost them more than that before the day was out. There were three big wild bastards working at the gates, two swinging heavy axes at the softened wood, the third trying to get a pry-bar in the gaps they'd made and tear the timbers apart.

'If we don't deal with them, they'll have those gates in!' Dogman shouted hoarse into the wet air.

'Uh,' said Grim, nodding his head, water flicking off his shaggy thatch of hair.

Took a good bit of bellowing and pointing from him and Tul, but Dogman got a crowd of his lads lined up by the slick parapet. Three score wet bows, all lowered at once, all drawn back creaking, all pointing down towards that gate. Three score men, frowning and taking aim, all dripping with water and getting wetter every minute.

'Alright then, loose!'

The bows went more or less together, the sounds muffled. The shafts spun down, bouncing off the wet wall, sticking in the rough wood of the gate, prickling the ground all round where the ditch used to be, before it became just another load of mud. Not what you'd call accurate, but there were a lot of shafts, and if you can't get quality, then numbers will have to do the job for you. The Easterner on the right dropped his axe, three arrows sticking out his chest, one through his leg. The one on the left slipped and fell on his side, went floundering for cover, an arrow in his shoulder. The one with the bar went down on his knees, thrashing around and grabbing behind him, trying to get at a shaft in the small of his back.

'Alright! Good!' the Dogman shouted. None of the rest of 'em seemed keen to try the gate for the moment, which was something to be grateful for. There were still plenty trying the ladders, but that was a harder task to deal with from up here. They might just as easily shoot their own boys on the walls as the enemy in this weather. Dogman gritted his teeth, and loosed a harmless, looping wet arrow down into the milling crowd. Nothing they could do. The walls was Shivers' job, and Dow's, and Red Hat's. The walls was Logen's job.

There was a crack, loud as the sky falling. The world went reeling bright, and soupy slow, sounds all echoing. Logen stumbled through this dream-place, the sword clattering out of his stupid fingers, lurched against the wall and grappled with it as it swayed around, trying to understand what had happened and not getting there.

Two men were struggling with each other over a spear, wrestling and jerking round and round, and Logen couldn't remember why. A man with long hair took a great slow blow with a club on his shield, a couple of splinters spinning, then he swept an axe round, teeth bared and shining, caught a wild-looking man in the legs and tore him off his feet. There were men everywhere, wet and furious, dirt and blood stained. A battle, maybe? Which side was he on?

Logen felt something warm tickling his eye, and he touched his hand to it. Frowned down at his red finger tips, turning pink as the rain pattered on them. Blood. Had someone hit him on the head, then? Or was he dreaming it? A memory, from long ago.

He spun round just before the club came down and crushed his skull like an egg, caught some hairy bastard's wrists with both hands. The world was suddenly fast, noisy, pain pulsing in his head. He lurched against the parapet, staring into a dirty, bearded, angry face, pressed up tight against his.

Logen let go the club with one hand, started snatching at his belt for a knife. He couldn't feel one. All that time spent sharpening all those blades, and now he needed one there was nothing to hand. Then he realised. The blade he was looking for was stuck in that ugly bastard, down in the mud somewhere at the base of the wall. He scrabbled round the other side of his belt, still wrestling at the club, but losing that battle now, given that he only had the one hand to work with. Logen got bent back, slowly, over the battlements. His fingers found the grip of a knife. The hairy Easterner tore his club free and lifted it up, opening his mouth wide and giving a stinking yell.

Logen stabbed him right through the face, and the blade went through one cheek and out the other and took a couple of teeth with it. Hairy's bellow turned to a high-pitched howl and he dropped his club and stumbled away, eyes bulging. Logen slid down and snatched his sword from under the trampling feet of the two fighting over the spear, waited a moment for the Easterner to come round close to him, then chopped through

269

the back of one thigh and brought him down with a scream where the Carl could see to him.

Hairy was still drooling blood, one hand on the grip of the knife through his face, trying to work it free. Logen's sword made a red gash through the wet furs on his side, brought him to his knees. The next swing split his head in half.

Not ten strides away Shivers was in bad trouble, backed up with three Easterners at him, another just getting to the top of a ladder, and all his boys kept busy behind. He winced as he took a hard blow from a hammer across his shield, stumbled back, his axe dropping from his hand and clattering on the stone. The thought did pass through Logen's mind that he'd be a deal better off if Shivers got his head flattened. But the odds were good that he'd be next.

So he took a great breath, and bellowed as he charged.

The first one turned just in time to get his face hacked open rather than the back of his skull. The second got his shield up, but Logen went low and chopped clean through his shin instead, sent him shrieking down on to his back, blood pumping out into the pools of water across the walkway. The third one was a big bastard, wild red hair sticking all ways off his head. He had Shivers stunned and on his knees by the parapet, his shield hanging down, blood running from a cut on his forehead. Red Hair raised a big hammer up to finish the job. Logen stabbed him through the back before he got the chance, the long blade sliding through him right to the hilt. Never take a man face to face if you can kill him from behind, Logen's father used to say, and that was one good piece of advice he'd always tried to follow. Red Hair thrashed and squealed, twisting madly with his last breaths, dragging Logen around after him by the hilt of his sword, but it wasn't long before he dropped.

Logen grabbed Shivers under the arm and hauled him up. He frowned hard as his eyes came back into focus, saw who was helping him. He leaned down and snatched his fallen axe up from the stones. Logen wondered for a moment if he was about to get it buried in his skull, but Shivers only stood there, blood running down his wet face from the cut across his head.

'Behind you,' said Logen, nodding past his shoulder. Shivers turned, Logen did the same, and they stood with their backs to each other. There were three or four ladders up now, around the gate, and the battle on the walls had broken up into a few separate, bloody little fights. There were Easterners clambering over the parapet, screaming their meaningless jabber, hard faces and hard weapons glistening wet, coming at Logen along the wall while more dragged themselves up. Behind him he heard the clash and grunt of Shivers fighting, but he paid it no mind. He could only deal with what was in front of him. You have to be realistic about these things.

He shuffled back, showing weariness that was only half-feigned, then as the first of them came on he gritted his teeth and leaped forward, cut him across the face and sent him screaming, hand clasped to his eyes. Logen stumbled into another and got barged in the chest with a shield, its rim catching him under the chin and making him bite his tongue.

Logen nearly tripped over the sprawled-out corpse of a dead Carl, righted himself just in time, flailed with his sword and hit nothing, reeled after it and felt something cut into his leg as he went. He gasped, and hopped, waving the sword around, all off-balance. He lunged at some moving fur, his leg gave under him and he piled into someone. They fell together and Logen's head cracked against the stone. They rolled and Logen struggled up on top, shouting and drooling, tangled his fingers in an Easterner's greasy hair and smashed his face into the stone, again and again until his skull went soft. He dragged himself away, heard a blade clang against the walkway where he'd been, hauled himself up to his knees, sword loose in one sticky hand.

He knelt there, water running down his face, dragging in air. More of them coming at him, and nowhere to go. His leg was hurting, no strength in his arms. His head felt light, like it might float away. No strength left to fight with, hardly. More of them coming at him, one at the front with thick leather gloves, a big maul in his hands, its heavy spiked head red with blood. Looked like he'd already broken one skull with it, and Logen's would be next. Then Bethod would've won, at last.

Logen felt a cold feeling stab at his gut. A hard, empty feeling. His knuckles clicked as the muscles in his hand went rigid, gripping the sword painful tight. 'No!' he hissed. 'No, no, no.' But he might as well have said no to the rain. That cold feeling spread out, up through Logen's face, tugging his mouth into a bloody smile. Gloves came closer, his maul scraping against the wet stone. He glanced over his shoulder.

His head came apart, spraying out blood. Crummock-i-Phail roared like an angry bear, fingerbones flying round his neck, his great hammer whirling round and round his head in huge circles. The next Easterner tried to back away, holding up his shield. Crummock's hammer swung two-handed, ripped his legs out from under him, sent him tumbling over and over and onto his face on the stone. The big hillman sprang up onto the walkway, nimble as a dancer for all his great bulk, caught the next man a blow in the stomach that hurled him through the air and left him crumpled against the battlements.

Logen watched one set of savages murdering another, breathing hard as Crummock's boys whooped and screamed, paint on their faces smeared in the rain. They flooded up onto the wall, hacking at the Easterners with their rough swords and their bright axes, driving them back and shoving their ladders away, flinging their bodies over the parapet and into the mud below.

He knelt there, in a puddle, leaning on the cold grip of Kanedias' sword, its point dug into the stone walkway. He bent over and breathed hard, his cold gut sucking in and out, his raw mouth salty, his nose full of the stink of blood. He hardly dared to look up. He clenched his teeth, and closed his eyes, and hawked sour spit up onto the stones. He forced that cold feeling in his stomach down and it slunk away, for now, at least, and left him with only pain and weariness to worry about.

'Looks like those bastards had enough,' came Crummock's laughing voice from out of the drizzle. The hillman tipped his head back, mouth open, stuck his tongue out into the rain, then licked his lips. 'That was some good work you put in today, Bloody-Nine. Not that it ain't my special pleasure to watch you at it, but I'm glad to get my share.' He hefted his great long hammer up in one hand and spun it round as if it was a willow switch, peering at a great bloody stain on the head with a clump of hair stuck to it, then grinning wide.

Logen looked up at him, hardly enough strength left to lift his head. 'Oh aye. Good work. We'll go at the back tomorrow though, eh, since you're that keen? You can take the fucking wall.'

The rain was slacking, down to a thin spit and drizzle. A glimmer of fading sunlight broke through the sagging clouds, bringing Bethod's camp back into view, his muddy ditch and his standards, tents scattered across the valley. Dogman squinted, thought he could see a few men stood around the front watching the Easterners run back, a glint of sunlight on something. An eye-glass maybe, like the Union used, usually to look the wrong way. Dogman wondered if it was Bethod down there, watching it all happen. It would be just like Bethod to have got himself an eye-glass.

He felt a big hand clap him on the shoulder. 'We gave 'em a slap, chief,' rumbled Tul, 'and a good 'un!'

There was small doubt o' that. There were a lot of dead Easterners scattered in the mud round the base of that wall, a lot of wounded carried by their mates, or dragging themselves slow and painful back towards their lines. But there were a fair few killed on their side of the wall as well. Dogman could see a stack of muddy corpses over near the back of the fortress where they were doing the burying. He could hear someone screaming. Hard and nasty screams, the kind a man makes when he needs a limb taken off, or he's had one off already.

'We gave 'em a slap, aye,' Dogman muttered, 'but they gave us one as well. I'm not sure how many slaps we'll stand.' The barrels that carried their arrows were no more'n half full now, the rocks close to run out. 'Best send some boys to pick over

273

the dead!' he shouted to the men over his shoulder. 'Get what we can while we can!'

'Can't have too many arrows at a time like this,' said Tul. 'Number o' those Crinna bastards we killed today, I reckon we'll have more spears tonight than we had this morning.'

Dogman managed to put a grin on his face. 'Nice of 'em to bring us something to fight with.'

'Aye. Reckon they'd get bored right quick if we ran out of arrows.' Tul laughed, and he clapped the Dogman on the back harder than ever, hard enough to make his teeth rattle. 'We did well! You did well! We're still alive, ain't we?'

'Some of us are.' Dogman looked down at the corpse of the one man who'd died up on the tower. An old boy, hair mostly grey, a rough-made arrow in his neck. Bad luck, that had been, to catch a shaft on a day as wet as today, but you're sure to get a measure of luck in a fight, both good and bad. He frowned down into the darkening valley. 'Where the hell are the Union at?'

At least the rain had stopped. You have to be grateful for the small things in life, like some smoky kind of a fire after the wet. You have to be grateful for the small things, when any minute might be your last.

Logen sat alone beside his scrub of a flame, and rubbed gently at his right palm. It was sore, pink, stiff from gripping the rough hilt of the Maker's sword all the long day, blistered round the joints of his fingers. His head was bruised all over. The cut on his leg was burning some, but he could still walk well enough. He could've ended up a lot worse. There were more than three score buried now, and they were putting them in pits for a dozen each, just as Crummock had said they would. Three score and more gone back to the mud, and twice that many hurt, a lot of them bad.

Over by the big fire, he could hear Dow growling about how he'd stabbed some Easterner in the fruits. He could hear Tul's rumbling laughter. Logen hardly felt like a part of it, any more. Maybe he never had been. A set of men he'd fought and beaten. Lives he'd spared, for no reason that made sense. Men who'd hated him worse than death, but been bound to follow. Hardly more his friends than Shivers was. Perhaps the Dogman was his only true friend in all the wide Circle of the World, and even in his eyes, from time to time, Logen thought he could see that old trace of doubt, that old trace of fear. He wondered if he could see it now, as the Dogman came up out of the darkness.

'You think they'll come tonight?' he asked.

'He'll give it a go in the dark sooner or later,' said Logen, 'but my guess is he'll leave it 'til we're a bit more worn down.'

'You get more worn down than this?'

'I guess we'll find out.' Logen grimaced as he stretched out his aching legs. 'It really seems like this shit used to be easier.'

Dogman gave a snort. Not a laugh, really. More just letting Logen know he'd heard. 'Memory can work some magic. You remember Carleon?'

'Course I do.' Logen looked down at his missing finger, and he bunched his fist, so it looked the same as it always had. 'Strange, how it all seemed so simple back in them days. Who you fought for, and why. Can't say it ever bothered me.'

'It bothered me,' said Dogman.

'It did? You should've said something.'

'Would you have listened?'

'No. I guess not.'

They sat there for a minute, in silence.

'You reckon we'll live through this?' asked the Dogman.

'Maybe. If the Union turns up tomorrow, or the day after.'

'You think they will?'

'Maybe. We can hope.'

'Hoping for a thing don't make it happen.'

'The opposite, usually. But every day we're still alive is a chance. Maybe this time it'll work.'

Dogman frowned at the shifting flames. 'That's a lot of maybes.'

'That's war.'

275

'Who'd have thought we'd be relying on a bunch of South-erners to solve our problems for us, eh?'

'I reckon you solve 'em any way you can. You have to be realistic.'

'Being realistic, then. You reckon we'll live through this?'

Logen thought about it for a while. 'Maybe.'

Boots squelched in the soft earth, and Shivers walked up quiet towards the fire. There was a grey bandage wrapped round his head, where he'd taken that cut, and his hair hung down damp and greasy from under it.

'Chief,' he said.

Dogman smiled as he got up, and clapped him on the shoulder. 'Alright, Shivers. That was good work, today. I'm glad you came over, lad. We all are.' He gave Logen a long look. 'All of us. Think I might try and get a rest for a minute. I'll see you boys when they come again. Most likely it'll be soon enough.' He walked off into the night, and left Shivers and Logen staring one at the other.

Probably Logen should have got his hand near to a knife, watched for sudden moves and all the rest. But he was too tired and too sore for it. So he just sat there, and watched. Shivers pressed his lips together, squatting down beside the fire oppos-ite, slow and reluctant, as if he was about to eat something he knew was rotten, but had no choice.

'If I'd have been in your place,' he said, after a while, 'I would've let those bastards kill me today.'

'Few years ago I'm sure I would've.'

'What changed?'

Logen frowned as he thought about it. Then he shrugged his aching shoulders. 'I'm trying to be better than I was.'

'You think that's enough?'

'What else can I do?'

Shivers frowned at the fire. 'I wanted to say . . .' He worked the words around in his mouth and spat them out. 'That I'm grateful, I guess. You saved my life today. I know it.' He wasn't happy about saying it, and Logen knew why. It's hard to be done a favour by a man you hate. It's hard to hate him so much afterwards. Losing an enemy can be worse than losing a friend, if you've had him for long enough.

So Logen shrugged again. 'It's nothing. What a man should do for his crew, that's all. I owe you a lot more. I know that. I can never pay what I owe you.'

'No. But it's some kind o' start at it, far as I'm concerned.' Shivers got up and took a step away. Then he stopped, and turned back, firelight shifting over one side of his hard, angry face. 'It ain't ever as simple, is it, as a man is just good or bad? Not even you. Not even Bethod. Not anybody.'

'No.' Logen sat and watched the flames moving. 'No, it ain't ever that simple. We all got our reasons. Good men and bad men. It's all a matter of where you stand.'

The Perfect Couple

One of Jezal's countless footmen perched on the stepladder, and lowered the crown with frowning precision onto his head, its single enormous diamond flashing pricelessly bright. He gave it the very slightest twist back and forth, the fur-trimmed rim gripping Jezal's skull. He climbed back down, whisked the stepladder away, and surveyed the result. So did half a dozen of his fellows. One of them stepped forward to tweak the precise positioning of Jezal's gold-embroidered sleeve. Another grimaced as he flicked an infinitesimal speck of dust from his pure white collar.

'Very good,' said Bayaz, nodding thoughtfully to himself. 'I believe that you are ready for your wedding.'

The peculiar thing, now that Jezal had a rare moment to think about it, was that he had not, in any way of which he was aware, agreed to get married. He had neither proposed nor accepted a proposal. He had never actually said 'yes' to anything. And yet here he was, preparing to be joined in matrimony in a few short hours, and to a woman he scarcely knew at all. It had not escaped his notice that in order to have been managed so quickly the arrangements must have been well underway before Bayaz had even suggested the notion. Perhaps before Jezal had even been crowned . . . but he supposed it was not so very surprising. Since his enthronement he had drifted helplessly through one incomprehensible event after another, like a man shipwrecked and struggling to keep his head above water, out of sight of land, dragged who knew where by unseen, irresistible currents. But considerably better dressed.

He was gradually starting to realise that the more powerful a man became, the fewer choices he really had. Captain Jezal dan Luthar had been able to eat what he liked, to sleep when he

278

liked, to see who he liked. His August Majesty King Jezal the First, on the other hand, was bound by invisible chains of tradition, expectation, and responsibility, that prescribed every aspect of his existence, however small.

Bayaz took a discerning step forward. 'Perhaps the top button undone here—'

Jezal jerked away with some annoyance. The attention of the Magus to every tiny detail of his life was becoming more than tiresome. It seemed that he could scarcely use the latrine without the old bastard poking through the results. 'I know how to button a coat!' he snapped. 'Should I expect to find you here tonight when I bring my new wife to our bed-chamber, ready to instruct me on how best to use my prick?'

The footmen coughed, and averted their eyes, and scraped away towards the corners of the room. Bayaz himself neither smiled nor frowned. 'I stand always ready to advise your Majesty, but I had hoped that might be one item of business you could manage alone.'

'I hope you're well prepared for our little outing. I've been getting ready all morn—' Ardee froze when she looked up and saw Glokta's face. 'What happened to you?'

'What, this?' He waved his hand at the mottled mass of bruises. 'A Kantic woman broke into my apartments in the night, punched me repeatedly and near drowned me in the bath.' *An experience I would not recommend.*

Evidently she did not believe him. 'What really happened?'

'I fell down the stairs.'

'Ah. Stairs. They can be brutal bastards when you're not that firm on your feet.' She stared at her half-full glass, her eyes slightly misty.

'Are you drunk?'

'It's the afternoon, isn't it? I try always to be drunk by now. Once you start a job you should give it your best. Or so my father liked to tell me.'

Glokta narrowed his eyes at her, and she stared back evenly over the rim of her glass. *No trembling lip, no tragic face, no streaks of bitter tears down the cheek.* She seemed no less happy than usual. *Or no more unhappy, perhaps. But Jezal dan Luthar's wedding day can be no joyous occasion for her. No one appreciates being jilted, whatever the circumstances. No one enjoys being abandoned.*

'We need not go, you know.' Glokta winced as he tried unsuccessfully to stretch some movement into his wasted leg, and the wince itself caused a ripple of pain through his split lips and across his battered face. 'I certainly won't complain if I do not have to walk another step today. We can sit here, and talk of rubbish and politics.'

'And miss the king's marriage?' gasped Ardee, one hand pressed to her chest in fake horror. 'But I really must see what the Princess Terez is wearing! They say she is the most beautiful woman in the world, and even scum like me must have someone to look up to.' She tipped back her head and swilled down the last of her wine. 'Having fucked the groom is really no excuse for missing a wedding, you know.'

The flagship of Grand Duke Orso of Talins ploughed slowly, deliberately, majestically forwards, under no more than quarter sail, a host of seabirds flapping and calling in the rich blue sky above. It was by far the largest ship that Jezal, or anyone among the vast crowds that lined the quay and crammed the roofs and windows of the buildings along the waterfront, had ever laid eyes upon.

It was decked out in its finest: coloured bunting fluttered from the rigging and its three towering masts were hung with bright flags, the sable cross of Talins and the golden sun of the Union, side by side in honour of the happy occasion. But it looked no less menacing for that. It looked as Logen Nine-fingers might have in a dandy's jacket. Unmistakably still a man of war, and appearing more savage rather than less for the gaudy finery in which it was plainly uncomfortable. As the means of bringing a single woman to Adua, and that woman Jezal's bride-to-be, this mighty vessel was anything but reassuring. It implied that Grand Duke Orso might be an intimidating presence as a father-in-law.

Jezal saw sailors now, crawling among the myriad ropes like ants through a bush, bringing the acres of sailcloth in with well-practised speed. They let the mighty ship plough forward under its own momentum, its vast shadow falling over the quay and plunging half the welcoming party into darkness. It slowed, the air full of the creaking of timbers and hawsers. It came to a deliberate stop, dwarfing the now tiny-seeming boats meekly tethered to either side as a tiger might dwarf kittens. The golden figurehead, a woman twice life-size thrusting a spear towards the heavens, glittered menacingly far over Jezal's head.

A huge wharf had been specially constructed in the middle of the quay where the draught was at its deepest. Down this gently sloping ramp the royal party of Talins descended into Adua, like visitors from a distant star where everyone was rich, beautiful, and obliviously happy.

To either side marched a row of bearded guardsmen, all dressed in identical black uniforms, their helmets polished to a painful pitch of mirror brightness. Between them, in two rows of six, came a dozen ladies-in-waiting, each one arrayed in red, or blue, or vivid purple silks, each one as splendid as a queen herself.

But not one of the awestruck multitude on the waterfront could have been in any doubt who was the centre of attention. The Princess Terez glided along at the fore: tall, slender, impossibly regal, as graceful as a circus dancer and as stately as an Empress of legend. Her pure white gown was stitched with glittering gold, her shimmering hair was the colour of polished bronze, a chain of daunting diamonds flashed and sparkled on her pale chest in the bright sunlight. The Jewel of Talins seemed at that moment an apt name indeed. Terez looked as pure and dazzling, as proud and brilliant, as hard and beautiful as a flawless gemstone.

As her feet touched the stones the crowds burst out into a tumultuous cheer, and flower petals began to fall in well-orchestrated cascades from the windows of the buildings high above. So it was that she advanced on Jezal with magnificent dignity, her head held imperiously high, her hands clasped proudly before her, over a soft carpet and through a sweet-smelling haze of fluttering pink and red.

To call it a breathtaking entrance would have been under-statement of an epic order.

'Your August Majesty,' she murmured, somehow managing to make him feel like the humble one as she curtsied, and behind her the ladies followed suit, and the guardsmen bowed low, all with impeccable co-ordination. 'My father, the Grand Duke Orso of Talins, sends his profound apologies,' and she rose up perfectly erect again as though hoisted by invisible strings, 'but urgent business in Styria prevents him from attending our wedding.'

'You are all we need,' croaked Jezal, cursing silently a moment later as he realised he had completely ignored the proper form of address. It was somewhat difficult to think clearly, under the circumstances. Terez was even more breathtaking now than when he had last seen her, a year or more ago, arguing savagely with Prince Ladisla at the feast held in his honour. The memory of her vicious shrieking did little to encourage him, but then Jezal would hardly have been de-lighted by the prospect of marrying Ladisla himself. After all, the man had been a complete ass. Jezal was an entirely different sort of person and could no doubt expect a different response. So he hoped.

'Please, your Highness,' and he held out his hand to her. She rested hers on it, seeming to weigh less than a feather.

'Your Majesty does me too much honour.'

The hooves of the grey horses crackled on the paving, the carriage-wheels whirred smoothly. They set off up the Kings-way, a company of Knights of the Body riding in tight forma-tion around them, arms and armour glinting, each stride of the great thoroughfare lined with appreciative commoners, each door and window filled with smiling subjects. All there to cheer for their new king, and for the woman soon to be their queen.

Jezal knew he must look an utter idiot next to her. A clumsy, low-born, ill-mannered oaf, who had not the slightest right to share her carriage, unless, perhaps, she was using him as a foot-rest. He had never in his life felt truly inferior before. He could scarcely believe that he was marrying this woman. Today. His hands were shaking. Positively shaking. Perhaps some heartfelt words might help them both relax.

'Terez . . .' She continued to wave imperiously to the crowds. 'I realise . . . that we do not know each other in the least, but . . . I would like to know you.' The slightest twitch of her mouth was the only sign that she had heard him. 'I know that this must have come as a terrible shock to you, just as it has to me. I hope, if there is anything I can do . . . to make it easier, that—'

'My father feels the interests of my country are best served by this marriage, and it is a daughter's place to obey. Those of us born to high station are long prepared to make sacrifices.'

Her perfect head turned smoothly on her perfect neck, and she smiled. A smile slightly forced, perhaps, but no less radiant for that. It was hard to believe that a face so smooth and flawless could be made of meat, like everybody else's. It seemed like porcelain, or polished stone. It was a constant, magical delight to see it move. He wondered if her lips were cool or warm. He would have liked very much to find out. She leaned close to him, and placed her hand gently on the back of his. Warm, undoubtedly warm, and soft, and very much made of flesh. 'You really should wave,' she murmured, her voice full of Styrian song.

'Er, yes,' he croaked, his mouth very dry, 'yes, of course.'

Glokta stood, Ardee beside him, and frowned at the doors of the Lords' Round. Beyond those towering gates, in the great circular hall, the ceremony was taking place. *Oh, joyous, joyous day!* High Justice Marovia's wise exhortations would be echoing from the gilded dome, the happy couple would be speaking their solemn vows with light hearts. Only the lucky few had been allowed within to bear witness. *The rest of us must worship from afar.* And quite a crowd had gathered to do just that. The wide Square of Marshals was choked with them. Glokta's ears were stuffed with their excited babbling. *A sycophantic throng, all eager for their divine Majesties to emerge.*

He rocked impatiently back and forth, from side to side, grimacing and hissing, trying to get the blood to flow in his aching legs, the cramps to be still. *But standing in one place for this length of time is, to put it simply, torture.*

'How long can a wedding take?'

Ardee raised one dark eyebrow. 'Perhaps they couldn't keep their hands off each other, and are busy consummating the marriage right there on the floor of the Lords' Round.'

'How bloody long can a consummation take?'

'Lean on me if you need to,' she said, holding out her elbow to him.

'The cripple using the drunk for support?' Glokta frowned. 'We make quite the couple.'

'Fall over if you prefer, and knock out the rest of your teeth. I'll lose no sleep over it.'

Perhaps I should take her up on the offer, if only for a moment. After all, where's the harm? But then the first shrill cheers began to float up, soon joined by more and more until a jubilant roar was making the air throb. The doors of the Lords' Round were finally being heaved open, and the High King and Queen of the Union emerged into the bright sunlight, hand in hand.

Even Glokta was forced to admit that they made a dazzling pair. Like monarchs of myth they stood arrayed in brilliant white, trimmed with twinkling embroidery, matching golden suns across the back of her long gown and his long coat, glittering as they turned to the crowds. Each tall, and slender, and graceful, each crowned with shining gold and a single flashing diamond. *Both so very young, and so very beautiful, and with all their happy, rich, and powerful lives ahead of them. Hurrah! Hurrah for them! My shrivelled turd of a heart bursts open with joy!*

Glokta rested his hand on Ardee's elbow, and he leaned towards her, and he smiled his most twisted, toothless, grotesque grin. 'Is it really true that our King is more handsome than I?'

'Offensive nonsense!' She thrust out her chest and tossed her head, giving Glokta a withering sneer down her nose. 'And I sparkle more brightly than the Jewel of Talins!'

'Oh, you do, my dear, you absolutely do. We make them look like beggars!'

'Like scum.'

'Like cripples.'

They chuckled together as the royal pair swept majestically across the square, accompanied by a score of watchful Knights of the Body. The Closed Council followed behind at a respectful distance, eleven stately old men with Bayaz among them in his arcane vestments, smiling almost as wide as the glorious couple themselves.

'I didn't even like him,' muttered Ardee under her breath, 'to begin with. Not really.' *That certainly makes two of us.*

'No need to weep. You're far too sharp to have been satisfied with a dullard like him.'

She breathed in sharply. 'I'm sure you're right. But I was so bored, and lonely, and tired.' *And drunk, no doubt.* She shrugged her shoulders hopelessly. 'He made me feel like I was something more than a burden. He made me feel . . . wanted.'

And what makes you suppose that I want to know about it? 'Wanted, you say? How wonderful. And now?'

She looked miserably down at the ground, and Glokta felt just the smallest trace of guilt. *But guilt only really hurts when there's nothing else to worry about.*

'It was hardly as if it was true love.' He saw the thin sinews in her neck moving as she swallowed. 'But somehow I always thought it would be me making a fool of him.'

'Huh.' *How rarely any of us get what we expect.*

The royal party processed gradually out of view, the last splendid courtiers and shining bodyguards tramping after them, the sound of rapturous applause creeping off towards the palace. *Towards their glorious futures, and we guilty secrets are by no means invited.*

'Here we stand,' murmured Ardee. 'The off-cuts.'

'The wretched leavings.'

'The rotten stalks.'

'I wouldn't worry over much.' Glokta gave a sigh. 'You are still young, clever, and passably pretty.'

'Epic praise indeed.'

'You have all your teeth and both your legs. A marked advantage over some of us. I do not doubt that you will soon find some other high-born idiot to entrap, and no harm done.'

She turned away from him, and hunched her shoulders, and he guessed that she was biting her lip. He winced, and lifted his hand to lay it on her shoulder . . . *The same hand that cut Sepp dan Teufel's fingers into slices, that pinched the nipples from Inquisitor Harker's chest, that carved one Gurkish emissary into pieces and burned another, that sent innocent men to rot in England, and so on, and so on . . .* He jerked it back, and let it fall. *Better to cry all the tears in the world than be touched by that hand. Comfort comes from other sources, and flows to other destinations.* He frowned out across the square, and left Ardee to her misery.

The crowd cheered on.

It was a magnificent event, of course. No effort or expense had been spared. Jezal would not have been at all surprised if he had five hundred guests, and no more than a dozen of them known to himself in any significant degree. The Lords and Ladies of the Union. The great men of Closed and Open Councils. The richest and the most powerful, dressed in their best and on their best behaviour.

The Chamber of Mirrors was a fitting venue. The most spectacular room in the entire palace, as big as a battlefield and made to seem larger yet by the great mirrors which covered every wall, creating the disconcerting impression of dozens of other magnificent weddings, in dozens of other adjoining ball-rooms. A multitude of candles flickered and waved on the tables, and in the sconces, and among the crystal chandeliers high above. Their soft light shone on the silverware, glittered on the jewels of the guests, and was reflected back from the dark walls, gleaming into the far, dim distance: a million points of light, like the stars in a dark night sky. A dozen of the Union's finest musicians played subtle and entrancing music, and it mingled with the swell of satisfied chatter, the clink and rattle of old money and new cutlery.

It was a joyous celebration. The evening of a lifetime. For the guests.

For Jezal it was something else, and he was not sure what. He sat at a gilded table with his queen beside him, the two of them outnumbered ten to one by fawning servants, displayed to the full view of the whole assembly as though they were a pair of prize exhibits in a zoo. Jezal sat in a haze of awkwardness, in a dreamlike silence, startling from time to time like a sick rabbit as a powdered footman blindsided him with vegetables. Terez sat on his right, occasionally spearing the slightest morsel with a discerning fork, lifting it, chewing it, swallowing it with elegant precision. Jezal had never thought that it was possible to eat beautifully. He now realised his mistake.

He could scarcely remember the ringing words of the High Justice that had, he supposed, bound the two of them irrevocably together. Something about love and the security of the nation, he vaguely recalled. But he could see the ring that he had handed numbly to Terez in the Lords' Round, its enormous blood-red stone glittering on her long middle finger. He chewed at a slice of the finest meat, and it tasted like mud in his mouth. They were man and wife.

He saw now that Bayaz had been right, as always. The people longed for something effortlessly higher than themselves. They might not all have had the king they would have asked for, but no one could possibly deny that Terez was all a queen should be and more. The mere idea of Ardee West sitting in that gilded chair was absurd. And yet Jezal felt a pang of guilt when the idea occurred, closely followed by a greater one of sadness. It would have been a comfort to have someone to talk to, then. He gave a painful sigh. If he was to spend his life with this woman, they would have to speak. The sooner they began, he supposed, the better.

'I hear that Talins . . . is a most beautiful city.'

'Indeed,' she said with careful formality, 'but Adua has its sights also.' She paused, and looked down unhopefully at her plate.

Jezal cleared his throat. 'This is somewhat . . . difficult to adjust to.' He ventured a fraction of a smile.

She blinked, and looked out at the room. 'It is.'

'Do you dance?'

She turned her head smoothly to look at him without the slightest apparent movement of her shoulders. 'A little.'

He pushed back his chair and stood up. 'Then shall we, your Majesty?'

'As you wish, your Majesty.'

As they made their way towards the middle of the wide floor, the chatter gradually diminished. The Chamber of Mirrors grew deathly quiet aside from the clicking of his polished boots, and her polished shoes, on the glistening stone. Jezal swallowed as they took their places, surrounded on three sides by the long tables, and the legions of magnificent guests, all watching. He had rather that same feeling of breathless anticipation, of fear and excitement, that he used to have when he stepped into the fencing circle against an unknown opponent, before the roaring crowd.

They stood still as statues, looking into each other's eyes. He held out his hand, palm up. She reached out, but instead of taking it she pressed the back of her hand firmly against the back of his and pushed it up so that their fingers were level. She lifted one eyebrow by the slightest margin. A silent challenge, that no one else in the hall could possibly have seen.

The first long drawn-out note sobbed from the strings and echoed around the chamber. They set off, circling each other with exaggerated slowness, the golden hem of Terez' dress swishing across the floor, her feet out of sight so that she appeared to glide rather than take steps, her chin held painfully high. They moved first one way and then the other, and in the mirrors around them a thousand other couples moved in time, stretching away into the shadowy distance, crowned and dressed in flawless white and gold.

As the second phrase began, and other instruments joined in, Jezal began to realise that he was utterly outclassed, worse than ever he had been by Bremer dan Gorst. Terez moved with such immaculate poise that he was sure she could have balanced a glass of wine on her head without spilling a drop. The music grew louder, faster, bolder, and Terez' movements came faster and bolder with it. It seemed as if she somehow controlled the musicians with her outstretched hands, the two were linked so perfectly. He tried to steer her and she stepped effortlessly around him. She feinted one way and whirled the other and Jezal almost went over on his arse. She dodged and spun with masterful disguise and left him lunging at nothing.

The music grew faster yet, the musicians sawed and plucked with furious concentration. Jezal made a vain attempt to catch her but Terez twisted away, dazzling him with a flurry of skirts that he could barely follow. She almost tripped him with a foot which was gone before he knew it, tossed her head and almost stabbed him in the eye with her crown. The great and good of the Union looked on in enchanted silence. Even Jezal found himself a dumbstruck spectator. It was the most he could do to remain in roughly the right positions to be made an utter fool of.

He was not sure whether he was relieved or disappointed when the music slowed again and she offered out her hand as though it were a rare treasure. He pressed the back of his against it and they circled each other, drawing closer and closer. As the last refrain wept from the instruments she pressed herself against him, her back to his chest. Slowly they turned, and slower still, his nose full of the smell of her hair. At the last long note she sank back and he lowered her gently, her neck stretching out, her head dropping, her delicate crown almost brushing the floor. And there was silence.

The room broke into rapturous applause, but Jezal hardly heard them. He was too busy staring at his wife. There was a faint colour to her cheek now, her lips slightly parted exposing flawless front teeth, and the lines of her jaw, and stretched-out neck, and slender collar-bones were etched with shadow and ringed with sparkling diamonds. Lower down her chest rose and fell imperiously in her bodice with her rapid breathing, the slightest, fascinating sheen of sweat nestling in her cleavage. Jezal would have very much liked to nestle there himself. He blinked, his own breath sharp in his throat.

'If it please your Majesty,' she murmured.

'Eh? Oh . . . of course.' He whisked her back to her feet as the applause continued. 'You dance . . . magnificently.'

'Your Majesty is too kind,' she replied, with the barest fragment of a smile, but a smile nonetheless. He beamed gormlessly back at her. His fear and confusion had, in the space of a single dance, smoothly transformed into a most pleasurable excitement. He had been gifted a glimpse beneath the icy shell, and plainly his new Queen was a woman of rare and fiery passion. A hidden side to her that he was now greatly looking forward to investigating further. Looking forward so sharply, in fact, that he was forced to avert his eyes and stare off into the corner, frowning and trying desperately to think of other things, lest the tightness of his trousers caused him to embarrass himself in front of the assembled guests.

The sight of Bayaz grinning in the corner was for once just what he needed to see, the old man's cold smile cooling his ardour as surely as a bucket of iced water.

Glokta had left Ardee in her over-furnished living room making every effort to get even more drunk, and ever since he had found himself in a black mood. *Even for me. There's nothing like the company of someone even more wretched than yourself to make you feel better. Trouble is, take their misery away and your own presses in twice as cold and dreary behind it.*

He slurped another half mouthful of gritty soup from his spoon, grimaced as he forced the over-salty slop down his throat. *I wonder how wonderful a time King Jezal is enjoying now? Lauded and admired by all, gorging himself on the best food and the best company.* He dropped the spoon into the bowl, his left eye twitching, and winced at a ripple of pain through his back and down into his leg. *Eight years since the Gurkish released me, yet I am still their prisoner, and always will be. Trapped in a cell no bigger than my own crippled body.*

The door creaked open and Barnam shuffled in to collect the bowl. Glokta looked from the half-dead soup to the half-dead old man. *The best food, and the best company.* He would have laughed if his split lips had allowed it.

'Finished, sir?' asked the servant.

'More than likely.' *I have been unable to pull the means of destroying Bayaz out of my arse, and so, of course, his Eminence will not be pleased. How displeased can he get, do we suppose, before he loses patience entirely? But what can be done?*

Barnam carried the bowl from the room, pulled the door shut behind him, and left Glokta alone with his pain. *What is it that I did to deserve this? And what is it that Luthar did? Is he not just as I was? Arrogant, vain, and selfish as hell? Is he a better man? Then why has life punished me so harshly, and rewarded him so richly?*

But Glokta already knew the answer. *The same reason that innocent Sepp dan Teufel languishes in Angland with his fingers shortened. The same reason that loyal General Vissbruck died in Dagoska, while treacherous Magister Eider was let live. The same reason that Tulkis, the Gurkish Ambassador, was butchered in front of a howling crowd for a crime he did not commit.*

He pressed his sore tongue into one of his few remaining teeth. *Life is not fair.*

Jezal pranced down the hallway in a dream, but no longer the panicked nightmare of the morning. His head was spinning from praise, and applause, and approval. His body was glowing with dancing, and wine, and, increasingly, lust. With Terez beside him, for the first time in his brief reign, he truly felt like a king. Gems and metal, silk and embroidery, and pale, smooth skin all shone excitingly in the soft candlelight. The evening had turned out to be a delight, and the night promised only to be better yet. Terez might have seemed as hard as a jewel from a distance, but Jezal had held her in his arms, and he knew better.

The great panelled doors of the royal bedchamber were held open by a pair of cringing footmen, then shut silently as the King and Queen of the Union swept past. The mighty bed dominated the far side of the room, sprays of tall feathers at the corners of its canopy casting long shadows up onto the gilded ceiling. Its rich green curtains hung invitingly wide, the silken space beyond filled with soft and tantalising shadows.

Terez took a few slow steps into the chamber ahead of him, her head bowed, while Jezal turned the key in the lock with a long, smooth rattling of wards. His breath came fast as he stepped up behind his wife, lifted his hand and placed it gently on her bare shoulder. He felt the muscles stiffen under her smooth skin, smiled at her nervousness, matching his own so closely. He wondered if he should say something to try and calm her, but what would have been the purpose? They both knew what had to happen now, and Jezal for one was impatient to begin.

He came closer, slipping his free hand around her waist, feeling his palm hiss over rough silk. He brushed the nape of her neck with his lips, once, twice, three times. He nuzzled against her hair, dragging in her fragrance and breathing it out softly against the side of her face. He felt her tremble at his breath upon her skin, but that only encouraged him. He slid his fingers over her shoulder and across her chest, her diamonds trailing over the back of his hand as he slipped it down into her bodice. He moved up closer yet, pressing himself against her, making a satisfied growl in his throat, his prick nudging pleasantly into her backside through their clothes—

In a moment she had torn away from him with a gasp, spun around and slapped him across the face with a smack that set his head ringing. 'You filthy bastard!' she shrieked in his face, spit flying from her twisted mouth. 'You son of a fucking whore! How dare you touch me? Ladisla was a cretin, but at least his blood was clean!'

Jezal gaped, one hand pressed against his burning face, his

whole body rigid with shock. He reached out feebly with his other hand. 'But I—ooof!'

Her knee caught him between the legs with pitiless accuracy, driving the wind from his chest, making him teeter for a breathless moment, then bringing him down like a sledgehammer to a house of cards. As he slid groaning to the carpet in that special, shooting agony that only a blow to the fruits can produce, it was little consolation that he had been right.

His Queen was quite evidently a woman of rare and fiery passion.

The tears flowing so liberally from his eyes were not just of pain, and awful surprise, and temporary disappointment, they were, increasingly, of deepening horror. It seemed that he had misjudged Terez' feelings most seriously. She had smiled for the crowds, but now, in private, she gave every indication of despising him and all he stood for. The fact that he had been born a bastard was hardly something he could ever change. For all he knew his wedding night was about to be spent on the royal floor. The queen had already hurried across the room, and the curtains of the bed were tightly drawn against him.

The Seventh Day

The Easterners had come again last night. Crept up by darkness, found a spot to climb in and killed a sentry. Then they'd set a ladder and a crowd of 'em had sneaked inside by the time they were found out. The cries had woken the Dogman, hardly sleeping anyway, and he'd scrabbled awake in the black, all tangled with his blanket. Enemies inside the fortress, men running and shouting, shadows in the dark, everything reeking of panic and chaos. Men fighting by star-light, and by torchlight, and by no light at all, blades swung with hardly a notion of where they were headed, boots stumbling and kicking showers of bright sparks out of the guttering campfires.

They'd driven 'em back in the end. They'd herded them to the wall, and cut them down in numbers, and only three had lived to drop their weapons and give up. A bad mistake for them, as it turned out. There were a lot of men dead, these seven days. Every time the sun went down there were more graves. No one was in much of a merciful mood, providing they'd been suited that way in the first place, and not many had. So when they'd caught these three, Black Dow had trussed 'em up on the wall where Bethod and all the rest could see. Trussed 'em up in the hard blue dawn, first streaks of light just stabbing across the black sky, and he'd doused them all with oil and set a spark to them. One by one he'd done it. So the others could see what was coming and set to screaming before their turn.

Dogman didn't much take to seeing men on fire. He didn't like hearing their shrieks and their fat crackling. He didn't smile at a nose-full of the sick-sweet stink of their burning meat. But he didn't think of trying to stop it neither. There was a time for soft opinions, and this weren't it. Mercy and weakness are the same thing in war, and there's no prizes for nice behaviour. He'd learned that from Bethod, a long time ago. Maybe now those Easterners would give it a second thought before they came again at night and fucked up everyone's breakfast.

Might help to put some steel in the rest of the Dogman's crew besides, because more than a few were getting itchy. Some lads had tried to get away two nights before. Given up their places and crept over the wall in the darkness, tried to get down into the valley. Bethod had their heads on spears out in front of his ditch now. A dozen battered lumps, hair blowing about in the breeze. You could hardly see their faces from the wall, but it seemed somehow they had an angry, upset sort of a look. Like they blamed the Dogman for leading them to this. As though he hadn't enough to worry about with the reproaches of the living.

He frowned down at Bethod's camp, the shapes of his tents and his signs just starting to come up black out of the mist and the darkness, and he wondered what he could do, except for stand there, and wait. All his boys were looking to him, hoping he'd pull some trick of magic to get them out of this alive. But Dogman didn't know any magic. A valley, and a wall, and no ways out. No ways out had been the whole point of the plan. He wondered if they could stand another day. But then he'd wondered that yesterday morning.

'What's Bethod planning for today, do we reckon?' he murmured to himself. 'What's he got planned?'

'A massacre?' grunted Grim.

Dogman gave him a hard look. 'Attack is the word I might've picked, but I wouldn't be surprised if we get it your way, before the day's out.' He narrowed his eyes and stared down into the shadowy valley, hoping to see what he'd been hoping for all the last seven long days. Some sign that the Union were coming. But there was nothing. Below Bethod's wide camp, his tents, and his standards, and his masses of men, there was nothing but the bare and empty land, mist clinging in the shady hollows.

Tul nudged him in the ribs with a great big elbow, and managed to make a grin. 'I don't know about this plan. Waiting for the Union, and all that. Sounds a bit risky, if you ask me. Any chance I can change my mind now?'

The Dogman didn't laugh. He hadn't any laughter left. 'Not much.'

'No.' The giant puffed out a weighty sigh. 'I don't suppose there is.'

Seven days, since the Shanka first came at the walls. Seven days, and it felt like seven months. Logen hardly had a muscle that didn't ache from hard use. He was covered in a legion of bruises, a host of scratches, an army of grazes, and knocks, and burns. He had the long cut down his leg bandaged, his ribs all bound up tight from getting kicked in them, a pair of good-sized scabs under his hair, his shoulder stiff as wood from where he'd got battered with a shield, his knuckles scraped and swollen from punching at an Easterner and catching stone instead. He was one enormous sore spot.

The rest of the crowd were little better off. There was hardly a man in the whole fortress without some kind of an injury. Even Crummock's daughter had picked up a scratch from somewhere. One of Shivers' boys had lost himself a finger the day before yesterday. Little one, on his left hand. He was looking at it now, wrapped up tight in dirty, bloody cloth, wincing.

'Burns, don't it?' he said, looking up at Logen, bunching up the rest of his fingers and opening them again.

Logen should've felt sorry for him, probably. He remembered the pain, and the disappointment even worse. Hardly able to believe that you wouldn't have that finger any more, for the whole rest of your life. But he'd got no pity left for anyone beyond himself. 'It surely does,' he grunted.

'Feels like it's still there.'

'Aye.'

'Does that feeling go away?'

'In time.'

'How much time?'

'More than we've got, most likely.'

The man nodded, slow and grim. 'Aye.'

Seven days, and even the cold stone and wet wood of the fortress itself seemed to have had enough. The new parapets were crumbled and sagging, shored up as best they could be, and crumbled again. The gates were chopped to rotten fire-wood, daylight showing through the hacked-out gaps, boulders piled in behind. A firm knock might have brought them down. A firm knock might have brought Logen down, for that matter, the way he was feeling.

He took a mouthful of sour water from his flask. They were getting to the rank stuff at the bottom of the barrels. Low on food too, and on everything else. Hope, in particular, was in short and dwindling supply. 'Still alive,' he whispered to himself, but there wasn't much triumph in it. Even less than usual. Civilisation might not have been all to his taste, but a soft bed, a strange place to piss, and a bit of scorn from some skinny idiots didn't seem like such a bad option right then. He was busy asking himself for the thousandth time why he came back at all when he heard Crummock-i-Phail's voice behind him.

'Well, well, Bloody-Nine. You look tired, man.'

Logen frowned up. The hillman's mad blather was starting to grate on him. 'It's been hard work these past days, in case you hadn't noticed.'

'I have, and I've had my part in it, haven't I, my beauties?' His three children looked at each other.

'Aye?' said the girl in a tiny voice.

Crummock frowned down at them. 'Don't like the way the game's played no more, eh? How about you, Bloody-Nine? The moon stopped smiling, has it? You scared, are you?'

Logen gave the fat bastard a long, hard look. 'Tired is what I am, Crummock. Tired o' your fortress, your food, and most of all I'm tired of your fucking talk. Not everyone loves the sound o' your fat lips flapping as much as you. Why don't you piss off and see if you can fit the moon up your arse.'

Crummock split a grin, a curve of yellow teeth standing out from his brown beard. 'That's the man I love, right there.' One of his sons, the one that carried the spear with him, was tugging at his shirt. 'What the hell is it, boy?'

'What happens if we lose, Da?'

'If we what?' growled Crummock, and he cuffed his son round the head with a great hand and knocked him on his face in the dirt. 'On your feet! There'll be no losing here, boy!'

'Not while the moon loves us,' muttered his sister, but not that loud.

Logen watched the lad struggling up, holding a hand to his bloody mouth and looking like he wanted to cry. He knew that feeling. Probably he should've said something about treating a child that way. Maybe he would've, on the first day, or the second even. Not now. He was too tired, and too sore, and too scared to care much about it.

Black Dow ambled up, something not too far from a smile across his face. The one man in the whole camp who might've been said to be in a better mood than usual, and you know you're in some sorry shit when Black Dow starts smiling.

'Ninefingers,' he grunted.

'Dow. Run out of men to burn, have you?'

'Reckon Bethod'll be sending me some more presently.' He nodded towards the wall. 'What d'you think he'll send today?'

'After what we gave 'em last night, I reckon those Crinna bastards are just about done.'

'Bloody savages. I reckon they are at that.'

'And there've been no Shanka for a few days now.'

'Four days, since he sent the Flatheads at us.'

Logen squinted up at the sky, slowly getting lighter. 'Looks like good weather today. Good weather for armour, and swords, and men walking shoulder to shoulder. Good weather to try and finish us. Wouldn't be surprised if he sends the Carls today.'

'Nor me.'

'His best,' said Logen, 'from way back. Wouldn't be surprised to see Whitesides, and Goring, and Pale-as-Snow, and fucking Littlebone and all the rest come strolling up to the gate after breakfast.'

Dow snorted. 'His best? Right crowd o' cunts, those.' And he turned his head and spat onto the mud.

'You'll get no argument from me.'

'That so? Didn't you fight alongside 'em, all those hard and bloody years?'

'I did. But I can't say I ever much liked 'em.'

'Well, if it's any consolation, I doubt they think too much o' you these days.' Dow gave him a long look. 'When did Bethod stop suiting you, eh, Ninefingers?'

Logen stared back at him. 'Hard to say. Bit by bit, I reckon. Maybe he got to be more of a bastard as time went on. Or maybe I got to be less of one.'

'Or maybe there ain't room on one side for two bastards as big as the pair o' you.'

'Oh, I don't know.' Logen got up. 'You and me work real sweet together.' He stalked away from Dow, thinking about what easy work Malacus Quai, and Ferro Maljinn, and even Jezal dan Luthar had been.

Seven days, and they were all at each other's throats. All angry, all tired. Seven days. The one consolation was that there couldn't be many more.

'They're coming.'

Dogman's eyes flicked sideways. Like most of the few things Grim said, it hardly needed saying. They could all see it as clearly as the sun rising. Bethod's Carls were on the move.

They were in no hurry. They came on stiff and steady, painted shields held up in front, eyes to the gateway. Standards flapped over their heads. Signs the Dogman recognised from way back. He wondered how many of those men down there he'd fought alongside. How many of their faces he could put a name to. How many he'd drunk with, eaten with, laughed with, that he'd have to do his best to put back in the mud. He took a long breath. The battlefield's no place for sentiment, Threetrees had told him once, and he'd taken it right to heart.

'Alright!' He lifted up his hand as the men around him on the tower readied their bows. 'Hold on to 'em for a minute yet!'

The Carls stomped on through the churned-up mud and the broken rocks where the valley narrowed, past the bodies of Easterners, and Shanka, left twisted where they lay, hacked, or crushed, or stuck with broken arrows. They didn't falter, or lose a step, the wall of shields shifted as they came, but didn't break. Not the slightest gap.

'They march tight,' muttered Tul.

'Aye. Too tight, the bastards.'

They were getting close, now. Close enough that Dogman had to try some arrows. 'Alright, boys! Aim high and let 'em drop!' The first flight went hissing from the tower, arced up high and started to fall on that tight column. They shifted their shields to meet them and arrows thudded into painted wood, spun off helmets and glanced off mail. A couple found marks, a shriek went up. Holes showed, here or there, but the rest just stepped on over, trudging up towards the wall.

Dogman frowned at the barrels where the shafts were kept. Less than quarter full, now, and most of those dug out from dead men. 'Careful now! Pick your marks, lads!'

'Uh,' said Grim, pointing down below. A good-sized pack o' men were scurrying out from the ditch, dressed in stiff leather and steel capped. They formed up in a few neat rows, kneeling down, tending to their weapons. Flatbows, like the Union used.

'Get down!' shouted Dogman.

Those nasty little bows rattled and spat. Most of the boys on the tower were well behind their parapet by then, but one optimist who'd been leaning out got a bolt through his mouth, swayed and toppled, silent, off the tower. Another took one in his chest, breathing with a wheeze like wind through a split pine.

'Alright! Give 'em something back!' They all came up at once and sent down a volley, strings humming, peppering those bastards with plunging shafts. Their bows might not have had the same spit to 'em, but with the height the arrows still came hard, and Bethod's archers had nothing to hide behind. More than a few fell back or started crawling away, screaming and squealing, but the rank behind pushed through, slow and steady, knelt down and aimed their flatbows.

Another flight of bolts came hissing up. Men ducked and threw themselves down. One zipped right past the Dogman's head and clicked off the rock face behind. Pure luck he didn't get pinned with it. A couple of the others were less lucky. One lad was lying on his back, a pair of bolts stuck in his chest, peering down at 'em and whispering, 'shit', to himself, over and over.

'Bastards!'

'Let 'em have it back!'

Shafts and bolts started flapping up both ways, men shouting and taking aim, all anger and gritted teeth. 'Steady!' shouted Dogman. 'Steady!' but no one hardly heard him. With the extra poke from the height and the cover they had from the walls, didn't take long for Dogman's boys to get the upper hand. Bethod's archers started scrambling back, then a couple dropped their flatbows and made a run for it, one getting a shaft right through his back. The rest started to break for the ditch, leaving their wounded crawling in the mud.

'Uh,' said Grim again. While they'd been busy trading shafts the Carls had made it right to the gate, shields up over their heads against the rocks and arrows the hillmen were chucking down. They'd got the ditch filled in a day or two before, and now the column opened up in the middle and those mailed men moved like they were passing something to the front. Dogman caught a glimpse of it. A long, thin tree trunk, cut down to use as a ram, branches left on short so men could give it a firm swing. Dogman heard the first tearing crash of it working at their sorry excuse for a gate.

'Shit,' he muttered.

Knots of Thralls were charging forward now, light-armed and light-armoured, carrying ladders between 'em, counting on speed to make it to the walls. Plenty fell, pricked with spear or arrow, knocked with rocks. Some of their ladders were pushed back, but they were quick and full of bones, and stuck to their task. Soon there were a couple of groups on the walls while more pressed up the ladders behind, fighting with Crummock's people and getting the better by pure freshness and weight of numbers.

Now there was a big crack and the gate went down. Dogman saw that tree-trunk swing one last time and cave one door right in. The Carls struggled with the other and heaved it open, a couple of stones bouncing from the shields and spinning away. The front few started pressing forwards through the gate.

'Shit,' said Grim.

'They're through,' breathed the Dogman, and he watched Bethod's Carls push on into that narrow gap in a mailed tide, trampling the shattered gates under their heavy boots, dragging the rocks behind out of the way, their bright-painted shields up, their bright-polished weapons ready. To either side the Thralls swarmed up their ladders and onto the wall, pressing Crummock's hillmen back down the walkways. Like a high river bursting a dam, Bethod's host flowed into the broken fortress, first in a trickle, and soon in a flood.

'I'm going down!' snarled Tul, dragging his great long sword out of its sheath.

Dogman thought about trying to stop him, but then he just nodded, tired, and watched the Thunderhead charge off down the steps, a few others following. There was no point getting in their way. Seemed like it was fast reaching that time.

Time for each man to choose where he'd die.

Logen saw them come through the gates, up the ramp and into the fortress. Time seemed to move slow. He saw each design on each shield picked out sharp in the morning sun – black tree, red bridge, two wolves on green, three horses on yellow. Metal glinted and flashed – shield's rim, mail's ring, spear's point, sword's edge. On they came, yelling their battle cries, high and thin, the way they'd done for years. The breath crawled in and out of Logen's nose. The Thralls and the hillmen fought on the walls as if they were underwater, their sounds dull and muffled. His palms sweated, and tickled, and itched as he watched the Carls break in. Hardly seemed as if it could be true that he had to charge into those bastards and kill as many as he could. What a damn fool notion.

He felt that powerful need, as he always had at times like that, to turn and run. All around he felt the fear of the others, their uncertain shuffling, their edging backwards. A sensible enough instinct, except there was nowhere now to run to. Nowhere except forwards, into the teeth of the enemy, and hope to drive them out before they could get a foothold. There was nothing to think about. It was their only chance.

So Logen lifted the Maker's sword high, and he gave a meaningless scream, and he started running. He heard the shouts around him, felt the men moving with him, the jostling and rattling of weapons. The ground, and the wall, and the Carls he ran at jolted and wobbled. His boots pounded on the earth, his own quick breath hissed and rushed with the wind.

He saw the Carls hurrying to set their shields, to form a wall, to make ready their spears and their weapons, but they were in a mess after coming through that narrow gate, flustered by the screaming mass of men charging down on them. The war-cries died in their throats and their faces sagged from triumph to shock. A couple at the edges started to have doubts, and they faltered, and shuffled back, and then Logen and the rest were on them.

He managed to twist around a wobbling spear and land a good hard chop on a shield with all the force of his charge, knock his man sprawling in the mud. Logen hacked at his leg as he tried to get up and the blade cut through mail and left a long gash in flesh, brought him shrieking down again. Logen swung at another Carl, felt the Maker's sword squeal against the metal rim of a shield and slide into flesh. A man gurgled, vomited blood down the front of his mail coat.

Logen saw an axe thud into a helmet and leave a dent the size of a fist in it. He reeled out of the way of a spear thrust and it stuck in the ribs of a man beside him. A sword hacked into a shield and sent splinters flying into Logen's eyes. He blinked, and dodged, slid in the muck, chopped at an arm as it tore at his coat and felt it break, flapping in its mail sleeve. Eyes rolled in a bloody face. Something shoved him in the back and nearly pushed him onto a sword.

There was hardly space to swing, then there was no space at all. Men crushed in from behind, crushed in through the gate, adding their straining, mindless weight to the press in the centre. Logen was squashed in tight, shoulder to shoulder. Men gasped and grunted, dug and elbowed at each other, stabbed with knives and gouged at faces with their fingers. He thought he saw Littlebone in the press, teeth bared in a snarl, long grey hair straggling out from under a helmet set with whirls of gold, spattered with streaks of red, shouting himself hoarse. Logen tried to press towards him but the blind currents of battle snatched him away and carried them far apart.

He stabbed at someone under a shield rim, winced as he felt something dig into his hip. A long, slow, burning, getting worse and worse. He growled as the blade cut, not swung, or thrust, just held there while he was squashed up against it. He thrashed with his elbows, with his head, managed to twist away from the pain, felt the wetness of blood down his leg. He found himself with room, got his sword-hand free, hacked at a shield, chopped a head open on the backswing then found himself shoved up against it, his face pressed into warm brains.

He saw a shield jerk up out of the corner of his eye. The edge caught him in the throat, under the chin, snapped his head back and filled his skull with blinding light. Before he knew it he was rolling, coughing, slithering in the filth down among the boots.

He dragged himself nowhere, clutching at dirt, spitting blood, boots squelching and straining in the mud all around him. Crawling through a dark, terrifying, shifting forest of legs, the screams of pain and rage filtering down from above with the flickering light. Feet kicked at him, stomped on him, battered at every part of him. He tried to struggle up and a boot in the mouth sent him limp again. He rolled over, gasping, saw a bearded Carl in the same state, impossible to say which side he was on, trying to push himself up out of the mud. Their eyes met, for a moment, then a glinting spear blade shot down from above and stabbed the Carl in the back, once, twice, three times. He went limp, blood gurgling down through his beard. There were bodies all around, on their faces and their sides, lying in amongst the dropped and broken gear, kicked and knocked around like children's dolls, some of them still twitching, clutching, grunting.

Logen squawked as a boot squelched down hard on his hand, crushing his fingers into the muck. He fumbled a knife from his belt and started slashing weakly at the leg above it, bloody teeth gritted. Something cracked him in the top of the head and sent him sprawling on his face again.

The world was a noisy blur, a painful smear, a mass of feet and anger. He didn't know which way he was facing, which way was up or down. His mouth tasted of metal, thirsty. There was blood in his eyes, mud in his eyes, his head was pounding, he wanted to be sick.

Back to the North, and get some vengeance. What the fuck had he been thinking?

Someone screamed, stuck with a flatbow bolt, but the Dogman had no time to worry about him.

Whitesides' Thralls were up on the wall under the tower, and a few had got around and onto the stairway. They were charging up it now, or as close as they could get to a charge on those narrow steps. Dogman dropped his bow and fumbled his sword out from its sheath, got a knife ready in the other hand. A few of the others took up spears, gathered round the head of the stairway as the Thralls came up. Dogman swallowed. He'd never been much for fights like this, toe to toe, no more'n the length of an axe from your enemies. He'd rather have kept things to a polite distance, but that didn't seem to be what these bastards had in mind.

An awkward kind of a fight started up at the top of the steps, defenders poking with spears, trying to shove the Thralls off, them poking back, shoving with shields, trying to get a foothold on the platform at the top, everyone taking care in case they took the long drop right back to the mud.

One charged through with a spear, screaming at the top of his lungs, and Grim shot him in the face, cool as you like, no more'n a stride or two distant. He staggered a step or two, bent right over with the flights of the arrows sticking out his mouth and the point out the back of his neck, then Dogman took the top of his head off with his sword and sent his corpse sprawling.

A big Thrall with wild red hair leaped up the steps, swinging a big axe, roaring like a madman. He got round a spear and felled an archer with a blow that spattered blood across the rock face, charged on through, folk scattering out o' the way.

Dogman dithered, trying to look like he was an idiot, then when the axe came down he dodged left and the blade missed him by a whisker. The red-haired Thrall stumbled, tired from getting over the wall and up all them steps, most likely. A long way to climb, especially with nothing but your death at the end of it. Dogman kicked hard at the side of his knee and his leg buckled, he yelled as he lurched towards the edge of the stairs. Dogman chopped at him with his sword, caught him a slash across the back, hard enough to send him over the edge. He dropped his axe, screamed as he tumbled through the empty air.

Dogman felt something move, turned just in time to see another Thrall coming at him from the side. He twisted round and knocked the first sword-cut clear, gasped as he felt the second thud cold into his arm, heard his sword clatter out of his limp hand. He jerked away from another swing, tripped and went down on his back. The Thrall came at him, lifting up his sword to finish the job, but before he got more'n a stride Grim loomed up quick from the side, caught hold of his sword-arm and held it pinned. Dogman scrambled up, taking a hard grip on his knife with his good hand, and stabbed the Thrall right in his chest. They stayed there, the three of 'em, tangled up tight together, still in the midst of all that madness, for as long as it took for the man to die. Then Dogman pulled his knife free and Grim let him fall.

They'd got the best of it up on the tower, at least for now. There was just one Thrall left on his feet, and while the Dogman watched a couple of his lads herded him up to the parapet and poked him off with spears. There were corpses scattered all about the place. A couple of dozen Thralls, maybe half that many of the Dogman's boys. One of 'em was propped against the cliff face, chest heaving as he breathed, face pasty pale, bloody hands clutched to his slashed guts.

Dogman's hand wouldn't work right, the fingers dangled useless. He tugged his shirtsleeve up, saw a long gash oozing from his elbow almost all the way to his wrist. His guts gave a heave and he coughed a bit of burning puke up and spat it out. Wounds on other people you can get used to. Cuts out of your own flesh always have a horror to 'em.

Down below, inside the wall, the fight was joined and nothing but a boiling, tight-pressed mass. Dogman could hardly tell which men were on which side. He stood frozen, bloody knife clutched in one bloody hand. There were no answers now, no plans. It was every man for himself. If they lived out the day it would be by luck alone, and he was starting to doubt he had that much luck left. He felt someone tugging at his sleeve. Grim. He followed his pointed finger with his eyes.

Beyond Bethod's camp, down in the valley, a great cloud of dust was coming up, a brown haze. Underneath, glittering in the morning sun, the armour of horsemen. His hand clamped tight round Grim's wrist, hope suddenly flickering alive again. 'Fucking Union!' he breathed, hardly daring to believe it.

West squinted through his eye-glass, lowered it and peered up the valley, squinted through it again. 'You're sure?'

'Yes, sir.' Jalenhorm's big, honest face was streaked with the dirt of eight days' hard riding. 'And it looks as if they're still holding out, just barely.'

'General Poulder!' snapped West.

'My Lord Marshal?' murmured Poulder with his newly acquired veneer of sycophancy.

'Are the cavalry ready to charge?'

The General blinked. 'They are not properly deployed, have been riding hard these past days, and would be charging uphill over broken ground and at a strong and determined enemy. They will do as you order, of course, Lord Marshal, but it might be prudent to wait for our infantry to—'

'Prudence is a luxury.' West frowned up towards that innocuous space between the two fells. Attack at once, while the Dogman and his Northmen still held out? They might enjoy the advantage of surprise, and crush Bethod between them, but the cavalry would be charging uphill, men and mounts disorganised and fatigued from hard marching. Or wait for the infantry to arrive, still some hours behind, and mount a well-planned assault? But by then would the Dogman and his friends have been slaughtered to a man, their fortress taken and Bethod well prepared to meet an attack from one side only?

West chewed at his lip, trying to ignore the fact that thousands of lives hung upon his decision. To attack now was the greater risk, but might offer the greater rewards. A chance to finish this war within a bloody hour. They might never again catch the King of the Northmen off guard. What was it that Burr had said to him, the night before he died? One cannot be a great leader without a certain . . . ruthlessness.

'Prepare the charge, and deploy our infantry across the mouth of the valley as soon as they arrive. We must prevent Bethod and any of his forces from escaping. If sacrifices are to be made, I intend that they be meaningful.' Poulder looked anything but convinced. 'Will you force me to agree with General Kroy's assessment of your fighting qualities, General Poulder? Or do you intend to prove the two of us wrong?'

The General snapped to attention, his moustaches vibrating with new eagerness. 'Respectfully, sir, to prove you wrong! I will order the charge immediately!'

He gave his black charger the spurs and flew off up the valley, towards the place where the dusty cavalry were massing, pursued by several members of his staff. West shifted in his saddle, chewing worriedly at his lip. His head was beginning to hurt again. A charge, uphill, against a determined enemy.

Colonel Glokta would no doubt have grinned at the prospect of such a deadly gamble. Prince Ladisla would have approved of such cavalier carelessness with other men's lives. Lord Smund would have slapped backs, and talked of vim and vigour, and called for wine.

And only look what became of those three heroes.

Logen heard a great roar, faint, and far away. Light came at his half-closed eyes, as though the fight was opened up wide. Shadows flickered. A great boot squelched in the filth in front of his face. Voices bellowed, far above. He felt himself grabbed by the shirt, dragged through the mud, feet and legs thrashing all around him. He saw the sky, painful bright, blinked and dribbled at it. He lay still, limp as a rag.

'Logen! You alright? Where you hurt?'

'I—' he croaked, then started coughing.

'D'you know me?' Something slapped at Logen's face, slapped some sluggish thought into his head. A shaggy shape loomed over him, dark against the bright sky. Logen squinted at it. Tul Duru Thunderhead, unless he was much mistaken. What the hell was he doing here? Thinking was painful. The more Logen thought, the more pain he was in. His jaw was on fire, feeling twice the size it usually did. His every breath was a shuddering, slavering gasp.

Above him the big man's mouth moved, and the words boomed and rang against Logen's ears, but they were nothing but noise. His leg prickled unpleasantly, far away, his own heartbeat leaped and jerked and pounded at his head. He heard sounds, clashing and rattling, coming at him from all sides, and the sounds themselves hurt him, made his jaw burn all the worse, unbearable.

'Get . . .' The air rasped and clicked, but no sound would

come. It wasn't his voice any longer. He reached out, with his last strength, and he put his palm against Tul's chest, and he tried to push him away, but the big man only caught his hand and pressed it with his own.

'It's alright,' he growled. 'I've got you.'

'Aye,' whispered Logen, and the smile spread out across his bloody mouth. He gripped that great hand with a sudden, terrible strength, and with his other fist he found the handle of a knife, tucked down warm against his skin. The good blade darted out, swift as the snake and just as deadly, and sank into the big man's thick neck to the hilt. He looked surprised, as the hot blood poured from his open throat, drooled from his open mouth, soaked his heavy beard, dribbled from his nose and down his chest, but he shouldn't have.

To touch the Bloody-Nine was to touch death, and death has no favourites, and makes no exceptions.

The Bloody-Nine rose up, shoving the great corpse away from him, and his red fist closed tight around the giant's sword, a heavy length of star-bright metal, dark and beautiful, a righteous tool for the work that awaited him. So much work.

But good work is the best of blessings. The Bloody-Nine opened his mouth, and shrieked out all his bottomless love and his endless hate in one long wail. The ground rushed underneath him, and the heaving, writhing, beautiful battle reached out and took him in its soft embrace, and he was home.

The faces of the dead shifted, blurred around him, roaring their curses and bellowing their anger. But their hate of him only made him stronger. The long sword flung men out of his path and left them twisted and broken, hacked and drooling, howling with happiness. Who fought who was none of his concern. The living were on one side, and he was on the other, and he carved a red and righteous way through their ranks.

An axe flashed in the sun, a bright curve like the waning moon, and the Bloody-Nine slid below it, kicked a man away with a heavy boot. He lifted up a shield, but the great sword split the painted tree, and the wood beneath it, and the arm beneath that, and tore open the mail behind as though it was nothing but a cobweb, and split his belly like a sack of angry snakes.

A boy-child cowered, and slithered away on his back, clutching at a great shield and an axe too big for him to lift. The Bloody-Nine laughed at his fear, teeth bared bright and smiling. A tiny voice seemed to whisper for restraint, but the Bloody-Nine hardly heard it. His sword hard-swung split big shield and small body together and sprayed blood across the dirt and the stone and the stricken faces of the men watching.

'Good,' he said, and he showed his bloody smile. He was the Great Leveller. Man or woman, young or old, all were dealt with exactly alike. That was the brutal beauty of it, the awful symmetry of it, the perfect justice of it. There could be no escape and no excuses. He came forward, taller than the mountains, and the men shuffled, and muttered, and spread out from him. A circle of shields, of painted designs, of flowering trees, and rippling water, and snarling faces.

Their words tickled at his ears.

'It's him.'

'Ninefingers.'

'The Bloody-Nine!'

A circle of fear, with him at the centre, and they were wise to fear.

Their deaths were written in the shapes of sweet blood on the bitter ground. Their deaths were whispered in the buzzing of the flies on the corpses beyond the wall. Their deaths were stamped on their faces, carried on the wind, held in the crooked line between the mountains and the sky. Dead men, all.

'Who's next to the mud?' he whispered.

A bold Carl stepped forward, a shield on his arm with a coiled serpent upon it. Before he could even lift his spear the Bloody-Nine's sword had made a great circle, above the top of his shield and below the bottom of his helmet. The point of the blade stole the jawbone from his head, cleaved into the shoulder of the next man, ate deep into his chest and drove him into the earth, blood flying from his silent mouth. Another man loomed up and the sword fell on him like a falling star, crushed his helmet and the skull beneath it down to his mouth. The body dropped on its back and danced a merry jig in the dirt.

'Dance!' laughed the Bloody-Nine, and the sword reeled around him. He filled the air with blood, and broken weapons, and the parts of men, and these good things wrote secret letters, and described sacred patterns that only he could see and understand. Blades pricked and nicked and dug at him but they were nothing. He repaid each mark upon his burning skin one-hundred fold, and the Bloody-Nine laughed, and the wind, and the fire, and the faces on the shields laughed with him, and could not stop.

He was the storm in the High Places, his voice as terrible as the thunder, his arm as quick, as deadly, as pitiless as the lightning. He rammed the sword through a man's guts, ripped it back and smashed a man's mouth apart with the pommel, snatched his spear away with his free hand and flung it through the neck of a third, split a Carl's side yawning open as he passed. He reeled, spun, rolled, drunken dizzy, spitting fire and laughter. He forged a new circle about him. A circle as wide as the giant's sword. A circle in which the world belonged to him.

His enemies lurked beyond its limit now, shuffled back from it, full of fear. They knew him, he could see it in their faces. They had heard whispers of his work, and now he had given them a bloody lesson, and they knew the truth of it, and he smiled to see them enlightened. The foremost of them held up his open hand, bent forward and laid his axe down on the ground.

'You are forgiven,' whispered the Bloody-Nine, and let his own sword clatter to the dirt. Then he darted forward and seized the man by his throat, lifting him up into the air with both his hands. He thrashed and kicked and wrestled, but the Bloody-Nine's red grip was the swelling ice that bursts the very bones of the earth apart.

'You are forgiven!' His hands were made of iron, and his thumbs sunk deeper and deeper into the man's neck until blood welled up from under them, and he lifted the kicking corpse out to arm's length and held it above him until it was still. He flung it away, and it fell upon the mud and flopped over and over in a manner that greatly pleased him.

'Forgiven . . .' He walked to the bright archway through a cringing crowd, shying away like sheep from the wolf, leaving a muddy path through their midst, strewn with their fallen shields and weapons. Beyond, in the sun, bright-armoured horsemen moved across the dusty valley, their swords twinkling as they rose and fell, herding running figures this way and that, riding between the high standards, rippling gently in the wind. He stood in that ragged gateway, with the splintered doors under his boots, and the corpses of his friends and of his enemies scattered about him, and he heard the sounds of men cheering victory.

And Logen closed his eyes, and breathed.

Too Many Masters

In spite of the hot summer day outside, the banking hall was a cool, dim, shadowy place. A place full of whispers, and quiet echoes, built of sharp, dark marble like a new tomb. Such thin shafts of sunlight as broke through the narrow windows were full of wriggling dust motes. There was no smell to speak of. *Except the stench of dishonesty, which even I find almost overpowering. The surroundings may be cleaner than the House of Questions, but I suspect there is more truth told among the criminals.*

There were no piles of shining gold ingots on display. There was not so much as a single coin in evidence. Only pens, and ink, and heaps of dull paper. Valint and Balk's employees were not swaddled in fabulous robes such as Magister Kault of the Mercers had worn. They did not sport flashing jewels as Magister Eider of the Spicers had. They were small, grey-dressed men with serious expressions. The only flashing was from the odd pair of studious eye-glasses.

So this is what true wealth looks like. This is how true power appears. The austere temple of the golden goddess. He watched the clerks working at their neat stacks of documents, at their neat desks arranged in neat rows. *There the acolytes, inducted into the lowest mysteries of the church.* His eyes flickered to those waiting. Merchants and moneylenders, shopkeepers and shysters, traders and tricksters in long queues, or waiting nervously on hard chairs around the hard walls. Fine clothes, perhaps, but anxious manners. *The fearful congregation, ready to cower should the deity of commerce show her vengeful streak.*

But I am not her creature. Glokta shouldered his way past the longest queue, the tip of his cane squealing loud against the tiles, snarling, 'I am crippled!' if one of the merchants dared to look his way.

The clerk blinked at him when he reached the front of the line. 'How may I—'

'Mauthis,' barked Glokta.

'And who shall I say is—'

'The cripple.' *Convey me to the high priest, that I might cleanse my crimes in banking notes.*

'I cannot simply—'

'You are expected!' Another clerk, a few rows back, had stood up from his desk. 'Please come with me.'

Glokta gave the unhappy queue a toothless leer as he limped out between the desks toward a door in the far, panelled wall, but his smile did not last. Beyond it, a set of high steps rose up, light filtering down from a narrow window at the top.

What is it about power, that it has to be higher up than everyone else? Can a man not be powerful on the ground floor? He cursed and struggled up after his impatient guide, then dragged his useless leg down a long hallway with many high doors on either side. The clerk leaned forward and humbly knocked at one, waited for a muffled 'Yes?' and opened it.

Mauthis sat behind a monumental desk watching Glokta hobble over the threshold. His face could have been carved from wood for all the warmth or welcome it displayed. On the expanse of blood-coloured leather before him pens, and ink, and neat piles of papers were arranged with all the merciless precision of recruits on a parade ground.

'The visitor you were expecting, sir.' The clerk hastened forward with a sheaf of documents. 'And there are also these for your attention.'

Mauthis turned his emotionless eyes to them. 'Yes . . . yes . . . yes . . . yes . . . all these to Talins . . .' Glokta did not wait to be asked. *And I've been in pain for far too long to pretend not to be.* He took a lurching step and sagged into the nearest chair, stiff leather creaking uncomfortably under his aching arse. *But it will serve.*

The papers crackled as Mauthis leafed through them, his pen

scratching his name at the bottom of each one. He paused at the last. 'And no. This must be called in at once.' He reached forward and took hold of a stamp, its wooden handle polished by long use, and rocked it carefully in its tray of red ink. It thumped down against the paper with a disturbing finality. *And is some merchant's life squashed out under that stamp, do we suppose? Is that ruin and despair, so carelessly administered? Is that wives and children, out upon the street? There is no blood here, there are no screams, and yet men are destroyed as completely as they are in the House of Questions, and with a fraction of the effort.*

Glokta's eyes followed the clerk as he hurried out with the documents. *Or is it merely a receipt for ten bits, refused? Who can say?* The door was pulled softly and precisely shut with the gentlest of smooth clicks.

Mauthis paused only to align his pen precisely with the edge of his desk, then he looked up at Glokta. 'I am truly grateful that you have answered promptly.'

Glokta snorted. 'The tone of your note did not seem to allow for delay.' He winced as he lifted his aching leg with both hands and heaved his dirty boot up onto the chair beside him. 'I hope you will return the favour and come promptly to the point. I am extremely busy.' *I have Magi to destroy, and Kings to bring down, and, if I cannot do one or the other, I have a pressing appointment to have my throat cut and be tossed in the sea.*

Mauthis' face did not so much as flicker. 'Once again, I find that my superiors are not best pleased with the direction of your investigations.'

Is that so? 'Your superiors are people of deep pockets and shallow patience. What now offends their delicate sensibilities?'

'Your investigation into the lineage of our new King, his August Majesty Jezal the First.' Glokta felt his eye twitch, and he pressed his hand against it with a sour sucking of his gums. 'In particular your enquiries into the person of Carmee dan Roth, the circumstances of her untimely demise, and the closeness of her friendship with our previous King, Guslav the Fifth. Do I come close enough to the point for your taste?'

A little closer than I would like, in fact. 'Those enquiries have scarcely even begun. I find it surprising that your superiors are so very well informed. Do they acquire their information from a crystal ball, or a magic mirror?' *Or from someone at the House of Questions who likes to talk? Or from someone closer to me even than that, perhaps?*

Mauthis sighed, or at least, he allowed some air to issue from his face. 'I told you to assume that they know everything. You will discover it is no exaggeration, particularly if you choose to try and deceive them. I would advise you very strongly against that course of action.'

'Believe me when I say,' muttered Glokta through tight lips, 'that I have no interest whatsoever in the King's parentage, but his Eminence has demanded it, and keenly awaits a report of my progress. What am I to tell him?'

Mauthis stared back with a face full of sympathy. *As much sympathy as one stone might have for another.* 'My employers do not care what you tell him, provided that you obey them. I see that you find yourself in a difficult position, but speaking plainly, Superior, I do not see a choice for you. I suppose you could go to the Arch Lector, and lay before him the whole history of our involvement. The gift you took from my employers, the conditions under which it was given, the consideration you have already extended to us. Perhaps his Eminence is more forgiving of divided loyalties than he appears to be.'

'Huh,' snorted Glokta. *If I did not know better, I might have almost taken that for a joke. His Eminence is only slightly less forgiving than a scorpion, and we both know it.*

'Or you could honour your commitment to my employers, and do as they demand.'

'They asked for favours, when I signed the damn receipt. Now they make demands? Where does it end?'

'That is not for me to say, Superior. Or for you to ask.' Mauthis' eyes flickered towards the door. He leaned across his desk and spoke soft and low. 'But if my own experience is anything to go by . . . it will not end. My employers have paid. And they always get what they have paid for. Always.'

Glokta swallowed. *It would seem that, in this case, they have paid for my abject obedience. It would not normally be a difficulty, of course, I am every bit as abject as the next man, if not more so. But the Arch Lector demands the same. Two well-informed and merciless masters in direct opposition begins too late to seem like one too many. Two too many, some might say. But as Mauthis so kindly explains, I have no choice.* He slid his boot off the chair, leaving a long streak of dirt across the leather, and shifted his weight painfully as he began the long process of getting up. 'Is there anything else, or do your employers merely wish me to defy the most powerful man in the Union?'

'They wish you also to watch him.'

Glokta froze. 'They wish me to what?'

'There has been a great deal of change of late, Superior. Change means new opportunities, but too much change is bad for business. My employers feel a period of stability is in everyone's best interests. They are satisfied with the situation.' Mauthis clenched his pale hands together on the red leather. 'They are concerned that some figures within the government may not be satisfied. That they may seek further change. That their rash actions might lead to chaos. His Eminence concerns them especially. They wish to know what he does. What he plans. They wish, in particular, to know what he is doing in the University.'

Glokta gave a splutter of disbelieving laughter. 'Is that all?'

The irony was wasted on Mauthis. 'For now. It might be best if you were to leave by the back entrance. My employers will expect news within the week.'

Glokta grimaced as he struggled down the narrow staircase at the back of the building, sideways on like a crab, the sweat standing out from his forehead, and not just from the effort. *How could they know? First that I was looking into Prince Raynault's death, against the Arch Lector's orders, and now that I am looking into our Majesty's mother, on the Arch Lector's behalf?*

Assume they know everything, of course, but no one knows anything without being told.

Who . . . told?

Who asked the questions, about the Prince and about the King? Whose first loyalty is to money? Who has already given me up once to save his skin? Glokta paused for a moment, in the middle of the steps, and frowned. *Oh, dear, dear. Is it every man for himself, now? Has it always been?*

The pain shooting up his wasted leg was the only reply.

Sweet Victory

West sat, arms crossed upon his saddle-bow, staring numbly up the dusty valley.

'We won,' said Pike, in a voice without emotion. Just the same voice in which he might have said, 'We lost.'

A couple of tattered standards still stood, hanging lifeless. Bethod's own great banner had been torn down and trampled beneath horses' hooves, and now its threadbare frame stuck up at a twisted angle, above the settling fog of dust, like clean-picked bones. A fitting symbol for the sudden fall of the King of the Northmen.

Poulder reined in his horse beside West, smiling primly at the carnage like a schoolmaster at an orderly classroom.

'How did we fare, General?'

'Casualties appear to have been heavy, sir, especially in our front ranks, but the enemy were largely taken by surprise. Most of their best troops were already committed to the attack on the fortress. Once our cavalry got them on the run, we drove them all the way to the walls! Picked their camp clean.' Poulder wrinkled his nose, moustaches trembling with distaste. 'Several hundred of those devilish Shanka we put to the sword, and a much greater number we drove off into the hills to the north, from whence, I do not doubt, they will be greatly reluctant to return. We wrought a slaughter among the Northmen to satisfy King Casamir himself, and the rest have laid down their arms. We guess at five thousand prisoners, sir. Bethod's army has been quite crushed. Crushed!' He gave a girlish chuckle. 'No one could deny that you have well and truly avenged the death of Crown Prince Ladisla today, Lord Marshal!'

West swallowed. 'Of course. Well and truly avenged.'

'A master-stroke, to use our Northmen as a decoy. A bold

and a decisive manoeuvre. I am, and will always be, honoured to have played my small part! A famous day for Union arms! Marshal Burr would have been proud to see it!'

West had never in his life expected to receive praise from General Poulder, but now the great moment had come he found that he could take no pleasure in it. He had performed no acts of bravery. He had taken no risks with his own life. He had done nothing but say charge. He felt saddle-sore and bone-weary, his jaw ached from being constantly clenched with worry. Even speaking seemed an effort. 'Is Bethod among the dead, or the captured?'

'As to specific prisoners, sir, I could not say. It may be that our Northern allies have him.' Poulder gave vent to a jagged chuckle. 'In which case I doubt he'll be with us much longer, eh, Marshal? Eh, Sergeant Pike?' He grinned as he drew his finger sharply across his belly and clicked his tongue. 'The bloody cross for him, I shouldn't wonder! Isn't that what they do, these savages? The bloody cross, isn't it?'

West did not see the funny side. 'Ensure that our prisoners are given food and water, and such assistance with their wounded as we are able to provide. We should be gracious in victory.' It seemed like the sort of thing that a leader should say, after a battle.

'Quite so, my Lord Marshal.' And Poulder gave a smart salute, the very model of an obedient underling, then reined his mount sideways and spurred away.

West slid down from his own horse, gathered himself for a moment, and began to trudge on foot up the valley. Pike came after him, sword drawn.

'Can't be too careful, sir,' he said.

'No,' murmured West. 'I suppose not.'

The long slope was scattered with men, alive and dead. The corpses of Union horsemen lay where they had fallen. Surgeons tended to the wounded with bloody hands and grim faces. Some men sat and wept, perhaps by fallen comrades. Some stared numbly at their own wounds. Others howled and gurgled, screamed for help, or water. Still others rushed to bring it to them. Final kindnesses, for the dying. A long procession of sullen prisoners was winding down the valley alongside the rock wall, watched carefully by mounted Union soldiers. Nearby were tangled heaps of surrendered weapons, piles of mail coats, stacks of painted shields.

West picked his way slowly through what had been Bethod's camp, rendered in one furious half-hour into a great expanse of rubbish, scattered across the bare rock and the hard earth. The twisted bodies of men and horses were mixed in with the trampled frames of tents, ripped and dragged-out canvas, burst barrels, broken boxes, gear for cooking, and mending, and fighting. All trodden into the churned mud, stamped with the smeared prints of hooves and boots.

In the midst of all this chaos there were strange islands of calm, where all seemed undisturbed, just as it must have been before West ordered the charge. A pot still hung over a smouldering fire, stew bubbling inside. A set of spears were neatly stacked against each other, with stool and whetstone beside, ready to be sharpened. Three bedrolls formed a perfect triangle, blankets well folded at the head of each one, all neat and orderly, except that a man lay sprawled across them, the contents of his gaping skull splattered across the pale wool.

Not far beyond a Union officer knelt in the mud, cradling another in his arms. West felt a sick twinge of recognition. The one on his knees was his old friend Lieutenant Brint. The one lying limp was his old friend Lieutenant Kaspa. For some reason, West felt an almost overpowering urge to walk away, off up the slope without stopping, and pretend not to have seen them. He had to force himself to stride over, his mouth filling with sour spit.

Brint looked up, pale face streaked with tears. 'An arrow,' he whispered. 'Just a stray. He never even drew his sword.'

'Bad luck,' grunted Pike. 'Bad luck.'

West stared down. Bad luck indeed. He could just see, snapped off at the edge of Kaspa's beard, under his jaw, the broken shaft of an arrow, but there was surprisingly little blood. Few marks of any kind. A splatter of mud down one sleeve of his uniform, and that was all. Despite the fact they were, in essence, staring cross-eyed at nothing, West could not help the feeling that Kaspa's eyes were looking directly into his. There was a peevish twist to his lip, an accusatory wrinkling of his brows. West almost wanted to take him up on it, demand to know what he meant by it, then had to remind himself that the man was dead.

'A letter, then,' muttered West, his fingers fussing with each other, 'to his family.'

Brint gave a miserable sniff which West found, for some reason, utterly infuriating. 'Yes, a letter.'

'Yes. Sergeant Pike, with me.' West could not stand there a moment longer. He turned away from his friends, one living and one dead, and strode off up the valley. He did his very best not to dwell on the fact that, had he not ordered the charge, one of the most pleasant and inoffensive men of his acquaintance would still be alive. One cannot be a leader without a certain ruthlessness, perhaps. But ruthlessness is not always easy.

He and Pike floundered over a crushed earth rampart and a trampled ditch, the valley growing steadily narrower, the high cliffs of stone pressing in on either side. More corpses here. Northmen, and wild men such as they found in Dunbrec, and Shanka too, all peppered liberally across the broken ground. West could see the wall of the fortress now, little more than a mossy hump in the landscape with more death scattered round its foot.

'They held out in there, for seven days?' muttered Pike.

'So it would seem.'

The one entrance was a rough archway in the centre of the wall, its gates torn off and lying ruined. There seemed to be three strange shapes within it. As he got closer, West realised with some discomfort what they were. Three men, hanging dead by their necks from ropes over the top of the wall, their limp boots swinging gently at about chest height. There were a lot of grim Northmen gathered around that gate, looking up at those dangling corpses with some satisfaction. One in particular turned a cruel grin on West and Pike as they came close.

'Well, well, well, if it ain't my old friend Furious,' said Black Dow. 'Turned up late to the party, eh? You always was a slow mover, lad.'

'There were some difficulties. Marshal Burr is dead.'

'Back to the mud, eh? Well, he's in good company, at least. Plenty of good men done that these past days. Who's your chief, now?'

West took a long breath. 'I am.'

Dow laughed, and West watched him laugh, feeling the slightest bit sick. 'Big chief Furious, what do you know?' and he stood up straight and made a mockery of a Union salute while the bodies turned slowly this way and that behind him. 'You should meet my friends. They're all big men too. This here is Crendel Goring, fought for Bethod from way back.' And he reached up and gave one of the bodies a shove, watched it sway back and forth.

'This here is Whitesides, and you couldn't have found a better man anywhere for killing folk and stealing their land.' And he gave the next a push and set it spinning round and round one way, then back the other, limbs all limp and floppy.

'And this one here is Littlebone. As hard a bastard as I've ever hung.' This last man was hacked near to meat, his gold-chased armour battered and dented, a great wound across his chest and his hanging grey hair thick with blood. One leg was off below his knee, and a pool of dry blood stained the ground underneath him.

'What happened to him?' asked West.

'To Littlebone?' The great fat hillman, Crummock-i-Phail, was one of the crowd. 'He got cut down in the battle, fighting to the last man, over yonder.'

'That he did,' said Dow, and he gave West a grin even bigger than usual. 'But that's no kind of a reason not to hang him now, I reckon.'

Crummock laughed. 'No kind of a reason!' And he smiled at the three bodies turning round and round, the ropes creaking.

'They make a pretty picture, don't they, hanging there? They say you can see all the beauty in the world in the way a hanged man swings.'

'Who does?' asked West.

Crummock shrugged his great shoulders. 'Them.'

'Them, eh?' West swallowed his nausea and pushed his way between the hanging bodies into the fortress. 'They surely are a bloodthirsty crowd.'

Dogman took another pull at the flask. He was getting good and drunk now. 'Alright. Let's get it done then.'

He winced as Grim stuck the needle in, curled his lips back and hissed through his teeth. A nice pricking and niggling to add to the dull throb. The needle went through the skin and dragged the thread after, and Dogman's arm started burning worse and worse. He took another swig, rocking back and forward, but it didn't help.

'Shit,' he hissed. 'Shit, shit!'

Grim looked up at him. 'Don't watch, then.'

Dogman turned his head. The Union uniform jumped out at him straight away. Red cloth in the midst of all that brown dirt. 'Furious!' shouted the Dogman, feeling a grin on his face even through the pain. 'Glad you could make it! Real glad!'

'Better to come late than not to come at all.'

'You'll get no trace of an argument from me. That is a fact.'

West frowned down at Grim sewing his arm up. 'You alright?'

'Well, you know. Tul's dead.'

'Dead?' West stared at him. 'How?'

'It's a battle, ain't it? Dead men are the point o' the fucking exercise.' He waved the flask around. 'I've been sat here, thinking about what I could've done differently. Stopped him going down them steps, or gone down with him to watch his back, or made the sky fall in, or all kind o' stupid notions, none of 'em any help to the dead nor the living. Seems I can't stop thinking, though.'

West frowned down at the rutted earth. 'Might be's a game with no winners.'

'Ah, fuck!' Dogman snarled as the needle jabbed into his arm again, and he flung the empty flask bouncing away. 'The whole fucking business has no winners, though, does it! Shit on it all, I say.'

Grim pulled his knife out and cut the thread. 'Move your fingers.' It burned all the way up Dogman's arm to make a fist, but he forced the fingers closed, growling at the pain as they bunched up tight.

'Looks alright,' said Grim. 'You're lucky.'

The Dogman stared round miserably at the carnage. 'So this is what luck looks like, is it? I've often wondered.' Grim shrugged his shoulders, ripped a piece of cloth for a bandage.

'Do you have Bethod?'

Dogman looked up at West, his mouth open. 'Don't you?'

'A lot of prisoners, but he wasn't among them.'

Dogman turned his head and spat his disgust out into the mud. 'Nor his witch, nor his Feared, nor neither one of his swollen up sons, I'll be bound.'

'I imagine they'll be riding for Carleon as swiftly as possible.'

'More'n likely.'

'I imagine he'll try to raise new forces, to find new allies, to prepare for a siege.'

'I shouldn't wonder.'

'We should follow him as soon as the prisoners are secure.'

Dogman felt a sudden wave of hopelessness, enough almost to knock him over. 'By the dead. Bethod got away.' He laughed, and felt tears prickling his eyes the next moment. 'Will there ever be an end to it?'

Grim finished wrapping the bandage and tied it up tight. 'You're done.'

Dogman stared back at him. 'Done? I'm starting to think I won't ever be done.' He held his hand out. 'Help me up, eh, Furious? I got a friend to bury.'

The sun was getting low when they put Tul in the ground, just peering over the tops of the mountains and touching the edges of the clouds with gold. Good weather, to bury a good man.

They stood round the grave, all packed in tight. There were plenty of others being buried, the sad words for them wept and whispered all around, but Tul had been well-loved, no man more, so there was quite the crowd. Even so, all round Logen there was a gap. An empty space a man wide. That space he used to have around him in the old days, where no one would dare to stand. Logen hardly blamed them. He'd have run away himself, if he could.

'Who wants to speak?' asked the Dogman, looking at them, one by one. Logen stared down at his feet, not even able to meet his eye, let alone say a word. He wasn't sure what had happened, in the battle, but he could guess. He could guess well enough, from the bits he did remember. He glanced around, licking at his split lips, but if anyone else guessed, they kept it to themselves.

'No one going to say a word?' asked Dogman again, his voice cracking.

'Guess it best be fucking me, then, eh?' And Black Dow stepped forward. He took a long look round at the gathering. Took a long look at Logen in particular, it seemed to him, but that was most likely just his own worries playing tricks.

'Tul Duru Thunderhead,' said Dow. 'Back to the mud. The dead know, we didn't always see things the same way, me and him. Didn't often agree on nothing, but maybe that was my fault, as I'm a contrary bastard at the best o' times. I regret it now, I reckon. Now it's too late.' He took a ragged breath.

'Tul Duru. Every man in the North knew his name, and every man said it with respect, even his enemies. He was the sort o' man . . . that gave you hope, I reckon. That gave you hope. You want strength, do you? You want courage? You want things done right and proper, the old way?' He nodded down at the new-turned earth. 'There you go. Tul Duru Thunderhead. Look no fucking further. I'm less, now that he's gone, and so are all o' you.' And Dow turned and stalked off away from the grave and into the dusk, his head down.

'We're all less,' muttered Dogman, staring down at the earth with the glimmer of a tear in his eye. 'Good words.' They all looked broken up, every one of them stood around the grave. West, and his man Pike, and Shivers, and even Grim. All broken up.

Logen wanted to feel as they did. He wanted to weep. For the death of a good man. For the fact that he might've been the one to cause it. But the tears wouldn't come. He frowned down at the fresh-turned earth, as the sun sank behind the mountains, and the fortress in the High Places grew dark, and he felt less than nothing.

If you want to be a new man you have to stay in new places, and do new things, with people who never knew you before. If you go back to the same old ways, what else can you be but the same old person? You have to be realistic. He'd played at being a different man, but it had all been lies. The hardest kind to see through. The kind you tell yourself. He was the Bloody-Nine. That was the fact, and however he twisted, and squirmed, and wished to be someone else, there was no escaping it. Logen wanted to care.

But the Bloody-Nine cares for nothing.

Rude Awakenings

Jezal was smiling when he began to wake. They were done with this madcap mission, and soon he would be back in Adua. Back in Ardee's arms. Warm and safe. He snuggled down into his blankets at the thought. Then he frowned. There was a knocking sound coming from somewhere. He opened his eyes a crack. Someone hissed at him from across the room, and he turned his head.

He saw Terez' face, pale in the darkness, glaring from between the bed curtains, and the last few weeks came back in a horrible rush. She looked just as she had the day he married her, surely, and yet the perfect face of his queen seemed now ugly and hateful to him.

The royal bedchamber had become a battlefield. The border, watched with iron determination, was an invisible line between door and fireplace which Jezal crossed at his peril. The far side of the room was Styrian territory, and the mighty bed itself was Terez' strongest citadel, its defences apparently impregnable. On the second night of their marriage, hoping perhaps that there had been some misunderstanding on the first, he had mounted a half-hearted assault which had left him with a bloody nose. Since then he had settled in hopelessly for a long and fruitless siege.

Terez was the very mistress of deception. He would sleep on the floor, or on some item of furniture never quite long enough, or wherever he pleased as long as it was not with her. Then at breakfast she would smile at him, and speak of nothing, sometimes even place her hand fondly on his when she knew they were being watched. Occasionally she would even have *him* believing that all was now well, but as soon as they were alone she would turn her back on him, and bludgeon him with silence, and stab him with looks of such epic scorn and disgust that he wanted to be sick.

Her ladies-in-waiting behaved towards him with scarcely less contempt whenever he had the misfortune to find himself in their whispering presence. One in particular, the Countess Shalere, apparently his wife's closest friend since a tender age, eyed him always with a murderous hatred. On one occasion he had blundered into the salon where all dozen of them were sitting arranged around Terez, muttering in Styrian. He had felt like a peasant boy stumbling upon a coven of extremely well-presented witches, chanting some dark curse. Probably one directed towards himself. He was made to feel like the lowest, most repulsive animal alive. And he was a king, in his own palace.

For some reason he lived in inexplicable horror that somebody would realise the truth, but if any of the servants noticed they kept it to themselves. He wondered if he should have told someone, but who? And what? Lord Chamberlain, good day. My wife refuses to fuck me. Your Eminence, well met. My wife will not look at me. High Justice, how are you? The Queen despises me, by the way. Most of all, he feared telling Bayaz. He had warned the Magus away from his personal affairs in no uncertain terms, and could scarcely go crawling for his help now.

And so he went along with the fiction, miserable and confused, and with every day that he pretended at marital bliss it became more and more impossible to see his way clear of it. His whole life stretched away before him – loveless, friendless, and sleeping on the floor.

'Well?' hissed Terez.

'Well what?' he snarled back.

'The door!'

As if on cue there was a brutal banging at the door, making it rattle in its frame. 'Nothing good ever comes from Talins,' Jezal whispered under his breath, as he flung back his blankets and struggled up from the carpet, stumbled angrily across the room and turned the key in the lock.

Gorst stood in the hallway outside, clad in full armour and with his sword drawn, a lantern held up in one hand, harsh light across one side of his heavy, worried face. From somewhere down the hall came the sound of echoing footsteps, of confused shouting, the flickering of distant lamps. Jezal frowned, suddenly wide awake. He did not like the feel of this.

'Your Majesty,' said Gorst.

'What the hell is going on?'

'The Gurkish have invaded Midderland.'

Ferro's eyes snapped open. She sprang up from the settle, her feet planted wide in a fighting stance, the torn-off table leg gripped tight in her fist. She cursed under her breath. She had fallen asleep, and nothing good ever happened when she did that. But there was no one in the room.

All dark and silent.

No sign of the cripple, or his black-masked servants. No sign of the armoured guards who watched her through narrowed eyes whenever she took a step down the tiled halls of this cursed place. Only the slightest chink of light under the panelled door that led through to Bayaz' room. That and a quiet murmuring of voices. She frowned, and padded over, kneeling silently beside the keyhole.

'Where have they landed?' Bayaz' voice, muffled through the wood.

'Their first boats came ashore in the grey dusk, on the empty beaches at the southwestern tip of Midderland, near to Keln.' Yulwei. Ferro felt a tingling thrill, her breath coming fast and cold in her nostrils. 'Are you prepared?'

Bayaz snorted. 'We could scarcely be less so. I was not expecting Khalul to move so soon, or so suddenly. They landed in the night, eh? Unannounced. Did Lord Brock not see them come?'

'My guess is that he saw them all too well, and welcomed them by previous arrangement. No doubt he has been promised the throne of the Union, once the Gurkish have crushed all resistance and hung your bastard from the gates of the Agriont.

He will be king – subject to the might of Uthman-ul-Dosht, of course.'

'Treachery.'

'Of an unremarkable kind. It should hardly shock such as we, eh, brother? We have seen worse, I think, and done worse too, perhaps.'

'Some things must be done.'

She heard Yulwei sigh. 'I never denied it.'

'How many Gurkish?'

'They never come in ones and twos. Five legions, perhaps, so far, but they are only the vanguard. Many more are coming. Thousands. The whole South moves to war.'

'Is Khalul with them?'

'Why would he be? He stays in Sarkant, in his sunny gardens upon the mountain terraces, and waits for news of your destruction. Mamun leads them. Fruit of the desert, thrice blessed and thrice—'

'I know the names he calls himself, the arrogant worm!'

'Whatever he calls himself, he is grown strong, and the Hundred Words are with him. They are here for you, brother. They are come. If I walked in your footsteps I would be away. Away to the cold North, while there is still time.'

'And then what? Will they not follow me? Should I flee to the edge of the World? I was there, not long ago, and it holds little appeal. I have yet a few cards left to play.'

A long pause. 'You found the Seed?'

'No.'

Another pause. 'I am not sorry. To tinker with those forces . . . to bend the First Law, if not to break it. The last time that thing was used it made a ruin of Aulcus and came near to making a ruin of the whole world. It is better left buried.'

'Even if our hopes are buried with it?'

'There are greater things at risk than my hopes, or yours.'

Ferro did not care a shit for Bayaz' hopes, or Yulwei's either if it came to that. They had both deceived her. She had swallowed a bellyful of their lies, and their secrets, and their promises. She had done nothing but talk, and wait, and talk again for far too long. She stood up, and lifted her leg, and gave a fighting scream. Her heel caught the lock and tore it from the frame, sent the door shuddering open. The two old men sat at a table nearby, a single lamp throwing light over the dark face, and the pale. A third figure sat in the shadows of the far corner. Quai, silent and sunk in darkness.

'Could you not have knocked?' asked Bayaz.

Yulwei's smile was a bright curve in his dark skin. 'Ferro! It is good to see you still—'

'When are the Gurkish coming?'

His grin faded, and he gave a long sigh. 'I see that you have not learned patience.'

'I learnt it, then ran out of it. When are they coming?'

'Soon. Their scouts are already moving through the country-side of Midderland, taking the villages and laying the fortresses under siege, making the country safe for the rest who will come behind.'

'Someone should stop them,' muttered Ferro, her nails digging into her palms.

Bayaz sat back in his chair, the shadows collecting in his craggy face. 'You speak my very thoughts. Your luck has changed, eh, Ferro? I promised you vengeance, and now it drops ripe and bloody into your lap. Uthman's army has landed. Thousands of Gurkish, and ready for war. They might be at the city gates within two weeks.'

'Two weeks,' whispered Ferro.

'But I have no doubt some Union soldiers will be going out to greet them sooner. I could find you a place with them, if you cannot wait.'

She had waited long enough. Thousands of Gurkish, and ready for war. The smile tugged at one corner of Ferro's mouth, then grew, and grew, until her cheeks were aching.

PART II

'Last Argument of Kings'

Inscribed on his cannons by Louis XIV

The Number of the Dead

I t was quiet in the village. The few houses, built from old stone with roofs of mossy slate, seemed deserted. The only life in the fields beyond, mostly fresh-harvested and ploughed over, were a handful of miserable crows. Next to Ferro the bell in the tower creaked softly. Some loose shutters on a window swung and tapped. A few curled-up leaves fell on a gust of wind and fluttered gently to the empty square. On the horizon three columns of dark smoke rose up just as gently into the heavy sky.

The Gurkish were coming, and they always had loved to burn.

'Maljinn!' Major Vallimir was below, framed by the trap-door, and Ferro scowled down. He reminded her of Jezal dan Luthar when she had first met him. A plump, pale face stuffed with that infuriating mixture of panic and arrogance. It was plain enough that he had never set an ambush for a goat before, let alone for Gurkish scouts. But still he pretended he knew best. 'Do you see anything?' he hissed at her, for the fifth time in an hour.

'I see them coming,' Ferro growled back.

'How many?'

'Still a dozen.'

'How far off?'

'Perhaps quarter of an hour's ride, now, and your asking will not make them come quicker.'

'When they are in the square, I will give the signal with two claps.'

'Make sure you do not miss one hand with the other, pink.'

'I told you not to call me that!' A brief pause. 'We must take one of them alive, to question.'

Ferro wrinkled her nose. Her taste did not lean towards taking Gurkish alive. 'We will see.'

She turned back to the horizon, and soon enough she heard the sound of Vallimir whispering orders to some of his men. The rest were scattered around the other buildings, hiding. An odd crowd of left-over soldiers. A few were veterans, but most of them were even younger and more twitchy than Vallimir himself. Ferro wished, and not for the first time, that they had Ninefingers with them. Like him or not, no one could have denied that the man knew his business. With him, Ferro had known what she would get. Solid experience or, on occasion, murderous fury. Either one would have been useful.

But Ninefingers was not there.

So Ferro stood in the wide window of the bell tower, alone, frowning out across the rolling fields of Midderland, and watched the riders come closer. A dozen Gurkish scouts, trotting in a loose group down a track. Wriggling specks on a pale streak between patchworks of dark earth.

They slowed as they passed the first wood-built barn, spreading out. A great Gurkish host would number soldiers from all across the Empire, fighters from a score of different conquered provinces. These twelve scouts were Kadiris, by their long faces and narrow eyes, their saddle-bags of patterned cloth, lightly armed with bows and spears. Killing them would not be much vengeance, but it would be some. It would fill the space for now. A space that had been empty far too long.

One of them startled as a crow flapped up from a scraggy tree. Ferro held her breath, sure that Vallimir or one of his blundering pinks would choose that moment to trip over one another. But there was only silence as the horsemen eased carefully into the village square, their leader with one hand raised for caution. He looked right up at her, but saw nothing. Arrogant fools. They saw only what they wanted to see. A village from which everyone had fled, crushed with fear of the Emperor's matchless army. Her fist clenched tight around her bow. They would learn.

She would teach them.

The leader had a square of floppy paper out in his hands, peering at it as though it was a message in a language he did not understand. A map, maybe. One of his men reined his horse in and slid from the saddle, took its bridle and led it towards a mossy trough. Two more sat loose on their mounts, talking and grinning, moving their hands, telling jokes. A fourth cleaned his fingernails with a knife. Another rode slowly round the edge of the square, leaning from his saddle and peering in through the windows of the houses. Looking for something to steal. One of the joke-tellers burst into a deep peal of laughter.

Then two sharp claps echoed from the buildings.

The scout by the trough was just filling his flask when Ferro's shaft sank into his chest. The canteen tumbled from his hand, shining drops spilling from the neck. Flatbows rattled in the windows. Scouts yelled and stared. One horse stumbled sideways and fell, puffs of dust rising from its flailing hooves, crushing its rider screaming underneath it.

Union soldiers charged from the buildings, shouting, spears ready. One of the riders had his sword half-drawn when he was nailed with a flatbow bolt, and fell lolling from the saddle. Ferro's second arrow took another in the back. The one who had been picking his fingernails was dumped from his horse, stumbled up in time to see a Union soldier coming at him with a spear. He threw down his knife and held his arms up too late, was run through anyway, the spear point sticking bloody out of his back as he fell.

Two of them made a dash the way they had come. Ferro took aim at one, but as they reached the narrow lane a rope was pulled tight across the gap. The pair of them were snatched from their saddles, dragging a Union soldier yelping from a building, bouncing along a few strides on his face, rope stuck tight round his arm. One of Ferro's arrows caught a scout between his shoulder-blades as he tried to push himself up from the dust. The other dragged himself a groggy few strides before a Union soldier hit him in the head with a sword and left the back of his skull hanging off.

Of the dozen, only the leader got away from the village. He

339

spurred his horse for a narrow fence between two buildings, jumping it with hooves clattering against the top rail. He galloped off across the coarse stubble of a harvested field, pressed low into his saddle, jerking his heels into his horse's flanks.

Ferro took a long, slow aim, feeling the smile tugging at the corners of her face. All in a moment she judged the way he was sitting in the saddle, the speed of the horse, the height of the tower, felt the wind on her face, the weight of the shaft, the tension in the wood, the string biting into her lip. She watched the arrow fly, a spinning black splinter against the grey sky, and the horse rushed forwards to meet it.

Sometimes, God is generous.

The leader arched his back and tumbled from the saddle, rolling over and over on the dusty earth, specks of mud and cut stalks flying up around him. His cry of agony came to Ferro's ear a moment later. Her lips curled back further from her teeth.

'Hah!' She threw the bow over her shoulder, slid down the ladder, vaulted through the back window and dashed out across the field. Her boots thudded in the soft soil between the clumps of stubble, her hand tightened around the grip of her sword.

The man mewled in the dirt as he tried to drag himself towards his horse. He got one desperate finger hooked over the stirrup as he heard Ferro's quick footsteps behind, but fell back with a squeal when he tried to lift himself. He lay on his side as she ran up, the blade hissing angry from its wooden sheath. His eyes rolled towards her, wild with pain and fear.

A dark face, like her own.

An unexceptional face of forty years old, with a patchy beard and a pale birth-mark on one cheek, dust caked to the other, beads of shining sweat across his forehead. She stood over him, and sunlight glinted on the edge of the curved sword.

'Give me a reason not to do it,' she found she had said. Strange, that she had said it, and to a soldier in the Emperor's army, of all people. In the heat and dust of the Badlands of Kanta she had not been in the habit of offering chances.

Perhaps something had changed in her, out there in the wet and ruined west of the world.

He stared up for a moment, his lip trembling. 'I . . .' he croaked, 'my daughters! I have two daughters. I pray to see them married . . .'

Ferro frowned. She should not have let him start talking. A father, with daughters. Just as she had once had a father, been a daughter. This man had done her no harm. He was no more Gurkish than she was. He had not chosen to fight, most likely, or had any choice but to do as the mighty Uthman-ul-Dosht commanded.

'I will go . . . I swear to God . . . I will go back to my wife and my daughters . . .'

The arrow had taken him just under the shoulder and gone clean through, snapped off when he hit the ground. She could see the splintered shaft under his arm. It had missed his lung, by the way he was talking. It would not kill him. Not right away, at least. Ferro could help him onto his horse and he would be gone, with a chance to live.

The scout held up a trembling hand, a spatter of blood on his long thumb. 'Please . . . this is not my war, I—'

The sword carved a deep wound out of his face, through his mouth, splitting his lower jaw apart. He made a hissing moan. The next blow cut his head half off. He rolled over, dark blood pouring out into the dark earth, clutching at the stubble of the shorn crop. The sword broke the back of his skull open and he was still.

It seemed that Ferro was not in a merciful mood that day.

The butchered scout's horse stared dumbly at her. 'What?' she snapped. Perhaps she had changed, out there in the west, but no one changes that much. One less soldier in Uthman's army was a good thing, wherever he came from. She had no need to make excuses for herself. Especially not to a horse. She grabbed at its bridle and gave it a yank.

Vallimir might have been a pink fool, but Ferro had to admit that he had managed the ambush well. Ten scouts lay dead in the village square, their torn clothes flapping in the breeze, their blood smeared across the dusty ground. The only Union casualty was the idiot who had been jerked over by his own rope, covered in dust and scratches.

A good day's work, so far.

A soldier poked at one of the corpses with his boot. 'So this is what the Gurkish look like, eh? Not so fearsome now.'

'These are not Gurkish,' said Ferro. 'Kadiri scouts, pressed into service. They did not want to be here any more than you wanted them here.' The man stared back at her, puzzled and annoyed. 'Kanta is full of people. Not everyone with a brown face is Gurkish, or prays to their God, or bows to their Emperor.'

'Most do.'

'Most have no choice.'

'They're still the enemy,' he sneered.

'I did not say we should spare them.' She shouldered past, back through the door into the building with the bell tower. It seemed Vallimir had managed to take a prisoner after all. He and some others were clustered nervously around one of the scouts, on his knees with his arms bound tightly behind him. He had a bloody graze down one side of his face, staring up with that look that prisoners tend to have.

Scared.

'Where . . . is . . . your . . . main . . . body?' Vallimir was demanding.

'He does not speak your tongue, pink,' snapped Ferro, 'and shouting it will not help.'

Vallimir looked angrily round at her. 'Perhaps we should have brought someone with us who speaks Kantic,' he said with heavy irony.

'Perhaps.'

There was a long pause, while Vallimir waited for her to say more, but she said nothing. Eventually, he gave a long sigh. 'Do you speak Kantic?'

'Of course.'

'Then would you be so kind as to ask him some questions for us?'

Ferro sucked her teeth. A waste of her time, but if it had to be done, it was best done quickly. 'What shall I ask him?'

'Well . . . how far away the Gurkish army is, how many are in it, what route they are taking, you know—'

'Huh.' Ferro squatted down in front of the prisoner and looked him squarely in the eyes. He stared back, helpless and frightened, no doubt wondering what she was doing with these pinks. She wondered herself.

'Who are you?' he whispered.

She drew her knife and held it up. 'You will answer my questions, or I will kill you with this knife. That is who I am. Where is the Gurkish army?'

He licked his lips. 'Perhaps . . . two days' march away, to the south.'

'How many?'

'More than I could count. Many thousands. People of the deserts, and the plains, and the—'

'What route are they taking?'

'I do not know. We were only told to ride to this village, and see whether it was empty.' He swallowed, the lump on the front of his sweaty throat bobbing up and down. 'Perhaps my Captain knows more—'

'Ssss,' hissed Ferro. His Captain would be telling nobody anything now she had carved up his head. 'A lot of them,' she snapped at Vallimir, in common, 'and many more to come, two days' march behind. He does not know their route. What now?'

Vallimir rubbed at the light stubble on his jaw. 'I suppose . . . we should take him back to the Agriont. Deliver him to the Inquisition.'

'He knows nothing. He will only slow us down. We should kill him.'

'He surrendered! To kill him would be no better than murder, war or no war.' Vallimir beckoned to one of the soldiers. 'I won't have that on my conscience.'

'I will.' Ferro's knife slid smoothly into the scout's heart, and out. His mouth and his eyes opened up very wide. Blood bubbled through the split cloth on his chest, spread out quickly in a dark ring. He gawped at it, making a long sucking sound.

'Glugh . . .' His head dropped back, his body sagged. She turned to see the soldiers staring at her, pale faces puffed up with shock. A busy day for them, maybe. A lot to learn, but they would soon get used to it.

That, or the Gurkish would kill them.

'They want to burn your farms, and your towns, and your cities. They want to make slaves of your children. They want everyone in the world to pray to God in the same way they do, with the same words they use, and for your land to be a province of their Empire. I know this.' Ferro wiped the blade of her knife on the sleeve of the dead man's tunic. 'The only difference between war and murder is the number of the dead.'

Vallimir stared down at the corpse of his prisoner for a moment, his lips thoughtfully pursed. Ferro wondered if he had more backbone than she had given him credit for. Finally, he turned towards her. 'What do you suggest?'

'We could wait for more here. Perhaps even get some real Gurkish this time. But that might mean too many for we few.'

'So?'

'East, or north, and set another trap like this one.'

'And defeat the Emperor's army a dozen men at a time? Small steps.'

Ferro shrugged. 'Small steps in the right direction. Unless you've seen enough, and want to go back to your walls.'

Vallimir gave her a long frown, then he turned to one of his men, a heavy-built veteran with a scar on his cheek. 'There is a village just east of here, is there not, Sergeant Forest?'

'Yes, sir. Marlhof is no more than ten miles distant.'

'Will that suit you?' asked Vallimir, raising one eyebrow at Ferro.

'Dead Gurkish suit me. That is all.'

Leaves on the Water

'Carleon,' said Logen.

'Aye,' said Dogman.

It squatted there, in the fork of the river, under the brooding clouds. Hard shapes of tall walls and towers on the sheer bluff above the fast-flowing water, up where Skarling's hall used to stand. Slate roofs and stone buildings squashed in tight on the long downward slope, clustered in round the foot of the hill and with another wall outside, everything leant a cold, sharp shine from the rain just finished falling. Dogman couldn't say he was glad to see the place again. Every visit yet had turned out badly.

'It's changed some, since the battle, all them years ago.' Logen was looking down at his spread-out hand, waggling the stump of his missing finger.

'There weren't no walls like that round it then.'

'No. But there weren't no Union army round it neither.'

Dogman couldn't deny it was a comforting fact. The Union pickets worked their way through the empty fields about the city, a wobbly line of earthworks, and stakes, and fences, with men moving behind 'em, dull sunlight catching metal now and then. Thousands of men, well-armed and vengeful, keeping Bethod penned up.

'You sure he's in there?'

'Don't see where else he's got to go. He lost most of his best boys up in the mountains. No friends left, I reckon.'

'We've all got less than we used to,' Dogman muttered. 'I guess we just sit here. We got time, after all. Lots of it. We sit here and watch the grass grow, and we wait for Bethod to give up.'

'Aye.' But Logen didn't look like he believed it.

'Aye,' said Dogman. But just giving up didn't sound much like the Bethod he knew.

He turned his head at the sound of hooves fast on the road, saw one of those messengers with a helmet like an angry chicken race from the trees and towards West's tent, horse well-lathered from hard riding. He reined up in a fumbling hurry, near fell out of his saddle in his rush to get down, wobbled past a few staring officers and in through the flap. Dogman felt that familiar weight of worry in his gut. 'That's got the taste o' bad news.'

'What other kind is there?'

There was some flutter down there now, soldiers shouting, throwing their arms around. 'Best go and see what's happened,' muttered Dogman, though he'd much rather have walked the other way. Crummock was stood near the tent, frowning at the commotion.

'Something's up,' said the hillman. 'But I don't understand a thing these Southerners say or do. I swear, they're all mad.'

Mad chatter came surging out of that tent alright, when Dogman pushed back the flap. There were Union officers all around the place and in a bastard of a muddle. West was in the midst of it, face pale as fresh milk, his fists clenched tight around nothing.

'Furious!' Dogman grabbed him by the arm. 'What the hell's happening?'

'The Gurkish have invaded Midderland.' West pulled his arm free and took to shouting.

'The who have done what now?' muttered Crummock.

'The Gurkish.' Logen was frowning deep. 'Brown folk, from way down south. Hard folk, by all accounts.'

Pike had come up now, his burned face grim. 'They landed an army by sea. They might have reached Adua already.'

'Hold on, now.' Dogman didn't know a thing about Gurkish, or Adua, or Midderland, but his bad feeling was getting worse every moment. 'What're you telling us, exactly?'

'We've been ordered home. Now.'

Dogman stared. He should've known all along it couldn't be

346

this simple. He grabbed West by the arm again, stabbing down towards Carleon with his dirty finger. 'We've nothing like the men we need to carry on a siege o' this place without you!'

'I know,' said West, 'and I'm sorry. But there's nothing I can do. Get over to General Poulder!' he snapped at a young lad with a squint. 'Tell him to get his division ready to march for the coast at once!'

Dogman blinked, feeling sick to his stomach. 'So we fought seven days in the High Places for nothing? Tul died, and the dead know how many more, for nothing?' It always took him by surprise, how fast something could fall apart once you were leaning on it. 'That's it, then. Back to woods, and cold, and running, and killing. No end to it.'

'Might be another way,' said Crummock.

'What way?'

The chief of the hillmen had a sly grin. 'You know, don't you Bloody-Nine?'

'Aye. I know.' Logen had a look like a man who knows he's about to hang, and he's staring at the tree they're going to do it from. 'When have you got to leave, Furious?'

West frowned. 'We have a lot of men and not a lot of road. Poulder's division tomorrow, I imagine, and Kroy's the day after.'

Crummock's grin got a shade wider. 'So all day tomorrow, there'll be piles o' men sat here, dug in round Bethod, looking like they're never going nowhere, eh?'

'I suppose there could be.'

'Give me tomorrow,' said Logen. 'Give me just that and maybe I can settle things. Then I'll come south with you if I'm still alive, and bring who I can. That's my word. We'll help you with the Gurkish.'

'What difference can one day make?' asked West.

'Aye,' muttered Dogman, 'what's one day?' Trouble was, he could already guess the answer.

Water trickled under the old bridge, past the trees and off down the green hillside. Down towards Carleon. Logen watched a few yellow leaves carried on it, turning round and round, dragged past the mossy stones. He wished that he could just float away, but it didn't seem likely.

'We fought here,' said the Dogman. 'Threetrees and Tul, Dow and Grim, and me. Forley's buried in them woods somewhere.'

'You want to go up there?' asked Logen. 'Give him a visit, see if—'

'What for? I doubt a visit'll do me any good, and I'm damn sure it won't do him any. Nothing will. That's what it is to be dead. You sure about this, Logen?'

'You see another way? The Union won't stick. Might be our last chance to finish with Bethod. Not that much to lose, is there?'

'There's your life.'

Logen took a long breath. 'Can't think of too many people who place much value on that. You coming down?'

Dogman shook his head. 'Reckon I'll stay up here. I had a belly full o' Bethod.'

'Alright then. Alright.' It was as if all the moments of Logen's life, things said and things done, choices he hardly remembered making, had led him to this. Now there was no choice at all. Maybe there never had been. He was like the leaves on the water – carried along, down towards Carleon, and nothing he could do about it. He gave his heels to his horse and off down the slope alone, down the dirt track, beside the gurgling stream.

Everything seemed picked out clearer than usual, as the day wore down. He rode past trees, damp leaves getting ready to fall – golden yellow, burning orange, vivid purple, all the colours of fire. Down towards the valley bottom through the heavy air, just a trace of autumn mist to it, sharp in his throat. The sounds of saddle creaking, harness rattling, hoofbeats in the soft ground all came muffled. He trotted through the empty fields, turned mud pocked with weeds, past the Union pickets, a ditch and a line of sharpened stakes, three times bow-shot from the walls. Soldiers there, in studded jackets and steel caps, watched him pass with frowns on their faces.

He pulled on the reins and slowed his horse to a walk. He clattered over a wooden bridge, one of Bethod's new ones, the river underneath surging with the autumn rain. Up the gentle rise, the wall looming over him. High, sheer, dark and solid looking. A threatening piece of wall if ever there'd been one. He couldn't see men at the slots in the battlements, but he guessed they had to be there. He swallowed, spit moving awkward in his throat, then made himself sit up tall, pretending he wasn't cut and aching all over from seven days of battle in the mountains. He wondered if he was about to hear a flatbow click, feel the stab of pain then drop into the mud, dead. Some kind of an embarrassing song that would make.

'Well, well, well!' came a deep voice, and Logen knew it right away. Who else would it be but Bethod?

The strange thing was that he was glad to hear it, for the quickest moment. Until he remembered all the blood between them. Until he remembered they hated each other. You can have enemies you never really meet, Logen had plenty. You can kill men you don't know, he'd done it often. But you can't truly hate a man without loving him first, and there's always a trace of that love left over.

'I'm taking a look down from my gates and who should ride up out of the past?' Bethod called to him. 'The Bloody-Nine! Would you believe it? I'd organise a feast, but we've no food to spare in here!' He stood there, at the parapet, high up above the doors, fists on the stone. He didn't sneer. He didn't smile. He didn't do much of anything.

'If it ain't the King o' the Northmen!' Logen shouted up. 'Still got your golden hat, then?'

Bethod touched the ring round his head, the big jewel on his brow glittering with the setting sun. 'Why wouldn't I have?'

'Let me see . . .' Logen looked left and right, up and down the bare walls. 'Just that you've got shit all left to be King of, far as I can tell.'

'Huh. I reckon we're both feeling lonely. Where are your

friends, Bloody-Nine? Those killers you liked around you. Where's the Thunderhead, and Grim, and the Dogman, and that bastard Black Dow?'

'All done with, Bethod. Dead, up in the mountains. Dead as Skarling. Them and Littlebone, and Goring, and Whitesides, and plenty more besides.'

Bethod looked grim at that. 'Not much to cheer about, if you're asking me. That's some useful men gone back to the mud, one way or another. Some friends of mine, and some of yours. There never is a happy outcome with we two, is there? Bad as friends, and worse as enemies. What did you come here for, Ninefingers?'

Logen sat there, for a moment, thinking of all the other times he'd done what he had to do now. The challenges he'd made, and their outcomes, and there were no happy memories among that lot. Say one thing for Logen Ninefingers, say he's reluctant. But there was no other way. 'I'm here to make a challenge!' he bellowed, and the sound of it echoed back from the damp, dark walls and died a slow death in the misty air.

Bethod tipped back his head and laughed. A laugh without much joy in it, Logen reckoned. 'By the dead, Ninefingers, but you never change. You're like some old dog no one can stop from barking. Challenge? What have we got left to fight over?'

'I win, you open the gates and belong to me. My prisoner. I lose, the Union pack up and sail for home, and you're free.'

Bethod's smile slowly faded and his eyes narrowed, suspicious. Logen knew that look from way back. Turning over the chances, sorting through the reasons why. 'That sounds like a golden offer, considering the fix I'm in. Hard to believe it. What's in it for your Southern friends up there?'

Logen snorted. 'They'll wait, if they have to, but they don't much care about you, Bethod. You're nothing to them, for all your bluster. They kicked your arse across the North already and they reckon you'll not be bothering them again either way. If I win, they get your head. If I lose, they can go home early.'

'I'm nothing to them, eh?' Bethod split a sad smile. 'Is that what it's come to, after all my work, and sweat, and pain? Are you happy, Ninefingers? To see all I've fought for put in the dust?'

'Why shouldn't I be? You've no one but yourself to blame for it. It was you brought us to this. Take my challenge, Bethod, then maybe one of us can have peace!'

The King of the Northmen gaped down, eyes wide. 'No one else to blame? Me? How soon we all forget!' He grabbed the chain round his shoulders and rattled it. 'You think I wanted this? You think I asked for any of it? All I wanted was a strip more land to feed my people, to stop the big clans squeezing me. All I wanted was to win a few victories to be proud of, to pass on something better to my sons than I got from my father.' He leaned forward, his hands clutching at the battlements. 'Who was it always had to push a step further? Who was it would never let me stop? Who was it had to taste blood, and once he'd tasted it got drunk on it, went mad with it, could never get enough?' His finger stabbed down. 'Who else but the Bloody-Nine?'

'That's not how it was,' growled Logen.

Bethod's laughter echoed harsh on the wind. 'Is it not? I wanted to talk with Shama Heartless, but you had to kill him! I tried to strike a deal at Heonan, but you had to climb up and settle your score, and start a dozen more! Peace, you say? I begged you to let me make peace at Uffrith, but you had to fight Threetrees! On my knees I begged you, but you had to have the biggest name in all the North! Then once you'd beaten him, you broke your word to me and let him live, as though there was nothing bigger to think about than your damn pride!'

'That's not how it was,' said Logen.

'There's not a man in the North that doesn't know the truth of it! Peace? Hah! What about Rattleneck, eh? I would have ransomed his son back to him, and we could all have gone home happy, but no! What did you say to me? Easier to stop the Whiteflow than to stop the Bloody-Nine! Then you had to nail his head to my standard for the whole world to see, so the vengeance would never find an end! Every time I tried to stop, you dragged me on, deeper and deeper into the mire! Until there could be no stopping any longer! Until it was kill or be killed! Until I had to put down the whole North! You made me King, Ninefingers. What other choices did you leave me?'

'That's not how it was,' whispered Logen. But he knew it had been.

'Tell yourself that I'm the cause of all your woes if it makes you happy! Tell yourself I'm the merciless one, the murderous one, the bloodthirsty one, but ask yourself who I learned it from. I had the best master! Play at being the good man if you please, the man with no choices, but we both know what you really are. Peace? You'll never have peace, Bloody-Nine. You're made of death!'

Logen would've liked to deny it, but it would just have been more lies. Bethod truly knew him. Bethod truly understood him. Better than anyone. His worst enemy, and still his best friend. 'Then why not kill me, when you had the chance?'

The King of the Northmen frowned, as though he couldn't understand something. Then he started to laugh again. He shrieked with it. 'You don't know why? You stood right beside him and you don't know? You learned nothing from me, Ninefingers! After all these years, you still let the rain wash you any way it pleases!'

'What're you saying?' snarled Logen.

'Bayaz!'

'Bayaz? What of him?'

'I was ready to put the bloody cross in you, sink your carcass in a bog with all the rest of your misfit idiots and was happy to do it, until that old liar came calling!'

'And?'

'I owed him, and he wanted you let go. It was that meddling old fuck that saved your worthless hide, and nothing else!'

'Why?' growled Logen, not knowing what to make of it, but not liking that he was learning about it so long after everyone else.

But Bethod only chuckled. 'Maybe I didn't grovel low enough for his taste. You're the one he saved, you ask him the whys, if you live long enough. But I don't think you will. I take

352

your challenge! Here. Tomorrow. At sunrise.' He rubbed his palms together. 'Man against man, with the future of the North hanging bloody on the outcome! Just as it used to be, eh, Logen? In the old days? In the sunny valleys of the past? Roll the dice together one more time, shall we?' The King of the Northmen stepped slowly back, away from the battlements. 'Some things have changed, though. I've a new champion now! If I was you, I'd say your goodbyes tonight, and get ready for the mud! After all . . . what was it you used to tell me . . . ?' His laughter faded slowly into the dusk. 'You have to be realistic!'

'Good piece o' meat,' said Grim.

A warm fire and a good piece of meat were two things to be thankful for, and there'd been times enough when Dogman had a lot less, but watching the blood drip from that chunk of mutton was making him feel sick. Reminded him of the blood that came out of Shama Heartless when Logen split him open. Years ago, maybe, but the Dogman could see it fresh as yesterday. He could hear the roars from the men, the shields crashing together. He could smell the sour sweat and the fresh blood on the snow.

'By the dead,' grunted Dogman, mouth watering like he was about to puke. 'How can you think about eating now?'

Dow gave a toothy grin. 'Us going hungry ain't going to help Ninefingers any. Nothing is. That's the point of a duel, ain't it? All about one man.' He poked at the meat with his knife and made the blood run sizzling into the fire. Then he sat back, thoughtful. 'You reckon he can do it? Really? You remember that thing?' Dogman felt a ghost of the sick fear he'd had in the mist, and he shuddered to his boots. He weren't likely ever to forget the sight of that giant coming through the murk, the sight of his painted fist rising, the sound of it crunching into Threetrees' ribs and crushing the life out of him.

'If anyone can do it,' he growled through his gritted teeth, 'I reckon Logen can.'

'Uh,' grunted Grim.

'Aye, but do you think he will? That's my question. That, and what happens if he don't?' It was a question that Dogman could hardly bear to think up an answer to. Logen would be dead, for a first thing. Then there'd be no siege of Carleon anymore. Dogman had too few men left after the mountains to keep a piss-pot surrounded, let alone the best walled city in the North. Bethod could do as he pleased – seek out help, and find new friends, and set to fighting again. There was no one tougher in a tight corner.

'Logen can do it,' he whispered, bunching his fists and feeling the long cut down his arm burning. 'He has to.'

He nearly fell in the fire when a great fat hand thumped him on the back. 'By the dead but I never seen such a fire-full o' long faces!' Dogman winced. The crazy hillman was hardly what he needed to lift his mood, grinning out of the night with his children behind him, great big weapons over their shoulders.

Crummock was down to just the two now, since one of his sons got killed up in the mountains, but he didn't seem so upset about it. He'd lost his spear too, snapped off in some Easterner, as he was fond of saying, so he still didn't have to carry aught himself. Neither one of the children had said much since the battle, or not in the Dogman's hearing, anyway. No more talk about how many men folk might've killed. The seeing of it close up could be a woeful drain on your enthusiasm for the business of war. Dogman knew well enough how that went.

But Crummock himself had no trouble keeping cheerful. 'Where's Ninefingers got himself off to?'

'Gone off on his own. Always liked to do that, before a duel.'

'Mmm.' Crummock stroked at the fingerbones round his neck. 'Speaking to the moon, I'll be bound.'

'Shitting himself is closer to it, I reckon.'

'Well, as long as you get the shitting done before the fight, I don't reckon anyone could grumble.' He grinned all across his face. 'No one's loved of the moon like the Bloody-Nine, I tell you! No one in all the wide Circle of the World. He's got some kind of chance at winning a fair fight, and that's the best a man could hope for against that devil-thing. There's only one problem.'

'Just one?'

'There'll be no fair fight as long as that damn witch is alive.'

The Dogman felt his shoulders slump even further. 'How d'you mean?'

Crummock spun one of the wooden signs on his necklace round and around. 'I can't see her letting Bethod lose, and herself along with him, can you? A witch as clever as that one? There's all kinds of magic she could mix. All kinds of blessings and curses. All kinds of ways that bitch could tilt the outcome, as though the chances weren't tilted enough already.'

'Eh?'

'My point is this. Someone needs to stop her.'

Dogman hadn't thought he could feel any lower. Now he knew better. 'Good luck with that,' he muttered.

'Ha ha, my lad, ha ha. I'd love to do it, too, but they've got an awful stretch of walls down there, and I'm not much for climbing over 'em.' Crummock slapped one fat hand against his fat belly. 'Twice too much meat for that. No, what we need for this task is a small man, but with great big fruits on him. No doubt we do, and the moon knows it. A man with a talent for creeping about, sharp-eyed and sure-footed. We need someone with a quick hand and a quick mind.' He looked at the Dogman, and he grinned. 'Now where is it that we'd find a man like that, do you reckon?'

'You know what?' Dogman put his face in his hands. 'I've no fucking idea.'

Logen lifted the battered flask to his lips and took a mouthful. He felt the sharp liquor tingling on his tongue, tickling at his throat, that old need to swallow. He leaned forward, pursed his lips, and blew it out in a fine spray. A gout of fire went up into the cold night. He peered into the darkness, saw nothing but the black outlines of tree-trunks, the shifting black shadows that his fire cast between them.

He shook the flask back and forth, heard the last measure sloshing inside. He shrugged his shoulders, put it to his mouth and tipped it all the way, felt it burn down to his stomach. The spirits could share with him tonight. Chances were good that, after tomorrow, he wouldn't be calling on them again.

'Ninefingers.' The voice rustled at him like the leaves falling.

One spirit slid out from the shadows, came up into the light from the fire. There was no trace of recognition about it, and Logen found he was relieved. There was no accusation either, no fear and no distrust. It didn't care what he was, or what he'd done.

Logen tossed the empty flask down beside him. 'On your own?'

'Yes.'

'Well, you're never alone if you bring laughter with you.' The spirit said nothing. 'Reckon laughter's a thing for men, not for spirits.'

'Yes.'

'Don't speak much, do you?'

'I did not call on you.'

'True.' Logen stared into the fire. 'I have to fight a man tomorrow. A man called Fenris the Feared.'

'He is not a man.'

'You know of him, then?'

'He is old.'

'By your reckoning?'

'Nothing is old by my reckoning, but he goes back to the Old Time and beyond. He had another master, then.'

'What master?'

'Glustrod.'

The name was like a knife in the ear. No name could've been less expected, or less welcome. The wind blew cold through the trees, and memories of the towering ruins of Aulcus crowded in on Logen, and made his back shiver. 'No chance it's some different Glustrod than the one came close to destroying half the world?'

'There is no other. He it was that wrote the signs upon the Feared's skin. Signs in the Old Tongue, the language of devils, across his left side. That flesh is of the world below. Where the word of Glustrod is written, the Feared cannot be harmed.'

'Cannot be harmed? Not at all?' Logen thought about it a moment. 'Why not write on both sides?'

'Ask Glustrod.'

'I don't think that's likely.'

'No.' A long pause. 'What will you do, Ninefingers?'

Logen peered off sideways into the trees. The notion of setting off running, and never looking back, seemed a pretty one, right then. Sometimes it can be better to live with the fear of it, than to die doing it, whatever Logen's father had told him.

'I ran before,' he muttered, 'and I only ran a circle. For me, Bethod's at the end of every path.'

'Then that is all our talk.' The spirit stood up from the fire.

'Perhaps I'll see you again.'

'I do not think so. The magic leaks from the world, and my kind sleep. I do not think so. Even if you beat the Feared, and I do not think you will.'

'Message o' hope then, eh?' Logen snorted. 'Luck go with you.'

The spirit faded back into the darkness, and was gone. It did not wish Logen luck. It did not care.

Authority

It was a dour and depressing meeting, even for the Closed Council. The weather beyond the narrow windows was sullen and overcast, promising storms but never delivering, casting the White Chamber into a chill gloom. From time to time heavy gusts of wind would rattle the old window panes, making Jezal start and shiver in his fur-trimmed robe.

The grim expressions of the dozen old faces did little to warm his bones. Lord Marshal Varuz was all clenched jaw and harsh determination. Lord Chamberlain Hoff clutched his goblet like a drowning man clinging to the last fragment of his boat. High Justice Marovia frowned as though he were about to pronounce the death sentence on the entire gathering, himself among them. Arch Lector Sult's thin lip was permanently curled as his cold eyes slid from Bayaz, to Jezal, to Marovia, and back.

The First of the Magi himself glared down the table. 'The situation, please, Lord Marshal Varuz.'

'The situation, honestly, is grim. Adua is in uproar. Perhaps one third of the population has already fled. The Gurkish blockade means that few supplies are making it to the markets. Curfews are in place but some citizens are still seizing the opportunity to rob, steal and riot while the authorities are occupied elsewhere.'

Marovia shook his head, grey beard swaying gently. 'And we can only expect the situation to deteriorate as the Gurkish come closer to the city.'

'Which they are,' said Varuz, 'at the rate of several miles a day. We are doing all we can to frustrate them, but with our resources so limited . . . they may well be outside the gates within the week.'

There were a few shocked gasps, breathed oaths, nervous sideways glances. 'So soon?' Jezal's voice cracked slightly as he said it.

'I am afraid so, your Majesty.'

'What is the Gurkish strength?' asked Marovia.

'Estimates vary wildly. At present however . . .' and Varuz sucked worriedly at his teeth, 'it appears they field at least fifty thousand.'

There were further sharp intakes of breath, not least from Jezal's own throat. 'So many?' muttered Halleck.

'And thousands more landing every day near Keln,' put in Admiral Reutzer, doing nothing to lift the mood. 'With the best part of our navy on its way to retrieve the army after its northern adventure, we are powerless to stop them.'

Jezal licked his lips. The walls of the wide room seemed to close in further with every moment. 'What of our troops?'

Varuz and Reutzer exchanged a brief glance. 'We have two regiments of the King's Own, one of foot and one of horse, some six thousand men in all. The Grey Watch, tasked with the defence of the Agriont itself, numbers four thousand. The Knights Herald and of the Body form an elite of some five hundred. In addition, there are non-combat soldiers – cooks, grooms, smiths, and so forth – who could be armed in an emergency—'

'I believe this qualifies,' observed Bayaz.

'—perhaps some few thousand more. The city watch might be of some use, but they are hardly professional soldiers.'

'What of the nobles?' asked Marovia. 'Where is their aid?'

'Some few have sent men,' said Varuz grimly, 'others only their regrets. Most . . . not even that.'

'Hedging their bets.' Hoff shook his head. 'Brock has let it be known there will be Gurkish gold for those who help him, and Gurkish mercy for those who stand with us.'

'It has ever been so,' lamented Torlichorm. 'The nobles are interested only in their own welfare!'

'Then we must open the armouries,' said Bayaz, 'and we must not be shy with their contents. We must arm every citizen who can hold a weapon. We must arm the labourers' guilds, and the craftsmen's guilds, and the veterans' associations. Even the beggars in the gutters must be ready to fight.'

All well and good, Jezal supposed, but he hardly cared to trust his life to a legion of beggars. 'When will Lord Marshal West return with the army?'

'If he received his orders yesterday, it will be a month at the very least before he is disembarked and ready to come to our aid.'

'Which means we must withstand several weeks of siege,' muttered Hoff, shaking his head. He leaned close to Jezal's ear and spoke softly, quite as if they were schoolgirls trading secrets. 'Your Majesty, it might be prudent for you and your Closed Council to leave the city. To relocate your government further north, outside the path of the Gurkish advance, where the campaign can be conducted in greater safety. To Holsthorm, perhaps, or—'

'Absolutely not,' said Bayaz sternly.

Jezal could scarcely deny that the notion held its attractions. The island of Shabulyan at that moment seemed an ideal place to relocate his government to – but Bayaz was right. Harod the Great would hardly have entertained the idea of retreat, and neither, unfortunately, could Jezal.

'We will fight the Gurkish here,' he said.

'Merely a suggestion,' muttered Hoff, 'merely prudence.'

Bayaz spoke over him. 'How do the defences of the city stand?'

'We have, in essence, three concentric lines of defence. The Agriont itself is, of course, our last bastion.'

'It will not come to that, though, eh?' chuckled Hoff, with far from total conviction.

Varuz decided not to answer. 'Arnault's Wall is beyond it, enclosing the oldest and most crucial parts of the city – the Agriont, the Middleway, the main docks and the Four Corners among them. Casamir's Wall is our outermost line of defence – weaker, lower, and a great deal longer than Arnault's. Smaller walls run between these two, like the spokes of a wheel, dividing the outer ring of the city into five boroughs, each of which can be sealed off, should it be captured by the enemy. There are some built-up areas beyond Casamir's Wall, but those must be immediately abandoned.'

Bayaz planted his elbows on the edge of the table, his meaty fists clasped together. 'Given the number and quality of our troops, we would be best served by evacuating the outer quarters of the city and concentrating our efforts around the much shorter and stronger length of Arnault's wall. We can continue to fight a rear-guard action in the outer boroughs, where our superior knowledge of the streets and buildings stands in our favour—'

'No,' said Jezal.

Bayaz fixed him with a brooding stare. 'Your Majesty?'

But Jezal refused to be overawed. It had been becoming clear for some time that if he allowed the Magus to rule him on every issue then he would never escape from under his boot. He might have seen Bayaz make a man explode with a thought, but he was hardly likely to do it to the King of the Union before his own Closed Council. Not with the Gurkish breathing down all their necks.

'I do not intend to give up the greater part of my capital to the Union's oldest enemy without giving battle. We will defend Casamir's Wall, and fight for every stride of ground.'

Varuz glanced across at Hoff, and the Chamberlain raised his eyebrows by the tiniest fraction. 'Er . . . of course, your Majesty. Every stride.' There was an uncomfortable silence, the displeasure of the First of the Magi hanging over the group as heavily as the storm clouds hung over the city.

'Does my Inquisition have anything to contribute?' croaked Jezal, doing his best to mount a diversion.

Sult's eyes darted coldly up to his. 'Of course, your Majesty. The Gurkish love of intrigue is well known. We have no doubt that there are already spies within the walls of Adua. Perhaps within the Agriont itself. All citizens of Kantic origin are now being interned. My Inquisitors are working day and night in the House of Questions. Several spies have already confessed.'

Marovia snorted. 'So we are expected to suppose that the Gurkish love of intrigue does not extend to the hiring of white-skinned agents?'

'We are at war!' hissed Sult, giving the High Justice a deadly glare. 'The very sovereignty of our nation is at risk! This is no time for your blather about freedom, Marovia!'

'On the contrary, this is precisely the time!'

The two old men bickered on, straining everyone's frayed nerves to breaking point. Bayaz, meanwhile, had sunk back into his chair and folded his arms, watching Jezal with an expression of calm consideration which was, if anything, even more fearsome than his frown. Jezal felt the worry weighing ever heavier upon him. However you looked at things, he was teetering on the verge of having the briefest and most disastrous reign in Union history.

'I am sorry that I had to send for your Majesty,' piped Gorst, in his girlish little voice.

'Of course, of course.' The clicking of Jezal's polished boot-heels echoed angrily around them.

'There is only so much that I can do.'

'Of course.'

Jezal shoved open the double doors with both hands. Terez sat bolt upright in the midst of the gilded chamber beyond, glaring at him down her nose in that manner with which he had become so infuriatingly familiar. As though he were an insect in her salad. Several Styrian ladies looked up, and then back to their tasks. Chests and boxes cluttered the room, clothes were being neatly packed within. Every impression was given that the Queen of the Union was planning to leave the capital, and without so much as informing her husband.

Jezal ground his already aching teeth. He was tormented by a disloyal Closed Council, a disloyal Open Council, and a disloyal populace. The poisonous disloyalty of his wife was almost too much to bear. 'What the hell is this?'

'I and my ladies can hardly assist you in your war with the

362

Emperor.' Terez turned her flawless head smoothly away from him. 'We are returning to Talins.'

'Impossible!' hissed Jezal. 'A Gurkish army of many thousands is bearing down upon the city! My people are fleeing Adua in droves and those that remain are a whisker from sliding into outright panic! Your leaving now would send entirely the wrong message! I cannot allow it!'

'Her Majesty is in no way involved!' snapped the Countess Shalere, gliding across the polished floor towards him.

As though Jezal had not enough to worry about with the Queen herself, he was now obliged to bandy words with her companions. 'You forget yourself,' he snarled at her.

'It is you who forgets!' She took a step towards him, her face twisted. 'You forget that you are a bastard son, and a scarred one at—'

The back of Jezal's hand cracked sharply into her sneering mouth and sent her reeling back with an ungainly gurgle. She tripped over her dress and collapsed on the floor, one shoe flying from her flailing foot and off into the corner of the room.

'I *am* a King, and in my own palace. I refuse to be spoken to in this manner by a glorified lady's maid.' The voice came out, flat, cold, and frighteningly commanding. It scarcely sounded like his own, but who else's could it be? He was the only man in the room. 'I see that I have been far too generous with you, and that you have mistaken my generosity for weakness.' The eleven ladies stared at him, and at their fallen comrade, crumpled on the ground with one hand to her bloody mouth. 'If any of your witches should desire to depart these troubled shores, I will arrange passage for them, and even pull an oar myself with a light heart. But you, your Majesty, will be going nowhere.'

Terez had leaped up from her seat and was glowering at him, body rigid. 'You heartless brute—' she began to hiss.

'We may both wholeheartedly wish it were otherwise,' he roared over her, 'but we are married! The time to raise objections to my parentage, or my person, or to any other facet of

363

our situation, was *before* you became Queen of the Union! Despise me all you wish, Terez, but you . . . go . . . nowhere.' And Jezal swept the dumbstruck ladies with a baleful glare, turned on his polished heel and stalked from the airy salon.

Damn it but his hand hurt.

The Circle

Dawn was coming, a grey rumour, the faintest touch of brightness around the solemn outline of the walls of Carleon. The stars had all faded into a stony sky, but the moon still hung there, just above the tree-tops, seeming almost close enough to try an arrow at.

West had not closed his eyes all night, and had passed into that strange realm of twitchy, dreamlike wakefulness that comes beyond exhaustion. Some time in the silent darkness, after all the orders had been given, he had sat by the light of a single lamp to write a letter to his sister. To vomit up excuses. To demand forgiveness. He had sat, he could not have said for how long, with the pen over the paper, but the words had simply not come. He had wanted to say all that he felt, but when it came to it, he felt nothing. The warm taverns of Adua, cards in the sunny courtyard. Ardee's one-sided smile. It all seemed a thousand years ago.

The Northmen were already busy, clipping at the grass in the shadow of the walls, the clicking of their shears a strange echo of the gardeners in the Agriont, shaving a circle a dozen strides across down to the roots. The ground, he supposed, on which the duel would take place. The ground where, in no more than an hour or two, the fate of the North would be decided. Very much like a fencing circle, except that it might soon be sprayed with blood.

'A barbaric custom,' muttered Jalenhorm, his thoughts evidently taking a similar course.

'Really?' growled Pike. 'I was just now thinking what a civilised one it is.'

'Civilised? Two men butchering each other before a crowd?'

'Better than a whole crowd butchering each other. A

problem solved with only one man killed? That's a war ended well, to my mind.'

Jalenhorm shivered and blew into his cupped hands. 'Still. A lot to hang on two men fighting one another. What if Nine-fingers loses?'

'Then I suppose that Bethod will go free,' said West, un-happily.

'But he invaded the Union! He caused the deaths of thousands! He deserves to be punished!'

'People rarely get what they deserve.' West thought of Prince Ladisla's bones rotting out in the wasteland. Some terrible crimes go unpunished, and a few, for no reason beyond the fickle movements of chance, are richly rewarded. He stopped in his tracks.

A man was sitting on his own on the long slope, his back to the city. A man hunched over in a battered coat, so still and quiet in the half-light that West had almost missed him. 'I'll catch you up,' he said as he left the path. The grass, coated with a pale fur of frost, crunched gently under his boots with each step.

'Pull up a chair.' Breath smoked gently round Ninefingers' darkened face.

West squatted down on the cold earth beside him. 'Are you ready?'

'Ten times before I've done this. Can't say I've ever yet been ready. Don't know that there is a way to get ready for a thing like this. The best I've worked out is just to sit, and let the time crawl past, and try not to piss yourself.'

'I imagine a wet crotch could be an embarrassment in the circle.'

'Aye. Better than a split head, though, I reckon.'

Undeniably true. West had heard tales of these Northern duels before, of course. Growing up in Angland, children whispered lurid stories of them to each other. But he had little idea how they were really conducted. 'How does this business work?'

'They mark out a circle. Round the edge men stand with

shields, half from one side, half from the other, and they make sure no one leaves before it's settled. Two men go into the circle. The one that dies there is the loser. Unless someone has it in mind to be merciful. Can't see that happening today, though, somehow.'

Also undeniable. 'What do you fight with?'

'Each one of us brings something. Could be anything. Then there's a spin of a shield, and the winner picks the weapon he wants.'

'So you might end up fighting with what your enemy brought?'

'It can happen. I killed Shama Heartless with his own sword, and got stuck through with the spear I brought to fight Harding Grim.' He rubbed at his stomach, as though the memory ached there. 'Still, don't hurt any worse, getting stuck with your own spear instead of someone else's.'

West laid a hand thoughtfully on his own gut. 'No.' They sat in silence for a while longer.

'There's a favour I'd like to ask you.'

'Name it.'

'Would you and your friends hold shields for me?'

'Us?' West blinked towards the Carls in the shadow of the wall. Their great round shields looked hard enough to lift, let alone to use well. 'Are you sure? I've never held one in my life.'

'Maybe, but you know whose side you're on. There ain't many folk among these that I can trust. Most of 'em are still trying to work out who they hate more, me or Bethod. It only takes one to give me a shove when I need a push, or let me fall when I need catching. Then we're all done. Me especially.'

West puffed out his cheeks. 'We'll do what we can.'

'Good. Good.'

The cold silence dragged out. Over the black hills, the black trees, the moon sank and grew dimmer.

'Tell me, Furious. Do you reckon a man has to pay for the things he's done?'

West looked up sharply, the irrational and sickly thought flashing through his mind that Ninefingers was talking of

367

Ardee, or of Ladisla, or both. Certainly, the Northman's eyes seemed to glint with accusation in the half-light – then West felt the surge of fear subside. Ninefingers was talking of himself, of course, as everyone always does, given the chance. It was guilt in his eyes, not accusation. Each man has his own mistakes to follow him.

'Maybe.' West cleared his dry throat. 'Sometimes. I don't know. I suppose we've all done things we regret.'

'Aye,' said Ninefingers. 'I reckon.'

They sat together in silence, and watched the light leak across the sky.

'Let's go, chief!' hissed Dow. 'Let's fucking go!'

'I'll say when!' Dogman spat back, holding the dewy branches out of the way and peering towards the walls, a hundred strides off, maybe, across a damp meadow. 'Too much light, now. We'll wait for that bloody moon to drop a touch further, then we'll make a run at it.'

'It ain't going to get any darker! Bethod can't have too many men left after all the ones we killed up in the mountains, and that's a lot o' walls. They'll be spread thin as cobwebs up there.'

'It only takes one to—'

And Dow was off across that field and running, as plain on the flat grass as a turd on a snow-field.

'Shit!' hissed Dogman, helpless.

'Uh,' said Grim.

There was nothing to do but stare, and wait for Dow to get stuck full of arrows. Wait for the shouts, and torches lit, and the alarm to go up, and the whole thing dumped right in the shit-hole. Then Dow dashed up the last bit of slope and was gone into the shadows by the wall.

'He made it,' said Dogman.

'Uh,' said Grim.

That ought to have been a good thing, but Dogman didn't feel too much like laughing. He had to make the run himself now, and he didn't have Dow's luck. He looked at Grim, and Grim shrugged. They burst out from the trees together, feet pounding across the soft meadow. Grim had the longer legs, started pulling away. The ground was a good deal softer than Dogman had—

'Gah!' His foot squelched to the ankle and he went flying over, splashed down in the mire and slid along on his face. He floundered up, cold and gasping, ran the rest of the way with his wet shirt plastered against his skin. He stumbled up the slope to the foot of the walls and bent over, hands to his knees, blowing hard and spitting out grass.

'Looks like you took a tumble there, chief.' Dow's grin was a white curve in the shadows.

'You mad bastard!' hissed Dogman, his temper flaring up hot in his cold chest. 'You could've been the deaths of all of us!'

'Oh, there's still time.'

'Shhhh.' Grim flailed one hand at them to say keep quiet. Dogman pressed himself tight to the wall, worry snuffing his anger out quick-time. He heard men moving up above, saw the glimmer of a lamp pass slow down the walls. He waited, still, no sound but Dow's quiet breath beside him and his own heart pounding, 'til the men above moved on and all was quiet again.

'Tell me that ain't got your blood flowing quick, chief,' whispered Dow.

'We're lucky it ain't flowing right out of us.'

'What now?'

Dogman gritted his teeth as he tried to scrape the mud out of his face. 'Now we wait.'

Logen stood up, brushed the dew from his trousers, took a long breath of the chill air. There could be no denying any longer that the sun was well and truly up. It might've been hidden in the east behind Skarling's Hill, but the tall black towers up there had bright golden edges, the thin, high clouds were pinking underneath, the cold sky between turning pale blue.

'Better to do it,' Logen whispered under his breath, 'than live with the fear of it.' He remembered his father telling him that. Saying it in the smoky hall, light from the fire shifting on his lined face, long finger wagging. Logen remembered telling it to his own son, smiling by the river, teaching him to tickle fish, Father and son, both dead now, earth and ashes. No one would learn it after Logen, once he was gone. No one would miss him much at all, he reckoned. But then who cared? There's nothing worth less than what men think of you after you're back in the mud.

He wrapped his fingers round the grip of the Maker's sword, felt the scored lines tickling at his palm. He slid it from the sheath and let it hang, worked his shoulders round in circles, jerked his head from side to side. One more cold breath in, and out, then he started walking, up through the crowd that had gathered in a wide arc around the gate. A mix of the Dogman's Carls and Crummock's hillmen, and a few Union soldiers given leave to watch the crazy Northerners kill each other. Some called to him as he came through, all knowing there were a lot more lives hanging on this than Logen's own.

'It's Ninefingers!'

'The Bloody-Nine.'

'Put an end to this!'

'Kill that bastard!'

They had their shields, all the men that Logen had picked to hold them, standing in a solemn knot near the walls. West was one, and Pike, and Red Hat, and Shivers too. Logen wondered if he'd made a mistake with the last of them, but he'd saved the man's life in the mountains and that ought to count for something. Ought to was a thin thread to hang your life on, but there it was. His life had been dangling from a thin thread ever since he could remember.

Crummock-i-Phail fell into step beside him, big shield looking small on one big arm, the other hand resting light on his fat belly. 'You looking forward to this then, Bloody-Nine? I am, I can tell you that!'

Hands slapped at his shoulders, voices called encouragement, but Logen said nothing. He didn't look left or right as he pushed past into the shaven circle. He felt men close in behind him, heard them set their shields in a half-ring round the edge of the short grass, facing the gates of Carleon. Further back the crowd pressed in tight. Whispering to each other. Straining to see. No way back now, that was a fact. But then there never had been. He'd been heading here all his days. Logen stopped, in the centre of the circle, and he turned his face up towards the battlements.

'It's sunrise!' he roared. 'Let's get to it!'

There was silence, while the echoes died, and the wind pushed some loose leaves around the grass. A silence long enough for Logen to start hoping no one would answer. To start hoping they'd all somehow slipped away in the night, and there'd be no duel after all.

Then faces appeared on the walls. One here, one there, then a whole crowd, lining the parapet as far as Logen could see in both directions. Hundreds of folk – fighting men, women, children even, up on shoulders. Everyone in the city, it looked like. Metal squealed, and wood creaked, and the tall gates ever so slowly swung apart, the glare of the rising sun spilling out the crack between, then pouring bright through the open archway. Two lines of men came tramping out. Carls, all hard faces and tangled hair, heavy mail jingling, painted shields on their arms.

Logen knew a few of them. Some of Bethod's closest, who'd been with him since the beginning. Hard men all, who'd held the shields for Logen more than once, back in the old days. They formed up in their own half-ring, closing the circle tight. A wall of shields – animal faces, trees and towers, flowing water, crossed axes, all of them scarred and scuffed from a hundred old fights. All of them turned in towards Logen. A cage of men and wood, and the only way out was to kill. Or to die, of course.

A black shape formed in the bright archway. Like a man, but taller, seeming to fill it all the way to the high keystone. Logen heard footsteps. Thumping footsteps, heavy as falling anvils. A strange kind of fear tugged at him. A mindless panic, as if he'd woken trapped under the snow again. He forced himself not to look over his shoulder at Crummock, forced himself to look ahead as Bethod's champion stepped out into the dawn.

'By the fucking dead,' breathed Logen.

He thought at first it must be some trick of the light that made him look the size he did. Tul Duru Thunderhead had been a big bastard, no doubt, big enough that some had called him a giant. But he'd still looked like a man. Fenris the Feared was built on such a scale that he seemed something else. A race apart. A giant indeed, stepped out from old stories and made flesh. A lot of flesh.

His face squirmed as he walked, great bald head jerking from side to side. His mouth sneered and grinned, his eyes winked and bulged by turns. One half of him was blue. No other way to put it. A neat line down his face divided blue skin from pale. His huge right arm was white. His left was blue all the long way from shoulder to the tips of his great fingers. In that hand he carried a sack, swinging back and forward with each step, bulging as if it was stuffed with hammers.

A couple of Bethod's shield-carriers cringed out of his way, looking like children beside him, grimacing as if death itself was breathing on their necks. The Feared stepped through into the circle, and Logen saw the blue marks were writing, just as the spirit had told him. Twisted symbols, scrawled over every part of his left side – hand, arm, face, lips even. The words of Glustrod, written in the Old Time.

The Feared stopped a few strides distant, and a sickly horror seemed to wash out from him and over the silent crowd, as if a great weight was pressing on Logen's chest, squeezing out his courage. But the task was simple enough, in its way. If the Feared's painted side couldn't be harmed, Logen would just have to carve the rest of him, and carve it deep. He'd beaten some hard men in the circle. Ten of the hardest bastards in all the North. This was just one more. Or so he tried to tell himself.

'Where's Bethod?' He'd meant to bellow it, all defiance, but it came out a tame, dry squawk.

'I can watch you die just as well from up here!' The King of the Northmen stood on the battlements above the open gate, well-groomed and happy, Pale-as-Snow and a few guards stood about him. If he'd had any trouble sleeping, Logen would never have known it. The morning breeze stirred his hair and the thick fur round his shoulders, the morning sun shone on the golden chain, struck sparks from the diamond on his brow. 'Glad you came! I was worried you'd make a run for it!' He gave a carefree sigh and it smoked on the sharp air. 'It's morning, like you said. Let's get started.'

Logen looked into the Feared's bulging, twitching, crazy eyes, and swallowed.

'We're gathered here to witness a challenge!' roared Crummock. 'A challenge to put an end to this war, and settle the blood between Bethod, who's taken to calling himself King of the Northmen, and Furious, who speaks for the Union. Bethod wins, the siege is lifted, and the Union leaves the North. Furious wins, then the gates of Carleon are opened, and Bethod stands at his mercy. Do I speak true?'

'You do,' said West, his voice sounding small in all that space.

'Aye.' Up on his walls, Bethod waved a lazy hand. 'Get to it, fat man.'

'Then name yourselves, champions!' shouted Crummock. 'And list your pedigree!'

Logen took a step forward. It was a hard step to take, as if he was pushing against a great wind, but he took it anyway, tilted his head back and looked the Feared full in his writhing face. 'I'm the Bloody-Nine, and there's no number on the men I've killed.' The words came out soft and dead. No pride in his empty voice, but no fear either. A cold fact. Cold as the winter. 'Ten challenges I've given, and I won 'em all. In this circle I beat Shama Heartless, Rudd Threetrees, Harding Grim, Tul Duru Thunderhead, Black Dow, and more besides. If I listed the Named Men I've put back in the mud we'd be here at sunrise tomorrow. There's not a man in the North don't know my work.'

Nothing changed in the giant's face. Nothing more than usual, at least. 'My name is Fenris the Feared. My achievements are all in the past.' He held up his painted hand, and squeezed the great fingers, and the sinews in his huge blue arm bulged like knotted tree roots. 'With these signs great Glustrod marked me out his chosen. With this hand I tore down the statues of Aulcus. Now I kill little men, in little wars.' Logen could just make out a tiny shrug of his massive shoulders. 'Such is the way of things.'

Crummock looked at Logen, and he raised his brows. 'Alright then. What weapons have you carried to the fight?'

Logen lifted the heavy sword, forged by Kanedias for his war against the Magi, and held it up to the light. A stride of dull metal, the edge glittered faintly in the pale sunrise. 'This blade.' He stabbed it down into the earth between them and left it standing there.

The Feared threw his sack rattling down and it sagged open. Inside were great black plates, spiked and studded, scarred and battered. 'This armour.' Logen looked at that vast weight of dark iron, and licked his teeth. If the Feared won the spin he could take the sword and leave Logen with a pile of useless armour way too big for him. What would he do then? Hide under it? He only had to hope his luck stuck out a few minutes longer.

'Alright, my beauties.' Crummock set his shield down on its rim and took hold of the edge. 'Painted or plain, Ninefingers?'

'Painted.' Crummock ripped the shield round and set it spinning. Round and round, it went – painted, plain, painted, plain. Hope and despair swapped with every turn. The wood started to slow, to wobble on its rim. It dropped down flat, plain side up, the straps flopping.

So much for luck.

Crummock winced. He looked up at the giant. 'You've got the choice, big lad.'

The Feared took hold of the Maker's blade and slid it from the earth. It looked like a toy in his monstrous hand. His bulging eyes rolled up to Logen's, and his great mouth twisted into a smile. He tossed the sword down at Logen's feet and it dropped in the dirt.

'Take your knife, little man.'

*

The sound of raised voices floated thin on the breeze. 'Alright,' hissed Dow, much too loud for the Dogman's nerves, 'they're getting started!'

'I can hear that!' Dogman snapped, coiling the rope round and round into easy circles, ready to throw.

'You know what you're doing with that? I could do without it dropping on me.'

'That so?' Dogman swung the grapple back and forward a touch, feeling the weight. 'I was just thinking that, after it sticking in that wall, it sticking in your fat head was the second best outcome.' He spun it round in a circle, then a wider one, letting some rope slip through his hand, then he hefted it all the way and let it fly. It sailed up, real neat, the rope uncoiling after it, and over the battlements. Dogman winced as he heard it clatter on the walkway, but no one came. He pulled on the rope. A stride or two slid down, and then it caught. Felt firm as a rock.

'First time,' said Grim.

Dogman nodded, hardly able to believe it himself. 'What are the odds? Who's first?'

Dow grinned at him. 'Whoever's got hold o' the rope now, I reckon.'

As the Dogman started climbing, he found he was going over all the ways a man could get killed going up this wall. Grapple slipped, and he fell. Rope frayed, and snapped, and he fell. Someone had seen the grapple, was waiting for him to get to the top before they cut the rope. Or they were waiting for him to get to the top before they cut his throat. Or they were just now calling for a dozen big men to take prisoner whatever idiot it was trying to climb into a city on his own.

His boots scuffled at the rough stone, the hemp bit at his hands, his arms burned at the work, and all the while he did his best to keep his rasping breath quiet. The battlements edged closer, then closer, then he was there. He hooked his fingers onto the stone and peered over. The walkway was empty, both ways. He slipped over the parapet, sliding a knife out, just in

375

case. You can never have too many knives, and all that. He checked the grapple was caught firm, then he leaned over, saw Dow at the bottom looking up, Grim with the rope in his hands, one foot on the wall, ready to climb. Dogman beckoned to him to say come, watched him start up, hand over hand, Dow holding to the bottom of the rope to stop it flapping. Soon enough he was halfway—

'What the fuck—'

Dogman jerked his head left. There were a pair of Thralls not far off, just stepped out from a door to the nearest tower and onto the wall. They stared at him, and he stared back, seemed like the longest time.

'There's a rope here!' he shouted, brandishing his knife around and making like he was trying to cut it away from the grapple. 'Some bastard's trying to climb in!'

'By the dead!' One came running, gawped down at Grim swinging around. 'He's coming up now!'

The other one pulled his sword out. 'Don't worry 'bout that.' He lifted it, grinning, ready to chop through the rope. Then he stopped. 'Here – why you all muddy?'

Dogman stabbed him in the chest, hard as he could, and again. 'Eeeeee!' wailed the Thrall, face screwed up, lurching back against the battlements and dropping his sword over the side. His mate came charging up, swinging a big mace. Dogman ducked under it, but the Thrall barrelled into him and brought him down on his back, head cracking on stone.

The mace clattered away and they wrestled around, the Thrall kicking and punching while Dogman tried to get his hands round his throat, stop him from calling out. They rolled over one way, then back the other, struggled up to standing and tottered about down the walkway. The Thrall got his shoulder in Dogman's armpit and shoved him back up against the battlements, trying to bundle him over.

'Shit,' gasped the Dogman as his feet left the ground. He could feel his arse scraping the stone, but still he clung on, hands tight round the Thrall's neck, stopping him getting a good breath. He went up another inch, felt his head forced back, almost more weight on the wrong side of the parapet than the right.

'Over you go, you fucker!' croaked the Thrall, working his chin away from Dogman's hands and pushing him a touch further. 'Over you—' His eyes went wide. He stumbled back, a shaft sticking out of his side. 'Oh, I don't—' Another thumped into his neck and he lurched a step, would've fallen off the back of the wall if the Dogman hadn't grabbed his arm and dragged him down onto the walkway, held him there while he slobbered his last breaths.

When he was finished, Dogman rolled up and stood bent over the corpse, breathing. Grim hurried over, taking a good look around to make sure no one else was likely to happen by. 'Alright?'

'Just once. Just once I'd like to get the help before I'm at the point o' getting killed.'

'Better'n after.' The Dogman had to admit there was some truth to that. He watched Dow pull himself over the battlements and roll down onto the walkway. The Thrall Dogman had stabbed was still breathing, just about, sat near the grapple. Dow chopped a piece out of his skull with his axe as he walked past, careless as if he was chopping logs.

He shook his head. 'I leave the two o' you alone for ten breaths together and look what happens. Two dead men, eh?' Dow leaned down, stuck two fingers in one of the holes Dogman's knife had made, pulled them out and smeared blood across one side of his face. He grinned up. 'What do you reckon we can do with two dead men?'

The Feared seemed to fill the circle, one half bare and blue, the other cased in black iron, a monster torn free from legends. There was nowhere to hide from his great fists, nowhere to hide from the fear of him. Shields rattled and clashed, men roared and bellowed, a sea of blurred faces twisted with mad fury.

Logen crept around the edge of the short grass, trying to keep light on his feet. He might've been smaller, but he was quicker, cleverer. At least he hoped he was. He had to be, or he was mud. Keep moving, rolling, ducking, stay out of the way and pick his moment. Above all, don't get hit. Not getting hit was the first thing.

The giant came at him out of nowhere, his great tattooed fist a blue blur. Logen threw himself out of the way but it still grazed his cheek and caught his shoulder, sent him stumbling. So much for not getting hit. A shield, and not a friendly one, shoved him in the back and he lurched the other way, head whipping forward. He pitched on his face, nearly cut himself on his own sword, rolled desperately to the side and saw the Feared's huge boot thud into the ground, soil flying where his skull had been a moment before.

Logen scrabbled up in time to see the blue hand coming at him again. He ducked underneath it, hacked at the Feared's tattooed flesh as he reeled past. The Maker's sword thudded deep into the giant's thigh like a spade into turf. The huge leg buckled and he dropped forward onto his armoured knee. It should have been a killing blow, right through the big veins, but there was hardly more blood than from a shaving-scratch.

Still, if one thing fails you try another. Logen roared as he chopped at the Feared's bald head. The blade clanged against the armour on the giant's right arm, raised just in time. It scraped down that black steel and slid off, harmless, chopping into the earth and leaving Logen's hands buzzing.

'Ooof!' The Feared's knee sank into his gut, folded him up and sent him staggering, needing to cough but not having the air to do it. The giant had already found his feet again, armoured hand swinging back, a lump of black iron the size of a man's head. Logen dived sideways, rolling across the short grass, felt the wind of the great arm ripping past him. It crashed into the shield where he'd been standing, broke it into splintered pieces, flung the man holding it wailing into the earth.

It seemed the spirit had been right. The painted side couldn't be hurt. Logen crouched, waiting for the clawing pain in his stomach to fade enough for him to breathe, trying to think of some trick to use and coming up with nothing. The Feared turned his writhing face towards Logen. Behind him on the ground the felled man whimpered under the wreckage of his shield. The Carls either side of him shuffled in to close the gap with some reluctance.

The giant took a slow step forwards, and Logen took a painful step back.

'Still alive,' he whispered to himself. But how long for, it was hard to say.

West had never in his life felt so scared, so exhilarated, so very much alive. Not even when he won the Contest with all the wide Square of Marshals cheering for him. Not even when he stormed the walls of Ulrioch, and burst out from the dust and chaos into the warm sunlight.

His skin tingled with hope and horror. His hands jerked helplessly with Ninefingers' movements. His lips murmured pointless advice, silent encouragement. Beside him Pike and Jalenhorm jostled, shoved, shouted themselves hoarse. Behind them the wide crowd roared, straining to see. On the walls they leaned out, screaming and shaking their fists in the air. The circle of men flexed with the movements of the fighters, never still, bowing out and sucking in as the champions came forward or fell back.

And almost always, so far, the one falling back was Ninefingers. A great brute of a man by most standards, he seemed tiny, weak and brittle in that terrifying company. To make matters a great deal worse, there was something very strange at work here. Something West could only have called magic. Great wounds, deadly wounds, closed in the Feared's blue skin before his very eyes. This thing was not a man. It could only be a devil, and whenever it towered over him West felt a fear as though he was standing at the very verge of hell.

West grimaced as Ninefingers lurched helplessly against the shields on the far side of the circle. The Feared raised his armoured fist to deliver a blow that could surely crush a skull to jelly. But it hit nothing but air. Ninefingers jerked away at the last moment and let the iron miss his jaw by a hair. His heavy sword slashed down, bounced off the Feared's armoured shoulder with a resounding clang. The giant stumbled back and Ninefingers came after him, pale scars stretched on his rigid face.

'Yes!' hissed West, the men around him bellowing their approval.

The next blow shrieked down the giant's armoured side, leaving a long, bright scratch and digging up a great sod of earth. The last chopped deep into his painted ribs and spat out a misty spray of blood, knocked him flailing off balance. West's mouth opened wide as the great shadow fell across him. The Feared toppled against his shield like a falling tree and drove him trembling to his knees, wilting under the great weight, his stomach rolling with horror and disgust.

Then he saw it. One of the buckles on the spiked and studded armour, just below the giant's knee, was inches from the fingers of West's free hand. All he could think of, in that moment, was that Bethod might escape, after all the dead men he had left, scattered up and down the length of Angland. He gritted his teeth and snatched hold of the end of the leather strap, thick as a man's belt. He dragged at it as the Feared shoved his huge bulk up. The buckle came jingling open, the armour on the mighty calf flapped loose as his foot thumped down again, as his arm lashed out and knocked Ninefingers stumbling away.

West struggled from the dirt, already greatly regretting his impulsiveness. He glanced around the circle, searching for any sign that someone had seen him, but all eyes were fixed on the fighters. It seemed now a tiny, petulant sort of sabotage that could never make the slightest difference. Beyond getting him killed, of course. It was a fact he had known from childhood. Catch you cheating in a Northern duel, and they'll cut the bloody cross in you and pull your guts out.

'Gah!' Logen jerked away from the armoured fist, tottered to his right as the blue one rushed past his face, dived to his left as the iron hand lashed at him again, slid and nearly fell. Any one of those blows had been hard enough to take his head off. He saw the painted arm go back, gritted his teeth as he dodged around another of the Feared's mighty punches, already swinging the sword up and over.

The blade sheared neatly through the blue arm, just below the elbow, sent it tumbling away across the circle along with a gout of blood. Logen heaved air into his burning lungs and raised the Maker's sword high, setting himself for one last effort. The Feared's eyes rolled up towards the dull grey blade. He jerked his head to one side and it chopped deep into his painted skull, showering out specks of dark blood and splitting his head down to the eyebrow.

The giant's armoured elbow crunched into Logen's ribs, half-lifted him off his feet and flung him kicking across the circle. He bounced from a shield and sprawled on his face, lay there spitting out dirt while the blurry world spun around him.

He winced as he pushed himself up, blinked the tears out of his eyes, and froze. The Feared stepped forward, sword still buried deep in his skull, and picked up his severed arm. He pressed it against the bloodless stump, twisted it to the right, then back to the left, and let it go. The great forearm was whole again, the letters ran from shoulder to wrist unbroken.

The men around the circle fell silent. The giant worked his blue fingers for a moment, then he reached up and closed his hand around the hilt of the Maker's sword. He turned it one way, then the other, his skull crunching as bone shifted. He dragged the blade free, shook his head as if to clear a touch of dizziness. Then he tossed the sword across the circle and it clattered down in front of Logen for the second time that day.

Logen stared at it, his chest heaving. It was getting heavier with each exchange. The wounds he'd taken in the mountains ached, the blows he'd taken in the circle throbbed. The air was still cold but his shirt was sticky with sweat.

The Feared showed no sign of tiring, even with half a ton of iron strapped to his body. There wasn't so much as a bead of sweat on his twisting face. Not so much as a scratch on his tattooed scalp.

Logen felt the fear pressing hard on him again. He knew

now how the mouse felt, when the cat had him between his paws. He should've run. He should've run and never looked back, but instead he'd chosen this. Say one thing for Logen Ninefingers, say that bastard never learns. The giant's mouth crawled up into a wriggling smile.

'More,' he said.

Dogman needed to piss as he walked up to the gate of Carleon's inner wall. Always needed to piss at times like this.

He had one of the dead Thrall's clothes on, big enough that he'd had to pull the belt too tight, cloak hanging over the bloody knife hole in the shirt. Grim was wearing the other's gear, bow over one shoulder, the big mace hanging from his free hand. Dow slumped between them, wrists tied at his back, feet scraping stupidly at the cobbles, bloody head hanging like they'd given him quite the beating.

Seemed a pitiful kind of a ruse, if the Dogman was being honest. There were fifty things he'd counted since they climbed off the walls that could've given them away. But there was no time for anything cleverer. Talk well, and smile, and no one would notice the clues. That's what he hoped anyway.

A guard stood each side of the wide archway, a pair of Carls in long mail coats and helmets, both with spears in their hands.

'What's this?' one asked, frowning as they walked up close.

'Found this bastard trying to creep in.' Dogman gave Dow a punch in the side of the head, just to make things look good. 'We're taking him down below, lock him up 'til after they're done.' He made to walk on past.

One of the guards stopped him cold with a hand on his chest, and the Dogman swallowed. The Carl nodded towards the city's gates. 'How's it going, down there?'

'Alright, I guess.' Dogman shrugged. 'It's going, anyway. Bethod'll come out on top, eh? He always does, don't he?'

'I don't know.' The Carl shook his head. 'That Feared puts the fucking wind up me. Him and that bloody witch. Can't say I'll cry too hard if the Bloody-Nine kills the pair of 'em.'

The other one chuckled, pushed his helmet onto the back of

his scalp, bringing up a cloth to wipe the sweat underneath. 'You got a—'

Dow sprang forward, loose bits of rope flapping round his wrists, and buried a knife all the way up to the hilt in the Carl's forehead. Dropped him like a chair with the legs kicked away. Same moment almost, Grim's borrowed mace clonked into the top of the other's helmet and left a great dent in it, jammed the rim right down almost to the tip of his nose. He dribbled some, stumbling back like he was drunk. Then blood came bubbling out of his ears and he fell down on his back.

Dogman turned round, trying to hold his stolen cloak out so no one would see Dow and Grim dragging the two corpses away, but the town seemed empty. Everyone watching the fight, no doubt. He wondered for a moment what was happening, out there in the circle. Long enough to get a nasty feeling in his gut.

'Come on.' He turned to see Dow grinning all across his bloody face. The two bodies he'd just wedged behind the gates, one of 'em staring cross-eyed at the knife hole in his head.

'That good enough?' asked Dogman.

'What, you want to say a few words for the dead, do you?'

'You know what I mean, if someone—'

'No time for clever, now.' Dow grabbed him by the arm and pulled him through the gate. 'Let's kill us a witch.'

The sole of the Feared's metal boot thudded into Logen's chest, ripped his breath out and rammed him into the earth, the sword tumbling from his clawing hand, puke burning at the back of his throat. Before he knew where he was a great shadow fell across him. Metal snapped shut round his wrist, tight as a vice. His legs were kicked away and he was on his face, arm twisted behind him and a mouthful of dirt to think about. Something pressed against his cheek. Cold at first, then painful. The Feared's great foot. His wrist was wrenched round, dragged up. His head was crushed further into the damp ground, short grass prickling up his nose.

The tearing pain in his shoulder was awful. Soon it was a lot worse. He was caught fast and helpless, stretched out like a rabbit for skinning. The crowd had fallen breathlessly silent, the only sound the battered flesh round Logen's mouth squelching, the air squeaking in one squashed nostril. He would've screamed if his face hadn't been so squeezed that he could scarcely wheeze in half a breath. Say one thing for Logen Ninefingers, say that he's finished. Back to the mud, and no one could've said he hadn't earned it. A fitting end for the Bloody-Nine, torn apart in the circle.

But the great arms didn't pull any further. Out the corner of one flickering eye, Logen could just see Bethod leaning against the battlements. The King of the Northmen waved his hand, round and round, in a slow wheel. Logen remembered what it meant.

Take your time. Make it last. Show them all a lesson they'll never forget.

The Feared's great boot slid off his jaw and Logen felt himself dragged into the air, limbs flopping like a puppet with the strings cut. The tattooed hand went up, black against the sun, and slapped Logen across the face. Open-handed, as a father might cuff a troublesome child. It was like being hit with a pan. Light burst open in Logen's skull, his mouth filled with blood. Things drew into focus just in time for him to see the painted hand swing back the other way. It came down with a terrible inevitability and cracked him a backhand blow, as a jealous husband might crack his helpless wife.

'Gurgh—' he heard himself say, and he was flying. Blue sky, blinding sun, yellow grass, staring faces, all meaningless smears. He crashed into the shields at the edge of the circle, flopped half-senseless to the earth. Far away men were shouting, screaming, hissing, but he couldn't hear the words, and hardly cared. All he could think about was the cold feeling in his stomach. As if his guts were stuffed with swelling ice.

He saw a pale hand, smeared with pink blood, white tendons starting from the scratched skin. His hand, of course. There was the stump. But when he tried to make the fingers open they only clutched tighter at the brown earth.

'Yes,' he whispered, and blood drooled out of his numb mouth and trickled into the grass. The ice spread out from his stomach, out to the very tips of his fingers and turned every part of him numb. It was well that it did. It was high time.

'Yes,' he said. Up, up onto one knee, his bloody lips curling back from his teeth, his bloody right hand snaking through the grass, seeking out the hilt of the Maker's sword, closing tight around it.

'Yes!' he hissed, and Logen laughed, and the Bloody-Nine laughed, together.

West had not expected Ninefingers to get up, not ever again, but he did, and when he did, he was laughing. It sounded almost like weeping at first, a slobbering giggle, shrill and strange, but it grew louder, sharper, colder as he rose. As if at a cruel joke that no one else could see. A fatal joke. His head fell sideways like a hanged man's, livid face all slack around a hacked-out grin.

Blood stained his teeth pink, trickled from the cuts on his face, seeped from his torn lips. The laughter gurgled up louder, and louder, ripping at West's ears, jagged as a saw-blade. More agonised than any scream, more furious than any war-cry. Awfully, sickeningly wrong. Chuckling at a massacre. Slaughterhouse giggling.

Ninefingers lurched forwards like a drunken man, swaying, wild, sword dangling from his bloody fist. His dead eyes glittered, wet and staring, pupils swollen to two black pits. His mad laughter cut, and grated, and hacked around the circle. West felt himself edging back, mouth dry. All the crowd edged back. They no longer knew who scared them more: Fenris the Feared, or the Bloody-Nine.

The world burned.

His skin was on fire. His breath was scalding steam. The sword was a brand of molten metal in his fist.

The sun stamped white-hot patterns into his prickling eyes, and the cold grey shapes of men, and shields, and walls, and of a giant made from blue words and black iron. Fear washed out from him in sickly waves, but the Bloody-Nine only smiled the wider. Fear and pain were fuel on the fire, and the flames surged high, and higher yet.

The world burned, and at its centre the Bloody-Nine burned hottest of all. He held out his hand, and he curled the three fingers, and he beckoned.

'I am waiting,' he said.

The great fists lashed at the Bloody-Nine's face, the great hands snatched at his body. But all the giant caught was laughter. Easier to strike the flickering fire. Easier to catch the rolling smoke.

The circle was an oven. The blades of yellow grass were tongues of yellow flame beneath it. The sweat, spit, blood dripped onto it like gravy from cooking meat.

The Bloody-Nine made a hiss, water on coals. The hiss became a growl, iron spattering from the forge. The growl became a great roar, the dry forest in flames, and he let the sword go free.

The grey metal made searing circles, hacked bloodless holes in blue flesh, rang on black iron. The giant faded away and the blade bit into the face of one of the men holding the shields. His head burst apart and sprayed blood across another, a hole torn from the wall around the circle. The others shuffled back, shields wavering, the circle swelling with their fear. They feared him more even than the giant, and they were wise to. Everything that lived was his enemy, and when the Bloody-Nine had made pieces of this devil-thing, he would set to work on them.

The circle was a cauldron. On the walls above the crowd surged like angry steam. The ground shifted and swelled under the Bloody-Nine's feet like boiling oil.

His roar became a scalding scream, the sword flashed down and clashed from spiked armour like a hammer on the anvil. The giant pressed his blue hand to the pale side of his head, face squirming like a nest of maggots. The blade had missed his skull, but stolen away the top half of his ear. Blood bubbled out from the wound, ran down the side of his great neck in two thin lines, and did not stop.

The great eyes went wide and the giant sprang forward with a thundering bellow. The Bloody-Nine rolled under his flailing fist and slid round behind him, saw the black iron on his leg flap away, the bright buckle dangling. The sword snaked out and slid into the gap, ate deep into the great pale calf inside it. The giant roared in pain, spun, lurched on his wounded leg and fell to his knees.

The circle was a crucible. The screaming faces of the men around its edge danced like smoke, swam like molten metal, their shields melting together.

Now was the time. The morning sun blazed down, glinted bright on the heavy chest-plate, marking the spot. Now was the beautiful moment.

The world burned, and like a leaping flame the Bloody-Nine reared up, arching back, raising high the sword. The work of Kanedias, the Master Maker, no blade forged sharper. Its bitter edge scored a long gash in the black armour, through the iron and into the soft flesh beneath, striking sparks and spattering blood, the shriek of tortured metal mingling with the wail of pain torn from the Feared's twisted mouth. The wound it left in him was deep.

But not deep enough.

The giant's great arms slid round the Bloody-Nine's back, folding him in a smothering embrace. The edges of the black metal pierced his flesh in a dozen places. Closer the giant drew him, and closer, and a ragged spike slid into the Bloody-Nine's face, cut through his cheek and scraped against his teeth, bit into the side of his tongue and filled his mouth with salt blood.

The Feared's grip was the weight of mountains. No matter how hot the Bloody-Nine's rage, no matter how he squirmed, and thrashed, and screamed in fury, he was held as tightly as the cold earth holds the buried dead. The blood trickling from his face, and from his back, and from the great gash in the Feared's armour soaked into his clothes and spread out blazing hot over his skin.

The world burned. Above the oven, the cauldron, the crucible, Bethod nodded, and the giant's cold arms squeezed tighter.

Dogman followed his nose. It rarely led him wrong, his nose, and he hoped to hell that it didn't fail him now. It was a sickly kind of a smell – like sweet cakes left too long in the oven. He led the others along an empty hallway, down a shadowy stair, creeping through the damp darkness in the knotty bowels of Skarling's Hill. He could hear something now, as well as smell it, and it sounded as bad as it smelled. A woman's voice, singing soft and low. A strange kind of singing, in no tongue the Dogman could understand.

'That must be her,' muttered Dow.

'Don't like the sound o' that one bit,' Dogman whispered back. 'Sounds like magic.'

'What d'you expect? She's a fucking witch ain't she? I'll go round behind.'

'No, wait on—' But Dow was already creeping off the other way, boots padding soft and silent.

'Shit.' Dogman followed the smell, creeping down the passageway with Grim at his back, the chanting coming louder and louder. A streak of light slunk out from an archway and he eased towards it, pressed his side to the wall and took a peer round the corner.

The room on the other side had about as witchy a look as a room could ever have. Dark and windowless, three other black doorways round the walls. It was lit just by one smoky brazier up at the far end, sizzling coals shedding a dirty red light on it all, giving off a sick, sweet stink. There were jars and pots scattered all round, bundles of twigs, and grass, and dried-out flowers hanging from the greasy rafters, casting strange shadows into the corners, like the shapes of hanged men swinging.

There was a woman standing over the brazier with her back to the Dogman. Her long, white arms were spread out wide, shining with sweat. Gold glinted round her thin wrists, black hair straggled down her back. The Dogman might not have known the words she was singing but he could guess it was some dark work she was up to.

Grim held up his bow, one eyebrow raised. Dogman shook his head, silently drew his knife. Tricky to kill her right off with a shaft, and who knew what she might do once she was shot? Cold steel in the neck left nothing to chance.

Together they crept into the room. The air was hot in there, thick as swamp water. Dogman sneaked forward, trying not to breathe, sure the reek would throttle him if he did. He sweated, or the room did, leastways his skin was beaded up with dew in no time. He picked his steps, finding a path between all the rubbish strewn across the floor – boxes, bundles, bottles. He worked his damp palm round the grip of his knife, fixed his eyes on the point between her shoulders, the point he'd stab it into—

His foot caught a jar and sent it clattering. The woman's head jerked round, the chant stopped dead on her lips. A gaunt, white face, pale as a drowned man's, black paint round her narrow eyes – blue eyes, cold as the ocean.

The circle was silent. The men around its edge were still, their faces and their shields hanging limp. The crowd at their backs, the people pressed to the parapet above, all held motionless, all quiet as the dead.

For all of Ninefingers' mad rage, for all his twisting and his struggling, the giant had him fast. Thick muscles squirmed under blue skin as the Feared's great arms tightened and slowly crushed the life from him. West's mouth was bitter with helpless disappointment. All that he had done, all that he had suffered, all those lives lost, for nothing. Bethod would go free.

Then Ninefingers gave an animal growl. The Feared held him still, but his blue arm was trembling with the effort. As if he was suddenly weakened, and could squeeze no further. Every sinew of West's own body was rigid as he watched. The thick strap of the shield bit into his palm. His jaw was clenched so tight that his teeth ached. The two fighters were locked together, straining against each other with every fibre and yet entirely still, frozen in the centre of the circle.

The Dogman sprang forward, knife raised and ready.

'Stop.'

He froze solid in a moment. He'd never heard a voice like it. One word and there was no thought in his head. He stared at the pale woman, his mouth open, his breath hardly moving, wishing that she'd say another.

'You too,' she said, glancing over at Grim, and his face went slack, and he grinned, halfway through drawing his bow.

She looked Dogman up and down, then pouted as if she was all disappointment. 'Is that any way for guests to behave?'

Dogman blinked. What the hell had he been thinking barging in here with a drawn blade? He couldn't believe he'd done such a thing. He blushed to the roots of his hair. 'Oh . . . I'm sorry . . . by the dead . . .'

'Gugh!' said Grim, throwing his bow into the corner of the room as if he'd suddenly realised he had a turd in his hand, then staring down at the arrow, baffled.

'That's better.' She smiled, and the Dogman found he was grinning like an idiot. Some spit might've come out of his mouth maybe, just a bit, but he weren't that bothered. As long as she kept talking nothing else seemed o' too much importance. She beckoned to them, long white fingers stroking at the thick air. 'No need to stand so far away from me. Come closer.'

Him and Grim stumbled towards her like eager children, Dogman near tripping over his feet in his hurry to please, Grim barging into a table on the way and coming close to falling on his face.

'My name is Caurib.'

'Oh,' said Dogman. Most beautiful name ever, no doubt about it. Amazing, that a single word could be so beautiful.

'Harding Grim's my name!'

'Dogman, they call me, 'count of a sharp sense o' smell, and . . . er . . .' By the dead, but it was hard to think straight.

There'd been something important he was meant to be doing, but for the life of him he couldn't think what.

'Dogman . . . perfect.' Her voice was soothing as a warm bath, as a soft kiss, as milk and honey . . . 'Don't sleep yet!' Dogman's head rolled, Caurib's painted face a black and white blur, swimming in front of him.

'Sorry!' he gurgled, blushing again and trying to hide the knife behind his back. 'Right sorry about the blade . . . no idea what—'

'Don't worry. I am glad that you brought it. I think it would be best if you used it to stab your friend.'

'Him?' Dogman squinted at Grim.

Grim grinned and nodded back at him. 'Aye, definitely!'

'Right, right, good idea.' Dogman lifted up the knife, seeming to weigh a ton. 'Er . . . anywhere you'd like him stabbed, in particular?'

'In the heart will do nicely.'

'Right you are. Right. The heart it is.' Grim turned front on to give him a better go at it. Dogman blinked, wiped some sweat from his forehead. 'Here we go, then.' Damn it but he was dizzy. He squinted at Grim's chest, wanting to make sure he got it right first time, and didn't embarrass himself again. 'Here we go . . .'

'Now!' she hissed at him. 'Just get it—'

The axe blade made a clicking sound as it split her head neatly down the middle, all the way to her chin. Blood sprayed out and spattered in Dogman's gawping face, and the witch's thin body slumped down on the stones like it was made of nothing but rags.

Dow frowned as he twisted the haft of his axe this way and that, until the blade came free of Caurib's ruined skull with a faint sucking sound. 'That bitch talks too much,' he grunted.

The Bloody-Nine felt the change. Like the first green shoot of spring. Like the first warmth on the wind as the summer comes. There was a message in the way the Feared held him.

His bones were no longer groaning, threatening to burst apart. The giant's strength was less, and his was more.

The Bloody-Nine sucked in the air and his rage burned hot as ever. Slowly, slowly, he dragged his face away from the giant's shoulder, felt the metal slide out from his mouth. He twisted, twisted until his neck was free. Until he was staring into the giant's writhing face. The Bloody-Nine smiled, then he darted forward, fast as a shower of sparks, and sank his teeth deep into that big lower lip.

The giant grunted, shifted his arms, tried to drag the Bloody-Nine's head away, tear the biting teeth out of his mouth. But he could more easily have shaken off the plague. His arms loosened and the Bloody-Nine twisted the hand that held the Maker's sword. He twisted it, as the snake twists in its nest, and slowly he began to work it free.

The giant's blue left arm uncoiled from the Bloody-Nine's body, his blue hand seized hold of the Bloody-Nine's wrist, but there could be no stopping it. When the sapling seed finds a crack in the mountain, over long years its deep roots will burst the very rock apart. So the Bloody-Nine strained with every muscle and let the slow time pass, hissing out his hatred into the Feared's twitching mouth. The blade crept onwards, slowly, slowly, and its very point bit into painted flesh, just below the giant's bottom rib.

The Bloody-Nine felt the hot blood trickling down the grip and over his bunched fist, trickling out of the Feared's mouth and into his, running down his neck, leaking from the wounds across his back, dripping to the ground, just as it should be. Softly, gently, the blade slid into the Feared's tattooed body, sideways, upwards, onwards.

The great hands clawed at the Bloody-Nine's arm, at his back, seeking desperately for some hold that might stop the terrible easing forward of that blade. But with every moment the giant's strength melted away, like ice before a furnace. Easier to stop the Whiteflow than to stop the Bloody-Nine. The movement of his hands was the growing of a mighty tree, one hair's breadth at a time, but no flesh, no stone, no metal could stop it.

The giant's painted side could not be harmed. Great Glustrod had made it so, long years ago, in the Old Time, when the words were written upon the Feared's skin. But Glustrod wrote on one half only. Slowly, now, softly, gently, the point of the Maker's sword crossed the divide and into the unmarked half of him, dug into his innards, spitted him like meat made ready for the fire.

The giant made a great, high shriek, and the last strength melted from his hands. The Bloody-Nine opened his jaws and let him free, one arm holding tight to his back while the other drove the sword on into him. The Bloody-Nine hissed laughter through his clenched teeth, dribbled laughter through the ragged hole in his face. He rammed the blade as far as it would go, and its point slid out between the plates of armour just beneath the giant's armpit and glinted red in the sun.

Fenris the Feared tottered backwards, still making his long squeal, his mouth hanging open and a string of red spit dangling from his lip, the painted half already healed over, the pale half tattered as mince-meat. The circle of men watched him, frozen, gaping over the tops of their shields. His feet shuffled in the dirt, one hand fumbling for the red hilt of the Maker's sword, buried to the cross-piece in his side, blood dripping from the pommel and leaving red spots scattered across the ground. His squeal became a rattling groan, one foot tripped the other and he toppled like a felled tree and crashed over on his back, in the centre of the circle, great arms and legs spread wide. The twitching of his face was finally still, and there was a long silence.

'By the dead.' It was spoken softly, thoughtfully. Logen squinted into the morning sun, saw the black shape of a man looking down at him from the high gatehouse. 'By the dead, I never thought you'd do it.' The world tipped from side to side as Logen began to walk, the breath hissing cold through the wound in his face, scraping in his raw throat. The men who'd made the circle moved out of his way, now, their voices fallen silent, their shields hanging from their hands.

'Never thought you could do it, but when it comes to killing, there's no man better! No man worse! I've always said so!'

Logen tottered through the open gates, found an archway and began to climb the lurching steps, round and round, his boots hissing against the stone and leaving dark smears behind. The blood dripped, tap, tap, tap from the dangling fingers of his left hand. Every muscle ached. Bethod's voice dug at him.

'But I get the last laugh, eh, Bloody-Nine? You're nothing but leaves on the water! Any way the rain washes you!'

Logen stumbled on, ribs burning, jaws locked tight together, shoulder scraping against the curved wall. Up, and up, and round, and round, his crackling breath echoing after.

'You'll never have anything! You'll never be anything! You'll never make anything but corpses!'

Out onto the roof, blinking in the morning brightness, spitting a mouthful of blood over his shoulder. Bethod stood at the battlements. The Named Men stumbled out of Logen's way as he strode towards him.

'You're made of death, Bloody-Nine! You're made of—'

Logen's fist crunched into his jaw and he took a flopping step back. Logen's other hand smashed into his cheek and he reeled against the parapet, a long string of bloody drool running from his split mouth. Logen caught the back of his head and jerked his knee up into Bethod's face, felt his nose crunch flat against it. Logen tangled his fingers in Bethod's hair, gripped it tight, pulled his head up high, and rammed it down into the stones.

'Die!' he hissed.

Bethod jerked, gurgled, Logen lifted his head and drove it down again, and again. The golden ring flew off his broken skull, bounced across the rooftop with a merry jingling.

'Die!'

Bone crunched, and blood shot out over the stone in fat drops and thin spatters. Pale-as-Snow and his Named Men stared, white-faced, helpless and fearful, horrified and delighted.

'Die, you fucker!'

And Logen hauled Bethod's ruined corpse into the air with one last effort and flung it tumbling over the battlements. He watched it fall. He watched it crunch to the ground and lie, on its side, arms and legs stuck out awkwardly, fingers curled as if they were grasping at something, the head no more than a dark smear on the hard earth. All the faces of the crowds of men standing below were turned towards that corpse, then slowly, eyes and mouths wide open, they lifted up to stare at Logen.

Crummock-i-Phail, standing in their midst, in the centre of the shaved circle beside the great body of the Feared, slowly raised his long arm, the fat forefinger on the end of it pointing upwards. 'The Bloody-Nine!' he screamed. 'King o' the Northmen!'

Logen gaped down at him, panting for breath, legs wobbling, trying to understand. The fury was gone and left nothing but terrible tiredness behind it. Tiredness and pain.

'King o' the Northmen!' someone shrieked, way back in the crowd.

'No,' croaked Logen, but no one heard him. They were all too drunk with blood and fury, or busy thinking what was easiest, or too scared to say any different. The chants broke out all over, first a trickle of them, then a flow, and then a flood, and all Logen could do was watch, clinging to the bloody stone and trying not to fall.

'The Bloody-Nine! King o' the Northmen!'

Pale-as-Snow was down on one knee beside him, spots of Bethod's blood sprayed across the white fur on his coat. He always had been one to lick whatever arse was nearest, but he wasn't alone. They were all kneeling, up on the walls and down on the grass. The Dogman's Carls and Bethod's. The men who'd held the shields for Logen and the ones who'd held the shields for the Feared. Maybe Bethod had taught them a lesson. Maybe they'd forgotten how to be their own men, and now they needed someone else to tell them what to do.

'No,' whispered Logen, but all that came out was a dull slurp. He had no more power to stop it than he had to make the sky fall in. Seemed to him then that men do pay for the things they've done, alright. But sometimes the payment isn't what they expected.

'The Bloody-Nine!' roared Crummock again, as he sank down on his knees and lifted up his arms towards the sky. 'King o' the Northmen!'

Greater Good

The room was another over-bright box. It had the same off-white walls, spotted with brown stains. *Mould, or blood, or both.* The same battered table and chairs. *Virtually instruments of torture in themselves.* The same burning pains in Glokta's foot, and leg, and back. *Some things never change.* The same prisoner, as far as anyone could have told, with the same canvas bag over their head. *Just like the dozens who have been through this room over the past few days, and just like the dozens more crammed into the cells beyond the door, waiting on our pleasure.*

'Very well,' Glokta waved a tired hand, 'let us begin.'

Frost dragged the bag from the prisoner's head. A long, lean Kantic face with deep creases around the mouth and a neatly trimmed black beard, streaked with grey. A wise, dignified face, deep-set eyes even now adjusting to the glare.

Glokta burst out laughing. Each chuckle stabbed at the base of his stiff spine and rattled his stiff neck, but he could not help himself. *Even after all these years, fate can still play jokes on me.*

'Wath futhy?' grunted Frost.

Glokta wiped his runny eye. 'Practical Frost, we are truly honoured. Our latest prisoner is none other than Master Farrad, formerly of Yashtavit in Kanta, and more recently of a magnificent address at the top of the Kingsway. We are in the presence of the finest dentist in the Circle of the World.' *And one must appreciate the irony.*

Farrad blinked into the glaring lamplight. 'I know you.'

'Yes.'

'You are the one who was a prisoner of the Gurkish.'

'Yes.'

'The one they tortured. I remember . . . you were brought to me.'

'Yes.'

Farrad swallowed. *As though the memory alone is enough to make him vomit.* He glanced up at Frost and the pink eyes glowered back, unblinking. He glanced round the grubby, bloodstained room, at the cracked tiles, at the scarred table-top. His eyes lingered on the paper of confession lying upon it. 'After what they did to you – how can you do this, now?'

Glokta showed Farrad his toothless grin. 'After what they did to me, how could I do anything else?'

'Why am I here?'

'For the same reason as everyone else who comes here.' Glokta watched Frost plant the heavy tips of his fingers on the paper of confession and slide it deliberately across the table towards the prisoner. 'To confess.'

'Confess to what?'

'Why, to spying for the Gurkish.'

Farrad's face creased up with disbelief. 'I am no spy! The Gurkish took everything from me! I fled my home when they came! I am innocent, you must know this!'

Of course. As have been all the spies who confessed in this room over the last few days. But they all confessed, without exception. 'Will you sign the paper?'

'I have nothing to confess to!'

'Why is it that no one can answer the questions I ask?' Glokta stretched out his aching back, worked his creaking neck from side to side, rubbed at the bridge of his nose with finger and thumb. Nothing helped. *But then nothing ever does. Why must they always make it so very difficult, for me and for themselves?* 'Practical Frost, would you show the good master our work so far?'

The albino slid a dented tin bucket out from under the table and dumped the contents without ceremony in front of the prisoner. Teeth clattered, and slid, and spun across the wood. Hundreds of them. Teeth of all shapes and sizes, from white, through all the shades of yellow, to brown. Teeth with bloody

398

roots and with shreds of flesh attached. A couple tumbled from the far end of the table and bounced from the grimy tiles, clicked away into the corners of the narrow room.

Farrad gaped down in horror at the bloody mess of dentistry before him. *And even the very Prince of Teeth can never have seen such a thing.* Glokta leaned forwards. 'I daresay you've pulled a tooth or two before yourself.' The prisoner nodded dumbly. 'Then you can probably imagine how tired I am after this lot. That's why I'd really like to be done with you as quickly as possible. I don't want you here, and you certainly don't want to be here. We can help each other.'

'What must I do?' muttered Farrad, his tongue moving nervously around his own mouth.

'It is not complicated. First you sign your confession.'

'Thorry,' mumbled Frost, leaning forward and brushing a couple of teeth off the document, one of them leaving a long, pink streak across the paper.

'Then you name two others.'

'Two other what?'

'Why, two other spies for the Gurkish, of course, from among your people.'

'But . . . I know no spies!'

'Then some other names will have to serve. You have been named already, several times.'

The dentist swallowed, then shook his head, and pushed the paper away. *A brave man, and a righteous one. But bravery and righteousness are bad virtues to have in this room.* 'I will sign. But I will not name innocent men. God have mercy on me, I will not.'

'God might have mercy on you. But he doesn't hold the pliers down here. Clamp him.'

Frost gripped Farrad's head from behind with one great white hand, tendons standing from the pale skin as he forced his mouth open. Then he shoved the clamp between Farrad's jaws and spun the nut round nimbly between finger and thumb until they were held wide open.

'Ah!' gurgled the dentist. 'Ayrh!'

'I know. And we're just getting started.' Glokta pushed back the lid of his case, watched the polished wood, the sharpened steel, the shining glass spread outwards. *What the . . .* There was a disconcerting gap in the tools. 'For pity's sake! Have you had the pliers out of here, Frost?'

'Nuh,' grunted the albino, shaking his head angrily.

'Damn it! Can none of these bastards keep their own instruments? Go next door and see if we can borrow some, at least.'

The Practical lumbered from the room, the heavy door hanging ajar behind him. Glokta winced as he rubbed at his leg. Farrad stared at him, spit running from one corner of his forced-open mouth. His bulging eyes rolled sideways as a howl of pain came muffled from the corridor outside.

'I do apologise for this,' said Glokta. 'We're usually a great deal more organised, but it's been busy as hell here the last few days. Such a lot to get through, you see.'

Frost pulled the door shut and handed Glokta a pair of rusty pliers, handles first. There was some dry blood and a couple of curly hairs caked to the jaws.

'Is this the best they could do? These are dirty!'

Frost shrugged. 'Whath a ifferenth?'

A fair point, I suppose. Glokta gave a long sigh, struggled up from his chair and leaned forwards to peer into Farrad's mouth. *And a sweet set he has, too. A pearly white complement. I suppose you'd expect prize-winning teeth from a prize-winning dentist. Anything else would be a poor advertisement for his trade.*

'I applaud your cleanliness. It's a rare privilege to question a man who appreciates the importance of washing the mouth out. I can't say I've ever seen a better set of teeth.' Glokta tapped at them happily with the pliers. 'It seems a shame to tear them all out, just so that you can confess in ten minutes' time instead of now, but there we are.' He closed the jaws around the nearest tooth, worked his hand around the handles.

'Gurlgh,' gurgled Farrad. 'Glaigh!'

Glokta pursed his lips, as though considering, then released the pliers. 'Let us give the good master one further chance to talk.' Frost unscrewed the clamp and pulled it from Farrad's mouth along with a string of drool. 'Is there something you wish to say?'

'I will sign!' gasped Farrad, a long tear running down one cheek. 'God help me, I will sign!'

'And you will name two accomplices?'

'Whatever you wish . . . please . . . whatever you wish.'

'Excellent,' said Glokta, as he watched the pen scratching against the paper of confession. 'Who's next?'

Glokta heard the lock behind him rattle. He scowled as he turned his head, preparing to scream at his presumptuous visitor.

'Your Eminence,' he whispered, with barely concealed dismay, grimacing as he struggled to get up from his chair.

'No need to rise, I do not have all day.' Glokta found himself frozen in the most painful possible position, bent somewhere between sitting and standing, and had to sag back into his chair with little grace as Sult swept into the room, three of his huge Practicals looming silently in the doorway behind him. 'You may ask your freak of nature to leave us.'

Frost's eyes narrowed, flickered over the other Practicals, then back to Sult. 'Very good, Practical Frost,' said Glokta hastily. 'You may remove our prisoner.'

The albino unlocked Farrad's manacles and dragged the dentist from his chair with one white fist, hauled him gasping by his collar to the door at the back of the room and ripped back the bolt with his free hand. He gave one pink glare over his shoulder and Sult glared back. Then he slammed the door behind him.

His Eminence slid into the chair opposite Glokta. *No doubt still warm from the sweating arse of the brave and righteous Master Farrad.* He brushed some of the teeth from the table-top before him with the side of one gloved hand and sent them clicking onto the floor. *And he could not have seemed to care less had they been breadcrumbs.* 'There is a deadly conspiracy afoot within the Agriont. Have we made progress in unmasking it?'

'I have interviewed most of the Kantic prisoners, extracted a suitable number of confessions, there should not be—'

Sult gave an angry wave of his hand. 'Not that, halfwit. I refer to that bastard Marovia and his pawns, the so-called First of the Magi and our so-called King.'

Even now, with the Gurkish knocking at the gates? 'Your Eminence, I had assumed the war would take precedence—'

'You have not the wit to assume,' sneered Sult. 'What evidence have you collected against Bayaz?'

I stumbled upon something I shouldn't have at the University, then was almost drowned in my bath. 'So far . . . nothing.'

'What of the parentage of King Jezal the First?'

'That avenue too appears . . . a dead end.' *Or an avenue with my own death at the end, if my owners at Valint and Balk were to hear of it. And they hear of everything.*

The Arch Lector's lips twisted. 'Then what the hell have you been doing lately?'

For the last three days I have been busy tearing meaningless confessions from the mouths of innocent men, so that we could appear effective. When was I supposed to find time to bring down the state, precisely? 'I have been occupied with seeking Gurkish spies—'

'Why do I never get anything from you but excuses? I have begun to wonder, since your effectiveness has so sharply declined, how you were able to keep Dagoska out of Gurkish hands so long. You must have needed a tremendous sum of money to strengthen the city's defences.'

It took all of Glokta's self-control to prevent his eye from twitching straight out of his head. *Still, now, you twitching jelly, or we are done.* 'The Guild of Spicers were persuaded to contribute when their own livelihoods were on the line.'

'How uncharacteristically generous of them. Now that I think of it, I find the whole business of Dagoska has a strange flavour. It has always struck me as odd that you chose to dispose of Magister Eider so privately, rather than sending her back to me.'

From very bad to an awful lot worse. 'A miscalculation on my part, your Eminence. I thought that I would spare you the trouble of—'

'Disposing of traitors is no trouble for me. You know that.' Angry creases spread out around Sult's hard blue eyes. 'Could it be, after all we have been through together, you might take me for a fool?'

Glokta's voice rasped uncomfortably in his dry throat. 'Absolutely not, Arch Lector.' *Merely a lethal megalomaniac. He knows. He knows that I am not entirely the dutiful slave. But how much does he know? And from whom did he learn it?*

'I gave you an impossible task, and so I have allowed you the benefit of the doubt. But your benefit will only last as long as your successes. I grow tired of putting the spur to you. If you do not solve my problems with our new King in the next two weeks, I will have Superior Goyle dig out the answers to my questions about Dagoska. I will have him dig them from your twisted flesh, if I must. Do I make myself clear?'

As Visserine glass. Two weeks to find the answers, or . . . fragments of a butchered corpse found floating by the docks. But if I even ask the questions, Valint and Balk will inform his Eminence of our arrangement and . . . bloated by seawater, horribly mutilated, far beyond recognition. Alas for poor Superior Glokta. A comely and a well-loved man, but such bad luck. Wherever will he turn?

'I understand, Arch Lector.'

'Then why ever are you still sitting here?'

It was Ardee West herself who opened the door, a half-full wine glass in one hand. 'Ah! Superior Glokta, what a delightful surprise. Do come in!'

'You sound almost pleased to see me.' *A rare response indeed to my arrival.*

'Why wouldn't I be?' She stepped graciously aside to allow him past. 'How many girls are lucky enough to have a torturer for a chaperone? There's nothing like it for encouraging the suitors.'

He hobbled over the threshold. 'Where is your maid?'

'She got herself all worked up about some Gurkish army or other, so I let her go. Went to her mother in Martenhorm.'

'And you are yourself ready to leave, I hope?' He followed her into the warm living room, shutters and curtains closed, illuminated by the shifting glow from the coals on the fire.

'In fact, I have decided to stay in the city.'

'Really? The tragic princess, pining in her empty castle? Abandoned by her faithless servants, wringing her helpless hands while her enemies surround the moat?' Glokta snorted. 'Are you sure you fit the role?'

'Better than you fit that of the knight on the white charger, come to rescue the damsel with blade a-flashing.' She looked him scornfully up and down. 'I'd hoped for a hero with at least half his teeth.'

'I thought you'd be used to getting less than you hoped for by now.' *I know that I am.*

'What can I say? I'm a romantic. Have you come here only to puncture my dreams?'

'No. I do that without trying. I had in mind a drink and a conversation which did not include the subtext of my mutilated corpse.'

'It is hard to say at this stage what direction our conversation might take, but the drink I can promise you.' She poured him a glass and he tossed it back in four long swallows. He held it out again, sucking his sweet gums.

'In all seriousness, the Gurkish are no more than a week from taking Adua under siege. You should leave as soon as possible.'

She filled his glass again, and then her own. 'Haven't you noticed that half the city has had the same idea? Such flea-bitten nags not requisitioned by the army are changing hands at five hundred marks a piece. Nervous citizens are pouring out to every corner of Midderland. Columns of defenceless refugees, wandering through a mass of mud at a mile a day as the weather turns cold, laden down with everything of value they possess, easy prey for every brigand within a hundred miles.'

'True,' Glokta had to admit as he wriggled his painful way into a chair near the fire.

'And where would I go to anyway? I swear I have not a single friend or relative anywhere in Midderland. Would you have me hide in the woods, lighting fires by rubbing sticks together and hunting down squirrels with my bare hands? How the hell would I stay drunk in those circumstances? No, thank you, I will be safer here, and considerably more comfortable. I have coal for the fire and the cellar is full to capacity. I can hold out for months.' She waved a floppy hand towards the wall. 'The Gurkish are coming from the west, and we are on the eastern side of town. I could not be safer in the palace itself, I daresay.'

Perhaps she is right. Here, at least, I can keep some kind of watch over her. 'Very well, I bow to your reasoning. Or I would, if my back allowed it.'

She settled herself opposite. 'And how is life in the corridors of power?'

'Chilly. As corridors often are.' Glokta stroked his lips with a finger. 'I find myself in a difficult situation.'

'I have some experience with those.'

'This one is . . . complicated.'

'Well then, in terms a dull wench like me might understand.'

Where's the harm? I stare death in the face already. 'In the terms of a dull wench, then, imagine this . . . desperately needing certain favours, you have promised your hand in marriage to two very rich and powerful men.'

'Huh. One would be a fine thing.'

'None would be a fine thing, in this particular case. They are both old and of surpassing ugliness.'

She shrugged. 'Ugliness is easily forgiven in the rich and powerful.'

'But both these suitors are prone to violent displays of jealousy. Dangerous displays, if your wanton faithlessness were to become common knowledge. You had hoped to extricate yourself from one promise or the other at some stage, but now the date of the weddings draws near, and you find that you are . . . still considerably entangled with both. More so than ever, in fact. Your response?'

She pursed her lips and took a long breath, considering it,

then tossed a strand of hair theatrically over her shoulder. 'I would drive them both near madness with my matchless wit and smouldering beauty, then engineer a duel between the two. Whichever won would be rewarded with the ultimate prize of my hand in marriage, never suspecting I was once promised also to his rival. Since he is old, I would earnestly hope for his imminent death, leaving me a wealthy and respected widow.' She grinned at him down her nose. 'What say you to that, sir?'

Glokta blinked. 'I fear the metaphor has lost its relevance.'

'Or . . .' Ardee squinted at the ceiling, then snapped her fingers. 'I might use my subtle feminine wiles . . .' thrusting back her shoulders and hitching up her bust, 'to entrap a third man, still more powerful and wealthy. Young, and handsome, and smooth of limb as well, I suppose, since this is a metaphor. I would marry him and with his help destroy those other two, and abandon them penniless and disappointed. Ha! What think you?'

Glokta felt his eyelid twitching, and he pressed one hand against it. *Interesting.* 'A third suitor,' he murmured. 'The idea had never even occurred.'

Skarling's Chair

Far below, the water frothed and surged. It had rained hard in the night, and now the river ran high with it, an angry flood chewing mindlessly at the base of the cliff. Cold black water and cold white spray against the cold black rock. Tiny shapes – golden yellow, burning orange, vivid purple, all the colours of fire, whisked and wandered with the mad currents, whatever way the rain washed them.

Leaves on the water, just like him.

And now it looked as if the rain would wash him south. To fight some more. To kill men who'd never heard of him. The idea of it made him want to be sick. But he'd given his word, and a man who doesn't keep his word isn't much of a man at all. That's what Logen's father used to tell him.

He'd spent a lot of long years not keeping to much of anything. His word, and the words of his father, and other men's lives, all meaning less than nothing. All the promises he'd made to his wife and to his children he'd let rot. He'd broken his word to his people, and his friends, and himself, more times than he could count. The Bloody-Nine. The most feared man in the North. A man who'd walked all his days in a circle of blood. A man who'd done nothing in all his life but evil. And all the while he'd looked at the sky and shrugged his shoulders. Blamed whoever was nearest, and told himself he'd had no choices.

Bethod was gone. Logen had vengeance, at last, but the world wasn't suddenly a better place. The world was the same, and so was he. He spread out the fingers of his left hand on the damp stone, bent and wonky from a dozen old breaks, knuckles scratched and scabbing, nails cracked and wedged under with dirt. He stared down at the familiar stump for a moment.

'Still alive,' he whispered, hardly able to believe it.

He winced at the pain in his battered ribs, groaned as he turned away from the window and back into the great hall. Bethod's throne room, and now his. The thought tugged a meagre belch of laughter out of his gut, but even that stabbed at the mass of stitches through his cheek and up the side of his face. He limped out across the wide floor, every step an ordeal. The sound of his scraping boots echoed in the high rafters, over the whispering of the river down below. Shafts of blurred light, heavy with floating dust, shone down and made criss-cross patterns across the boards. Near to Logen, on a raised-up dais, stood Skarling's Chair.

The hall, and the city, and the land around it had all changed far beyond recognition, but Logen reckoned the chair itself was much the same as it had been when Skarling lived. Skarling Hoodless, greatest hero of the North. The man who'd united the clans to fight against the Union, long ago. The man who'd drawn the North together with words and gestures, for a few brief years, at least.

A simple seat for a simple man – big, honest chunks of old wood, faded paint around the edges, polished smooth by Skarling's sons, and grandsons, and the men who'd led his clan since. Until the Bloody-Nine came knocking at the gates of Carleon. Until Bethod took the chair for his own, and pretended that he was all that Skarling had been, while he forced the North together with fire, and fear, and steel.

'Well then?' Logen jerked his head round, saw Black Dow leaning in the doorway, arms folded across his chest. 'Ain't you going to sit in it?'

Logen shook his head, even though his legs were aching so bad he could hardly bear to stand a moment longer. 'Mud always did for me to sit on. I'm no hero, and Skarling was no king.'

'Turned down a crown, as I heard it told.'

'Crowns.' Logen spat onto the straw, spit still pink from the

408

cuts in his mouth. 'Kings. The whole notion's shit, and me the worst choice there could be.'

'You ain't saying no, though, eh?'

Logen frowned up at him. 'So some other bastard even worse'n Bethod can sit in that chair, make the North bleed some more? Maybe I can do some good with it.'

'Maybe.' Dow looked straight back. 'But some men aren't made for doing good.'

'You talking 'bout me again?' chuckled Crummock, striding in through the doorway, Dogman and Grim at his shoulder.

'Not all talk's about you, Crummock,' said Dogman. 'You sleep alright, Logen?'

'Aye,' he lied. 'Like the dead.'

'What now?'

Logen stared at that chair. 'South, I reckon.'

'South,' grunted Grim, giving no clue whether he thought it was a good idea or a bad.

Logen licked at the ragged flesh at the side of his mouth, checking again, for no reason that made any sense, just how much it hurt. 'Calder and Scale are still out there, somewhere. No doubt Bethod sent 'em to find some help. From out past the Crinna, or up in the high valleys, or wherever.'

Crummock chuckled softly. 'Ah, the good work's never done.'

'They'll be causing mischief sooner or later,' said Dogman, 'small doubt o' that.'

'Someone needs to stay back here and keep a watch on things. Hunt those two bastards out if they can.'

'I'll do it,' said Black Dow.

'You sure?'

Dow shrugged. 'I don't like boats and I don't like the Union. Don't need to take no voyage to work that out. And I've got scores enough to settle with Calder and Scale. I'll pick me some Carls out o' what's left, and I'll pay 'em a visit.' He flashed his nasty grin, and clapped Dogman on the arm. 'Good luck to the rest o' you down there with the Southerners, eh? Try not to get yourselves killed.' He narrowed his eyes at

Logen. 'You especially, eh, Bloody-Nine? Wouldn't want to lose us another King o' the Northmen, now, would we?' And he sauntered out, arms folded.

'How many men we got left over?'

'Might be three hundred, now, if Dow takes a few.'

Logen gave a long sigh. 'Best get 'em ready to leave then. Wouldn't want Furious to go without us.'

'Who'll want to go?' asked Dogman. 'After what they been through these past months? Who'll want more killing now?'

'Men who don't know how to do much else, I guess.' Logen shrugged. 'Bethod had gold down there, didn't he?'

'Aye, some.'

'Then share it out. Plenty for each man comes with us. Some now, some when we get back. Reckon a good few'll take the offer.'

'Maybe. Men'll talk hard for gold. Not sure they'll fight hard for it, when the time comes.'

'I reckon we'll see.'

Dogman stared at him for a long moment. Stared him right in the eye. 'Why?'

'Because I gave my word.'

'And? Never bothered you before, did it?'

'Can't say it did, and there's the problem.' Logen swallowed, and his mouth tasted bad. 'What else can you do, but try and do better?'

Dogman nodded, slow, his eyes not leaving Logen's face. 'Right you are then, chief. South it is.'

'Uh,' said Grim, and the two of them walked out the doorway, leaving just Crummock behind.

'Off to the Union for you is it, your Majesty? South and kill you some brown men in the sun?'

'South.' Logen worked one sore shoulder beside his sore neck, and then the other. 'You coming?'

Crummock pushed himself away from the wall and walked forward, finger bones clicking round his thick neck. 'No, no, no, not me. I've relished our time together, so I have, but everything's got an end, don't it. I've been away from my

410

mountains for far too long, and my wives'll be missing me.' The chief of the hillmen held his arms out wide, took a step forward, and hugged Logen tight. A little too tight for comfort, if he was being honest.

'They can have a king if they want one,' whispered Crummock in his ear, 'but I can't say I do. Especially not the man who killed my son, eh?' Logen felt himself go cold, from the roots of his hair to the tips of his fingers. 'What did you think? That I wouldn't know?' The hillman leaned back to look Logen in the eye. 'You slaughtered him before the whole world, now, didn't you? You butchered little Rond like a sheep for the pot, and him just as helpless as one.'

They were alone in that wide hall, just the two of them, and the shadows, and Skarling's chair. Logen winced as Crummock's arms squeezed tighter, round the bruises and the wounds the Feared's arms had left him. Logen hadn't the strength left now to fight a cat, and they both knew it. The hillman could've crushed him flat, and finished the job the Feared had started. But he only smiled.

'Don't you worry, now, Bloody-Nine. I've got what I wanted, haven't I? Bethod's dead and gone, and his Feared, and his witch, and his whole bastard notion of clans united, all back to the mud where they belong. With you in charge, I daresay it'll be a hundred years before folk in the North stop killing each other. Meantime maybe we up in the hills can have some peace, eh?'

'Course you can,' croaked Logen, through his gritted teeth, grimacing as Crummock pressed him even tighter.

'You killed my son, that's true, but I've got plenty more. You have to weed the weak ones out, don't you know? The weak and the unlucky. You don't put a wolf amongst your sheep then cry when you find one eaten, do you?'

Logen could only stare. 'You really are mad.'

'Maybe I am, but there's worse than me out there.' He leaned close again, soft breath in Logen's ear. 'I'm not the one killed the boy, am I?' He let Logen free, and he slapped him on the shoulder. The way a friend might, but there was no

411

friendship in it. 'Don't ever come up in the High Places again, Ninefingers, that's my advice. I might not be able to give you another friendly reception.' He turned and walked away, slowly, waving one fat finger over his shoulder. 'Don't come up in the High Places again, Bloody-Nine! You're beloved o' the moon just a little too much for my taste!'

Leadership

Jezal clattered through the cobbled streets astride a magnificent grey, Bayaz and Marshal Varuz just behind him, a score of Knights of the Body, led by Bremer dan Gorst, following in full war gear. It was strangely unsettling to see the city, usually so brimful with humanity, close to deserted. Only a scattering of threadbare urchins, of nervous city watchmen, of suspicious commoners remained to hurry out of the way of the royal party as they passed. Most of those citizens who had stayed in Adua were well barricaded in their bedrooms, Jezal imagined. He would have been tempted to do the same, had Queen Terez not beaten him to it.

'When did they arrive?' Bayaz was demanding over the clatter of hooves.

'The vanguard appeared before dawn,' Jezal heard Varuz shout back. 'And more Gurkish troops have been pouring in down the Keln road all morning. There were a few skirmishes in the districts beyond Casamir's Wall, but nothing to slow them significantly. They are already halfway to encircling the city.'

Jezal jerked his head round. 'Already?'

'The Gurkish always liked to come prepared, your Majesty.' The old soldier urged his horse up beside him. 'They have started to construct a palisade around Adua, and have brought three great catapults with them. The same ones that proved so effective in their siege of Dagoska. By noon we will be entirely surrounded.' Jezal swallowed. There was something about the word 'surrounded' that caused an uncomfortable tightening in his throat.

The column slowed to a stately walk as they approached the city's westernmost gate. It was, in an irony that gave Jezal little pleasure, the very same gate through which he had entered the city in triumph before he was crowned High King of the Union. A crowd had gathered in the shadow of Casamir's Wall, larger even than the one that had greeted him after his strange victory over the peasants. Today, however, there was hardly a mood of celebration. Smiling girls had been replaced by frowning men, fresh flowers with old weapons. Polearms stuck up above the press at all angles in an unruly forest, points and edges glinting. Pikes and pitch-forks, bill hooks and boat hooks, brooms with the twigs removed and knives nailed in their places.

There was a smattering of King's Own padded out by some squinting members of the city watch, a few puffed-up tradesmen with leather jerkins and polished swords, some slouching labourers with antique flatbows and tough expressions. These were the very best of what was on offer. They were accompanied by a random assortment of citizens of both sexes and all ages, equipped with a bewildering range of mismatched armour and weapons. Or nothing at all. It was difficult to tell who was supposed to be a soldier and who a citizen, if, indeed, there was still a difference. Every one of them was looking at Jezal as he smartly dismounted, his golden spurs jingling. Looking *to* him, he realised, as he began to walk out among them, his well-armoured bodyguard clanking behind.

'These are the defenders of this borough?' murmured Jezal to Lord Marshal Varuz, following at his shoulder.

'Some of them, your Majesty. Accompanied by some enthusiastic townsfolk. A touching spectacle.'

Jezal would happily have traded a touching crowd for an effective one, but he supposed a leader had always to appear indomitable before his followers. Bayaz had told him so often. How doubly, how triply true of a king before his subjects? Especially a king whose grip on his recently won crown might be thought of as slippery at best.

So he stood tall, pointed his scarred chin as high as he dared, flicked out his gilt-edged cloak with one gauntleted hand. He strode through the crowd with the confident swagger he had always used to have, one hand resting on the jewelled pommel of his sword, hoping with every step that no one caught an inkling of the cauldron of fear and doubt behind his eyes. The crowd muttered as he swept past, Varuz and Bayaz hurrying behind. Some made attempts at bows, others did not bother.

'The king!'

'I thought he'd be taller . . .'

'Jezal the Bastard.' Jezal snapped his head round, but there was no way of telling who spoke.

'That's Luthar!'

'A cheer for 'is Majesty!' Followed by a half-hearted murmur.

'This way,' said a pale-looking officer before the gate, indicating a staircase with one apologetic hand. Jezal climbed manfully, two stone steps at a time, spurs jingling. He came out onto the roof of the gatehouse and froze, his lip curling with distaste. Who should be standing there but his old friend Superior Glokta, bent over on his cane, his repulsive toothless smile on his face?

'Your Majesty,' he leered, voice heavy with irony. 'What an almost overwhelming honour.' He lifted his cane to point towards the far parapet. 'The Gurkish are that way.'

Jezal was attempting to frame a suitably acidic reply as his eyes followed Glokta's stick. He blinked, the muscles of his face going slack. He stepped past the cripple without saying a word. His scarred jaw crept gradually open, and stayed there.

'The enemy,' growled Varuz. Jezal tried to imagine what Logen Ninefingers would have said faced with the sight below him now.

'Shit.'

In the patchwork of damp fields, over the roads and through the hedgerows, between the farms and villages and the few coppices of old trees beyond the city walls, Gurkish troops swarmed in their thousands. The wide paved road towards Keln, curving away southwards through the flat farmland, was a single crawling, glittering, heaving river of marching men. Gurkish soldiers, in column, flooding up and flowing smoothly out to encircle the city in a giant ring of men, wood, and steel. Tall standards stood out above the boiling throng, golden symbols flashing in the watery autumn sunlight. The standards of the Emperor's legions. Jezal counted ten at his first glance.

'A considerable body of men,' said Bayaz, with awesome understatement.

Glokta grinned. 'The Gurkish hate to travel alone.'

The fence that Marshal Varuz had referred to earlier was already rising, a dark line winding through the muddy fields a few hundred strides from the walls, a shallow ditch in front of it. More than adequate to prevent supplies or reinforcements reaching the city from outside. Further away several camps were taking shape: vast bodies of white tents erected in neatly ordered squares, several with tall columns of dark smoke already floating up into the white sky from cook-fires and forges. There was a deeply worrying feeling of permanence about the whole arrangement. Adua might still have been in Union hands, but even the most patriotic liar could not have denied that the city's hinterland already belonged firmly to the Emperor of Gurkhul.

'You have to admire their organisation,' said Varuz grimly.

'Yes . . . their organisation . . .' Jezal's voice was suddenly creaky as old floorboards. Putting a brave face on this seemed more like insanity than courage.

A dozen horsemen had detached themselves from the Gurkish lines and now rode forward at a steady trot. Two long flags streamed above their heads, red and yellow silk, worked with Kantic characters in golden thread. There was a white flag too, so small as to be barely noticeable.

'Parleys,' growled the First of the Magi, slowly shaking his head. 'What are they but an excuse for old fools who love to hear their own voices to prattle about fair treatment before they start on the butchery?'

'I suppose on the subject of old fools who love to hear their own voices, you are the absolute expert.' That was what Jezal thought but he kept it to himself, watching the Gurkish party approach in brooding silence. A tall man came at their head, gold shining on his sharply pointed helmet and his polished armour, riding with that upright arrogance that shouts, even from a distance, of high command.

Marshal Varuz frowned. 'General Malzagurt.'

'You know him?'

'He commanded the Emperor's forces, during the last war. We grappled with each other for months. We parleyed more than once. A most cunning opponent.'

'You got the better of him though, eh?'

'In the end, your Majesty.' Varuz looked far from happy. 'But I had an army then.'

The Gurkish commander clattered up the road, through the jumble of deserted buildings scattered beyond Casamir's wall. He reined in his horse before the gate, staring proudly upwards, one hand resting casually on his hip.

'I am General Malzagurt,' he called in a sharp Kantic accent, 'the chosen representative of his magnificence, Uthman-ul-Dosht, Emperor of Gurkhul.'

'I am King Jezal the First.'

'Of course. The bastard.'

It was pointless to deny it. 'That's right. The bastard. Why don't you come in, General? Then we can speak face to face, like civilised men.'

Malzagurt's eyes flickered across to Glokta. 'Forgive me, but the response of your government to unarmed emissaries of the Emperor has not always been . . . civilised. I think I will remain outside the walls. For now.'

'As you wish. I believe you are already acquainted with Lord Marshal Varuz?'

'Of course. It seems an age since we tussled in the dry wastelands. I would say that I have missed you . . . but I have not. How are you, my old friend, my old enemy?'

'Well enough,' grunted Varuz.

Malzagurt gestured towards the vast array of manpower deploying behind him. 'Under the circumstances, eh? I do not know your other—'

'He is Bayaz. First of the Magi.' A smooth, even voice. It

417

came from one of Malzagurt's companions. A man dressed all in simple white, somewhat in the manner of a priest. He seemed hardly older than Jezal, and very handsome, with a dark face, perfectly smooth. He wore no armour, carried no weapon. There was no adornment on his clothes or his simple saddle. And yet the others in the party, even Malzagurt himself, seemed to look at him with great respect. With fear, almost.

'Ah.' The General peered up, stroking thoughtfully at his short grey beard. 'So this is Bayaz.'

The young man nodded. 'This is he. It has been a long time.'

'Not long enough, Mamun, you damned snake!' Bayaz clung to the parapet, teeth bared. The old Magus was so good at playing the kindly uncle that Jezal had forgotten how terrifying his sudden fury could be. He took a shocked step away, half raising a hand to shield his face. The Gurkish aides and flag-carriers cringed, one going so far as to be noisily sick. Even Malzagurt lost a sizeable chunk of his heroic bearing.

But Mamun gazed up just as levelly as before. 'Some among my brothers thought that you would run, but I knew better. Khalul always said your pride would be the end of you, and here is the proof. It seems strange to me, now, that I once thought you a great man. You look old, Bayaz. You have dwindled.'

'Things seem smaller when they are far above you!' growled the First of the Magi. He ground the toe of his staff into the stones under his feet, his voice carrying now a terrible menace. 'Come closer, Eater, and you can judge my weakness while you burn!'

'The time was you could have crushed me with a word, I do not doubt it. But now your words are only empty air. Your power has leaked away with the slow years, while mine has never been greater. I have a hundred brothers and sisters behind me. What allies have you, Bayaz?' He swept the battlements with a mocking smile. 'Only such as you deserve.'

'I may yet find allies to surprise you.'

'I doubt it. Long ago, Khalul told me what your final, desperate hope would be. Time proved him right, as it always

418

has. So you went to the very edge of the World, chasing shadows. Dark shadows indeed, for one who calls himself righteous. I know that you failed.' The priest showed two rows of perfect white teeth. 'The Seed passed out of history, long ago. Interred, dark leagues beneath the earth. Sunk, far below the bottomless ocean. Your hopes are sunk with it. You have only one choice left to you. Will you come with us willingly, and be judged by Khalul for your betrayal? Or must we come in and take you?'

'You dare to speak to me of betrayal? You who betrayed the highest principals of our order, and broke the sacred law of Euz? How many have you murdered, so that you could be powerful?'

Mamun only shrugged. 'Very many. I am not proud. You left us a choice of dark paths, Bayaz, and we made the sacrifices we had to. There is no purpose in our arguing over the past. After these long centuries, standing on opposite sides of a great divide, I think neither one of us will convince the other. The victors can decide who was right, just as they always have, since long before the Old Time. I know your answer already, but the Prophet would have me ask the question. Will you come to Sarkant, and answer for your great crimes? Will you be judged by Khalul?'

'Judged?' snarled Bayaz. '*He* will judge *me*, the swollen-headed old murderer?' He barked harsh laughter down from the walls. 'Come and take me if you dare, Mamun, I will be waiting!'

'Then we will come,' murmured Khalul's first apprentice, frowning up from under his fine black brows. 'We have been preparing long years to do it.'

The two men fell to sullen glaring, and Jezal frowned with them. He resented the sudden feeling that the whole business was somehow an argument between Bayaz and this priest and that he, although a king, was like a child eavesdropping on his parents' conversation, and with just as little say in the outcome.

'Speak your terms, General!' he bellowed down.

Malzagurt cleared his throat. 'Firstly, if you surrender the

419

city of Adua to the Emperor, he is prepared to allow you to retain your throne, as his subject, of course, paying regular tribute.'

'How generous of him. What of the traitor, Lord Brock? We understood that you have promised him the crown of the Union.'

'We are not altogether committed to Lord Brock. He does not hold the city, after all. You do.'

'And we have scant respect for those who turn on their own masters,' added Mamun, with a dark look up at Bayaz.

'Secondly, the citizens of the Union will be permitted to continue to live according to their own laws and customs. They will continue to live in freedom. Or as close to it as they have ever really been, at least.'

'Your generosity is astonishing.' Jezal had meant to sneer it, but in the end it escaped without much irony.

'Thirdly,' shouted the General, with a nervous glance sideways towards Mamun, 'the man known as Bayaz, the First of the Magi, be delivered over to us, bound and in chains, that he may be conveyed to the Temple of Sarkant, for judgement by the Prophet Khalul. Those are our terms. Refuse them, and the Emperor has decreed that Midderland shall be treated as any other conquered province. Many will be killed, and many more made slaves, Gurkish governors will be installed, your Agriont will be made a temple, and your current rulers . . . conveyed to cells beneath the Emperor's palace.'

Jezal half opened his mouth to refuse on an instinct. Then he paused. Harod the Great, no doubt, would have spat his defiance at any odds, and probably pissed on the emissary to boot. The slightest notion of negotiating with the Gurkish was against every long-held belief he possessed.

But, thinking about it, the terms were far more generous than he had ever expected. Jezal would probably have enjoyed more authority as a subject of Uthman-ul-Dosht than he did with Bayaz staring over his shoulder every moment of every day. He could save lives by saying a word. Real lives, of real people. He reached up and rubbed gently at his scarred lips with a fingertip. He had experienced enough suffering on the endless plains of the Old Empire to think long and hard about risking so much pain to so many, and himself in particular. The notion of cells beneath the Emperor's palace caused him some pause.

It was bizarre that such a vital decision should fall to him. A man who, no more than a year ago, had proudly confessed to knowing nothing about anything, and caring still less. But then Jezal was beginning to doubt that anyone in a position of high authority ever really knew what they were doing. The best one could hope for was to maintain some shred of an illusion that one might. And occasionally, perhaps, try to give the mindless flood of events the slightest push in one direction or another, hoping desperately that it would turn out to be the right one.

But what was the right one?

'Give me your answer!' shouted Malzagurt. 'I have preparations to make!'

Jezal frowned. He was sick of being dictated to by Bayaz, but at least the old bastard had played some role in his ascension to the throne. He was sick of being slighted by Terez, but at least she was his wife. Quite aside from any other consideration, his patience was stretched very thin. He simply refused to be ordered around at sword-point by some posturing Gurkish General and his damn fool priest.

'I reject your terms!' he called airily down from the walls. 'I reject them utterly and completely. I am not in the habit of surrendering my advisers, or my cities, or my sovereignty simply when asked. Particularly not to a pack of Gurkish curs with small manners and even smaller wits. You are not in Gurkhul now, General, and here your arrogance becomes you even less than that absurd helmet. I suspect that you will learn a harsh lesson before you leave these shores. Might I add, before you scuttle off, that I encourage you and your priest to fuck each other? Who knows? Perhaps you could persuade the great Uthman-ul-Dosht – and the all-knowing Prophet Khalul too for that matter – to join you!'

General Malzagurt frowned. He conferred quickly with an

aide, evidently having not entirely understood the finer points of that last utterance. Once he had finally taken them in he gave an angry slash of his dark hand and barked an order in Kantic. Jezal saw men moving among the buildings scattered outside the walls, torches in their hands. The Gurkish General took one last look up at the gatehouse. 'Damn pinks!' he snarled. 'Animals!' And he tore at the reins of his horse and sprang away, his officers clattering after him.

The priest Mamun sat there a moment longer, a sadness on his perfect face. 'So be it. We will put on our armour. May God forgive you, Bayaz.'

'You need forgiveness more than I, Mamun! Pray for yourself!'

'So I do. Every day. But I have seen no sign in all my long life that God is the forgiving kind.' Mamun turned his horse away from the gates and rode slowly back towards the Gurkish lines, through the abandoned buildings, flames already licking hungrily at their walls.

Jezal took a long, ragged breath as his eyes flicked up to the mass of men moving through the fields. Damn his mouth, it got him in all kinds of trouble. But it was a little late now for second thoughts. He felt Bayaz' fatherly touch on his shoulder, that steering touch that had become so very annoying to him over the past few weeks. He had to grit his teeth to keep from shaking free.

'You should address your people,' said the Magus.

'What?'

'The right words could make all the difference. Harod the Great could speak at a moment's notice. Did I tell you of the time he—'

'Very well!' snapped Jezal, 'I am going.'

He walked towards the opposite parapet with all the enthusiasm of a condemned man to his scaffold. The crowd was spread out below in all its disturbing variety. Jezal had to stop himself fussing with his belt-buckle. He kept worrying for some reason that his trousers would fall down in front of all those people. A ridiculous notion. He cleared his throat. Someone saw him, pointed.

'The king!'

'King Jezal!'

'The king speaks!'

The crowd shifted and stretched, drawn towards the gatehouse, a sea of hopeful, fearful, needy faces. The noise in the square slowly died and a breathless silence fell.

'My friends . . . my countrymen . . . my subjects!' His voice rang out with pleasing authority. A good beginning, very . . . rhetorical. 'Our enemies may be many . . . very many . . .' Jezal cursed to himself. That was hardly an admission to give courage to the masses. 'But I urge you to take heart! Our defences are strong!' He slapped at the firm stones under his hand. 'Our courage is indomitable!' He thumped at his polished breastplate. 'We will hold firm!' This was better! He had discovered a natural talent for speaking. The crowd was warming to him now, he could feel it. 'We need not hold out forever! Lord Marshal West is even now bringing his army to our assistance—'

'When?' someone screamed out. There was a wave of angry muttering.

'Er . . .' Jezal, wrong-footed, glanced nervously across at Bayaz, 'er . . .'

'When will they come? When?' The First of the Magi hissed at Glokta, and the cripple made a sharp gesture to someone below.

'Soon! You may depend upon it!' Curse Bayaz, this had been an awful notion. Jezal did not have the ghost of an idea of how to put heart into a rabble.

'What about our children? What about our homes? Will your house burn? Will it?' A swell of unhappy calls went up.

'Do not fear! I beg you . . . please . . .' Damn it! He had no business pleading, he was a king. 'The army is on its way!' Jezal noticed black figures forcing through the press. Practicals of the Inquisition. They converged, somewhat to his relief, on the point where the heckles were coming from. 'They are even now leaving the North! Any day they will come to our aid, and teach these Gurkish dogs a—'

'When? When will—' Black sticks rose and fell in the midst of the crowd and the question was cut off in a high-pitched shriek.

Jezal did his best to shout over it. 'In the meantime, will we let these Gurkish scum ride free over our fields? Over the fields of our fathers?'

'No!' someone roared, to Jezal's great relief.

'No! We will show these Kantic slaves how a free Union citizen can fight!' A volley of lukewarm agreements. 'We will fight as bravely as lions! As fiercely as tigers!' He was warming to his work, now, the words were spilling out as if he really meant them. Perhaps he did. 'We will fight as we did in the days of Harod! Of Arnault! Of Casamir!' A rousing cheer went up. 'We will not rest until these Gurkish devils are driven back across the Circle Sea! There will be no negotiation!'

'No negotiation!' someone called.

'Damn the Gurkish!'

'We will never surrender!' Jezal bellowed, striking the parapet with his fist. 'We will fight for every street! For every house! For every room!'

'For every house!' someone squealed with rabid excitement, and the citizens of Adua bellowed their approval.

Feeling the moment upon him, Jezal slid his sword from its sheath with a suitably warlike ringing and held it high above his head. 'And I will be proud to draw my sword beside you! We will fight for each other! We will fight for the Union! Every man . . . every woman . . . a hero!'

There was a deafening cheer. Jezal waved his sword and a glittering wave surged out among the spears as they were shaken in the air, thumped against armoured chests, hammered down against the stone. Jezal smiled wide. The people loved him, and were more than willing to fight for him. Together they would be victorious, he felt it. He had made the right decision.

'Nicely done,' murmured Bayaz in his ear. 'Nicely—'

Jezal's patience was worn out. He rounded on the Magus with his teeth bared. 'I know how it was done! I have no need of your constant—'

'Your Majesty.' It was Gorst's piping voice.

'How dare you interrupt me? What the hell is—'

Jezal's tirade was cut off by a ruddy glare at the corner of his eye, followed a moment later by a roaring detonation. He jerked his head round to see flames springing up above the jumble of roofs some distance away on his right. Below in the square there was a collective gasp, a wave of nervous movement through the crowd.

'The Gurkish bombardment has begun,' said Varuz.

A streak of fire shot up into the white sky above the Gurkish lines. Jezal watched it open-mouthed as it plummeted down towards the city. It crashed into the buildings, this time on Jezal's left, bright fire shooting high into the air. The terrifying boom assaulted his ears an instant afterward.

Shouts came from below. Orders, perhaps, or screams of panic. The crowd began to move in every direction at once. People rushed for the walls, or for their homes, or nowhere in particular, a chaotic tangle of pressing bodies and waving polearms.

'Water!' someone shouted.

'Fire!'

'Your Majesty.' Gorst was already leading Jezal back towards the stairway. 'You should return to the Agriont at once.'

Jezal started at another thunderous explosion, this one even closer. Smoke was already rising in oily smudges over the city. 'Yes,' he muttered, allowing himself to be led to safety. He realised that he still had his sword drawn, and sheathed it somewhat guiltily. 'Yes of course.'

Fearlessness, as Logen Ninefingers had once observed, is a fool's boast.

A Rock and a Hard Place

Glokta shook with laughter, wheezing gurgles slobbering through his empty gums, the hard chair creaking under his bony arse. His coughs and his whimpers echoed dully from the bare walls of his dim living room. In a way, it sounded very much like weeping. *And perhaps it is, just a little.*

Every shake of his twisted shoulders drove nails into his neck. Every jerk of his rib-cage sent flashes of pain down to the very tips of such toes as he had left. He laughed, and the laughter hurt, and the pain made him laugh all the more. *Oh, the irony! I titter with hopelessness. I chuckle with despair.*

Bubbles of spit blew from his lips as he gave one last long whine. *Like a sheep's death rattle, but less dignified.* Then he swallowed, and wiped his running eyes. *I have not laughed so hard in years. Since before the Emperor's torturers did their work, I shouldn't wonder. And yet it is not so very difficult to stop. After all, nothing is really very funny here, is it?* He lifted the letter, and read it again.

Superior Glokta,

My employers at the banking house of Valint and Balk are more than disappointed with your progress. It is some time now since I asked you, in person, to inform us of Arch Lector Sult's plans. In particular, the reasons for his continuing interest in the University. Since then we have received no communication from you.

It may be that you believe the sudden arrival of the Gurkish beyond the city walls has altered the expectations of my employers.

It has not, in any way whatsoever. Nothing will.

You will report to us within the week, or his Eminence will be informed of your divided loyalties.

I need hardly add that it would be wise for you to destroy this letter.

Mauthis.

Glokta stared at the paper for a long while by the light of the single candle, his ruined mouth hanging open. *For this, I lived through months of agony in the darkness of the Emperor's prisons? Tortured my savage way through the Guild of Mercers? Slaughtered my bloody path through the city of Dagoska? To end my days in ignominy, trapped between a bitter old bureaucrat and a bankful of treacherous swindlers? All my twisting, my lying, my bargains, and my pain. All those corpses left beside the road . . . for this?*

A new wave of laughter rocked his body, twisted him up and made his aching back rattle. *His Eminence and these bankers deserve each other! Even with the city burning down around them, their games cannot stop for an instant. Games which may very well prove fatal to poor Superior Glokta, who only tried to do his crippled best.* He had to wipe a little snot from under his nose he laughed so hard at that last thought.

It almost seems a shame to burn such a horribly hilarious document. Perhaps I should take it to the Arch Lector instead? Would he see the funny side, I wonder? Would we chuckle over it together? He reached out and held the corner of the letter to the twisting candle flame, watched fire flicker up the side, creep out through the writing, white paper curling up into black ashes.

Burn, as my hopes, and my dreams, and my glorious future burned beneath the Emperor's palace! Burn, as Dagoska did and Adua surely will before the Emperor's fury! Burn, as I would love to burn King Jezal the Bastard, and the First of the Magi, and Arch Lector Sult, and Valint and Balk, and the whole damned—

'Gah!' Glokta flailed his singed fingertips in the air then stuck them in his toothless mouth, his laughter quickly cut off. *Strange. However much pain we experience, we never become used to it. We always scramble to escape it. We never become resigned to more.* The corner of the letter was still smouldering on the floor. He frowned, and ground it out with a savage poke of his cane.

The air was heavy with the sharp tang of wood smoke. *Like a hundred thousand burnt dinners.* Even here in the Agriont, there was the slightest grey haze of it, a messy blending together of the buildings at the end of each street. Fires had been raging in the outer districts for several days now, and the Gurkish bombardment had not let up a hair, night or day. Even as Glokta walked, the breath wheezing through the gaps in his teeth with the effort of putting one foot in front of the other, there came the muffled boom of an incendiary landing somewhere in the city, the tiniest murmur of vibration through the soles of his boots.

The people in the lane froze, staring up in alarm. *Those few unlucky folk who found themselves without excuses to flee the city when the Gurkish came. Those unlucky folk who were too important, or not important enough. An optimistic handful who thought the Gurkish siege would be another passing fad – like a rain storm or short trousers. Too late they discover their grave error.*

Glokta kept hobbling, head lowered. He had not lost a wink of sleep for the explosions rocking the city in the darkness the past week. *I was too busy losing sleep for my mind spinning round and round like a cat in a sack, trying to find some way clear of this trap. I became well-used to explosions during my holiday in charming Dagoska.* For him, the pain lancing through his arse and up his spine was considerably more worrisome.

Oh, arrogance! Who would ever have dared suggest that Gurkish boots would one day trample across the fertile fields of Midderland? That the pretty farms and sleepy villages of the Union would dance with Gurkish fire? Who could ever have expected that beautiful, thriving Adua would turn from a little piece of heaven into a little piece of hell? Glokta felt himself smiling. *Welcome, everyone! Welcome! I've been here all along. How nice of you to join me.*

He heard armoured boots tramping down the road behind him, shuffled too late out of the way of a hurrying column of soldiers and was barged roughly onto the grassy verge, left foot sliding in the mud and sending a stab of agony up his leg. The column clattered past, heedless, and Glokta grimaced after them. *People no longer have the proper level of fear for the Inquisition. They are all a great deal too afraid of the Gurkish for that.* He stepped away from the wall with a wince and a curse, stretched his neck out and carried on limping.

High Justice Marovia was framed in the largest window of his echoing office, hands clasped behind his back. His windows faced west. *The direction of the main Gurkish assault.* Above the rooftops in the distance, columns of dark smoke rose into the pale sky, blending together into a gritty pall that rendered the autumn half-light still more funereal. Marovia turned when he heard Glokta's toeless foot creaking on the dark boards, his lined old face alive with a welcoming smile.

'Ah, Superior Glokta! You cannot imagine my delight to hear you announced! I have missed you since your last visit. I do so enjoy your . . . forthright style. I do so admire your . . . commitment to your work.' He flapped one lazy hand towards the window. 'The law, I must admit, tends to be sleepy in times of war. But even with the Gurkish at the gates the noble business of his Majesty's Inquisition continues, eh? I assume you have come once again on behalf of his Eminence?'

Glokta paused. *But only out of habit. I must turn my twisted back on the Inquisition. What would Sult call me? A traitor? No doubt, and worse besides. But every man's first loyalty must be to himself. I have made my sacrifices.* 'No, your Worship. I have come on behalf of Sand dan Glokta.' He limped up to a chair, slid it out and dumped himself into it without being asked. *I am far past the niceties, now.* 'Frankly, I need your help.' *Frankly, you are my last hope.*

'My help? Surely you are not without powerful friends of your own?'

'It is my regrettable experience that powerful men can afford no friends.'

'All too unfortunately true. You do not reach my position, or even yours, without understanding that each man stands alone, in the end.' Marovia gazed down beneficently as he settled into his own tall chair. *Though I am far from put at ease. His smiles are every bit as deadly as Sult's frowns, I think.* 'Our friends must be those that can make themselves useful to us. With that in mind, what help can I offer you? And more importantly, what can you offer me in return?'

'That may take some explaining.' Glokta winced at a cramp in his leg and forced it out straight under the table. 'May I speak entirely honestly with you, your Worship?'

Marovia stroked thoughtfully at his beard. 'The truth is a very rare and valuable commodity. I am astonished that a man of your experience would simply give it away. Especially to someone on the other side of the fence, so to speak.'

'I was once told that a man lost in the desert must take such water as he is offered, regardless of the source.'

'Lost, are you? Speak honestly, then, Superior, and we will see if I can spare something from my canteen.'

Hardly a promise of succour, but the best I might have hoped for from a man so recently a bitter enemy. And so . . . my confession. Glokta turned over the memories of the last couple of years in his mind. *And a filthy, a shameful, an ugly set they are. Where to begin?* 'It is some time ago, now, that I began to examine irregularities in the business of the Honourable Guild of Mercers.'

'I well remember the unfortunate affair.'

'During my investigations I discovered that the Mercers were financed by a bank. A very wealthy and powerful bank. Valint and Balk.'

Glokta watched carefully for a reaction, but Marovia's eyes did not so much as flicker. 'I am aware of the existence of such an institution.'

'I suspected that they were implicated in the Mercers' crimes. Magister Kault told me as much before his unfortunate demise. But his Eminence did not wish me to investigate further. Too many complications at a complicated time.' Glokta's left eye twitched and he felt it beginning to run. 'My apologies,' he muttered as he wiped it with a finger. 'Shortly afterwards I was dispatched to Dagoska, to take charge of the defence of the city.'

'Your particular diligence in that matter was a source of some discomfort to me.' Marovia worked his mouth sourly. 'My congratulations. You did an extraordinary job.'

'I cannot entirely take the credit. The task the Arch Lector had given me was impossible. Dagoska was riddled with treason and surrounded by the Gurkish.'

Marovia snorted. 'One sympathises.'

'If only anyone had sympathised then, but they were busy here, trying to get the better of each other, as they always are. Dagoska's defences were in a state entirely inadequate for the task. I could not strengthen them without money—'

'His Eminence was not forthcoming.'

'His Eminence would not part with a single mark. But an unlikely benefactor stepped forward in my time of need.'

'A rich uncle? What a happy chance.'

'Not entirely.' Glokta licked at the salty space where his front teeth had once been. *And the secrets begin to spill like turds from a draining latrine-pit.* 'My rich uncle was none other than the banking house of Valint and Balk.'

Marovia frowned. 'They advanced you money?'

'It was thanks to their generosity that I was able to keep the Gurkish out as long as I did.'

'Bearing in mind that powerful people have no friends, what did Valint and Balk get in return?'

'In essence?' Glokta gave the High Justice an even stare. 'Whatever they wanted. Shortly after returning from Dagoska I was investigating the death of Crown Prince Raynault.'

'A terrible crime.'

'Of which the Gurkish ambassador who hung for it was innocent.'

Marovia registered the tiniest hint of surprise. 'You say so?'

'Undoubtedly. But the death of the heir to the throne created other problems, problems relating to votes in the Open Council, and his Eminence was happy with the easy answer. I tried to pursue the matter, but was prevented. By Valint and Balk.'

'You suspect that these bankers were involved in the death of the Crown Prince, then?'

'I suspect them of all manner of things, but proof is in short supply.' *Always too many suspicions, and not enough proof.*

'Banks,' grunted Marovia. 'They are made of air. They spin money out of guesses, and lies, and promises. Secrets are their currency, even more than gold.'

'So I have discovered. But men lost in the desert—'

'Yes, yes! Please continue.'

Glokta found, to his surprise, that he was greatly enjoying himself. He was almost tripping over his own tongue in his eagerness to blurt it all out. *Now I begin throwing away the secrets I have hoarded for so long, I find I cannot stop. I feel like a miser on a spending spree. Horrified, yet liberated. Agonised, yet delighted. Something like cutting your own throat, I imagine – a glorious release, but one you can enjoy only once. And like cutting my own throat, it will very likely end in my ugly death. Ah well. It has been coming some time, has it not? And not even I could claim I don't deserve it ten times over.*

Glokta leaned forwards. *Even here, even now, I somehow need to speak it softly.* 'Arch Lector Sult is not happy with our new king. Most particularly, he is not happy with the influence that Bayaz exerts over him. Sult finds his powers much curtailed. He believes, in fact, that you are somehow behind the whole business.'

Marovia frowned. 'Does he now?'

He does, and I am not entirely sure that I discount the possibility. 'He has asked me to find some means of removing Bayaz . . .' His voice dropped almost to a whisper. 'Or removing the king. I suspect, should I fail, that he has other plans. Plans which somehow involve the University.'

'You would seem to be accusing his Eminence the Arch Lector of high treason against the state.' Marovia's eyes were bright and hard as a pair of new nails. *Suspicious, and yet terribly eager.* 'Have you uncovered anything to use against the king?'

'Before I could even consider doing so, Valint and Balk quite forcibly dissuaded me.'

'They knew so quickly?'

'I am forced to concede that someone close to me may not be as reliable as I have always hoped. The bankers not only demanded that I disobey his Eminence, they also insisted that I investigate *him*. They want to know his plans. I have only a few days to satisfy them, and Sult no longer trusts me enough to share the contents of his latrine with me, let alone the contents of his mind.'

'Oh dear, dear.' Marovia slowly shook his head. 'Oh dear, dear.'

'To add to my woes, I believe that the Arch Lector is considerably less ignorant of what occurred in Dagoska than he at first appeared. If somebody is talking, it may well be that they are talking to both sides.' *If you can betray a man once, after all, it is not so very difficult to do it twice.* Glokta gave a long sigh. *And there we are. The secrets are all spilled. The turd-pit is emptied. My throat is slashed from ear to ear.* 'That is the whole story, your Worship.'

'Well, Superior, you certainly find yourself in quite a pickle.' *Quite a fatal one, in fact.* Marovia got up and wandered slowly around the room. 'Let us suppose, for the moment, that you truly have come for my help, and not to lead me into some manner of embarrassment. Arch Lector Sult has the means to cause a most serious problem. And the towering self-obsession necessary to try it at a time like this.' *You'll get no argument from me there.* 'If you could obtain compelling evidence, I would, of course, be willing to present it to the king. But I cannot move against a member of the Closed Council, and the Arch Lector in particular, without firm proof. A signed confession would be best.'

'Sult's signed confession?' murmured Glokta.

'Such a document would seem to solve some problems for both of us. Sult would be gone, and the bankers would have lost their hold over you. The Gurkish would still be camped outside our walls of course, but one can't have everything.'

'The Arch Lector's signed confession.' *And shall I pluck the moon from the sky while I'm about it?*

'Or a big enough stone to start the landslide – perhaps the confession of someone suitably close to him. I understand that you are expert at obtaining them.' The High Justice peered at Glokta from under his heavy brows. 'Was I misinformed?'

'I cannot conjure evidence from thin air, your Worship.'

'Those lost in the desert must take the chances they are offered, however slender. Find evidence, and bring it to me. Then I can act, and not one moment before. You understand that I cannot take any risks for you. It is difficult to trust a man who chose his master, and now chooses another.'

'Chose?' Glokta felt his eyelid twitching again. 'If you believe that I chose any part of the pitiful shadow of a life you see before you, you are very much mistaken. I chose glory and success. The box did not contain what was written on the lid.'

'The world is full of tragic tales.' Marovia walked to the window, turning his back and staring out at the darkening sky. 'Especially now. You can hardly expect them to make any difference to a man of my experience. I wish you good day.'

Further comment seems pointless. Glokta rocked forwards, pushed himself painfully up to standing with the aid of his cane, and limped for the door. *But the tiniest glimmer of hope has come creeping into the dank cellar of my despair . . . I need only obtain a confession to High Treason from the head of his Majesty's Inquisition—*

'And Superior!' *Why can no one ever finish talking before I get up?* Glokta turned back into the room, his spine burning. 'If someone close to you is talking, you need to shut them up. Now. Only a fool would consider uprooting treason from the Closed Council before he had cut the weeds from his own lawn.'

'Oh, you need not worry about my garden, your Worship.' Glokta treated the High Justice to his most repulsive grin. 'I am even now sharpening my shears.'

Charity

Adua burned.

The two westernmost districts – the Three Farms, at the south-western corner of the city, and the Arches, further north – were hacked with black wounds. Smoke was still pouring up from some of them, great columns lit in faint orange near the base. They spread out in oily smears, dragged away to the west by a stiff wind, drawing a muddy curtain across the setting sun.

Jezal watched in solemn silence, his hands bunched into numb fists on the parapet of the Tower of Chains. There was no sound up here but for the wind fumbling at his ears and, just occasionally, the slightest hint of distant battle. A war cry, or the screams of the wounded. Or perhaps only a sea-bird calling, high on the breeze. Jezal wished for a maudlin moment that he were a bird, and could simply fly from the tower and off over the Gurkish pickets, away from this nightmare. But escape would not be so easy.

'Casamir's Wall was first breached three days ago,' Marshal Varuz was explaining in a monotonous drone. 'We drove back the first two assaults, and held the Three Farms that night, but the next day there was another breach, and another. This damn fire-powder has changed all the bloody rules. A wall that would have stood a week they can bring down in an hour.'

'Khalul always loved to tinker with his dust and his bottles,' muttered Bayaz, unhelpfully.

'They were in the Three Farms in force that night, and carried the gates into the Arches soon afterwards. Ever since, the whole western part of the city has been one running battle.' The tavern where Jezal had celebrated his victory over Filio in the Contest was in that district. The tavern where he had sat with West and Jalenhorm, Kaspa and Brint, before they went away to the North, and he to the Old Empire. Was that building now burning? Was it already a blackened shell?

'We're fighting them hand to hand in the streets by daylight. We're mounting raids in the darkness, every night. Not a stride of ground is given up without it being soaked with Gurkish blood.' Perhaps Varuz hoped to be inspiring, but he was only succeeding in making Jezal feel sick. The streets of his capital soaked in blood, whoever's blood it might have been, was hardly his first aim as king of the Union. 'Arnault's Wall still stands firm, though there are fires burning in the centre of town. The flames almost reached the Four Corners last night, but the rain doused them down, at least for now. We're fighting for every street, every house, every room. Just as you said we should, your Majesty.'

'Good,' Jezal managed to croak, but he almost choked on the word.

When he so blithely turned down General Malzagurt's terms, he was not sure what he had been expecting. He had dimly imagined that someone would soon come to the rescue. That something heroic would occur. Only now the bloody business was well underway, and there was no sign of instant deliverance. Probably there was heroism going on down there in the smoke. Soldiers hauling injured comrades to safety through the sooty darkness. Nurses stitching wounds by screaming candlelight. Townsfolk plunging into burning buildings to drag out coughing children. Heroism of an every-day and unglamorous kind. A kind that made no difference to the overall outcome.

'Are those our ships in the bay?' he asked quietly, already afraid of the answer.

'I wish they were, your Majesty. I never thought I'd say it, but they have the best of us by sea. You never saw so many damn ships. Even if most of our navy weren't ferrying the army back from Angland, I'm not sure what they could do. As it is, the men will have to be landed outside the city. It's a damned inconvenience, and it could get to be a great deal more than that. The docks are a weak spot. Sooner or later they may try to land men there.'

Jezal looked nervously towards the water. Armies of Gurkish, pouring from their ships and into the heart of the city. The Middleway cut straight through the centre of Adua from the bay to the Agriont. A road invitingly wide enough to march an entire Gurkish legion straight down in a twinkling. He shut his eyes and tried to breathe evenly.

Before the arrival of the Gurkish he had hardly been able to have a moment's silence for the opinions of his councillors. Now that he actually needed advice, the torrent had suddenly run dry. Sult rarely appeared in the Closed Council, and then only to glare at Marovia. The High Justice himself had little to offer beyond bemoaning the fix they were all in. Even Bayaz' stock of historical examples seemed finally to be exhausted. Jezal was left to carry the responsibility alone, and he was finding it quite a weight. He supposed it was a good deal more unpleasant for those that were actually wounded, or homeless, or killed, but that was slender consolation.

'How many are dead already?' he found himself asking, like a child picking at a scab. 'How many have we lost?'

'The fighting along Casamir's Wall was fierce. The fighting throughout the occupied districts has been fiercer yet. Casualties on both sides are heavy. I would guess at a thousand dead at least on our side.'

Jezal swallowed sour spit. He thought about the mismatched defenders he had seen near the western gate, in a square now presumably overrun by Gurkish legions. Ordinary people, who had looked to him with hope and pride. Then he tried to picture what a thousand corpses might look like. He imagined a hundred of them, side by side, in a row. Then ten such rows, one above the other. A thousand. He gnawed at his thumbnail, already down to the painful quick.

'And many more wounded, of course,' added Varuz, in a sudden twist of the knife. 'We are very short of space for them, in fact. Two districts are at least partly occupied by the Gurkish and the enemy are landing incendiaries almost in the heart of the city.' Jezal's tongue sought out the still sore gap in his teeth. He remembered his own pain, out on the endless plain under the merciless sky, the stabs through his face as the cartwheels squeaked and jolted.

'Open the Agriont to the wounded, to the homeless. With the army away there is room to spare. Barracks for thousands, and ample provisions.'

Bayaz was shaking his bald head. 'A risk. We have no way of knowing who we would be letting in. Gurkish agents. Spies of Khalul. Not all of them are what they appear.'

Jezal ground his teeth. 'I am prepared to take the risk. Am I king here, or not?'

'You are,' growled Bayaz, 'and you would be well advised to act like it. This is no time for sentiment. The enemy are closing on Arnault's Wall. In places they might be within two miles of where we stand.'

'Two miles?' murmured Jezal, his eyes flickering nervously towards the west again. Arnault's Wall was a fine grey line through the buildings, looking a terribly frail sort of a barrier from up here, and worryingly close. A sudden fear gripped him. Not the guilty concern he felt for the theoretical people down there in the smoke, but a real and very personal fear for his own life. Like the one he had felt among the stones, when the two warriors advanced on him with murder in mind. Perhaps he had made a mistake not leaving the city when he had the chance. Perhaps it was not too late to—

'I will stand or fall alongside the people of the Union!' he shouted, as angry at his own cowardice as he was at the Magus. 'If they are willing to die for me, then I am willing to die for them!' He turned his shoulder towards Bayaz and quickly looked away. 'Open the Agriont, Marshal Varuz. You can fill the palace with wounded too, if you have to.'

Varuz glanced nervously sideways at Bayaz, then gave a stiff bow. 'Hospitals will be set up in the Agriont, then, your Majesty. The barracks will be opened to the people. The palace we had probably better leave sealed, at least until things get worse.'

Jezal could hardly bear to imagine what worse might look like. 'Good, good. See it done.' He had to wipe a tear from under his eye as he turned away from the smouldering city and made for the long stair. The smoke, of course. Nothing but the smoke.

Queen Terez sat alone, framed in the window of their vast bed-chamber.

The Countess Shalere was still lurking around the palace somewhere, but it seemed she had learned to keep her scorn well out of Jezal's way. The rest of Terez' ladies she had sent back to Styria before the Gurkish blockaded the harbour. Jezal rather wished that he could have returned the queen herself along with the rest but that, unfortunately, was not an option.

Terez did not so much as glance in his direction as Jezal shut the door. He had to stifle a heavy sigh as he trudged across the room, his boots muddy from the spitting rain, his skin greasy from the soot in the air outside.

'You are treading dirt with you,' said Terez, without looking round, her voice as icy as ever.

'War is a dirty business, my love.' He saw the side of her face twitch with disgust when he said the last two words, and hardly knew whether he wanted to laugh or cry at it. He dropped down heavily in the chair opposite her without touching his boots, knowing all the while that it would infuriate her. There was nothing he could do that would not.

'Must you come to me in this manner?' she snapped.

'Oh, but I could not stay away! You are my wife, after all.'

'Not by choice.'

'It was not my choice either, but I am willing to make the best of things! Believe it or not I would rather have married someone who did not hate me!' Jezal shoved one hand through his hair and pressed his anger down with some difficulty. 'But let us not fight, please. I have enough fighting to do out there. More than I can stand! Can we not, at least . . . be civil to one another?'

She looked at him for a long moment, a thoughtful frown on her face. 'How can you?'

'How can I what?'

'Keep trying.'

Jezal ventured a fragment of a grin. 'I had hoped that you might come to admire my persistence, if nothing else.' She did not smile, but he sensed, perhaps, the slightest softening of the hard line of her mouth. He hardly dared suppose that she might have finally begun to thaw, but he was willing to seize on the slightest shred of hope. Hope was in short supply, these days. He leaned towards her, staring earnestly into her eyes. 'You have made it clear that you think very little of me, and I suppose that I hardly blame you. I do not think so very much of myself, believe me. But I am trying . . . I am trying very hard . . . to be a better man.'

The corner of Terez' mouth twitched up in a sad kind of smile, but a kind of smile nonetheless. To his great surprise she reached out, and placed one hand tenderly on his face. His breath caught in his throat, skin tingling where her fingertips rested.

'Why can you not understand that I despise you?' she asked. He felt himself go very cold. 'I despise the look of you, the feel of you, the sound of your voice. I despise this place and its people. The sooner the Gurkish burn it all to the ground the happier I'll be.' She took her hand away and turned back to the window, a glimmering of light down her perfect profile.

Jezal slowly stood up. 'I think I will find another room to sleep in tonight. This one is altogether too cold.'

'At last.'

It can be a terrible curse for a man to get everything he ever dreamed of. If the shining prizes turn out somehow to be empty baubles, he is left without even his dreams for comfort. All the things that Jezal had thought he wanted – power, fame, the beautiful trappings of greatness – they were nothing but dust. All he wanted now was for things to be as they had been, before he got them. But there was no way back. Not ever.

He really had nothing further to say. He turned stiffly and trudged for the door.

Better Left Buried

When the fighting is over you dig, if you're still alive. You dig graves for your dead comrades. A last mark of respect, however little you might have had for them. You dig as deep as you can be bothered, you dump them in, you cover them up, they rot away and are forgotten. That's the way it's always been.

There would be a lot of digging when this fight was done. A lot of digging for both sides.

Twelve days, now, since the fire started falling. Since the wrath of God began to rain on these arrogant pinks, and lay blackened waste to their proud city. Twelve days since the killing started – at the walls, and in the streets, and through the houses. For twelve days in the cold sunlight, in the spitting rain, in the choking smoke, and for twelve nights by the light of flickering fires, Ferro had been in the thick of it.

Her boots slapped against the polished tiles, leaving black marks down the immaculate hallway behind her. Ash. The two districts where the fighting was raging were covered in it, now. It had mingled with the thin rain to make a sticky paste, like black glue. The buildings that still stood, the charred skeletons of the ones that did not, the people who killed and the people who died, all coated in it. The scowling guards and the cringing servants frowned at her and the marks she left, but she had never cared a shit for their opinions, and was not about to start. They would have more ash than they knew what to do with soon. The whole place would be ash, if the Gurkish got their way.

And it looked very much as if they might. Each day and each night, for all the efforts of the rag-tag defenders, for all the dead they left among the ruins, the Emperor's troops worked their way further into the city.

Towards the Agriont.

Yulwei was sitting in the wide chamber when she got there, shrunken into a chair in one corner, the bangles hanging from his limp arms. The calmness which had always seemed to swaddle him like an old blanket was stripped away. He looked worried, worn, eyes sunken in dark sockets. A man looking defeat in the face. A look that Ferro was getting used to seeing over the past few days.

'Ferro Maljinn, back from the front. I always said that you would kill the whole world if you could, and now you have your chance. How do you like war, Ferro?'

'Well enough.' She tossed her bow rattling onto a polished table, dragged her sword out of her belt, shrugged off her quiver. She had only a few shafts left. Most of them she had left stuck through Gurkish soldiers, out there in the blackened ruins at the edge of the city.

But Ferro could not bring herself to smile.

Killing Gurkish was like eating honey. A little only left you craving more. Too much could become sickening. Corpses had always been a poor reward for all the effort it took to make them. But there was no stopping now.

'You are hurt?'

Ferro squeezed at the filthy bandage round her arm, and watched the blood seep out into the grey cloth. There was no pain. 'No,' she said.

'It is not too late, Ferro. You do not need to die here. I brought you. I can still take you away. I go where I please, and I take who I please with me. If you stop killing now, who knows? Perhaps God will still find a place in heaven for you.'

Ferro was becoming very tired of Yulwei's preaching. She and Bayaz might not have trusted each other a finger's breadth, but they understood each other. Yulwei understood nothing.

' "Heaven"?' she sneered as she turned away from him. 'Perhaps hell suits me better, did you think of that?'

She hunched up her shoulders as footsteps echoed down the

hallway outside. She felt Bayaz' anger even before the door was flung open and the old bald pink stormed into the room.

'That little bastard! After all that I have given him, how does he repay me?' Quai and Sulfur slunk through the doorway behind him like a pair of dogs creeping after their master. 'He defies me before the Closed Council! He tells me to mind my business! Me! How would that cringing dunce know what is my business and what is not?'

'Trouble with King Luthar the Magnificent?' grunted Ferro.

The Magus narrowed his eyes at her. 'A year ago there was no emptier head in the whole Circle of the World. Stick a crown on him and have a crowd of old liars tongue his arse for a few weeks and the little shit thinks he's Stolicus!'

Ferro shrugged. Luthar had never lacked a high opinion of himself, king or not. 'You should be more careful who you stick crowns on.'

'That's the trouble with crowns, they have to go on someone. All you can do is drop them in a crowd and hope for the best.' Bayaz scowled over at Yulwei. 'What of you brother? Have you been walking outside the walls?'

'I have.'

'And what have you seen?'

'Death. Much of that. The Emperor's soldiers flood into the western districts of Adua, his ships choke the bay. Every day more troops come up the road from the south, and tighten the Gurkish grip on the city.'

'That much I can learn from those halfwits on the Closed Council. What of Mamun and his Hundred Words?'

'Mamun, the thrice blessed and thrice cursed? Wondrous first apprentice of great Khalul, God's right hand? He is waiting. He and his brothers, and his sisters, they have a great tent outside the bounds of the city. They pray for victory, they listen to sweet music, they bathe in scented water, they laze naked and enjoy the pleasures of the flesh. They wait for the Gurkish soldiers to carry the walls of the city, and they eat.' He looked up at Bayaz. 'They eat night and day, in open defiance of the Second Law. In brazen mockery of the solemn word of

Euz. Making ready for the moment when they will come to seek you out. The moment for which Khalul made them. They think it will not be long, now. They polish their armour.'

'Do they indeed?' hissed Bayaz. 'Damn them then.'

'They have damned themselves already. But that is no help to us.'

'Then we must visit the House of the Maker.' Ferro's head jerked up. There was something about that great, stark tower that had fascinated her ever since she first arrived in Adua. She found her eyes always drawn towards its mountainous bulk, rising untouchable, high above the smoke and the fury.

'Why?' asked Yulwei. 'Do you plan to seal yourself inside? Just as Kanedias did, all those years ago, when we came seeking our vengeance? Will you cower in the darkness, Bayaz? And this time, will you be the one thrown down, to break upon the bridge below?'

The First of the Magi snorted. 'You know me better than that. When they come for me I will face them in the open. But there are still weapons in the darkness. A surprise or two from the Maker's forge for our cursed friends beyond the walls.'

Yulwei looked even more worried than before. 'The Divider?'

'One edge here,' whispered Quai from the corner. 'One on the Other Side.'

Bayaz, as usual, ignored him. 'It can cut through anything, even an Eater.'

'Will it cut through a hundred?' asked Yulwei.

'I will settle for Mamun alone.'

Yulwei slowly unfolded himself from the chair, stood with a sigh. 'Very well, lead on. I will enter the Maker's House with you, one last time.'

Ferro licked her teeth. The idea of going inside was irresistible. 'I will come with you.'

Bayaz glared back. 'No, you will not. You can stay here and sulk. That has always been your special gift, has it not? I would hate to deny you the opportunity to make use of it. You will come with us,' he snapped at Quai. 'You have your business, eh, Yoru?'

'I do, Master Bayaz.'

'Good.' The First of the Magi strode from the room with Yulwei at his shoulder, his apprentice trudging at the rear. Sulfur did not move. Ferro frowned at him, and he grinned back, his head tipped against the panelled wall, his chin pointed towards the moulded ceiling.

'Are these Hundred Words not your enemies too?' Ferro demanded.

'My deepest and most bitter enemies.'

'Why do you not fight, then?'

'Oh, there are other ways to fight than struggling in the dirt out there.' There was something in those eyes, one dark, one bright, that Ferro did not like the look of. There was something hard and hungry behind his smiles. 'Though I would love to stay and chat, I must go and give the wheels another push.' He turned a finger round and round in the air. 'The wheels must keep turning, eh, Maljinn?'

'Go then,' she snapped. 'I will not stop you.'

'You could not if you wanted to. I would bid you a good day. But I'd wager you've never had one.' And he sauntered out, the door clicking to behind him.

Ferro was already across the room, shooting back the bolt on the window. She had done as Bayaz told her once before, and it had brought her nothing but a wasted year. She would make her own choices now. She jerked the hangings aside and slipped out onto the balcony. Curled-up leaves blew on the wind, whipping around the lawns below along with the spitting rain. A quick glance up and down the damp paths showed only one guard, and he was looking the wrong way, huddled in his cloak.

Sometimes it is best to seize the moment.

Ferro swung her legs over the rail, gathered herself, then sprang out into the air. She caught a slippery tree branch, swung to the trunk, slid down it to the damp earth and crept behind a neatly clipped hedge, low to the ground.

She heard footsteps, then voices. Bayaz' voice, and Yulwei's, speaking soft into the hissing wind. Damn, but these old fools of Magi loved to flap their lips.

'Sulfur?' came Yulwei's voice. 'He is still with you?'

'Why would he not be?'

'His studies ran in . . . dangerous directions. I told you this, brother.'

'And? Khalul is not so picky with his servants . . .'

They passed out of earshot and Ferro had to rush along behind the hedge to keep pace, staying bent double.

'. . . I do not like this habit,' Yulwei was saying, 'of taking forms, of changing skin. A cursed discipline. You know what Juvens' feelings were on it—'

'I have no time to worry on the feelings of a man centuries in his grave. There is no Third Law, Yulwei.'

'Perhaps there should be. Stealing another's face . . . the tricks of Glustrod and his devil-bloods. Arts borrowed from the Other Side—'

'We must use such weapons as we can find. I have no love for Mamun, but he is right. They are called the Hundred Words because they are a hundred. We are two, and time has not been kind to us.'

'Then why do they wait?'

'You know Khalul, brother. Ever careful, watchful, deliberate. He will not risk his children until he must . . .'

Through the chinks in the bare twigs Ferro watched the three men pass between the guards and out of the gate in the high palace wall. She gave them a few moments, then she started up and strode after, shoulders back, as though she was about important business. She felt the hard stares of the armoured men flanking the gate, but they were used to her coming and going now. For once they kept their silence.

Between the great buildings, around the statues, through the dull gardens she followed the two Magi and their apprentice across the Agriont. She kept her distance, loitering in doorways, under trees, walking close behind those few people hurrying down the windy streets. Sometimes, above the buildings in a square, or at the end of a lane, the top of the great mass of the

447

Maker's House reared up. Hazy grey through the drizzle to begin with, but growing more black, vast and distinct with each stride she took.

The three men led her to a ramshackle building with crumbling turrets sticking from its sagging roof. Ferro knelt and watched from behind a corner while Bayaz beat on the rickety door with the end of his staff.

'I am glad you did not find the Seed, brother,' said Yulwei, while they waited. 'That thing is better left buried.'

'I wonder if you will still think so when the Hundred Words swarm through the streets of the Agriont, howling for our blood?'

'God will forgive me, I think. There are worse things than Khalul's Eaters.'

Ferro's nails dug into her palms. There was a figure standing at one of the grimy windows, peering out at Yulwei and Bayaz. A long, lean figure with a black mask and short hair. The woman who had chased her and Ninefingers, long before. Ferro's hand strayed on an instinct towards her sword, then she realised she had left it in the palace, and cursed her foolishness. Ninefingers had been right. You could never have too many knives.

The door wobbled open, some words were muttered, the two old men went through, Quai at their back, head bowed. The masked woman watched for a while longer, then stepped back from the window into the darkness. Ferro sprang over a hedge as the door wobbled closed, wedged her foot in the gap and slid through sideways, stealing into the deep shadows on the other side. The door clattered shut on its creaking hinges.

Down a long hallway, dusty paintings on one wall, dusty windows in the other. All the way the back of Ferro's neck prickled, waiting for the black masks to come boiling out of the shadows. But nothing came besides the echoing footsteps up ahead, the mindless droning of the old men's voices.

'This place has changed,' Yulwei was saying. 'Since that day we fought Kanedias. The day the Old Time ended. It rained, then.'

'I remember it.'

'I lay wounded on the bridge, in the rain. I saw them fall, the Maker and his daughter. From on high, they tumbled down. Hard to believe, that I smiled to see it, then. Vengeance is a fleeting thrill. The doubts, we carry to our graves.' Ferro sneered at that. If she could have the vengeance she would live with the doubts.

'Time has brought us both regrets,' muttered Bayaz.

'More of them with every passing year. A strange thing, though. I could have sworn, as I lay there, that it was Kanedias who fell first, and Tolomei second.'

'Memory can tell lies, especially to men who have lived as long as we. The Maker threw down his daughter, then I him. And so the Old Time ended.'

'So it did,' murmured Yulwei. 'So much lost. And now we are come to this . . .'

Quai's head snapped round and Ferro plastered herself against the wall behind a leaning cabinet. He stood there, for a long moment, frowning towards her. Then he followed the others. Ferro waited, holding her breath, until the three of them turned a corner and passed out of sight.

She caught them up in a crumbling courtyard, choked with dead weeds, littered with broken slates fallen from the roofs above. A man in a stained shirt led them up a long stairway, towards a dark arch high in the high wall of the Agriont. He had a bunch of jingling keys in his gnarled hands, was muttering something about eggs. Once they had passed into the tunnel Ferro padded across the open space and up the steps, pausing near the top.

'We will come back shortly,' she heard Bayaz growling. 'Leave the door ajar.'

'It's always kept locked,' a voice answered. 'That's the rule. It's been kept locked all my life, and I don't plan to—'

'Then wait here until we come back! But go nowhere! I have many better things to do than sit waiting on the wrong side of your locked doors!' Keys turned. Old hinges squealed. Ferro's fingers slid round a loose lump of stone and gripped it tightly.

The man in the dirty shirt was pulling the gates shut as she crept to the top of the steps. He muttered angrily as he fumbled with his keys, metal clinking. There was a dull thump as the stone clubbed him across his bald spot. He gasped, lurched forward, Ferro caught his limp body under the arms and lowered him carefully to the ground.

Then she set the rock down and relieved him of his keys with a hooked finger.

As Ferro lifted her hand to push the doors open, a strange sensation washed over her. Like a cool breeze on a hot day, surprising, at first, then delightful. A shiver, not at all unpleasant, worked its way up her spine and made her breath catch. She pressed her hand to the weathered wood, the grain brushing warm and welcoming against her palm. She eased the door open just wide enough to peer through.

A narrow bridge sprang out from the wall of the Agriont, no more than a stride across, without rail or parapet. At the far end it met the side of the Maker's House – a soaring cliff of bare rock, shining black with the rain. Bayaz, Yulwei and Quai stood before a gate at the end of that strip of stone. A gate of dark metal, marked in the centre with bright circles. Rings of letters that Ferro did not understand. She watched Bayaz pull something out from the collar of his shirt. She watched the circles begin to move, to turn, to spin, her heart pounding in her ears. The doors moved silently apart. Slowly, reluctantly, almost, the three men passed into that square of blackness, and were gone.

The House of the Maker stood open.

Grey water slapped at hard stone below as Ferro followed them across the bridge. The rain kissed and the wind nipped at her skin. In the distance, smudges of smoke rose from the smouldering city and into the muddy sky, but her eyes were fixed on the yawning portal straight ahead. She loitered on the threshold for a moment, her hands clenched into fists.

Then she stepped into the darkness.

It was neither cold nor warm on the other side of the gate. The air was so still, and flat, and silent that it seemed to weigh heavily on Ferro's shoulders, to press at her ears. A few muffled steps and the light had all faded. Wind, and rain, and the open sky were dimly remembered dreams. She felt she walked a hundred miles beneath the dead earth. Time itself seemed to have stopped. Ferro crept up to a wide archway and peered through.

The hall beyond was like a temple, but it would have swallowed whole even the great temple in Shaffa, where thousands called hourly out to God. It dwarfed the lofty dome where Jezal dan Luthar had been given a crown. It was an expanse that made even the vastness of ruined Aulcus seem petty. A place crowded with solemn shadows, peopled with sullen echoes, bounded by angry, unyielding stone. The tomb of long-dead giants.

The grave of forgotten gods.

Yulwei and Bayaz stood at its centre. Tiny, insect figures in an ocean of gleaming darkness. Ferro pressed herself to the cold rock, striving to pick their words out from the sea of echoes.

'Go to the armoury and find some of the Maker's blades. I will go up, and bring . . . that other thing.'

Bayaz turned away, but Yulwei caught him by the arm. 'First answer me one question, brother.'

'What question?'

'The same one I always ask.'

'Again? Even now? Very well, if you must. Ask.'

The two old men stood still for the longest time. Until the last echoes had faded and left only a silence as heavy as lead. Ferro held her breath.

'Did you kill Juvens?' Yulwei's whisper hissed through the darkness. 'Did you kill our master?'

Bayaz did not flinch. 'I made mistakes, long ago. Many mistakes, I know. Some out in the ruined west. Some here, in this place. The day does not pass when I do not regret them. I fought with Khalul. I ignored my master's wisdom. I trespassed in the House of the Maker. I fell in love with his daughter. I was proud, and vain, and rash, all this is true. But I did not kill Juvens.'

'What happened that day?'

The First of the Magi spoke the words as though they were lines long rehearsed. 'Kanedias came to take me. For seducing his daughter. For stealing his secrets. Juvens would not give me up. They fought, I fled. The fury of their battle lit the skies. When I returned, the Maker was gone, and our master was dead. I did not kill Juvens.'

Again a long silence, and Ferro watched, frozen. 'Very well.' Yulwei let fall his hand from Bayaz' arm. 'Mamun lied, then. Khalul lied. We will fight against them together.'

'Good, my old friend, good. I knew that I could trust you, as you can trust me.' Ferro curled her lip. Trust. It was a word that only liars used. A word the truthful had no need of. The First of the Magi's footsteps rang out as he strode towards one of the many archways and vanished into the gloom.

Yulwei watched him go. Then he gave a sharp sigh, and padded off in the other direction, his bangles jingling on his thin arms. The echoes of his passing slowly faded, and Ferro was left alone with the shadows, wrapped in silence.

Slowly, carefully, she crept forwards into that immense emptiness. The floor glittered – snaking lines of bright metal, set into the black rock. The ceiling, if there was one, was shrouded in darkness. A high balcony ran around the walls a good twenty strides up, another far above that, then another, and another, vague in the half-light. Above all, a beautiful device hung. Rings of dark metal, great and small, gleaming discs and shining circles, marked with strange writings. All moving. All revolving, one ring about the other, and at their centre a black ball, the one point of perfect stillness.

She turned round, and round, or perhaps she stood still and the room turned about her. She felt dizzy, drunken, breathless. The bare rock soared away into the black, rough stones without mortar, no two alike. Ferro tried to imagine how many stones the tower was made of.

Thousands. Millions.

What had Bayaz said, on the island at the edge of the World? Where does the wise man hide a stone? Among a thousand.

Among a million. The rings high above shifted gently. They pulled at her, and the black ball in the centre pulled at her most of all. Like a beckoning hand. Like a voice calling out her name.

She dug her fingers into the dry spaces between the stones and began to climb, hand over hand, up and up. It was easily done. As though the wall was meant to be climbed. Soon she swung her legs over the metal rail of the first balcony. On again, without pausing for breath, up and up. She reached the second balcony, sticky with sweat in the dead air. She reached the third, breath rasping. She gripped the rail of the fourth, and pulled herself over. She stood, staring down.

Far below, at the bottom of a black abyss, the whole Circle of the World lay on the round floor of the hall. A map, the coastlines picked out in shining metal. Level with Ferro, filling almost all the space within the gently curving gallery, suspended on wires no thicker than threads, the great mechanism slowly revolved.

She frowned at the black ball in its centre, her palms tingling. It seemed to hover there, without support. She should have wondered how that could be, but all she could think about was how much she wanted to touch it. Needed to. She had no choice. One of the metal circles drifted close to her, gleaming dully.

Sometimes it is best to seize the moment.

She sprang up onto the rail, crouched there for an instant, gathering herself. She did not think. Thinking would have been madness. She leapt into empty space, limbs flailing. The whole machine wobbled and swayed as she caught hold of its outermost ring. She swung underneath, hanging breathless. Slowly, delicately, her tongue pressed into the roof of her mouth, she pulled herself up by her arms, hooked her legs over the metal and dragged herself along it. Soon it brought her close to a wide disc, scored with grooves, and she clambered from one to the other, body trembling with effort. The cool metal quivered under her weight, twisting and flexing, wobbling with her every movement, threatening to shrug her off into the empty void. Ferro might have had no fear in her.

But plunges of a hundred strides onto the hardest of hard rock still demanded her deep respect.

So she slithered out, from one ring to another, hardly daring even to breathe. She told herself there was no drop. She was only climbing trees, sliding between their branches, the way she had when she was a child, before the Gurkish came. Finally she caught hold of the innermost ring. She clung to it, furious tight, waiting until its own movement brought her close to the centre. She hung down, legs crossed around the frail metal, one hand gripping it, the other reaching out towards that gleaming black ball.

She could see her rigid face reflected in its perfect surface, her clawing hand, swollen and distorted. She strained forward with every nerve, teeth gritted. Closer, and closer yet. All that mattered was to touch it. The very tip of her middle finger brushed against it and, like a bubble bursting, it vanished into empty mist.

Something dropped free, falling, slowly, as if it sank through water. Ferro watched it tumble away from her, a darker spot in the inky darkness, down, and down. It struck the floor with a boom that seemed to shake the very foundations of the Maker's House, filled the hall with crashing echoes. The ring that Ferro clung to trembled and for a giddy instant she nearly lost her grip. When she managed to haul herself back she realised that it had stopped moving.

The whole device was still.

It seemed to take her an age to clamber back across the motionless rings to the topmost gallery, to make the long descent down the towering walls. When she finally dropped to the floor of the cavernous chamber her clothes were torn, her hands, elbows, knees grazed and bloody, but she scarcely noticed. She ran across the wide floor, her footsteps ringing out. Towards the very centre of the hall, where the thing that had fallen from above still lay.

It looked like nothing more than an uneven chunk of dark

stone the size of a big fist. But this was no stone, and Ferro knew it. She felt something leaking from it, pouring from it, flooding out in thrilling waves. Something that could not be seen, or touched, and yet filled the whole space to its darkest reaches. Invisible, yet irresistible, it flowed tingling around her and dragged her forwards.

Ferro's heart thumped at her ribs as her footsteps drew close. Her mouth flooded with hungry spit as she knelt beside it. Her breath clawed in her throat as she reached out, palm itching. Her hand closed around its pocked and pitted surface. Very heavy, and very cold, as if it were a chunk of frozen lead. She lifted it slowly up, turning it in her hand, watching it glitter in the darkness, fascinated.

'The Seed.'

Bayaz stood in one of the archways, face trembling with an ugly mixture of horror and delight. 'Leave, Ferro, now! Take it to the palace.' He flinched, raised one arm, as if to shield his eyes from a blinding glare. 'The box is in my chambers. Put it inside, and seal it tight, do you hear me? Seal it tight!'

Ferro turned away, scowling, not sure now which of the archways led out of the Maker's House.

'Wait!' Quai was padding across the floor towards her, his gleaming eyes fixed on her hand. 'Stay!' He showed no trace of fear as he came closer. Only an awful kind of hunger, strange enough that Ferro took a step away. 'It was here. Here, all along.' His face looked pale, slack, full of shadows. 'The Seed.' His white hand crept through the darkness towards her. 'At last. Give it to—'

He crumpled up like discarded paper, was ripped from his feet and flung away the whole width of the vast room in the time it took Ferro to drag in one stunned breath. He hit the wall just below the lowest balcony with an echoing crunch. She watched open-mouthed as his shattered body bounced off and tumbled to the ground, broken limbs flopping.

Bayaz stepped forward, his staff clenched tightly in his fist. The air around his shoulders was still shimmering ever so slightly. Ferro had killed many men, of course, and shed no tears. But the speed of this shocked even her.

'What did you do?' she hissed, the echoes of Quai's fatal impact with the far wall still thudding about them.

'What I had to. Get to the palace. Now.' Bayaz stabbed at one of the archways with a heavy finger, and Ferro saw the faintest glimmer of light inside it. 'Put that thing into the box! You cannot imagine how dangerous it is!'

Few people liked taking orders less, but Ferro had no wish to stay in this place. She stuffed the lump of rock down inside her shirt. It felt right there, pressed against her stomach. Cool and comforting, for all Bayaz called it dangerous. She took one step, and as her boot slapped down a grating chuckle floated up from the far side of the hall.

From where Quai's ruined corpse had fallen.

Bayaz did not seem surprised. 'So!' he shouted. 'You show yourself at last! I have suspected for some time that you were not who you appeared to be! Where is my apprentice, and when did you replace him?'

'Months ago.' Quai was still chuckling as he pushed himself slowly up from the polished floor. 'Before you left on your fool's errand to the Old Empire.' There was no blood on his smiling face. Not so much as a graze. 'I sat beside you, at the fire. I watched you while you lay helpless in that cart. I was with you all the way, to the edge of the World and back. Your apprentice stayed here. I left his half-eaten corpse in the bushes for the flies, not twenty strides from where you and the North-man soundly slept.'

'Huh.' Bayaz tossed his staff from one hand to the other. 'I thought I noted a sharp improvement in your skills. You should have killed me then, when you had the chance.'

'Oh, there is time now.' Ferro shivered as she watched Quai stand. The hall seemed to have grown suddenly very cold.

'A hundred words? Perhaps. One word?' Bayaz' lip curled. 'I think not. Which of Khalul's creatures are you? The East Wind? One of those damned twins?'

'I am not one of Khalul's creatures.'

The faintest flicker of doubt passed over Bayaz' face. 'Who, then?'

'We knew each other well, in times long past.'

The First of the Magi frowned. 'Who are you? Speak!'

'Taking forms.' A woman's voice, soft and low. Something was happening to Quai's face as he paced slowly forward. His pale skin drooped, twisted. 'A dread and insidious trick.' His nose, his eyes, his lips began to melt, running off his skull like wax down a candle. 'Do you not remember me, Bayaz?' Another face showed itself beneath, a hard face, white as pale marble. 'You said that you would love me forever.' The air was icy chill. Ferro's breath was smoking before her mouth. 'You promised me that we would never be parted. When I opened my father's gate to you . . .'

'No!' Bayaz took a faltering step back.

'You look surprised. Not as surprised as I was, when instead of taking me in your arms you threw me down from the roof, eh, my love? And why? So that you could keep your secrets? So that you could seem noble?' Quai's long hair had turned white as chalk. It floated now about a woman's face, terribly pale, eyes two bright, black points. Tolomei. The Maker's daughter. A ghost, stepped out of the faded past. A ghost that had walked beside them for months, wearing a stolen shape. Ferro could almost feel her icy breath, cold as death on the air. Her eyes flickered from that pale face to the archway, far away across the floor, caught between wanting to run, and needing to know more.

'I saw you in your grave!' whispered Bayaz. 'I piled the earth over you myself!'

'So you did, and wept when you did, as though you had not been the one to throw me down.' Her black eyes swivelled to Ferro, to where the Seed lay tingling against her belly. 'But I had touched the Other Side. In these two hands I had held it, while my father worked, and it had left me altered. There I lay, in the earth's cold embrace. Between life and death. Until I heard the voices. The voices that Glustrod heard, long ago. They offered me a bargain. My freedom for theirs.'

'You broke the First Law!'

'Laws mean nothing to the buried! When I finally clawed my way from the grasping earth the human part of me was gone. But the other part, the part that belongs to the world below – that cannot die. It stands before you. Now I will complete the work that Glustrod began. I will throw open the doors that my grandfather sealed. This world and the Other Side shall be one. As they were before the Old Time. As they were always meant to be.' She held out her open hand, and a bitter chill flowed from it and sent shivers across Ferro's back to the tips of her fingers. 'Give me the Seed, child. I made a promise to the Tellers of Secrets, and I keep the promises I make.'

'We shall see!' snarled the First of the Magi. Ferro felt the tugging in her stomach, saw the air around Bayaz begin to blur. Tolomei stood ten strides away from him. The next instant she struck him with a sound like a thunderclap. His staff burst apart, splintered wood flying. He gave a shocked splutter as he flew through the darkness, rolled over and over across the cold stone to lie face down in a crumpled heap. Ferro stared as a wave of freezing air washed over her. She felt a sick and terrible fear, all the worse for being unfamiliar. She stood frozen.

'The years have made you weak.' The Maker's daughter moved slowly now, silently towards Bayaz' senseless body, her white hair flowing out behind her like the ripples on a frosty pool. 'Your Art cannot harm me.' She stood over him, her dry white lips spreading into an icy smile. 'For all you took from me. For my father.' She raised her foot above Bayaz' bald head. 'For myself—'

She burst into brilliant flames. Harsh light flickered to the furthest corners of the cavernous chamber, brightness stabbed into the very cracks between the stones. Ferro stumbled back, holding one hand over her eyes. Between her fingers she saw Tolomei reel madly across the floor, thrashing and dancing, white flames wreathing her body, her hair a coiling tongue of fire.

She flopped to the ground, the darkness closing back in, smoke pouring up in a reeking cloud. Yulwei padded out from one of the archways, his dark skin shining with sweat. He held a bundle of swords under one scrawny arm. Swords of dull metal, like the one that Ninefingers had carried, each marked with a single silver letter. 'Are you alright, Ferro?'

'I . . .' The fire had brought no warmth with it. Ferro's teeth were rattling, the hall had grown so cold. 'I . . .'

'Go.' Yulwei frowned at Tolomei's body as the last flames died. Ferro finally found the strength to move, began to back away. She felt a bitter sinking in her gut as she watched the Maker's daughter climb up, the ash of Quai's clothes sliding from her body. She stood, tall and deathly lean, naked and as bald as Bayaz, her hair all seared away to grey dust. There was not so much as a mark on her corpse-pale skin, gleaming flawless white.

'Always there is something more.' She glared at Yulwei with her flat black eyes. 'No fire can burn me, conjuror. You cannot stop me.'

'But I must try.' The Magus flung his swords into the air. They turned, spun, edges glittering, spreading apart in the darkness, drifting impossibly sideways. They began to fly around Yulwei and Ferro in a whirling circle. Faster and faster until they were a blur of deadly metal. Close enough that if Ferro had reached out, her hand would have been snatched off at the wrist.

'Stand still,' said Yulwei.

That hardly needed saying. Ferro felt a surge of anger, hot and familiar. 'First I should run, then stand still? First the Seed is at the Edge of the World, and now it is here at the centre? First she is dead and now she has stolen another's face? You old bastards need to get your stories straight.'

'They are liars!' snarled Tolomei, and Ferro felt the cold of her freezing breath wash over her cheek and chill her to the bone. 'Users! You cannot trust them!'

'But I can trust you?' Ferro snorted her contempt. 'Fuck yourself!'

Tolomei nodded slowly. 'Then die, along with the rest.' She padded sideways, balanced on her toes, rings of white frost

459

spreading out wherever her bare feet touched the ground. 'You cannot keep juggling your knives forever, old man.'

Over her white shoulder, Ferro saw Bayaz get slowly to his feet, holding one arm with the other, rigid face scratched and bloody. Something dangled from his limp fist – a long mass of metal tubes with a hook on the end, dull metal gleaming in the darkness. His eyes rolled to the far-off ceiling, veins bulging from his neck with effort as the air began to twist around him. Ferro felt that sucking in her gut and her eyes were drawn upwards. Up to the great machine that hung above their heads. It began to tremble.

'Shit,' she muttered, starting to back away.

If Tolomei noticed, she showed no sign. She bent her knees and sprang high into the air, a white streak over the spinning swords. She hung above for an instant, then plummeted down towards Yulwei. She crashed into the floor, knees first, the impact making the ground shake. A splinter of stone grazed Ferro's cheek and she felt a blast of icy wind against her face, lurched a step back.

The Maker's daughter frowned up. 'You do not die easily, old man,' she snarled as the echoes faded.

Ferro could not tell how Yulwei had avoided her, but now he danced away, his hands moving in slow circles, bangles jingling, swords still tumbling through the air behind him. 'I have been working at it all my life. You do not die easily either.'

The Maker's daughter stood and faced him. 'I do not die.'

High above the huge device lurched, cables pinging as they snapped, whipping in the darkness. With an almost dreamlike slowness, it began to fall. Glittering metal twisted, flexed, shrieked as it tumbled down. Ferro turned and ran. Five breathless strides and she flung herself down, sliding flat on her face across the polished rock. She felt the Seed digging into her stomach, the wind of the spinning swords ripping close to her back as she passed just beneath them.

The great machine hit the floor behind her with a noise like the music of hell. Each ring made a vast cymbal, a giant's gong. Each struck its own mad note, a screaming, clanging, booming of tortured metal, loud enough to make every one of Ferro's bones buzz. She looked up to see one great disc reel past her, clattering on its edge, striking bright sparks from the floor. Another flew into the air, spinning crazily like a flipped coin. She gasped as she rolled out of its way, scrambled back as it crashed into the ground beside her.

Where Yulwei and Tolomei had faced each other there was a hill of twisted metal, of broken rings and leaning discs, bent rods and tangled cables. Ferro struggled dizzily to her feet, a fury of discordant echoes ripping about the hall. Splinters dropped around her, pinging from the polished floor. Fragments were scattered the width of the hall, glinting in the shadows like stars in the night sky.

She had no idea who was dead and who alive.

'Out!' Bayaz growled at her through gritted teeth, face a twisted mask of pain. 'Out! Go!'

'Yulwei,' she muttered, 'is he—'

'I will come back for him!' Bayaz flailed at her with his good arm. 'Go!'

There are times to fight, and there are times to run, and Ferro knew well the difference. The Gurkish had taught it to her, deep in the Badlands. The archway jerked and wobbled as she sprinted towards it. Her own breath roared in her ears. She leaped over a gleaming wheel of metal, boots slapping at the smooth stone. She was almost at the archway. She felt a bitter chill at her side, a rush of sick terror. She flung herself forwards.

Tolomei's white hand missed Ferro by a whisker, tore a great chunk of stone from the wall and filled the air with dust.

'You go nowhere!'

Time to run, perhaps, but Ferro's patience was all worn down. As she sprang up her fist was already swinging, all the fury of her wasted months, her wasted years, her wasted life behind it. Her knuckles hit Tolomei's jaw with a sharp crunch. It was like punching a block of ice. There was no pain as her hand broke, but she felt her wrist buckle, her arm go numb. Too late to worry on it. Her other fist was on its way.

Tolomei snatched her arm from the air before it touched

her, dragged Ferro close, twisting her helpless onto her knees with awful, irresistible strength. 'The Seed!' The hissing words froze across Ferro's face, snatching her breath out in a sick groan, her skin burning where Tolomei held her. She felt her bones twist, then snap, her forearm clicking sideways like a broken stick. A white hand crept through the shadows towards the lump in Ferro's shirt.

There was a sudden light, a brilliant curve of it that lit the whole chamber for a blinding instant. Ferro heard a piercing shriek and she was free, sprawling on her back. Tolomei's hand was sliced off cleanly just above the wrist, leaving a bloodless stump. A great wound was scored down the smooth wall and deep into the floor, molten stone running from it, bubbling and sizzling. Smoke curled from the strange weapon in Bayaz' hand as he lurched from the shadows, the hook at its end still glowing orange. Tolomei gave an icy scream, one hand clawing at him.

Bayaz roared mindlessly back at her, his eyes narrowed, his bloody mouth wide open. Ferro felt a twisting at her stomach, so savage she was bent over, almost dragged to her knees. The Maker's daughter was snatched up and blasted away, one white heel tearing a long scar through the map on the floor, gouging through rock and ripping up metal.

The wreck of the grand device was blown apart behind her, its ruined pieces scattered glittering in the darkness like leaves on the wind. Tolomei was a flailing shape in a storm of flying metal. She hit the distant wall with an earth-shaking boom, flinging out chunks of broken stone. A hail of twisted fragments rattled, rang, clanged against the rock around her. Rings, pins, slivers like dagger blades wedged into the wall, making the whole great curve of stone a giant bed of nails.

Bayaz' eyes bulged, his gaunt face wet with sweat. 'Die, devil!' he bellowed.

Dust filtered down, rock began to shift. Cold laughter echoed out across the hall. Ferro scrambled back, heels kicking at the smooth stone, and she ran. Her broken hand shuddered over the wall of the tunnel, her broken arm dangled. A square of light came jolting towards her. The door of the Maker's House.

She tottered out into the air, stinging bright after the shadows, the thin rain warm after Tolomei's freezing touch. The Seed still weighed heavy in her shirt, rough and comforting against her skin.

'Run!' came Bayaz' voice from the darkness. 'To the palace!' Ferro tottered across the bridge, clumsy feet slipping on wet stone, cold water lurching far below. 'Put it in the box, and seal it tight!' She heard an echoing boom behind her, metal clashing against metal, but she did not look back.

She shouldered her way through the open doors in the wall of the Agriont, nearly tripping over the doorman, sitting against the wall where she had left him with one hand clasped to his head. She sprang over him as he cringed away, flew down the steps three at a time, across the crumbling courtyard, down the dusty corridors, sparing no thought for masked figures or for anyone else. They seemed a pitiful, everyday sort of threat, now. She could still feel the icy breath on her neck.

Nothing mattered but to put it far behind her.

She slid up to the door, fumbled at the bolt with the heel of her broken hand, burst out into the drizzle and pounded down the wet streets the way she had come. The people in the lanes and squares stumbled back out of her way, shocked at the sight of her, desperate and bloody. Angry voices echoed after her but she ignored them, turned a corner onto a wide street between grey buildings and nearly slid right over on the wet stones.

A great crowd of dishevelled people were choking the road. Women, children, old men, dirty and shambling.

'Out of my way!' she screamed, and started to force a path through. 'Move!' The story Bayaz had told on the endless plain nagged at the back of her mind. How the soldiers had found the Seed in the ruins of Aulcus. How they had withered and died. She pushed and kicked and shouldered her way through the press. 'Move!' She tore free of them and sprinted off down the empty street, her broken arm held against her body, against the thing inside her shirt.

She ran across the park, leaves fluttering down from the trees with each chilly gust. The high wall of the palace rose up where the lawns ended and Ferro made for the gate. The two guards still flanked it just as they always did, and she knew they were watching her. They might have let her out, but they were not so keen on letting her in, especially filthy, bloody, covered in dirt and sweat, and running as if she had a devil at her heels.

'Wait, you!' Ferro made to duck past them but one grabbed hold of her.

'Let me go you fucking pink fools!' she hissed. 'You don't understand!' She tried to twist away, and a gilded halberd fell to the ground as one of the guards wrapped his arms around her.

'Explain it, then!' snapped out from behind the visor of the other. 'Why the hurry?' His gauntleted fist reached out towards the bulge in her shirt. 'What have you got—'

'No!' Ferro hissed and squirmed, stumbled against the wall bearing one guard clanking back into the archway. The halberd of the other swung down smoothly, its glittering point levelled at Ferro's chest.

'Hold still!' he growled. 'Before I—'

'Let her in! Now!' Sulfur stood on the other side of the gates, and for once he was not smiling. The guard's head turned doubtfully towards him. 'Now!' he roared. 'In the name of Lord Bayaz!'

They let her free and Ferro tore away, cursing. She ran through the gardens, into the palace, boots echoing in the hallways, servants and guards moving suspiciously out of her way. She found the door of Bayaz' rooms and fumbled it open, stumbled through. The box sat open on a table near the window, an unremarkable block of dark metal. She strode across to it, unbuttoned her shirt and pulled out the thing inside.

A dark, heavy stone, the size of a fist. Its dull surface was still cold, no warmer than when she had first picked it up. Her hand tingled pleasantly, as if at the touch of an old friend. It made her angry, somehow, to even think of letting go.

So this, at last, was the Seed. The Other Side, made flesh. The very stuff of magic. She remembered the blighted ruins of Aulcus. The dead expanse of the land around it, for a hundred miles in every direction. Power enough to send the Emperor, and the Prophet, and his cursed Eaters, and the whole nation of Gurkhul to hell, and more besides. Power so terrible that it should have belonged to God alone, held now, in her frail fist. She stared down at it for a long time. Then, slowly, Ferro began to smile.

Now she would have vengeance.

The sound of heavy footsteps in the corridor outside brought her suddenly to her senses. She dropped the Seed into its resting place, jerked her hand away with an effort and snapped the lid of the box closed. As if a candle flame had been suddenly blown out in a darkened room, the world seemed dimmer, weaker, robbed of excitement. It was only then that she realised her hand was whole. She frowned down at it, working her fingers. They moved as easily as ever, not the slightest swelling around knuckles she had been sure were shattered. Her other arm too, the forearm straight and smooth, no sign of a mark where Tolomei's freezing fingers had crushed it. Ferro looked towards the box. She had always healed quickly. But bones set, within an hour?

That was not right.

Bayaz dragged himself grimacing through the doorway. There was dry blood caked to his beard, a sheen of sweat across his bald head. He was breathing hard, skin pale and twitching, one arm pressed to his side. He looked like a man who had spent the afternoon fighting a devil, and had only just survived.

'Where is Yulwei?'

The First of the Magi stared back at her. 'You know where he is.'

Ferro remembered the echoing bang as she ran from the tower. Like the sound of a door being shut. A door that no blade, no fire, no magic could open. Bayaz alone had the key. 'You did not go back. You sealed the gates with them inside.'

'Sacrifices must be made, Ferro, you know this. I have made

a great sacrifice today. My own brother.' The First of the Magi hobbled across the room towards her. 'Tolomei broke the First Law. She struck a deal with the Tellers of Secrets. She meant to use the Seed to open the gates to the world below. She could be more dangerous than all of Khalul's Eaters. The House of the Maker must remain sealed. Until the end of time, if need be. An outcome not without irony. She began her life imprisoned in that tower. Now she has returned. History moves in circles, just as Juvens always said.'

Ferro frowned. 'Fuck your circles, pink. You lied to me. About Tolomei. About the Maker. About everything.'

'And?'

She frowned even harder. 'Yulwei was a good man. He helped me in the desert. He saved my life.'

'And mine, more than once. But good men will only go so far along dark paths.' Bayaz' bright eyes slid down to rest on the cube of dark metal under Ferro's hand. 'Others must walk the rest of the way.'

Sulfur stepped through the doorway, and Bayaz pulled the weapon he had brought from the House of the Maker from under his coat, grey metal glinting in the soft light from the windows. A relic of the Old Time. A weapon that Ferro had seen cut stone as if it was butter. Sulfur took it from him with a nervous respect, wrapped it carefully in an old oilskin. Then he flipped open his satchel and slid out the old black book that Ferro had seen once before. 'Now?' he muttered.

'Now.' Bayaz took it from him, placed his hand gently on the scarred cover, closed his eyes and took a long breath. When he opened them he was looking straight at Ferro. 'The paths we must walk now, you and I, are dark indeed. You have seen it.'

She had no answer. Yulwei had been a good man, but the gate of the Maker's House was sealed, and he was gone to heaven, or to hell. Ferro had buried many men, in many ways. One more pile of dirt in the desert was nothing to remark upon. She was sick of stealing her revenge one grain at a time. Dark paths did not scare her. She had been walking them all her life. Even through the metal of the box, she thought that she heard the barest hint of a whisper, calling to her. 'All I want is vengeance.'

'And you shall have it, just as I promised.'

She stood face to face with Bayaz, and she shrugged. 'Then what does it matter now, who killed who a thousand years ago?'

The First of the Magi smiled a sickly smile, his eyes bright in his pale and bloody face. 'You speak my very thoughts.'

Tomorrow's Hero

The hooves of Jezal's grey charger clopped obediently in the black mud. It was a magnificent beast, the very kind he had always dreamed of riding. Several thousand marks-worth of horse flesh, he did not doubt. A steed that could give any man who sat on it, however worthless, the air of royalty. His shining armour was of the best Styrian steel, chased with gold. His cloak was of the finest Suljuk silk, trimmed with ermine. The hilt of his sword was crusted with diamonds, twinkling as the clouds flowed overhead to let the sun peep through. He had foregone the crown today in favour of a simple golden circlet, its weight considerably less wearisome on the sore spots he had developed round his temples.

All the trappings of majesty. Ever since he was a child, Jezal had dreamed of being exalted, worshipped, obeyed. Now the whole business made him want to be sick. Although that might only have been because he had scarcely slept last night, and scarcely eaten that morning.

Lord Marshal Varuz rode on Jezal's right, looking as if age had suddenly caught up with him. He seemed shrunken in his uniform, stooped and slump-shouldered. His movements had lost their steely precision, his eyes their icy focus. He had developed, somehow, the very slightest hint of not knowing what to do.

'Fighting still continues in the Arches, your Majesty,' he was explaining, 'but we have only toe-holds there. The Gurkish have the Three Farms under firm control. They moved their catapults forward to the canal, and last night they threw incendiaries far into the central district. As far as the Middleway and beyond. Fires were burning until dawn. Still are burning, in some parts. The damage has been . . . extensive.'

A crashing understatement. Whole sections of the city had been devastated by fire. Whole rows of buildings, that Jezal remembered as grand houses, busy taverns, clattering workshops, reduced to blackened wreckage. Looking at them was as horrifying as seeing an old lover open their mouth to reveal two rows of shattered teeth. The reek of smoke, and burning, and death clawed constantly at Jezal's throat and had reduced his voice to a gravelly croak.

A man streaked with ash and dirt looked up from picking through the wreckage of a still-smoking house. He stared at Jezal and his guards as they trotted past.

'Where is my son?' he shrieked suddenly. 'Where is my son?'

Jezal carefully looked away and gave his horse the slightest suggestion of a spur. He did not need to offer his conscience any further weapons with which to stab at him. It was already exceedingly well armed.

'Arnault's Wall still holds, though, your Majesty.' Varuz spoke considerably louder than was necessary in a futile effort to smother the heartbroken wails still ringing through the ruins behind them. 'Not a single Gurkish soldier has yet set foot in the central district of the city. Not one.'

Jezal wondered how much longer they would be able to make that boast. 'Have we received any news from Lord Marshal West?' he demanded for the second time that hour, the tenth time that day.

Varuz gave Jezal the same answer he would no doubt receive ten times more before descending into a fitful sleep that night. 'I regret that we are almost utterly cut off, your Majesty. News arrives but rarely through the Gurkish cordon. But there have been storms off Angland. We must face the possibility that the army will be delayed.'

'Black luck,' murmured Bremer dan Gorst from the other side, his narrow eyes flickering endlessly over the ruins for the slightest sign of any threat. Jezal chewed worriedly at the salty remnant of his thumbnail. He could scarcely remember the last shred of good news. Storms. Delays. Even the elements were ranged against them, it seemed.

Varuz had nothing to lift the mood. 'And now illness has broken out in the Agriont. A swift and merciless plague. A large group of the civilians to whom you opened the gates have succumbed, all at once. It has extended to the palace itself. Two Knights of the Body have already died from it. One day they were standing guard at the gate, as always. The next night they were in their coffins. Their bodies withered, their teeth rotted, their hair fell out. The corpses are burned, but more cases appear. The physicians have never seen the like before, have no notion of a cure. Some are saying it is a Gurkish curse.'

Jezal swallowed. The magnificent city, the work of so many pairs of hands over long centuries, it had taken only a few short weeks of his tender care to transform into charred wreckage. Its proud people were mostly reduced to stinking beggars, to shrieking wounded, to wailing mourners. Those who had not been reduced to corpses. He was the most pathetic excuse for a king the Union could ever have spawned. He could not bring happiness to his own bitter sham of a marriage, let alone a nation. His reputation was all based on lies that he had not the courage to deny. He was a powerless, spineless, helpless cipher.

'Whereabouts are we now?' he mumbled as they rode out into a great, windswept space.

'Why, this is the Four Corners, your Majesty.'

'This? This cannot . . .' He trailed off, recognition coming as sharply as a slap in the face.

Only two walls of the building that had once been the Mercers' guildhall still stood, windows and doorways gaping like the stricken features of corpses, frozen at the moment of their deaths. The paving where hundreds of merry stalls had once been set out was cracked and caked with sticky soot. The gardens were leafless patches of mud and burned briar. The air should have been ringing with the calls of traders, the prattle of servants, the laughter of children. Instead it was deadly silent but for a cold wind hissing through the wreckage, sweeping waves of black grit through the heart of the city.

Jezal pulled on his reins, and his escort of some twenty Knights of the Body, five Knights Herald, a dozen of Varuz' staff and a nervous page or two clattered to a halt around him. Gorst frowned up towards the sky. 'Your Majesty, we should move on. It is not safe here. We do not know when the Gurkish will begin their bombardment again.'

Jezal ignored him, swung down from his saddle and walked out into the wreckage. It was difficult to believe that it was the same place where he had once bought wine, shopped for trinkets, been measured for a new uniform. Not one hundred strides away, on the other side of a row of smoking ruins, stood the statue of Harod the Great where he had met Ardee in the darkness, it seemed a hundred years ago.

A sorry group were clustered near there now, round the edge of a trampled garden. Women and children, mostly, and a few old men. Dirty and despairing, several with crutches or bloody bandages, clutching salvaged oddments. Those rendered homeless in last night's fires, last night's fighting. Jezal's breath caught in his throat. Ardee was one of them, sitting on a stone in a thin dress, shivering and staring at the ground, her dark hair fallen across half of her face. He started towards her, the first time he had smiled in what felt like weeks.

'Ardee.' She turned, eyes wide open, and Jezal froze. A different girl, younger and considerably less attractive. She blinked up at him, rocking slowly back and forward. His hands twitched ineffectually, he mumbled something incoherent. They were all watching him. He could hardly just walk off. 'Please, take this.' He fumbled with the gilded clasps on his crimson cloak and held it out to her.

She said nothing as she took it from him, only stared. A ridiculous, worthless gesture, almost offensive in its burning hypocrisy. But the rest of the homeless civilians did not seem to think so.

'A cheer for King Jezal!' someone shouted, and a rousing clamour went up.

A young lad on a crutch gazed at him with moon-eyed desperation. A soldier had a bloody bandage over one eye, the other rimmed with proud moisture. A mother clutched a baby wrapped in what looked horribly like a shred of cloth from a fallen Union flag. It was as if the whole scene had been carefully posed for the greatest emotional impact. A set of painter's models for a lurid and ham-fisted piece on the horrors of war.

'King Jezal!' came the shout again, accompanied by a weak, 'Hurrah!'

Their adulation was like poison to him. It only made the great weight of responsibility press down all the heavier. He turned away, unable to maintain his twisted mockery of a smile one instant longer.

'What have I done?' he whispered, his hands tugging ceaselessly at each other. 'What have I done?' He clambered back up into the saddle, guilt picking at his guts. 'Take me closer to Arnault's Wall.'

'Your Majesty, I hardly think that—'

'You heard me! Closer to the fighting. I want to see it.'

Varuz frowned. 'Very well.' He turned his horse, led Jezal and his bodyguard off in the direction of the Arches, down routes that were so familiar, and yet so horribly changed. After a few nervous minutes the Lord Marshal pulled up his mount, pointing down a deserted lane to the west. He spoke softly, as though worried the enemy might hear them.

'Arnault's Wall is no more than three hundred strides that way, and the Gurkish are crawling on the other side. We really should turn—'

Jezal felt a faint vibration through his saddle, his horse started, dust filtered from the roofs of the houses on one side of the street.

He was just opening his mouth to ask what had happened when the air was ripped open by a thunderous noise. A crushing, terrifying wall of sound that left Jezal's ears humming. Men gasped and gaped. The horses milled and kicked, their eyes rolling with fear. Varuz' mount reared up, dumping the old soldier unceremoniously from his saddle.

Jezal paid him no mind, he was too busy urging his own horse keenly in the direction of the blast, seized by an awful curiosity. Small stones had started raining down, pinging from the roofs and clattering into the road like hailstones. A great cloud of brown dust was rising up into the sky to the west.

'Your Majesty!' came Gorst's plaintive cry. 'We should turn back!' But Jezal took no notice.

He rode out into a wide square, a great quantity of rubble scattered across the broken paving, some of it in chunks big as sheds. As the choking dust slowly settled in an eerie silence, Jezal realised that he knew the place. Knew it well. There was a tavern he had used to visit on the north side, but something was changed – it was more open than it had been . . . his jaw fell. A long stretch of Arnault's Wall had formed the western boundary of the square. Now there was nothing but a yawning crater.

The Gurkish must have dug a mine and filled it with their damned blasting powder. The sun chose that moment to break through the clouds above and Jezal could see all the way across the gaping fissure and into the ruined Arches district. There, crowding at the far edge, clambering down the rubble strewn slope with armour glinting and spears waving, was a sizeable body of Gurkish soldiers.

The first of them were already climbing up out of the crater and into the remains of the shattered square. A few semi-conscious defenders were crawling through the dust, choking and spitting. Others were not moving at all. There was no one to turn the Gurkish back, that Jezal could see. No one but him. He wondered what Harod the Great would have done in this spot.

The answer was not so very hard to find.

Courage can come from many places, and be made of many things, and yesterday's coward can become tomorrow's hero in an instant if the time is right. The giddy flood of bravery which Jezal experienced at that moment consisted largely of guilt and fear, and shame at his fear, swollen by a peevish frustration at nothing having turned out the way he had hoped, and a sudden vague awareness that being killed might solve a great number of irritating problems to which he saw no solution. Not noble ingredients, to be sure. But no one ever asks what the baker put in his pie as long as it tastes well.

He drew his sword and held it up to the sunlight. 'Knights of the Body!' he roared. 'With me!'

Gorst made a despairing grab at his reins. 'Your Majesty! You cannot put yourself in—'

Jezal gave his mount the spurs. It sprang forward with unexpected vigour, and his head snapped painfully back almost causing him to lose his grip on the reins. He rolled in the saddle, hooves hammering, the dirty paving flying by beneath him. He was dimly aware of his escort following, some distance behind, but his attention was rather drawn to the ever-increasing body of Gurkish soldiers directly ahead.

His horse carried him forwards with gut-churning speed, directly at a man at the very front of the crowd, a standard-bearer with a tall staff, golden symbols shining on it. His bad luck, Jezal supposed, to have been given such a prominent task. The man's eyes went wide as he saw an enormous weight of horse bearing down on him. He flung away his standard and tried to throw himself aside. The edge of Jezal's steel bit deep into his shoulder with the full force of the charge, ripped him open and flung him onto his back. More men went down screaming under the hooves of his mount as it crashed into their midst, he could not have said how many.

Then all was chaos. He sat above a mass of snarling dark faces, glinting armour, jabbing spears. Wood cracked, metal clanged, men shouted words he did not understand. He hacked around him, on one side then the other, yelling mindless curses. A spear tip shrieked along his armoured leg. He chopped at a hand as it seized his reins and a couple of fingers flew off it. Something crunched into his side and nearly threw him from the saddle. His sword caved in a helmet with a hollow bonk and knocked the man under it down into the press of bodies.

Jezal's horse gave a shriek, reared up, twisting. He felt a terrible lurch of fear as he came away from the saddle, the world turning over. He crunched down, dust in his eyes, dust in his mouth, coughing and struggling. He rolled up to his knees. Hooves crashed against the broken ground. Boots slid and stomped. He fumbled in his hair for his circlet, but it must have come off somewhere. How would anyone know he was king? Was he still king? His head was all sticky. A helmet would have been a damn good thing to have brought with him, but it was a little late now. He plucked weakly at the rubble, turned over a flat stone. He had forgotten what he was looking for. He stumbled up, something caught his foot and snatched it painfully away, dumping him on his face again. He waited to have the back of his head broken, but it was only his stirrup, still strapped to his horse's magnificent corpse. He dragged his boot free, gasping for air, reeled a couple of drunken steps under the weight of his armour, his sword dangling from one limp hand.

Someone lifted a curved blade and Jezal stabbed him through the chest. He vomited blood in Jezal's face, fell and twisted the steel from his hand. Something thumped into Jezal's breastplate with a dull clang and knocked him sideways, right into a Gurkish soldier with a spear. He dropped it and they clawed at each other, tottering pointlessly around. Jezal was getting terribly, terribly tired. His head hurt a lot. Just dragging the breath in was a tremendous effort. The whole heroic charge idea seemed as if it had been a bad one. He wanted to lie down.

The Gurkish soldier tore one arm free and raised it up high, a knife clutched in his fist. It flew off at the wrist, a long gout of blood spurting after it. He started to slide to the ground, staring at the stump and wailing. 'The king!' piped Gorst's boyish little voice. 'The king!'

His long steel described a wide arc and whipped the screaming soldier's head away. Another leaped forward, a curved sword raised. Before he got a stride Gorst's heavy blade split his skull wide open. An axe clanged into his armoured shoulder and he shrugged it away as if it was a fly, chopped the man who had swung it down in a shower of gore. A fourth got the short steel through his neck, staggered forward, eyes bulging, one bloody hand clutched to his throat.

Jezal, swaying numbly back and forward, almost felt sorry for the Gurkish. Their numbers might have been impressive from a distance, but close up these men were evidently auxiliaries, thrown forward into the crater as a forlorn hope. They were scrawny, dirty, helplessly disorganised, lightly armed and barely armoured. Many of them, he realised, looked extremely scared. Gorst hacked his way impassively through them like a bull through a flock of sheep, growling as his scything steels opened gaping wounds with sickening fleshy sounds. Other armoured figures crowded in after him, shoving with shields, chopping with their bright swords, clearing a bloody space in the Gurkish crowd.

Gorst's hand slid under Jezal's armpit and dragged him backwards, his heels kicking at the rubble. He was vaguely aware that he had dropped his sword somewhere, but it seemed foolish to go looking for it now. Some beggar would no doubt receive a priceless windfall while he hunted among the bodies, later. Jezal saw a Knight Herald still mounted, an outline with a winged helmet in the choking dust, his long axe chopping around him.

He was half-carried back, out of the press. Some of the city's regular defenders had regrouped, or were coming in from other parts of the walls. Men with steel caps started to kneel at the lip of the crater, shooting flatbows down into the heaving mass of Gurkish in the bottom, all tangled up with the mud and the rubble. Others dragged up a cart and tipped it onto its side to form a temporary rampart. A Gurkish soldier sobbed as he was cut open, tumbled over the ragged edge of the crater and back down into the mud. More Union flatbows appeared at the edge of the square, more spears. Barrels, masonry, broken spars came with them until an improvised barricade was built up all across the wide gap in Arnault's wall, bristling with men and weapons.

Peppered with bolts and chunks of fallen masonry, the Gurkish faltered, then fell back, scrambling through the debris to their side of the crater and up towards safety, leaving the bottom strewn with corpses.

'To the Agriont, your Majesty,' said Gorst. 'At once.'

Jezal made no effort to resist. He had done more than enough fighting for today.

Something strange was happening in the Square of Marshals. Labourers were working at the paving stones with pick and chisel, digging up shallow trenches, apparently at random. Smiths sweated at temporary forges, pouring iron into moulds, lit by the glow of molten metal. The din of clanging hammers and crashing stone was enough to make Jezal's teeth hurt, yet somehow the voice of the First of the Magi managed to be louder still.

'No! A circle, dunce, from here to there!'

'I must return to the Halls Martial, your Majesty,' said Varuz. 'Arnault's Wall is breached. It will not be long until the Gurkish try to push through once again. They would already be at the Middleway if it hadn't been for that charge of yours, though, eh? I see now how you won your reputation in the west! As noble a business as I ever saw!'

'Uh.' Jezal watched the dead being dragged away. Three Knights of the Body, one of Varuz' staff and a page-boy no older than twelve, the last with his head hanging off by a flap of gristle. Three men and a child he had led to their deaths. And that was without even considering the wounds the rest of his faithful entourage had gathered on his behalf. A noble business indeed.

'Wait here,' he snapped at Gorst, then he threaded his way through the sweating workmen towards the First of the Magi. Ferro sat cross-legged nearby on a row of barrels, her hands dangling loose, the same utter contempt she had always shown him written plainly on her dark face. It was almost comforting to see that some things never changed. Bayaz was glaring grimly down into the pages of a large black book, evidently of great age, its leather covers cracked and torn. He looked gaunt and pale, old and withered. One side of his face was covered in scabbed-over scratches.

'What happened to you?' asked Jezal.

Bayaz frowned, a muscle trembling under one dark-ringed eye. 'I could ask you the same question.'

Jezal noted that the Magus had not even bothered with a 'your Majesty'. He touched a hand to the bloody bandage round his skull. 'I was involved in a charge.'

'In a what?'

'The Gurkish brought down a section of Arnault's Wall while I was surveying the city. There was no-one to turn them back, and so . . . I did it myself.' He was almost surprised to hear himself saying the words. He was far from proud of the fact, certainly. He had done little more than ride, fall, and hit his head. Bremer dan Gorst and his own dead horse had done the majority of the fighting, and against meagre opposition to boot. But he supposed he had done the right thing, for once, if there was any such a thing.

Bayaz did not agree. 'Have what little brains fate saved for you turned to shit?'

'Have they . . .' Jezal blinked as the meaning of Bayaz' words soaked slowly into his consciousness. 'How dare you, you meddling old turd? You are talking to a king!' That was what he wanted to say, but his head was pounding, and something in the Magus' twitching, wasted face prevented him. Instead he found himself mumbling in a tone almost apologetic. 'But . . . I don't understand. I thought . . . isn't that what Harod the Great would have done?'

'Harod?' Bayaz sneered in Jezal's face. 'Harod was an utter coward, and an utter fathead to boot! That idiot could scarcely dress himself without my help!'

'But—'

'It is easy to find men to lead charges.' The Magus pronounced each word with exaggerated care, as though addressing a simpleton. 'Finding men to lead nations is considerably more difficult. I do not intend that the effort I have put into you should be wasted. Next time you experience a yearning to risk your life, perhaps you might lock yourself in the latrine instead. People respect a man with a fighter's reputation, and that you have been fortunate enough to have been gifted. People do not respect a corpse. Not there!' roared Bayaz, limping past Jezal and waving one arm angrily at one of the smiths. The poor man started like a frightened rabbit, glowing embers spattering from his crucible. 'I told you, fool! You must follow the charts precisely! Exactly as I have drawn it! One mistake could be worse than fatal!'

Jezal stared after him, outrage, guilt, and simple exhaustion fighting for control of his body. Exhaustion won. He trudged over to the barrels and slumped down next to Ferro.

'Your fucking Majesty,' she said.

He rubbed at his eyes with finger and thumb. 'You do me too much honour with your kind attentions.'

'Bayaz not happy, eh?'

'It seems not.'

'Well. When is that old bastard happy with anything?'

Jezal gave a grunt of agreement. He realised that he had not spoken to Ferro since he was crowned. It was not as though they had been fast friends before, of course, but he had to admit that he was finding her utter lack of deference to him an unexpected tonic. It was almost like being, for a brief moment, the vain, idle, worthless, happy man he used to be. He frowned over at Bayaz, stabbing his finger at something in his old book. 'Whatever is he up to, anyway?'

'Saving the world, he tells me.'

'Ah. That. He's left it a little late, don't you think?

She shrugged. 'I'm not in charge of the timing.'

'How does he plan to do it? With picks and forges?'

Ferro watched him. He still found those devil-yellow eyes as off-putting as ever. 'Among other things.'

Jezal planted his elbows on his knees, his chin drooping down onto his palms, and gave vent to a long sigh. He was so very, very tired. 'I seem to have done the wrong thing,' he muttered.

'Huh.' Ferro's eyes slid away. 'You've got a knack for it.'

479

Nightfall

General Poulder squirmed in his field chair, moustaches quivering, as though he could only just control his body so overpowering was his fury. His ruddy complexion and snorting breath seemed to imply that he might spring from the tent at any moment and charge the Gurkish positions alone. General Kroy sat rigidly erect on the opposite side of the table, clenched jaw-muscles bulging from the side of his close-cropped skull. His murderous frown clearly demonstrated that his anger at the invader, while no less than anyone else's, was kept under iron command, and if any charging was to be done it would be managed with fastidious attention to detail.

In their first briefings West had found himself outnumbered twenty to one by the two Generals' monstrous staffs. He had reduced them, by a relentless process of attrition, to a meagre two officers a piece. The meetings had lost the charged atmosphere of a tavern brawl and instead taken on the character of a small and bad-tempered family event – perhaps the reading of a disputed will. West was the executor, trying to find an acceptable solution for two squabbling beneficiaries to whom nothing was acceptable. Jalenhorm and Brint, sitting to either side of him, were his dumbstruck assistants. What role the Dogman played in the metaphor it was hard to judge, but he was adding to the already feverish pitch of worry in the tent by picking at his fingernails with a dagger.

'This will be a battle like no other!' Poulder was frothing, pointlessly. 'Never since Harod forged the Union has an invader set foot upon the soil of Midderland!'

Kroy growled his agreement.

'The Gurkish mean to overturn our laws, smother our

culture, make slaves of our people! The very future of our nation hangs in the—'

The tent flap snapped back and Pike ducked through, his melted face expressionless. A tall man shuffled behind, stooped over and wobbly with fatigue, a heavy blanket wrapped round his shoulders, his face smeared with dirt.

'This is Fedor dan Hayden,' said Pike. 'A Knight Herald. He was able to swim from the docks in Adua under cover of night, and slip around the Gurkish lines.'

'An action of conspicuous bravery,' said West, to grumbles of grudging agreement from Poulder and Kroy. 'You have all of our thanks. How do things stand inside the city?'

'Frankly, my Lord Marshal, they are dire.' Hayden's voice was scratchy with weariness. 'The western districts – the Arches and the Three Farms – belong to the Emperor. The Gurkish breached Arnault's Wall two days ago, and the defences are stretched to breaking point. At any moment they could burst through, and threaten the Agriont itself. His Majesty asks that you march on Adua with all possible speed. Every hour could be vital.'

'Does he have any particular strategy in mind?' asked West. Jezal dan Luthar never used to have anything in mind beyond getting drunk and bedding his sister, but he hoped that time might have wrought changes.

'The Gurkish have the city surrounded, but they are spread thin. On the eastern side, particularly. Lord Marshal Varuz believes you could break through with a sharp attack.'

'Though the western districts of the city will still be crawling with Gurkish swine,' growled Kroy.

'Bastards,' whispered Poulder, his jowls twitching. 'Bastards.'

'We have no choice but to march on Adua immediately,' said West. 'We will make use of every road and move with all possible speed to take up a position east of the city, marching by torchlight if necessary. We must assault the Gurkish encirclement at dawn and break their hold on the walls. Admiral Reutzer will meanwhile lead the fleet in an attack against the Gurkish ships in the harbour. General Kroy, order some cavalry forward to scout the way and screen our advance. I want no surprises.'

For once, there was no sign of reluctance. 'Of course, my Lord Marshal.'

'Your division will approach Adua from the north-east, break through the Gurkish lines and enter the city in force, pushing westward towards the Agriont. If the enemy have reached the centre of the city, you will engage them. If not, you will bolster the defences at Arnault's Wall and prepare to flush them from the Arches district.'

Kroy nodded grimly, a single vein bulging on his forehead, his officers like statues of military precision behind him. 'By this time tomorrow, not one Kantic soldier will be left alive in Adua.'

'Dogman, I would like you and your Northmen to support General Kroy's division in their attack. If your . . .' West wrestled with the word, '. . . king has no objections.'

The Dogman licked his sharp teeth. 'Reckon he'll go which-ever way the wind blows. That's always been his style.'

'The wind blows towards Adua tonight.'

'Aye.' The Northman nodded. 'Towards Adua, then.'

'General Poulder, your division will approach the city from the south-east, participate in the battle for the walls, then enter the city in force and move on the docks. If the enemy has made it that far, you will clear them away, then turn northwards and follow the Middleway to the Agriont.'

Poulder hammered the table with his fist, his officers growl-ing like prize-fighters. 'Yes, damn it! We'll paint the streets with Gurkish blood!'

West gave Poulder, and then Kroy, each a hard frown. 'I hardly need to emphasise the importance of victory tomorrow.'

The two Generals rose without a word and moved for the tent flap together. They faced each other before it. For a moment West wondered if, even now, they would fall back into their familiar bickering.

Then Kroy held out his hand. 'The best of luck, General Poulder.'

Poulder seized the hand in both of his. 'And to you, General Kroy. The very best of luck to all of us.' The two of them stepped smartly out into the dusk, their officers following, Jalenhorm and Brint close behind.

Hayden coughed. 'Lord Marshal . . . four other Knights Herald were sent with me. We split up, in the hopes that one of us at least would make it through the Gurkish lines. Have any of the others arrived?'

'No . . . not yet. Perhaps later . . .' West did not think it terribly likely, and neither did Hayden, he could see it in his eyes.

'Of course. Perhaps later.'

'Sergeant Pike will find you some wine and a horse. I imagine you would very much like to see us attack the Gurkish in the morning.'

'I would.'

'Very good.' The two men left the way they had come, and West frowned after them. A shame about the man's comrades, but there would be many more deaths to mourn before tomorrow was done. If there was anyone left to do the mourning. He pushed aside the tent flap and stepped out into the chill air.

The ships of the fleet were anchored in the narrow harbour down below, rocking slowly on the waves, tall masts waving back and forth against the darkening clouds – hard blue, and cold grey, and angry orange. West fancied he could see a few boats crawling closer to the black beach, still ferrying the last of the army to the shore.

The sun was dropping fast towards the horizon, a final muddy flare above the hills in the west. Somewhere under there, just out of sight, Adua was burning. West worked his shoulders round in circles, trying to force the knotted muscles to relax. He had heard no word since before they left Angland. As far as he was aware Ardee was still inside its walls. But there was nothing he could do. Nothing beyond ordering an immediate attack and hoping, against the general run of luck, for the best. He rubbed unhappily at his stomach. He had been suffering with indigestion ever since the sea journey. The pressures of command, no doubt. A few more weeks of it would probably see him vomiting blood over his maps, just like his predecessor. He took a long, ragged breath and blew it out.

'I know how you feel.' It was the Dogman, sitting on a rickety bench beside the tent flap, elbows on his knees, staring down towards the sea.

West sagged down beside him. Briefings with Poulder and Kroy were always a terrible drain. Play the man of stone for too long and you are left a man of straw. 'I'm sorry,' he found himself saying.

Dogman looked up at him. 'You are? For what?'

'For all of it. For Threetrees, for Tul . . . for Cathil.' West had to swallow an unexpected lump in his throat. 'For all of it. I'm sorry.'

'Ah, we're all sorry. I don't blame you. I don't blame no one, not even Bethod. What good does blame do? We all do what we have to. I gave up looking for reasons a long time ago.'

West thought about that for a moment. Then he nodded. 'Alright.' They sat and watched the torches being lit around the bay below, like glittering dust spreading out across the dark country.

Night time, and a grim one. Grim for the cold, and the drip, drip of thin rain, and all the hard miles that needed slogging over before dawn. Grim most of all for what waited at the end of it, when the sun came up. Marching to a battle only got harder each time. When Logen had been a young man, before he lost a finger and gained a black reputation, there'd at least been some trace of excitement to it, some shadow of a thrill. Now there was only the sick fear. Fear of the fight, and worse still, fear of the results.

Being king was no kind of help. It was no help to anything, far as he could see. It was just like being chief, but worse. Made him think there was something he should be doing that he wasn't. Made the gap between him and everyone else that bit wider. That bit more unbridgeable.

Boots squelched and sucked, weapons and harness clattered and jingled, men grunted and cursed in the darkness. A few of them had spitting torches now, to light the muddy way, streaks of rain flitting down in the glow around them. The rain fell on Logen too, a feathery kiss at his scalp, and his face, the odd pit and patter on the shoulders of his old coat.

The Union army was spread out down five roads, all heading east, all pointing towards Adua and what sounded like a hard reckoning with the Gurkish. Logen and his crew were on the northernmost one. Off to the south he could see a faint line of flickering lights, floating disembodied in the black country, stretching away out of sight. Another column. Another few thousand men, cursing through the mud towards a bloody dawn.

Logen frowned. He saw the side of Shivers' lean face, up ahead, by the flickering light of a torch, a scowl full of hard shadows, one eye glinting. They watched each other for a moment, then Shivers turned his back, hunched up his shoulders and carried on walking.

'He still don't like me much, that one, and never will.'

'Careless slaughter ain't necessarily the high road to popularity,' said Dogman. 'Especially in a king.'

'But that one there might have the bones to do something about it.' Shivers had a grudge. One that wasn't going away with time, or kindness, or even lives saved. There aren't many wounds that ever heal all the way, and there are some that hurt more with every day that passes.

The Dogman seemed to guess at Logen's thoughts. 'Don't worry about Shivers. He's alright. We've got plenty to worry about with these Gurkish, or whatever.'

'Uh,' said Grim.

Logen wasn't so sure about that. The worst enemies are the ones that live next door, his father always used to tell him. Back in the old days he'd just have murdered the bastard where he stood and problem solved. But he was trying to be a better man now. He was trying hard.

'By the dead, though,' Dogman was saying. 'Fighting against brown men, now, for the Union? How the bloody hell did that all happen? We shouldn't be down here.'

Logen took a long breath, and he let Shivers walk away. 'Furious stuck around for us. Wasn't for him we'd never have been done with Bethod. We owe him. It's just this one last fight.'

'You ever noticed how one fight has a habit of leading on to another? Seems like there's always one fight more.'

'Uh,' said Grim.

'Not this time. This is the last, then we're done.'

'That so? And what happens then?'

'Back to the North, I guess.' Logen shrugged his shoulders. 'Peace, isn't it?'

'Peace?' grunted the Dogman. 'Just what is that, anyway? What do you do with it?'

'I reckon . . . well . . . we'll make things grow, or something.'

'Make things grow? By all the fucking dead! What do you, or I, or any one of us know about making things grow? What else have we done, all our lives, but kill?'

Logen wriggled his shoulders, uncomfortable. 'Got to keep some hope. A man can learn, can't he?'

'Can he? The more you kill, the better you get at it. And the better you get at killing, the less use you are for anything else. Seems to me we've lived this long 'cause when it comes to killing we're the very best there is.'

'You're in a black mood, Dogman.'

'I been in a black mood for years. What worries me is that you ain't. Hope don't much suit the likes of us, Logen. Answer me this. You ever touched a thing that wasn't hurt by it? What have you ever had, that didn't turn to dirt?'

Logen thought about that. His wife and his children, his father and his people, all back to the mud. Forley, Threetrees and Tul. All good folk, and all dead, some of them by Logen's own hand, some of them by his neglect, and his pride, and his foolishness. He could see their faces, now, in his thoughts, and they didn't look happy. The dead don't often. And that was without looking to the dark and sullen crew lurking behind. A crowd of ghosts. A hacked and bloody army. All the folk he'd chosen to kill. Shama Heartless, his guts hanging out of his split stomach. Blacktoe, with his crushed legs and his burned hands. That Finnius bastard, one foot cut off and his chest slashed open. Bethod, even, right at the front with his skull pounded to mush, his frowning face twisted sideways, Crummock's dead boy peering from around his elbow. A sea of murder. Logen squeezed his eyes shut then prised them wide open, but the faces still lingered at the edge of his mind. There was nothing he could say.

'Thought so.' Dogman turned away from him, wet hair dripping round his face. 'You have to be realistic, ain't you always told me? You have to be that.' He strode off up the road, under the cold stars. Grim lingered next to Logen for a moment, then he shrugged his damp shoulders and followed the Dogman, taking his torch with him.

'A man can change,' whispered Logen, not sure whether he was talking to the Dogman, or to himself, or to those corpse-pale faces waiting in the darkness. Men clattered down the track all round him, and yet he stood alone. 'A man can change.'

Questions

A trace of autumn fog had slunk off the restless sea as the sun went down over crippled Adua, turning the chill night ghostly. A hundred strides distant the houses were indistinct. Two hundred and they were spectral, the few lights in the windows floating wraiths, hazy through the gloom. *Good weather for bad work, and we have much of that ahead of us.*

No distant explosions had rattled the still darkness so far. The Gurkish catapults had fallen silent. *At least for the moment, and why not? The city almost belongs to them, and why burn your own city?* Here, on the eastern side of Adua, far from the fighting, all seemed timelessly calm. *Almost as if the Gurkish had never come.* So when a vague clattering filtered through the gloom, as of the boots of a body of well-armed men, Glokta could not help a pang of nervousness, and pressed himself into the deeper shadows against the hedge by the road. Faint, bobbing lights filtered through the murk. Then the outline of a man, one hand resting casually on the pommel of a sword, walking with a loose, strutting slouch that bespoke extreme over-confidence. Something tall appeared to stick from his head, waving with his movements.

Glokta peered into the murk. 'Cosca?'

'The very same!' laughed the Styrian. He was affecting a fine leather cap with a ludicrously tall plume, and he flicked at it with a finger. 'I bought a new hat. Or should I say you bought me one, eh, Superior?'

'So I see.' Glokta glared at the long feather, the flamboyant golden basketwork on the hilt of Cosca's sword. 'I thought we said inconspicuous.'

'In . . . con . . . spicuous?' The Styrian frowned, then

shrugged his shoulders. 'Ah, so that was the word. I remember something was said, and I remember I didn't understand it.' He winced, and scratched at his crotch with one hand. 'I think I picked up some passengers from one of those women at the tavern. Little bastards don't half give a man an itch.' *Huh. The women are paid to go there. One might have thought the lice would have better taste.*

A shadowy crowd began to form out of the darkness behind Cosca, a few carrying hooded lanterns. A dozen shaggy outlines, then a dozen more, menace floating silently from each one of them like the stink floating from a turd. 'Are these your men?'

The nearest sported perhaps the worst facial boils that Glokta had ever seen. The man beside him had only one hand, the other having been replaced with a savage-looking hook. A huge fat fellow came next, his pale neck blue with a confusion of badly drawn tattoos. A man almost dwarfish, with a face like a rat and only one eye accompanied him. He had not bothered with a patch, and the socket yawned open under his greasy hair. The list of villainy went on. Two dozen, perhaps, all told, of the most savage-looking criminals Glokta had ever laid eyes on. *And I've laid eyes on a few in my time. Strangers to bathwater, certainly. Not a one of them looks like he wouldn't sell his sister for a mark.* 'They appear somewhat unreliable,' he murmured.

'Unreliable? Nonsense, Superior! Out of luck is all, and we both know how that goes, no? Why, there's not a man of them I wouldn't trust my mother to.'

'Are you sure?'

'She's been dead these twenty years. What harm could they do her now?' Cosca flung his arm round Glokta's twisted shoulders and drew him close, causing a painful twinge to jab at his hips. 'I'm afraid that pickings are slim.' His warm breath smelled strongly of spirits and corruption. 'Every man not desperate fled the city the moment the Gurkish arrived. But who cares, eh? I hired them for their guts and their sinews, not their looks. Desperate men are the kind I like! We can

489

understand them, no, you and I? Some jobs call for desperate men only, eh, Superior?'

Glokta frowned briefly over that collection of gaunt, of bloated, of scarred and ruined faces. *How could it possibly be that promising Colonel Glokta, dashing commander of the King's Own first regiment, came to be in charge of such a rabble?* He gave a long sigh. *But it is a little late now to be finding fine-looking mercenaries, and I suppose these will fill a pit as well as better.* 'Very well. Wait here.'

Glokta looked up at the dark house as he swung the gate open with his free hand and hobbled through. A chink of light peeped out from between the heavy hangings in the front window. He rapped at the door with the handle of his cane. A pause, then the sound of reluctant footsteps shuffling up the hall.

'Who is it?'

'Me. Glokta.'

Bolts drew back and light spilled out into the chill. Ardee's face appeared, lean-looking, grey round the eyes and pink round the nose. *Like a dying cat.*

'Superior!' She grinned as she took him by the elbow and half-dragged him over the threshold. 'What a delight! Some conversation at last! I'm so toweringly bored.' Several empty bottles were gathered in the corner of the living room, made to glint angrily by smoky candles and a smouldering log in the grate. The table was cluttered with dirty plates and glasses. The place smelled of sweat and wine, old food and new desperation. *Can there be a more miserable occupation than getting drunk on one's own? Wine can keep a happy man happy, on occasion. A sad one it always makes worse.*

'I've been trying to get through this damn book again.' Ardee slapped at a heavy volume lying open, face down, on a chair.

'*The Fall of the Master Maker*,' muttered Glokta. 'That rubbish? All magic and valour, no? I couldn't get through the first one.'

'I sympathise. I'm onto the third and it doesn't get any

490

easier. Too many damn wizards. I get them mixed up one with another. It's all battles and endless bloody journeys, here to there and back again. If I so much as glimpse another map I swear I'll kill myself.'

'Someone might save you the trouble.'

'Eh?'

'I'm afraid you are no longer safe here. You should come with me.'

'Rescue? Thank the fates!' She waved a dismissive hand. 'We've been over this. The Gurkish are away on the other side of the city. You're in more danger in the Agriont I shouldn't—'

'The Gurkish are not the threat. My suitors are.'

'Your gentleman-friends are a threat to me?'

'You underestimate the extent of their jealousy. I fear they will soon become a threat to everyone I have known, friend or enemy, my whole sorry life.' Glokta jerked a hooded cloak from a peg on the wall and held it out to her.

'Where are we going?'

'A charming little house down near the docks. A little past its best, but plenty of character. Like the two of us, you could say.'

There were heavy footsteps in the hallway and Cosca stuck his head into the room. 'Superior, we should leave if we want to reach the docks by—' He stopped, staring at Ardee. There was an uncomfortable silence.

'Who is this?' she murmured.

Cosca pushed flamboyantly into the room, swept off his hat, displaying his scabrous bald patch, and bowed low, low, low. *Any lower and his nose would scrape the floorboards.* 'Forgive me, my lady. Nicomo Cosca, famed soldier of fortune, at your service. Abject, in fact, at your feet.' His throwing knife dropped out of his coat and rattled against the boards.

They all stared at it for a moment, then Cosca grinned up. 'You see that fly, against the wall?'

Glokta narrowed his eyes. 'Perhaps not the best moment for—'

The blade spun across the room, missed the target by a

stride, hit the wall handle-first and gouged out a lump of plaster, bounced back and clattered across the floor.

'Shit,' said Cosca. 'I mean . . . damn.'

Ardee frowned down at the knife. 'I'd say shit.'

Cosca passed it off with a rotten smile. 'I must be dazzled. When the Superior described to me your beauty I thought he must have . . . how do you say . . . exaggerated? Now I see that he came short of the mark.' He retrieved his knife and jammed his hat back on, slightly askew. 'Please allow me to declare myself in love.'

'What did you tell him?' asked Ardee.

'Nothing.' Glokta sucked sourly at his gums. 'Master Cosca has a habit of overstating the case.'

'Especially when in love,' threw in the mercenary. 'Especially then. When I fall in love, I fall hard, and, as a rule, I do it no more than once a day.'

Ardee stared at him. 'I don't know whether to feel flattered or scared.'

'Why not be both?' said Glokta. 'But you will have to do it on the way.' *We are short of time, and I have a rank garden to weed.*

The gate came open with an agonised shrieking of rusted metal. Glokta lurched over the decaying threshold, his leg, his hip, his back all stabbing at him from the long limp to the docks. The ruined mansion loomed out of the gloom at the far end of the shattered courtyard. *Like a mighty mausoleum. A suitable tomb for all my dead hopes.* Severard and Frost waited in the shadows on the broken steps, dressed all in black and masked, as usual. *But not at all alike.* A burly man and a slender, one white haired and one dark, one standing, arms folded, the other sitting, cross-legged. *One is loyal, the other . . . we shall find out.*

Severard unravelled himself and got up with the usual grin around his eyes. 'Alright, chief, so what's all the—'

Cosca stepped through the gate and wandered lazily across the broken paving, tapping a few lumps of masonry away with the toe of one shabby boot. He stopped beside a ruined fountain and scraped some muck out of it with a finger. 'Nice place. Nice and . . .' He waved the finger around, and the muck with it. 'Crumbly.' His mercenaries were already spreading out slowly around the rubble-strewn courtyard. Patched coats and tattered cloaks twitched back to display weapons of every size and shape. Edges, points, spikes and flanges glinted in the shifting light from their lanterns, their steel as smooth and clean as their faces were rough and dirty.

'Who the hell are these?' asked Severard.

'Friends.'

'They don't look too friendly.'

Glokta showed his Practical the yawning hole in his front teeth. 'Well. I suppose that all depends whose side you're on.'

The last traces of Severard's smile had vanished. His eyes flickered nervously around the yard. *The eyes of the guilty. How well we know them. We see them on our prisoners. We see them in the mirror, when we dare to look. One might have hoped for better from a man of his experience, but holding the blade is a poor preparation for being cut by it. I should know.* Severard dashed towards the house, quick as a rabbit, but he only got a step before a heavy white hand chopped into the side of his neck and flung him senseless on the broken paving.

'Take him downstairs, Frost. You know the way.'

'Downthtairth. Unh.' The hulking albino dragged Severard's limp body over his shoulder and set off towards the front door.

'I have to say,' said Cosca, flicking the scum carelessly off his finger, 'that I like your way with your men, Superior. Discipline, I've always admired it.'

'Fine advice from the least disciplined man in the Circle of the World.'

'I have learned all kinds of things from my many mistakes.' Cosca stretched his chin up and scratched at his scabby neck. 'The one thing I never learn is to stop making them.'

'Huh,' grunted Glokta as he laboured up the steps. *A curse we all have to bear. Round and round in circles we go, clutching at successes that we never grasp, endlessly tripping over the same*

493

old failures. Truly, life is the misery we endure between disappointments.

They stepped through the empty doorway and into the deeper darkness of the entrance hall. Cosca held his lamp high, staring up towards the ragged roof, his boots squelching heedless in the bird droppings spattering the floor. 'A palace!' His voice echoed back from the shattered staircases, the empty doorways, the naked rafters high above.

'Please make yourselves comfortable,' said Glokta. 'But out of sight, perhaps. We can expect visitors some time tonight.'

'Excellent. We love company, don't we lads?'

One of Cosca's men gave a wet-lunged chuckle, displaying two rows of shit-coloured teeth. *A set so incredibly rotten I am almost glad to have my own.* 'These visitors will come from his Eminence the Arch Lector. Perhaps you could take a firm hand with them, while I'm downstairs?'

Cosca glanced round approvingly at the crumbling hall. 'A nice place for a warm welcome. I'll let you know when our guests have been. I doubt they'll stay long.'

Ardee had found a place near the wall, her hood up, her eyes on the floor. *Trying to fade into the plaster, and who could blame her? Hardly the most pleasant company for a young woman, or the most reassuring setting. But better than a slit throat, I suppose.* Glokta held his hand out to her. 'It would be best if you were to come with me.'

She hesitated. *As though not entirely sure that it would, in fact, be best to come with me.* But a brief glance at some of the ugliest men in one of the world's ugliest professions evidently persuaded her. Cosca handed her his lamp, making sure his fingers lingered on hers for an uncomfortably long moment.

'Thank you,' she said, jerking her hand away.

'My particular pleasure.'

Sheets of hanging paper, broken laths, lumps of fallen plaster cast strange shadows as they left Cosca and his thugs behind and picked their way into the guts of the dead building. Doorways passed by, squares of blackness, yawning like graves.

'Your friends seem a charming crowd,' murmured Ardee.

'Oh indeed, the brightest stars in the social firmament. Some tasks demand desperate men, apparently.'

'You must have some truly desperate work in mind, then.'

'When don't I?'

Their lamp barely lit the rotting drawing room, panelling sagging from the cheap brickwork, the best part of the floor a single festering puddle. The hidden door stood open in the far wall and Glokta shuffled round the edge of the room towards it, his hips burning with the effort.

'What did your man do?'

'Severard? He let me down.' *And we will soon find out how badly.*

'I hope I never let you down, then.'

'You, I am sure, have better sense. I should go first, then if I fall at least I fall alone.' He winced his way down the steps while she followed with the light.

'Ugh. What's that smell?'

'The sewers. There's an entrance to them down here, somewhere.' Glokta stepped past the heavy door and into the converted wine cellar, the bright steel grilles on the cells to either side glimmering as they passed, the whole place reeking of damp and fear.

'Superior!' came a voice from the darkness. Brother Longfoot's desperate face appeared, pressed up against one set of bars.

'Brother Longfoot, my apologies! I have been so very busy. The Gurkish have laid siege to the city.'

'Gurkish?' squeaked the man, his eyes bulging. 'Please, if you release me—'

'Silence!' hissed Glokta in a voice that brooked no dallying. 'You should stay here.'

Ardee glanced nervously towards the Navigator's cell. 'Here?'

'He isn't dangerous. I think you'll be more comfortable than you would be . . .' and he nodded his head towards the open doorway at the end of the vaulted hall, 'in there.'

She swallowed. 'Alright.'

'Superior, please!' One despairing arm stuck from

Longfoot's cell. 'Please, when will you release me? Superior, please!' Glokta shut the door on his begging with a gentle click. *We have other business today, and it will not wait.*

Frost already had Severard manacled to the chair beside the table, still unconscious, and was lighting the lamps one by one with a flaming taper. The domed chamber gradually grew bright, the colour leaking into the mural across the round walls. Kanedias frowned down, arms outstretched, the fire burning behind him. *Ah, our old friend the Master Maker, always disapproving.* Opposite him his brother Juvens still bled his lurid last across the wall. *And not the only blood that will be spilled in here tonight, I suspect.*

'Urr,' groaned Severard, his lank hair swaying. Glokta lowered himself slowly into his chair, the leather creaking under him. Severard grunted again, his head dropped back, eyelids flickering. Frost lumbered over, reached out and undid the buckles on Severard's mask, pulled it off and tossed it away into the corner of the room. *From a fearsome Practical of the Inquisition to . . . nothing much.* He stirred, wrinkled his nose, twitching like a boy asleep.

Young. Weak. Helpless. One could almost feel sorry for him, if one had a heart. But now is not the time for sentiment and soft feelings, for friendship and forgiveness. The ghost of happy and promising Colonel Sand dan Glokta has been clinging to me for far too long. Farewell, my old friend. You cannot help us today. Now is the time for the ruthless Superior Glokta to do what he does best. To do the only thing that he does well. Now is the time for hard heads, hard hearts and even harder edges.

Time to cut the truth out.

Frost jabbed Severard in the stomach with two fingers and his eyes snapped open. He jerked in his chair, the manacles rattling. He saw Glokta. He saw Frost. His eyes went wide as they darted round the room. They went wider still when he realised where he was. He snorted in air, the quick, hard breath of abject terror, the greasy strands of hair across his face blowing this way and that with the force of it. *And how will we begin?*

496

'I know . . .' he croaked. 'I know I told that woman who you were . . . I know . . . but I had no choice.' *Ah, the wheedling. Every man, more or less, behaves the same way when he's chained to a chair.* 'What could I do? She would've fucking killed me! I had no choice! Please—'

'I know what you told her, and I know you had no choice.'

'Then . . . then why—'

'Don't give me that, Severard. You know why you're here.' Frost stepped forward, as impassive as ever, and lifted the lid on Glokta's wonderful case. The trays inside opened up like an exotic flower, proffering out the polished handles, the gleaming needles, the shining blades of his instruments.

Glokta puffed out his cheeks. 'I had a good day, today. I woke up clean, and made it to the bath on my own. Not too much pain.' He wrapped his fingers around the grip of the cleaver. 'Something to celebrate, a good day. I get so very few of them.' He slid it from its sheath, the heavy blade flashing in the harsh lamplight. Severard's eyes followed it all the way, bulging with fear and fascination, beads of sweat glittering on his pale forehead.

'No,' he whispered. *Yes.* Frost unlocked the cuff around Severard's left wrist, lifted his arm in both meaty hands. He took the fingers and spread them out one by one until they were flattened on the wood in front of him, wrapping his other arm around Severard's shoulders in a tight embrace.

'I think we can dispense with the preamble.' Glokta rocked forward, got up and limped slowly around the table, his cane clicking on the tiles, his left leg dragging behind it, the corner of the cleaver's blade scraping gently across the wood of the table-top. 'I need not explain how this will work to you. You, who have assisted me so very ably, on so very many occasions. Who could know better how we will proceed?'

'No,' whimpered Severard, trying half a desperate smile, but with a tear leaking from the corner of his eye nonetheless. 'No, you wouldn't! Not to me! You wouldn't!'

'Not to you?' Glokta gave a sad smile of his own. 'Oh,

Practical Severard, please . . .' He let the grin slowly fade as he lifted the cleaver. 'You know me so much better than that.'

Bang! The heavy blade flashed down and hacked into the table-top, paring the slightest sliver of skin from the end of Severard's middle finger.

'No!' he squawked. 'No!' *You don't admire my precision any longer, then?*

'Oh, yes, yes.' Glokta tugged at the smooth handle and dragged the blade free. 'How did you think this would end? You've been talking. You've been saying things you shouldn't, to people you had no business saying anything to. You will tell me what. You will tell me who.' The cleaver glimmered as he raised it again. 'And you had better tell me soon.'

'No!' Severard thrashed and wriggled in the chair but Frost had him as tightly as a fly in honey. *Yes.*

The blade sliced cleanly through the end of Severard's middle finger and took it off at the first joint. The end of his index finger spun across the wood. The tip of his ring finger stayed where it was, wedged into a joint in the table top. With Frost's hand still clamped tight as a vice round his wrist the blood only dribbled gently from the three wounds and spread out in slow rivulets down the grain.

There was a breathless pause. *One, two, three . . .* Severard screamed. He wailed, and jerked, and trembled, his face quivering. *Painful, eh? Welcome to my world.*

Glokta worked his aching foot around in his boot. 'Who would ever have thought that our charming association, so enjoyable and profitable to us both, could possibly end like this? Not my choice. Not mine. Tell me who you spoke to. Tell me what you said. Then this unpleasantness will all be over. Otherwise . . .'

Bang! The end of his little finger, now, and three more pieces of the rest. His middle finger was down to the knuckle, almost. Severard stared, his eyes wide with horror, his breath coming in short, fast gasps. *Shock, amazement, stunned terror.* Glokta leaned down to his ear. 'I hope you weren't planning to take up the violin,' Severard. You'll be lucky if you can play a fucking gong by the time we're done here.' He winced at a spasm in his neck as he lifted the cleaver again.

'Wait!' sobbed Severard. 'Wait! Valint and Balk! The bankers! I told them . . . I told them . . .'

I knew it. 'What did you tell them?'

'That you were still looking for Raynault's murderer when we'd already hung the Emperor's emissary!' Glokta met Frost's eyes, and the albino stared back, emotionless. *And another secret is dragged kicking into the merciless light. How disappointingly right I was. It always amazes me, how swiftly problems can be solved, once you start cutting things off people.* 'And . . . and . . . I told them that you wanted to know about our bastard king, and about Bayaz, and I told them you weren't checking up on Sult like they asked, and I told them . . . I told them . . .'

Severard stuttered to a halt, staring at the remains of his fingers, scattered out across the table in a spreading slick of blood. *That mixture of unbearable pain, even more unbearable loss, and total disbelief. Am I dreaming? Or have I really lost half my fingers, forever?*

Glokta nudged Severard with the end of the cleaver. 'What else?'

'I told them anything I could. I told them . . . everything I knew . . .' The words came spitting and drooling from his lips, curled back with agony. 'I had no choice. I had debts, and . . . they offered to pay. I had no choice!'

Valint and Balk. Debts, and blackmail, and betrayal. How horribly banal it all is. That's the trouble with answers. They're never as exciting as the questions, somehow. Glokta's lips twitched into a sad smile. 'No choice. I know exactly how you feel.' He lifted the cleaver again.

'But—'

Bang! The heavy blade scraped against the table-top as Glokta swept four more neat slices of flesh carefully out of the way. Severard screamed, and gasped, and screamed some more. Desperate, slobbering screams, his face screwed up tight. *Just like the prunes I sometimes have for breakfast.* He still had half his little finger, but the other three were nothing more than oozing stumps. *But we cannot stop now, not after we have come so far. We cannot stop for anything, can we? We must know it all.*

'What about the Arch Lector?' asked Glokta, stretching his neck to the side and working his stiff shoulder. 'How did he know what went on in Dagoska? What did you tell him?'

'How did he . . . what . . . I told him nothing! I told him—'

Bang! Severard's thumb flew off, spinning across the table, leaving behind a spiralling trail of bloody spots. Glokta worked his hips back and forth, trying to wriggle out of the aches down his legs, the aches up his back. *But there is no escaping them. Every possible position, a little worse than the one before.* 'What did you tell Sult?'

'I . . . I . . .' Severard stared up, his mouth hanging open, a long string of drool dangling from his bottom lip. 'I . . .'

Glokta frowned. *That is not an answer.* 'Tie it off at the wrist and get the other hand ready. We've nothing left to work with here.'

'No! No! Please . . . I didn't . . . please . . .' *How I tire of the pleading. The words 'no' and 'please' lose all meaning after half an hour of this. They begin to sound like a sheep bleating. We are all lambs to the slaughter, in the end.* He stared at the pieces of finger scattered across the bloody table. *Meat for the butcher.* Glokta's head hurt, the room was too bright. He put the cleaver down and rubbed at his sore eyes. *A draining business, mutilating your closest friends.* He realised he had smeared blood across his eyelids. *Damn it.*

Frost had already tightened a tourniquet round Severard's wrist and manacled the bloody remains of his left hand back to the chair. He unfastened his right arm and guided it carefully to the table. Glokta watched him do it. *All neat, and business-like, and ruthlessly efficient. Does his conscience nag at him, I wonder, when the sun goes down? I doubt it. I give the orders after all. And I act on orders from Sult, on advice from Marovia, on the demands of Valint and Balk. What choice do any of us have, in the end? Why, the excuses almost make themselves.*

Frost's white face was dusted with bloody red specks as he

spread Severard's right hand out on the table, just where the left one had been. He did not even struggle this time. *You lose the will, after a while. I remember.* 'Please . . .' he whispered.

It would be so very nice to stop. Most likely the Gurkish will burn the whole city and kill us all, and then who will care who told who what? If by some miracle they fail, no doubt Sult will finish me, or Valint and Balk will collect their debt in my blood. What will it matter when I am floating face-down in the docks whether certain questions were ever answered? Then why do I do this? Why?

The blood reached the edge of the wood and started dripping to the floor with a steady tap, tap, tap. No other answer. Glokta felt a flurry of twitches run up the side of his face. He took hold of the cleaver again.

'Look at this.' He gestured at the pieces of bloody flesh scattered across the table. 'Look what you've lost here, already. All because you won't tell me what I need to know. Do you not value your own fingers? They're no use to you now, are they? They're no use to me, I can tell you that. They're no use to anyone, besides a hungry dog or two, maybe.' Glokta bared the yawning hole in his front teeth, and ground the point of the cleaver into the wood between Severard's outspread fingers. 'One more time.' He pronounced the words with icy precision. 'What . . . did you tell . . . his Eminence?'

'I . . . told him . . . nothing!' The tears ran down Severard's hollow cheeks, his chest shuddered with sobs. 'I told him nothing! Valint and Balk, I had no choice! I've never spoken to Sult in my fucking life! Not a word! Never!'

Glokta looked into his Practical's eyes, his prisoner's eyes, for a long moment, trying to see the truth. All was silent except for Severard's gurgling, agonised breath. Then Glokta wrinkled his lip and tossed the cleaver down rattling on the table. *Why give up your other hand, when you have confessed already?* He gave a long sigh, reached out and gently wiped the tears from Severard's pale face. 'Alright. I believe you.'

But what then? We are left with more questions than before, and nowhere to look for the answers. He arched his back, wincing at the aches in his twisted spine, down his twisted leg, through his toeless foot. *Sult must have gained his information elsewhere. Who else survived Dagoska, who else saw enough? Eider? She would never dare reveal herself. Vitari? If she wanted to spill her guts she could have done it at the time. Cosca? His Eminence would never work with a man that unpredictable. I only use him myself because I have no other choice. Then who?*

Glokta's eyes met Frost's. Pink eyes, unblinking. They stared at him, bright and hard as pink gemstones. And the wheels clicked into place.

I see.

Neither one of them spoke. Frost reached out, without much haste, his eyes never leaving Glokta's, and wrapped both his thick arms around Severard's neck. The ex-Practical could only stare, helpless.

'What're—' Frost frowned slightly. There was a sharp crunching sound as he wrenched Severard's head sideways. *As simple and careless as killing a chicken.* Severard's skull flopped backwards as Frost let him go, and far past backwards, unnatural knobbly shapes sticking from the pale skin of his twisted neck.

The albino stood up, between Glokta and the door, hanging ajar. *No way out.* Glokta winced as he stumbled backwards, the tip of his cane scraping against the floor. 'Why?' Frost came on, slowly and surely, his white fists clenched tight, his white face expressionless behind his mask. Glokta held up one hand. 'Just tell me why, damn it!'

The albino shrugged. *I suppose some questions have no answers, after all.* Glokta's twisted back hit the curved wall. *And my time is up. Ah well.* He took a long breath. *The odds were always stacked against me. I do not mind dying, so very much.*

Frost raised his white fist, then grunted. The cleaver sank deep into his heavy shoulder with a dull smack. Blood began to leak out from it into his shirt. Frost turned. Ardee stood behind him. The three of them stared at each other for a moment. Then Frost punched her in the face. She reeled away and crashed into the side of the table, slid limp to the floor, dragging it over on its side, Glokta's case clattering down beside her, instruments tumbling, blood and bits of flesh scattering. Frost started to turn back, the cleaver still wedged in his flesh, his left arm hanging limp.

Glokta's lips curled away from his empty gums. *I do not mind dying. But I refuse to be beaten.*

He set his feet as best he could, ignoring the pain that stabbed through his toeless foot and up his front leg. He brought up his cane and jammed his thumb into its hidden catch. It had been made to his precise instructions by the same man who had made the case for his instruments. *And is an even finer piece of craftsmanship.*

There was a gentle click as the wood sprang open on secret hinges and dropped away revealing a two-foot needle of mirror-bright metal. He let go a piercing shriek.

Jab, jab, Glokta. Jab, jab.

The steel was a blur. The first thrust ran Frost neatly through the left side of his chest. The second darted silently through the right side of his neck. The third punctured his mask and scraped against his jaw bone, the glinting point showing itself just under his white ear for an instant before it whipped back out.

Frost stood, motionless, his white eyebrows going up with mild surprise. Then blood welled from the tiny wound on his throat and ran down into his shirt in a black line. He reached out with one big white hand. He wobbled, blood bubbling from under his mask.

'Futh,' he breathed.

He crumpled to the ground as though his legs had been snatched suddenly from under him. He put out an arm to push himself up, but there was no strength in it. His breaths gurgled noisily, then quietly, and he was still. *And that is all.*

Ardee was sitting up near the table, blood running out of her nose and down her top lip. 'He's dead.'

'I used to fence,' murmured Glokta. 'It seems the trick never entirely leaves you.' He stared from one corpse to the other. Frost lay in a slowly widening dark pool, one pink eye staring ahead, still unblinking, even in death. Severard's head was hanging back over the chair, mouth yawning wide open in a silent scream, his mutilated hand still manacled, the other hanging limp. *My boys. My eyes. My hands. All finished.* He frowned at the bloody length of metal in his fist. *Well. We must fumble onwards as best we can without them.*

He winced as he reached down and picked up the fallen piece of his cane between two fingers, snapped it shut around the bloody steel. 'If you wouldn't mind closing that case for me.' Ardee stared wide-eyed at the instruments, at Severard's yawning corpse, at the blood-stained table on its side and the fragments of flesh scattered across the floor. She coughed, and pressed the back of her hand to her mouth. *One forgets that some people are not used to dealing with these matters. But we need such help as we can get, and it is a little late for easing anyone into this gently. If she can chop into a man with a cleaver, she can carry a blade or two for me without swooning.* 'The case,' he snapped. 'I will still need my instruments.'

Ardee blinked, collected the few scattered tools with trembling hands and put them back in their places. She wedged the box under her arm and stood up, somewhat unsteadily, wiping the blood from her nose on her white sleeve. Glokta noticed that she had a piece of one of Severard's fingers caught in her hair.

'You have something . . .' he pointed at his head, 'just here.'

'What? Gah!' She tore the dead thing out and flung it on the ground, gave a shiver of disgust. 'You should find another way to make a living.'

'I have been thinking that for some time. But there are still a few more questions I must have answered.'

The door creaked and Glokta felt a sudden stab of panic. Cosca stepped through into the room. He whistled softly as he surveyed the carnage, pushed his cap back on his head, its feather casting a spray of long shadows across the mural behind him. 'You've made quite a mess, Superior, quite a mess.'

Glokta fingered his cane. His leg was on fire, his heart was thumping dully at his temples, he was damp with cold sweat under his scratchy clothes. 'Unavoidable.'

'I thought you'd want to know that we had our visitors. Six Practicals of the Inquisition. I rather suspect they may have been sent here to kill you.' *Undoubtedly. On the Arch Lector's orders, acting on information from the late Practical Frost.*

'And?' asked Glokta. After the events of the past hour he was almost expecting Cosca to come at him, sword swinging.

But if the last hour has taught us anything, it is that the least trusted henchman is not always the least reliable. 'And we cut them to pieces, of course.' The Styrian grinned. 'I'm insulted you might think otherwise.'

'Good. Good.' *At least something has gone to plan.* Glokta wanted nothing more than to slide to the floor and lie there, screaming. *But there is work to do.* He winced as he limped for the door. 'We need to head for the Agriont immediately.'

The first traces of dawn were leaking into the cold, clear sky as Glokta hobbled out onto the Middleway, Ardee at his shoulder. There was still mist on the air, but it was fading, now. *A fine day in prospect, it would appear. A fine day for bloodshed, treachery, and—*

Shapes were moving in the mist, away south down the wide cobbled road, towards the sea. There were noises too. Rattling, jingling. It sounded very much like a body of armoured men on the move. Further off, someone was shouting. A bell began to clang, sullen and muffled. *A warning bell.*

Cosca frowned into the thinning mist. 'What is that?'

The shapes grew more distinct. Armoured men, carrying spears, and in numbers. Their tall helmets were plainly not of Union design.

Ardee touched Glokta on the arm. 'Are they—'

'Gurkish.' Their armour glinted in the thin, grey light as the fog drifted aside. A vast body of them, marching north up the Middleway. *They must finally have landed men at the docks, broken through into the centre of the city. What astonishingly poor timing.* 'Back!' Glokta turned towards the alley, slipped and nearly fell, grimacing as Ardee caught him by the elbow and dragged him up straight.

'Back to the mansion!' *And hope we weren't seen already.* 'And keep those lamps with you, we'll need them.' He hurried to the stinking alley as best he could, barged and jostled by Cosca's mercenaries.

'Damn these Gurkish,' hissed the Styrian. 'I don't know for the life of me what I did to upset them so.'

'You have my sympathy.' The gate squealed shut and a couple of the mercenaries started dragging a broken fountain behind it. *I'm not sure how long that will keep out one of the Emperor's legions.*

'Might I ask what the plan is now, exactly, Superior? Charming though your palace is, sitting here and waiting for relief would hardly seem to be an option.'

'No.' Glokta struggled up the steps and through the open front door. 'We need to get to the Agriont.'

'Something tells me our Gurkish friends will have had the same idea. We will not be getting there overground, that is certain.'

'Then we must go underground.' Glokta limped into the guts of the building as smartly as he could, Ardee and the mercenaries following behind in a worried crowd. 'There is an entrance to the sewers here. One can get all the way to the Agriont, if one knows the route.'

'Sewers?' Cosca grinned. 'I like nothing more than wading through life's filth, as you well know, but sewers can be quite . . . confusing. Do you know the route?'

'Actually, no.' *But I know a man who says he can find a way through anything, even a river of shit.* 'Brother Longfoot!' he called out as he hobbled towards the steps. 'I have a proposition for you!'

The Day of Judgement

Lord Marshal West stood in the shadow of an abandoned barn, up on a rise above the fertile plains of Midderland, his eye-glass clutched tightly in one gloved hand. There was still a trace of morning mist clinging to the flat autumn fields – patchworks of brown, green, yellow, stabbed with trees, slashed with bare hedgerows. In the distance West could see the outermost walls of Adua, a stern grey line pimpled with towers. Behind, in a lighter grey, the vague shapes of buildings jutted skywards. Above them loomed the towering ghost of the House of the Maker, stark and unrepentant. All in all, it was a grim homecoming.

There was not so much as a breath of wind. The crisp air was strangely still. Just as if there was no war, no rival armies drawing up, no bloody battles scheduled to begin. West swept his eye-glass back and forth, but he could scarcely see any hint of the Gurkish. Perhaps he imagined a tiny fence, down there before the walls, perhaps the outlines of pin-prick spears, but at this distance, in this light, he could be sure of nothing.

'They must be expecting us. They must be.'

'Maybe they're sleeping late,' said Jalenhorm, ever the optimist.

Pike was more direct. 'What difference if they are?'

'Not much,' West admitted. King Jezal's orders had been specific. The city was infested with Gurkish troops and the defences were close to complete collapse. There was no time for clever stratagems, for careful approaches, for probing the enemy for weak spots. Prince Ladisla, ironically, would probably have been as good a commander for this particular situation as anyone else. For once, circumstances called for a magnificent charge, followed closely by death or glory. The only thing under West's control was the timing.

Brint pulled up his horse nearby, sending a shower of grit into the cold air. He swung down from the saddle and gave a smart salute. 'General Kroy's cavalry is in position on the right wing, Lord Marshal, and ready to charge at your order.'

'Thank you, Captain. His foot?'

'Perhaps halfway to deploying. Some companies are still spread out down the roads.'

'Still?'

'Muddy-going, sir.'

'Huh.' Armies left mud behind them like a slug left a trail. 'What about Poulder?'

'A similar position, as far as I can tell,' said Brint. 'No messages?'

Jalenhorm shook his head. 'General Poulder has not been forthcoming this morning.'

West stared towards the city, that distant grey line beyond the fields. 'Soon.' He chewed at his lip, already raw from his constant worrying. 'Very soon. Mustn't let fly half-drawn. When a little more of the foot comes up . . .'

Brint was frowning off to the south. 'Sir, is that . . .' West followed his pointing finger. Over on the left wing, where Poulder had been gathering his division, the cavalry were already moving smartly forward.

West stared as the riders gathered pace. 'What the . . .'

Two full regiments of heavy horse broke into a majestic gallop. Thousands of them, streaming forwards across the open farmland, surging round the trees and the scattered farmhouses, throwing up a wake of dusty earth. West could hear the hammering of their hooves now, like distant thunder, could almost feel the vibration of it through his boots. The sun glinted on raised sword and lance, on shield and full armour. Banners streamed and snapped in the wind. It was quite the display of martial grandeur. A scene from a lurid storybook with a muscular hero in which meaningless words like honour and righteousness were often repeated.

'Shit,' growled West through gritted teeth, feeling the familiar pulsing coming up behind his eyes. General Poulder had been itching to mount one of his fabled cavalry charges all across the North and back. There the harsh terrain, or the harsh weather, or the harsh circumstances had all prevented it. Now, with the perfect conditions, it seemed he had been unable to resist the opportunity.

Jalenhorm slowly shook his head. 'Bloody Poulder.'

West gave a snarl of frustration, raised up his eye-glass to dash it on the ground. He managed to stop himself at the last moment, forced in a heavy breath, and slapped the thing angrily closed. He could not afford to indulge himself today. 'Well, that's it then, isn't it? Order the charge, all across the line!'

'Sound the charge!' roared Pike. 'The charge!'

The sharp bugle call rang out, blaringly loud on the chill morning air, doing nothing to ease West's throbbing headache. He stuck one muddy boot in his stirrup and dragged himself reluctantly up into his saddle, already sore from riding all night. 'I suppose we must follow General Poulder to glory. At a less honourable distance, though, perhaps. Someone still needs to co-ordinate this shambles.' The sounds of answering bugles further down the line floated up to them, and on the right Kroy's horsemen began to trot forwards.

'Major Jalenhorm, order the foot forward in support as soon as they come up.' West worked his mouth. 'Piecemeal if need be.'

'Of course, Lord Marshal.' The big man was already turning his horse to give the orders.

'War,' muttered West. 'A noble business.'

'Sir?' asked Pike.

'Nothing.'

Jezal took the last few steps two at a time, Gorst and a dozen of his Knights clattering after him, sticking to his heels as tightly as his shadow. He swept imperiously past the guard and into the bright morning light at the top of the Tower of Chains, high above the stricken city. Lord Marshal Varuz was already at the parapet, surrounded by a gaggle of his staff, all glaring out across Adua. The old soldier stood stiffly, his hands clasped behind him, just the way he had always done at fencing practice, long ago. Jezal had never noticed his hands shake in the old days, however. They shook now, and badly. High Justice Marovia stood beside him, black robes stirred by the gentle breeze.

'The news?' demanded Jezal.

The Lord Marshal's tongue darted nervously over his lips. 'The Gurkish mounted an assault before dawn. The defenders of Arnault's wall were overwhelmed. Not long afterwards they managed to land men at the docks. A great number of men. We have been fighting a rearguard action with the greatest courage, but . . . well . . .'

There was really no need to say more. As Jezal moved closer to the parapet, and wounded Adua came into view, he could plainly see the Gurkish flooding down the Middleway, the tiny golden standards of the Emperor's legions bobbing above the mass of humanity like flotsam on a glittering tide. Like seeing one ant on the carpet, then gradually becoming aware of hundreds all across his living room, Jezal began to notice movement elsewhere, then everywhere. The very centre of the city was infested with Gurkish soldiers.

'Fighting a rearguard action with . . . mixed success,' finished Varuz lamely.

Down below, a few men burst out from the buildings near the western gate of the Agriont, ran across the cobbled square before the moat, heading for the bridge.

'Gurkish?' someone squealed.

'No,' muttered the Lord Marshal. 'Those are ours.' Men doing their very best to escape the slaughter that was no doubt taking place down in the ruined city. Jezal had faced death often enough to guess at how they felt.

'Have those men brought to safety,' he said, voice cracking slightly.

'I am afraid . . . the gates have been sealed, your Majesty.'

'Then unseal them!'

Varuz' dewy eyes wandered nervously to Marovia. 'That would . . . not be wise.'

A dozen or more had made it to the bridge now, were shouting and waving their arms. Their words were lost over the distance, but the tone of helpless, abject terror was impossible to miss.

'We should do something.' Jezal's hands gripped tight to the parapet. 'We must do something! There will be others out there, many more!'

Varuz cleared his throat. 'Your Majesty—'

'No! Have my horse saddled. Gather the Knights of the Body. I refuse to—'

High Justice Marovia had moved to block the door to the stairs, and now looked calmly, sadly into Jezal's face. 'If you were to open the gates now, you would be putting everyone in the Agriont at risk. Many thousands of citizens, all looking to you for protection. Here we can keep them safe, at least for now. We must keep them safe.' His eyes slid sideways to the streets. Different-coloured eyes, Jezal noticed, one blue, one green. 'We must weigh the greater good.'

'The greater good.' Jezal looked the other way, into the Agriont. Brave defenders were ranged around the walls, he knew, ready to fight to the death for king and country, however undeserving. He pictured civilians too, scurrying for safety through the narrow lanes. Men, women, children, the old and the young, driven from their ruined homes. People to whom he had promised safety. His eyes flickered across the high white buildings around the green park, the wide Square of Marshals, the long Kingsway with its tall statues. They were filled, he knew, with the helpless and the needy. Those unlucky enough to have no one better to rely on than the gutless fraud, Jezal dan Luthar.

It stuck in his throat, but he knew the old bureaucrat was right. There was nothing he could do. He had been shockingly lucky to survive his last magnificent charge, and it was far too late for another. Outside the Agriont, Gurkish soldiers were beginning to boil into the square before the gate. A few of them knelt, bows in hand, and sent a flight of arrows arcing across onto the bridge. Tiny figures tumbled and fell, splashed into the moat. Tiny screams wafted gently up to the top of the Tower of Chains.

An answering volley rattled from the walls, peppered the Gurkish with flatbow bolts. Men dropped, others faltered and fell back, leaving a few bodies scattered across the cobbles. They scurried for cover in the buildings around the edge of the square, men darting through the shadows from house to house. A Union soldier jumped from the bridge and splashed along in the moat for a few strokes before disappearing. He did not resurface. Behind him a last handful of the stranded defenders were still crawling, desperately holding up their arms. The notion of the greater good was likely to be scant consolation for them as they choked their last breaths. Jezal squeezed his eyes shut and looked away.

'There! To the east!'

Varuz and a few members of his staff had clustered around the far parapet, gazing out past the House of the Maker and towards the distant fields outside the city. Jezal strode over to them, shielded his eyes against the rising sun. Beyond the great wall of the Agriont, beyond the shining river and the wide curve of the city, he thought he caught some trace of movement. A wide crescent of movement, crawling slowly towards Adua.

One of the officers lowered an eye-glass. 'Cavalry! Union Cavalry!'

'Are you sure?'

'The Army!'

'Late to the party,' muttered Varuz, 'but no less welcome for that.'

'Hurrah for Marshal West!'

'We are delivered!'

Jezal was in no mood to whoop for joy. Hope was a fine thing, of course, and had long been in short supply, but celebrations were decidedly premature. He crossed back to the other side of the tower and frowned down.

More Gurkish were surging into the square outside the citadel, and more still, and they were coming well prepared. They wheeled great sloping wooden screens forward, each one big enough for a score of men or more to hide behind. The foremost of them already bristled with flatbow bolts, but they continued to creep towards the bridge. Arrows flitted up and down. The wounded fell, did their best to crawl for the rear. One of the buildings at the side of the square had already caught fire, flames licking hungrily round the eaves of its roof.

'The army!' someone whooped from the opposite battlement. 'Marshal West!'

'Indeed.' Marovia frowned down at the carnage below, the sounds of battle growing steadily more frantic. 'Let us hope he has not come too late.'

The noise of fighting crept up through the cool air. Clashing and clicking, echoing calls. Logen glanced left and right at the men around him, jogging forward over the open fields, quick breath hissing, gear rattling, all blunt frowns and sharp weapons.

Hardly a heartening thing, to be part of all this again.

The sad fact was that Logen had felt more warmth and more trust with Ferro and Jezal, Bayaz and Quai than he did with his own kind now. They'd been a difficult set of bastards, each in their own way. It wasn't that he'd really understood them, or even liked them much. But Logen had liked himself when he was with them. Out there in the deserted west of the World, he'd been a man you could rely on, like his father had been. A man with no bloody history breathing on his shoulder, no name blacker than hell, no need to watch his back every moment. A man with hopes for something better.

The thought of seeing those folk again, the chance at being that man again, put the spur to him, made Logen want to run at the grey wall of Adua all the faster. It seemed, in that moment anyway, as if he might be able to leave the Bloody-Nine outside it.

But the rest of the Northmen didn't share his eagerness. It was closer to a stroll than a charge. They ambled up to a stand of trees, a couple of birds went flapping into the white sky, and they stopped altogether. No one said anything. One lad even sat down, with his back to a tree, and started supping water from a flask.

Logen stared at him. 'By the dead, I don't reckon I ever saw such a piss-weak charge as this. Did you leave your bones back in the North?'

There was a bit of mumbling, a few shifty looks. Red Hat glanced sideways, his tongue wedged into his bottom lip. 'Maybe we did. Don't get me wrong, chief, or your Royal Highness, or whatever it is now.' He bowed his head to show he meant no disrespect by it. 'I've fought before and hard enough, had my life balanced on a sword's edge, and all o' that. Just, well . . . why fight now, is what I'm saying. What we're all thinking, I reckon. Ain't none of our business, is it? Ain't our fight, this.'

Dogman shook his head. 'The Union are going to take us for a right crowd o' cowards.'

'Who cares what they think?' someone said.

Red Hat stepped up close. 'Look, chief, I don't care much of a shit whether some fool I don't know thinks I'm a coward. I've spilled enough blood for that. We all have.'

'Huh,' grunted Logen. 'So your vote's to stay here, then, is it?'

Red Hat shrugged. 'Well, I guess—' He squawked as Logen's forehead crunched into his face, smashing his nose like a nut on an anvil. He dropped hard on his back in the mud, spluttering blood down his chin.

Logen turned round, and he let his face hang on one side, the way he used to. The Bloody-Nine's face – cold and dead, caring for nothing. It was easy to do it. Felt as natural on him as a favourite pair of boots. His hand found the cold grip of the

Maker's sword, and all around him men eased back, shuffled away, muttered and whispered.

'Any other one o' you cunts want a vote?'

The lad dropped his flask in the grass and jumped up from where he'd been sitting. Logen gave a few of them his eye, one by one, whoever looked hardest, and one by one they looked at the ground, at the trees, at anything but him. Until he looked at Shivers. That long-haired bastard stared straight back at him. Logen narrowed his eyes. 'How about you?'

Shivers shook his head, hair swaying across his face. 'Oh no. Not now.'

'When you're ready, then. When any one o' you are ready. Until then, I'll have some work out o' you. Weapons,' he growled.

Swords and axes, spears and shields were all made ready quick-time. Men fussed about, finding their places, competing all of a sudden to be the first to charge. Red Hat was just getting up, wincing with one hand to his bloody face. Logen looked down at him. 'If you're feeling hard done by, think on this. In the old days you'd be trying to hold your guts in about now.'

'Aye,' he grunted, wiping his mouth. 'Right y'are.' Logen watched him walk off back to his boys, spitting blood. Say one thing for Logen Ninefingers, say he's got a talent for turning a friend into an enemy.

'Did you have to?' asked the Dogman.

Logen shrugged. He hadn't wanted it, but he was leader now. Always a disaster, but there it was, and a man in charge can't have men putting questions. Just can't have it. They come with questions first, then they come with knives. 'Couldn't see another way. That's how it's always been, ain't it?'

'I was hoping times changed.'

'Times never change. You have to be realistic, Dogman.'

'Aye. Shame, though.'

A lot of things were a shame. Logen had given up trying to put them right a long time ago. He slid out the Maker's sword and held it up. 'Let's go, then! And this time like we care a shit!'

He started off through the trees, hearing the rest of the lads following. Out into the open air, and the walls of Adua loomed up, a sheer grey cliff at the top of a grassy rise, studded with round towers. There were quite a number of corpses lying around. Enough to give even a battle-hardened Carl some cold feelings. Gurkish corpses mostly, from the colour of their skin, sprawled among all kinds of broken gear, squashed into muddy earth, trampled with hoof-prints.

'Steady!' shouted Logen as he jogged on through them. 'Steady!' He caught sight of something up ahead, a fence of sharpened stakes, the body of a horse hanging dead from one of them. Behind the stakes, men moved. Men with bows.

'Cover up!' A few arrows came zipping down. One thudded into Shivers' shield, a couple more into the ground round Logen's feet. A Carl not a stride from him got one in the chest and tumbled over.

Logen ran. The fence came wobbling towards him, a good bit slower than he'd have liked. Someone stood between two of the stakes, dark-faced, with a shining breastplate, a red plume on his pointed helmet. He was shouting to a crowd of others gathered behind him, waving a curved sword. A Gurkish officer, maybe. As good a thing to charge at as any. Logen's boots squelched at the churned-up ground. A couple more arrows spun past him, hastily aimed. The officer's eyes went wide. He took a nervous step back, raised his sword.

Logen jerked to his left and the curved blade thudded into the turf at his feet. He growled as he swung the Maker's sword round and the heavy length of metal clanged deep into the officer's bright breastplate, left a great dent in it. He screeched, then tottered forwards, all doubled up and hardly able to gasp in a breath. His sword spun out of his hand and Logen hit him on the back of his head, crushed his helmet and sent him sprawling in the mud.

He looked to the others, but not one of them had moved. They were a tattered-looking set, like a dark-skinned version of the weakest kind of Thralls. Hardly the ruthless bastards he'd expected from the way that Ferro had always talked about the

Gurkish. They huddled together, spears sticking out this way and that. A couple even had bows with arrows nocked, probably could have stuck him like a hedgehog, but they didn't. Still, charging right at them might well have been the very thing to wake them up. Logen had taken an arrow or two in his time and he didn't fancy another.

So instead of coming forward, he stood up tall, and he gave a roar. A fighting roar, like the one he'd given when he charged down the hill at Carleon, all those years ago, when he still had all his fingers and all his hopes intact. He felt the Dogman come up beside him, and lift his sword, and give a scream of his own. Then Shivers was up with them, bellowing like a bull and smashing the head of his axe against his shield. Then Red Hat, with his bloody face, and Grim, and all the rest, yelling their war cries.

They stood in a long line, shaking their weapons, beating them crashing together, roaring and screaming and whooping at the tops of their voices, making a sound as if hell itself had opened up and a crowd of devils was singing welcome. The brown men watched them, staring and trembling, their mouths and their eyes wide open. Logen didn't reckon they'd ever seen anything like this before.

One of them dropped his spear. Didn't mean to, maybe, just so struck with the noise and the sight of all these crazy hairy bastards his fingers came open. It fell anyway, whether he meant it or not, and that was it, they all started dropping their gear. Fast as they could, it clattered down in the grass. Seemed stupid to keep shouting, and the war cries died out, left the two groups of men staring at each other in silence across that stretch of mud, planted with bent stakes and twisted corpses.

'Strange kind o' battle, that,' muttered Shivers.

The Dogman leaned towards Logen. 'What do we do with 'em now we've got 'em?'

'We can't just sit hear minding 'em.'

'Uh,' said Grim.

Logen chewed at his lip, spun his sword round and round in his hand, trying to think of some clever way to come at this. He couldn't see one. 'Might as well just let 'em go.' He jerked his head away north. None of them moved, so he tried it again, and pointed with his sword. They cringed and muttered to each other when he lifted it, one of them falling over in the mud. 'Just piss off that way,' he said, 'and we've got no argument. Just piss . . . off . . . that way!' He stabbed with the sword again.

One of them got the idea now, took a cautious step away from the group. When no one struck him dead, he started running. Soon enough the others followed him. Dogman watched the last of them shamble off. Then he shrugged his shoulders. 'Good luck to 'em, then, I guess.'

'Aye,' muttered Logen. 'Good luck.' Then, so quiet that no one could hear, 'Still alive, still alive, still alive . . .'

Glokta limped through the reeking gloom, down a fetid walk-way half a stride across, his tongue squirming into his empty gums with the effort of staying upright, wincing all the way as the pain in his leg grew worse and worse, doing his best not to breathe through his nose. *I thought when I lay crippled in bed after I came back from Gurkhul I could sink no lower. When I presided over the brutality of a stinking prison in Angland I thought the same again. When I had a clerk slaughtered in an abattoir I imagined I had reached the bottom. How wrong I was.*

Cosca and his mercenaries formed a single file with Glokta in their midst, their cursing, grumbling, slapping footfalls echoing up and down the vaulted tunnel, the light from their swinging lamps casting swaying shadows over the glistening stone. Rotten black water dripped from above, trickled down the mossy walls, gurgled in slimy gutters, rushed and churned down the reeking channel beside him. Ardee shuffled along behind with his instruments clasped under one arm. She had abandoned any attempt to hold up the hem of her dress and the fabric was well stained with black slurry. She looked up at him, damp hair hanging across her face, and made a weak effort at a smile. 'You certainly do take a girl to the very best places.'

'Oh, indeed. My knack for finding romantic settings no doubt explains my continuing popularity with the fairer sex.' Glokta winced at a painful twinge. 'Despite being a crippled monstrosity. Which way are we heading, now?'

Longfoot hobbled along in front, tethered by a rope to one of the mercenaries. 'North! Due north, give or take. We are just beside the Middleway.'

'Huh.' *Above us, not ten strides distant, are some of the most fashionable addresses in the city. The shimmering palaces and a river of shit, so much closer together than most would ever like to believe. Everything beautiful has a dark side, and some of us must dwell there, so that others can laugh in the light.* His snort of laughter turned to a squeak of panic as his toeless foot slid on the sticky walkway. He flailed at the wall with his free hand, fumbled his cane and it clattered to the slimy stones. Ardee caught his elbow before he fell and pulled him upright. He could not stop a girlish whimper of pain hissing out from the gaps in his teeth.

'You're really not enjoying yourself, are you?'

'I've had better days.' He smacked the back of his head against the stone as Ardee leaned down to retrieve his cane. 'To be betrayed by both,' he found himself muttering. 'That hurts. Even me. One I expected. One I could have taken. But both? Why?'

'Because you're a ruthless, plotting, bitter, twisted, self-pitying villain?' Glokta stared at her, and she shrugged. 'You asked.' They set off once again through the nauseating darkness.

'The question was meant to be rhetorical.'

'Rhetoric? In a sewer?'

'Wait up, there!' Cosca held up his hand and the grumbling procession shuffled to a halt again. A sound filtered down from above, softly at first, then louder – the rhythmic boom of tramping feet, seeming to come, disconcertingly, from everywhere at once. Cosca pressed himself to the sticky wall, stripes of daylight falling across his face from a grate above, the long feather on his cap drooping with slime. Voices settled through the murk. *Kantic voices.* Cosca grinned, and jabbed one finger up towards the roof. 'Our old friends the Gurkish. Those bastards don't give up, eh?'

'They've moved quickly,' grunted Glokta as he tried to catch his breath.

'No one much fighting in the streets any more, I imagine. All pulled back to the Agriont, or surrendered.'

Surrendering to the Gurkish. Glokta winced as he stretched out his leg. *Rarely a good idea, and not one a man would ever consider twice.* 'We must hurry, then. Move along there, Brother Longfoot!'

The Navigator hobbled on. 'Not much further, now! I have not led you wrong, oh no, not I! That would not have been my way. We are close now, to the moat, very close. If there is a way inside the walls, I will find it, on that you may depend. I will have you inside the walls in a—'

'Shut your mouth and get on with it,' growled Glokta.

One of the workmen shook the last of the wood shavings from his barrel, another raked the heap of pale powder smooth, and they were done. The whole Square of Marshals, from the towering white walls of the Halls Martial on Ferro's right to the gilded gates of the Lords' Round on her left, was entirely covered in sawdust. It was as if snow had come suddenly, only here, and left a thin blanket across the smooth flags. Across the dark stone, and across the bright metal.

'Good.' Bayaz nodded with rare satisfaction. 'Very good!'

'Is that all, my Lord?' called their foreman from the midst of their cringing group.

'Unless any of you wish to stay, and witness the destruction of the indestructible Hundred Words?'

The foreman squinted sideways at one of his fellows with some confusion. 'No. No, I think we'll just . . . you know . . .' He and the rest of the workmen began to back off, taking their empty barrels with them. Soon they were away between the white palaces. Ferro and Bayaz were left alone in all that flat expanse of dust.

Just the two of them, and the Maker's box, and the thing that it contained.

'So. The trap is set. We need merely wait for our quarry.' Bayaz tried his knowing grin, but Ferro was not fooled. She saw his gnarled hands fussing with each other, the muscles clenching and unclenching on the side of his bald head. He was not sure if his plans would work. However wise he was, however subtle, however cunning, he could not be sure. The thing in the box, the cold and heavy thing that Ferro longed to touch, was an unknown. The only precedent for its use was far away, in the empty wastes of the Old Empire. The vast ruin of blighted Aulcus.

Ferro frowned, and loosened her sword in its scabbard.

'If they come, that will not save you.'

'You can never have too many knives,' she growled back. 'How do you know they will even come this way?'

'What else can they do? They must come to wherever I am. That is their purpose.' Bayaz pulled in a ragged breath through his nose, and blew it out. 'And I am here.'

Sacrifices

Dogman squeezed through the gate along with a rush of others, some Northmen and an awful lot of Union boys, all pouring into the city after that excuse for a battle outside. There were a few folk scattered on the walls over the archway, cheering and whooping like they were at a wedding. A fat man in a leather apron was standing on the other side of the tunnel, clapping folk on the back as they came past. 'Thank you, friend! Thank you!' He shoved something into Dogman's hand, grinning like a madman all the way. A loaf of bread.

'Bread.' Dogman sniffed at it, but it smelled alright. 'What the hell's all that about?' The man had a whole heap of loaves on a cart. He was handing them out to any soldier that came past, Union or Northman. 'Who's he, anyway?'

Grim shrugged. 'A baker?'

There weren't much time to think on it. They were all getting shoved together into a big space full of men pushing, and grumbling, and making mess. All kind of soldiers and some old men and women round the edge, starting to get tired of cheering. A well-clipped lad in a black uniform was standing on top of a cart in the midst of this madness and screeching like a lost goat.

'Eighth regiment, towards the Four Corners! Ninth towards the Agriont! If you're with the tenth you came through the wrong damn gate!'

'Thought we were to the docks, Major!'

'Poulder's division are dealing with the docks! We're for the north part of the city! Eighth regiment towards the Four Corners!'

'I'm with the Fourth!'

'Fourth? Where's your horse?'

'Dead!'

'What about us?' roared Logen. 'Northmen!'

The lad stared at them, wide-eyed, then he threw up his hands. 'Just get in there! If you see any Gurkish, kill them!' He turned back towards the gate, jerking his thumb over his shoulder into the city. 'Ninth regiment towards the Agriont!'

Logen scowled. 'We'll get no sense here.' He pointed down a wide street, full of walking soldiers. Some great tall tower poked up above the buildings. Huge thing, must've been built on a hill. 'We get split up, we'll just aim at that.' He struck off down that street and Dogman came after, Grim behind with Shivers and his boys, Red Hat and his crew further back. Wasn't long before the crowds thinned out and they were marching down empty streets, quiet except for some birds calling, happy as ever, not caring a thing for there having been a battle just now, and caring even less that there was another one coming.

Dogman wasn't giving it a lot of thought either, for all he had his bow loose in one hand. He was too busy staring at the houses down either side of the road. Houses the like of which he'd never seen in his life. Made of little square, red stones, and black wood filled in with white render. Each one of 'em was big enough for a chieftain to be happy with, most with glass windows in as well.

'Bloody palaces, eh?'

Logen snorted. 'You think this is something? You should see this Agriont we're aiming at. The buildings they got there. You never dreamed o' the like. Carleon's a pigsty beside this place.'

Dogman had always found Carleon a good bit too built-up. This was downright ridiculous. He dropped back a way, found he was walking next to Shivers. He tore the loaf and held one half out.

'Thanks.' Shivers took a bite out of the end, then another. 'Not bad.'

'Ain't nothing quite like it, is there? That taste o' new bread? Tastes like . . . peace, I guess.'

'If you say so.' They chewed together for a while, saying nothing.

Dogman looked sideways. 'I think you need to put this feud o' yours behind you.'

'What feud's that?'

'How many you got? The one with our new king up there. Ninefingers.'

'Can't say I haven't tried.' Shivers frowned up the road at Logen's back. 'But whenever I turn around, there it is beside me.'

'Shivers, you're a good man. I like you. We all do. You got bones, lad, and brains too, and men'll follow you. You could go a long way if you don't get yourself killed, and there's the problem. I don't want to see you start up something you can't put a good end to.'

'You needn't worry then. Anything I start I'll make sure I finish.'

Dogman shook his head. 'No, no, that ain't my point, lad, not at all. Maybe you come out on top, maybe you don't. My point is neither one's a victory. Blood makes blood, and nothing else. My point is it ain't too late for you. It ain't too late for you to be better'n that.'

Shivers frowned at him. Then he tossed the heel of bread away, turned his big shoulder and headed off without another word. Dogman sighed. Some things can't be put right just with talk. Some things can't be put right at all.

They came out from the maze of buildings and onto a river. It must've been as wide as the Whiteflow, only the banks on each side were made of stone. The biggest bridge the Dogman had ever seen spanned it, railings made of curly iron, wide enough to drive two carts across side by side. Another wall stood at the far end, even bigger than the one they came through first. Dogman took a few gawping steps forward, and he looked up and down the gleaming water, and he saw that there were more bridges. A lot more, and some even bigger, standing out from a great forest of walls, and towers, and soaring high buildings.

A lot of the others were staring too, eyes wide open like they'd stepped out onto the moon. Even Grim had a twist to his face that might've been surprise.

'Bloody hell,' said Shivers. 'You ever see the like o' this?'

Dogman's neck was aching from staring round at it all. 'They've got so much here. Why do they even want bloody Angland? Place is a shit-hole.'

Logen shrugged. 'Couldn't say. Some men always want more, I guess.'

'Some men always want more, eh, Brother Longfoot?' Glokta gave a disapproving shake of his head. 'I spared your other foot. I spared your life. Now you want freedom, too?'

'Superior,' he wheedled. 'If I may, you did undertake to release me . . . I have upheld my side of the bargain. That door should open onto a square not far from the House of Questions—'

'We shall see.'

One last splintering blow of the axe and the door shuddered back on its rusty hinges, daylight spilling into the narrow cellar. The mercenary with the tattooed neck stood aside and Glokta limped up and peered out. *Ah, fresh air. A gift we so often take for granted.* A short set of steps led up to a cobbled yard, hemmed in by the grubby backs of grey buildings. Glokta knew it. *Just round the corner from the House of Questions, as promised.*

'Superior?' murmured Longfoot.

Glokta curled his lip. *But where's the harm? The chances are none of us will live out the day in any case, and dead men can afford to be merciful. The only kind of men that can, in fact.* 'Very well. Let him go.' The one-eyed mercenary slid out a long knife and sawed through the rope round Longfoot's wrists. 'It would be best if I didn't ever see you again.'

The Navigator had the ghost of a grin on his face. 'Don't worry, Superior. I was only this moment thinking the very same thing.' He hobbled back the way they had come, down the dank stairway towards the sewers, rounded a corner and was gone.

'Tell me you brought the things,' said Glokta.

'I'm untrustworthy, Superior. Not incompetent.' Cosca flicked a hand at the mercenaries. 'Time, my friends. Let's black up.'

As a unit they pulled out black masks and buckled them on, pulled off their ragged coats, their torn clothes. Every man wore clean black underneath, from head to toe, with weapons carefully stowed. In a few moments a crowd of criminal villains was transformed into a well-ordered unit of Practicals of his Majesty's Inquisition. *Not that there's too much of a leap from one to the other.*

Cosca himself whisked his coat off, pulled it quickly inside out and dragged it back on. The lining was black as night. 'Always wise to wear a choice of colours,' he explained. 'In case one should be called upon to change sides in a pinch.' *The very definition of a turncoat.* He took off his hat, flicked at the filthy feather. 'Can I keep it?'

'No.'

'You're a hard man, Superior.' He grinned as he tossed the cap away into the shadows. 'And I love you for it.' He pulled his own mask on, then frowned at Ardee, standing, confused and exhausted in a corner of the store-room. 'What about her?'

'Her? A prisoner, Practical Cosca! A spy in league with the Gurkish. His Eminence expressed his desire to question her personally.' Ardee blinked at him. 'It's easy. Just look scared.'

She swallowed. 'That shouldn't be a problem.'

Wandering through the House of Questions with the aim of arresting the Arch Lector? I should say not. Glokta snapped his fingers. 'We need to move.'

'We need to move,' said West. 'Have we cleared the docks? Where the hell is Poulder?'

'Nobody seems to know, sir.' Brint tried to push his horse further, but they were squashed in by a grumbling throng. Spears waved, their points flailing dangerously close. Soldiers cursed. Sergeants bellowed. Officers clucked like frustrated chickens. It was hard to imagine more difficult terrain than the narrow streets behind the docks through which to man-oeuvre an army of thousands. To make matters worse there was now an ominous flow of wounded, limping or being carried, in the opposite direction.

'Make some room for the Lord Marshal!' roared Pike. 'The Lord Marshal!' He lifted his sword as though he was more than willing to lay about him with the flat, and men rapidly cleared out of the way, a valley forming through the rattling spears. A rider came clattering up out of their midst. Jalenhorm, a bloody cut across his forehead.

'Are you alright?'

The big man grinned. 'It's nothing, sir. Caught my head on a damn timber.'

'Progress?'

'We're forcing them back towards the western side of the city. Kroy's cavalry made it to the Four Corners, as far as I can tell, but the Gurkish still have the Agriont well surrounded, and now they're regrouping, counterattacking from the west. A lot of Kroy's foot are still all caught up in the streets on the other side of the river. If we don't get reinforcement there soon—'

'I need to speak to General Poulder,' snapped West. 'Where the hell is bloody Poulder? Brint?'

'Sir?'

'Take a couple of these fellows and bring Poulder here, right away!' He stabbed at the air with a finger. 'In person!'

'Yes, sir!' Brint did his best to turn his horse around.

'What about at sea? Is Reutzer up?'

'As far as I'm aware he's engaged the Gurkish fleet, but I've no idea how . . .' The smell of rotting salt and burning wood intensified as they emerged from the buildings and onto the harbour. 'Bloody hell.'

West could only agree.

The graceful curve of Adua's docks had been transformed into a crescent of carnage. Near to them the quay was

527

blackened, wasted, scattered with broken gear and broken bodies. Further off, crowds of men were struggling in ill-formed groups, polearms sticking up in all directions like hedgehog's spines, the air heavy with their noise. Union battle-flags and Gurkish standards flailed like scarecrows in the breeze. The epic conflict covered almost the entire long sweep of the shoreline. Several warehouses were in flames, sending up a shimmering heat-haze, lending a ghostly air to the hundreds of men locked in battle beyond them. Long smears of choking smoke, black, grey, white, rolled from the burning buildings and out into the bay. There, in the churning harbour, a host of ships were engaged in their own desperate struggle.

Vessels ploughed this way and that under full sail, turning, tacking, jockeying for position, flinging glittering spray high into the air. Catapults hurled flaming missiles, archers on the decks loosed flaming volleys, sailors crawled high in the cobwebs of rigging. Other ships were locked together in ungainly pairs by rope and grapple, like fighting dogs snapping at one another, glinting sunlight showing men in savage mêlée on their decks. Stricken vessels limped vainly, torn sailcloth hanging, slashed rigging dangling. Several were burning, sending up brown columns of smoke, turning the low sun into an ugly smudge. Wreckage floated everywhere on the frothing water – barrels, boxes, shivered timbers and dead sailors.

West knew the familiar shapes of the Union ships, yellow suns stitched into their sails, he could guess which were the Gurkish vessels. But there were others there too – long, lean, black-hulled predators, each one of their white sails marked with a black cross. One in particular towered far over every other vessel in the harbour, and was even now being secured at one of the few wharves still intact.

'Nothing good ever comes from Talins,' muttered Pike.

'What the hell are Styrian ships doing here?'

The ex-convict pointed to one in the very act of ramming a Gurkish ship in the side. 'Fighting the Gurkish, by the look of it.'

'Sir,' somebody asked. 'What shall we do?'

The eternal question. West opened his mouth, but nothing came out. How could one man hope to exert any measure of control over the colossal chaos spread out before him? He remembered Varuz, in the desert, striding around with his huge staff crowding after him. He remembered Burr, thumping at his maps and wagging his thick finger. The greatest responsibility of a commander was not to command, but to look like he knew how to. He swung his sore leg over the saddle bow and slid down to the sticky cobbles.

'We will set up our headquarters here, for the time being. Major Jalenhorm?'

'Sir?'

'Find General Kroy and tell him to keep pressing north and west, towards the Agriont.'

'Yes, sir.'

'Somebody get some men together and start clearing this rubbish from the docks. We need to get our people through quicker.'

'Yes, sir.'

'And somebody find me General Poulder, damn it! Each man has to do his part!'

'What's this now?' grunted Pike.

A strange procession was sweeping down the blasted quay towards them, almost dreamily out of place amongst the wreckage. A dozen watchful guards in black armour flanked a single man. He had black hair streaked with grey, sported a pointed beard, immaculately trimmed. He wore black boots, a fluted breastplate of black steel, a cloak of black velvet flowing majestically from one shoulder. He was dressed, in fact, like the world's richest undertaker, but walked with the kind of steely self-importance reserved for the highest royalty. He plotted a direct course towards West, looking neither left nor right, the dumbfounded guards and staff forced effortlessly aside by his air of command like iron filings parted by magnetic repulsion.

He held out his black-gauntleted hand. 'I am Grand Duke Orso, of Talins.'

The idea, perhaps, was that West should kneel and kiss it.

Instead he seized it with his own and gave it a firm shake. 'Your Excellency, an honour.' He had no idea if that was even the proper form of address. He had scarcely been expecting to encounter one of the most powerful men in the world in the midst of a bloody battle on the docks of Adua. 'I am Lord Marshal West, commander of his Majesty's Army. Not to appear ungrateful, but you are far from home—'

'My daughter is your Queen. On her behalf, the people of Talins are prepared to make any sacrifice. As soon as I heard of the . . .' He arched one black eyebrow at the burning harbour. 'Troubles, here, I prepared an expedition. The ships of my fleet, as well as ten thousand of my best troops, stand at your disposal.'

West hardly knew how to respond. 'They do?'

'I have taken the liberty of disembarking them. They are engaged in clearing the Gurkish from the south-western quarter of the city. The Three Farms, is it called?'

'Er . . . yes.'

Duke Orso gave the thinnest of smiles. 'A picturesque name for an urban area. You need no longer trouble yourself with your western flank. I wish you the best of luck with your endeavours, Lord Marshal. If fate is willing, we will meet each other afterward. Victorious.' He bowed his magnificent head and swept away.

West stared after him. He knew that he really should have been grateful for the sudden appearance of ten thousand helpful Styrian troops, but he could not escape the nagging feeling that he would have been happier if Grand Duke Orso had never arrived. For the time being, however, he had more pressing worries.

'Lord Marshal!' It was Brint, hurrying down the quay at the front of a group of officers. One side of his face was covered in a long smear of ash. 'Lord Marshal, General Poulder—'

'At long bloody last!' snapped West. 'Now perhaps we'll have some answers. Where the hell is that bastard?' He shouldered Brint aside, and froze. Poulder lay on a stretcher held by four muddy and miserable-looking members of his staff. He had the expression of a man in peaceful sleep, to the degree that West kept expecting to hear him snore. A huge, ragged wound in his chest rather spoiled the effect, however.

'General Poulder led the charge from the front,' said one of the officers, swallowing his tears. 'A noble sacrifice . . .'

West stared down. How often had he wished that man dead? He jerked one hand over his face at a sudden wave of nausea. 'Damn it,' he whispered.

'Damn it!' hissed Glokta as he twisted his trembling ankle on the topmost step and nearly pitched onto his face. A bony Inquisitor coming the other way gave him a long look. 'Is there a problem?' he snarled back. The man lowered his head and hurried past without speaking.

Click, tap, pain. The dim hallway slid by with agonising slowness. Every step was an ordeal, now, but he forced himself on, legs burning, foot throbbing, neck aching, sweat running down his twisted back under his clothes, a rictus of toothless nonchalance clamped onto his face. At every gasp and grunt through the building he had expected a challenge. With each twinge and spasm he had been waiting for the Practicals to flood from the doorways and butcher him and his thinly disguised hirelings like hogs.

But those few nervous people they had passed had scarcely looked up. *Fear has made them sloppy. The world teeters at a precipice. All scared to take a step in case they put a foot into empty air. The instinct of self-preservation. It can destroy a man's efficiency.*

He lurched through the open doors and into the ante-room outside the Arch Lector's office. The secretary's head jerked angrily up. 'Superior Glokta! You cannot simply . . .' He stumbled on the words as the mercenaries began to tramp into the narrow room behind him. 'I mean to say . . . you cannot . . .'

'Silence! I am acting on the express orders of the king himself.' *Well, everyone lies. The difference between a hero and a villain is whether anyone believes him.* 'Step aside!' he hissed at the two Practicals flanking the door, 'or be prepared to answer for it.' They glanced at each other, then, as more of Cosca's men appeared, raised their hands together and allowed themselves to be disarmed. *The instinct of self-preservation. A decided disadvantage.*

Glokta paused before the doorway. *Where I have cringed so often at the pleasure of his Eminence.* His fingers tingled against the wood. *Can it possibly be this easy? To simply walk up in broad daylight and arrest the most powerful man in the Union?* He had to suppress a smirk. *If only I had thought of it sooner.* He wrenched the doorknob round and lurched over the threshold.

Sult's office was much as it had always been. The great windows, with their view of the University, the huge round table with its jewelled map of the Union, the ornate chairs and the brooding portraits. It was not Sult sitting in the tall chair, however. It was none other than his favourite lapdog, Superior Goyle. *Trying the big seat out for size, are we? Far too big for you, I'm afraid.*

Goyle's first reaction was outrage. *How dare anyone barge in here like this?* His second was confusion. *Who would dare to barge in here like this?* His third was shock. *The cripple? But how?* His fourth, as he saw Cosca and four of his men follow Glokta through the door, was horror. *Now we're getting somewhere.*

'You!' he hissed. 'But you're—'

'Slaughtered? Change of plans, I'm afraid. Where's Sult?'

Goyle's eyes flickered around the room, over the dwarfish mercenary, the one with a hook for a hand, the one with the hideous boils, and came to rest on Cosca, swaggering round the edge of the chamber with one fist on his sword-hilt.

'I'll pay you! Whatever he's paying you, I'll double it!'

Cosca held out his open palm. 'I prefer cash in hand.'

'Now? I don't have . . . I don't have it with me!'

'A shame, but I work on the same principle as a whore. You'll buy no fun with promises, my friend. No fun at all.'

'Wait!' Goyle stumbled up and took a step back, his trembling hands held up in front of him. *But there's nowhere to go but out the window. That's the trouble with ambition. It's easy to forget, when you're always looking upwards, that the only way down from the dizzy heights is a long drop.*

'Sit down, Goyle,' growled Glokta.

Cosca grabbed his wrist, twisted his right arm savagely behind him and made him squeal, forced him back into the chair, clamped one hand round the back of his head and smashed his face into the beautiful map of the Union. There was a sharp crunch as his nose broke, spattering blood across the western part of Midderland.

Hardly subtle, but then the time for subtlety is behind us. The Arch Lector's confession, or someone close to him . . . Sult would have been better, but if we cannot have the brains, I suppose we must make do with the arsehole. 'Where is that girl with my instruments?' Ardee crept cautiously into the room, came slowly across to the table and put the case down.

Glokta snapped his fingers, pointed. The fat mercenary ambled up and took a firm grip on Goyle's free arm, dragged it sharply out across the table. 'I expect you think you know an awful lot about torture, eh, Goyle? Believe me, though, you don't really understand a thing until you've spent some time on both sides of the table.'

'You mad bastard!' The Superior squirmed, smearing blood across the Union with his face. 'You've crossed the line!'

'Line?' Glokta spluttered with laughter. 'I spent the night cutting the fingers from one of my friends and killing another, and you dare to talk to me about *lines*?' He pushed open the lid of the case and his instruments offered themselves up. 'The only line that matters is the one that separates the strong from the weak. The man who asks the questions from the man who answers them. There are no other lines.' He leaned forward and ground the tip of his finger into the side of Goyle's skull. 'That's all in your head! The manacles, if you please.'

'Eh?' Cosca looked to the fat mercenary, and the man shrugged, the blurred tattoos on his thick neck squirming.

'Pffft,' said the dwarf. Boil-face was silent. The one-handed mercenary had pulled down his mask and was busy picking his nose with his hook.

Glokta arched his back and gave a heavy sigh. *There really is no replacement for experienced help.* 'Then I suppose we must improvise.' He scooped up a dozen long nails and scattered them jingling across the table-top. He slid out the hammer, its polished head shining. 'I think you can see where we're going with this.'

'No. No! We can work something out, we can—' Glokta pressed the point of one nail into Goyle's wrist. 'Ah! Wait! Wait—'

'Would you be good enough to hold this? I have only one hand to spare.'

Cosca took the nail gingerly between finger and thumb. 'Mind where you aim with the hammer, though, eh?'

'Don't worry. I am quite precise.' *An awful lot of practice.*

'Wait!' screeched Goyle.

The hammer made three metallic clicks, almost disappointingly quiet, as it drove the nail cleanly between the bones of Goyle's forearm and into the table beneath. He roared with pain, spraying bloody spit over the table.

'Oh, come now, Superior, compared to what you did to your prisoners in Angland this is really quite infantile. Try to pace yourself. If you scream like that now, you'll have nowhere to go later.' The fat mercenary seized Goyle's other wrist in his pudgy hands and dragged it out across the map of the Union.

'Nail?' asked Cosca, raising an eyebrow.

'You're getting the hang of it.'

'Wait! Ah! Wait!'

'Why? This is the closest I've come to enjoying myself in six years. Don't begrudge me my little moment. I get so very few of them.' Glokta raised the hammer.

'Wait!'

Click. Goyle roared with pain again. Click. And again. Click. The nail was through, and the one-time scourge of Angland's penal colonies was pinned flat by both arms. *I suppose that's where ambition gets you without the talent.*

Humility is easier to teach than one would think. All it takes to puncture our arrogance is a nail or two in the right place. Goyle's breath hissed through his bloody teeth, pinioned fingers clawing at the wood. Glokta disapprovingly shook his head. 'I would stop struggling if I was you. You'll only tear the flesh.'

'You'll pay for this, you crippled bastard! Don't think you won't!'

'Oh, I've paid already.' Glokta turned his neck around in a slow circle, trying to make the grumbling muscles in his shoulders unclench just a fraction. 'I was kept, I am not sure for how long, but I would guess at several months, in a cell no bigger than a chest of drawers. Far too small to stand, or even to sit up straight in. Every possible position twisted, bent, agonising. Hundreds of interminable hours in the pitch darkness, the stifling heat. Kneeling in a stinking slurry of my own shit, wriggling, and squirming, and gasping for air. Begging for water which my jailers let drip down through a grate above. Sometimes they would piss through it, and I would be grateful. I have never stood up straight since. I really have no idea how I remained sane.' Glokta thought about it for a moment, then shrugged. 'Perhaps I didn't. In any case, these are the kind of sacrifices I have made. What sacrifices will you make, just to keep Sult's secrets?'

No answer but the blood running out from under Goyle's forearms, pooling around the glittering stone that marked the House of Questions in the city of Keln.

'Huh.' Glokta gripped his cane hard and leaned down to whisper in Goyle's ear. 'There's a little bit of flesh, between your fruits and your arsehole. You never really see it, unless you're a contortionist, or unnaturally fond of mirrors. You know the one I'm talking about. Men spend hours thinking about the area in front of it, and almost as long on the area behind, but that little patch of flesh? Unfairly ignored.' He scooped up a few nails and jingled them gently in Goyle's face. 'I mean to set that right, today. I'm going to start there, and work outwards, and believe me, once I'm done, you'll be thinking about that patch of flesh for the rest of your life. Or you'll be thinking about where it used to be, at least. Practical Cosca, would you be kind enough to help the Superior out of his trousers?'

'The University!' bellowed Goyle. He had a sheen of sweat all over his balding head. 'Sult! He's in the University!'

So soon? Almost disappointing. But then few bullies take a beating well. 'What's he doing there, at a time like this?'

'I . . . I don't—'

'Not good enough. Trousers, please.'

'Silber! He's with Silber!'

Glokta frowned. 'The University Administrator?'

Goyle's eyes darted from Glokta, to Cosca, and back again. He squeezed them shut. 'The Adeptus Demonic!'

There was a long pause. 'The what?'

'Silber, he doesn't just run the University! He conducts . . . experiments.'

'Experiments of what nature?' Glokta jabbed sharply at Goyle's bloody face with the head of the hammer. 'Before I nail your tongue to the table.'

'Occult experiments! Sult has been giving him money, for a long time! Since the First of the Magi came calling! Before, maybe!'

Occult experiments? Funding from the Arch Lector? It hardly seems Sult's style, but it explains why those damn Adepti were expecting money from me when I first visited the place. And why Vitari and her circus have set up shop there now. 'What experiments?'

'Silber . . . he can make contact . . . with the Other Side!'

'What?'

'It's true! I have seen it! He can learn things, secrets, there is no other way of knowing, and now . . .'

'Yes?'

'He says he has found a way to bring them through!'

'Them?'

'The Tellers of Secrets, he calls them!'

Glokta licked at his dry lips. 'Demons?' *I thought his*

536

Eminence had no patience with superstition, when all this time . . . The nerve of the man!

'He can send them against his enemies, he says. Against the Arch Lector's enemies! They are ready to do it!'

Glokta felt his left eye twitching, and he pressed the back of his hand against it. *A year ago I would have laughed to my boots and nailed him to the ceiling. But things are different, now. We passed inside the House of the Maker. We saw Shickel smile as she burned. If there are Eaters? If there are Magi? Why should there not be demons? How could there not be?* 'What enemies?'

'The High Justice! The First of the Magi!' Goyle squeezed his eyes shut again. 'The king,' he whimpered.

Ahhhh. The. King. Those two little words are my kind of magic. Glokta turned to Ardee, and showed her the yawning gap in his front teeth. 'Would you be so kind as to prepare a Paper of Confession?'

'Would I . . .' She stared at him for a moment, eyes wide in her pale face, then hurried to the Arch Lector's desk, snatched up a sheet of paper and a pen, dipped it rattling in a bottle of ink. She paused, her hand trembling. 'What should I write?'

'Oh, something like, "I, Superior Goyle, confess to being an accomplice in a treasonous plot of his Eminence Arch Lector Sult, to . . ."' *How to phrase it?* He raised his brows. *How else but call it what it is?* ' "To use diabolical arts against his Majesty the king and members of his Closed Council." '

The nib scratched clumsily over the paper, scattering specks of ink. Ardee held it crackling out to him. 'Good enough?'

He remembered the beautiful documents that Practical Frost used to prepare. The elegant, flowing script, the immaculate wording. *Each Paper of Confession, a work of art.* Glokta stared sadly down at the ink-spotted daub in his hand.

'But a brief step from unreadable, but it will serve.' He slid the paper under Goyle's trembling hand, then took the pen from Ardee and wedged it between his fingers. 'Sign.'

Goyle sobbed, sniffed, scrawled his name at the bottom of the page as best he could with his arm nailed down. *I win, and for once the taste is almost sweet.*

'Excellent,' said Glokta. 'Pull those nails, and find some sort of bandage. It would be a shame if he bled to death before he had the chance to testify. Gag him, though, I've heard enough for now. We'll take him with us to the High Justice.'

'Wait! Wait! Wurghh—!' Goyle's cries were sharply cut off as the mercenary with the boils wedged a wad of dirty cloth in his mouth. The dwarf slid the pliers from the case. *So far, and we are still alive. Whatever are the odds of that?* Glokta limped to the window and stood, stretching his aching legs. There was a muffled shriek as the first nail was ripped from Goyle's arm, but Glokta's thoughts were elsewhere. He stared out towards the University, its spires looming up through the smoky murk like clawing fingers. *Occult experiments? Summonings and sendings?* He licked sourly at his empty gums. *What is going on in there?*

'What is going on out there?' Jezal strode up and down the roof of the Tower of Chains in a manner which he hoped was reminiscent of a caged tiger, but probably was closer to a criminal on the morning of his own hanging.

Smoke had drawn a sooty veil across the city and made it impossible to tell what was happening any further than a half mile distant. Members of Varuz' staff, scattered around the parapets, would occasionally call out useless and wildly contradictory news. There was fighting in the Four Corners, up the Middleway, throughout the central part of the city. There was fighting on land and on sea. By turns all hope was lost and they were on the verge of deliverance. But one thing was in no doubt. Below, beyond the moat of the Agriont, the Gurkish efforts continued ominously unabated.

A rain of flatbow bolts continued to pepper the square outside the gates, but for every corpse the Gurkish left, for every wounded man dragged away, five more would vomit out from the burning buildings like bees from a broken hive. Soldiers swarmed down there in teeming hundreds, enclosing the whole circuit of the Agriont in an ever-strengthening ring of men and steel. They squatted behind their wooden screens, they shot arrows up towards the battlements. The pounding of drums had drawn steadily closer and now echoed out around the city. Peering through his eye-glass, with every muscle tensed to try and hold it steady, Jezal had begun to notice strange figures scattered below.

Tall and graceful figures, conspicuous in pearly white armour edged with glinting gold, they moved among the Gurkish soldiers, pointing, ordering, directing. Often, now, they were pointing towards the bridge that led to the west gate of the Agriont. Dark thoughts niggled at the back of Jezal's mind. Khalul's Hundred Words? Risen up from the shadowy corners of history to bring the First of the Magi to justice?

'If I didn't know better, I would have said that they were preparing for an assault.'

'There is no cause for alarm,' croaked Varuz, 'our defences are impregnable.' His voice quavered, then cracked entirely at the final word, doing little to give anyone the slightest reassurance. Only a few short weeks ago, nobody would have dared to suggest that the Agriont could ever fall. But nobody would ever have dreamed that it would be surrounded by legions of Gurkish soldiers, either. Very plainly, the rules had changed. A deep blast of horns rang out.

'Down there,' muttered one of his staff.

Jezal peered through his borrowed eye-glass. Some form of great cart had been drawn up through the streets, like a wooden house on wheels, covered by plates of beaten metal. Even now, Gurkish soldiers were loading barrels into it under the direction of two men in white armour.

'Explosive powder,' someone said, unhelpfully.

Jezal felt Marovia's hand on his arm. 'Your Majesty, it might be best if you were to retire.'

'And if I am not safe here? Where, precisely, will I be out of danger, do you suppose?'

'Marshal West will soon deliver us, I am sure. But in the meantime the palace is much the safest place. I will accompany you.' He gave an apologetic smile. 'At my age, I fear I will be little use on the walls.'

Gorst held out one gauntleted hand towards the stairs. 'This way.'

'This way,' growled Glokta, limping up the hall as swiftly as his ruined feet would carry him, Cosca ambling after. *Click, tap, pain.*

Only one secretary remained outside the office of the High Justice, peering disapprovingly over his twinkling eye-glasses. *No doubt the rest have donned ill-fitting armour and are manning the walls. Or, more likely, have locked themselves in cellars. If only I were with them.*

'I am afraid his Worship is busy.'

'Oh, he will see me, don't worry about that.' Glokta hobbled past without stopping, placed his hand on the brass doorknob of Marovia's office, and almost jerked it back in surprise. The metal was icy cold. *Cold as hell.* He turned it with his fingertips and opened the door a crack. A breath of white vapour curled out into the hall, like the freezing mist that would hang over the snowy valleys in Angland in the midst of winter.

It was deathly cold in the room beyond. The heavy wooden furniture, the old oak panelling, the grubby window panes, all glittered with white hoar-frost. The heaps of legal papers were furry with it. A bottle of wine on a table by the door had shattered, leaving behind a bottle-shaped block of pink ice and a scattering of sparkling splinters.

'What in hell . . .' Glokta's breath smoked before his smarting lips. Mysterious articles were scattered widely about the wintry room. A long, snaking length of black tubing was frozen to the panelling, like a string of sausages left in the snow. There were patches of black ice on the books, on the desk, on the crunching carpet. There were pink fragments frozen to the ceiling, long white splinters frozen to the floor . . .

Human remains?

A large chunk of icy flesh, partly coated in rime, lay in the middle of the desk. Glokta turned his head sideways to better take it in. There was a mouth, still with some teeth attached, an ear, an eye. Some strands of a long beard. Enough, in the end, for Glokta to recognise whose parts were scattered so widely around the freezing room. *Who else but my last hope, my third suitor, High Justice Marovia?*

Cosca cleared his throat. 'It seems there is something to your friend Silber's claims after all.'

An understatement of devilish proportions. Glokta felt the muscles round his left eye twitching with a painful intensity. The secretary fussed up to the door behind them, peered through, gasped, and reeled away. Glokta heard him being noisily sick outside. 'I doubt the High Justice will be lending us much assistance.'

'True. But isn't it getting a little late in the day for your papers and so forth anyway?' Cosca gestured towards the windows, flecked and spotted with frozen blood. 'The Gurkish are coming, remember? If you've scores to settle, get them settled now, before our Kantic friends tear up all the bills. When plans fail, swift action must serve, eh, Superior?' He reached behind his head, unbuckled his mask, and let it drop to the floor. 'Time to laugh in your enemy's face! To risk all on one final throw! You can pick up the pieces afterward. If they don't go back together, well, what's the difference? Tomorrow we might all be living in a different world.'

Or dying in one. Not the way we wanted it, maybe, but he is right. Perhaps we might borrow one final shred of Colonel Glokta's dash before the game is over? 'I hope I can still count on your help?'

Cosca clapped him on the shoulder and sent a painful shudder through his twisted back. 'A noble last effort, against all the odds? Of course! Though I should mention that I usually charge double once the diabolical arts are involved.'

'How does triple sound?' *After all, Valint and Balk have deep pockets.*

Cosca's grin grew wider. 'It sounds well.'

'And your men? Are they reliable?'

'They are still waiting for four fifths of their pay. Until they receive it I would trust any one of them with my life.'

'Good. Then we are prepared.' Glokta worked his aching

foot around in his boot. *Just a little further now, my toeless beauty. Just a few shuddering steps more, and one way or another, we both can rest.* He opened his fingers and let Goyle's confession float down to the frosty floor. 'To the University, then! His Eminence has never liked to be kept waiting.'

Open the Box

Logen could feel the doubt in the men around him, could see the worry on their faces, in the way they held their weapons, and he didn't blame them. A man can be fearless on his own doorstep, against enemies he understands, but take him long miles over the salty sea to strange places he never dreamed of, he'll take fright at every empty doorway. And there were an awful lot of those, now.

The city of white towers, where Logen had hurried after the First of the Magi, amazed at the scale of the buildings, the strangeness of the people, the sheer quantity of both, had become a maze of blackened ruins. They crept down empty streets, lined with the outsize skeletons of burned-out houses, charred rafters stabbing at the sky. They crept across empty squares, scattered with rubble and dusted with ash. Always the sounds of battle echoed, ghostly – near, far, all around them.

It was as if they crept through hell.

'How d'you fight in this?' whispered the Dogman.

Logen wished he had an answer. Fighting in forests, in mountains, in valleys, they'd done it all a hundred times, and knew the rules, but this? His eyes flickered nervously over the gaping windows and doorways, the piles of fallen stones. So many places for an enemy to hide.

All Logen could do was aim at the House of the Maker and hope for the best. What would happen when they got there, he wasn't sure, but it seemed a safe bet there'd be blood involved. Nothing that would do anyone the slightest good, most likely, but the fact was he'd said go, and the one thing a leader can't do is change his mind.

The clamour of fighting was getting louder, now, and louder. The stink of smoke and anger was picking at his nose, scratching at his throat. The scored metal of the Maker's sword was slippery in his sweaty palm. He crept low to the ground, over a heap of rubble and along beside a shattered wall, his hand held flat behind him to say go careful. He eased up to the edge, and peered around it.

The Agriont rose up just ahead, great walls and towers black against the white sky, a second set reflected in the moat below. A lot of men were gathered near the water, crowded up and down the cobbled space as far as Logen could see. It didn't take a sharp mind to realise they were Gurkish. Arrows flitted up towards the battlements, bolts flitted back down, spinning from the cobbles, sticking wobbling into wooden screens.

Not thirty strides away they'd drawn up a line, facing into the city. A good, clean line, bristling with spears, set out on either side of a tall standard, golden letters twinkling on it. A tough-looking line of hard men, well armed and well armoured, nothing like the rubbish they'd faced outside the walls. Logen didn't reckon shouting was going to get this lot moving anywhere. Except straight at him, maybe.

'Whoa,' muttered the Dogman as he crept up. A few more Northmen followed him, spreading out in the mouth of the street, staring stupidly around.

Logen waved an arm at them. 'Might be best if we stay out of sight for the—'

An officer in the midst of the Gurkish line barked in his harsh tongue, pointed towards them with his curved sword. Armour rattled as the men set their spears.

'Ah, shit,' hissed Logen. They came forward, fast, but organised. A mass of them, and bristling with bright, sharp, deadly metal.

There are only three choices when you get charged. Run away, stand, or charge yourself. Running away isn't usually a bad option, but given the way the rest of the boys were feeling, if they ran they wouldn't stop running until they fell in the sea. If they stood, all in a puzzled mess from coming through the city, the chances were good they'd break, and that would leave some dead and do nothing for the rest. Which left one choice, and that's no choice at all.

Two charges in one day. Shitty luck, that, but there was no use crying about it. You have to be realistic about these things. Logen started running. Not the way he wanted to, but forward, out from the buildings and across the cobbles towards the moat. He didn't give too much thought to whether anyone was following. He was too busy screaming and waving his sword around. The first into the killing, just like in the old days. A fitting end for the Bloody-Nine. Be a good song, maybe, if anyone could be bothered finding a tune for it. He gritted his teeth, waiting for the terrible impact.

Then a crowd of Union soldiers came pouring from the buildings on the left, shouting like madmen themselves. The Gurkish charge faltered, their line began to break up, spears swinging wildly as men turned to face the sudden threat. An unexpected bonus, and no mistake.

The Union crashed into the end of the line. Men screeched and bellowed, metal shrieked on metal, weapons flashed, bodies dropped, and Logen fell into the midst of it. He slid past a wobbling spear, slashed at a Gurkish soldier. He missed and hit another, sent him screaming, blood bubbling down chain-mail. He rammed into a third with his shoulder and flung him on his back, stomped on the side of his jaw and felt it crunch under his boot.

The Gurkish officer who'd led the charge was only a stride away, his sword ready. Logen heard a bow string behind and an arrow took the officer near the collar bone. He dragged in a shuddering breath to scream, half spinning round. Logen chopped a deep gash through his back-plate, spots of blood jumping. Men crunched into the remains of the line around him. A spear shaft bent up and shattered sending splinters flying in Logen's face. Someone roared right next to him and made his ear buzz. He jerked his head away to see a Carl throw a desperate hand up, a curved sword sliced into it and sent a thumb spinning. Logen hacked the Gurkish soldier who'd swung it in the face, the heavy blade of the Maker's sword catching him across the cheek and splitting his skull wide.

A spear flashed at him. Logen tried to turn sideways, gasped as the point slid through his shirt and down his right side, leaving a cold line under his ribs. The man who held it stumbled on towards him, moving too quick to stop. Logen stabbed him right through, just under his breastplate, ended up blinking in his face. A Union soldier with a patchy ginger beard on his cheeks.

The man frowned, puzzled at seeing another white face. 'Wha . . .' he croaked, clutching at him. Logen tore away, one hand pressed to his side. It was wet there. He wondered if the spear had nicked him or run him right through. He wondered if it had killed him already, and he had just a last few bloody moments left.

Then something hit him on the back of his head and he was reeling, bellowing, not knowing what was happening. His limbs were made of mud. The world wobbled about, full of flying dirt and flying edges. He hacked at something, kicked at something else. He grappled with someone, snarling, tore his hand free and fumbled out a knife, stabbed at a neck, black blood flowing. The sounds of battle roared and hummed in his ears. A man staggered past with part of his face hanging off. Logen could see right inside his mangled mouth from the side, bits of teeth falling out.

The cut down his side burned, and burned, and sucked his breath out. The knock on his head made the pulse pound in his skull, made the blurry world slide from side to side. His mouth was full of the salt metal taste of blood. He felt a touch on his shoulder and lurched around, teeth bared, fingers tight round the grip of the Maker's blade.

Dogman let go of him and held up his hands. 'It's me! It's me!'

Logen saw who it was. But it wasn't his hand that held the sword, now, and the Bloody-Nine saw only work that needed doing.

*

What a curious flock this crippled shepherd has acquired. Two dozen fake Practicals followed Glokta through the deserted lanes of the Agriont, Nicomo Cosca, infamous soldier of fortune, swaggering at their head. *My hopes all entrusted to the world's least trustworthy man.* One of them dragged the bound and gagged Superior Goyle stumbling along by a rope. *Like an unwilling dog being taken for a walk.* Ardee West shuffled in their midst, her white dress stained with the filth of the sewers and the blood of several men, her face stained with darkening bruises and a haunted slackness. *No doubt the result of the several horrors she has already witnessed today. All capering through the Agriont after the Inquisition's only crippled Superior. A merry dance to hell, accompanied by the sounds of distant battle.*

He lurched to a sudden halt. An archway beside him led through into the Square of Marshals and, for some reason beyond his comprehension, the whole wide space had been covered with sawdust. In the middle of that yellow-white expanse, perfectly recognisable even over this distance, the First of the Magi stood, waiting. Beside him was the dark-skinned woman who had nearly drowned Glokta in his bath. *My two favourite people in all the world, I do declare.*

'Bayaz,' hissed Glokta.

'No time for that.' Cosca caught him by the elbow and pulled him away, and the First of the Magi and his sullen companion passed out of view. Glokta limped on, down the narrow lane, winced as he turned a corner, and found himself staring directly into the face of his old acquaintance Jezal dan Luthar. *Or, should I say, the High King of the Union. I am painfully honoured.*

'Your Majesty,' he said, lowering his head and causing a particularly unpleasant stabbing through his neck. Cosca, just appearing beside him, gave an extravagant bow, reaching for his cap to sweep it from his head. It was gone. He shrugged his shoulders apologetically, and tugged at his greasy forelock.

Luthar frowned at him, and at each member of his strange group as they appeared. Someone seemed to be lurking at the back of the royal entourage. A robe of black and gold in amongst all that polished steel. *Could that be . . . our old friend the High Justice? But surely he is in frozen pieces—* Then Ardee shuffled around the corner.

Luthar's eyes went wide. 'Ardee . . .'

'Jezal . . .' She looked every bit as amazed as he did. 'I mean—'

And the air was ripped apart by a colossal explosion.

The Middleway was not what it used to be.

West and his staff rode northwards in stunned silence. Their horses' hooves tapped at the cracked road. A sorry bird cheeped from the bare rafters of a burned-out house. Someone in a side street squealed for help. From the west the vague sounds of fighting still echoed, like the noise of a distant sporting event, but one with no winners. Fire had swept through the centre of the city, turning whole swathes of buildings to blackened shells, the trees to grey claws, the gardens to patches of withered slime. Corpses were the only addition. Corpses of every size and description.

The Four Corners was a slaughter-yard, scattered with all the ugly garbage of war, bounded by the ruined remains of some of Adua's finest buildings. Near at hand, the wounded were laid out in long rows on the dusty ground, coughing, groaning, calling for water, bloody surgeons moving helplessly among them.

A few grim soldiers were already piling the Gurkish dead into formless heaps, masses of tangled arms, legs, faces. They were watched over by a tall man with his hands clenched behind his back. General Kroy, always quick to put things in order. His black uniform was smudged with grey ash, one torn sleeve flapping around his wrist. The fighting must have been savage indeed to make a mark on his perfect presentation, but his salute was unaffected. It could not have been more impeccable if they stood on a parade ground.

'Progress, General?'

'Bitter fighting through the central district, Lord Marshal! Our cavalry broke through this morning and we took them by surprise. Then they counterattacked while we were waiting for the foot. I swear, this weary patch of ground has changed hands a dozen times. But we have the Four Corners, now! They're fighting hard for every stride, but we're driving them back towards Arnault's wall. Look at that, now!' He pointed to a pair of Gurkish standards leaning against a length of crumbling masonry, their golden symbols gleaming in the midst of that drab destruction. 'They'll make a fine centrepiece to anyone's living room, eh, sir?'

West could not stop his eyes wandering down to a group of groaning wounded lolling against the wall below. 'I wish you joy of them. The Agriont?'

'The news is less good there, I'm afraid. We're pushing them hard, but the Gurkish are up in numbers. They still have the citadel entirely surrounded.'

'Push harder, General!'

Kroy snapped out another salute. 'Yes, sir, we'll break them, don't you worry. Might I ask how General Poulder is doing with the docks?'

'The docks are back in our hands, but General Poulder . . . is dead.'

There was a pause. 'Dead?' Kroy's face had turned deathly pale. 'But how did he—'

There was a rumble, like thunder in the distance, and the horses shied, pawed at the ground. West's face, and Kroy's, and the faces of their officers, all turned as one to the north. There, over the tops of the blackened ruins at the edge of the square, a great mass of dust was rising high above the Agriont.

The bright world spun and throbbed, full of the beautiful song of battle, the wonderful taste of blood, the fine and fruitful stink of death. In the midst of it, no further than arms' length away, a small man stood, watching him.

To come so close to the Bloody-Nine? To ask for death as surely as to step into the searing fire. To beg for death. To demand it.

Something about his pointed teeth seemed familiar. A faint

memory, from long ago. But the Bloody-Nine pushed it away, shook it off, sunk it in the bottomless sea. It meant nothing to him who men were, or what they had done. He was the Great Leveller, and all men were equal before him. His only care was to turn the living into the dead, and it was past time for the good work to begin. He raised the sword.

The earth shook.

He stumbled, and a great noise washed over him, tore between the dead men and the living, split the world in half. He felt it knock something loose inside his skull. He snarled as he righted himself, lifted the blade high . . .

Except the arm would not move.

'Bastard . . .' snarled the Bloody-Nine, but the flames were all burned out. It was Logen who turned towards the noise.

A vast cloud of grey smoke was rising up from the wall of the Agriont a few hundred strides away. Spinning specks flew up high, high above it leaving arching trails of brown dust in the sky, like the tentacles of some vast sea-monster. One seemed to reach its peak just above them. Logen watched it fall. It had looked like a pebble at first. As it tumbled slowly down he realised it was a chunk of masonry the size of a cart.

'Shit,' said Grim. There was nothing else to say. It crashed through the side of a building right in the midst of the fight. The whole house burst apart, flinging broken bodies in every direction. A broken timber whirred past the Dogman and splashed into the moat. Specks of grit nipped at the back of Logen's head as he flung himself to the ground.

Choking dirt billowed out across the road. He retched, one hand over his face. He wobbled up to standing, the dusty world lurching around him, using his sword as a crutch, ears still ringing from the noise, not sure who he was, let alone where.

The bones had gone right out of the battle by the moat. Men coughed, stared, wandered in the gloom. There were a lot of bodies, Northmen, Gurkish, Union, all mixed up together. Logen saw a dark-skinned man staring at him, blood running down his dusty face from a cut above one eye.

Logen lifted his sword, gave a throaty roar, tried to charge and ended up staggering sideways and nearly falling over. The Gurkish soldier dropped his spear and ran off into the murk.

There was a second deafening detonation, this one even closer, off to the west. A sudden blast of wind ripped at Jezal's hair, nipped at his eyes. Swords rang from sheaths. Men stared up, faces slack with shock.

'We must go,' piped Gorst, taking a firm grip on Jezal's elbow.

Glokta and his henchmen were already making off down a cobbled lane, as quickly as the Superior could limp. Ardee gave one brief look over her shoulder, eyes wide.

'Wait . . .' Seeing her like that had given Jezal a sudden and painful rush of longing. The idea of her in the thrall of that disgusting cripple was almost too much to bear. But Gorst was having none of it.

'The palace, your Majesty.' He ushered Jezal away towards the park without a backward glance, the rest of the royal bodyguard clattering after. Fragments of stone began to click off the roofs around them, to bounce from the road, to ping from the armour of the Knights of the Body.

'They are coming,' muttered Marovia, staring grimly off towards the Square of Marshals.

Ferro squatted, hands held over her head, the monstrous echoes still booming from the high white walls. A stone the size of a man's head fell out of the sky and burst apart on the ground a few strides away, black gravel scattering across the pale sawdust. A boulder ten times as big crashed through the roof of a building, sent glass tinkling from shattered windows. Dust billowed out from the streets and into the square in grey clouds. Gradually the noise faded. The man-made hailstorm rattled to a stop, and there was a pregnant silence.

'What now?' she growled at Bayaz.

'Now they will come.' There was a crash somewhere in the streets, the sound of men shouting, then a long scream suddenly cut off. He turned towards her, his jaw working nervously. 'Once we begin, do not move from the spot. Not a hair. The circles have been carefully—'

'Keep your mind on your own part, Magus.'

'Then I will. Open the box, Ferro.'

She stood, frowning, her fingertips rubbing at her thumbs. Once it was opened, there would be no going back, she felt it.

'Now!' snapped Bayaz. 'Now, if you want your vengeance!'

'Sssss.' But the time for going back was far behind her. She squatted down, laying her hand on the cool metal of the lid. A dark path was the only choice, and always had been. She found the hidden catch and pressed it in. The box swung silently open, and that strange thrill seeped, then flowed, then poured out over her and made the air catch in her throat.

The Seed lay inside, nestling on its metal coils, a dull, grey, unremarkable lump. She closed her fingers round it. Lead-heavy and ice-cold, she lifted it from the box.

'Good.' But Bayaz was wincing as he watched her, face twisted with fear and disgust. She held it out towards him and he flinched back. There were beads of sweat across his forehead. 'Come no closer!'

Ferro slammed the box shut. Two Union guards, clad in full armour, were backing into the square, heavy swords in their fists. There was a fear in the way they moved, as if they were retreating from an army. But only one man rounded the corner. A man in white armour, worked with designs of shining metal. His dark face was young, and smooth, and beautiful, but his eyes seemed old. Ferro had seen such a face before, in the wastelands near Dagoska.

An Eater.

The two guards came at him together, one shouting a shrill battle-cry. The Eater shrugged effortlessly around their swords, came forward in a sudden blur, caught one of the Union men with a careless flick of his open hand. There was a hollow clang as it caved in his shield and breastplate both, lifted him flailing into the air. He crunched down some twenty strides from where he had been standing, rolled over and over leaving dark marks in the pale sawdust. He flopped to rest not far from Ferro, coughed out a long spatter of blood and was still.

The other guard backed away. The Eater looked at him, a sadness on his perfect face. The air around him shimmered, briefly, the man's sword clattered down, he gave a long squeal and clutched at his head. It burst apart, showering fragments of skull and flesh across the walls of the white building beside him. The headless corpse slumped to the ground. There was a pause.

'Welcome to the Agriont!' shouted Bayaz.

Ferro's eyes were drawn up by a flash of movement. High above, a figure in white armour dashed across a roof. They made an impossible leap across the wide gap to the next building and vanished from sight. In the street below a woman flowed out of the shadows and into the square, dressed in glittering chain-mail. Her hips swayed as she sauntered forwards, a happy smile on her flawless face, a long spear carried loose in one hand. Ferro swallowed, shifted her fist around the Seed, gripping it tight.

Part of a wall collapsed behind her, blocks of stone tumbling out across the square. A huge man stepped through the ragged gap, a great length of wood in his hands, studded with black iron, his armour and his long beard coated in dust. Two others followed, a man and a woman, all with the same smooth skin, the same young faces and the same old, black eyes. Ferro scowled round at them as she slid her sword out, the cold metal glinting. Useless, maybe, but holding it was some kind of comfort.

'Welcome to you all!' called Bayaz. 'I have been waiting for you, Mamun!'

The first of the Eaters frowned as he stepped carefully over the headless corpse. 'And we for you.' White shapes flitted from the roofs of the buildings, thumped down into the square in crouches, and stood tall. Four of them, one to each corner. 'Where is that creeping shadow, Yulwei?'

'He could not be with us.'

'Zacharus?'

553

'Mired in the ruined west, trying to heal a corpse with a bandage.'

'Cawneil?'

'Too much in love with what she used to be to spare a thought for what comes.'

'You are left all alone, then, in the end, apart from this.' Mamun turned his empty gaze on Ferro. 'She is a strange one.'

'She is, and exceptionally difficult, but not without resources.' Ferro scowled, and said nothing. If anything needed saying, she could talk with her sword. 'Ah, well.' Bayaz shrugged. 'I have always found myself my own best council.'

'What choice have you? You destroyed your own order with your pride, and your arrogance, and your hunger for power.' More figures stepped from doorways round the square, strolled unhurried from the streets. Some strutted like lords. Some held hands like lovers. 'Power is all you ever cared for, and you are left without even that. The First of the Magi, and the last.'

'So it would seem. Does that not please you?'

'I take no pleasure in this, Bayaz. This is what must be done.'

'Ah. A righteous battle? A holy duty? A crusade, perhaps? Will God smile on your methods, do you think?'

Mamun shrugged. 'God smiles on results.' More figures in white armour spilled into the square and spread out around its edge. They moved with careless grace, with effortless strength, with bottomless arrogance. Ferro frowned around at them, the Seed clutched tight at one hip, her sword at the other.

'If you have a plan,' she hissed. 'Now might be the time.'

But the First of the Magi only watched as they were surrounded, the muscles twitching on the side of his face, his hands clenching and unclenching by his sides. 'A shame that Khalul himself could not pay a visit, but you have brought some friends with you, I see.'

'One hundred, as I promised. Some few have other tasks about the city. They send their regrets. But most of us are here for you. More than enough.' The Eaters were still. They stood facing inwards, spread out in a great ring with the First of the Magi at their centre. Ferro Maljinn felt no fear, of course.

But these were poor odds.

'Answer me one thing,' called Mamun, 'since we are come to the end. Why did you kill Juvens?'

'Juvens? Ha! He thought to make the world a better place with smiles and good intentions. Good intentions get you nothing, and the world does not improve without a fight. I say I killed no one.' Bayaz looked sideways at Ferro. His eyes were feverish bright, now, his scalp glistened with sweat. 'But what does it matter who killed who a thousand years ago? What matters is who dies today.'

'True. Now, at last, you will be judged.' Slowly, very slowly, the circle of Eaters began to contract, stepping gently forward as one, drawing softly inwards.

The First of the Magi gave a grim smile. 'Oh, there will be a judgement here, Mamun, on that you can depend. The magic has drained from the world. My Art is a shadow of what it was. But you forgot, while you were gorging yourselves on human meat, that knowledge is the root of power. High Art I learned from Juvens. Making I took from Kanedias.'

'You will need more than that to defeat us.'

'Of course. For that I need some darker medicine.'

The air around Bayaz' shoulders shimmered. The Eaters paused, some of them raised their arms in front of their faces. Ferro narrowed her eyes, but there was only the gentlest breath of wind. A subtle breeze, that washed out from the First of the Magi in a wave, that lifted the sawdust from the stones and carried it out in a white cloud to the very edge of the Square of Marshals.

Mamun looked down, and frowned. Set into the stone beneath his feet, metal shone dully in the thin sunlight. Circles, and lines, and symbols, and circles within circles, covering the entire wide space in a single vast design.

'Eleven wards, and eleven wards reversed,' said Bayaz. 'Iron. Quenched in salt water. An improvement suggested by Kanedias' researches. Glustrod used raw salt. That was his mistake.'

Mamun looked up, the icy calmness vanished from his face.

'You cannot mean . . .' His black eyes flickered to Ferro, then down to her hand, clenched tight around the Seed. 'No! The First Law—'

'The First Law?' The Magus showed his teeth. 'Rules are for children. This is war, and in war the only crime is to lose. The word of Euz?' Bayaz' lip curled. 'Hah! Let him come forth and stop me!'

'Enough!' One of the Eaters leaped forward, flashing across the metal circles towards their centre. Ferro gasped as the stone in her hand turned suddenly, terribly cold. The air about Bayaz twisted, danced, as though he was reflected in a rippling pool.

The Eater sprang up, mouth open, the bright blade of his sword shining. Then he was gone. So were two others behind him. A long spray of blood was smeared across the ground where one of them had been standing. Ferro's eyes followed it, growing wider and wider. Her mouth fell open.

The building that had stood behind them had a giant, gaping hole torn out of it from ground to dizzy roof. A great canyon lined with broken stone and hanging plaster, with splintered spars and dangling glass. Dust showered from the shattered edges and into the yawning hole below. A flock of torn papers fluttered down through the empty air. From out of the carnage a thin and agonised screaming came. A sobbing. A screech of pain. Many voices. The voices of those who had been using that building as a refuge.

Poor luck for them.

Bayaz' mouth slowly curled up into a smile. 'It works,' he breathed.

Dark Paths

Jezal hurried through the tall archway and into the gardens of the palace, his Knights around him. It was remarkable that High Justice Marovia had been able to keep pace with them on their dash through the Agriont, but the old man scarcely seemed out of breath. 'Seal the gates!' he bellowed. 'The gates!'

The huge doors were heaved shut, two beams the thickness of ships' masts swung into position behind them. Jezal allowed himself to breathe a little easier. There was a reassuring feeling to the weight of those gates, to the height and thickness of the walls of the palace compound, to the sizeable host of well trained and armoured men defending it.

Marovia laid his hand gently on Jezal's shoulder, began to steer him down the cobbled path towards the nearest door into the palace. 'We should find the safest place possible, your Majesty—'

Jezal shook him off. 'Would you lock me in my bedroom? Or should I hide in the cellar? I will remain here, and co-ordinate the defence of—'

A long, blood-chilling scream came from the other side of the wall and echoed around the bare gardens. It was as if that shriek made a hole in him through which all confidence quickly leaked away. The gates rattled slightly against the mighty beams, and the notion of hiding in the cellar gained appeal with astonishing speed.

'A line!' barked Gorst's shrill voice. 'To the King!' A wall of heavily-armoured men clustered instantly around Jezal, swords drawn, shields raised. Others kneeled in front, pulling bolts from quivers, turning the cranks of their heavy flatbows. All eyes were fixed on the mighty double doors. They rattled gently again, wobbled slightly.

'Down there!' someone called from the walls above. 'Down—' There was a screech and an armoured man plummeted from the battlements and crunched into the turf. His body trembled, then fell limp.

'How . . .' someone muttered.

A white figure dived from the walls, gracefully turned over in the air and thudded onto the pathway in front of them. It stood up. A dark-skinned man, arrayed in armour of white and gold, his face smooth as a boy's. He held a spear of dark wood with a long, curved blade in one hand. Jezal stared at him, and he looked back, expressionless. There was something in those black eyes, or rather there was something missing from them. Jezal knew that this was not a man. It was an Eater. A breaker of the Second Law. One of Khalul's Hundred Words, come to settle ancient scores with the First of the Magi. It seemed, rather unfairly, that their score had somehow come to include Jezal. The Eater raised one hand, as if in blessing.

'May God admit us all to heaven.'

'Loose!' squealed Gorst. Flatbows rattled and popped. A couple of bolts glanced off the Eater's armour, a couple more thudded into flesh, one under the breastplate, another in the shoulder. One bolt caught it right through the face, the flights sticking out just below the eye. Any man should have dropped dead before them. The Eater sprang forwards with shocking speed.

One of the Knights raised his flatbow in a feeble attempt to defend himself. The spear split it in two and sliced him cleanly in half at the belly, chopped into another man with an echoing clang and sent him tumbling through the air into a tree ten strides away. Fragments of dented armour and splintered wood flew. The first Knight made a strange whistling sound as his top half tumbled to the path, showering his dumbstruck comrades with gore.

Jezal was jostled back, could see nothing more than flashes of movement between his bodyguards. He heard screams and

558

groans, clashing metal, saw swords glinting, gouts of blood flying. An armoured body flew into the air, flopping like a rag-doll, crunched into a wall on the other side of the gardens.

The bodies swayed apart. The Eater was surrounded, swinging its spear in blinding circles. One ripped into a man's shoulder and knocked him shrieking to the ground, the shaft splintering with the force of the blow and the blade spinning away edge-first into the turf. A Knight charged in from behind and spitted the Eater through the back, the glittering point of his halberd sliding bloodless through the white armour on its chest. Another Knight struck its arm off with an axe and dust showered from the stump. The Eater screeched, hit him across the chest with a backhanded blow that crushed his breastplate and drove him sighing into the dirt.

A sword-cut squealed through the white armour, sending dust flying up as if from a beaten carpet. Jezal stared dumbly as the Eater reeled towards him. Gorst shoved him out of the way, growling as he brought his long steel round to hack deep into the Eater's neck with a meaty thud. It flailed, silently, its head hanging off by a flap of gristle, brown dust pouring from its yawning wounds. It clutched at Gorst with its remaining hand and he staggered, face twisted with pain, sank to his knees as it wrenched his arm around.

'Here's heaven, bastard!' Jezal's sword chopped through the last bit of neck and the Eater's head dropped onto the grass. It let go of Gorst and he clutched at his mangled forearm, the shape of the Eater's hand dented into his heavy armour. The headless body slowly toppled over. 'Cursed thing!' Jezal took one step and kicked its head across the garden, watched it bounce and roll into a flower bed leaving a trail of dust through the grass. Three men stood over the body, their heavy breath echoing from inside their helmets, their swords flashing in the sun as they hacked it into pieces. Its fingers were still twitching.

'They're made of dust,' someone whispered.

Marovia frowned at the remains. 'Some are. Some bleed. Each one is different. We should get inside the palace!' he shouted as he hurried across the gardens. 'There will be more of them!'

'More?' Twelve Knights of the Body lay dead. Jezal swallowed as he counted their broken and bloody, dented and battered corpses. The best men the Union had to offer, scattered around the palace gardens like heaps of scrap metal among the brown leaves. 'More? But how do we—?' The gates shuddered. Jezal's head snapped towards them, the blind courage of the fight fading quickly and sick panic rushing in behind it.

'This way!' roared Marovia, holding open a door and beckoning desperately. It was not as though there were other choices. Jezal rushed towards him, caught one gilded boot with the other three steps in, and went sprawling painfully on his face. There was a cracking, a tearing, a squealing of wood and metal behind. He clawed his way onto his back to see the gates torn apart in a cloud of flying timber. Broken planks spun through the air, bent nails pinged from the pathways, splinters settled gently across the lawns.

A woman sauntered through the open gateway, the air still shimmering gently around her tall, thin body. A pale woman with long, golden hair. Another walked beside her, just the same except that her left side was spattered from head to toe with red blood. Two women, happy smiles on their beautiful, perfect, identical faces. One of them slapped a Knight Herald across the head as he charged up, tearing his winged helmet from his shattered skull and sending it spinning high into the air. The other turned her black, empty eyes on Jezal. He struggled up and ran, wheezing with fear, slid through the door beside Marovia and into the shadowy hallway, lined with ancient arms and armour.

Gorst and a few Knights of the Body tumbled through after him. Over their shoulders the one-sided battle in the gardens continued. A man raised a flatbow only to explode in a shower of blood. An armoured corpse crashed into a Knight just as he turned to run, sent him hurtling sideways through a window, sword spinning from his hand. Another ran towards them, arms pumping, tumbled down a few strides away, thrashing on the ground, flames spurting from the joints in his armour.

'Help me!' someone wailed. 'Help me! Help—' Gorst slammed the heavy doors shut with his one good arm, one of his fellows dropped the thick bar into the brackets. They tore old polearms from the walls, one with a tattered battle-flag attached, and started wedging them in the doorway.

Jezal was already backing away, cold sweat tickling at his skin under his armour, gripping tight to the hilt of his sword more for reassurance than defence. His drastically denuded entourage stumbled back with him – Gorst, Marovia, and but five others, their gasping, horrified breath echoing in the dim corridor, all staring towards the door.

'The last gate did not hold them,' Jezal whispered. 'Why should this one?'

No one answered.

'Keep your wits about you, gentlemen,' said Glokta. 'The door, please.'

The fat mercenary took his axe to the front gate of the University. Splinters flew. It wobbled at the first blow, shuddered at the second, tore open at the third. The one-eyed dwarf slithered through, a knife in either hand, closely followed by Cosca, sword drawn.

'Clear,' came his Styrian drawl from inside, 'if fusty.'

'Excellent.' Glokta looked at Ardee. 'It might be best if you stayed towards the back.'

She gave an exhausted nod. 'I was thinking the same.'

He limped painfully over the threshold, black-clad mercenaries pouring through the doorway behind him, the last of them dragging Goyle reluctantly by his bandaged wrists. *And along the very paths I took the first time I visited this heap of dust, so many months ago. Before the vote. Before Dagoska, even. How lovely to be back . . .*

Down the dark hallway, past the dirty paintings of forgotten Adepti, tortured floorboards groaning under the boots of the mercenaries. Glokta lurched out into the wide dining hall.

The freak-show of Practicals was scattered about the dim chamber just as it had been when he last visited. The two identical men from Suljuk, with their curved swords. The tall, thin one, the dark men with their axes, the vast Northman with the ruined face. *And so on.* A good score of them in all. *Have they been sitting here all this time, I wonder, just being menacing to each other?*

Vitari was already up from her chair. 'I thought I told you to keep away from here, cripple.'

'I tried, indeed I did, but I could not banish the memory of your smile.'

'Ho, ho, Shylo!' Cosca strolled out from the hallway, twiddling at the waxed ends of his moustache with one hand, sword drawn in the other.

'Cosca! Don't you ever die?' Vitari let a cross-shaped knife tumble from her hand to clatter across the boards on the end of a long chain. 'Seems a day for men I hoped I'd seen the last of.' Her Practicals spread out around her, swords sliding from sheaths, axes, maces, spears scraping off the table. The mercenaries clomped into the hall, their own weapons at the ready. Glokta cleared his throat. 'I think it would be better for all concerned if we could discuss this like civilised—'

'You see anyone civilised?' snarled Vitari.

A fair point. One Practical sprang up on the table making the cutlery jump. The one-handed mercenary waved his hook in the air. The two heavily-armed groups edged towards each other. It looked very much as if Cosca and his hired hands would be earning their pay. *A merry bloodbath I daresay it will be, and the outcome of a bloodbath is notoriously hard to predict. All in all, I would rather not take the gamble.*

'A shame about your children! A shame for them, that there's no one civilised around!'

Vitari's orange eyebrows drew furiously inwards. 'They're far away!'

'Oh, I'm afraid not. Two girls and a boy? Beautiful, flaming red hair, just like their mother's?' *Which gate would they go through? The Gurkish came from the west, so . . .* 'They were stopped at the east gate, and taken into custody.' Glokta stuck out his bottom lip. 'Protective custody. These are dangerous times for children to be wandering the streets, you know.'

Even with her mask on Glokta could see her horror. 'When?' she hissed.

When would a loving mother send her children to safety? 'Why, the very day the Gurkish arrived, of course, you know that.' The way her eyes widened told him that he had guessed right. *Now to twist the blade.* 'Don't worry though, they're tucked up safe. Practical Severard is acting as nurse. But if I don't come back . . .'

'You wouldn't hurt them.'

'What is it with everyone today? Lines I won't cross? People I won't hurt?' Glokta showed his most revolting leer. 'Children? Hope, and prospects, and all that happy life ahead of them? I despise the little bastards!' He shrugged his twisted shoulders. 'But perhaps you know me better. If you're keen to play dice with your children's lives, I suppose we can find out. Or we could reach an understanding, as we did in Dagoska.'

'Shit on this,' growled one of the Practicals, hefting his axe and taking a step forward. *And the atmosphere of violence lurches another dizzy step towards the brink . . .*

Vitari shoved out her open hand. 'Don't move.'

'You've got children, so what? Means nothing to me. It'll mean nothing to Sult eeeeeee—' There was a flash of metal, the jingling of a chain, and the Practical staggered forward, blood pouring from his opened throat.

Vitari's cross-shaped knife slapped back into her palm and her eyes flicked back to Glokta. 'An understanding?'

'Exactly. You stay here. We go past. You didn't see nothing, as they say in the older parts of town. You know well enough that you can't trust Sult. He left you to the dogs in Dagoska, didn't he? And he's all done, anyway. The Gurkish are knocking at the door. Time we tried something new, don't you think?'

Vitari's mask shifted as she worked her mouth. *Thinking,*

thinking. The eyes of her killers sparkled, the blades of their weapons glinted. *Don't call the bluff, bitch, don't you dare . . .*

'Alright!' She gestured with her arm and the Practicals edged unhappily back, still glaring at the mercenaries across the room. Vitari nodded her spiky head towards a doorway at the end of the chamber. 'Down that hall, down the stairs at the end, and there's a door. A door with black iron rivets.'

'Excellent.' *A few words can be more effective than a lot of blades, even in such times as these.* Glokta began to hobble away, Cosca and his men following.

Vitari frowned after them, her eyes deadly slits. 'If you so much as touch my—'

'Yes, yes.' Glokta waved his hand. 'My terror is boundless.'

There was a moment of stillness, as the remains of the gutted building settled across one side of the Square of Marshals. The Eaters stood, as shocked as Ferro, a circle of amazement. Bayaz appeared to be the only one not horrified by the scale of the destruction. His harsh chuckling echoed out and bounced back from the walls. 'It works!' he shouted.

'No!' screamed Mamun, and the Hundred Words came rushing forward.

Closer they came, the polished blades of their beautiful weapons flashing, their hungry mouths hanging open, their white teeth gleaming. Closer yet, streaming inwards with terrible speed, shrieking out a chorus of hate that made even Ferro's blood turn cold.

But Bayaz only laughed. 'Let the judgement begin!'

Ferro growled through clenched teeth as the Seed burned cold at her palm. A mighty blast of wind swept out across the square from its centre, sent Eaters tumbling like skittles, rolling and flailing. It shattered every window, ripped open every door, stripped the roofs of every building bare.

The great inlaid gates of the Lords' Round were sucked open, then torn from their hinges, careering across the square. Tons of wood, spinning over and over like sheets of paper in a gale. They carved a crazy swathe through the helpless Eaters.

They ripped white-armoured bodies apart, sending parts of limbs flying, blood and dust going up in sprays and spatters.

Ferro's hand was shimmering, and half her forearm. She gasped quick breaths as the cold spread through her veins, out to every part of her, burning at her insides. The Seed blurred and trembled as if she looked at it through fast flowing water. The wind whipped at her eyes as white figures were flung through the air like toys, writhing in a storm of shattered glass, shredded wood, splintered stone. No more than a dozen of them kept their feet, reeling, clutching at the ground, shining hair streaming from their heads, straining desperately against the blast.

One of them reached for Ferro, snarling into the wind. A woman, her glittering chain-mail thrashing, her hands clawing at the screaming air. She edged closer, and closer. A smooth, proud face, stamped with contempt.

Like the faces of the Eaters who had come for her near Dagoska. Like the faces of the slavers who had stolen her life from her. Like the face of Uthman-ul-Dosht, who had smiled at her anger and her helplessness.

Ferro's shriek of fury merged with the shrieking of the wind. She had not known that she could swing a sword so hard. The look of shock only just had time to form on the Eater's perfect face before the curved blade sliced through her outstretched arm and took her head from her shoulders. The corpse was plucked flopping away, dust flying from its gaping wounds.

The air was full of flashing shapes. Ferro stood frozen as debris whirred past her. A beam crashed through a struggling Eater's chest and carried it screaming away, high into the air, spitted like a locust on a skewer. Another burst suddenly apart in a cloud of blood and flesh, the remains sucked spiralling up into the trembling sky.

The great Eater with the beard struggled forward, lifting his huge club above his head, bellowing words no one could hear. Through the pulsing, twisting air Ferro saw Bayaz raise one eyebrow at him, saw his lips make one word.

'Burn.'

For a single moment he blazed as brightly as a star, the image of him stamped white into Ferro's eyes. Then his blackened bones were snatched away into the storm.

Only Mamun remained. He strained forwards, dragging his feet across the stone, across the iron, inch by desperate inch towards Bayaz. One armoured greave tore from his leg and flew back spinning through the maddened air, then a plate from his shoulder followed it. Torn cloth flapped. The skin on his snarling face began to ripple and stretch.

'No!' One clutching, clawing arm stretched desperately out towards the First of the Magi, fingertips straining.

'Yes,' said Bayaz, the air around his smiling face trembling like the air above the desert. The nails tore from Mamun's fingers, his outstretched arm bent back, snapped, was ripped from his shoulder. Flawless skin peeled from bone, flapping like sailcloth in a squall, brown dust flying out of his torn body like a sandstorm over the dunes.

He was dashed suddenly away, crashed through a wall near the top of one of the tall buildings. Blocks were sucked from the edges of the ragged hole he left and tumbled outwards, upwards. They joined the whipping paper, thrashing rock, spinning planks, flailing corpses that reeled through the air around the edge of the square, faster and faster, a circle of destruction that followed the iron circles on the ground. It reached now as high as the tall buildings, and now higher yet. It flayed and scoured at everything it passed, tearing up more stone, glass, wood, metal, flesh, growing darker, faster, louder and more powerful with every moment.

Over the mindless anger of the wind Ferro could just hear Bayaz' voice.

'God smiles on results.'

Dogman got up, and shook his sore head, dirt flying from his hair. There was blood running down his arm, red on white. Seemed as if the world hadn't ended after all.

Looked like it had come close, though.

Bridge and gatehouse both had disappeared. Where they'd

stood there was nothing but a great heap of broken stone and a yawning chasm carved out of the walls. That and a whole lot of dust. There were still some folk killing, but there were a lot more rolling about, choking and groaning, staggering through the rubbish, the fight all gone out of 'em. Dogman knew how they felt.

Someone was clambering up onto that mass of junk where the moat used to be, heading towards the breach. Someone with a tangled mess of hair and a long sword in one hand.

Who else but Logen Ninefingers?

'Ah, shit,' cursed Dogman. He'd got some damn fool ideas all of a sudden, had Logen, but that wasn't halfway the worst of it. There was someone following him across that bridge of rubble. Shivers, axe in hand, shield on arm, and a frown on his dirty face like a man with some dark work in mind.

'Ah, shit!'

Grim shrugged his dusty shoulders. 'Best get after 'em.'

'Aye.' Dogman jerked his thumb at Red Hat, just getting up from the ground and shaking a pile of grit off his coat. 'Get some lads together, eh?' He pointed off towards the breach with the blade of his sword. 'We're going that way.'

Damn it but he needed to piss, just like always.

Jezal backed away down the shadowy hall, hardly daring even to breathe, feeling the sweat prickle at his palms, at his neck, at the small of his back.

'What are they waiting for?' someone muttered.

There was a gentle creaking sound above. Jezal looked up towards the black rafters. 'Did you hear—'

A shape burst through the ceiling and hurtled down into the hallway in a white blur, flattening one of the Knights of the Body, her feet leaving two great dents in his breastplate, blood spraying from his visor.

She smiled up at Jezal. 'Greetings from the Prophet Khalul.'

'The Union!' roared another Knight, charging forward. One moment his sword whistled towards her. The next she was on the other side of the corridor. The blade clanged harmlessly into the stone floor and the man tottered forward. She seized him under the armpit, bent her knees slightly, and flung him shrieking through the ceiling. Broken plaster rained down as she grabbed another Knight round the neck and smashed his head into the wall with such force that he was left embedded in the shattered stonework, armoured legs dangling. Antique swords tumbled from their brackets and clattered down into the hallway around his limp corpse.

'This way!' The High Justice dragged Jezal, numb and helpless, towards a pair of gilded double doors. Gorst lifted up one heavy boot, gave them a shivering kick and sent them flying open. They burst through into the Chamber of Mirrors, cleared of the many tables that had stood there on Jezal's wedding night, an empty acre of polished tiles.

He ran for the far door, his slapping footfalls and his heaving, wheezing, horrified breath echoing out around the huge room. He saw himself running, distorted, in the mirrors far ahead of him, the mirrors to each side. A ludicrous sight. A clown-king, fleeing though his own palace, crown askew, his scarred face beaded with sweat, slack with terror and exhaustion. He skidded to a halt, almost fell over backwards in his haste to stop, Gorst nearly ploughing into his back.

One of the twins was sitting on the floor beside the far doorway, leaning back against the mirrored wall, reflected in it, as though she were leaning against her sister. She lifted up one languorous hand, daubed crimson with blood, and she waved.

Jezal spun towards the windows. Before he could even think of running one of them burst into the room. The other twin came tumbling through in a shower of glittering glass, rolled over and over across the polished floor, unfolded to her feet and slid to a stop.

She ran one long hand through her golden hair, yawned, and smacked her lips. 'Have you ever had the feeling that someone else is having all the fun?' she asked.

Reckonings

R ed Hat had been right. There was no reason for anyone to die here. No-one but the Bloody-Nine, at least. It was high time that bastard took his share of the blame.

'Still alive,' Logen whispered, 'still alive.' He crept around the corner of a white building and into the park.

He remembered this place full of people. Laughing, eating, talking. There was no laughter here now. He saw bodies scattered on the lawns. Some armoured, some not. He could hear a distant roar – far-off battle, maybe. Nothing nearer except the hissing of the wind through the bare branches and the crunching of his own footsteps in the gravel. His skin prickled as he crept towards the high wall of the palace.

The heavy doors were gone, only the twisted hinges left hanging in the archway. The gardens on the other side were full of corpses. Armoured men, all dented and bloody. There was a crowd of them on the path before the gate, crushed and broken as though they'd been smashed with a giant hammer. One was sliced clean in half, the two pieces lying in a slick of dark blood.

A man stood in the midst of all this. He had white armour on, speckled and dusted with red. A wind had blown up in the gardens, and his black hair flicked around his face, dark skin smooth and flawless as a baby's. He was frowning down at a body near his feet, but he looked up at Logen as he came through the gate. Without hatred or fear, without happiness or sadness. Without anything much.

'You are a long way from home,' he said, in Northern.

'You too.' Logen looked into that empty face. 'You an Eater?'

'To that crime I must confess.'

'We're all guilty o' something.' Logen hefted his sword in one hand. 'Shall we get to it, then?'

'I came here to kill Bayaz. No one else.'

Logen glanced round at the ruined corpses scattered across the gardens. 'How's that working out for you?'

'Once you set your mind on killing, it is hard to choose the number of the dead.'

'That is a fact. Blood gets you nothing but more blood, my father used to tell me.'

'A wise man.'

'If only I'd listened.'

'It is hard, sometimes, to know what is . . . the truth.' The Eater lifted up his bloody right hand and frowned at it. 'It is fitting that a righteous man should have . . . doubts.'

'You tell me. Can't say I know too many righteous men.'

'I once thought I did. Now I am not sure. We must fight?'

Logen took a long breath. 'Looks that way.'

'So be it.'

He came so fast there was hardly time to lift a sword, let alone swing it. Logen threw himself out of the way but still got caught in the ribs with something – elbow, knee, shoulder. It can be hard to tell when you're flopping over and over on the grass, everything tumbling around you. He tried to get up, found that he couldn't. Raising his head an inch was almost more than he could manage. Every breath was painful. He dropped back, staring up at the white sky. Maybe he should've stayed outside the walls. Maybe he should've just let the lads rest in the trees, until after it was all settled.

The tall shape of the Eater swam into his blurry vision, black against the clouds. 'I am sorry for this. I will pray for you. I will pray for us both.' He lifted up his armoured foot.

An axe chopped into his face and sent him staggering. Logen shook the light out of his head, dragged some air in. He forced himself up onto one elbow, clutching at his side. He saw a white-armoured fist flash down and crash onto Shivers' shield. It ripped a chunk out of the edge and knocked Shivers onto his knees. An arrow pinged off the Eater's shoulder-plate and he turned, one side of his head hanging bloodily open. A second shaft stuck him neatly through the neck. Grim and the Dogman stood in the archway, their bows raised.

The Eater went pounding towards them with huge strides, the wind of his passing tearing at the grass.

'Huh,' said Grim. The Eater rammed into him with an armoured elbow. He crashed into a tree ten strides away and flopped down onto the grass. The Eater raised its other arm to chop at Dogman and a Carl stabbed a spear into him, carried him thrashing backwards. More Northmen charged through the gate, crowding round, screaming and shouting, hacking with axes and swords.

Logen rolled over, crawled across the lawn and seized hold of his sword, tearing a wet handful of grass up with it. A Carl tumbled past him, broken head covered in blood. Logen squeezed his jaws together and charged, lifting his sword in both hands.

It bit into the Eater's shoulder, sheared through his armour and split him open down as far as his chest, showering blood in the Dogman's face. Same time, almost, one of the Carls caught him full in the side with a maul, smashed his other arm and left a great dent in his breastplate.

The Eater stumbled and Red Hat hacked a gash in one of his legs. He lurched to his knees, blood spilling from his wounds and running down his dented white armour, pooling on the path underneath him. He was smiling, so far as Logen could tell with half his face hanging off. 'Free,' he whispered.

Logen raised the Maker's blade and hacked his head from his shoulders.

A wind had blown up suddenly, swirling through the stained streets, hissing out of the burned-out buildings, whipping ash and dust in West's face as he rode towards the Agriont. He had to shout over it. 'How do we fare?'

'The fight's gone out of 'em!' bellowed Brint, his hair dragged sideways by another gust. 'They're in full retreat! Seems as if they were too keen to get the Agriont surrounded and they weren't ready for us! Now they're falling over each other to get away to the west. Still some fighting around Arnault's Wall, but Orso has them on the run in the Three Farms!'

West saw the familiar shape of the Tower of Chains over the top of a ruin, and he urged his horse towards it. 'Good! If we can just clear them away from the Agriont we'll have the best of it! Then we can . . .' He trailed off as they rounded the corner and could see all the way to the west gate of the citadel. Or, more accurately, where the west gate had once been.

It took him a moment to make sense of it. The Tower of Chains loomed up to one side of a monumental breach in the wall of the Agriont. The entire gatehouse had somehow been brought down, along with large sections of the wall to either side, the remains choking the moat below or distributed widely around the ruined streets in front.

The Gurkish were inside the Agriont. The very heart of the Union lay exposed.

Not far ahead, now, a formless battle was still raging before the citadel. West urged his horse closer, through the stragglers and the wounded, into the very shadow of the walls. He saw a line of kneeling flatbow-men deliver a withering volley into a crowd of Gurkish, bodies toppling. Beside him a man screamed into the wind as another tried to secure a tourniquet on the bloody stump of his leg.

Pike's face was grimmer even than usual. 'We should be further back, sir. This isn't safe.'

West ignored him. Each man had to do his part, without exception. 'We need a line formed up here! Where is General Kroy?' The Sergeant was no longer listening. His eyes had drifted upwards, his mouth dropping stupidly open. West turned around in his saddle.

A black column was rising above the western end of the citadel. It seemed at first to be made of swirling smoke, but as West gained some sense of scale he realised it was spinning matter. Masses of it. Countless tons of it. His eyes followed it upwards, higher and higher. The clouds themselves were moving, whipped round in a spiral at the centre, shifting in a slow circle above them. The fighting sputtered, as Union and Gurkish alike gaped up at the writhing pillar above the Agriont, the Tower of Chains a black finger in front of it, the House of the Maker an insignificant pin-prick behind.

Things began to rain from the sky. Small things, at first – splinters, dust, leaves, fragments of paper. Then a chunk of wood the size of a chair leg plummeted down and bounced spinning from the paving. A soldier squealed as a stone big as a fist smashed into his shoulder. Those who were not fighting were backing away, crouching to the ground, holding shields above their heads. The wind was growing more savage, clothes whipping in the storm, men stumbling against it, leaning into it, teeth gritted and eyes narrowed. The spinning pillar was growing wider, darker, faster, higher, touching the very sky. West could see specks around its edge dancing against the white clouds like swarms of midges on a summer's day.

Except that these were tumbling blocks of stone, wood, earth, metal, by some freak of nature sucked into the heavens and set flying. He did not know what was happening, or how. All he could do was stare.

'Sir!' bellowed Pike in his ear. 'Sir, we must go!' He seized hold of West's bridle. A great chunk of masonry crashed into the paving not far from them. West's horse reared up, screaming in panic. The world lurched, spun, was black, he was not sure how long for.

He was on his face, mouth full of grit. He raised his head, wobbled drunkenly up to his hands and knees, wind roaring in his ears, flying grit stinging at his face. It was dark as dusk. The air was full of tumbling rubbish. It ripped at the ground, at the buildings, at the men, huddled now like sheep, all thoughts of battle long forgotten, the living sprawled on their faces with the dead. The Tower of Chains was scoured by debris, the slates flying from its rafters, then the rafters torn away into the storm. A giant beam plummeted down and crashed into the cobbles, spun end over end, flinging corpses out of its path to slice through the wall of a house and send its roof sliding inwards.

West trembled, tears snatched away from his stinging eyes, utterly helpless. Was this how the end would come? Not covered in blood and glory at the head of a fool's charge like General Poulder. Not passing quietly in the night like Marshal Burr. Not even hooded on the scaffold for the murder of Crown Prince Ladisla.

Crushed at random by a giant piece of rubbish falling from the sky.

'Forgive me,' he whispered into the tempest.

He saw the black outline of the Tower of Chains shifting. He saw it lean outwards. Chunks of stone rained down, splashed into the churning moat. The whole vast edifice lurched, bulged, and toppled outwards, with ludicrous slowness, through the flailing storm and into the city.

It broke into monstrous sections as it fell, crashing down upon the houses, crushing cowering men like ants, throwing deadly missiles in every direction.

And that was all.

There were no buildings, now, around the space that had once been the Square of Marshals. The gushing fountains, the stately statues in the Kingsway, the palaces full of soft pinks.

All snatched away.

The gilded dome had lifted from the Lords' Round, cracked, split, and been ripped into chaff. The high wall of the Halls Martial was a ravaged ruin. The rest of the proud buildings were nothing more than shattered stumps, torn down to their very foundations. They had all melted away before Ferro's watering eyes. Dissolved into the formless mass of fury that whirled shrieking around the First of the Magi, endlessly hungry from the ground to the very heavens.

'Yes!' She could hear his delighted laughter, over the noise of the storm. 'I am greater than Juvens! I am greater than Euz himself!'

Was this vengeance? Then how much of it would make her whole? Ferro wondered dumbly how many people had been cowering in those vanished buildings. The shimmering around the Seed was swelling, up to her shoulder, then to her neck, and it engulfed her.

The world grew quiet.

Far away the destruction continued, but it was blurred now, the sounds of it came to her muffled, as if through water. Her hand was beyond cold. She was numb to the shoulder. She saw Bayaz, smiling, his arms raised. The wind ripped about them, a wall of endless movement.

But there were shapes within it.

They grew sharper even as the rest of the world grew less distinct. They gathered around the outside of the outermost circle. Shadows. Ghosts. A hungry crowd of them.

'Ferro . . .' came their whispering voices.

A storm had blown up sudden in the gardens, more sudden even than the storms in the High Places. The light had faded, then stuff had started tumbling down from the dark sky. Dogman didn't know where it was coming from and he didn't much care. He had other things more pressing to worry on.

They dragged the wounded in through a high doorway, groaning, cursing, or worst of all, saying nothing. A couple they left outside, back to the mud already. No point wasting breath on them who were far past helping.

Logen had Grim under his armpits, the Dogman had him by the boots. His face was white as chalk but for the red blood on his lips. You could see it plain on his face that it was bad, but he didn't complain any, not Harding Grim. Dogman wouldn't have believed it if he had.

They set him down on the floor, in the gloom on the other side of the door. Dogman could hear things rattling against the windows, thumping against the turf outside, clattering on the roofs above. More men were carried in – broken arms and broken legs and worse besides. Shivers came after, bloody axe in one hand and his shield-arm dangling useless.

Dogman had never seen a hallway like it. The floor was made of green stone and white stone, polished up smooth and shining bright as glass. The walls were hung with great paintings. The ceiling was crusted with flowers and leaves, carved so fine they looked almost real, except that they were made from gold, glittering in the dim light leaking through the windows.

Men bent down, tending to fellows injured, giving them water and soft words, a splint or two being fixed. Logen and Shivers just stood there, giving each other a look. Not hatred, exactly, and not respect. It was hard for the Dogman to say what it was, and he didn't much care about that either.

'What were you thinking?' he snapped. 'Pissing off on your own like that? Thought you were supposed to be chief, now! That's a poor effort, ain't it?'

Logen only stared back, eyes gleaming in the gloom. 'Got to help Ferro,' he muttered, half to himself. 'Jezal too.'

Dogman stared at him. 'Got to help who? There's real folk here in need o' help.'

'I ain't much with the wounded.'

'Only with the making of 'em! Go on then, Bloody-Nine, if you must. Get to it.'

Dogman saw Logen's face flinch when he heard that name. He backed away, one hand clamped to his side and his sword gripped bloody in the other. Then he turned and limped off down the glittering hallway.

'Hurts,' said Grim, as Dogman squatted down next to him.

'Where?'

He gave a bloody smile. 'Everywhere.'

'Right, well . . .' Dogman pulled his shirt up. One side of his chest was caved in, a great blue-black bruise spread out all across it like a tar-stain. He could hardly believe a man could still be breathing with a wound like that. 'Ah . . .' he muttered, not having a clue where to start even.

'I think . . . I'm done.'

'What, this?' Dogman tried to grin but didn't have it in him. 'No more'n a scratch.'

'Scratch, eh?' Grim tried to lift his head, winced and fell back, breathing shallow. He stared up, eyes wide open. 'That's a fucking beautiful ceiling.'

The Dogman swallowed. 'Aye. I reckon.'

'Should've died fighting Ninefingers, long time ago. The rest was all a gift. Grateful for it, though, Dogman. I've always loved . . . our talks.'

He closed his eyes, and he stopped breathing. He'd never said much, Harding Grim. Famous for it. Now he'd stay silent forever. A pointless sort of a death, a long way from home. Not for anything he'd believed in, or understood, or stood to gain from. Nothing more'n a waste. But then Dogman had seen a lot of men go back to the mud, and there was never anything fine about it. He took a long breath, and stared down at the floor.

A single lamp cast creeping shadows across the mouldering hallway, over rough stone and flaking plaster. It made sinister outlines of the mercenaries, turned Cosca's face and Ardee's into unfamiliar masks. The darkness seemed to gather inside the heavy stonework of the archway and around the door within – ancient-looking, knotted and grained, studded with black iron rivets.

'Something amusing, Superior?'

'I stood here,' murmured Glokta. 'In this exact spot. With Silber.' He reached out and brushed the iron handle with his fingertips. 'My hand was on the latch . . . and I moved on.' *Ah, the irony. The answers we seek so long and far for – so often at our fingertips all along.*

Glokta felt a shiver down his twisted spine as he leaned close to the door. He could hear something from beyond, a muffled droning in a language he did not recognise. *The Adeptus Demonic calls upon the denizens of the abyss?* He licked his lips, the image of High Justice Marovia's frozen remains fresh in his mind. *It would be rash to plunge straight through, however keen we are to put our questions to rest. Very rash . . .*

'Superior Goyle, since you have led us here, perhaps you would care to go first?'

'Geegh?' squeaked Goyle through his gag, his already bulging eyes going even wider. Cosca took the Superior of Adua by his collar, seized the iron handle with his other hand, thrust it swiftly open and applied his boot to the seat of Goyle's trousers. He stumbled through, bellowing meaningless nonsense into his gag. The metallic sound of a flatbow being discharged issued from the other side of the door, along with the chanting, louder and harsher now by far.

What would Colonel Glokta have said? Onwards to victory, lads! Glokta lurched through the doorway, almost tripping over his own aching foot on the threshold, and gazed about him in surprise. A large, circular hall with a domed ceiling, its shadowy walls painted with a vast, exquisitely detailed mural. *And one that seems uncomfortably familiar.* Kanedias, the Master Maker, loomed up over the chamber with arms outspread, five times life-size or more, fire blazing from behind him in vivid crimson, orange, white. On the opposite wall lay his brother Juvens, stretched out on the grass beneath flowering trees, blood running from his many wounds. In between the two men, the Magi marched to take their revenge, six on one side, five on the other, bald Bayaz in the lead. *Blood, fire, death, vengeance. How wonderfully appropriate, given the circumstances.*

An intricate design had been laid out with obsessive care, covering wide floor. Circles within circles, shapes, symbols, figures of frightening complexity, all described in neat lines of white powder. *Salt, unless I am much mistaken.* Goyle lay on his chest a stride or two from the door, at the edge of the outermost ring, his hands still tied behind him. Dark blood spread out from under him, the point of a flatbow bolt sticking out of his back. *Just where his heart should be. I would never have taken that for his weak spot.*

Four of the University's Adepti stood in various stages of amazement. Three of them: Chayle, Denka, and Kandelau, held candles in both hands, their sputtering wicks giving off a choking corpse-stink. Saurizin, the Adeptus Chemical, clutched an empty flatbow. The faces of the old men, lit in bilious yellow from beneath, were pantomime masks of fear.

At the far side of the room Silber stood behind a lectern, a great book open before him, staring down with intense concentration by the light of a single lamp. His finger hissed across the page, his thin lips moving ceaselessly. Even at this distance, and despite the fact the room was icy cold, Glokta could see fat beads of sweat running down his thin face. Beside him, painfully upright in his pure white coat and glaring blue daggers across the width of the chamber, stood Arch Lector Sult.

'Glokta, you crippled bastard!' he snarled. 'What the hell are you doing here?'

'I could well ask you the same question, your Eminence.' He waved his cane at the scene. 'Except the candles, the ancient books, the chanting and the circles of salt rather give the game away, no?' *And a rather infantile game it seems, suddenly. All that time, while I was torturing my way through the Mercers, while I was risking my life in Dagoska, while I was blackmailing votes in your name, you were up to . . . this?*

But Sult seemed to be taking it seriously enough. 'Get out, you fool! This is our last chance!'

'This? Seriously?' Cosca was already through the door, masked mercenaries following. Silber's eyes were still fixed on the book, lips still moving, more sweat on his face than ever. Glokta frowned. 'Someone shut him up.'

'No!' shouted Chayle, a look of utter horror on his tiny face. 'You mustn't stop the incantations! It is a profoundly dangerous operation! The consequences could be . . . could be—'

'Disastrous!' shrieked Kandelau. One of the mercenaries took a step towards the middle of the room nonetheless.

'Don't tread near the salt!' screeched Denka, wax dripping from his wobbling candle. 'Whatever you do!'

'Wait!' snapped Glokta, and the man paused at the edge of the circle, peering at him over his mask. The room was growing colder even as they spoke. Unnaturally cold. Something was happening in the centre of the circles. The air was trembling, like the air above a bonfire, more and more as Silber's harsh voice droned on. Glokta stood frozen, his eyes flicking between the old Adepti. *What to do? Stop him, or don't stop him? Stop him, or—*

'Allow me!' Cosca stepped forwards, delving into his black coat with his spare left hand. *But you can't be—* He whipped his arm out with a careless flourish and his throwing knife came with it. The blade flashed in the candlelight, spun directly through the shimmering air in the centre of the room, and imbedded itself to the hilt in Silber's forehead with a gentle thud.

'Ha!' Cosca seized Glokta by the shoulder. 'What did I tell you? Have you ever seen a knife thrown better?'

Blood ran down the side of Silber's face in a red trickle. His eyes rolled upwards, flickered, then he sagged sideways, dragging over his lectern, and crashed to the floor. His book tumbled down on top of him, aged pages flapping, the lamp spilled over and sprayed streaks of burning oil across the floor.

'No!' shrieked Sult.

Chayle gasped, his mouth falling open. Kandelau threw his candle aside and sank grovelling to the floor. Denka gave a terrified squeak, one hand over his face, staring out pop-eyed from between his fingers. There was a long pause while everyone except Cosca stared, horrified, towards the corpse of the Adeptus Demonic. Glokta waited, his few teeth bared, his eyes almost squeezed shut. *Like that horrible, beautiful moment between stubbing your toe and feeling the hurt. Here it comes. Here it comes.*

Here comes the pain . . .

But nothing came. No demonic laughter echoed through the chamber. The floor did not fall in to expose a gate to hell. The shimmering faded, the room began to grow warmer. Glokta raised his brows, almost disappointed. 'It would seem the diabolical arts are decidedly overrated.'

'No!' snarled Sult again.

'I am afraid so, your Eminence. And to think I used to respect you.' Glokta grinned at the Adeptus Chemical, still clinging weakly to his empty flatbow. He waved a hand at Goyle's body. 'A good shot. I congratulate you. One less mess for me to tidy up.' He waved a finger at the crowd of mercenaries behind him. 'Now seize that man.'

'No!' bellowed Saurizin, throwing his flatbow to the floor. 'None of it was my idea! I had no choice! It was him!' He stabbed a thick finger at Silber's lifeless body. 'And . . . and him!' He pointed to Sult with a trembling arm.

'You've got the right idea, but it can wait for the interrogation. Would you be kind enough to take his Eminence into custody?'

'Happily.' Cosca strolled across the floor of the wide room, his boots sending up puffs of white powder, leaving a trail of ruination through the intricate patterns.

'Glokta, you blundering idiot!' shrieked Sult. 'You have no idea of the danger Bayaz poses! This First of the Magi and his bastard king! Glokta! You have no right! Gah!' He yelped as Cosca dragged his arms behind his back and forced him to his knees, his white hair in disarray. 'You have no idea—'

'If the Gurkish don't kill the lot of us, you'll get ample time to explain it to me. Of that I assure you.' Glokta leered his toothless smile as Cosca drew the rope tight around Sult's wrists. *If you only knew how long I have dreamed of saying these words.* 'Arch Lector Sult. I arrest you for high treason against his Majesty the King.'

Jezal could only stand and stare. One of the twins, the one spattered in blood, lifted her long arms slowly over her head and gave a long, satisfied stretch. The other raised an eyebrow.

'How would you like to die?' she asked.

'Your Majesty, get behind me.' Gorst hefted his long steel in his one good hand.

'No. Not this time.' Jezal pulled the crown from his head, the crown that Bayaz had been so particular in designing, and tossed it clattering away. He was done with being a king. If he was to die, he would die a man, like any other. He had been given so many advantages, he realised now. Far more than most men could ever dream of. So many chances to do good, and he had done nothing besides whine and think of himself. Now it was too late. 'I've lived my life leaning on others. Hiding behind them. Climbing on their shoulders. Not this time.'

One of the twins raised her hands and started slowly to clap, the regular tap, tap, echoing from the mirrors. The other giggled. Gorst raised his sword. Jezal did the same, one last act of pointless defiance.

Then High Justice Marovia flashed between them. The old man moved with impossible speed, his dark robe snapping around him. He had something in his hand. A long rod of dark metal with a hook on the end.

'What—' muttered Jezal.

The hook blazed suddenly, searingly white, bright as the sun on a summer's day. A hundred hooks burned like stars, reflected back from the mirrors round the walls, and back, and back, into the far distance. Jezal gasped, squeezed his eyes shut, holding one hand over his face, the long trail left by that brilliant point burned fizzing into his vision.

He blinked, gaped, lowered his arm. The twins stood, the High Justice beside them, just where they had before, still as statues. Tendrils of white steam hissed up from vents in the end of the strange weapon and curled around Marovia's arm. For a moment, nothing moved.

Then a dozen of the great mirrors at the far end of the hall fell in half across the middle, as though they were sheets of paper slashed suddenly by the world's sharpest knife. A couple of the bottom halves and one of the top toppled slowly forwards into the room and shattered, scattering bright fragments of glass across the tiled floor.

'Urgggh,' breathed the twin on the left. Jezal realised that blood was spurting out from under her armour. She lifted one hand towards him and it dropped off the end of her arm and thudded to the tiles, blood squirting from the smoothly severed stump. She toppled to the left. Or her body did, at least. Her legs fell the other way. The bigger part of her crashed to the ground, and her head came off and rolled across the tiles in a widening pool. Her hair, trimmed off cleanly at the neck, fluttered down into the bloody mess in a golden cloud.

Armour, flesh, bone, all divided into neat sections as perfectly as cheese by a cheese wire. The twin on the right frowned, took a wobbling step towards Marovia. Her knees gave out and she fell in half at the waist. The legs slumped down and lay still, dust sliding out in a brown heap. The top half dragged itself forward by the nails, lifted its head, hissing.

The air around the High Justice shimmered and the Eater's severed body burst into flames. It thrashed, for a while, making a long squealing sound. Then it was still, a mass of smoking black ash.

Marovia lifted up the strange weapon, whistling softly as he smiled at the hook on the end, a last few traces of vapour still drifting from it. 'Kanedias. He certainly knew how to make a weapon. The Master Maker indeed, eh, your Majesty?'

'What?' muttered Jezal, utterly dumbfounded.

Marovia's face melted slowly away as he crossed the floor towards them. Another began to show itself beneath. Only his eyes remained the same. Different-coloured eyes, happy lines around the corners, grinning at Jezal like an old friend.

Yoru Sulfur bowed. 'Never any peace, eh, your Majesty? Never the slightest peace.'

There was a crash as one of the doors burst open. Jezal raised his sword, heart in his mouth. Sulfur whipped round, the Maker's weapon held down by his side. A man stumbled into the room. A big man, his grimacing face covered in scars, his chest heaving, a heavy sword hanging from one hand, the other clutched to his ribs.

Jezal blinked, hardly able to believe it. 'Logen Ninefingers. How the hell did you get here?'

The Northman stared for a moment. Then he leaned back against a mirror by the door, let his sword drop to the tiles. He slid down, slowly, until he hit the floor, and sat there with his head leaning back against the glass. 'Long story,' he said.

'Listen to us . . .'

The wind was full of shapes, now. Hundreds of them. They crowded in around the outermost circle, the bright iron turned misty, gleaming with cold wet.

'. . . we have things to tell you, Ferro . . .'

'Secrets . . .'

'What can we give you?'

'We know . . . everything.'

'You need only let us in . . .'

So many voices. She heard Aruf among them, her old teacher. She heard Susman the slaver. She heard her mother and her father. She heard Yulwei, and Prince Uthman. A hundred voices. A thousand. Voices she knew and had forgotten. Voices of the dead and of the living. Shouts, mutters, screams. Whispers, in her ear. Closer still. Closer than her own thoughts.

'You want vengeance?'

'We can give you vengeance.'

'Like nothing you have dreamed of.'

'All you want. All you need.'

'Only let us in . . .'

'That empty space in you?'

'We are what is missing!'

The metal rings had turned white with frost. Ferro kneeled at one end of a dizzying tunnel, its walls made from rushing, roaring, furious matter, full of shadows, its end far beyond the dark sky. The laughter of the First of the Magi echoed faintly in her ears. The air hummed with power, twisted, shimmered, blurred.

'You need do nothing.'

'Bayaz.'

'He will do it.'

'Fool!'

'Liar!'

'Let us in . . .'

'He cannot understand.'

'He uses you!'

'He laughs.'

'But not for long.'

'The gates strain.'

'Let us in . . .'

If Bayaz heard the voices he gave no sign. Cracks ran

through the quivering paving, branching out from his feet, splinters floating up around him in whirling spirals. The iron rings began to shift, to buckle. With a grinding of tortured metal they twisted out from the crumbling stones, bright edges shining.

'The seals break.'

'Eleven wards.'

'And eleven wards reversed.'

'The doors open.'

'Yes,' came the voices, speaking together.

The shadows crowded in closer. Ferro's breath came short and fast, her teeth rattled, her limbs trembled, the cold was on her very heart. She knelt at a precipice, bottomless, limitless, full of shadows, full of voices.

'Soon we will be with you.'

'Very soon.'

'The time is upon us.'

'Both sides of the divide, joined.'

'As they were meant to be.'

'Before Euz spoke his First Law.'

'Let us in . . .'

She needed only to cling to the Seed a moment longer. Then the voices would give her vengeance. Bayaz was a liar, she had known it from the start. She owed him nothing. Her eyelids flickered, closed, her mouth hung open. The noise of the wind grew fainter yet, until she could hear only the voices.

Whispering, soothing, righteous.

'We will take the world and make it right.'

'Together.'

'Let us in . . .'

'You will help us.'

'You will free us.'

'You can trust us.'

'Trust us . . .'

Trust?

A word that only liars used. Ferro remembered the wreckage of Aulcus. The hollow ruins, the blasted mud. The creatures of the Other Side are made of lies. Better to have an empty space in her, than to fill it with this. She wedged her tongue between her teeth and bit down hard, felt her mouth fill up with salty blood. She sucked in breath, forced her eyes open.

'Trust us . . .'

'Let us in!'

She saw the Maker's box, a shifting, swimming outline. She bent down over it, digging at it with her numb fingertips while the air lashed at her. She would be no one's slave. Not for Bayaz, not for the Tellers of Secrets. She would find her own path. A dark one, perhaps, but her own.

The lid swung open.

'No.' The voices hissed together in her ear.

'No!'

Ferro ground her bloody teeth, growled with fury as she forced her fingers to unclench. The world was a melting, screaming, formless mass of darkness. Gradually, gradually, her dead hand came open. Here was her revenge. Against the liars, the users, the thieves. The earth shook, crumbled, tore, as thin and fragile as a sheet of glass, and with an empty void beneath it. She turned her trembling hand and the Seed dropped from her palm.

All as one, the voices screamed their harsh command. *'No!'*

She blindly seized hold of the lid. 'Fuck yourselves!' she hissed.

And with her last grain of strength she forced the box closed.

After the Rains

Logen leaned on the parapet, high up on a tower at one side of the palace, and frowned into the wind. He'd done the same, it felt an age ago now, from the top of the Tower of Chains. He'd stared out dumbstruck at the endless city, wondering if he could ever have dreamed of a man-made thing so proud, and beautiful, and indestructible as the Agriont.

By the dead, how times change.

The green space of the park was scattered with fallen rubbish, trees broken, grass gouged, half the lake leaked away and sunken to a muddy bog. At its western edge a sweep of fine white buildings still stood, even if the windows gaped empty. Further west, and they had no roofs, bare rafters hanging. Further still their walls were torn and scoured, empty shells, choked with rubble.

Beyond that, there was nothing. The great hall with the golden dome, gone. The square where Logen had watched the sword-game, gone. The Tower of Chains, the mighty wall under it, and all the grand buildings over which Logen had fled with Ferro. All gone.

A colossal circle of destruction was carved from the western end of the Agriont, and only acres of formless wreckage remained. The city beyond was torn with black scars, smoke still rising from a few last fires, from smouldering hulks still drifting in the bay. The House of the Maker loomed over the scene, a sharp black mass under the brooding clouds, uncaring and untouched.

Logen stood there, scratching at the scarred side of his face, over and over. His wounds ached. So many of them. Every part of him was battered and bruised, slashed and torn. From the fight with the Eater, from the battle beyond the moat, from the duel with the Feared, from seven days of slaughter in the High Places. From a hundred fights, and skirmishes, and old campaigns. Too many to remember. So tired, and sore, and sick.

He frowned down at his hands on the parapet in front of him. The bare stone looked back where his middle finger used to be. He was Ninefingers still. The Bloody-Nine. A man made of death, just as Bethod had said. He'd nearly killed the Dogman yesterday, he knew it. His oldest friend. His only friend. He'd raised the sword, and if it wasn't for a trick of fate, he would have done it.

He remembered standing high up, on the side of the Great Northern library, looking out over the empty valley, the still lake like a great mirror beneath it. He remembered feeling the wind on his fresh-shaved jaw, and wondering whether a man could change.

Now he knew the answer.

'Master Ninefingers!'

Logen turned quickly, hissed through his teeth as the stitches down his side burned. The First of the Magi stepped through the doorway and out into the open air. He was changed, somehow. He looked young. Younger even than when Logen first met him. There was a sharpness to his movements, a gleam in his eye. It even seemed that there were a few dark hairs in the grey beard round his friendly grin. The first smile Logen had seen in a good while.

'You are hurt?' he asked.

Logen sucked sourly at his teeth. 'Hardly the first time.'

'And yet it gets no easier.' Bayaz placed his meaty fists on the stone next to Logen's and stared out happily at the view. Just as if it was a field of flowers instead of a sweep of epic ruin. 'I hardly expected to see you again so soon. And to see you so very far advanced. I understand that your feud is over. You defeated Bethod. Threw him from his own walls, the way I heard it. A nice touch. Always thinking of the song they will sing, eh? And then you took his place. The Bloody-Nine, King of the Northmen! Imagine that.'

Logen frowned. 'That wasn't how it happened.'

'Details. The result is the same, is it not? Peace in the North, at last? Either way, I congratulate you.'

'Bethod had a few things to say.'

'Did he?' asked Bayaz, carelessly. 'I always found his conversation rather drab. All about himself, his plans, his achievements. It is so very tiresome when men think never of others. Poor manners.'

'He said you're the reason why he didn't kill me. That you bargained for my life.'

'True, I must confess. He owed me, and you were the price I demanded. I like to keep one eye on the future. Even then, I knew I might have need of a man who could speak to the spirits. It was an unexpected bonus that you turned out to be such a winning travelling companion.'

Logen found he was talking through gritted teeth. 'Would have been nice to know is all.'

'You never asked, Master Ninefingers. You did not want to know my plans, as I recall, and I did not want to make you feel indebted. "I saved your life once" would have been a poor start to our friendship.'

All reasonable enough, like everything Bayaz ever said, but it left a sour taste still, to have been traded like a hog. 'Where's Quai? I'd like to—'

'Dead.' Bayaz pronounced the word smartly, sharp as a knife thrust. 'We feel his loss most keenly.'

'Back to the mud, eh?' Logen remembered the effort he'd made to save that man's life. The miles he'd slogged through the rain, trying to do the right thing. All wasted. Perhaps he should've felt more. But it was hard with so much death spread out in front of him. Logen was numb, now. Either that, or he really didn't care a shit. It was hard to say which.

'Back to the mud,' he muttered again. 'You carry on, though, don't you.'

'Of course.'

'That's the task that comes with surviving. You remember them, you say some words, then you carry on, and hope for better.'

'Indeed.'

'You have to be realistic about these things.'

'True.'

Logen worked at his sore side with one hand, trying to make himself feel something. But a scrap of extra pain helped no one. 'I lost a friend yesterday.'

'It was a bloody day. But a victorious one.'

'Oh aye? For who?' He could see people moving among the ruins, insects picking at the rubble, searching for survivors and finding the dead. He doubted many of them were feeling the flush of victory right now. He knew he wasn't. 'I should be with my own kind,' he muttered, but without moving. 'Helping with the burying. Helping with the wounded.'

'And yet you are here, looking down.' Bayaz' green eyes were hard as stones. That hardness that Logen had noticed from the very start, and had somehow forgotten. Somehow grown to overlook. 'I entirely understand your feelings. Healing is for the young. As one gets older, one finds one has less and less patience with the wounded.' He raised his eyebrows as he turned back towards the horrible view. 'I am very old.'

He lifted his fist to knock, then paused, fingers rubbing nervously against his palm.

He remembered the sour-sweet smell of her, the strength of her hands, the shape of her frown in the firelight. He remembered the warmth of her, pressed up close to him in the night. He knew there had been something good between them, even if all the words they had said had been hard. Some people don't have soft words in them, however much they try. He didn't hold much hope, of course. A man like him was better off without it. But you get nothing out if you put nothing in.

So Logen gritted his teeth and knocked. No reply. He chewed at his lip, and knocked again. Nothing. He frowned, twitchy and suddenly out of patience, wrenched the knob round and shoved the door open.

Ferro spun about. Her clothes were rumpled and dirty, even more than usual. Her eyes were wide, wild even, her fists clenched. But her face quickly fell when she saw it was him, and his heart sank with it.

'It's me, Logen.'

'Uh,' she grunted. She jerked her head sideways, frowning at the window. She took a couple of steps towards it, eyes narrowed. Then she snapped round suddenly the other way. 'There!'

'What?' muttered Logen, baffled.

'Do you not hear them?'

'Hear what?'

'Them, idiot!' She crept over to one wall and pressed herself up against it.

Logen hadn't been sure how it would go. You could never be sure of anything with her, he knew that. But he hadn't been expecting this. Just plough ahead, he reckoned. What else could he do?

'I'm a king, now.' He snorted. 'King of the Northmen, would you believe it?' He was thinking she'd laugh in his face, but she just stood, listening to the wall. 'Me and Luthar, both. A pair of kings. Can you think of two more worthless bastards to put crowns on, eh?' No answer.

Logen licked his lips. No choice but to get straight to it, maybe. 'Ferro. The way things turned out. The way we . . . left it.' He took a step towards her, and another. 'I wish I hadn't . . . I don't know . . .' He put one hand on her shoulder. 'Ferro, I'm trying to tell you—'

She turned, quickly, plastered her hand over his mouth. 'Shhhhh.' She grabbed his shirt and pulled him down, down onto his knees. She pressed her ear against the tiles, eyes moving back and forward as if she was listening for something. 'Do you hear that?' She let go of him and pushed herself into the corner. 'There! Do you hear them?'

He reached out, slowly, and touched the back of her neck, ran his rough fingertips over her skin. She shook him off with a jerk of her shoulders, and he felt his face twist. Perhaps that good thing between them had been only in his mind, and never in hers. Perhaps he had wanted it so badly that he had let himself imagine it.

He stood up, cleared his dry throat. 'Never mind. I'll come back later, maybe.' She was still on her knees, her head against the floor. She did not even watch him leave.

Logen Ninefingers was no stranger to death. He'd walked among it all his days. He'd watched the bodies burned by the score after the battle at Carleon, long ago. He'd seen them buried by the hundred up in the nameless valley in the High Places. He'd walked on a hill of men's bones under ruined Aulcus.

But even the Bloody-Nine, even the most feared man in the North, had never looked on anything like this.

Bodies were stacked beside the wide avenue in heaps, chest-high. Sagging mounds of corpses, on and on. Hundreds upon hundreds. Too many for him to guess at the numbers. Some-one had made an effort at covering them, but not that great an effort. The dead give no thanks for it, after all. Ragged sheets flapped in the breeze, weighted down with broken wood, limp hands and feet hanging out from underneath.

At this end of the road a few statues still stood. Once-proud kings and their advisers, stone faces and bodies scarred and pitted, stared sadly down at the bloody waste heaped round their feet. Enough of them for Logen to recognise that this truly was the Kingsway, and that he hadn't somehow stumbled into the land of the dead.

A hundred strides further and there were only empty plinths, one with broken legs still attached. A strange group were clustered around them. Withered-looking. Somewhere between dead and alive. A man sat on a block of stone, staring numbly as he pulled handfuls of hair out of his head. Another was coughing into a bloody rag. A woman and a man lay side by side, gawping at nothing, faces shrivelled to little more than skulls. Her breath came crackling short and fast. His did not come at all.

Another hundred strides and it was as if Logen walked

through some ruined hell. There was no sign that statues, buildings, or anything else had ever stood there. In their place were only tangled hills of strange rubbish. Broken stone, splintered wood, twisted metal, paper, glass, all crushed together and bound up with tons of dust and mud. Things stuck from the wreckage, strangely intact – a door, a chair, a carpet, a painted plate, the smiling face of a statue.

Men and women struggled everywhere among this chaos, streaked with dirt, picking at the rubbish, throwing it down to the road, trying to clear paths through it. Rescuers, workmen, thieves, who knew? Logen passed by a crackling bonfire high as a man, felt the kiss of its heat on his cheek. A big soldier in armour stained with black soot stood beside it. 'You find anything in white metal?' he was roaring at the searchers. 'Anything at all? It goes in the fire! Flesh in white metal? Burn it! Orders of the Closed Council!'

A few strides further on, someone was on top of one of the highest mounds, straining at a great length of wood. He turned round to get a better grip. None other than Jezal dan Luthar. His clothes were torn and grubby, his face was smudged with mud. He barely looked any more like a king than Logen did.

A thickset man stood staring up, one arm in a sling. 'Your Majesty, this is not safe!' he piped in an oddly girlish voice. 'We really should be—'

'No! This is where I'm needed!' Jezal bent back over the beam, straining at it, veins bulging from his neck. There was no way he was going to get it shifted on his own, but still he tried. Logen stood watching him. 'How long's he been like this?'

'All night, and all day,' said the thickset man, 'and no sign of stopping. Those few we've found alive, nearly all of them have this sickness.' He waved his good arm towards the pitiful group beside the statues. 'Their hair falls out. Their nails. Their teeth. They wither. Some have died already. Others are well on the way.' He slowly shook his head. 'What crime did we commit to deserve this punishment?'

'Punishment doesn't always come to the guilty.'

'Ninefingers!' Jezal was looking down, the watery sun behind him. 'There's a strong back! Grab the end of that beam there!'

It was hard to see what good shifting a beam might do, in all of this. But great journeys start with small steps, Logen's father had always told him. So he clambered up, wood cracking and stones sliding underneath his boots, hauled himself to the top and stood there, staring.

'By the dead.' From where he was standing, the hills of wreckage seemed to go on forever. People crawled over them, dragging frantically at the rubble, sorting carefully through it, or simply standing like him, stunned by the scale of it. A circle of utter waste, a mile across or more.

'Help me, Logen!'

'Aye. Right.' He bent down and dug his hands under one end of the great length of scarred wood. Two kings, dragging at a beam. The kings of mud.

'Pull, then!' Logen heaved, his stitches burning. Gradually he felt the wood shift. 'Yes!' grunted Jezal through gritted teeth. Together they lifted it, hauled it to one side. Jezal reached down and dragged away a dry tree-branch, tore back a ripped sheet. A woman lay beneath, staring sideways. One broken arm was wrapped around a child, curly hair dark with blood.

'Alright.' Jezal wiped slowly at his mouth with the back of one dirty hand. 'Alright. Well. We'll put them with the rest of the dead.' He clambered further over the wreckage. 'You! Bring that crowbar up here! Up here, and a pick, we need to clear this stone! Stack it there. We'll need it, later. To rebuild!'

Logen put a hand on his shoulder. 'Jezal, wait. Wait. You know me.'

'Of course. I like to think so.'

'Alright. Tell me something, then. Am I . . .' He struggled to find the right words. 'Am I . . . an evil man?'

'You?' Jezal stared at him, confused. 'You're the best man I know.'

They were gathered under a broken tree in the park, a shadowy crowd of them. Black outlines of men, standing calm and still, red clouds and golden spread out above, around the setting sun. Logen could hear their slow voices as he walked up. Words for the dead, soft and sad. He could see the graves at their feet. Two dozen piles of fresh turned earth, set out in a circle so each man was equal. The Great Leveller, just as the hillmen say. Men put in the mud, and men saying words. Could've been a scene out of the old North, long ago in the time of Skarling Hoodless.

'. . . Harding Grim. I never saw a better man with a bow. Not ever. Can't count the number o' times he saved my life, and never expected thanks for it. Except maybe that I'd do the same for him. Guess I couldn't, this time. Guess none of us could . . .'

The Dogman's voice trailed off. A few heads turned to look at Logen as his footsteps crunched in the gravel. 'If it ain't the King o' the Northmen,' someone said.

'The Bloody-Nine his self.'

'We should bow, shouldn't we?'

They were all looking at him now. He could see their eyes gleaming in the dusk. Nothing more than shaggy outlines, hard to tell one man from another. A crowd of shadows. A crowd of ghosts, and just as unfriendly.

'You got something you want to say, Bloody-Nine?' came a voice from near the back.

'I don't reckon,' he said. 'You're doing alright.'

'Was no reason for us to be here.' A few mumbles of agreement.

'Not our bloody fight.'

'No need for them to have died.' More mutters.

'Should be you we're burying.'

'Aye, maybe.' Logen would have liked to weep at that. But instead he felt himself smiling. The Bloody-Nine's smile. That grin that skulls have, with nothing inside but death. 'Maybe. But you don't get to pick who dies. Not unless you've got the bones to put your own hand to it. Have you? Have any of you?' Silence. 'Well, then. Good for Harding Grim. Good for the rest o' the dead, they'll all be missed.' Logen spat onto the

Answers

So much to do.

The House of Questions still stood, and someone had to take the reins. *Who else will do it? Superior Goyle? A flatbow bolt through the heart prevents him, alas.* Someone had to look to the internment and questioning of the many hundreds of Gurkish prisoners, more captured every day as the army drove the invaders back to Keln. *And who else will do it? Practical Vitari? Left the Union forever with her children in tow.* Someone had to examine the treason of Lord Brock. To dig him up, and root out his accomplices. To make arrests, and obtain confessions. *And who else is there, now? Arch Lector Sult? Oh, dear me, no.*

Glokta wheezed up to his door, his few teeth bared at the endless pains in his legs. *A fortunate decision, at least, to move to the eastern side of the Agriont. One should be grateful for the small things in life, like a place to rest one's crippled husk. My old lodgings are no doubt languishing under a thousand tons of rubble, just like the rest of—*

His door was not quite shut. He gave it the gentlest of pushes and it creaked open, soft lamplight spilling out into the corridor, a glowing stripe over the dusty floorboards, over the foot of Glokta's cane and the muddy toe of one boot. *I left no door unlocked, and certainly no lamps burning.* His tongue slithered nervously over his empty gums. *A visitor, then. An uninvited one. Do I go in, and welcome them to my rooms?* His eyes slid sideways into the shadows of the corridor. *Or do I make a run for it?* He was almost smiling as he shuffled over the threshold, cane first, then the right foot, then the left, dragging painfully behind him.

Glokta's guest sat by the window in the light of a single

lamp, brightness splashed across the hard planes of his face, cold darkness gathered in the deep hollows. The squares board was set before him, just as Glokta left it, the pieces casting long shadows across the chequered wood.

'Why, Superior Glokta. I have been waiting for you.'

And I for you. Glokta limped over to the table, his cane scraping against the bare boards. *As reluctantly as a man limping to the gallows. Ah, well. No one tricks the hangman forever. Perhaps we'll have some answers, at least, before the end. I always dreamed of dying well-informed.* Slowly, ever so slowly, he lowered himself grunting into the free chair.

'Do I have the pleasure of addressing Master Valint, or Master Balk?'

Bayaz smiled. 'Both, of course.'

Glokta wrapped his tongue round one of his few remaining teeth and dragged it away with a faint sucking sound. 'And to what do I owe the overpowering honour?'

'I said, did I not, that day we visited the Maker's House, that we should have a talk at some point? A talk about what I want, and about what you want? That point has come.'

'Oh joyous day.'

The First of the Magi watched him, the same look in his bright eyes that a man might have while watching an interesting beetle. 'I must admit that you fascinate me, Superior. Your life would seem to be entirely unbearable. And yet you fight so very, very hard to stay alive. With every weapon and stratagem. You simply refuse to die.'

'I am ready to die.' Glokta returned his gaze, like for like. 'But I refuse to lose.'

'Whatever the cost, eh? We are two of a kind, you and I, and we are a rare kind indeed. We understand what must be done, and we do not flinch from doing it, regardless of sentiment. You remember Lord Chancellor Feekt, of course.'

If I cast my mind a long way back . . . 'The Golden Chancellor? They say he ran the Closed Council for forty years. They say he ran the Union.' *Sult said so. Sult said his death left a hole, into which he and Marovia were both keen to step. That is where this ugly dance began, for me. With a visit from the Arch Lector, with the confession of my old friend Salem Rews, with the arrest of Sepp dan Teufel, Master of the Mints . . .*

Bayaz let one thick fingertip trail across the pieces on the squares board, as though considering his next move. 'We had an agreement, Feekt and I. I made him powerful. He served me, utterly.'

Feekt . . . the foundation on which the nation rested . . . served you? I expected delusions of grandeur, but this will take some beating. 'You would have me suppose that you controlled the Union all that time?'

Bayaz snorted. 'Ever since I forced the damn thing together in the time of Harod the Great, so-called. It has sometimes been necessary for me to take a hand myself, as in this most recent crisis. But mostly I have stood at a distance, behind the curtain, as it were.'

'A little stuffy back there, one imagines.'

'An uncomfortable necessity.' The lamplight gleamed on the Magus' white grin. 'People like to watch the pretty puppets, Superior. Even a glimpse of the puppeteer can be most upsetting for them. Why, they might even suddenly notice the strings around their own wrists. Sult caught a glimpse of something, behind the curtain, and only look at the trouble he caused for everyone.' Bayaz flicked one of the pieces over and it clattered onto its side, rocked gently back and forth.

'Let us suppose you are indeed the great architect, and you have given us . . .' Glokta waved his hand towards the window. *Acres of charming devastation.* 'All this. Why such generosity?'

'Not entirely selfless, I must confess. Khalul had the Gurkish to fight for him. I needed soldiers of my own. Even the greatest of generals needs little men to hold the line.' He absently nudged one of the smallest pieces forward. 'Even the greatest of warriors needs his armour.'

Glokta stuck out his bottom lip. 'But then Feekt died, and you were left naked.'

'Naked as a babe, at my age.' Bayaz gave a long sigh. 'And in poor weather too, with Khalul making ready for war. I should

599

have arranged a suitable successor more quickly, but my thoughts were elsewhere, deep in my books. The older you get, the more swiftly the years pass. It's easy to forget how quickly people die.'

And how easily. 'The death of the Golden Chancellor left a vacuum,' muttered Glokta, thinking it through. 'Sult and Marovia saw a chance to take power for themselves, and advance their own notions of what the nation should be.'

'Exceptionally cock-eyed notions, as it happens. Sult wanted to return to an imaginary past where everyone kept their place and always did as they were told, and Marovia? Hah! Marovia wanted to piss power away to the people. Votes? Elections? The voice of the common man?'

'He aired some such notion.'

'I hope you aired the suitable level of contempt. Power for the people?' sneered Bayaz. 'They don't want it. They don't understand it. What the hell would they do with it if they had it? The people are like children. They *are* children. They need someone to tell them what to do.'

'Someone like you, I suppose?'

'Who better suited? Marovia thought to use me in his petty schemes, and all the while I made good use of him. While he tussled with Sult over scraps the game was already won. A move I had prepared some time before.'

Glokta slowly nodded. 'Jezal dan Luthar.' *Our little bastard.*

'Your friend and mine.'

But a bastard is no use unless . . . 'Crown Prince Raynault stood in the way.'

The Magus flicked a piece over and it rolled slowly from the board and rattled to the table. 'We talk of great events. There is sure to be some wastage.'

'You made it seem that he was killed by an Eater.'

'Oh, he was.' Bayaz watched smugly from the shadows. 'Not all who break the Second Law serve Khalul. My apprentice, Yoru Sulfur, has long been partial to a bite or two.' And he snapped his two rows of smooth and even teeth together.

'I see.'

'This is war, Superior. In war one must make use of every weapon. Restraint is folly. Worse. Restraint is cowardice. But only look who I am lecturing. You need no lessons in ruthlessness.'

'No.' *They cut them into me in the Emperor's prisons, and I have been practising them ever since.*

Bayaz nudged one of the pieces gently forward. 'A useful man, Sulfur. A man who long ago accepted the demands of necessity, and mastered the discipline of taking forms.' *He was the guard, weeping outside Prince Raynault's door. The guard who vanished into thin air the next day . . .*

'A shred of cloth taken from the Emissary's bed-chamber,' murmured Glokta. 'Blood daubed on his robe.' *And so an innocent man went to the gallows, and the war between Gurkhul and the Union blossomed. Two obstacles swept neatly away with one sharp flick of the broom.*

'Peace with the Gurkish did not suit my purposes. It was sloppy of Sulfur to leave such blatant clues. But then he never expected you to care about the truth when there was a convenient explanation to hand.'

Glokta nodded, slowly, as the shape of things unfolded in his mind. 'He heard of my investigations from Severard, and I received a charming visit from your walking corpse, Mauthis, telling me to halt or die.'

'Exactly so. On other occasions Yoru took another face, and called himself the Tanner, and incited a few peasants to some rather unbecoming behaviour.' Bayaz examined his fingernails. 'All in a good cause, though, Superior.'

'To lend glamour to your latest puppet. To make him a favourite with the people. To make him familiar to the nobles, to the Closed Council. You were the source of the rumours.'

'Heroic acts in the ruined west? Jezal dan Luthar?' Bayaz snorted. 'He did little more than whine about the rain.'

'Amazing the rubbish idiots will believe if you shout it loudly enough. And you rigged the Contest too.'

'You noticed that?' Bayaz' smile grew wider. 'I am impressed, Superior, I am most impressed. You have fumbled so very close to the truth this whole time.' *And yet so very far away.* 'I wouldn't feel badly about it. I have many advantages. Sult groped towards the answers, in the end, but far too late. I suspected from the first what his plans might be.'

'Which is why you asked me to investigate?'

'The fact that you did not oblige me until the very last moment was the source of some annoyance.'

'Asking nicely might have helped.' *It would have been refreshing, at least.* 'I regret that I found myself in a difficult position. A case of too many masters.'

'No longer, though, eh? I was almost disappointed when I found out how limited Sult's studies were. Salt, and candles, and incantations? How pathetically adolescent. Enough to put a timely end to that would-be democrat Marovia, perhaps, but nothing to pose the slightest threat to me.'

Glokta frowned down at the squares board. *Sult and Marovia. For all their cleverness, for all their power, their ugly little struggle was an irrelevance. They were small pieces in this game. So small they never even guessed how vast the board truly was. Which makes me what? A speck of dust between the squares, at best.*

'What of the mysterious visitor to your chambers the day I first met you?' *A visitor to my chambers too, perhaps? A woman, and cold . . .*

Angry lines cut across Bayaz' forehead. 'A mistake made in my youth. You will speak no more of it.'

'Oh, as you command. And the Great Prophet Khalul?'

'The war will continue. On different battlefields, with different soldiers. But this will be the last battle fought with the weapons of the past. The magic leaks from the world. The lessons of the Old Time fade into the darkness of history. A new age dawns.'

The Magus made a careless movement with one hand and something flickered into the air, clattered to the centre of the board and spun round and round until it lay flat, with the unmistakable sound of falling money. A golden fifty-mark piece, glinting warm and welcoming in the lamplight. Glokta almost laughed. *Ah, even now, even here, it always comes down to this. Everything has a price.*

'It was money that bought victory in King Guslav's half-baked Gurkish war,' said Bayaz. 'It was money that united the Open Council behind their bastard king. It was money that brought Duke Orso rushing to the defence of his daughter and tipped the balance in our favour. All my money.'

'It was money that enabled me to hold Dagoska as long as I did.'

'And you know whose.' *Who would have thought? More first of the moneylenders than First of the Magi. Open Council and Closed, commoners and kings, merchants and torturers, all caught up in a golden web. A web of debts, and lies, and secrets, each strand plucked in its proper place, played like a harp by a master. And what of poor Superior Glokta, fumbling buffoon? Is there a place for his sour note in this sweet music? Or is the loan of my life about to be called in?*

'I suppose I should congratulate you on a hand well played,' muttered Glokta bitterly.

'Bah.' Bayaz dismissed it with a wave. 'Forcing a clutch of primitives together under that cretin Harod and making them act like civilised men. Keeping the Union in one piece through the civil war and bringing that fool Arnault to the throne. Guiding that coward Casamir to the conquest of Angland. Those were hands well played. This was nothing. I hold all the cards and always will do. I have—'

I tire of this. 'And blah, blah, fucking blah. The stench of self-satisfaction is becoming quite suffocating. If you mean to kill me, blast me to a cinder now and let's be done, but, for pity's sake, subject me to no more of your boasting.'

They sat still for a long moment, gazing at each other in silence across the darkened table. Long enough for Glokta's leg to start trembling, for his eye to start blinking, for his toothless mouth to turn dry as the desert. *Sweet anticipation. Will it be now? Will it be now? Will it be—* 'Kill you?' asked Bayaz mildly. 'And rob myself of your winning sense of humour?'

Not now. 'Then . . . why reveal your game to me?'

'Because I will soon be leaving Adua.' The Magus leaned forwards, his hard face sliding into the light. 'Because it is necessary that you understand where the power lies, and always will lie. It is necessary that you, unlike Sult, unlike Marovia, have a proper perspective. It is necessary . . . if you are to serve me.'

'To serve you?' *I would sooner spend two years in the stinking darkness. I would sooner have my leg chopped to mincemeat. I would sooner have my teeth pulled from my head. But since I have done all those things already . . .*

'You will take the task that Feekt once had. The task that a score of great men bore before him. You will be my representative, here in the Union. You will manage the Closed Council, the Open Council, and our mutual friend the king. You will ensure him heirs. You will maintain stability. In short, you will watch the board, while I am gone.'

'But the rest of the Closed Council will never—'

'Those that survive have been spoken to. They all will bow to your authority. Under mine, of course.'

'How will I—'

'I will be in touch. Frequently. Through my people at the bank. Through my apprentice, Sulfur. Through other means. You will know them.'

'I don't suppose I have any choice in the matter?'

'Not unless you can repay the million marks I leant you. Plus interest.'

Glokta patted at the front of his shirt. 'Damn it. I left my purse at work.'

'Then I fear you have no choice. But why would you refuse me? I offer you the chance to help me forge a new age.' *To bury my hands to the elbow in your dirty work.* 'To be a great man. The very greatest of men.' *To bestride the Closed Council like a crippled colossus.* 'To leave your likeness set in stone on the Kingsway.' *Where its hideousness can make the children cry. Once they clear away the rubble and the corpses, of course.* 'To shape the course of a nation.'

'Under your direction.'

604

'Naturally. Nothing is free, you know that.' Again the Magus flicked his hand and something clattered spinning across the squares board. It came to rest in front of Glokta, gold glinting. The Arch Lector's ring. *So many times I bent to kiss this very jewel. Who could have dreamed that I might one day wear it?* He picked it up, turned it thoughtfully round and round. *And so I finally shake off a dark master, only to find my leash in the fist of another, darker and more powerful by far. But what choice do I have? What choices do any of us truly have?* He slid the ring onto his finger. The great stone shone in the lamplight, full of purple sparks. *From a dead man to the greatest in the realm, and all in one evening.*

'It fits,' murmured Glokta.

'Of course, your Eminence. I always knew it would.'

The Wounded

West woke with a start and tried to jerk up to sitting. Pain shot up one leg, across his chest, through his right arm, and stayed there, throbbing. He dropped back with a groan and stared at the ceiling. A vaulted stone ceiling, covered in thick shadows.

Sounds crept at him now from all around. Grunts and whimpers, coughs and sobs, quick gasping, slow growling. The occasional outright shriek of pain. Sounds between men and animals. A voice whispered throatily from somewhere to his left, droning endlessly away like a rat scratching at the walls. 'I can't see. Bloody wind. I can't see. Where am I? Somebody. I can't see.'

West swallowed, feeling the pain growing worse. In the hospitals in Gurkhul there had been sounds like that, when he had come to visit wounded soldiers from his company. He remembered the stink and noise of those horrible tents, the misery of the men in them, and above all the overpowering desire to leave and be among the healthy. But it was already awfully clear that leaving would not be so easy this time.

He was one of the wounded. A different, contemptible and disgusting species. Horror crept slowly through his body and mingled with the pain. How badly was he injured? Did he have all his limbs, still? He tried to move his fingers, wriggle his toes, clenched his teeth as the aching in his arm and leg grew worse. He brought his left hand trembling up before his face, turned it over in the dimness. It seemed intact, at least, but it was the only limb that he could move, and even that was a crushing effort. Panic slithered up his throat and clutched at him.

'Where am I? Bloody wind. I can't see. Help. Help. Where am I?'

'Fucking shut up!' West shouted, but the words died in his dry throat. All that came up was a hollow cough that set his ribs on fire again.

'Shhhh.' A soft touch on his chest. 'Just be still.'

A blurry face swam into view. A woman's face, he thought, with fair hair, but it was hard to focus. He closed his eyes and stopped trying. It hardly seemed to matter that much. He felt something against his lips, the neck of a bottle. He drank too thirstily, spluttered and felt cold water running down his neck.

'What happened?' he croaked.

'You were wounded.'

'I know that. I mean . . . in the city. The wind.'

'I don't know. I don't think anyone knows.'

'Did we win?'

'I suppose that . . . the Gurkish were driven out, yes. But there are a lot of wounded. A lot of dead.'

Another swallow of water. This time he managed it without gagging. 'Who are you?'

'My name is Ariss. Dan Kaspa.'

'Ariss . . .' West fumbled with the name. 'I knew your cousin. Knew him well . . . a good man. He always used to talk about . . . how beautiful you were. And rich,' he muttered, vaguely aware he should not be saying this, but unable to stop his mouth from working. 'Very rich. He died. In the mountains.'

'I know.'

'What are you doing here?'

'Trying to help with the wounded. It would be best for you to sleep now, if you—'

'Am I whole?'

A pause. 'Yes. Sleep now, if you can.'

Her dark face grew blurry, and West let his eyes close. The noises of agony slowly faded around him. He was whole. All would be well.

Someone was sitting next to his bed. Ardee. His sister. He blinked, worked his sour mouth, unsure where he was for a moment.

'Am I dreaming?' She reached forward and dug her nails into his arm. 'Ah!'

'Painful dream, eh?'

'No,' he was forced to admit. 'This is real.'

She looked well. Far better than the last time he had seen her, that was sure. No blood on her face for one thing. No look of naked hatred, for another. Only a thoughtful frown. He tried to bring himself up to sitting, failed, and slumped back down. She did not offer to help. He had not really expected her to. 'How bad is it?' he asked.

'Nothing too serious, apparently. A broken arm, a few broken ribs, and a leg badly bruised, they tell me. Some cuts on your face that may leave a scar or two, but then I got all the looks in the family anyway.'

He gave a snort of laughter and winced at the pain across his chest. 'True enough. The brains too.'

'Don't feel badly about it. I've used them to make the towering success of my life that you see before you. The kind of achievement that you, as a Lord Marshal of the Union, can only dream of.'

'Don't,' he hissed, clamping his good hand across his ribs. 'It hurts.'

'No less than you deserve.'

His laughter quickly stuttered out, and they were silent for a moment, looking at each other. Even that much was difficult. 'Ardee . . .' His voice caught in his sore neck. 'Can you . . . forgive me?'

'I already did. The first time I heard you were dead.' She was trying to smile, he could tell. But she still had that twist of anger to her mouth. Probably she would have liked to dig her nails into his face rather than his arm. He was almost glad then, for a moment, that he was wounded. She had no choice but to be soft with him. 'It's good that you're not. Dead, that is . . .' She frowned over her shoulder. There was some manner of commotion at one end of the long cellar. Raised voices, the clatter of armoured footsteps.

'The king!' Whoever it was nearly squealed it in their excitement. 'The king is come again!'

In the beds all around men turned their heads, propped themselves up. A nervous excitement spread from cot to cot. 'The king?' they whispered, faces anxious and expectant, as though they were privileged to witness a divine visitation.

Several figures moved through the shadows at the far end of the hall. West strained to look, but could see little more than metal gleaming in the darkness. The foremost shape stopped beside a wounded man a few beds down.

'They are treating you well?' A voice strangely familiar, strangely different.

'Yes, sir.'

'Is there anything you need?'

'A kiss from a good woman?'

'I would love to oblige you, but I fear I'm only a king. We're a great deal more common than good women.' Men laughed, even though it was not funny. West supposed that people laughing at your poor jokes was one advantage of being a monarch. 'Anything else?'

'Maybe . . . maybe another blanket, sir. Getting cold down here, at night.'

'Of course.' The figure jerked his thumb at a man behind. Lord Hoff, West realised now, dragging along at a respectful distance. 'Another blanket for every man here.'

The Lord Chamberlain, that fearsome scourge of the audience chamber, humbly nodded his head like a meek child. The king stood, and moved into the light.

Jezal dan Luthar, of course, and yet it was hard to believe that it was the same man, and not only because of the rich fur mantle and the golden circlet on his forehead. He seemed taller. Handsome, still, but no longer boyish. A deep scar on his bearded jaw had given him an air of strength. The sneer of arrogance had become a frown of command. The carefree swagger had become a purposeful stride. He worked his way on slowly down the aisle between the cots, speaking to each man, pressing their hands, giving them thanks, promising them help. No one was overlooked.

'A cheer for the king!' someone gurgled through gritted teeth.

'No! No. The cheering should be for you, my brave friends! You who have made sacrifices in my name. I owe you everything. It was only with your help that the Gurkish were defeated. Only with your help that the Union was saved. I do not forget a debt, that I promise you!'

West stared. Whoever this strange apparition was who looked so like Jezal dan Luthar, he spoke like a monarch. West almost felt a preposterous desire to drag himself from his bed and kneel. One casualty was trying to do just that as the king passed his bed. Jezal restrained him with a gentle hand on his chest, smiled and patted his shoulder as though he had been offering succour to the wounded his entire life, instead of getting drunk in shit-holes with the rest of the officers, and whining about such meagre tasks as he was given.

He drew close and saw West, lying there. His face lit up, though there was a tooth missing from his smile. 'Collem West!' he said, hastening over. 'I can honestly say that I have never in my life been so pleased to see your face.'

'Er . . .' West moved his mouth around a bit, but hardly knew what to say.

Jezal turned to his sister. 'Ardee . . . I hope you are well.'

'Yes.' She said nothing else. They stared at each other, for a long and intensely awkward moment, not speaking.

Lord Hoff frowned at the king, then at West, then at Ardee. He insinuated himself somewhat between the two of them. 'Your Majesty, we should—'

Jezal silenced him effortlessly with one raised hand. 'I trust that you will soon join me in the Closed Council, West. I am in some need of a friendly face there, in truth. Not to mention good advice. You always were a mine of good advice. I never did thank you for it. Well, I can thank you now.'

'Jezal . . . I mean, your Majesty—'

'No, no. Always Jezal to you, I hope. You will have a room

in the palace, of course. You will have the royal surgeon. Everything possible. See to that, please, Hoff.'

The Lord Chamberlain bowed. 'Of course. Everything will be arranged.'

'Good. Good. I am glad you are well, West. I cannot afford to lose you.' The king nodded, to him, and to his sister. Then he turned and moved on, pressing hands, speaking soft words. A pool of hope seemed to surround him as he passed. Despair crowded in behind it. Smiles faded as he moved away. Men dropped back onto their beds, faces clouding over with pain.

'Responsibility seems to have improved him,' muttered West. 'Almost beyond recognition.'

'How long will it last, do you think?'

'I'd like to think that it could stick, but then I've always been an optimist.'

'That's good.' Ardee watched the magnificent new king of the Union striding away, wounded men straining from their cots for the slightest touch of his cloak. 'That one of us can be.'

'Marshal West!'

'Jalenhorm. Good to see you.' West pulled back the blankets with his good hand, eased his legs over the edge of the bed and winced his way up to sitting. The big man reached out and gave his hand a squeeze, clapped him on the shoulder.

'You're looking well!'

West smiled weakly. 'Better ever day, Major. How's my army?'

'Fumbling on without you. Kroy's holding things together. Not such a bad sort, the General, once you get used to him.'

'If you say so. How many did we lose?'

'Still hard to say. Things are somewhat chaotic. Whole companies missing. Impromptu units still chasing Gurkish stragglers across half the countryside. I don't think we'll have numbers for a while. I don't know if we'll ever get them. No one did well, but the ninth regiment were the ones fighting at the western end of the Agriont. They took the worst of . . .' He fumbled for the words. 'It.'

West grimaced. He remembered that black column of whirling matter reaching from the tortured earth to the circling clouds. The debris lashing at his skin, the screaming of the wind all around him. 'What was . . . it?'

'I'm damned if I know.' Jalenhorm shook his head. 'Damned if anyone does. But the rumour is that this Bayaz was involved, somehow. Half the Agriont's in ruins, and they've barely started shifting the rubble. You never saw anything like it, that I promise you. A lot of people dead in all that. Bodies stacked up in the open . . .' Jalenhorm took a long breath. 'And there are more dying every day. A lot of people getting ill.' He shuddered. 'This . . . sickness.'

'Disease. Always a part of war.'

'Not like this. Hundreds of cases, now. Some die in a day, almost before your eyes. Some take longer. They wither to skin and bone. They have whole halls full of them. Stinking, hopeless places. But you don't need to worry about that.' He shook himself. 'I have to go.'

'Already?'

'Flying visit, sir. I'm helping to arrange Poulder's funeral, would you believe? He's being buried in state, by order of the king . . . that is to say Jezal. Jezal dan Luthar.' He blew out his cheeks. 'Strange business.'

'The strangest.'

'All that time. A king's son sitting in the midst of us. I knew there had to be a reason why he was so bloody good at cards.' He slapped West on the back again. 'Good to see you looking so well, sir. Knew they wouldn't be able to keep you down for long!'

'Keep out of trouble!' West called after him as he made for the door.

'Always!' The big man grinned as he pulled it shut.

West took his stick from the side of the bed, gritted his teeth as he pushed himself up to standing. He hobbled across the expanse of chequered tiles to the window, one painstaking step at a time, and finally stood blinking into the morning sunlight.

Looking down on the palace gardens it was hard to believe

that there had been any war, that there were any acres of ruins, any heaps of dead. The lawns were neatly trimmed, the gravel well-raked. The last few brown leaves had fallen from the trees, leaving the smooth wood black and bare.

It had been autumn when he set out for Angland. Could it really have been only a year ago? He had lived through four great battles, a siege, an ambush, a bloody mêlée. He had witnessed a duel to the death. He had stood at the centre of great events. He had survived a slog of hundreds of miles through the bleak Angland winter. He had found new comrades in unlikely places, and he had seen friends dead before his eyes. Burr, Kaspa, Cathil, Threetrees, all back to the mud, as the Northmen said. He had faced death, and he had delivered it. He shifted his aching arm uncomfortably in the sling. He had murdered the heir to the throne of the Union with his own hands. He had risen, by a stroke of chance that verged on the impossible, to one of the highest posts in the nation.

Busy year.

And now it was over. Peace, of a kind. The city was in ruins, and every man had to do his part, but he owed himself a rest. Surely no one would begrudge him that. Perhaps he could insist on Ariss dan Kaspa to tend him to health. A rich and beautiful nurse seemed like just the thing he needed . . .

'You shouldn't be up.' Ardee stood in the doorway.

He grinned. It was good to see her. For the last few days they had been close. Almost as it had been long ago, when they were children. 'Don't worry. Getting stronger every day.'

She walked across to the window. 'Oh yes, in a few weeks time you'll be strong as a little girl. Back to bed.' She slid one arm under his and took the cane from his hand, started to guide him back across the room. West made no effort to resist. If he was being honest, he was starting to feel tired anyway. 'We're taking no chances,' she was saying. 'You're all I have, I'm sorry to say. Unless you count that other invalid, my good friend Sand dan Glokta.'

West almost snorted with laughter. 'That worked out?'

'The man is utterly loathsome, of course, in a way.

613

Terrifying and pitiful at once. And yet . . . having had no one else to talk to, I find that I've strangely warmed to him.'

'Huh. He used to be loathsome in an entirely different way. I've never been sure quite why I warmed to him then. And yet I did. I suppose there's no—'

He felt a sudden wave of sickness cramp up his guts, stumbled and almost fell, sank onto the bed, stiff leg stretched out in front of him. His vision was blurry, his head spun. He pressed his face into his palms, teeth gritted, as spit rushed into his mouth. He felt Ardee's hand on his shoulder.

'Are you alright?'

'Ah, yes, it's just . . . I've been having these sick spells.' The feeling was already passing. He rubbed at his sore temples, then the back of his skull. He lifted his head, and smiled up at her again. 'I'm sure it's nothing.'

'Collem . . .'

There was hair wedged between his fingers. A lot of hair. His own, by the colour. He blinked at it, mystified, then coughed with disbelieving laughter. A wet, salty cough from down under his ribs. 'I know it's been thinning for years,' he croaked, 'but really, this is too much.'

Ardee did not laugh. She was staring at his hands, eyes wide with horror.

Patriotic Duties

Glokta winced as he carefully lowered himself into his chair. There was no fanfare to mark the moment when his aching arse touched the hard wood. No round of applause. Only a sharp clicking in his burning knee. *And yet it is a moment of the greatest significance, and not only for me.*

The designers of the White Chamber's furniture had ventured beyond austerity and into the realm of profound discomfort. *One would have thought that they could have stretched to some upholstery for the most powerful men in the realm. Perhaps the intention was to remind the occupants that one should never become too comfortable at the pinnacle of power.* He glanced sideways, and saw Bayaz watching him. *Well, uncomfortable is about as good as I ever get. Have I not often said so?* He winced as he tried to worm his way forwards, the legs of his chair squealing noisily against the floor.

Long ago, when I was handsome, young, and promising, I dreamed of one day sitting at this table as a noble Lord Marshal, or a respected High Justice, or even an honourable Lord Chamberlain. Who could ever have suspected, even in their darkest moments, that beautiful Sand dan Glokta would one day sit on the Closed Council as the feared, the abhorred, the all-powerful Arch Lector of the Inquisition? He could scarcely keep the smile from his toothless mouth as he slumped back against the unyielding wood.

Not everyone appeared amused by his sudden elevation, however. King Jezal in particular glowered at Glokta with the most profound dislike. 'Remarkable that you are confirmed already in your position,' he snapped.

Bayaz interposed. 'Such things can happen quickly when there is the will, your Majesty.'

'After all,' observed Hoff, stealing a rare moment away from his goblet to sweep the table with a melancholy glance, 'our numbers are most sadly reduced.'

All too true. Several chairs loomed significantly empty. Marshal Varuz was missing, presumed dead. *Certainly dead, given that he was conducting the defence from the Tower of Chains, a structure now scattered widely over the streets of the city. Farewell, my old fencing master, farewell.* High Justice Marovia had also left a vacant seat. *No doubt they are still trying to scrape the frozen meat from the walls of his office. Adieu to my third suitor, I fear.* Lord Valdis, Commander of the Knights Herald, was not in attendance. *Keeping watch on the southern gate, I understand, when the Gurkish detonated their explosive powder. Body never found, nor ever will be, one suspects.* Lord Admiral Reutzer too, was absent. *Wounded at sea by a cutlass to the guts. Not expected to survive, alas.*

Truly, the pinnacle of power is less crowded than it used to be.

'Marshal West could not be with us?' asked Lord Chancellor Halleck.

'He regrets that he cannot.' General Kroy seemed to pinch off each word with his teeth. 'He has asked me to take his place, and speak for the army.'

'And how is the Marshal?'

'Wounded.'

'And further afflicted by the wasting illness that has recently swept the Agriont,' added the king, frowning grimly down the table at the First of the Magi.

'Regrettable.' Bayaz' face showed not the slightest sign of regret or anything else.

'A terrible business,' lamented Hoff. 'The physicians are utterly baffled.'

'Few survive.' Luthar's glare had become positively deadly.

'Let us ardently hope,' gushed Torlichorm, 'that Marshal West is one of the lucky ones.' *Let us hope so indeed. Although hope changes nothing.*

'To business, then?' Wine gurgled from the pitcher as Hoff

filled his goblet for the second time since entering the room. 'How fares the campaign, General Kroy?'

'The Gurkish army is utterly routed. We have pursued them towards Keln, where some few managed to flee on the remnant of their fleet. Duke Orso's ships soon put an end to that, however. The Gurkish invasion is over. Victory is ours.' *And yet he frowns as though he is admitting defeat.*

'Excellent.'

'The nation owes a debt of thanks to its brave soldiers.'

'Our congratulations, General.'

Kroy stared down at the table-top. 'The congratulations belong to Marshal West, who gave the orders, and to General Poulder and the others who gave their lives carrying them out. I was no more than an observer.'

'But you played your part, and admirably.' Hoff raised his goblet. 'Given the unfortunate absence of Marshal Varuz, I feel confident his Majesty will soon wish to confer a promotion upon you.' He glanced towards the king, and Luthar grunted his unenthusiastic assent.

'I am honoured to serve in whatever capacity his Majesty should decide, of course. The prisoners are a more urgent matter, however. We have many thousands of them, and no food with which to—'

'We have not enough food for our own soldiers, our own citizens, our own wounded,' said Hoff, dabbing at his wet lips.

'Ransom any men of quality back to the Emperor?' suggested Torlichorm.

'There were precious few men of quality among their entire damn army.'

Bayaz frowned down the table. 'If they are of no value to the Emperor they are certainly of no value to us. Let them starve.'

A few men shifted uncomfortably. 'We are talking of thousands of lives, here—' began Kroy.

The gaze of the First of the Magi fell upon him like a great stone and squashed his objections flat. 'I know what we are talking of, General. Enemies. Invaders.'

'Surely we can find a way?' threw in the king. 'Could we not ship them back to Kantic shores? It would be a shameful epilogue to our victory if—'

'Each prisoner fed is one citizen that must go hungry. Such is the terrible arithmetic of power. A difficult decision, your Majesty, but those are the only kind we have in this room. What would your opinion be, Arch Lector?'

The eyes of the king, and the old men in the high chairs, all turned towards Glokta. *Ah, we know what must be done, and we do not flinch, and so forth. Let the monster pronounce the sentence, so the rest can feel like decent men.* 'I have never been a great admirer of the Gurkish.' Glokta shrugged his aching shoulders. 'Let them starve.'

King Jezal settled further into his throne with an even grimmer frown. *Could it be that our monarch is a touch less house-broken than the First of the Magi would like to believe?* Lord Chancellor Halleck cleared his throat. 'Now that victory is ours, our first concern, without question, is the clearing of the ruins, and the rebuilding of the damage caused by . . .' his eyes shifted nervously sideways to Bayaz, and back. 'Gurkish aggression.'

'Hear, hear.'

'Rebuilding. We are all agreed.'

'The costs,' and Halleck winced as if the word caused him pain, 'even of clearing the wreckage in the Agriont alone, may run to many tens of thousands of marks. The price of rebuilding, many millions. When we consider the extensive damage to the city of Adua besides . . . the costs . . .' Halleck scowled again and rubbed at his ill-shaved jaw with one hand. 'Difficult even to guess at.'

'We can only do our best.' Hoff sadly shook his head. 'And find one mark at a time.'

'I, for one, suggest we look to the nobles,' said Glokta. There were several grumbles of agreement.

'His Eminence makes a fine point.'

'A sharp curtailment of the powers of the Open Council,' said Halleck.

'Harsh taxes on those who did not provide material support in the recent war.'

'Excellent! Trim the nobles' sails. Damn parasites.'

'Sweeping reforms. Lands returned to the crown. Levies on inheritance.'

'On inheritance! An inspired notion!'

'The Lord Governors too must be brought into the fold.'

'Skald and Meed. Yes. They have long enjoyed too much independence.'

'Meed can hardly be blamed, his province is a wreck—'

'This is not a question of blame,' said Bayaz. *No indeed, we all know where that lies.* 'This is a question of control. Victory has given us the opportunity for reform.'

'We need to centralise!'

'Westport as well. Too long they have played us off against the Gurkish.'

'They need us now.'

'Perhaps we should extend the Inquisition to their city?' suggested Glokta.

'A foothold in Styria!'

'We must rebuild!' The First of the Magi thumped at the table with one meaty fist. 'Better and more glorious even than before. The statues in the Kingsway may have fallen, but they have left space for new ones.'

'A new era of prosperity,' said Halleck, eyes shining.

'A new era of power,' said Hoff, raising his goblet.

'A golden age?' Bayaz looked up the table at Glokta.

'An age of unity and opportunity for all!' said the king.

His offering fell somewhat flat. Eyes swivelled uncomfortably toward the king's end of the table. *Quite as if he noisily farted, rather than spoke.* 'Er . . . yes, your Majesty,' said Hoff. 'Opportunities.' *For anyone lucky enough to sit on the Closed Council, that is.*

'Perhaps heavier taxes on the merchant guilds?' proffered Halleck. 'As our last Arch Lector had in mind. The banks also. Such a move could produce vast incomes—'

'No,' said Bayaz, offhand. 'Not the guilds, not the banks.

The free operation of those noble institutions provides wealth and security to all. The future of the nation lies in commerce.'

Halleck humbly inclined his head. *With more than a hint of fear, do I detect?* 'Of course, Lord Bayaz, you are right. I freely admit my mistake.'

The Magus moved smoothly on. 'Perhaps the banks would be willing to extend a loan to the crown, however.'

'An excellent idea,' said Glokta without hesitation. 'The banking house of Valint and Balk are a trustworthy and long-founded institution. They were of profound value during my attempts to defend Dagoska. I am sure we could count on their help again.' Bayaz' smile was almost imperceptible. 'In the meantime the lands, assets, and titles of the traitor Lord Brock have been requisitioned by the crown. Their sale will raise a considerable sum.'

'And what of the man himself, Arch Lector?'

'It would appear he fled the nation along with the last of the Gurkish. We assume that he is still their . . . guest.'

'Their puppet, you mean.' Bayaz sucked at his teeth. 'Unfortunate. He may continue to be a focus for discontent.'

'Two of his children are under lock and key in the House of Questions. His daughter and one of the sons. An exchange might be possible—'

'Brock? Ha!' barked Hoff. 'He wouldn't swap his own life for the whole world and everything in it.'

Glokta raised his eyebrows. 'Then perhaps a demonstration of intent? A clear message that treason will not and will never be tolerated?'

'Never a bad message to send,' growled Bayaz to affirmative mutterings from the old men.

'A public declaration of Brock's guilt, then, and his responsibility for the ruin of the city of Adua. Accompanied by a pair of hangings.' *A shame for them, to have been born to such an ambitious father, but everyone loves a public killing.* 'Does anyone have a preference for a certain day or—'

'There will be no hangings.' The king was frowning levelly at Bayaz.

Hoff blinked. 'But your Majesty, you cannot allow—'

'There has been enough bloodshed. Far more than enough. Release Lord Brock's children.' There were several sharp intakes of breath around the table. 'Allow them to join their father, or remain in the Union as private citizens, as they desire.' Bayaz glared balefully from the far end of the room, but the king did not appear intimidated. 'The war is over. We won.' *The war never ends, and victory is temporary.* 'I would rather try to heal wounds than deepen them.' *A wounded enemy is the best kind, they are the easiest to kill.* 'Sometimes mercy buys you more than ruthlessness.'

Glokta cleared his throat. 'Sometimes.' *Though I myself have yet to see the circumstance.*

'Good,' said the king in a voice that brooked no argument. 'Then it is decided. Have we other pressing business? I need to make a tour of the hospitals, and then once more to clearing the wreckage.'

'Of course, your Majesty.' Hoff gave a sycophantic bow. 'Your care for your subjects does you much credit.'

Jezal stared at him for a moment, then snorted, and got up. He had already left the room before most of the old men had struggled to their feet. *And I take even longer.* When Glokta had finally wrestled his chair out of the way and grimaced to standing, he found Hoff was beside him, a frown on his ruddy face. 'We have a small problem,' he muttered.

'Indeed? Something we cannot raise with the rest of the Council?'

'I fear so. Something which, in particular, it would be better not to discuss before his Majesty.' Hoff looked quickly over his shoulder, waited for the last of the old men to pull the heavy door shut behind him and leave the two of them unobserved. *Secrets, then? How tremendously exciting.* 'Our absent Lord Marshal's sister.'

Glokta frowned. *Oh dear.* 'Ardee West? What of her?'

'I have it on good authority, that she finds herself in . . . a delicate condition.'

The familiar flurry of twitches ran up the left side of Glokta's face. 'Is that so?' *What a shame.* 'You are remarkably well informed about that lady's personal business.'

'It is my duty to be so.' Hoff leaned close and blasted Glokta with wine-stinking breath as he whispered. 'When you consider who the father might very well be.'

'And that is?' *Though I think we both already guess the answer.*

'Who else but the king?' hissed Hoff under his breath, a note of panic in his voice. 'You must be well aware that they were involved in . . . a liaison, to put it delicately, prior to his coronation. It is scarcely a secret. Now this? A bastard child! When the king's own claim to the throne is not of the purest? When he has so many enemies still on the Open Council? Such a child could be used against us, if it became known of, and it will, of course!' He leaned closer yet. 'Such a thing would constitute a threat to the state.'

'Indeed,' said Glokta icily. *All too unfortunately true. What a terrible, terrible shame.*

Hoff's fat fingers fussed nervously with each other. 'I realise that you have some association with the lady and her family. I understand entirely if this is one responsibility that you would rather be free of. I can make the arrangements with no—'

Glokta flashed his craziest grin. 'Are you implying that I lack sufficient ruthlessness for the murder of a pregnant mother, Lord Chamberlain?' His voice bounced loud from the hard white walls, merciless as a knife-thrust.

Hoff winced, his eyes darting nervously towards the door. 'I am sure you would not flinch from any patriotic duty—'

'Good. You may rest easy, then. Our mutual friend did not select me for this role because of my soft heart.' *Anything but.* 'I will deal with the matter.'

The same small, brick-built house in the same unremarkable street that Glokta had visited so often before. *The same house where I spent so many enjoyable afternoons. As close as I have come to comfort since I was dragged drooling from the Emperor's prisons.* He slid his right hand into his pocket, felt the cold metal brush against his fingertips. *Why do I do this? Why? So that drunken arsehole Hoff can mop his brow at a calamity averted? So that Jezal dan Luthar can sit a hair more secure on his puppet throne?* He twisted his hips one way and then the other until he felt his back click. *She deserves so much better. But such is the terrible arithmetic of power.*

He pushed back the gate, hobbled up to the front door, and gave it a smart knock. It was a moment before the cringing maid answered. *Perhaps the one who alerted our court drunkard Lord Hoff to the unfortunate situation?* She showed him through into the over-furnished sitting room with little more than a mumble and left him there, staring at a small fire in the small grate. He caught a glimpse of himself in the mirror above the fireplace, and frowned.

Who is that man? That ruined shell? That shambling corpse? Can you even call it a face? So twisted and so lined, so etched with pain. What is this loathsome, pitiable species? Oh, if there is a God, protect me from this thing!

He tried to smile. Savage grooves cut through his corpse-pale skin, the hideous gap in his teeth yawned. The corner of his mouth trembled, his left eye twitched, narrower than the other, rimmed with angry red. *The smile seems to promise horrors more surely even than the frown.*

Has any man ever looked more of a villain? Has any man ever been more of a monster? Could any vestige of humanity possibly remain behind such a mask? How did beautiful Sand dan Glokta become . . . this? Mirrors. Even worse than stairs. His lip curled with disgust as he turned away.

Ardee stood in the doorway, watching him in silence. She looked well, to his mind, once he got over the awkward surprise of being observed. *Very well, with perhaps the slightest swelling about her stomach already? Three months along now? Four perhaps? Soon there will be no disguising it.*

'Your Eminence.' She gave him an appraising glance as she stepped into the room. 'White suits you.'

'Truly? You do not feel it makes the skull-like rings about my feverish eyes look all the darker?'

'Why, not at all. It perfectly matches your ghoulish pallor.'

Glokta leered his toothless grin. 'The very effect I was hoping for.'

'Have you come to take me on another tour of sewers, death and torture?'

'A repeat of that performance will probably never be possible, alas. I seem to have used up all my friends and most of my enemies in that one throw.'

'And regrettably the Gurkish army can no longer be with us.'

'Busy elsewhere, I understand.' He watched her cross to the table, look out of the window towards the street, the daylight glowing through her dark hair, down the edge of her cheek.

'I trust that you are well?' she asked.

'Busier even than the Gurkish. A great deal to do. How is your brother? I have been meaning to visit him, but . . .' *But I doubt even I could stand the stink of my own hypocrisy if I did. I cause pain. The easing of it is a foreign tongue to me.*

Ardee looked at her feet. 'He is always sick now. Every time I visit he is thinner. One of his teeth fell out while I was with him.' She shrugged her shoulders. 'It just came out while he was trying to eat. He nearly choked on it. But what can I do? What can anyone?'

'I am truly sorry to hear it.' *But it changes nothing.* 'I am sure that you are a great help to him.' *I am sure that there can be no help for him.* 'And how are you?'

'Better than most, I suppose.' She gave a long sigh, shook herself and tried to smile. 'Will you take some wine?'

'No, but don't let me stop you.' *I know you never have.*

But she only held the bottle for a moment, then set it down again. 'I have been trying to drink less, lately.'

'I have always felt that you should.' He took a slow step towards her. 'You feel sick, then, in the mornings?'

She looked sharply sideways, then swallowed, the thin muscles standing out from her neck. 'You know?'

'I am the Arch Lector,' he said as he came closer. 'I am supposed to know everything.'

Her shoulders sagged, her head dropped, she leaned forwards, both hands on the edge of the table. Glokta could see her eyelids fluttering, from the side. *Blinking back the tears. For all of her anger, and her cleverness, she's just as much in need of saving as anyone could be. But there is no one to come to the rescue. There is only me.*

'I suppose I made quite a mess of things, just as my brother said I would. Just as you said I would. You must be disappointed.'

Glokta felt his face twisting. *Something like a smile, perhaps. But not much joy in it.* 'I've spent most of my life disappointed. But not in you. It's a hard world. No one gets what they deserve.' *How long must we drag this out before we find the courage? It will not get any easier to do it. It must be now.*

'Ardee . . .' his voice sounded rough in his own ears. He took another limping step, his palm sweaty on the handle of his cane. She looked up at him, wet eyes gleaming, one hand on her stomach. She moved as if to take a step back. *A trace of fear, perhaps? And who can blame her? Can it be that she guesses at what is coming?*

'You know that I have always had a great liking and respect for your brother.' His mouth was dry, his tongue slurped awkwardly against his empty gums. *Now is the time.* 'Over the past months I have developed a great liking and respect for you.' A flurry of twitches ran up the side of his face and made a tear leak from his flickering eye. *Now, now.* 'Or . . . as close to such feelings as a man like myself can come, at least.' Glokta slid his hand into his pocket, carefully, so she would not notice. He felt the cold metal, the hard, merciless edges brushing against his skin. *It must be now.* His heart was pounding, his throat so tight that he could barely speak. 'This is difficult. I am . . . sorry.'

'For what?' she said, frowning at him.

Now.

He lurched towards her, snatching his hand from his pocket. She stumbled back against the table, eyes wide . . . and they both froze.

The ring glittered between them. A colossal, flashing diamond so large it made the thick golden band look flimsy. *So large it looks a joke. A fake. An absurd impossibility. The biggest stone that Valint and Balk had to offer.*

'I have to ask you to marry me,' he croaked. The hand that held the ring was trembling like a dry leaf. *Put a cleaver in it and it's steady as a rock, but ask me to hold a ring and I nearly wet myself. Courage, Sand, courage.*

She stared down at the glittering stone, her mouth hanging stupidly open. *With shock? With horror? Marry this . . . thing? I would rather die!* 'Uh . . .' she muttered. 'I . . .'

'I know! I know, I'm as disgusted as you are, but . . . let me speak. Please.' He stared down at the floor, his mouth twisting as he said the words. 'I am not stupid enough to pretend that you might ever come to love . . . a man like me, or think of me with anything warmer than pity. This is a question of necessity. You should not flinch from it because . . . of what I am. They know you are carrying the king's child.'

'They?' she muttered.

'Yes. They. The child is a threat to them. You are a threat to them. This way I can protect you. I can give your child legitimacy. It must be our child, now and forever.' Still she stared at the ring in silence. *Like a prisoner staring horrified upon the instruments, and deciding whether to confess. Two awful choices, but which is the worse?*

'There are many things that I can give you. Safety. Security. Respect. You will have the best of everything. A high place in society, for what such things are worth. No one will dream of laying a finger upon you. No one will dare to talk down to you. People will whisper behind your back, of course. But they will whisper of your beauty, your wit, and your surpassing virtue.' Glokta narrowed his eyes. 'I will see to it.'

She looked up at him, and swallowed. *And now comes the refusal. My thanks, but I would rather die.* 'I should be honest with you. When I was younger . . . I did some foolish things.' Her mouth twisted. 'This isn't even the first bastard I've carried. My father threw me down the stairs and I lost it. He nearly killed me. I didn't think that it could happen again.'

'We have all done things we are not proud of.' *You should*

hear my confessions, some time. Or rather no one ever should. 'That changes nothing. I promised that I would look to your welfare. I see no other way.'

'Then yes.' She took the ring from him without any ceremony and slid it onto her finger. 'There is nothing to think about, is there?' *Scarcely the gushing acceptance, the tearful acquiescence, the joyful surrender that one reads of in the story books. A reluctant business arrangement. An occasion for sad reflection on all that might have been, but is not.*

'Who would have thought,' she murmured, staring at the jewel on her finger, 'when I watched you fence with my brother, all those years ago, that I would one day wear your ring? You always were the man of my dreams.'

And now of your nightmares. 'Life takes strange turns. The circumstances are not quite what anyone would have predicted.' *And so I save two lives. How much evil can that possibly outweigh? Yet it is something on the right side of the scales, at least. Every man needs something on the right side of the scales.*

Her dark eyes rolled up to his. 'Could you not have afforded a bigger stone?'

'Only by raiding the treasury,' he croaked. *A kiss would be traditional, but under the circumstances—*

She stepped towards him, lifting one arm. He lurched back, winced at a twinge in his hip. 'Sorry. Somewhat . . . out of practice.'

'If I am to do this, I mean to do it properly.'

'To make the best of it, do you mean?'

'To make something of it, anyway.' She drew closer still. He had to force himself to stay where he was. She looked into his eyes. She reached up, slowly, and touched his cheek, and set his eyelid flickering. *Foolishness. How many women have touched me before? And yet that was another life. Another—*

Her hand slid round his face, her fingertips pressing tight into his jaw. His neck clicked as she pulled him close. He felt her breath warm on his chin. Her lips brushed against his, gently, and back the other way. He heard her make a soft grunt in her throat, and it made his own breath catch. *Pretence, of*

627

course. How could any woman want to touch this ruined body? Kiss this ruined face? Even I am repulsed at the thought of it. Pretence, and yet I must applaud her for the effort.

His left leg trembled and he had to cling tight to his cane. The breath hissed fast through his nose. Her face was sideways on to his, their mouths locked together, sucking wetly. The tip of his tongue licked at his empty gums. *Pretence, of course, what else could it be? And yet she does it so very, very well . . .*

The First Law

Ferro sat, and she stared at her hand. The hand that had held the Seed. It looked the same as ever, yet it felt different. Cold, still. Very cold. She had wrapped it in blankets. She had bathed it in warm water. She had held it near the fire, so near that she had burned herself.

Nothing helped.

'Ferro . . .' Whispered so quiet it could almost have been the wind around the window-frame.

She jerked to her feet, knife clutched in her fist. She stared into the corners of her room. All empty. She bent down to look under the bed, under the tall cupboard. She tore the hangings out of the way with her free hand. No one. She had known there would be no one.

Yet she still heard them.

A thumping at the door and she whipped round again, breath hissing through her teeth. Another dream? Another ghost? More heavy knocks.

'Come in?' she growled.

The door opened. Bayaz. He raised one eyebrow at her knife. 'You are altogether too fond of blades, Ferro. You have no enemies here.'

She glared at the Magus through narrowed eyes. She was not so sure. 'What happened, in the wind?'

'What happened?' Bayaz shrugged. 'We won.'

'What were those shapes? Those shadows.'

'I saw nothing, aside from Mamun and his Hundred Words receiving the punishment they deserved.'

'Did you not hear voices?'

'Over the thunder of our victory? I heard nothing.'

'I did.' Ferro lowered the knife and slid it into her belt. She worked the fingers of her hand, the same, and yet changed. 'I still hear them.'

'And what do they tell you, Ferro?'

'They speak of locks, and gates, and doors, and the opening of them. Always they talk of opening them. They ask about the Seed. Where is it?'

'Safe.' Bayaz gazed blankly at her. 'Remember, if you truly hear the creatures of the Other Side, that they are made of lies.'

'They are not alone in that. They ask me to break the First Law. Just as you did.'

'Open to interpretation.' Bayaz had a proud twist to the corner of his mouth. As if he had achieved something wonderful. 'I tempered Glustrod's disciplines with the techniques of the Master Maker, and used the Seed as the engine for my Art. The results were . . .' He took a long, satisfied breath. 'Well, you were there. It was, above all, a triumph of will.'

'You tampered with the seals. You put the world at risk. The Tellers of Secrets . . .'

'The First Law is a paradox. Whenever you change a thing you borrow from the world below, and there are always risks. If I have crossed a line it is a line of scale only. The world is safe, is it not? I make no apologies for the ambition of my vision.'

'They are burying men, and women, and children, in pits for a hundred. Just as they did in Aulcus. This sickness . . . it is because of what we did. Is that ambition, then? The size of the graves?'

Bayaz gave a dismissive toss of his head. 'An unexpected side-effect. The price of victory, I fear, is the same now as it was in the Old Time, and always will be.' He fixed her with his eye, and there was a threat in it. A challenge. 'But if I broke the First Law, what then? In what court will you have me judged? By what jury? Will you release Tolomei from the darkness to give evidence? Will you seek out Zacharus to read the charge? Will you drag Cawneil from the edge of the World to deliver the verdict? Will you bring great Juvens from the land of the dead to pronounce the sentence? I think not. I am First of the Magi. I am the last authority and I say . . . I am righteous.'

'You? No.'

'Yes, Ferro. Power makes all things right. That is my first law, and my last. That is the only law that I acknowledge.'

'Zacharus warned me,' she murmured, thinking of the endless plain, the wild-eyed old man with his circling birds. 'He told me to run, and never stop running. I should have listened to him.'

'To that bloated bladder of self-righteousness?' Bayaz snorted. 'Perhaps you should have, but that ship has sailed. You waved it away happily from the shore, and chose instead to feed your fury. Gladly you fed it. Let us not pretend that I deceived you. You knew we were to walk dark paths.'

'I did not expect . . .' she worked her icy fingers into a trembling fist. 'This.'

'What did you expect, then? I must confess I thought you made of harder stuff. Let us leave the philosophising to those with more time and fewer scores to settle. Guilt, and regret, and righteousness? It is like talking with the great King Jezal. And who has the patience for that?' He turned towards the door. 'You should stay near me. Perhaps, in time, Khalul will send other agents. Then I will have need of your talents once again.'

She snorted. 'And until then? Sit here with the shadows for company?'

'Until then, smile, Ferro, if you can remember how.' Bayaz flashed his white grin at her. 'You have your vengeance.'

The wind tore around her, rushed around her, full of shadows. She knelt at one end of a screaming tunnel, touching the very sky. The world was thin and brittle as a sheet of glass, ready to crack. Beyond it a bottomless void, filled with voices.

'Let us in . . .'

'No!' She thrashed her way free and struggled up, stood panting on the floor beside her bed, every muscle rigid. But there was no one to fight. Another dream, only.

Her own fault, for letting herself sleep.

A long strip of moonlight reached towards her across the

tiles. The window at its end stood ajar, a cold night breeze washed through and chilled her sweat-beaded skin. She walked to it, frowning, pushed it shut and slid the bolt. She turned around.

A figure stood in the thick shadows beside the door. A one-armed figure, swathed in rags. The few pieces of armour still strapped to him were scuffed and gouged. His face was a dusty ruin, torn skin hanging in scraps from white bone, but even so, Ferro knew him.

Mamun.

'We meet again, devil-blood.' His dry voice rustled like old paper.

'I am dreaming,' she hissed.

'You will wish that you were.' He was across the room in a breathless instant. His one hand closed round her throat like a lock snapping shut. 'Digging my way out of that ruination one handful of dirt at a time has given me a hunger.' His dry breath tickled at her face. 'I will make myself a new arm from your flesh, and with it I will strike down Bayaz and take vengeance for great Juvens. The Prophet has seen it, and I will turn his vision into truth.' He lifted her, effortlessly, crushed her back against the wall, her heels kicking against the panelling.

The hand squeezed. Her chest heaved, but no air moved inside her neck. She struggled with the fingers, ripped at them with her nails, but they were made of iron, made of stone, tight as a hanged man's collar. She fought and twisted but he did not shift a hair's breadth. She fiddled with Mamun's ruined face, her fingers worked their way into his ripped cheek, tore at the dusty flesh inside but his eyes did not even blink. It had grown cold in the room.

'Say your prayers, child,' he whispered, broken teeth grinding, 'and hope that God is merciful.'

She was growing weaker now. Her lungs were bursting. She tore at him still, but each effort was less. Weaker and weaker. Her arms drooped, her legs dangled, her eyelids were heavy, heavy. All was terrible cold.

'Now,' he whispered, breath smoking. He brought her

down, opening his mouth, his torn lips sliding back from his splintered teeth. 'Now.'

Her finger stabbed into his neck. Through his skin and into his dry flesh, up to the knuckle. It drove his head away. Her other hand wormed round his, prised it from her throat, bent his fingers backwards. She felt the bones in them snap, crunch, splinter as she dropped to the floor. White frost crept out across the black window-panes beside her, squeaked under her bare feet as she twisted Mamun round and rammed him against the wall, crushed his body into the splintering panels, the cracking plaster. Dust showered down from the force of it.

She drove her finger further into his throat, upwards, inwards. It was easy to do it. There was no end to her strength. It came from the other side of the divide. The Seed had changed her, as it had changed Tolomei, and there could be no going back.

Ferro smiled.

'Take my flesh, would you? You have had your last meal, Mamun.'

The tip of her finger slid out between his teeth, met her thumb and hooked him like a fish. With a jerk of her wrist she ripped the jaw-bone from his head and tossed it clattering away. His tongue lolled inside a ragged mass of dusty flesh.

'Say your prayers, Eater,' she hissed, 'and hope that God is merciful.' She clamped her palms around either side of his head. A long squeak came from his nose. His shattered hand pawed at her, uselessly. His skull bent, then flattened, then burst apart, splinters of bone flying. She let the body fall, dust sliding out across the floor, curling round her feet.

'Yes . . .'

She did not startle. She did not stare. She knew where the voice came from. Everywhere and nowhere.

She stepped to the window and pulled it open. She jumped through, dropped a dozen strides down to the turf, and stood. The night was full of sounds, but she was silent. She padded across the moonlit grass, crunching frozen where her bare feet fell, crept up a long stair and onto the walls. The voices followed her.

'Wait.'

'The Seed!'

'Ferro.'

'Let us in . . .'

She ignored them. An armoured man stared out into the night, out towards the House of the Maker, a blacker outline against the black sky. A wedge of darkness over the Agriont within which there were no stars, no moonlit clouds, no light at all. Ferro wondered if Tolomei was lurking in the shadows inside, scratching at its gates. Scratching, scratching, forever. She had wasted her chance at vengeance.

Ferro would not do the same.

She slid down the battlements, around the guard, hugging his cloak tight about his shoulders as she passed. Up onto the parapet and she leaped, the wind rushing against her skin. She cleared the moat, creaking ice spreading out across the water beneath her. The cobbled ground beyond rushed up. Her feet thumped into it and she rolled over, over, away into the buildings. Her clothes were torn from the fall but there was no mark on her skin. Not so much as a bead of blood.

'No, Ferro.'

'Back, and find the Seed!'

'It is near him.'

'Bayaz has it.'

Bayaz. Perhaps when she was done in the South, she would return. When she had buried the great Uthman-ul-Dosht in the ruins of his own palace. When she had sent Khalul, and his Eaters, and his priests to hell. Perhaps then she would come back, and teach the First of the Magi the lesson that he deserved. The lesson that Tolomei meant to teach him. But then, liar or not, he had kept his word to her, in the end. He had given her the means of vengeance.

Now she would take it.

Ferro stole through the silent ruins of the city, quiet and

quick as a night breeze. South, towards the docks. She would find a way. South, across the sea to Gurkhul, and then . . .

The voices whispered to her. A thousand voices. They spoke of the gates that Euz closed, and of the seals that Euz put upon them. They begged her to open them. They told her to break them. They told her how, and they commanded her to do it.

But Ferro only smiled. Let them speak.

She had no masters.

Tea and Threats

Logen frowned.

He frowned at the wide hall, and its glittering mirrors, and the many powerful people in it. He scowled at the great Lords of the Union facing him. Two hundred of them or more, sitting in a muttering crowd around the opposite side of the room. Their false talk, and their false smiles, and their false faces cloyed at him like too much honey. But he felt no better about the folk on his side of the hall, sharing the high platform with him and the great King Jezal.

There was the sneering cripple who'd asked all the questions that day in the tower, dressed now all in white. There was a fat man with a face full of broken veins, looked as if he started each day with a bottle. There was a tall, lean bastard in a black breastplate covered in fancy gold, with a soft smile and hard little eyes. As shifty a pack of liars as Logen had ever laid eyes on, but there was one worse than all the rest together.

Bayaz sat with an easy grin on his face, as if everything had turned out just the way he'd planned. Maybe it had. Damn wizard. Logen should have known better than to trust a man with no hair. The spirits had warned him that Magi have their own purposes, but he'd taken no notice, plunged on blindly, hoping for the best, just like always. Say one thing for Logen Ninefingers, say he never listens. One fault among many.

His eyes swivelled the other way, towards Jezal. He looked comfortable enough in his kingly robes, golden crown gleaming on his head, golden chair even bigger than the one that Logen was sitting in. His wife sat beside him. She had a frosty pride about her, maybe, but no worse for that. Beautiful as a winter morning. And she had this look on her face, when she looked at Jezal. A fierce kind of look, as if she could hardly stop herself tearing into him with her teeth. That lucky bastard always seemed to come out alright. She could've had a little bite out of Logen if she'd wanted, but what woman in her right mind did?

He frowned most of all at himself in the mirrors opposite, raised up on the high platform beside Jezal and his queen. He looked a sullen and brooding, scarred and fearsome monster beside that beautiful pair. A man made of murder, then swaddled in rich coloured cloth and rare white furs, set with polished rivets and bright buckles, all topped off with a great golden chain around his shoulders. That same chain that Bethod had worn. His hands stuck from the ends of his fur-trimmed sleeves, marked and brutal, one finger missing, grasping at the arms of his gilded chair. King's clothes, maybe, but killer's hands. He looked like the villain in some old children's story. The ruthless warrior, clawed his way to power with fire and steel. Climbed to a throne up a mountain of corpses. Maybe he was that man.

He squirmed around, new cloth scratching at his clammy skin. He'd come a long way, since he dragged himself out of a river without even a pair of boots to his name. Dragged himself across the High Places with nothing but a pot for company. He'd come a long way, but he wasn't sure he hadn't liked himself better before. He'd laughed when he'd heard that Bethod was calling himself a king. Now here he was, doing the same, and even worse suited to the job. Say one thing for Logen Ninefingers, say he's a cunt. Simple as that. And that's not something any man likes to admit about himself.

The drunkard, Hoff, was doing most of the talking. 'The Lords' Round lies in ruins, alas. For the time being, therefore, until a venue of grandeur suitable for this noble institution has been built – a new Lords' Round, richer and greater than the last – it has been decided that the Open Council will stand in recess.'

There was a pause. 'In recess?' someone muttered.

'How will we be heard?'

'Where will the nobles have their voice?'

'The nobles will speak through the Closed Council.' Hoff had that tone a man uses talking down to a child. 'Or may apply to the Under-Secretary for Audiences to obtain a hearing with the king.'

'But any peasant may do so!'

Hoff raised his eyebrows. 'True.'

A ripple of anger spread out through the Lords in front of them. Logen might not have understood too much about politics, but he could recognise one set of men getting stood on by another. Never a nice thing to be part of, but at least he was on the side doing the standing, for once.

'The king and the nation are one and the same!' Bayaz' harsh voice cut over the chatter. 'You only borrow your lands from him. He regrets that he requires some portion of them back, but such is the spur of necessity.'

'A quarter.' The cripple licked at his empty gums with a faint sucking sound. 'From each one of you.'

'This will not stand!' shouted an angry old man in the front row.

'You think not, Lord Isher?' Bayaz only smiled at him. 'Those who do not think so may join Lord Brock in dusty exile, and surrender all their lands to the crown instead of just a portion.'

'This is an outrage!' shouted another man. 'Always, the king has been first among equals, the greatest of nobles, not above them. Our votes brought him to the throne, and we refuse—'

'You dance close to a line, Lord Heugen.' The cripple's face twitched with ugly spasms as he frowned across the room. 'You might wish to remain on that side of it, where it is safe, and warm, and loyal. The other side will not suit you so well, I think.' A long tear ran from his flickering left eye and down his hollow cheek. 'The Surveyor General will be assessing your estates over the coming months. It would be wise for you all to lend him your fullest assistance.'

A lot of men were on their feet now, scowling, shaking fists. 'This is outrageous!'

'Unprecedented!'

'Unacceptable!'

'We refuse to be intimidated!'

Jezal sprang from his throne, raising his jewelled sword high, and struck at the platform again and again with the end of the scabbard, filling the room with booming echoes. 'I am the king!' he bellowed at the suddenly silent chamber. 'I am not offering a choice, I am issuing a royal decree! Adua will be rebuilt, and more glorious than ever! This is the price! You have grown too used to a weak crown, my Lords! Believe me when I say that those days are now behind us!'

Bayaz leaned sideways to mutter in Logen's ear. 'Surprisingly good at this, isn't he?'

The Lords grumbled, but they sat back down as Jezal spoke on, voice washing around the room with easy confidence, sheathed sword still held firmly in one fist. 'Those who lent me their wholehearted support in the recent crisis will be exempt. But that list, to your shame, is all too brief. Why, it was friends from outside the borders of the Union who sustained us in our time of need!'

The man in black swept from his chair. 'I, Orso of Talins, stand always at the side of my royal son and daughter!' He seized Jezal's face and kissed both his cheeks. Then he did the same with the queen. 'Their friends are my friends.' He said it with a smile, but the meaning was hard to miss. 'Their enemies? Ah! You all are clever men. You can guess the rest.'

'I thank you for your part in our deliverance,' said Jezal. 'You have our gratitude. The war between the Union and the North is at an end. The tyrant Bethod is dead, and there is a new order. I am proud to call the man who threw him down my friend. Logen Ninefingers! King of the Northmen!' He beamed, holding out his hand. 'It is fitting that we should stride into this bold new future as brothers.'

'Aye,' said Logen, pushing himself painfully up from his chair. 'Right.' He folded Jezal in a hug, slapped him on the back with a thump that echoed round the great chamber. 'Reckon we'll be staying our side of the Whiteflow from now on. Unless my brother has trouble down here, of course.' He swept the sullen old men in the front row with a graveyard scowl. 'Don't make me fucking come back here.' He sat down in the big chair and frowned out. The Bloody-Nine might not have known too much about politics, but he knew how to make a threat alright.

'We won the war!' Jezal rattled the golden hilt of his sword, then slid it smoothly back through the clasp on his belt. 'Now we must win the peace!'

'Well said, your Majesty, well said!' The red-faced drunkard stood, not giving anyone the chance to get a word in. 'Then only one order of business remains before the Open Council stands in recess.' He turned with an oily smile and a hand-rubbing bow. 'Let us offer our thanks to Lord Bayaz, the First of the Magi, who, by the wisdom of his council and the power of his Art, drove out the invader and saved the Union!' He began to clap. The cripple Glokta joined him, then Duke Orso.

A burly lord in the front row sprang up. 'Lord Bayaz!' he roared, smashing his fat hands together. Soon the whole hall was resounding with reluctant applause. Even Heugen joined in. Even Isher, although he had a look on his face as if he was clapping at his own burial. Logen let his hands stay where they were. If he was honest, he felt a touch sick even being there. Sick and angry. He slumped back in his chair, and kept on frowning.

Jezal watched the great worthies of the Union file unhappily out of the Chamber of Mirrors. Great men. Isher, Barezin, Heugen, and all the rest. Men that he had once gaped at the sight of. All humbled. He could hardly keep the smile from his face as they grumbled their helpless discontent. It felt almost like being a king, until he caught sight of his queen.

Terez and her father, the Grand Duke Orso, were engaged in what appeared to be a heartfelt argument, carried out in expressive Styrian, accentuated on both sides by violent hand movements. Jezal might have been relieved that he was not the only family member she appeared to despise, had he not suspected that he was the subject of their argument. He heard

640

a soft scraping behind him, and was mildly disgusted to see the twisted face of his new Arch Lector.

'Your Majesty.' Glokta spoke softly, as if he planned to discuss secrets, frowning towards Terez and her father. 'Might I ask . . . is all well between you and the queen?' His voice dropped even lower. 'I understand that you rarely sleep in the same room.'

Jezal was on the point of giving the cripple a backhanded blow across the face for his impudence. Then he caught Terez looking at him, out of the corner of his eye. That look of utter contempt that was his usual treatment as a husband. He felt his shoulders sag. 'She can scarcely stand to be in the same country as me, let alone the same bed. The woman's an utter bitch!' he snarled, then hung his head and stared down at the floor. 'What am I to do?'

Glokta worked his neck to one side, then the other, and Jezal suppressed a shudder as he heard a loud click. 'Let me speak to the queen, your Majesty. I can be quite persuasive when I have the mind. I understand your difficulties. I am myself but recently married.'

Jezal dreaded to think what manner of monster might have accepted this monster as a husband. 'Truly?' he asked, feigning interest. 'Who is the lady?'

'I believe that the two of you are distantly acquainted. Ardee is her name. Ardee dan Glokta.' And the cripple's lips slid back to display the sickening hole in his front teeth.

'But not—'

'My old friend Collem West's sister, yes.' Jezal stared, speechless. Glokta gave a stiff bow. 'I accept your congratulations.' He turned away, limped to the edge of the platform, and began to lurch down the steps, leaning heavily on his cane.

Jezal could hardly contain his cold shock, his crushing disappointment, his utter horror. He could not conceive of what blackmail that shambling monstrosity might have employed to trap her. Perhaps she had simply been desperate when Jezal abandoned her. Perhaps, with her brother ill, she had been left with nowhere else to turn. Only the other morning, in the hospital, the sight of her had tugged at something in him, just the way it used to. He had been thinking to himself that perhaps, one day, with time . . .

Now even such pleasurable fancies were brought crashing to the ground. Ardee was married, and to a man that Jezal despised. A man who sat on his own Closed Council. To make matters even worse, a man to whom he had, in a moment of madness, just now confessed the total emptiness of his own marriage. He had made himself appear weak, vulnerable, absurd. He cursed bitterly under his breath.

It seemed now that he had loved Ardee with an unbearable passion. That they had shared something he would never find again. How could he not have realised it at the time? How could he have allowed it all to fall apart, for this? The sad fact was, he supposed, that love on its own was nothing like enough.

Logen felt a lurch of disappointment as he opened the door, and close behind it an ugly wave of anger. The room was empty, neat and clean, as though no one had ever slept there. Ferro was gone.

Nothing had worked out the way he'd hoped. He should've expected it by now, maybe. After all, things never had before. And yet he kept on pissing into the wind. He was like a man whose door's too low, but instead of working out how to duck, keeps on smacking his head into the lintel every day of his miserable life. He wanted to feel sorry for himself, but he knew he deserved no better. A man can't do the things he'd done, and hope for happy endings.

He strode out into the corridor and down the hallway, his jaw clenched. He shouldered open the next door without knocking. The tall windows stood open, sunlight pouring into the airy room, hangings stirring in the breeze. Bayaz sat in a carved chair in front of one of them, a teacup in his hand. A fawning servant in a velvet jacket was pouring into it from a silver pot, a tray and cups balanced on his outspread fingertips.

'Ah, the King of the Northmen!' called Bayaz. 'How are—'

'Where is Ferro?'

'Gone. She left something of a mess behind, in fact, but I have tidied up, as I so often find myself—'

'Where?'

The Magus shrugged. 'South, I would imagine. Vengeance, or some such, if I was forced to guess. She always said a very great deal about vengeance. A most ill-tempered woman.'

'She is changed.'

'Great events, my friend. None of us are quite the same. Now, will you take tea?'

The servant pranced forward, silver tray bobbing. Logen seized him by his velvet jacket and flung him across the room. He squealed as he crashed into the wall and sprawled on the carpet, cups clattering around him.

Bayaz raised an eyebrow. 'A simple "no" would have sufficed.'

'Shit on that, you old bastard.'

The First of the Magi frowned. 'Why, Master Ninefingers, you seem in bullish mood this morning. You are a king now, and it ill becomes you to let your baser passions rule you in this manner. Kings of that sort never last. You have enemies still in the North. Calder and Scale, up in the hills causing trouble, I am sure. Manners should be repaid by like manners, I have always thought. You have been helpful to me, and I can be helpful in return.'

'As you were to Bethod?'

'Just so.'

'Much good it did him.'

'When he had my help, he prospered. Then he became proud, and unruly, and demanded things all his own way. Without my help . . . well, you know the rest.'

'Stay out of my business, wizard.' Logen let his hand fall onto the hilt of the Maker's blade. If swords have voices, as the Magus had once told him, he made it give a grim threat now.

But Bayaz' face showed only the slightest trace of annoyance. 'A lesser man might find himself upset. Did I not buy your life from Bethod? Did I not give you purpose when you had nothing? Did I not take you to the very edge of the World, show you wonders few men have seen? These are poor manners. Why, the very sword with which you threaten me was my gift to you. I had hoped we might come to a—'

'No.'

'I see. Not even—'

'We are done. Looks as if I'll never be a better man, but I can try not to be a worse. I can try that much, at least.'

Bayaz narrowed his eyes. 'Well, Master Ninefingers, you surprise me to the last. I thought you a courageous yet restrained man, a calculating yet compassionate one. I thought you, above all, a realistic man. But the Northmen have ever been prone to petulance. I observe in you now an obstinate streak and a destructive temper. I see the Bloody-Nine at last.'

'I'm happy to disappoint you. Seems we misjudged each other entirely. I took you for a great man. Now I realise my mistake.' Logen slowly shook his head. 'What have you done here?'

'What have I done?' Bayaz snorted with disbelieving laughter. 'I combined three pure disciplines of magic, and I forged a new one! It seems you do not understand the achievement, Master Ninefingers, but I forgive you. I realise that book-learning has never been your strongest suit. Such a thing has not been contemplated since before the Old Time, when Euz split his gifts among his sons.' Bayaz sighed. 'None will appreciate my greatest achievement, it seems. None except Khalul, perhaps, and it is unlikely he will ever proffer his congratulations. Why, such power has not been released within the Circle of the World since . . . since . . .'

'Glustrod destroyed himself and Aulcus with him?'

The Magus raised his eyebrows. 'Since you mention it.'

'And the results are pretty much the same, it seems to me, except you wrought a touch less careless slaughter, and ruined a smaller part of a smaller city, in a smaller, meaner time. Otherwise what's the difference, between you and him?'

'I would have thought that was entirely obvious.' Bayaz lifted his tea-cup, gazing mildly over the rim. 'Glustrod lost.'

Logen stood there for a long while, thinking on that. Then he turned and stalked from the room, the servant cringing out of his way. Into the corridor, footsteps clapping from the gilded ceiling, Bethod's heavy chain jingling round his shoulders like laughter in his ear.

He probably should've kept the ruthless old bastard on his side. Chances were that Logen would need his help, the way things were like to be in the North, once he got back. He probably should've sucked up that stinking piss he called tea and smiled as if it was honey. He probably should've laughed, and called Bayaz old friend, so he could come crawling to the Great Northern Library when things turned sour. That would have been the clever thing to do. That would have been the realistic thing. But it was just the way that Logen's father had always said . . .

He'd never been that realistic.

Behind the Throne

As soon as he heard the door open, Jezal knew who his visitor must be. He did not even have to look up. Who else would have the temerity to barge into a king's own chambers without so much as knocking? He cursed, silently, but with great bitterness.

It could only be Bayaz. His jailer. His chief tormentor. His ever-present shadow. The man who had destroyed half the Agriont, and made a ruin of beautiful Adua, and now smiled and revelled in the applause as though he were the saviour of the nation. It was enough to make a man sick to the pit of his guts. Jezal ground his teeth, staring out of the window towards the ruins, refusing to turn round.

More demands. More compromises. More talk of what had to be done. Being the head of state, at least with the First of the Magi at his shoulder, was an endlessly frustrating and disempowering experience. Getting his own way on even the tiniest of issues, an almost impossible struggle. Wherever he looked he found himself staring directly into the Magus' disapproving frown. He felt like nothing more than a figurehead. A fine-looking, a gilded, a magnificent yet utterly useless chunk of wood. Except a figurehead at least gets to go at the front of the ship.

'Your Majesty,' came the old man's voice, the usual thin veneer of respect scarcely concealing the hard body of disdain beneath.

'What now?' Jezal finally turned to face him. He was surprised to see that the Magus had shed his robes of state in favour of his old travel-stained coat, the heavy boots he had worn on their ill-fated journey into the ruined west. 'Going somewhere?' asked Jezal, hardly daring even to hope.

'I am leaving Adua. Today.'

'Today?' It was the most Jezal could do to stop himself leaping in the air and screaming for joy. He felt like a prisoner stepping from his stinking dungeon and into the bright sunlight of freedom. Now he could rebuild the Agriont as he saw fit. He could reorganise the Closed Council, pick his own advisers. Perhaps even rid himself of that witch of a wife Bayaz had saddled him with. He would be free to do the right thing, whatever that was. He would be free to try and find out what the right thing might be, at least. Was he not the High King of the Union, after all? Who would refuse him? 'We will be sorry to lose you, of course.'

'I can imagine. There are some arrangements that we must make first, however.'

'By all means.' Anything if it meant he was rid of the old bastard.

'I have spoken with your new Arch Lector, Glokta.'

The name alone produced a shiver of revulsion. 'Have you indeed?'

'A sharp man. He has greatly impressed me. I have asked him to speak in my stead while I am absent from the Closed Council.'

'Truly?' asked Jezal, wondering whether to toss the cripple from his post directly after the Magus left the gates or to leave it a day.

'I would recommend,' Bayaz said in very much the tone of an order, 'that you listen closely to his opinions.'

'Oh I will, of course. The best of luck on your journey back to . . .'

'I would like you, in fact, to do as he says.'

A cold knot of anger pressed at Jezal's throat. 'You would have me, in effect . . . obey him?'

Bayaz' eyes did not deviate from his own. 'In effect . . . yes.'

Jezal was left momentarily speechless. For the Magus to suppose that he could come and go as he pleased, leaving his maimed lackey in charge? Above a king, in his own kingdom? The overwhelming arrogance of the man! 'You have taken a

647

high hand of late in my affairs!' he snapped. 'I am in no mind to trade one overbearing adviser for another.'

'That man will be very useful to you. To us. Decisions will have to be made that you would find difficult. Actions will have to be taken which you would rather not take yourself. People who would live in sparkling palaces need others willing to carry away their ordure, lest it pile up in the polished corridors and one day bury them. All this is simple, and obvious. You have not attended to me.'

'No! You are the one who has failed to attend! Sand dan Glokta? That crippled bastard . . .' he realised his unfortunate choice of words, but had to forge on regardless, growing angrier than ever, 'sitting beside me at the Closed Council? Leering over my shoulder every day of my life? And now you would have him dictate to me? Unacceptable. Insufferable. Impossible! We are no longer in the time of Harod the Great! I have no notion of what causes you to suppose that you could speak to me in such a manner. I am king here, and I refuse to be steered!'

Bayaz closed his eyes, and drew a slow breath through his nose. Quite as though he were trying to find the patience for the education of a moron. 'You cannot understand what it is to live as long as I have. To know all that I know. You people are dead in the blink of an eye, and have to be taught the same old lessons all over again. The same lessons that Juvens taught Stolicus a thousand years ago. It becomes extremely tiresome.'

Jezal's fury was steadily building. 'I apologise if I bore you!'

'I accept your apology.'

'I was joking!'

'Ah. Your wit is so very sharp I hardly noticed I was cut.'

'You mock me!'

'It is easily done. Every man seems a child to me. When you reach my age you see that history moves in circles. So many times I have guided this nation back from the brink of destruction, and on to ever greater glory. And what do I ask in return? A few little sacrifices? If you only understood the sacrifices that I have made on behalf of you cattle!'

648

Jezal stabbed one finger furiously towards the window. 'And what of all those dead? What of all those who have lost everything? Those cattle, as you put it! Are they happy with their sacrifices, do you suppose? What of all those who have suffered from this illness? That still suffer? My own close friend among them! I cannot but notice it seems similar to that illness you described to us in ruined Aulcus. I cannot help thinking that your magic might be the cause!'

The Magus made no effort to deny it. 'I deal in the momentous. I cannot concern myself with the fate of every peasant. Neither can you. I have tried to teach you this, but it seems you have failed to learn the lesson.'

'You are mistaken! I refuse to learn it!' Now was his chance. Now, while he was angry enough, for Jezal to step forever from the shadow of the First of the Magi and stand a free man. Bayaz was poison, and he had to be cut out. 'You helped me to my throne, and for that I thank you. But I do not care for your brand of government, it smacks of tyranny!'

Bayaz narrowed his eyes. 'Government is tyranny. At its best it is dressed in pretty colours.'

'Your callous disregard for the lives of my subjects! I will not stand for it! I have moved beyond you. You are no longer wanted here. No longer needed. I will find my own way from now on.' He waved Bayaz away with what he hoped was a regal gesture of dismissal. 'You may leave.'

'May . . . I . . . indeed?' The First of the Magi stood in silence for a long time, his frown growing darker and darker. Long enough for Jezal's rage to begin to wilt, for his mouth to go dry, for his knees to feel weak. 'I perceive that I have been far too soft with you,' said Bayaz, each word sharp as a razor-cut. 'I have coddled you, like a favourite grandchild, and you have grown wilful. A mistake that I shall not make again. A responsible guardian should never be shy with the whip.'

'I am a son of kings!' snarled Jezal, 'I will not—'

He was doubled over by a spear of pain through his guts, stunningly sudden. He tottered a step or two, scalding vomit spraying from his mouth. He crashed onto his face, scarcely able even to breathe, his crown bouncing off and rolling away into the corner of the room. He had never known agony like it. Not a fraction of it.

'I have no notion . . . of what causes you to suppose . . . that you could speak to me in such a manner. To me, the First of the Magi!' Jezal heard Bayaz' footsteps thumping slowly towards him, voice picking at his ears as he squirmed helplessly in his own sick.

'Son of kings? I am disappointed, after all that we have been through together, that you would so readily believe the lies I have spread on your behalf. That nonsense was meant for the idiots in the streets, but it seems that idiots in palaces are lulled by sweet slop just as easily. I bought you from a whore. You cost me six marks. She wanted twenty, but I drive a hard bargain.'

The words were painful, of course. But far, far worse was the unbearable stabbing that cut up Jezal's spine, that tore at his eyes, burned his skin, seared the very roots of his hair and made him thrash like a frog in boiling water.

'I had others waiting, of course. I know better than to trust all to one throw of the dice. Other sons of mysterious parentage, ready to step into the role. There was a family called Brint, as I recall, and plenty more besides. But you floated to the top, Jezal, like a turd in the bath. When I crossed that bridge into the Agriont and saw you grown, I knew you were the one. You simply looked right, and you can't teach that. You have even come to speak like a king, which is a bonus I never expected.'

Jezal moaned and slobbered, unable even to scream. He felt Bayaz' boot slide under him and kick him over onto his back. The Magus' scowling face loomed down towards him, blurred by tears.

'But if you insist on being difficult . . . if you insist on going your own way . . . well, there are other options. Even kings die unexplained deaths. Thrown by a horse. Choked on an olive-pit. Long falls to the hard, hard cobble-stones. Or simply found dead in the morning. Life is always short for you insects. But it can be very short for those who are not useful. I made you out of nothing. Out of air. With a word I can unmake you.' Bayaz snapped his fingers, and the sound was like a sword through Jezal's stomach. 'Like that you can be replaced.'

The First of the Magi leaned down further. 'Now, dolt, bastard, son of a whore, consider carefully your answers to these questions. You will do as your Arch Lector advises, yes?'

The cramps relaxed a merciful fraction. Enough for Jezal to whisper, 'yes.'

'You will be guided by him in all things?'

'Yes.'

'You will abide by his orders, in public and in private?'

'Yes,' he gasped, 'yes.'

'Good,' said the Magus, straightening up, towering over Jezal as his statue had once towered over the people on the Kingsway. 'I knew that you would say so, because although I know that you are arrogant, ignorant, and ungrateful, I know this also . . . you are a coward. Remember that. I trust that this is one lesson you will not ignore.' The agony ebbed suddenly away. Enough for Jezal to lift his spinning head from the tiles.

'I hate you,' he managed to croak.

Bayaz spluttered with laughter. 'Hate me? The arrogance of you! To suppose that I might care. I, Bayaz, first apprentice of great Juvens! I, who threw down the Master Maker, who forged the Union, who destroyed the Hundred Words!' The Magus slowly lifted his foot and planted it on the side of Jezal's jaw. 'I don't care whether you like me, fool.' He ground Jezal's face into the vomit-spattered floor with his boot. 'I care that you obey. And you will. Yes?'

'Yes,' Jezal slobbered through his squashed mouth.

'Then, your Majesty, I take my leave. Pray that you never give me cause to return.' The crushing pressure on his face released and Jezal heard the Magus' footsteps tap away to the far side of the room. The door creaked open, and then clicked firmly shut.

He lay on his back, staring at the ceiling, his breath heaving quickly in and out. After a while he drew up the courage to roll over, dragged himself dizzily up to his hands and knees. There was an unpleasant stink, and not just from the vomit smeared across his face. He realised with a meagre flicker of shame that he had soiled himself. He crawled across to the window, still limp as a wrung-out rag, drew himself gasping up to his knees, and looked down into the chilly gardens.

It only took a moment for Bayaz to come into view, striding down the gravel path between the neat lawns, the back of his bald pate shining. Yoru Sulfur walked behind him, staff in one hand, a box of dark metal held under the other arm. The same box that had followed Jezal, and Logen, and Ferro in a cart across half the Circle of the World. What happy days those seemed now.

Bayaz stopped, suddenly, turned, raised his head. He looked up, straight towards the window.

Jezal pressed himself into the hangings with a whimper of terror, his whole body trembling, the after-image of that unbearable pain still stamped, cold as ice, into his guts. The First of the Magi stood there for a moment longer, the faintest hint of a smile on his face. Then he turned away smartly, strode between the bowing Knights of the Body flanking the gate, and was gone.

Jezal knelt there, clinging to the curtains like a child to his mother. He thought about how happy he had once been, and how little he had realised it. Playing cards, surrounded by friends, a bright future ahead of him. He dragged in a heavy breath, the tightness of tears creeping up his throat, spreading out around his eyes. Never in his life had he felt so alone. Son of Kings? He had no one and nothing. He spluttered and sniffed. His vision grew blurry. He shook with hopeless sobs, his scarred lip trembling, the tears dripping down and spattering on the tiles.

He wept with pain and fear, with shame and anger, with disappointment and helplessness. But Bayaz had been right. He was a coward. So most of all he wept with relief.

Good Men, Evil Men

Grey morning time, out in the cold, wet gardens, and the
Dogman was just stood there, thinking about how
things used to be better. Stood there, in the middle of
that circle of brown graves, staring at the turned earth over
Harding Grim. Strange, how a man who said so little could
leave such a hole.

It was a long journey that Dogman had taken, the last few
years, and a strange one. From nowhere to nowhere, and he'd
lost a lot of friends along the way. He remembered all those
men gone back to the mud. Harding Grim. Tul Duru
Thunderhead. Rudd Threetrees. Forley the Weakest. And
what for? Who was better off because of it? All that waste. It
was enough to make a man sick to the soles of his boots. Even
one who was famous for having a flat temper. All gone, and left
Dogman lonely. The world was a narrower place without 'em.

He heard footsteps through the wet grass. Logen, walking up
through the misty rain, breath smoking round his scarred face.
Dogman remembered how happy he'd been, that night, when
Logen had stepped into the firelight, still alive. It had seemed
like a new beginning, then. A good moment, promising better
times. Hadn't quite worked out that way. Strange, how the
Dogman didn't feel so happy at the sight of Logen Ninefingers
no more.

'The King o' the Northmen,' he muttered. 'The Bloody-
Nine. How's the day?'

'Wet is how it is. Getting late in the year.'

'Aye. Another winter coming.' Dogman picked at the hard
skin on his palm. 'They come quicker and quicker.'

'Reckon it's high time I got back to the North, eh? Calder

and Scale still loose, making mischief, and the dead know what type o' trouble Dow's cooked up.'

'Aye, I daresay. High time we left.'

'I want you to stay.'

Dogman looked up. 'Eh?'

'Someone needs to talk to the Southerners, make a deal. You've always been the best man I knew for talking. Other than Bethod, maybe, but . . . he ain't an option now, is he?'

'What sort of a deal?'

'Might be we'll need their help. There'll be all kind o' folk in the North not too keen about the way things have gone. Folk don't want a king, or don't want this one, leastways. The Union on our side'll be a help. Wouldn't hurt if you brought some weapons back with you too, when you come.'

Dogman winced. 'Weapons, is it?'

'Better to have 'em and not want 'em, than to need 'em but—'

'I know the rest. What happened to one more fight, then we're done? What happened to making things grow?'

'They might have to grow without us, for now. Listen, Dogman, I never looked for a fight, you know that, but you have to be—'

'Don't. Even. Bother.'

'I'm trying to be a better man, here, Dogman.'

'That so? I don't see you trying that hard. Did you kill Tul?'

Logen's eyes went narrow. 'Dow been talking, has he?'

'Never mind who said what. Did you kill the Thunderhead or did you not? Ain't a hard one to come at. It's just a yes or a no.'

Logen made a kind of snort, like he was about to start laughing, or about to start crying, but didn't do either one. 'I don't know what I did.'

'Don't know? What use is don't know? Is that what you'll say after you've stabbed me through the back, while I'm trying to save your worthless life?'

Logen winced down at the wet grass. 'Maybe it will be. I

don't know.' His eyes slid back up to the Dogman's, and stuck there, hard. 'But that's the price, ain't it? You know what I am. You could have picked a different man to follow.'

Dogman watched him go, not knowing what to say, not knowing what to think even. Just standing there, in the midst of the graves, getting wetter. He felt someone come up beside him. Red Hat, looking off into the rain, watching after Logen's black shape growing fainter and fainter. He shook his head, mouth pursed up tight.

'I never believed the stories they told about him. About the Bloody-Nine. All bluster, I thought. But I believe 'em now. I heard he killed Crummock's boy, in that fight in the mountains. Carved him careless as you'd crush a beetle, no reason. That's a man there cares for nothing. No man worse, I reckon, ever, in all the North. Not even Bethod. That's an evil bastard, if ever there was one.'

'That so?' Dogman found he was right up in Red Hat's face, and shouting. 'Well piss on you, arsehole! Who made you the fucking judge?'

'Just saying, is all.' Red Hat stared at him. 'I mean . . . I thought we had the same thing in mind.'

'Well, we don't! You need a mind bigger'n a pea to hold something in it and you're lacking the equipment, idiot! You wouldn't know a good man from an evil if he pissed on you!'

Red Hat blinked. 'Right y'are. I see I got the wrong notion.' He backed off a stride, then walked away through the drizzle, shaking his head.

Dogman watched him go, teeth gritted, thinking how he wanted to hit someone, but not sure who. There was no one here but him, now, anyway. Him and the dead. But maybe that's what happens once the fighting stops, to a man who knows nothing but fighting. He fights himself.

He took a long breath of the cold, wet air, and he frowned down at the earth over Grim's grave. He wondered if he'd know a good man from an evil, any more. He wondered what the difference was.

Not What You Wanted

Glokta woke to a shaft of soft sunlight spilling through the hangings and across his wrinkled bed-clothes, full of dancing dust-motes. He tried to turn over, winced at a click in his neck. *Ah, the first spasm of the day.* The second was not long coming. It flashed through his left hip as he wrestled his way onto his back and snatched his breath away. The pain crept down his spine, settled in his leg, and stayed there.

'Ah,' he grunted. He tried, ever so gently, to turn his ankle round, to work his knee. The pain instantly grew far worse. 'Barnam!' He dragged the sheet to one side and the familiar stink of ordure rose up to his nostrils. *Nothing like the stench of your own dung to usher in a productive morning.*

'Ah! Barnam!' He whimpered, and slobbered, and clutched at his withered thigh, but nothing helped. The pain grew worse, and worse. The fibres started from his wasted flesh like metal cables, toeless foot flopping grotesquely on the end, entirely beyond his control.

'Barnam!' he screamed. 'Barnam, you fucker! The door!' Spit dribbled from his toothless mouth, tears ran down his twitching face, his hands clawed, clutching up fistfuls of brown-stained sheet.

He heard hurried footsteps in the corridor, the lock scraping. 'Locked you fool!' he squealed through his gums, thrashing with pain and anger. The knob turned and the door opened, much to his surprise. *What the . . .*

Ardee hurried over to the bed. 'Get out!' he hissed, holding one arm pointlessly over his face, clutching at his bedclothes with the other. 'Get out!'

'No.' She tore the sheet away and Glokta grimaced, waiting for her face to go pale, waiting for her to stagger back, one hand across her mouth, eyes wide with shock and disgust. *I am married . . . to this shit-daubed monstrosity?* She only frowned down, for a moment, then took hold of his ruined thigh and pressed her thumbs into it.

He gasped and flailed and tried to twist away but her grip was merciless, two points of agony stabbing right into the midst of his cramping sinews. 'Ah! You fucking . . . you . . .' The wasted muscle went suddenly soft, and he went soft with it, dropping back against the mattress. *And now being splattered with my own shit begins to seem just the slightest bit embarrassing.*

He lay there for a moment, helpless. 'I didn't want you to see me . . . like this.'

'Too late. You married me, remember. We're one body, now.'

'I think I got the better part of that deal.'

'I got my life, didn't I?'

'Hardly the kind of life that most young women hanker for.' He watched her, the strip of sunlight wandering back and forth across her darkened face as she moved. 'I know that I'm not what you wanted . . . in a husband.'

'I always dreamed of a man I could dance with.' She looked up and held his eye. 'But I think, perhaps, that you suit me better. Dreams are for children. We both are grownups.'

'Still. You see now that not dancing is the least of it. You should not have to do . . . this.'

'I want to do it.' She took a firm grip on his face and twisted it, somewhat painfully, so he was looking straight into hers. 'I want to do something. I want to be useful. I want someone to need me. Can you understand that?'

Glokta swallowed. 'Yes.' *Few better.* 'Where's Barnam?'

'I told him he could have the mornings off. I told him I'd be doing this from now on. I've told him to move my bed in here, as well.'

'But—'

'Are you telling me I can't sleep in the same room as my husband?' Her hands slid slowly over his withered flesh, gentle, but firm, rubbing at the scarred skin, pressing at the ruined muscles. *How long ago? Since a woman looked at me with anything but horror? Since a woman touched me with anything but violence?* He lay back, his eyes closed and his mouth open, tears running from his eye and trickling down the sides of his head into the pillow. *Almost comfortable. Almost . . .*

'I don't deserve this,' he breathed.

'No one gets what they deserve.'

Queen Terez looked down her nose at Glokta as he lurched into her sunny salon, without the slightest attempt to hide her utter disgust and contempt. *As though she saw a cockroach crawling into her regal presence. But we will see. We know well the path, after all. We have followed it ourselves, and we have dragged so many others after. Pride comes first. Then pain. Humility follows hard upon it. Obedience lies just beyond.*

'My name is Glokta. I am the new Arch Lector of his Majesty's Inquisition.'

'Ah, the cripple,' she sneered. *With refreshing directness.* 'And why do you disrupt my afternoon? You will find no criminals here.' *Only Styrian witches.*

Glokta's eyes flickered to the other woman, standing bolt upright near one of the windows. 'It is a matter we had better discuss alone.'

'The Countess Shalere has been my friend since birth. There is nothing you can say to me that she cannot hear.' The Countess glared at Glokta with a disdain little less piercing than the queen's.

'Very well.' *No delicate way to say it. I doubt that delicacy will serve us here in any case.* 'It has come to my attention, your Majesty, that you have not been performing your duties as a wife.'

Terez' long, thin neck seemed to stretch with indignation. 'How dare you? That is none of your concern!'

'I am afraid that it is. Heirs for the king, you see. The future of the state, and so forth.'

'This is insufferable!' The queen's face was white with fury. *The Jewel of Talins flashes fire indeed.* 'I must eat your repulsive

659

food, I must tolerate your dreadful weather, I must smile at the rambling mutterings of your idiot king! Now I must answer to his grotesque underlings? I am kept prisoner here!'

Glokta looked round at the beautiful room. The opulent hangings, the gilt furnishings, the fine paintings. The two beautiful women in their beautiful clothes. He dug one tooth sourly into the underside of his tongue. 'Believe me. This is not what a prison looks like.'

'There are many kinds of prison!'

'I have learned to live with worse, and so have others.' *You should see what my wife has to put up with.*

'To share my bed with some disgusting bastard, some scarred son of who knows what, to have some stinking, hairy man pawing at me in the night!' The queen gave a shiver of revulsion. 'It is not to be borne!'

Tears shone in her eyes. Her lady-in-waiting rushed forward, dress rustling, and knelt beside her, putting a comforting hand on her shoulder. Terez reached up, pressed her own hand on top of it. The queen's companion stared at Glokta with naked hatred. 'Get out! Out, cripple, and never come back! You have upset her Majesty!'

'I have a gift for it,' muttered Glokta. 'One reason why I am so widely hated . . .' He trailed off, frowning. He stared at their two hands on Terez' shoulder. There was something in that touch. *Comforting, soothing, protective. The touch of the committed friend, the trusted confidante, the sisterly companion. But there is more than that. Too familiar. Too warm. Almost like the touch of . . . Ah.*

'You don't have much use for men, do you?'

The two women looked up at him together, then Shalere snatched her hand away from the queen's shoulder. 'I will have your meaning!' barked Terez, but her voice was shrill, almost panicked.

'I think you know my meaning well enough.' *And my task is made a great deal easier.* 'Some help here!' Two hulking Practicals barged through the doors. *And as quickly as that, everything is changed. Amazing, the spice that two big men can add to a conversation. Some kinds of power are only tricks of the mind. I learned that well, in the Emperor's prisons, and my new master has only reinforced the lesson.*

'You would not dare!' shrieked Terez, staring at the masked arrivals with wide eyes. 'You would not dare to touch me!'

'As luck would have it, I doubt it will be necessary, but we will see.' He pointed at the Countess. 'Seize that woman.'

The two black-masked men tramped across the thick carpet. One moved a chair out of his way with exaggerated care.

'No!' The queen sprang up, grabbing Shalere's hand in hers. 'No!'

'Yes,' said Glokta.

The two women backed away, clinging to each other, Terez in front, shielding the Countess with her body, teeth bared in a warning snarl as the two great shadows approached. *One might almost be touched by their evident care for one another, if one was capable of being touched at all.* 'Take her. But no marks on the queen, if you please.'

'No!' screamed Terez. 'I'll have your heads for this! My father . . . my father is—'

'On his way back to Talins, and I doubt he'll be starting a war over your friend since birth, in any case. You are bought and paid for, and Duke Orso does not strike me as the type to renege on a deal.'

The two men and the two women lurched around the far end of the room in an ungainly dance. One of the Practicals seized the Countess by one wrist, dragged her away from the queen's clutching hand and forced her down onto her knees, twisting her arms behind her, snapping heavy irons shut on her wrists. Terez shrieked, punched, kicked, clawed at the other, but she might as well have vented her fury on a tree. The huge man barely moved, his eyes every bit as emotionless as the mask below them.

Glokta found that he was almost smiling as he watched the ugly scene. *I may be crippled, and hideous, and in constant pain, but the humiliation of beautiful women is one pleasure I can still enjoy. I do it now with threats and violence, instead of with soft words and entreaties, but still. Almost as much fun as it ever was.*

One of the Practicals forced a canvas bag over Shalere's head, turning her cries to muffled sobs, then marched her helplessly across the room. The other stayed where he was for a moment, keeping the queen herded into the corner. Then he backed off towards the door. On his way he picked up the chair he had moved and carefully put it back exactly as he had found it.

'Curse you!' Terez screeched, her clenched fists trembling as the door clicked shut and left the two of them alone. 'Curse you, you twisted bastard! If you harm her—'

'It will not come to that. Because you have the means of her deliverance well within your grasp.'

The queen swallowed, chest heaving. 'What must I do?'

'Fuck.' The word somehow sounded twice as ugly in the beautiful surroundings. 'And bear children. I will give the Countess seven days in the darkness, unmolested. If, at the end of that time, I do not hear that you have set the king's cock on fire every night, I will introduce her to my Practicals. Poor fellows. They get so little exercise. Ten minutes each should do the trick, but there are plenty of them, in the House of Questions. I daresay we can keep your childhood friend quite busy night and day.'

A spasm of horror passed over Terez' face. *And why not? This is a low chapter even for me.* 'If I do as you ask?'

'Then the Countess will be kept quite safe and sound. Once you are verifiably with child, I will return her to you. Things can be as they are now, during the period of your confinement. Two boys, as heirs, two girls, to marry off, and we can be done with one another. The king can find his entertainment elsewhere.'

'But, that will take years!'

'You could get it done in three or four, if you really ride him hard. And you might find it makes everyone's lives easier if you at least pretend to enjoy it.'

'Pretend?' she breathed.

'The more you seem to like it, the quicker it will be over.

662

The cheapest whore on the docks can squeal for her coppers when the sailors stick her. Are you telling me you cannot squeal for the king of the Union? You offend my patriotic sensibilities! Uh!' he gasped, rolling his eyes in a parody of ecstasy. 'Ah! Yes! Just there! Don't stop!' He curled his lip at her. 'You see? Even I can do it! A liar of your experience should have no difficulty.'

Her teary eyes darted round the room, as though she were looking for some way out. *But there is none. The noble Arch Lector Glokta, protector of the Union, great heart of the Closed Council, paragon of the gentlemanly virtues, displays his flair for politics and diplomacy.* He felt some tiny stirring within him as he watched her wretched desperation, some negligible flutter in his guts. *Guilt, perhaps? Or indigestion? It hardly matters which, I have learned my lesson. Pity never works for me.*

He took one more slow step forward. 'Your Majesty, I hope you fully understand the alternative.'

She nodded, and wiped her eyes. Then she proudly raised up her chin. 'I will do as you ask. Please, I beg of you, do not hurt her . . . please . . .'

Please, please, please. Many congratulations, your Eminence. 'You have my word. I will see the Countess has only the best of treatment.' He licked gently at the sour gaps in his teeth. 'And you will do the same with your husband.'

Jezal sat in the darkness. He watched the fire dance in the great hearth, and he thought about what might have been. He thought about it with some bitterness. All the paths his life could have taken, and he had ended up here. Alone.

He heard hinges creaking. The small door that connected to the queen's bedchamber crept slowly open. He had never bothered to lock it, from his side. He had not foreseen any circumstance under which she would ever want to use it. Some error of etiquette that he had made, no doubt, for which she could not wait even until morning to admonish him.

He stood up, quickly, stupidly nervous.

Terez stepped through the shadowy doorway. She looked so different that at first he hardly recognised her. Her hair was loose, she wore only her shift. She looked humbly towards the ground, her face in darkness. Her bare feet padded across the boards, across the thick carpet towards the fire. She seemed very young, suddenly. Young and small, weak and alone. He watched her, mostly confused, somewhat scared, but also, as she came closer and the firelight caught the shape of her body, ever so slightly aroused.

'Terez, my . . .' he fumbled for the word. Darling scarcely seemed to cover it. Nor did love. Worst enemy might have, but it hardly would have helped matters. 'Can I—'

She cut him off, as ever, but not with the tirade he was expecting. 'I'm sorry for the way that I have treated you. For the things that I have said . . . you must think me . . .'

There were tears in her eyes. Actual tears. He would hardly have believed until that moment that she could cry. He took a hurried step or two towards her, one hand out, no idea of what to do. He had never dared to hope for an apology, and certainly not one so earnestly and honestly delivered.

'I know,' he stuttered, 'I know . . . I'm not what you wanted in a husband. I'm sorry for that. But I'm as much a prisoner in this as you are. I only hope . . . that perhaps we can make the best of it. Perhaps we might find a way . . . to care for one another? We have no one else, either of us. Please, tell me what I have to do—'

'Shhhh.' She touched one finger to his lips, looking into his eyes, one half of her face glowing orange from the fire, the other half black with shadow. Her fingers worked through his hair and drew him towards her. She kissed him, gently, awkwardly, almost, their lips brushing, then pressing clumsily together. He slid one hand round behind her neck, under her ear, his thumb stroking at her smooth cheek. Their mouths worked mechanically, accompanied by the soft squeak of breath in his nose, the gentle squelch of spit moving. Hardly the most passionate kiss he had ever enjoyed, but it was a great deal more than he had ever expected to get from her. There was a pleasant tingling building in his crotch as he pushed his tongue into her mouth.

He ran his other palm down her back, feeling the bumps of her spine under his fingers. He grunted softly as he slid his hand over her arse, down the side of her thigh then up between her legs, the hem of her shift gathering round his wrist. He felt her shudder, felt her flinch, and bite her lip in shock, it seemed, or even in disgust. He jerked his hand back, and they broke apart, both looking at the floor. 'I'm sorry,' he muttered, inwardly cursing his eagerness. 'I—'

'No. It's my fault. I'm not . . . experienced . . . with men . . .' Jezal blinked for a moment, then almost smiled at a surge of relief. Of course. Now everything was clear. She was so assured, so sharp, it had never even occurred to him that she might be a virgin. It was simple fear that made her tremble so. Fear of disappointing him. He felt a rush of sympathy.

'Don't worry,' he murmured it softly, stepping forward and taking her in his arms. He felt her stiffen, no doubt with nervousness, and he gently stroked her hair. 'I can wait . . . we don't have to . . . not yet.'

'No.' She said it with a touching determination, looking him fearlessly in the eye. 'No. We do.'

She dragged her shift up and over her head, let it drop to the floor. She came close to him, took hold of his wrist, guided it back to her thigh, then upwards.

'Ah,' she whispered, urgent and throaty, her lips brushing his cheek, her breath hot in his ear. 'Yes . . . just there . . . don't stop.' She led him breathless to the bed.

'If that is all?' Glokta looked around the table, but the old men were silent. *All waiting for my word.* The king was absent again, so he made them wait an unnecessarily long time. *Just to stab home to any doubters who is in charge. Why not, after all? The purpose of power is not to be gracious.* 'Then this meeting of the Closed Council is over.'

They rose, quickly, quietly, and in good order. Torlichorm, Halleck, Kroy and all the rest filed slowly from the room. Glokta himself struggled up, his leg still aching with the memory of the morning's cramps, only to find that the Lord

Chamberlain had, once again, remained behind. *And he looks far from amused.*

Hoff waited until the door shut before he spoke. 'Imagine my surprise,' he snapped, 'to hear of your recent marriage.'

'A swift and understated ceremony.' Glokta showed the Lord Chamberlain the wreckage of his front teeth. 'Young love, you understand, brooks no delays. I apologise if the lack of an invitation offended you.'

'An invitation?' growled Hoff, frowning mightily. 'Hardly! This is not what we discussed!'

'Discussed? I believe we have a misunderstanding. Our mutual friend,' and Glokta let his eyes move significantly to the empty thirteenth chair at the far end of the table, 'left me in charge. Me. No other. He deems it necessary that the Closed Council speak with one voice. From now on, that voice will sound remarkably like mine.'

Hoff's ruddy face had paled slightly. 'Of course, but—'

'You are aware, I suppose, that I lived through two years of torture? Two years in hell, so I can stand before you now. Or lean before you, twisted as an old tree root. A crippled, shambling, wretched mockery of a man, eh, Lord Hoff? Let us be honest with one another. Sometimes I lose control of my own leg. My own eyes. My own face.' He snorted. 'If you can call it a face. My bowels too, are rebellious. I often wake up daubed in my own shit. I find myself in constant pain, and the memories of everything that I have lost nag at me, endlessly.' He felt his left eye twitching. *Let it twitch.* 'So you can see how, despite my constant efforts to be a man of sunny temper, I find that I despise the world, and everything in it, and myself most of all. A regrettable state of affairs, for which there is no remedy.'

The Lord Chamberlain licked his lips uncertainly. 'You have my sympathy, but I fail to see the relevance.'

Glokta came suddenly very close, ignoring a spasm up his leg, pressing Hoff back against the table. 'Your sympathy is less than worthless, and the relevance is this. Knowing what I am, what I have endured, what I still endure . . . can you suppose there is anything in this world I fear? Any act I will shrink from? The most unbearable pain of others is at the worst . . . an irritation to me.' Glokta jerked even closer, letting his lips work back from his ruined teeth, letting his face tremble, and his eye weep. 'Knowing all that . . . can you possibly think it wise . . . for a man to stand where you stand now . . . and make threats? Threats against my wife? Against *my* unborn child?'

'No threat was intended, of course, I would never—'

'That simply would not do, Lord Hoff! That simply would not do. At the very slightest breath of violence against them . . . why, I would not wish you even to imagine the inhuman horror of my response.' Closer yet, so close that his spit made a soft mist across Hoff's trembling jowls. 'I cannot permit any further *discussion* of this issue. Ever. I cannot permit even the rumour that there might be an issue. Ever. It simply . . . would . . . not . . . do, Lord Hoff, for an eyeless, tongueless, faceless, fingerless, cockless bag of meat to be occupying your chair on the Closed Council.' He stepped away, grinning his most revolting grin. 'Why, my Lord Chamberlain . . . who would drink all the wine?'

It was a beautiful autumn day in Adua, and the sun shone pleasantly through the branches of the fragrant fruit trees, casting a dappled shade onto the grass beneath. A pleasing breeze fluttered through the orchard, stirring the crimson mantle of the king as he strode regally around his lawn, and the white coat of his Arch Lector as he hobbled doggedly along at a respectful distance, stooped over his cane. Birds twittered from the trees, and his Majesty's highly polished boots crunched in the gravel and made faint, agreeable echoes against the white buildings of the palace.

From the other side of the high walls came the faint sound of distant work. The clanking of picks and hammers, the scraping of earth and the clattering of stone. The faint calls of the carpenters and the masons. These were the most pleasant sounds of all, to Jezal's ear. The sounds of rebuilding.

'It will take time, of course,' he was saying.

'Of course.'

'Years, perhaps. But much of the rubble is already cleared. The repair of some of the more lightly damaged buildings has already begun. The Agriont will be more glorious than ever before you know it. I have made it my highest priority.'

Glokta bowed his head even lower. 'And therefore mine, and that of your Closed Council. Might I enquire . . .' he murmured, 'after the health of your wife, the queen?'

Jezal worked his mouth. He hardly liked discussing his personal business with this man, of all people, but it could not be denied that whatever the cripple had said, there had been a most dramatic improvement.

'A material change.' Jezal shook his head. 'I find now that she is a woman of almost . . . insatiable appetites.'

'I am delighted that my entreaties have had an effect.'

'Oh, they have, they have, only there is still a certain . . .' Jezal waved his hand in the air, searching out the right word. 'Sadness in her. Sometimes . . . I hear her crying, in the night. She stands at the open window, and she weeps, for hours at a time.'

'Crying, your Majesty? Perhaps she is merely homesick. I always suspected she was a much gentler spirit than she appears to be.'

'She is! She is. A gentle spirit.' Jezal thought about it for a moment. 'Do you know, I think you may be right. Homesick.' A plan began to take shape in his mind. 'Perhaps we should have the gardens of the palace redesigned, to give a flavour of Talins? We could have the stream altered, in the likeness of canals, and so forth!'

Glokta leered his toothless grin. 'A sublime idea. I shall speak to the Royal Gardener. Perhaps another brief word with her Majesty as well, to see if I can staunch her tears.'

'I would appreciate whatever you can do. How is your own wife?' he tossed over his shoulder, hoping to change the subject, then realising he had strayed onto one even more difficult.

But Glokta only showed his empty smile again. 'She is a

tremendous comfort to me, your Majesty. I really don't know how I ever managed without her.'

They moved on in awkward silence for a moment, then Jezal cleared his throat. 'I've been thinking, Glokta, about that scheme of mine. You know, about a tax on the banks? Perhaps to pay for a new hospital near the docks. For those who cannot afford a surgeon. The common folk have been good to us. They have helped us to power, and suffered in our name. A government should offer something to all its people, should it not? The more mean, the more base, the more they need our help. A king is only truly as rich as his poorest subject, do you not think? Would you have the High Justice draw something up? Small to begin with, then we can go further. Free housing, perhaps, for those who find themselves without a home. We should consider—'

'Your Majesty, I have spoken to our mutual friend of this.'

Jezal stopped dead, a cold feeling creeping up his spine. 'You have?'

'I fear that I am obliged to.' The cripple's tone was that of a servant, but his sunken eyes did not stray from Jezal's for a moment. 'Our friend is . . . not enthusiastic.'

'Does he rule the Union, or do I?' But they both knew the answer to that question well enough.

'You are king, of course.'

'Of course.'

'But our mutual friend . . . we would not wish to disappoint him.' Glokta came a limping step closer, his left eye giving a repulsive flutter. 'Neither one of us, I am sure, would want to encourage a visit to Adua . . . on his part.'

Jezal's knees felt suddenly very weak. The faint memory of that awful, unbearable pain nagged at his stomach. 'No,' he croaked, 'no, of course not.'

The cripple's voice was only just above a whisper. 'Perhaps, in time, funds could be found for some small project. Our friend cannot see everything, after all, and what he does not see will do no harm. I am sure between the two of us, quietly . . . we could do some little good. But not yet.'

'No. You are right, Glokta. You have a fine sense for these things. Do nothing that would cause the least offence. Please inform our friend that his opinions will always be valued above all others. Please tell our good friend that he can rely on me. Will you tell him that, please?'

'I will, your Majesty. He will be delighted to hear it.'

'Good,' murmured Jezal. 'Good.' A chilly breeze had blown up, and he turned back towards the palace, pulling his cloak around him. It was not, in the end, quite so pleasant a day as he had hoped it might be.

Loose Ends

A grubby white box with two doors facing each other. The ceiling was too low for comfort, the room too brightly lit by blazing lamps. Damp was creeping out of one corner and the plaster had erupted with flaking blisters, speckled with black mould. Someone had tried to scrub a long bloodstain from the wall, but hadn't tried nearly hard enough.

Two huge Practicals stood against the wall, their arms folded. One of the chairs at the bolted-down table was empty. Carlot dan Eider sat in the other. *History moves in circles, so they say. How things have changed. And yet, how they have stayed the same.* Her face was pale with worry, there were dark rings of sleeplessness around her eyes, but she still seemed beautiful. *More than ever, in a way. The beauty of the candle-flame that has almost burned out. Again.*

Glokta could hear her scared breathing as he settled himself in the remaining chair, leaned his cane against the scarred table-top, and frowned into her face. 'I am still wondering whether, in the next few days, I will receive that letter you spoke of. You know the one. The one you meant for Sult to read. The one that lays out the history of my self-indulgent little mercy to you. The one that you made sure will be sent to the Arch Lector . . . in the event of your death. Will it find its way onto my desk, now, do you suppose? A final irony.'

There was a pause. 'I realise that I made a grave mistake, when I came back.' *And an even worse one when you didn't leave fast enough.* 'I hope you will accept my apology. I only wanted to warn you about the Gurkish. If you can find it in your heart to be merciful—'

'Did you expect me to be merciful once?'

'No,' she whispered.

'Then what, do you suppose, are the chances of my making the same mistake twice? Never come back, I said. Not ever.' He waved with his hand and one of the monstrous Practicals stepped forward and lifted the lid of his case.

'No . . . no.' Her eyes darted over his instruments, and back. 'You won. You won, of course. I should have been grateful, the first time. Please.' She leaned forward, looking him in the eyes. Her voice dropped, grew husky, 'Please. Surely there must be . . . something that I can do . . . to make up for my foolishness . . .'

A peculiar mixture of feigned desire and genuine disgust. Fake longing and genuine loathing. And rendered still more distasteful by the edge of mounting terror. It makes me wonder why I was merciful in the first place.

Glokta snorted. 'Must this be embarrassing as well as painful?'

The effort at seduction leaked quickly away. *But I note that the fear is going nowhere.* It was joined now by a rising note of desperation. 'I know that I made a mistake . . . I was trying to help . . . please, I meant you no real harm . . . I caused you no harm, you know it!' He reached out slowly towards the case, watched her horrified eyes follow his white-gloved hand, her voice rising to a squeal of panic. 'Only tell me what I can do! Please! I can help you! I can be useful! Tell me what I can do!'

Glokta's hand paused on its remorseless journey across the table. He tapped one finger against the wood. The finger on which the Arch Lector's ring glittered in the lamplight. 'Perhaps there is a way.'

'Anything,' she gurgled, teary eyes gleaming. 'Anything, only name it!'

'You have contacts in Talins?'

She swallowed. 'In Talins? Of . . . of course.'

'Good. I, and some colleagues of mine on the Closed Council, are concerned about the role that Grand Duke Orso means to play in Union politics. Our feeling – our very strong feeling – is that he should stick to bullying Styrians, and keep his nose out of our business.' He gave a significant pause.

'How do I—'

'You will go to Talins. You will be my eyes in the city. A traitor, fleeing for her life, friendless and alone, seeking only a place for a new beginning. A beautiful yet wretched traitor, in desperate need of a strong arm to protect her. You get the idea.'

'I suppose . . . I suppose that I could do that.'

Glokta snorted. 'You had better.'

'I will need money—'

'Your assets have been seized by the Inquisition.'

'Everything?'

'You may have noticed that there is a great deal of rebuilding to do. The king needs every mark he can lay his hands on, and confessed traitors can hardly expect to keep their chattels in such times as these. I have arranged passage for you. When you arrive, make contact with the banking house of Valint and Balk. They will arrange a loan to get you started.'

'Valint and Balk?' Eider looked even more scared than before, if that was possible. 'I would rather be in debt to anyone but them.'

'I know the feeling. But it's that or nothing.'

'How will I—'

'A woman of your resourcefulness? I am sure that you will find a way.' He winced as he pushed himself up from his chair. 'I want to be snowed in by your letters. What happens in the city. What Orso is about. Who he makes war with, who he makes peace with. Who are his allies and his enemies. You leave on the next tide.' He turned back, briefly, at the door. 'I'll be watching.'

She nodded dumbly, wiping away the tears of relief with the back of one trembling hand. *First it is done to us, then we do it to others, then we order it done. Such is the way of things.*

'Are you always drunk by this time in the morning?'

'Your Eminence, you wound me.' Nicomo Cosca grinned. 'Usually I have been drunk for hours by now.'

Huh. We each find our ways of getting through the day. 'I should thank you for all your help.'

The Styrian gave a flamboyant wave of one hand. A hand, Glokta noticed, flashing with a fistful of heavy rings. 'To hell with your thanks, I have your money.'

'And I think every penny well spent. I hope that you will remain in the city, and enjoy Union hospitality for a while longer.'

'Do you know? I believe I will.' The mercenary scratched thoughtfully at the rash on his neck leaving red fingernail marks through the flaky skin. 'At least until the gold runs out.'

'How quickly can you possibly spend what I have paid you?'

'Oh, you would be amazed. I have wasted ten fortunes in my time and more besides. I look forward to wasting another.' Cosca slapped his hands down on his thighs, pushed himself up, strolled, somewhat unsteadily, to the door, and turned with a flourish. 'Make sure you call on me when you next have a desperate last stand organised.'

'My first letter will bear your name.'

'Then I bid you . . . farewell!' Cosca swept off his enormous hat and bowed low. Then, with a knowing grin, he stepped through the doorway, and was gone.

Glokta had moved the Arch Lector's office to a large hall on the ground floor of the House of Questions. *Closer to the real business of the Inquisition – the prisoners. Closer to the questions, and the answers. Closer to the truth. And, of course, the real clincher . . . no stairs.*

There were well-tended gardens outside the large windows. The faint sound of a fountain splashing beyond the glass. But inside the room there was none of the ugly paraphernalia of power. The walls were plastered and painted simple white. The furniture was hard and functional. *The whetstone of discomfort has kept me sharp this long. No reason to let the edge grow dull, simply because I have run out of enemies. New enemies will present themselves, before too long.*

There were some heavy bookcases of dark wood. Several leather-covered desks, already stacked high with documents requiring his attention. Aside from the great round table with its map of the Union and its pair of bloody nail-marks, there was only one item of Sult's furniture that Glokta had brought downstairs with him. The dark painting of bald old Zoller glowered down from above the simple fireplace. *Bearing an uncanny resemblance to a certain Magus I once knew. It is fitting, after all, that we maintain the proper perspective. Every man answers to somebody.*

There was a knocking at the door, and the head of Glokta's secretary appeared at the gap. 'The Lord Marshals have arrived, Arch Lector.'

'Show them in.'

Sometimes, when old friends meet, things are instantly as they were, all those years before. The friendship resumes, untouched, as though there had been no interruption. *Sometimes, but not now.* Collem West was scarcely recognisable. His hair had fallen out in ugly patches. His face was shrunken, had a yellow tinge about it. His uniform hung slack from his bony shoulders, stained around the collar. He shuffled into the room, bent over in an old man's stoop, leaning heavily on a stick. He looked like nothing so much as a walking corpse.

Glokta had expected something of the kind, of course, from what Ardee had told him. But the sick shock of disappointment and horror he felt at the sight still caught him by surprise. *Like returning to the happy haunt of one's youth, and finding it all in ruins. Deaths. They happen every day. How many lives have I wrecked with my own hands? What makes this one so hard to take?* And yet it was. He found himself lurching up from his chair, starting painfully forwards as if to lend some help.

'Your Eminence.' West's voice was fragile and jagged as broken glass. He made a weak effort at a smile. 'Or I suppose . . . I should call you brother.'

'West . . . Collem . . . it is good to see you.' *Good, and awful both at once.*

A cluster of officers followed West into the room. *The wonderfully competent Lieutenant Jalenhorm I remember, of course, but a Major now. And Brint too, made a Captain by his friend's swift advancement. Marshal Kroy we know and love from the Closed Council. Congratulations, all, on your promotions.*

Another man brought up the rear of the party. A lean man with a face horribly burned. *But we, of all people, should hardly hold a repulsive disfigurement against him.* Each one of them frowned nervously towards West, as though ready to pounce forward if he should slump to the floor. Instead he shuffled to the round table and sagged trembling into the nearest chair.

'I should have come to you,' said Glokta. *I should have come to you far sooner.*

West made another effort at a smile, even more bilious than the last. Several of his teeth were missing. 'Nonsense. I know how busy you are, now. And I am feeling much better today.'

'Good, good. That is . . . good. Is there anything that I can get you?' *What could possibly help?* 'Anything at all.'

West shook his head. 'I do not think so. These gentlemen you know, of course. Apart from Sergeant Pike.' The burned man nodded to him.

'A pleasure.' *To meet someone even more maimed than myself, always.*

'I hear . . . happy news, from my sister.'

Glokta winced, almost unable to meet his old friend's eye. 'I should have sought your permission, of course. I surely would have, had there been time.'

'I understand.' West's bright eyes were fixed on his. 'She has explained it all. It is some kind of comfort to know that she'll be well taken care of.'

'On that you can depend. I will see to it. She will never be hurt again.'

West's gaunt face twisted. 'Good. Good.' He rubbed gently at the side of his face. His fingernails were black, edged with dried blood, as though they were peeling from the flesh beneath. 'There's always a price to be paid, eh, Sand? For the things we do?'

Glokta felt his eye twitching. 'It would seem so.'

'I have lost some of my teeth.'

'I see that, and can sympathise. Soup, I find . . .' *I find utterly disgusting.*

'I am . . . scarcely able to walk.'

676

'I sympathise with that also. Your cane will be your best friend.' *As it will soon be mine, I think.*

'I am a pitiable shell of what I was.'

'I truly feel your pain.' *Truly. Almost more keenly than my own.*

West slowly shook his withered head. 'How can you stand it?'

'One step at a time, my old friend. Steer clear of stairs where possible, and mirrors, always.'

'Wise advice.' West coughed. An echoing cough, from right down beneath his ribs. He swallowed noisily. 'I think my time is running out.'

'Surely not!' Glokta's hand reached out for a moment, as if to rest on West's shrunken shoulder, as if to offer comfort. He jerked it back, awkwardly. *It is not suited to the task.*

West licked at his empty gums. 'This is how most of us go, isn't it? No final charge. No moment of glory. We just . . . fall slowly apart.'

Glokta would have liked to say something optimistic. *But that rubbish comes from other mouths than mine. Younger, prettier mouths, with all their teeth, perhaps.* 'Those who die on the battlefield are in some ways the lucky few. Forever young. Forever glorious.'

West nodded, slowly. 'Here's to the lucky few, then . . .' His eyes rolled back, he swayed, then slumped sideways. Jalenhorm was the first forward, catching him before he hit the ground. He flopped in the big man's arms, a long string of thin vomit splattering against the floor.

'Back to the palace!' snapped Kroy. 'At once!'

Brint hurried to swing the doors open while Jalenhorm and Kroy steered West out of the room, draped between them with his arms over their shoulders. His limp shoes scraped against the floor, his piebald head lolling. Glokta watched them go, standing helpless, his toothless mouth half open, as if to speak. As if to wish his friend good luck, or good health, or a merry afternoon. *None of them seem quite to fit the circumstance, however.*

677

The doors clattered shut and Glokta was left staring at them. His eyelid flickered, he felt wet on his cheek. *Not tears of compassion, of course. Not tears of grief. I feel nothing, fear nothing, care for nothing. They cut away the parts of me that could weep in the Emperor's prisons. This can only be salt water, and nothing more. Merely a broken reflex in a mutilated face. Farewell, brother. Farewell, my only friend. And farewell to the ghost of beautiful Sand dan Glokta, too. Nothing of him remains. All for the best, of course. A man in my position can afford no indulgences.*

He took a sharp breath, and wiped his face with the back of his hand. He limped to his desk, sat, composed himself for a moment, assisted by a sudden twinge in his toeless foot. He turned his attention to his documents. *Papers of confession, tasks outstanding, all the tedious business of government—*

He looked up. A figure had detached itself from the shadows behind one of the high book-cases and now stepped out into the room, arms folded. The man with the burned face who had come in with the officers. In the excitement of their exit, it seemed that he had remained behind.

'Sergeant Pike, was it?' murmured Glokta, frowning.

'That's the name I've taken.'

'Taken?'

The scarred face twisted into a mockery of a smile. *One even more hideous than my own, if that's possible.* 'Not surprising, that you shouldn't recognise me. My first week, there was an accident in a forge. Accidents often happen, in Angland.' *Angland? That voice . . . something about that voice . . .* 'Still nothing? Perhaps if I come closer?'

He sprang across the room without warning. Glokta was still struggling up from his seat as the man dived across the desk. They tumbled to the floor together in a cloud of flying paper, Glokta underneath, the back of his skull cracking against the stone, his breath all driven out in a long, agonised wheeze.

He felt the brush of steel against his neck. Pike's face was no more than a few inches from his, the mottled mass of burns picked out in particularly revolting detail.

678

'How about now?' he hissed. 'Anything seem familiar?'

Glokta felt his left eye flickering as recognition washed over him like a wave of freezing water. *Changed, of course. Changed utterly and completely. And yet I know him.*

'Rews,' he breathed

'None other.' Rews bit off the words with grim satisfaction.

'You survived.' Glokta whispered it, first with amazement, then with mounting amusement. 'You survived! You're a far harder man than I gave you credit for! Far, far harder.' He started to chuckle, tears running down the side of his cheek again.

'Something funny?'

'Everything! You have to appreciate the irony. I have overcome so many powerful enemies, and it's Salem Rews with the knife at my neck! It's always the blade you don't see coming that cuts you deepest, eh?'

'You'll get no deeper cuts than this one.'

'Then cut away, my man, I am ready.' Glokta tipped his head back, stretched his neck out, pressing it up against the cold metal. 'I've been ready for a long time.'

Rews' fist worked around the grip of his knife. His burned face trembled, eyes narrowing to bright slits in their pink sockets. *Now.*

His mottled lips slid back from his teeth. The sinews in his neck stood out as he made ready to wield the blade. *Do it.*

Glokta's breath hissed quickly in and out, his throat tingling with anticipation. *Now, at last . . . now . . .*

But Rews' arm did not move.

'And yet you hesitate,' whispered Glokta through his empty gums. 'Not out of mercy, of course, not out of weakness. They froze all that out of you, eh? In England? You pause because you realise, in all that time dreaming of killing me, you never thought of what would be next. What will you truly have gained, with all your endurance? With all your cunning and your effort? Will you be hunted? Will you be sent back? I can offer you so much more.'

Rews' melted frown grew even harder. 'What could you give me? After this?'

'Oh, this is nothing. I suffer twice the pain and ten times the humiliation getting up in the morning. A man like you could be very useful to me. A man . . . as hard as you have proved yourself to be. A man who has lost everything, including all his scruples, all his mercy, all his fear. We both have lost everything. We both have survived. I understand you, Rews, as no one else ever can.'

'Pike is my name, now.'

'Of course it is. Let me up, Pike.'

Slowly the knife slid away from his throat. The man who had been Salem Rews stood over him, frowning down. *Who could ever anticipate the turns that fate can take?* 'Up, then.'

'Easier said than done.' Glokta dragged in a few sharp breaths, then growling with a great and painful effort he rolled over onto all fours. *A heroic achievement indeed.* He slowly tested his limbs, wincing as his twisted joints clicked. *Nothing broken. No more broken than usual, anyway.* He reached out and took the handle of his fallen cane between two fingers, dragged it towards him through the scattered papers. He felt the point of the blade pressing into his back.

'Don't take me for a fool, Glokta. If you try anything—'

He clutched at the edge of the desk and dragged himself up. 'You'll cut my liver out and all the rest. Don't worry. I am far too crippled to try anything worse than shit myself. I have something to show you, though. Something that I feel sure you will appreciate. If I'm wrong, well . . . you can slit my throat a little later.'

Glokta lurched out of the heavy door of his office, Pike sticking as close to his shoulder as a shadow, the knife kept carefully out of sight.

'Stay,' he snapped at the two Practicals in the ante-room, hobbling on past the frowning secretary at the huge desk. Out into the wide hallway running through the heart of the House of Questions and Glokta limped faster, cane clicking against the tiles. It hurt him to do it, but he held his head back, gave a cold wrinkle to his lip. Out of the corners of his eyes he saw the Clerks, the Practicals, the Inquisitors, bowing, sliding backwards, clearing away. *How they fear me. More than any man in Adua, and with good reason. How things have changed. And yet, how they have stayed the same.* His leg, his neck, his gums. These things were as they had always been. *And always will be. Unless I am tortured again, of course.*

'You look well,' Glokta tossed over his shoulder. 'Aside from your hideous facial burns, of course. You lost weight.'

'Starving can do that.'

'Indeed, indeed. I lost a great deal of weight in Gurkhul. And not just from the pieces they cut out of me. This way.'

They turned through a heavy door flanked by frowning Practicals, past an open gate of iron bars. Into a long and windowless corridor, sloping steadily downwards, lit by too few lanterns and filled with slow shadows. The walls were rendered and whitewashed, though none too recently. There was a seedy feel to the place, and a smell of damp. *Just as there always is.* The clicking of Glokta's cane, the hissing of his breath, the rustling of his white coat, all fell dead on the chill, wet air.

'Killing me will bring you scant satisfaction, you know.'

'We shall see.'

'I doubt it. I was hardly the one responsible for your little trip northwards. I did the work perhaps, but others gave the orders.'

'They were not my friends.'

Glokta snorted. 'Please. Friends are people one pretends to like in order to make life bearable. Men like us have no need of such indulgences. It is our enemies by which we are measured.' *And here are mine.* Sixteen steps confronted him. *That old, familiar flight.* Cut from smooth stone, a little worn towards the centre.

'Steps. Bastard things. If I could torture one man, do you know who it would be?' Pike's face was a single, expressionless scar. 'Well, never mind.' Glokta struggled to the bottom without incident, limped on a few more painful strides to a heavy wooden door, bound with iron.

'We are here.' Glokta slid a bunch of keys from the pocket of his white coat, flicked through them until he found the right one, unlocked the door, and went in.

Arch Lector Sult was not the man he used to be. *But then none of us are, quite.* His magnificent shock of white hair was plastered greasily to his gaunt skull, dry blood matted in a yellow-brown mass on one side. His piercing blue eyes had lost their commanding sparkle, sunken as they were in deep sockets and rimmed with angry pink. He had been relieved of his clothes, and his sinewy old man's body, somewhat hairy around the shoulders, was smeared with the grime of the cells. He looked, in fact, like nothing so much as a mad old beggar. *Can this truly once have been one of the most powerful men in the wide Circle of the World? You would never guess. A salutary lesson to us all. The higher you climb, the further there is to fall.*

'Glokta!' he snarled, thrashing helplessly, chained to his chair. 'You treacherous, twisted bastard!'

Glokta held up his white-gloved hand, the purple stone on his ring of office glinting in the harsh lamplight. 'I believe *your Eminence* is the proper term of address.'

'You?' Sult barked sharp laughter. 'Arch Lector? A withered, pitiable husk of a man? You disgust me!'

'Don't give me that.' Glokta lowered himself, wincing, into the other chair. 'Disgust is for the innocent.'

Sult glared up at Pike, looming menacingly over the table, his shadow falling across the polished case containing Glokta's instruments. 'What is this thing?'

'This is an old friend of ours, Master Sult, but recently returned from the wars in the North, and seeking new opportunities.'

'My congratulations! I never believed that you could find an assistant even more hideous than yourself!'

'You are unkind, but thankfully we are not easily offended. Let us call him equally hideous.' *And just as ruthless, too, I hope.*

'When will be my trial?'

'Trial? Why ever would I want one of those? You are presumed dead and I have made no effort to deny it.'

'I demand the right to address the Open Council!' Sult struggled pointlessly with his chains. 'I demand . . . curse you! I demand a hearing!'

Glokta snorted. 'Demand away, but look around you. No one is interested in listening, not even me. We all are far too busy. The Open Council stands in indefinite recess. The Closed Council is all changed, and you are forgotten. I run things now. More completely than you could ever have dreamed of doing.'

'On the leash of that devil Bayaz!'

'Correct. Maybe in time I'll work some looseness into his muzzle, just as I did into yours. Enough to get things my own way, who knows?'

'Never! You'll never be free of him!'

'We'll see.' Glokta shrugged. 'But there are worse fates than being the first among slaves. Far worse. I have seen them.' *I have lived them.*

'You fool! We could have been free!'

'No. We couldn't. And freedom is far overrated in any case. We all have our responsibilities. We all owe something to someone. Only the entirely worthless are entirely free. The worthless and the dead.'

'What does it matter now?' Sult grimaced down at the table. 'What does any of it matter? Ask your questions.'

'Oh, we're not here for that. Not this time. Not for questions, not for truth, not for confessions. I have my answers already.' *Then why do I do this? Why?* Glokta leaned slowly forwards across the table. 'We are here for our amusement.'

Sult stared at him for a moment, then he shrieked with wild laughter. 'Amusement? You'll never have your teeth back! You'll never have your leg back! You'll never have your life back!'

'Of course not, but I can take yours.' Glokta turned, stiffly, slowly, painfully, and he gave a toothless grin. 'Practical Pike, would you be so good as to show our prisoner the instruments?'

Pike frowned down at Glokta. He frowned down at Sult. He stood there for a long moment, motionless.

Then he stepped forward, and lifted the lid of the case.

'Does the devil know
he is a devil?'

Elizabeth Madox Roberts

The Beginning

The sides of the valley were coated in white snow. The black road ran through it like an old scar, down to the bridge, over the river, up to the gates of Carleon. Black sprouts of sedge, tufts of black grass, black stones poked up through the clean white blanket. The black branches of the trees were each picked out on top with their own line of white. The city was a huddle of white roofs and black walls, crowded in around the hill, pressed into the fork in the black river under a stony grey sky.

Logen wondered if this was how Ferro Maljinn saw the world. Black and white, and nothing else. No colours. He wondered where she was now, what she was doing. If she thought about him.

Most likely not.

'Back again.'

'Aye,' said Shivers. 'Back.' He hadn't had much to say the whole long ride from Uffrith. They might have saved each other's lives, but conversation was another matter. Logen reckoned he still wasn't Shivers' favourite man. Doubted that he ever would be.

They rode down in silence, a long file of hard riders beside the black stream, no more than an icy trickle. Horses and men snorted out smoke, harness jingled sharp on the cold air. They rode over the bridge, hooves thumping on the hollow wood, on to the gate where Logen had spoken to Bethod. The gate he'd thrown him down from. The grass had grown back, no doubt, in the circle where he'd killed the Feared, then the snow had fallen down and covered it. So it was with all the acts of men, in the end. Covered over and forgotten.

There was no-one out to cheer for him, but that was no

surprise. The Bloody-Nine arriving was never any cause for celebration, especially not in Carleon. Hadn't turned out too well for anyone the first time he visited. Nor any of the times after. Folk were no doubt barred into their houses, scared that they'd be the first to get burned alive.

He swung down from his horse, left Red Hat and the rest of the boys to see to themselves. He strode up through the cobbled street, up the steep slope towards the gateway of the inner wall, Shivers at his shoulder. A couple of Carls watched him come. A couple of Dow's boys, rough-looking bastards. One of them gave him a grin with half the teeth missing. 'The king!' he shouted, waving his sword in the air.

'The Bloody-Nine!' shouted the other, rattling his shield. 'King o' the Northmen!'

He crunched across the quiet courtyard, snow piled up into the corners, over to the high doors of Bethod's great hall. He raised his hands and pushed them creaking open. It wasn't much warmer inside than out in the snow. The high windows were open at the far end, the noise of the cold, cold river roaring from far below. Skarling's Chair stood on its raised-up platform, at the top of the steps, casting a long shadow across the rough floorboards towards him.

Someone was sitting in it, Logen realised, as his eyes got used to the dark. Black Dow. His axe and his sword leaned up against the side of the chair, the glint of sharpened metal in the darkness. Just like him, that. Always kept his weapons close to hand.

Logen grinned at him. 'Getting comfortable, Dow?'

'Bit hard on the arse, being honest, but it's better'n dirt for sitting in.'

'Did you find Calder and Scale?'

'Aye. I found 'em.'

'Dead, then, are they?'

'Not yet. Thought I'd try something different. We been talking.'

'Talking is it? To those two bastards?'

'I can think o' worse. Where's the Dogman at?'

'Still back there, trading words with the Union, sorting out an understanding.'

'Grim?'

Logen shook his head. 'Back to the mud.'

'Huh. Well, there it is. Makes this easier, anyway.' Dow's eyes flickered sideways.

'Makes what easier?' Logen looked round. Shivers was standing right at his shoulder, scowling as if he had someone's murder in mind. No need to ask whose. Steel gleamed beside him in the shadows. A blade, out and ready. He could've stabbed Logen in the back with time to spare. But he hadn't done, and he didn't now. It seemed as if they all stayed still for quite a while, frozen as the cold valley out beyond the windows.

'Shit on this.' Shivers tossed the knife away clattering across the floor. 'I'm better'n you, Bloody-Nine. I'm better than the pair o' you. You can get your own work done, Black Dow. I'm done with it.' He turned round and strode out, shoving his way past the two Carls from the gate, just now coming the other way. One of them hefted his shield as he frowned at Logen. The other one pulled the doors shut, swung the bar down with a final-sounding clunk.

Logen slid the Maker's sword out of its sheath, turned his head and spat on the boards. 'Like that, is it?'

'Course it is,' said Dow, still sat in Skarling's chair. 'If you'd ever looked a stride further than the end o' your nose you'd know it.'

'What about the old ways, eh? What about your word?'

'The old ways are gone. You killed 'em. You and Bethod. Men's words ain't worth much these days. Well then?' he called over his shoulder. 'Now's your chance, ain't it?'

Logen felt the moment. A lucky choice, maybe, but he'd always had plenty of luck, good and bad. He dived sideways, heard the rattle of the flatbow at the same moment, rolled across the floor and came up in a crouch as the bolt clattered against the wall behind him. He saw a figure in the dark now, kneeling up at the far end of the hall. Calder. Logen heard his curse, fishing for another bolt.

'Bloody-Nine, you broken dog!' Scale came pounding out of the shadows, boots battering the floorboards, an axe in his great fists with a blade big as a cart-wheel. 'Here's your death!'

Logen stayed where he was, crouching loose and ready, and he felt himself smile. The odds were against him, maybe, but that was nothing new. It was almost a relief, not to have to think. Fine words and politics, none of that meant anything to him. But this? This he understood.

The blade crashed into the boards, sent splinters flying. Logen had already rolled out of the way. Now he backed off, watching, moving, letting Scale cleave the air around him. The air healed quick, after all. The next blow flashed sideways and Logen dodged back, let it chop a great lump of plaster from the wall. He stepped in closer as Scale snarled again, his furious little eyes bulging, ready to swing his axe round in a blow to split the world.

The pommel of the Maker's sword crunched into his mouth before he got the chance, jerked his head up, spots of black blood and a chunk of white tooth flying. He staggered back and Logen followed him. Scale's eyes rolled down, axe going up high, opening his bloody mouth to make another bellow. Logen's boot rammed hard into the side of his leg. His knee bent back the wrong way with a sharp pop and he dropped to the boards, axe flying from his hands, his roar turning to a shriek of pain.

'My knee! Ah! Fuck! My knee!' He thrashed on the floor, blood running down his chin, trying to kick his way back with only one good leg.

Logen laughed at him. 'You bloated pig. I warned you, didn't I?'

'By the fucking *dead*!' barked Dow. He sprang up out of Skarling's chair, axe and sword in his hands. 'If you want a thing done fucking right, you'd best get ready to set your own hand to it!'

Logen would've liked to stab Scale right through his fat

head, but there were too many other men needed watching. The two Carls were still standing by the door. Calder was loading up his next bolt. Logen sidled into space, trying to keep his eye on all of them at once, and Dow most of all. 'Aye, you faithless bastard!' he shouted. 'Let's have you!'

'Faithless, me?' Dow snorted as he came on slow down the steps, one at a time. 'I'm a dark bastard, aye, I know what I am. But I'm nothing to you. I know my friends from my enemies. I never killed my own. Bethod was right about one thing, Bloody-Nine. You're made of death. If I can put an end to you, d'you know what? That'll be the best thing I've done in my life.'

'That all?'

Dow showed his teeth. 'That, and I'm just plain sick o' taking your fucking say-so.'

He came on fast as a snake, axe swinging over, sword flashing across waist high. Logen dodged the axe, met the blade with his own, metal clanging on metal. Dow caught him in his sore ribs with his knee and sent him gasping back towards the wall, then came at him again, blades leaving bright traces in the darkness. Logen sprang out of the way, rolled and came up, strutting out into the middle of the hall again, sword hanging loose from his hand.

'That it?' he asked, smiling through the pain in his side.

'Just getting the blood flowing.'

Dow leaped forward, made to go right and came left instead, sword and axe sweeping down together. Logen saw them coming, weaved away from the axe, turned the sword off his own and stepped in, growling. Dow jerked back as the Maker's blade hissed through the air right in front of his face, stumbled away a step or two. His eye twitched, some red leaking down his cheek from a nick just under it. Logen grinned, spun the grip of his sword round in his hand. 'Blood's flowing now, eh?'

'Aye.' Dow gave a grin of his own. 'Just like old times.'

'I should've killed you then.'

'Damn right you should've.' Dow circled round him, always moving, weapons gleaming in the cold light from the tall windows. 'But you love to play the good man, don't you? Do you know what's worse than a villain? A villain who thinks he's a hero. A man like that, there's nothing he won't do, and he'll always find himself an excuse. We've had one ruthless bastard make himself King o' the North, and I'll be damned before I see a worse.' He feinted forward and Logen jerked back.

He heard the click of Calder's flatbow again and saw the bolt flash right between them. Dow scowled over at him. 'You trying to kill me? You loose another bolt and you're spitted, you hear?'

'Stop pissing around and kill him, then!' snapped Calder, cranking away at his flatbow.

'Kill him!' bellowed Scale, from somewhere in the shadows.

'I'm working at it, pig.' Dow jerked his head at the two Carls by the door. 'You two going to pitch in or what?' They looked at each other, none too keen. Then they came forward into the hall, their round shields up, their eyes on Logen, herding him towards one corner.

Logen bared his teeth as he backed off. 'That's how you'll get it done, is it?'

'I'd rather kill you fair. But kill you crooked?' Dow shrugged his shoulders. 'Just as good. I ain't in the business o' giving chances. Go on then! At him!'

The two of them closed in, cautious, Dow moving off to the side. Logen scrambled back, trying to look scared and waiting for some kind of chance. It wasn't long coming. One of the Carls stepped a touch too close, let his shield drop low. He chose a bad moment to raise his axe and a bad way to do it. There was a click as the Maker's sword took his forearm off, left it hanging from his elbow by a scrap of chain-mail. He stumbled forward, dragging in a great wheezing breath, making ready to scream, blood spurting out of the stump of his arm and splattering on the boards. Logen chopped a great gash out of his helmet and he dropped down on his knees.

'Gwarghh . . .' he muttered, blood pouring down the side of his face. His eyes rolled up to the ceiling and he flopped on his side. The other Carl jumped over his body, roaring at the top of his lungs. Logen caught his sword, their blades scraping together, then he barged into the man's shield with his shoulder, sent him sprawling on his arse. He gave a wail, the Carl, one boot sticking up. Logen swung the Maker's sword down and split that foot in half up to his ankle.

Quick footsteps came up under the Carl's shriek. Logen spun, saw Black Dow charging at him, face crushed up into a killing grin.

'Die!' he hissed. Logen lurched away, the blade just missing him on one side, the axe on the other. He tried to swing the Maker's sword but Dow was too quick and too clever, shoved Logen back with his boot and sent him staggering.

'Die, Bloody-Nine!' Logen dodged, parried, stumbled as Dow came on again, no pauses and no mercy. Steel glinted in the darkness, blades lashing, killing blows, every one.

'Die, you evil fucker!' Dow's sword chopped down and Logen only just brought his own round in time to block it. The axe came out of nowhere, up from underneath, clattered into the crosspiece and tore Logen's blade spinning from his numb hand. He wobbled back a couple of strides and stood, heaving in air, sweat tickling at his neck.

It was quite a scrape he was in. He'd been in some bad ones alright, and lived to sing the songs, but it was hard to see how this could get much worse. Logen nodded towards the Maker's sword, lying on the boards just next to Dow's boot. 'Don't suppose you fancy giving a man a fair chance, and letting me have that blade, eh?'

Dow grinned wider than ever. 'What's my name? White Dow?'

Logen had a knife to hand, of course. He always did, and more than one. His eyes flickered from the notched blade of Dow's sword to the glinting edge of his axe and back. No amount of knives were going to be a match for those, not in Black Dow's hands. Then there was Calder's flatbow still rattling away as he tried to load the bastard thing again. He wouldn't miss forever. The Carl with the split foot was dragging himself squealing towards the door, on his way to let some more men in and finish the job. If Logen stood and fought he was a dead man, Bloody-Nine or not. So it came to a choice between dying and a chance at living, and that's no choice at all.

Once you know what has to be done, it's better to do it, than to live with the fear of it. That's what Logen's father would have said. So he turned towards the tall windows. The tall, open windows with the bright white sunlight and the cold wind pouring through, and he ran at them.

He heard men shouting behind, but he paid them no mind. He kept running, breath hissing, long strips of light wobbling closer. He was up the steps in a couple of bounds, flashed past Skarling's Chair, faster and faster. His right foot clomped down on the hollow floorboards. His left foot slapped down on the stone window sill. He sprang out into empty space with all the strength he had left, and for a moment he was free.

Then he began to fall. Fast. The rough walls, then the steep cliff face flashed past – grey rock, green moss, patches of white snow, all tumbling around him.

Logen turned over slowly in the air, limbs flailing pointlessly, too scared to scream. The rushing wind whipped at his eyes, tugged at his clothes, plucked the breath out of his mouth. He'd chosen this? Didn't seem like such a clever choice, right then, as he plunged down towards the river. But then say one thing for Logen Ninefingers, say that—

The water came up to meet him. It hit him in the side like a charging bull, punched the air out of his lungs, knocked the sense out of his head, sucked him in and down into the cold darkness . . .

Acknowledgments

Four people without whom:

Bren Abercrombie, whose eyes are sore from reading it
Nick Abercrombie, whose ears are sore from hearing about it
Rob Abercrombie, whose fingers are sore from turning the pages
Lou Abercrombie, whose arms are sore from holding me up

Then, at the House of Questions,
all those who assisted in this testing interrogation,
but particularly:

Superior Spanton, Practical Weir,
and, of course, Inquisitor Redfearn.

You can put away the instruments.

I confess . . .

Turn the page for a sneak preview of:

Best Served Cold

The fantastic standalone novel from Joe Abercrombie

Available now from Gollancz

Benna Murcatto Saves a Life

The sunrise was the colour of bad blood. It leaked out of the east and stained the dark sky red, marked the scraps of cloud with stolen gold. Underneath it the road twisted up the mountainside towards the fortress of Fontezarmo – a cluster of sharp towers, ash-black against the wounded heavens. The sunrise was red, black and gold.

The colours of their profession.

'You look especially beautiful this morning, Monza.'

She sighed, as if that was an accident. As if she hadn't spent an hour preening herself before the mirror. 'Facts are facts. Saying them isn't a gift. You only prove you're not blind.' She yawned, stretched in her saddle, made him wait a moment longer.

He noisily cleared his throat and held up one hand, a bad actor preparing for his grand speech. 'Your hair is like to . . . a veil of shimmering sable!'

'You pompous cock. What was it yesterday? A curtain of midnight. I liked that better, it had some poetry to it. Bad poetry, but still.'

'Women and their money.' He squinted up at the clouds. 'Your eyes, then, gleam like piercing sapphires, beyond price!'

'I've got stones in my face, now?'

'Lips like rose petals?'

She spat at him, but he was ready and dodged it, the phlegm clearing his horse and spattering on the dry stones beside the track. 'That's to make your roses grow, arsehole. You can do better.'

'Harder every day,' he muttered. 'That jewel I bought looks wonderful well on you.'

She held her right hand up to admire it, a ruby the size of an almond, catching the first glimmer of sunlight and glistening the colour of a slit throat. 'I've had worse gifts.'

'It matches your fiery temper.'

She snorted. 'And my bloody reputation.'

'Piss on your reputation! Nothing but idiot's chatter! You're a dream. A vision. You look like . . .' He snapped his fingers. 'The very Goddess of War!'

'Goddess, eh?'

'Of War. You like it?'

'It'll do. If you can kiss Duke Orso's arse half so well we might even get a bonus.'

Benna puckered his lips at her. 'I love nothing more of a morning than a mouthful of his Excellency's rich, round buttocks. They taste like . . . power.'

Hooves crunched on the dusty track, saddle creaked and harness rattled. The road turned back on itself, and again. The rest of the world dropped away below them. The eastern sky bled out from red to butchered pink. The river crept slowly into view, winding through the autumn woods at the base of the steep valley. Glittering like an army on the march, flowing swift and merciless towards the sea. Towards Talins.

'I'm waiting,' he said.

'For what?'

'My share of the compliments, of course.'

'If your head swells any further it'll fucking burst.'

She twitched her silken cuffs up. 'And I don't want your brains on my new shirt.'

'Stabbed!' Benna clutched one hand to his chest. 'Right here! Is this how you repay my years of devotion, you heartless bitch?'

'How dare *you* presume to be devoted to *me*, peasant? You're like a tick devoted to a tiger!'

'Tiger? Hah. When they compare you to an animal they usually pick a snake.'

'Snake? Hah! Better than a maggot.'

'Whore.'

'Coward.'

'Murderer.'

She could hardly deny that one. Silence settled on them again. A bird trilled from a thirsty tree beside the road. Benna's horse drew gradually up beside hers, and ever so gently, sweetly, he murmured.

'You look especially beautiful this morning, Monza.'

That brought a smile to the corner of her mouth. The corner he couldn't see. 'Well. Facts are facts.'

She spurred ahead, round one more steep bend, and the outermost wall of the citadel of Fontezarmo thrust up ahead of them. A narrow bridge crossed a dizzy ravine to the gatehouse, water sparkling as it fell away beneath. At the far end an archway yawned, welcoming as a grave.

'They've strengthened the walls since last year,' muttered Benna. 'I wouldn't fancy trying to storm the place.'

'Don't pretend you'd have the guts to climb the ladder.'

'I wouldn't fancy telling someone else to storm the place.'

'Don't pretend you'd have the guts to give the orders.'

'I wouldn't fancy watching you tell someone else to storm the place.'

'No.' She leaned gingerly from her saddle and frowned down at the plummeting drop on her left. Then she peered up at the sheer wall on her right, battlements a jagged black edge against the brightening sky. 'It's almost as if Orso's worried someone might try to kill him.'

'He's got enemies?' breathed Benna, eyes round as saucers with mock amazement.

'Only half of Styria.'

'Then . . . we have enemies?'

'More than half of Styria.'

'But I've tried so hard to be popular . . .' They trotted between two dour-faced soldiers, spears and steel caps polished to a murderous glint. Hoofbeats echoed in the darkness of the long tunnel, sloping gradually upwards. 'You have that look, now.'

'What look?'

'No more fun today.'

'Huh.' She felt the familiar frown gripping her face. 'You can afford to smile. You're the good one.'

It was a different world beyond the gates, air heavy with lavender, shining green after the grey mountainside. A world of close-clipped lawns, of hedges tortured into wondrous shapes, of fountains throwing up glittering spray. Grim guardsmen, the black cross of Talins stitched into their white surcoats, spoiled the mood at every doorway.

'Monza . . .'

'Yes?'

'Let's make this the last season on campaign,' Benna wheedled. 'The last summer in the dust. Let's find something more comfortable to do. Now, while we're young.'

'What about the Thousand Swords? Closer to ten thousand now, all looking to us for orders.'

'They can look elsewhere. They joined us for plunder and we've given them plenty. They've no loyalty beyond their own profit.'

She had to admit the Thousand Swords had never represented the best of mankind, or even the best of mercenaries. Most of them were a step above the criminal. Most of the rest were a step below. But that wasn't the point. 'You have to stick at something in your life,' she grunted.

'I don't see why.'

'That's you all over. One more season, and Visserine will fall, and Rogont will surrender, and the League of Eight will all be done. Orso can crown himself King of Styria, and we can melt away and be forgotten.'

'We deserve to be remembered. We could have our own city. You could be the noble Duchess Monzcarro of . . . wherever—'

'And you the fearless Duke Benna?' She laughed at that. 'You stupid arse. You can scarcely govern your own bowels without my help. War's a dark enough trade, I draw the line at politics. Orso crowned, then we're done.'

Benna sighed. 'I thought we were mercenaries? Cosca never stuck to an employer like this.'

'I'm not Cosca. And it's not wise to say no to the Lord of Talins.'

'You just love to fight.'

'No. I love to win. Just one more season, then we can see the world. Visit the Old Empire. Tour the Thousand Isles. Off to Adua and stand in the shadow of the House of the Maker. Everything we talked about.' Benna pouted, the way he always did when he didn't get his way. He pouted, but he never said no. It scratched at her, sometimes, that she always had to make the choices. 'Since we've clearly only got one pair of balls between us, don't you ever feel the need to borrow them yourself?'

'They look better on you. Besides, you've got all the brains, it's best they stay together.'

'What do you get from the deal?'

Benna grinned at her. 'The winning smile.'

'Smile, then. For one more season.' She swung down from her saddle, jerked her sword-belt straight, tossed the reins at the groom and strode for the inner gatehouse. Benna had to hurry to catch up, getting tangled with his own sword on the way. For a man who earned his living from war, he'd always been an embarrassment where weapons were concerned.

The inner courtyard was split into wide terraces at the summit of the mountain, planted with exotic palms and even more heavily guarded than the outer. An ancient column said to come from the palace of Scarpius stood tall in the centre, casting a shimmering reflection in a round pool, teeming with silvery fish. The immensity of glass, bronze and marble that was Duke Orso's palace towered around it on three sides like a monstrous cat with a mouse between its paws.

Since the spring they'd built a vast new wing along the northern wall, its festoons of decorative stonework still half-shrouded in scaffolding.

'They've been building,' she said.

'Of course. How could Prince Ario manage with only ten halls for his shoes?'

'A man can't be fashionable these days without at least twenty rooms of footwear.'

Benna frowned down at his own gold-buckled boots. 'I've no more than thirty pairs all told. I feel my shortcomings most keenly.'

'As do we all,' she muttered. A half-finished set of statues stood along the roofline. Duke Orso giving alms to the poor. Duke Orso gifting knowledge to the ignorant. Duke Orso shielding the weak from harm.

'I'm surprised he hasn't got one of the whole of Styria tongueing his arse,' whispered Benna in her ear.

She pointed to a partly chiselled block of marble. 'That's next.'

'Benna!'

Count Foscar, Orso's younger son, rushed round the pool like an eager puppy, shoes crunching on the fresh-raked gravel, freckled face all lit up. He'd made an ill-advised attempt at a beard since Monza last saw him but the sprinkling of sandy hairs only made him look the more boyish. He might've inherited all the honesty in his family, but the looks had gone elsewhere. Benna grinned, threw one arm around Foscar's shoulders and ruffled his hair. An insult from anyone else, from Benna it was effortlessly charming. He had a knack of making people happy that always seemed like magic to Monza. Her talents lay elsewhere.

'Your father here yet?' she asked.

'Yes, and my brother too. They're with their banker.'

'How's his mood?'

'Good, so far as I can tell, but you know my father. Still, he's never angry with you two, is he? You always bring good news. You bring good news today, yes?'

'Shall I tell him, Monza, or—'

'Borletta's fallen. Cantain's dead.'

Foscar didn't celebrate. He hadn't his father's appetite for corpses. 'Cantain was a good man.'

That was a long way from the point, as far as Monza could see. 'He was your father's enemy.'

'A man you could respect, though. There are precious few of them left in Styria. He's really dead?'

Benna blew out his cheeks. 'Well his head's off, and spiked above the gates, so unless you know one hell of a physician . . .'

They passed through a high archway, the hall beyond dim and echoing as an emperor's tomb, light filtering down in dusty columns and pooling on the marble floor. Suits of old armour stood gleaming to silent attention, antique weapons clutched in steel fists. The sharp clicking of boot heels snapped from the walls as a man in a dark uniform paced towards them.

'Shit,' Benna hissed in her ear. 'That reptile Ganmark's here.'

'Leave it be.'

'There's no way that cold-blooded bastard's as good with a sword as they say—'

'He is.'

'If I was half a man, I'd—'

'You're not. So leave it be.'

706

General Ganmark's face was strangely soft, his moustaches limp, his pale grey eyes always watery, lending him a look of perpetual sadness. The rumour was he'd been thrown out of the Union army for a sexual indiscretion involving another officer, and crossed the sea to find a more broad-minded master. The breadth of Duke Orso's mind was infinite where his servants were concerned, provided they were effective. She and Benna were proof enough of that.

Ganmark nodded stiffly to Monza. 'General Murcatto.' He nodded stiffly to Benna. 'General Murcatto. Count Foscar, you are keeping to your exercises, I hope?'

'Sparring every day.'

'Then we will make a swordsman of you yet.'

Benna snorted. 'That, or a bore.'

'Either one would be something,' droned Ganmark in his clipped Union accent. 'A man without discipline is no better than a dog. A soldier without discipline is no better than a corpse. Worse, in fact. A corpse is no threat to his own comrades.'

Benna opened his mouth but Monza talked over him. He could make an arse of himself later, if he pleased. 'How was your season?'

'I played my part, keeping your flanks free of Rogont and his Osprians.'

'Stalling the Duke of Delay?' Benna smirked. 'Quite the challenge.'

'No more than a supporting role. A comic turn in a great tragedy, but one appreciated by the audience, I hope.'

The echoes of their footsteps swelled as they passed through another archway and into the towering rotunda at the heart of the palace. The curving walls were vast panels of sculpture showing scenes from antiquity. Wars between Demons and Magi, and other such rubbish. High above, the great dome was frescoed with seven winged women against a stormy sky – armed, armoured, and angry-looking. The fates, bringing destinies to earth. Aropella's greatest work, she'd heard it had taken him eight years to finish. Monza never got over how tiny, weak, utterly insignificant this space made her feel. That was the point of it.

The four of them climbed a sweeping staircase, wide enough for twice as many to walk abreast. 'And where have your comic talents taken you?' she asked Ganmark.

'Fire and murder, to the gates of Puranti and back.'

Benna curled his lip. 'Any actual fighting?'

'Why ever would I do that? Have you not read your Stolicus? "An animal fights his way to victory—"'

'"A general marches there,"' Monza finished for him. 'Did you raise many laughs?'

'Not for the enemy, I suppose. Precious few for anyone, but that is war.'

'I find time to chuckle,' threw in Benna.

'Some men laugh easily. It makes them winning dinner companions.' Ganmark's soft eyes moved across to Monza's. 'I note that you are not smiling.'

'I will. Once the League of Eight are finished and Orso is King of Styria. Then we can all hang up our swords.'

'In my experience swords do not hang comfortably from hooks. They have a habit of finding their way back into one's hands.'

'I daresay Orso will keep you on,' said Benna. 'Even if it's only to polish the tiles.'

Ganmark did not give so much as a sharp breath. 'Then his Excellency will have the cleanest floors in all of Styria.'

A pair of high doors faced the top of the stairs, gleaming with inlaid wood, carved with lion's faces. A thick-set man paced up and down before them like a loyal old hound before his master's bedchamber. Faithful Carpi, the longest-serving Captain in the Thousand Swords, the scars of a hundred engagements marked out on his broad, weathered, honest face.

'Faithful!' Benna seized the old mercenary by his big slab of a hand. 'Climbing a mountain, at your age? Shouldn't you be in a brothel somewhere?'

'If only.' Carpi shrugged. 'But his Excellency sent for me.'

'And you, being an obedient sort . . . obeyed.'

'That's why they call me Faithful.'

'How did you leave things in Borletta?' asked Monza.

'Quiet. Most of the men are quartered outside the walls with Andiche and Victus. Best if they don't set fire to the place, I thought. I left some of the more reliable ones in Cantain's palace with Sesaria watching over them. Old timers, like me, from back in Cosca's day. Seasoned men, not prone to impulsiveness.'

Benna chuckled. 'Slow thinkers, you mean?'

'Slow but steady. We get there in the end.'

'Going in, then?' Foscar set his shoulder to one of the doors and heaved it open. Ganmark and Faithful followed. Monza paused a moment on the threshold, trying to find her hardest face. She looked up and saw Benna smiling at her. Without thinking, she found herself smiling back. She leaned and whispered in his ear.

'I love you.'

'Of course you do.' He stepped through the doorway, and she followed.

Duke Orso's private study was a marble hall the size of a market square. Lofty windows marched in bold procession down one side, standing open, a keen breeze washing through and making the vivid hangings twitch and rustle. Beyond them a terrace seemed to hang in empty air, overlooking the steepest drop from the mountain's summit.

The opposite wall was covered with towering panels, painted by the foremost artists of Styria, displaying the great battles of history. The victories of Stolicus, of Harod the Great, of Farans and Verturio, all preserved in sweeping oils. The message that Orso was the latest in a line of royal winners was hard to miss, even though his great-grandfather had been a usurper, and a common criminal besides.

The largest painting of them all faced the door, ten strides high at the least. Who else but Grand Duke Orso? He was seated upon a rearing charger, his shining sword raised high, his piercing eye fixed on the far horizon, urging his men to victory at the Battle of Etrea. The painter seemed to have been unaware that Orso hadn't come within fifty miles of the fighting.

But then fine lies beat tedious truths every time.

The Duke of Talins himself sat crabbed over a desk, wielding a pen rather than a sword. A tall, gaunt, hook-nosed man stood at his elbow, staring down as keenly as a vulture waiting for thirsty travellers to die. A great shape lurked near them, in the shadows against the wall. Gobba, Orso's bodyguard, fat-necked as a great hog. Prince Ario, the Duke's eldest son and heir, lounged in a gilded chair nearer at hand. He had one leg crossed over the other, a wine glass dangling carelessly, a bland smile balanced on his blandly handsome face.

'I found these beggars wandering the grounds!' called Foscar. 'And thought I'd commend them to your charity, father!'

'Charity?' Orso's sharp voice echoed around the cavernous room. 'I'm not a great admirer of the stuff. Make yourselves comfortable, my friends, I will be with you shortly.'

'If it isn't the Butcher of Caprile,' murmured Ario, 'and her little Benna too.'

'Your Highness. You look well.' Monza thought he looked an indolent cock, but kept it to herself.

'You too, as ever. If all soldiers looked as you did I might even be tempted to go on campaign myself. A new bauble?' Ario waved his own jewel-encrusted hand limply towards the ruby on Monza's finger.

'Just what was to hand when I was dressing.'

'I wish I'd been there. Wine?'

'Just after dawn?'

He glanced heavy-lidded towards the windows. 'Still last night as far as I'm concerned.' As if staying up late was a heroic achievement.

'I will.' Benna was already pouring himself a glass, never to be outdone as far as showng off went. Most likely he'd be drunk within the hour, and embarrass

711

himself, but Monza was tired of playing his mother. She strolled past the monumental fireplace held up by carven figures of Juvens and Kanedias, and towards Orso's desk.

'Sign here, and here, and here,' the gaunt man was saying, one bony finger hovering over the documents.

'You know Mauthis, do you?' Orso gave a sour glance in his direction. 'My leash-holder.'

'Always your humble servant, your Excellency. The banking house of Valint and Balk agree to this further loan for the period of one year, after which they regret they must charge interest.'

Orso snorted. 'As the plague regrets the dead, I'll be bound.' He scratched out a parting swirl on the last signature and tossed down his pen. 'Everyone must kneel to someone, eh? Make sure you extend to your superiors my infinite gratitude for their indulgence.'

'I shall do so.' Mauthis collected up the documents. 'That concludes our business, your Excellency. I must leave at once if I mean to catch the evening tide for Westport—'

'No. Stay a while longer. We have one other matter to discuss.'

Mauthis' dead eyes moved towards Monza, then back to Orso. 'As your Excellency desires.'

The Duke rose smoothly from his desk. 'Now to happier business. You do bring happy news, eh, Monzcarro?'

'I do, your Excellency.'

'Ah, whatever would I do without you?' There was a trace of iron grey in his black hair since she saw him last, perhaps some deeper lines at the corners of his eyes, but his air of complete command was impressive as ever. He leaned forwards and kissed her on both cheeks, then whispered in her ear. 'Ganmark can lead soldiers well enough, but for a man who sucks cocks he hasn't the slightest sense of humour. Come, tell me of your victories in the open air.' He left one arm draped around her shoulders and guided her, past the sneering Prince Ario, through the open windows onto the high terrace.

The sun was climbing, now, and the bright world was full of colour. The blood had drained from the sky and left it a vivid blue, white clouds crawling high above. Below, at the very bottom of a dizzy drop, the river wound through the wooded base of the valley, autumn leaves pale green, burnt orange, faded yellow, angry red, light glinting silver on fast-flowing water. To the east, the forest crumbled away into a patch-work of fields – squares of fallow green, rich black earth, golden crop. Further still and the river met the grey sea, branching out in a wide delta, choked with islands. Monza could just make out the suggestion of tiny towers there, buildings, bridges, walls. Great Talins, no bigger than her thumbnail.

She narrowed her eyes against the stiff breeze, pushed some stray hair out of her face. 'I never tire of this view.'

'How could you? It's why I built this damn place. Here I can keep one eye always on my subjects, as a watchful parent should upon his children. Just to make sure they don't hurt themselves while they play, you understand.'

'Your people are lucky to have such a just and caring father,' she lied smoothly.

'Just and caring.' Orso frowned thoughtfully

towards the distant sea. 'Do you think that is how history will remember me?'

Monza thought it incredibly unlikely. 'What did Bialoveld say? "History is written by the victors."'

The Duke squeezed her shoulder again. 'All this, and well-read into the bargain. Ario is ambitious enough, but he has no insight. I'd be surprised if he could read to the end of a signpost in one sitting. All he cares about is whoring. And shoes. My daughter Terez, meanwhile, weeps most bitterly because I married her to a king. I swear, if I had offered great Euz as the groom she would have whined for a husband better fitting her station.' He gave a heavy sigh. 'None of my children understand me. My great-grandfather was a mercenary, you know. A fact I do not like to advertise.' Though he told her every other time they met. 'A man who never shed a tear in his life, and wore on his feet whatever was to hand. A low-born fighting man, who seized power in Talins by the sharpness of his mind and sword together.' More by blunt ruthlessness and brutality the way Monza had heard the tale. 'We are from the same stock, you and I. We have made ourselves, out of nothing.'

Orso had been born to the wealthiest dukedom in Styria and never done a hard day's work in his life, but Monza bit her tongue. 'You do me too much honour, your Excellency.'

'Less than you deserve. Now tell me of Borletta.'

'You heard about the battle on the High Bank?'

'I heard you scattered the League of Eight's army, just as you did at Sweet Pines! Ganmark says Duke Salier had three times your number!'

'Numbers are a hindrance if they're lazy, ill-prepared, and led by idiots. An army of farmers from Borletta, cobblers from Affoia and merchants from Visserine. Amateurs. They camped by the river, thinking we were far away, scarcely posted guards. We came up through the woods at night and caught them at sunrise, not even in their armour.'

'I can see Salier now, the fat pig, waddling from his bed to run!'

'Faithful led the charge. We broke them quickly, captured their supplies.'

'Turned the golden cornfields crimson, I was told.'

'They hardly even fought. Ten times as many drowned trying to swim the river as died fighting. More than four thousand prisoners. Some ransoms were paid, some not, some men were hanged.'

'And few tears shed, eh, Monza?'

'Not by me. If they were so keen to live they could've surrendered.'

'As they did at Caprile?'

She stared straight back into Orso's black eyes. 'Just as they did at Caprile.'

'Borletta is besieged, then?'

'Fallen already.'

The Duke's face lit up like a boy's on his birthday. 'Fallen? Cantain surrendered?'

'When his people heard of Salier's defeat they lost hope.'

'And people without hope are a dangerous crowd, even in a republic.'

'Especially in a republic. A mob dragged Cantain from the palace, hung him from the highest tower, opened the gates and threw themselves on the mercy of the Thousand Swords.'

'Hah! Slaughtered by the very people he laboured to keep free. There's the gratitude of the common man, eh, Monza? Cantain should have taken my money when I offered. It would have been cheaper for both of us.'

'The people are falling over themselves to become your subjects. I've given orders they should be spared, where possible.'

'Mercy, eh?'

'Mercy and cowardice are the same,' she snapped out. 'But you want their land, not their lives, no? Dead men can't obey.'

Orso smiled. 'Why can my sons not mark my lessons as you have? I entirely approve. Hang only the leaders. And Cantain's head above the gates. Nothing encourages obedience like a good example.'

'Already rotting, with those of his sons.'

'Fine work!' The Lord of Talins clapped his hands, as though he never heard such pleasing music as the news of rotting heads. 'What of the takings?'

The accounts were Benna's business, and he came forward now, sliding a folded paper from his inside pocket. 'The city was scoured, your Excellency. Every building stripped, every floor dug up, every person searched. The usual rules apply, according to our terms of engagement. Quarter for the man that finds it, quarter for his captain, quarter for the generals,' and he bowed low, unfolding the paper and offering it out, 'and quarter for our noble employer.'

Orso's smile spread as his eyes scanned down the figures. 'My blessing on the Rule of Quarters! Enough to keep you both in my service a little longer.' He stepped between Monza and Benna, placed a gentle

716

hand on each of their shoulders and led them back through the open windows. Towards the great round table of black marble that stood in the centre of the room and the great map spread out upon it. Ganmark, Ario, and Faithful had already gathered there. Gobba still lurked in the shadows, thick arms folded across his chest. 'What of our one-time friends and now our bitter enemies, the treacherous citizens of Visserine?'

'The fields round the city are burned up to the gates, almost.' Monza scattered carnage across the countryside with a few waves of her finger. 'Farmers driven off, livestock slaughtered. It'll be a lean winter for the good people of Visserine, and a leaner spring.'

'They will have to rely on the noble Duke Rogont and his Osprians,' said Ganmark, with the faintest of smiles.

Prince Ario snickered. 'Much talk blows down from Ospria, always, but little help.'

'Visserine is poised to drop into your lap next year, your Excellency.'

'And with it the heart is torn from the League of Eight.'

'The crown of Styria will be yours.'

The mention of crowns teased Orso's smile still wider. 'And we have you to thank, Monzcarro. I do not forget that.'

'Not only me.'

'Curse your modesty. Benna has played his part, and our good friend General Ganmark, and Faithful too, but no one could deny this is your work. Your commitment, your single-mindedness, your swiftness to act! You shall have a great triumph, just as the heroes of ancient Aulcus did. You shall ride through the streets of Talins and my people will shower you with flower petals in honour of your many victories.' Benna grinned, but Monza couldn't join him. She'd never had much taste for congratulations. 'They will cheer far louder for you, I think, than they ever will for my own sons. They will cheer far louder even than they do for me, their rightful lord, to whom they owe so much.' It seemed that Orso's smile slipped, and his face looked tired, and sad, and worn without it. 'They will cheer, in fact, a little too loudly for my taste.'

There was the barest flash of movement at the corner of her eye, enough to make her bring up her hand on an instinct.

The wire hissed taught around it, snatching it up under her chin, crushing it chokingly tight against her throat.

Benna started forward. 'Mon—' Metal glinted as Prince Ario stabbed him in the neck. He missed his throat, caught him just under the ear.

Orso carefully stepped back as blood speckled the tiles with red. Foscar's mouth fell open, wine glass dropping from his hand, shattering on the floor.

Monza tried to scream, but only spluttered through her half-shut windpipe, made a sound like a honking pig. She fished at the hilt of her dagger with her free hand but someone caught her wrist, held it fast. Faithful Carpi, pressed up tight against her left side.

'Sorry,' he muttered in her ear, pulling her sword from its scabbard and flinging it clattering across the room.

Benna stumbled, gurgling red drool, one hand clutched to the side of his face, black blood leaking

718

out between white fingers. His other hand fumbled for his sword while Ario watched him, frozen. He drew a clumsy foot of steel before General Ganmark stepped forward and stabbed him, smoothly and precisely – once, twice, three times. The thin blade slid in and out of Benna's body, the only sound the soft breath from his gaping mouth. Blood shot across the floor in long streaks, began to leak out into his white shirt in dark circles. He tottered forwards, tripped over his own feet and crashed down, half drawn sword scraping against the marble underneath him.

Monza strained, every muscle trembling, but she was held helpless as a fly in honey. She heard Gobba grunting with effort in her ear, his stubbly face rubbing against her cheek, his great body warm against her back. She felt the wire cut slowly into the sides of her neck, deep into the side of her hand, caught fast against her throat. She felt the blood running down her forearm, into the collar of her shirt.

One of Benna's hands crawled across the floor, reaching out for her. He lifted himself an inch or two, veins bulging from his neck. Ganmark leaned forwards and calmly ran him through the heart from behind. Benna quivered for a moment, then sagged down and was still, pale cheek smeared with red. Dark blood crept out from under him, worked its way along the cracks between the tiles.

'Well.' Ganmark leaned down and wiped his sword on the back of Benna's shirt. 'That's that.'

Mauthis watched, frowning. Slightly puzzled, slightly irritated, slightly bored. As though examining a set of figures that wouldn't quite add.

Orso gestured at the body. 'Get rid of that, Ario.'

'Me?' The Prince's lip curled even further.

'Yes, you. And you can help him, Foscar. The two of you must learn what needs to be done to keep our family in power.'

'No!' Foscar stumbled away. 'I'll have no part of this!' He turned and ran from the room, his boots slapping against the marble floor.

'That boy is soft as syrup,' muttered Orso at his back. 'Ganmark, help him.'

Monza's bulging eyes followed them as they dragged Benna's corpse out through the doors to the terrace, Ganmark grim and careful at the head end, Ario cursing as he daintily took the boots. They heaved Benna up onto the balustrade and rolled him off. Like that he was gone.

'Ah!' squawked Ario, waving one hand. 'Damn it! You scratched me!'

Ganmark stared back at him. 'I apologise, your Highness. Murder can be a painful business.'

The Prince looked round for something to wipe his bloody hands on. He reached for the rich hangings beside the window.

'Not there!' snapped Orso. 'That's Kantic silk, at fifty scales a piece!'

'Where, then?'

'Find something else, or leave them red! Sometimes I wonder if your mother told the truth about your paternity, boy.' Ario wiped his hands sulkily on the front of his shirt while Monza stared, helpless, face burning from lack of air. Orso frowned over at her, a blurred black figure through the wet in her eyes, the hair tangled across her face. 'Is she still alive? What ever are you about, Gobba?'

'Fucking wire's caught on her hand,' hissed the bodyguard.

'Find another way to be done with her, then, lackwit.'

'I'll do it.' Faithful pulled the dagger from her belt, still pinning her wrist with his other hand. 'I really am sorry.'

'Just get to it!' growled Gobba.

The blade went back, steel glinting in a shaft of light. Monza stomped down on Gobba's foot with all the strength she had left. The bodyguard grunted, grip slipping on the wire, and she dragged it away from her neck, growling, twisting hard as Carpi stabbed at her.

The blade went well wide of the mark, slid in under her bottom rib. Cold metal, but it felt burning hot, a line of fire from her stomach to her back. It slid right through and the point pricked Gobba's gut.

'Gah!' He let go the wire and Monza whooped in air, started shrieking mindlessly, lashed at him with her elbow and sent him staggering. Faithful was caught off-guard, fumbled the knife as he pulled it out of her and sent it spinning across the floor. She kicked at him, missed his groin and caught his hip, bent him over. She snatched at a dagger on his belt, pulled it from its sheath, but her cut hand was clumsy and he caught her wrist before she could ram the blade into him. They wrestled with it, teeth bared, gasping spit in each others' faces, lurching back and forward, their hands sticky with her blood.

'Kill her!'

There was a crunch and her head was full of light. The floor cracked against her skull, slapped her in the back. She spat blood, mad screams guttering to a long drawn croak, clawing at the smooth floor with her nails.

'Fucking bitch!' The heel of Gobba's big boot cracked down on her right hand and sent pain lancing up her forearm, tore a sick gasp from her. His boot crunched down again across her knuckles, then her fingers, then her wrist. At the same time Faithful's foot was thudding into her ribs, over and over, making her cough and shudder. Her shattered hand twisted, turned sideways on. Gobba's heel crashed down and crushed it flat into the cold marble with a splintering of bone. She flopped back, hardly able to breathe, the room turning over, history's painted winners grinning down.

'You stabbed me, you dumb old bastard! You stabbed me!'

'You're hardly even cut, fathead! You should've kept a hold on her!'

'I should stab the useless pair of you!' hissed Orso's voice. 'Just get it done!'

Gobba's great fist came down, dragged Monza up by her throat. She tried to grab at him with her left hand but all her strength had leaked out through the hole in her side, the cuts in her neck. Her clumsy fingertips only smeared red traces across his stubbly face. Her arm was dragged away, twisted sharply behind her back.

'Where's Hermon's gold?' came Gobba's rough voice. 'Eh, Murcatto? What did you do with the gold?'

Monza forced her head up. 'Lick my arse, cocksucker.' Not clever, perhaps, but from the heart.

'There never was any gold!' snapped Faithful. 'I told you that, pig!'

'There's this much.' One by one, Gobba twisted the battered rings from her dangling fingers, already bloating, turning angry purple, bent and shapeless as rotten sausages. 'Good stone, that,' he said, peering at the ruby. 'Seems a waste of decent flesh, though. Why not give me a moment with her? A moment's all it would take.'

Prince Ario tittered. 'Speed isn't always something to be proud of.'

'For pity's sake!' Orso's voice. 'We're not animals. Off the terrace and let us be done. I am late for breakfast.'

She felt herself dragged, head lolling. Sunlight stabbed at her. She was lifted, limp, boots hissed against stone. Blue sky turning. Up onto the balcony. The breath scraped at her nose, shuddered in her chest. She twisted, kicked. Her body, struggling vainly to stay alive.

'Let me make sure of her.' Ganmark's voice.

'How sure do we need to be?' Blurry through the bloody hair across her eyes she saw Orso's lined face. 'I hope you understand. My great-grandfather was a mercenary. A low-born fighting man, who seized power by the sharpness of his mind and sword together. I cannot allow another mercenary to seize power in Talins.'

She meant to spit in his face, but all she did was blow bloody drool down her own chin. 'Fuck yourse—'

Then she was flying.

Her torn shirt billowed and flapped against her

tingling skin. She turned over, and over, and the world tumbled around her. Blue sky with shreds of cloud, black towers at the mountain top, grey rock face rushing past, yellow-green trees and sparkling river, blue sky with shreds of cloud, and again, and again, faster, and faster.

Cold wind ripped at her hair, roared in her ears, whistled between her teeth along with her terrified breath. She could see each tree, now, see each branch, each leaf. They surged up towards her. She opened her mouth to scream—

Twigs snatched, grabbed, lashed at her. A broken branch knocked her spinning. Wood cracked and tore around her as she plunged down, down, and crashed into the mountainside. Her legs splintered under her plummeting weight, her shoulder broke apart against firm earth. But rather than dashing her brains out on the rocks, she only shattered her jaw against her brother's bloody chest, his mangled corpse wedged against the base of a tree.

Which was how Benna Murcatto saved his sister's life.

She bounced from the corpse, three-quarters sense-less, and down the steep mountainside, over and over, flailing like a broken doll. Rocks, and roots, and hard earth clubbed and battered, punched and crushed her, as if she was broken apart with a hundred hammers.

She tore through a patch of bushes, thorns whip-ping and clutching. She rolled, and rolled, down the sloping earth in a cloud of dirt and leaves. She tumbled over a tree root, crumpled on a mossy rock. She slid slowly to a stop, on her back, and was still.

'Huuuurrrrhhh . . .'

Stones clattered down around her, sticks and gravel. Dust slowly settled. She heard wind, creaking in the branches, crackling in the leaves. Or her own breath, creaking and crackling in her broken throat. The sun flickered through the black trees, jabbing at one eye. The other was dark. Flies buzzed, zipping and swimming in the warm morning air. She was down with the waste from Orso's kitchens. Sprawled out helpless in the midst of the rotten vegetables, and the cooking slime, and the stinking offal left over from the last month's magnificent meals. Tossed out with the rubbish.

'Huuurrhhh . . .'

A jagged, mindless sound. She was embarrassed by it, almost, but couldn't stop making it. Animal horror. Mad despair. The groan of the dead, in hell. Her eye darted desperately around. She saw the wreck of her right hand, a shapeless, purple glove with a bloody gash in the side. One finger trembled slightly. Its tip brushed against torn skin on her elbow. The forearm was folded in half, a broken-off twig of grey bone sticking through bloody silk. It didn't look real. Like a cheap theatre prop.

'Huurrhhh . . .'

The fear had hold of her now, swelling with every breath. She couldn't move her head. She couldn't move her tongue in her mouth. She could feel the pain, gnawing at the edge of her mind. A terrible mass, pressing up against her, crushing every part of her, worse, and worse, and worse.

'Huurhh . . . uurh . . .'

Benna was dead. A streak of wet ran from her flickering eye and she felt it trickle slowly down her

725